VOYAGE

By the same author:

The Xeelee Sequence Novels:

RAFT
TIMELIKE INFINITY
FLUX
RING

THE TIME SHIPS
ANTI-ICE

Voyager

STEPHEN BAXTER

VOYAGE

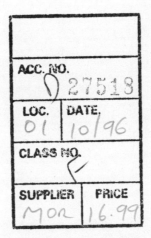

HarperCollinsPublishers

Voyager
An imprint of HarperCollins*Publishers*
77–85 Fulham Palace Road,
Hammersmith, London W6 8JB

Published by HarperCollins*Publishers* 1996
1 3 5 7 9 8 6 4 2

A catalogue record for this book
is available from the British Library

ISBN 0 00 224616 3

Set in Sabon by Rowland Phototypesetting Ltd,
Bury St Edmunds, Suffolk

Printed and bound in Great Britain by
Caledonian International Book Manufacturing Ltd, Glasgow

This is Ares Launch Control, Jacqueline B. Kennedy Space Center.

We have passed the six-minute mark in our countdown. Now at T minus five minutes, fifty-one seconds and counting.

Ares waits ready for launch on Launch Complex 39A.

We are on schedule at the present time for the planned lift-off at thirty-seven minutes past the hour.

Spacecraft test conductor has now completed the status check of his personnel in the control room. All report that they are go for the mission and this has been reported to the test supervisor.

The test supervisor is now going through some more status checks.

Launch operations manager reports go for launch.

Mission Control at Houston reports that all systems on the Ares orbital booster cluster are also nominal and ready to support the mission. The need to be in plane with the cluster, to enable the docking, is imposing a tight window on today's launch.

Launch director now gives the go. We are at T minus four minutes, fifty seconds and counting.

At launch time, you may wish to look out for flights of pelicans, egrets and herons, from the marshy land here on Merritt Island. Forty years ago Merritt pretty much belonged to the birds, and they're still here, although nowadays they're disturbed every few months by a new launching.

It has taken nine Saturn VB launches so far to put the Ares complex into orbit. Today's will be the tenth. So nesting isn't so good any more.

T minus four minutes and counting. As a preparation for main engine ignition, the fuel valve heaters have been turned on. T minus three minutes fifty-four seconds and counting. The final fuel purge on the main engines has been started. That's the vapor you can see there, billowing across the launch pad, away from the Saturn booster.

The liquid oxygen replenish system has been turned off, so we can pressurize the tanks for the launch.

The wind is below ten knots, and we have a thin cloud layer. That's pretty nearly perfect launch weather, well within mission rules.

1

It is typically hot, humid Florida weather here, on this historic day, Thursday March 21, 1985.

T minus three minutes forty seconds and counting.

I am told that there are an estimated one million here with us today, the largest turnout for a launch since Apollo 11. Welcome to all of you. You might like to know that among the celebrities watching the launch today in the VIP enclosure are Apollo 11 astronauts Neil Armstrong, Joe Muldoon and Michael Collins, cosmonaut Vladimir Viktorenko, along with Liza Minnelli, Clint Eastwood, Steven Spielberg, George Lucas, William Shatner, sci fi authors Arthur C. Clarke, Ray Bradbury and Isaac Asimov, and singer John Denver. We're sure you aren't going to be disappointed.

T minus three minutes twenty seconds and counting. Ares is now on internal power.

Coming up on T minus three minutes.

T minus three minutes and counting.

The engine gimbal check is underway, to ensure that the engines are moving freely, ready for flight control.

T minus two minutes fifty-two seconds. The liquid oxygen valves on both stages have been closed and pressurization of fuel and oxidizer tanks has begun.

T minus two minutes twenty-five seconds and counting. The liquid oxygen tanks are now at flight pressure.

Coming up on two minutes away from launch.

T minus two minutes mark, and counting. Two minutes from launch.

The liquid hydrogen vent valves have been closed and the hydrogen tanks' flight pressurization is underway.

T minus one minute fifty seconds and counting. No holds so far.

Capcom John Young has just said, 'Smooth ride, baby,' to astronauts Phil Stone, Ralph Gershon and Natalie York. Mission Commander Stone has replied, 'Thank you very much, we know it will be a good flight.'

T minus one minute thirty-five seconds and counting.

T minus one minute ten seconds and counting. All liquid hydrogen tanks are at flight pressure.

T minus one minute, mark, and counting.

The firing system for the sound suppression water system will be armed just a couple of seconds from now.

The firing system has now been armed.

T minus forty-five seconds and counting.

T minus forty seconds and counting. The development flight

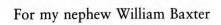

For my nephew William Baxter

AUTHOR'S NOTE

In 1996, evidence of life on Mars has ignited interest in manned missions to the red planet, but such missions are many years, perhaps decades away. But NASA could have sent astronauts to Mars as long ago as 1986.

Voyage depicts an alternate history: a timeline identical to our own up to a crucial moment in the autumn of 1963, and diverging thereafter.

This novel is a work of fiction. Because of the nature of the plot certain real people associated with the US manned space program are referred to in the story by their real names. For the purposes of weaving my story into the fabric of our own history I have replaced some historical personages with fictional characters. In particular, the second American to orbit Earth was Scott Carpenter, not Chuck Jones as portrayed in the novel; and the second man to walk on the Moon was Buzz Aldrin, not Joe Muldoon as portrayed here. All other characters are fictional constructs, in which case any resemblance to any real individual is wholly unintentional and coincidental.

I would like to acknowledge the invaluable help of Simon Bradshaw, Eric Brown and Calvin Johnson, all of whom read and commented on versions of the manuscript; and the staff at NASA's Johnson Space Center, Houston, who were extremely generous of their time and energy in support of my research for this book, particularly Eileen Hawley, Paul Dye, Frank Hughes, astronaut Michael Foale, and especially Kent Joosten of JSC's Solar System Exploration Division who scrutinized my Mars mission with great attention and care. The assistance of these friends has greatly improved the accuracy of my depiction, and any remaining errors and omissions are my responsibility.

In our history, Americans have not traveled to Mars. But in 1969 the US came as close as it ever has to assembling the will and resources for such a mission. Diagrams at the end of the book show how the mission might have been assembled. In an afterword, for interested readers, I have set out my understanding of the crucial historical points at which America turned away from Mars.

In 1996 we need scientists on Mars. They could have been there a decade ago. My novel may be the closest thing to a history of that lost, alternate universe ever to be written, and I have striven to make it as 'true' as possible.

It really would have been like this.

Stephen Baxter
Great Missenden
August 1996

instrumentation recorders are on. We are still go *with* Ares.

Astronaut Stone reports: 'It feels good.'

T *minus thirty seconds.*

We are just a few seconds away from switching on the redundant sequence. This is the automatic system for engine cut-off.

T minus twenty-seven seconds and counting.

We have gone for redundant sequence start.

T minus twenty seconds and counting. Sound suppression system fired. Solid Rocket Boosters armed.

T minus fifteen, fourteen, thirteen.

T minus ten, nine, eight.

Main engine start.

Book 1

DECISION

THE WHITE HOUSE
WASHINGTON

Thursday, February 13, 1969

MEMORANDUM for

The Vice President
The Secretary of Defense
The Acting Administrator, National Aeronautics
   and Space Administration
The Science Adviser

It is necessary for me to have in the near future a definitive recommendation on the direction which the US space program should take in the post-Apollo period. I, therefore, ask the Secretary of Defense, the Acting Administrator of NASA, and the Science Adviser each to develop proposed plans and to meet together as a Space Task Group, with the Vice President in the chair, to prepare for me a coordinated program and budget proposal. In developing your proposed plans, you may wish to seek advice from the scientific, engineering and industrial communities, from the Congress and the public.

   I would like to receive the coordinated proposal by September 1, 1969.

[signature]

Richard M. Nixon

Handwritten addendum: Spiro, do we have to go to Mars? What options have we got? RMN.

Public Papers of the Presidents of the United States: Richard M. Nixon, 1969 (Washington DC: Government Printing Office, 1969)

In their orange pressure suits, York, Gershon and Stone were jammed together so close they were rubbing elbows. They were enclosed from daylight; small fluorescent floods lit up the Command Module's cramped cabin.

There was a powerful thump. York, startled, glanced at her crewmates.

'Fuel pumps,' Stone said.

Now York heard a dull rumbling – like faraway thunder – a shudder that transmitted itself through the padded couch to her body.

Hundreds of feet below York, liquid oxygen and hydrogen were rushing together, mingling in the big first stage engines' combustion chambers.

She could feel her heartbeat rising, clattering within her chest. *Take it easy, damn it.*

A small metal model of a cosmonaut, squat and Asiatic, dangled from a chain fixed above her head. This was Boris, the gift from Vlad Viktorenko. The toy swung back and forth, its grotesque features leering at her out of a sketch of a helmet. *Good luck, Bah-reess.*

The noise began, cacophonous, a steady roar. It was like being inside the mouth of some huge, bellowing giant.

Phil Stone shouted, 'All five at nominal. Stand by for the stretch.'

The five liquid rocket engines of the Saturn VB booster's first stage, the MS-IC, had ignited a full eight seconds ahead of the enhanced Saturn's four Solid Rocket Boosters. And now came the 'stretch,' as the stack reached up under the pressure of that immense thrust. She could *feel* the ship pushing upwards, hear the groan of strained metal as the joints of the segmented solid boosters flexed.

It was all supposed to happen this way. But still . . . *Jesus. What a design.*

Stone said, 'Three, two. SRB ignition.'

Now they were committed. The solid boosters were big fire-crackers; once the SRBs were ignited, nothing could stop them until they burned out.

'Clock is running –'

Zero.

There was a jolt: mild, easy. The explosive pins holding down the boosters had snapped.

Nothing as heavy as a Saturn VB was going to leap into the air.

The cabin started to shake, the couch restraints and fittings rattling.

'Climbout,' Stone said evenly. 'Here we go.'

Ralph Gershon whooped. 'Rager! Going full bore!'

Liftoff. Good God. I'm off the ground.

She felt excitement surge in her; the grainy reality of the motion pressed in on her. '*Poyekhali!*' she shouted. *Let's go!* – the spontaneous cry of an excited Yuri Gagarin.

The lurching continued.

York was thrown against her harness, to the right; and then to the left, so that she jammed up against Gershon.

The Saturn VB was inching its way upwards past the launch tower, almost skittishly, its automated controls swiveling its five first stage engines to correct for wind shear. Right, left, forward, back, in a series of spasmodic jerks hard enough to bruise her.

No simulation had even hinted at this violence. It was like riding out of an explosion.

'Access arm,' Stone called. 'Clear of the tower.'

John Young, Houston capcom for the launch, came on line.

'Ares, Houston. Copy. You are clear of the tower.'

York felt a lurch forwards. The whole stack had pitched over; she was sitting up in her couch now, the huge rattling thrust of the first stage pushing at her back.

'Houston, we have a good roll program,' Stone said.

'Roger the roll.'

The Saturn was arcing over the Florida coast, toward the Atlantic.

Down there on the beaches, she knew, children had written huge good luck messages into the Florida sand. GODSPEED ARES. York looked up and to her right, toward the tiny square window there. But there was nothing to see. They were cocooned; the boost protective cover, a solid cone, lay over the Command Module.

The Command Module's interior was the size of a small car. It was small, dingy, mechanical, metallic. Very 1960s, York thought. The walls, painted gray and yellow, were studded with gauges, dials, control switches and circuit breakers. There were scraps of notes, from the crew to themselves, and emergency checklists, and hundreds of tiny round-cornered squares of blue Velcro stuck to the walls.

The three crew couches were just metal frames with canvas supports. York lay on her back, in the Command Module's right hand seat. Stone, as commander, was in the left hand seat; Ralph Gershon

9

was in the center couch. The main hatch, behind Gershon's head, had big chunky levers on its inside, like a submarine's hatch.

'Ares, Houston. You're right smack dab on the trajectory.'

'Roger, John,' Stone said. 'This baby is really going.'

'Roger that.'

'Go, you mother,' Gershon shouted. 'Shit hot!' York could hear his voice shaking with the oscillation.

'Ten thousand and Mach point five,' Young said.

Mach point five. Less than thirty seconds into the mission, and I'm already hitting half the speed of sound.

John Young didn't sound scared, or nervous. Just another day at the office, for him.

John had ridden around the Moon in Apollo 10, back in 1969; and if the later Apollos hadn't been canned, he probably would have commanded a mission to the lunar surface.

In fact, if he hadn't been so critical of NASA following Apollo-N, Young might have been sitting in here himself.

The vibration worsened. Her head rattled in her helmet, like a seed in a gourd. The whole cabin was shaking, and she couldn't focus on the oscillating banks of instruments in front of her.

'Mach point nine,' Stone said. 'Forty seconds. Mach one. Going through nineteen thousand.'

'Ares, you are go at forty.'

Abruptly the ride smoothed out; it was like passing onto a smoother road surface. Even the engine noise was gone; they were moving so fast they were leaving their own sound behind.

'Ares, you're looking good.'

'Rog,' Stone said. 'Okay, we're throttling down.'

The engines cut down to ease the stack through max-q, the point when air density and the boosters' velocity combined to exert maximum stress on the airframe.

'You are go at throttle up.'

'Roger. Go at throttle up.'

The pressure on York's chest seemed to be growing; it was becoming more difficult to breathe, as her lungs labored against the thrust of the stack.

Stone said, 'Thirty-five thousand feet. Going through one point nine Mach. SRB combustion chamber pressure down to fifty pounds per square inch.'

'Copy,' John Young said from the ground. 'You are go for SRB separation.'

'Rog.'

She heard a faint, muffled bang; the cabin shuddered, rattling her against her restraints. Separation squibs had fired, pushing the exhausted solid boosters away from the main stack. She felt a dip in the thrust; but then the acceleration of the MS-IC's central liquid boosters picked up again, and she was pressed back into her seat.

'Roger on the sep,' Young said.

'Smooth as glass, John.'

The solid boosters would be falling away like matchsticks, dribbling smoke and flames. The strap-on solid boosters were the most visible enhancement of the VB over the core Saturn V design; with their help the VB was capable of carrying twice the payload of the V to Earth orbit.

'Five thousand one hundred feet per second,' Stone said. 'Thirty-three miles down range.'

She glanced at the G-meter. Three times the force of gravity. It wasn't comfortable, but she had endured a lot worse in the centrifuge.

Cool air played inside her helmet, bringing with it the smell of metal and plastic.

With the SRBs gone, the ride was a lot easier. Liquid motors were fundamentally smoother burners than solids. She could hear the mounting, steady roar of the MS-IC's engines, the continuing purring of the Command Module's equipment.

Everything was smooth, ticking, regular. Right now, inside the cosy little cabin, it was like being inside a huge sewing machine. Whir, purr. Save for the press of the acceleration it was unreal: as if this was, after all, just another sim.

'Three minutes,' Stone said. 'Altitude forty-three miles, down-range seventy miles.'

'Coming up on staging,' Gershon said. 'Stand by for the train wreck.'

Right on schedule the first stage engines shut down.

The acceleration vanished.

It was as if they were sitting in a catapult. She was thrown forward, toward the instrument panel, and slammed up against her restraints. The canvas straps hauled her back into her seat, and then she was shoved forward again.

The first stage engines had compressed the whole stack like an accordion; when the engines cut, the accordion just stretched out and rebounded. It was incredibly violent.

Just like a train wreck, in fact. *Another thing they didn't tell me about in the sims.*

She heard the clatter of explosive bolts, blowing away the dying MS-IC. And now there were more bangs, thumps in her back transmitted through her couch: small ullage rockets, firing to settle the liquid oxygen and hydrogen in the huge second stage tanks.

Vibration returned as the second stage engines ignited, and she was shoved back into her seat.

There was a loud bang over her head, startling her, as if someone was hammering on the skin of the Command Module. Flame and smoke flared beyond her window.

'Tower,' Stone reported.

'Roger, tower.'

The emergency escape rocket had blown itself away, taking the conical cap over the Command Module with it. Daylight, startlingly brilliant, streamed into the cabin, lapping over their orange pressure suits, dimming the instruments.

York peered through her window. There was a darkening blue sky above, a vivid bright segment of clouds and wrinkled ocean below.

Stone said dryly, 'Ah, Houston, we advise the visual is go today.'

There was a lot of debris coming past York's exposed window now, from the jettisoned escape tower and the MS-IC. It looked like confetti, floating away from the vehicle, turning and sparkling in the sun.

Young said: 'Press for engine cutoff.'

'Rog,' Stone said. 'Press to ECO.'

Whatever else happened now, Ares was to continue on, up to cutoff of the MS-II's main engines. On to orbit.

'Ares, you are go at five plus thirty, with ECO eight plus thirty-four.'

Ares had reached Mach 15, at an altitude of eighty miles. And still the engines burned; still they climbed upwards. Earth's gravity well was *deep*.

'Eight minutes. Ares, Houston, you are go at eight.'

'Looking good,' Stone said.

The residual engine noise and vibration died, suddenly. The recoil was powerful. York was thrown forward again, and bounced back in her canvas restraints.

'ECO!' Stone called.

Engine cutoff; the MS-II stage was spent.

. . . And this time, the weight didn't come back. It was like taking a fast car over a bump in the road, and never coming back down again.

12

'Standing by for MS-II sep.'

There was another muffled bang, a soft jolt.

John Young said, 'Roger, we confirm the sep, Ares.'

'Uh, we are one zero one point four by one zero three point six.'

'Roger, we copy, one zero one point four by one zero three point six . . .'

The parameters of an almost perfect circular orbit about the Earth, a hundred miles high.

Phil Stone's voice was as level as Young's. *Just another day at the office.* But now, the stack he commanded was moving at five miles per second.

York gazed at the glistening curvature of Earth, the crumpled skin of ocean, the clouds layered on like whipped cream.

I'm in orbit. My God. She felt a huge relief that she was still alive, that she had survived that immense expenditure of energy.

Above her head, the little cosmonaut was floating, his chain slack and coiling up.

Sunday, July 20, 1969
Tranquillity Base

Joe Muldoon peered through the Lunar Module's triangular window.

Muldoon was fascinated by the play of light and color on the lunar surface. If he looked straight ahead, to the west, away from the rising sun, the flat landscape reflected back the light in a shimmering golden brown sheen. But to either side there was a softer tan. And if he leaned forward to look off to the side, away from the line of the sun, the surface looked a dull ash gray, as if he was looking through a polarizing filter.

Even the light here wasn't Earth-like.

Outside, Armstrong was moving about with what looked like ease, bouncing across the beach-like lunar surface like a balloon. His white suit gleamed in the sunlight, the brightest object on the surface of the Moon, but his lower legs and light blue overshoes were already stained dark gray by dust. Muldoon couldn't see Armstrong's face, behind his reflective golden sun-visor.

He checked the time. It was fourteen minutes after the commander's egress.

13

'Neil, are you ready for me to come out?'

Armstrong called back. 'Yes. Just stand by a second. First let me move the LEC over the edge for you.'

Armstrong floated about the LM, pushing aside the LEC, the crude rope-and-pulley Lunar Equipment Conveyor which Muldoon had been using to pass equipment down to his commander on the surface.

Muldoon turned around in the evacuated cabin and got to his knees. He crawled backwards, out through the LM's small hatch, and over the porch, the platform which bridged to the egress ladder fixed to the LM's front leg. The pressurized suit seemed to resist every movement, as if he were enclosed in a form-fitting balloon; he even had trouble closing his gloved fingers around the porch's handles.

Armstrong guided him out. 'Okay, you saw what difficulties I was having. I'll try to watch your PLSS from underneath here. Your PLSS looks like it's clearing okay. The shoes are about to come over the sill . . . Okay, now drop your PLSS down. There you go, you're clear and spidery, you're good. About an inch of clearance on top of your PLSS.'

When he got to the ladder's top rung, Muldoon took hold of the handrails and pulled himself upright. He could see the small TV camera, sitting on its stowage tray hinged out from the LM, which Armstrong had deployed to film his own egress. The camera watched him silently. He said, 'Now I want to back up and partially close the hatch. Making sure I haven't left the key in the ignition, and the handbrake is on . . .'

'A particularly good thought.'

'We'd walk far to find a rental car around here.'

He was ten feet or so above the lunar surface, with the gaunt planes of the LM's ascent stage before him, the spider-like descent stage below. 'Okay, I'm on the top step and I can look down over the pads. It's a simple matter to hop down from one step to the next.'

'Yeah,' Armstrong said. 'I found it to be very comfortable, and walking is also very comfortable. Joe, you've got three more rungs and then a long one.'

'I'm going to leave one foot up there and move both hands down to the fourth rung up . . .'

It was routine, like a sim in the Peter Pan rig back at MSC. He didn't find it hard to report his progress down the ladder to Houston.

But once he was standing on *Eagle*'s footpad, he found words fleeing from him.

Morning on the Moon:

Holding onto the ladder, Muldoon turned slowly. His suit was a warm, comforting bubble around him; he heard the hum of pumps and fans in the PLSS – his backpack, the Portable Life Support System – and he felt the soft breeze of oxygen across his face.

The LM was standing on a broad, level plain. There were craters everywhere, ranging from several yards to a thumbnail width, the low sunlight deepening their shadows. There were even tiny micrometeorite craters, zap pits, punched in the sides of the rocks littering the surface.

There were rocks and boulders scattered about, and ridges that might have been twenty feet high – but it was hard to judge distance, because there were no plants, no buildings, no people to give him any sense of scale: it was more barren than the high desert of the Mojave, with not even the haze of an atmosphere, so that rocks at the horizon were just as sharp as those near his feet.

Muldoon was overwhelmed. The sims – even his previous spaceflight in Earth orbit on Gemini – hadn't prepared him for the strangeness of this place, the jewel-like clarity about the airless view, with its sharp contrast between the darkness of the sky and the lunar plain beneath, jumbled with rocks and craters.

Holding the ladder with both hands, Muldoon swung his feet off the pad and onto the Moon.

It was like walking on snow.

There was a firm footing beneath a soft, resilient layer a few inches thick. Every time he took a step a little spray of dust particles sailed off along perfect parabolae, like tiny golf balls. He understood how this had implications for the geology: no atmospheric winnowing here, no gravitational sorting.

In some of the smaller zap craters he saw small, shining fragments, with a metallic sheen. Like bits of mercury on a bench. And here and there he saw transparent crystals lying on the surface, like fragments of glass. He wished he had a sample collector. He would have to remember to come back for these glass beads, during the documented sampling later.

His footprints were miraculously sharp, as if he'd placed his

15

ridged overshoes in fine, damp sand. He took a photograph of one particularly well-defined print; it would persist here for millions of years, he realized, like the fossilized footprint of a dinosaur, to be eroded away only by the slow rain of micrometeorites, that echo of the titanic bombardments of the deep past.

Muldoon's job now was to check his balance and stability. He did turns and leaps like a dancer. The pull of this little world was so gentle that he couldn't tell when he stood upright, and the inertia of the PLSS at his back was a disconcerting drag at his changes of motion.

'. . . Very powdery surface,' he reported back to Houston. 'My boot tends to slide over it easily . . . You have to be careful about where your center of mass is. It takes two or three paces to bring you to a smooth stop. And to change direction you have to step out to the side and cut back a little bit. Like a football player. Moving your arms around doesn't lift your feet off the surface. We're not quite that light-footed . . .'

There was a pressure in his kidneys. He stood still and let go, into the urine collection condom; it was like wetting his pants. *Well, Neil might have been the first man to walk on the Moon. But I'm the first to take a leak here.*

He looked up. A star was climbing out of the eastern sky, unblinking, hauling its way toward the zenith, directly over his head. It was Apollo, waiting in orbit to take him home.

Armstrong peeled away silver plastic and read out the inscription on the plaque on the LM's front leg. 'First, there's the two hemispheres of the Earth. Underneath it says, "Here Man from the planet Earth first set foot upon the Moon, July 1969 A.D. We came in peace for all mankind." It has the crew members' signatures and the signature of the President of the United States.'

They unfurled the Stars and Stripes. The flag had been stiffened with wire so it would fly here, without any wind.

The two of them tried to plant the pole in the dust. But as hard as they pushed, the flagpole would only go six or eight inches into the ground, and Muldoon worried that the flag would fall over in front of the huge TV audience.

At last they got the pole steady, and backed away.

Muldoon set off on some more locomotion experiments.

He tried a slow-motion jog. His steps took him so high that time seemed to slow during each step. On Earth he would descend sixteen feet in the first second of a fall; here, he would fall only two. So he was suspended in each mid-stride, waiting to come down.

He started to evolve a better way of moving. He bent, and rocked from side to side as he ran. It was more of a lope than a run: push with one foot, shift your weight, land on the other.

He was breathing hard; he heard the hiss of water through the suit's cooling system, the pipes that curled around his limbs and chest.

He felt buoyant, young. A line from an old novel floated into his mind: *We are out of Mother Earth's leading-strings now . . .*

The capcom's voice startled him.

'Tranquillity Base, this is Houston. Could we get both of you on the camera for a minute please?'

Muldoon stumbled to a halt.

Armstrong had been erecting a panel of aluminum foil that he unrolled from a tube; the experiment was designed to trap particles emanating from the sun. 'Say again, Houston.'

'Rog. We'd like to get both of you in the field of view of the camera for a minute. Neil and Joe, the President of the United States is in his office now and would like to say a few words to you.'

The President? Goddamn it, I bet Neil knew about this.

He heard Armstrong say formally: 'That would be an honor.'

'Go ahead, Mr President. This is Houston. Over.'

Muldoon floated over to Armstrong and faced the TV camera.

Hello, Neil and Joe. I'm talking to you by telephone from the Oval Room at the White House. And this certainly has to be the most historic phone call ever made. I just can't tell you how proud we all are of what you have achieved. For every American, this has to be the proudest moment of our lives, and for all people all over the world, I am sure they too join with Americans in recognizing what a feat this is. Because of what you have done, the heavens have become part of man's world . . .

What Muldoon mostly felt as Nixon rambled on was impatience. He and Armstrong had little enough time here as it was – no more than two and a half hours for their single moonwalk – and every second had been choreographed, in the endless sims back in Houston, and detailed in the little spiral-bound checklists fixed to their cuffs. Nixon's speech hadn't been rehearsed in the simulations, though, and Muldoon felt a mounting anxiety as he thought ahead over the tasks they still had to complete. They would have to skip something. He could see them returning to Earth with fewer samples than had been anticipated, and maybe they would have to skip documenting them, and just grab what they could . . . The scientists wouldn't be pleased.

He would like to have got a sample of one of those glittering fragments in the crater bottoms, or one of the crystals. There just wouldn't be time.

Muldoon didn't really care about the science, if truth be told. But he felt a gnawing anxiety about completing the checklist. Getting through your checklist was the way to get on another flight.

With these thoughts, some of the lightness he'd enjoyed earlier began to dissipate.

. . . For one priceless moment, in the whole history of man, all the people on this Earth are one. One in their pride in what you have done, and one in our prayers that you will return safely to Earth.

Armstrong responded: 'Thank you, sir. It's a great honor and privilege for us to be here, representing not only the United States but men of peace of all nations – and with interest and curiosity, and men with a vision for the future.'

And thank you very much. Now I want to pass you on briefly to a special guest I have here with me in the Oval Office today.

Muldoon thought, *A guest? My God. Has he any idea of how much this call is costing?*

And then familiar tones – that oddly clipped Bostonian accent – sounded in his headset, and Muldoon felt a response rising within him, a thrill deep and atavistic.

Hello, gentlemen. How are you today? I won't take up your precious time on the Moon. I just want to quote to you what I said to Congress, on May 25, 1961 – just eight short years ago . . .

'Now is the time to take longer strides – time for a great new American enterprise – time for this nation to take on a clearly leading role in space achievement, which in many ways may hold the key to our future on Earth.

'I believe this nation should commit itself to achieving the goal, before this decade is out, of landing a man on the Moon and returning him safely to Earth. No single space project in this period will be more impressive to mankind, or more important for the long-range exploration of space; and none will be so difficult or expensive to accomplish . . .'

My God, Muldoon thought. *Nixon hates Kennedy; everyone knows that.* Muldoon wondered what calculations – PR, political, even geopolitical – lay behind Nixon letting old JFK back into the limelight now, today of all days.

18

It was hard to concentrate on Kennedy's words.

Fifty feet from him the LM looked like a gaunt spider, twenty feet tall, resting there in the glaring sunlight. The *Eagle* was complex and delicate, a filmy construct of gold leaf and aluminum, the symmetry of the ascent stage spoiled by the bulbous fuel tank to the right. The craft bristled with antennae, docking targets, and reaction control thruster assemblies. He saw how dust had splashed up over the skirt of the descent stage's engine, and the gold leaf which coated it. In the sunlight the LM looked fragile. And so it was, he knew, just a taut bubble of aluminum, shaved to the minimum weight by Grumman engineers. But here, on this small, static, delicate world, the LM didn't seem at all out of place.

I want to tell you now how nervous I was that day, gentlemen. I wasn't sure if I was right to ask that august body for such huge sums of money, indeed for a transformation of our national economy. But now that goal is accomplished, thanks to the courage of you, Neil and Joe, and so many of your colleagues, and the dedication of many skilled people all across our great county, in NASA and its contractor allies . . . Muldoon glanced uneasily at the mute TV camera on its tripod. *He said 'the goal is accomplished.'* He knew that on a hot July evening in Houston it was around ten forty. He wondered how many moonwalk parties would already be breaking up.

Maybe it really was just about footprints and flags after all.

But, back in Clear Lake, Jill would still be watching – wouldn't she?

. . . Apollo has energized the American spirit, after a difficult decade at home and abroad. Now that we have reached the Moon, I believe we must not let our collective will dissipate. I believe we must look further. Here, at this moment of Apollo's triumph, I would like to set my country a new challenge: to go further and farther than most of us have dreamed – to continue the building of our great ships, and to fly them onwards to Mars.

Mars?

The clipped voice was an insect whisper in his headset, remote and meaningless.

Maybe it was true what they whispered: that the bullets Kennedy had survived in Texas six years ago had damaged more than his body . . .

Standing silently, he saw now that the land *curved*, gently but noticeably, all the way to the horizon, and in every direction from him. It was a little like standing at the summit of a huge, gentle hill. He could actually see that he and Armstrong were two people standing on a ball floating in space. It was vertiginous, a kind of science-fiction feeling, something he'd never experienced on Earth.

... This will certainly be the most arduous journey since the great explorers set sail to map our own planet over three centuries ago: it is a journey which will take a new generation of heroes to a place so far away that the Earth itself will be diminished to a point of light, indistinguishable from the stars themselves ... We will go to Mars because it is the most likely abode of life beyond our Earth. And we will make that world into a second Earth, and so secure the survival of humankind as a species for the indefinite future ...

The Earth, floating above him, was huge, a ball, blue and complex; it was much more obviously a three-dimensional world than the Moon ever looked from home. He was aware of the sun, fat and low, its light slanting across this desolate place. Suddenly he got a sense of perspective of the distance he'd traveled, to come here: so far that the trinity of lights that had always dominated human awareness – Earth, Moon and sun – had moved around him in a complex dance, to these new relative positions in his sensorium.

And yet his sense of detachment was all but gone. He was as locked to Earth as if this was all just another sim at JSC. *I guess you don't throw off four billion years of evolution in a week.*

He found himself wondering about his own future.

All his life, someone – some outside agency – had directed him toward *goals.* It had started with his father, and later – *what a place to remember such a thing!* – summer camp, where winning teams got turkey, and losers got beans. Then there had been the Academy, and the Air Force, and NASA ...

He'd always been driven by a strong sense of purpose, a purpose that had brought him far – all the way to the Moon itself.

But now, his greatest goal was achieved.

He remembered how his mood had taken a dip, after returning from his Gemini flight. How tough was this new return going to be for him?

Kennedy had finished speaking. There was a silence that stretched awkwardly; Muldoon wondered if he should say something.

Armstrong said, 'We're honored to talk to you, sir.'

Thank you very much. I'm grateful to President Nixon for his hospitality toward me today, and I'll ask him to pass on my very best regards when he sees you on the Hornet *on Thursday.*

Muldoon steeled himself to speak. 'I look forward to that very much, sir.'

Then, following Armstrong's lead, he raised his gloved hand in salute, and turned away from the camera.

He felt perplexed, troubled. It was as if Earth, above, was working on him already, its huge gravity pushing down on him.

He would have to find a new goal, that was all.

What, he mused, if Kennedy's fantastic Mars vision came to reality? Now, that would be a project to work on.

Maybe he could join that new program. Maybe he could be the first man to walk on three worlds. That would be one hell of a goal to work toward: fifteen, twenty more years of direction, of shape to his life . . .

But to do that, he knew, he'd have to get out from under all the PR hoopla that was going to follow the splashdown.

For him, he suspected, returning to Earth was going to be harder than journeying to the Moon ever was.

He loped away from the TV camera, back toward the glittering, toy-like LM.

Saturday, October 4, 1969
Nuclear Rocket Development Station, Jackass Flats, Nevada

A smell of burning came on the breeze off the desert, and mixed with the test rig's faint stench of oil and paint. The scents were unearthly, as if York had been transported away from Nevada.

I read somewhere that moondust smells like this, she thought. *Of burning, of ash, an autumn scent.*

In 1969, Natalie York was twenty-one years old.

In Ben Priest's Corvette they'd made the ninety-mile journey from Vegas to Jackass Flats in under an hour.

At the Flats, Mike Conlig was there to meet them and wave them through security. This late in the evening, the site was deserted save for a handful of security guys. When the three of them – York, Priest, and Petey, Priest's son – climbed out of Ben's Corvette, York noticed how the car was coated with dust, and popped as it cooled.

Nevada was huge, empty, its topography complex and folded, cupped by misshapen hills. The sun was hanging over the western horizon, fat and red, and the day's heat was leaching quickly out of the air. The ground was all but barren. York recognized salt-resistant shadscale and creosote bushes clinging here and there, and the occasional pocket of sagebrush. *Good place to test out a nuclear rocket,* York thought. *But – my God – what soul-crushing desolation.*

In bursts of quick jargon, Mike and Ben started discussing some aspect of the test results they'd been reviewing that day. If York had learned one skill in too many hours in college bars and common rooms – she was finishing up her own BS in geology at UCLA – it was how to tune out someone else's specialty. So she let Mike and Ben talk themselves out, and walked a little way away from them.

Ben Priest's son Petey, at ten, was a lanky framework of muscle and energy; he ran ahead of the others, his blond hair a shining flag in the last of the daylight.

The test site was laid out as a rectangle confined by roads, to the south, and rail tracks, to the north. They were walking out west – away from the control buildings where the car was parked – toward the static test site, Engine Test Facility One.

This test station was cupped in an immense dip in the land delimited by two great fault blocks: the Colorado Plateau and Wasatch Range to the east, the Sierra Nevada range to the west. The station – with its isolated test stands and bits of rail track and handful of shabby tar-paper shacks – looked overwhelmed by the echoing geology of the desert, reduced to something shabby, trivial.

They reached the test facility. The assembly was maybe thirty feet high, its geometry crude, complex and mysterious. York made out a sleek, upright cylindrical form enclosed by a gantry, a boxy thing of girders. The stack was scuffed, patchy, unpainted. The whole thing was mounted on a flatwagon on the rail track, hooked up to a rudimentary locomotive. Big pipes ran out of the rig and off to other parts of the test station; in the distance she saw the gleam of spherical cryogenic tanks: liquid hydrogen, she guessed.

Petey Priest had his face pressed to the fence around the test facility, so that the wire mesh made patterned indentations on his face; he stared at the rig, evidently captivated.

York watched Conlig and Priest together.

Mike Conlig was a native Texan. At twenty-seven he was a little shorter than York; his build was stocky, his engineer's hands callused and scarred, and his jet-black hair, which he wore tied back in a pony-tail, showed his Irish extraction. Just now, a slight paunch was pushing out his T-shirt.

York had met Mike half a year ago, at a party at Ricketts House at Caltech, which was a half-hour drive from UCLA. York had gone out there on a kind of dare; women weren't admitted to Caltech. Natalie enjoyed his fast, lively mind, his genuine readiness to respect her for her intellect . . . and the compact muscles of his body.

She'd finished up in bed with Mike within a couple of hours.

Mike was quite a contrast to Ben Priest, she thought, looking at them together.

At thirty-one, Ben Priest was tall, wiry, and with an ear-to-ear, kindly grin. He was a Navy aviator with a dozen years' experience, including two at the Navy's prime flight test center at Patuxent River, Maryland – and, since 1965, he'd been a NASA astronaut, although he hadn't yet flown in space.

York knew Mike and Ben had struck up a close relationship since Ben's assignment here as astronaut representative on the project. She'd no doubt Mike was throwing himself into the camaraderie of the station here – guys together in their prefabricated shacks, at the frontier of technology, playing with NERVA all day, and knocking back a few each evening.

It was having a visible physical effect on Mike, she thought, if not on Ben . . .

Security lights were coming on all over the nuclear test rig now; they made it into a sculpture of shadows and glimmering reflections, an angular, deformed representation of a true spacecraft. As if the ambitions driving the men and women who worked here had actually shaped the geometry of the place, making it into something not quite of the Earth.

While he was talking to Priest about the day's events, Mike Conlig tried to keep a hawkeye on Natalie. She was gazing around the plant. Natalie was a little too tall, slim, intense, her hair jet-black and tied back; right now, those big Romanian-peasant eyebrows she hated so much were creased in concentration.

This visit was important to Conlig.

Strictly speaking, he and Priest were breaking NASA and AEC regs by bringing her here, to see their work close up; and certainly a kid like Petey shouldn't be allowed here. But regulations got replaced by realism in a place as remote as this. *We're all good old boys together out here*, he thought.

Anyhow, he was keen to show Natalie this place: where he worked, what he did with his life. It was worth breaking a few rules to achieve that. He wanted Natalie to see Jackass Flats through his eyes.

Natalie's head was habitually full of suspicion and disapproval of Big Government Science like this. But the world looked different to Conlig. To him, this shabby test site was the gateway to the future: to other worlds, colonies on the Moon.

Even Mars itself.

Ben Priest was trying to explain the test rig to Natalie. He made her look more closely at the object inside the gantry, trying to get her to make sense of it. A nozzle, gracefully shaped, flared from the top toward the sky . . .

'Oh,' she said. 'I've got it. It's a *rocket*. There's the nozzle, at the top of the stack. It's a rocket, on its launch gantry. Gee. Just like Cape Kennedy.'

Ben Priest laughed. 'Except it's upside down.'

'One day we'll see this at Kennedy,' Conlig said, aware he sounded a little defensive. 'One day soon. Its descendants, anyhow; this poor bird is never going to fly.'

'This is actually a late generation engine,' Ben said. 'Our newest pride and joy. The XE-Prime: quite close to a flight configuration. The first rigs here, ten years ago, were called Kiwis.'

'Oh,' York said. 'Flightless birds.'

'Now,' said Ben, 'there are a string of projects working under the generic title NERVA. For "Nuclear Engine –"'

'"– for Rocket Vehicle Application." I know.'

'But we're still restricted to building flightless birds,' Priest mused. 'We're proud of this baby, Natalie. We've managed to get close to fifty thousand pounds of thrust with her. And we managed *twenty-eight* restarts. Reliability is going to be a key factor in long-haul space travel . . .'

Conlig watched Natalie, trying to gauge her reaction.

All of six years older than Natalie, Conlig had finished his PhD – on exotic, heat-tolerant refractory materials for lightweight fission reactors – in a near-record time.

Conlig was certain – so was Natalie, come to that – that he was heading for the top of his chosen profession. And since, if Spiro Agnew could be believed, nuclear rockets were going to be the Next Big Thing in space, that top could be a very high summit indeed. Meanwhile, York's geology was likely to take her away for months at a time. Their relationship was going to be odd, to say the least.

It was odd to know that his whole life might be shaped by the

24

success, or failure, of a nuclear rocket. *I really am living in the future*, he thought.

To Conlig, nuclear rockets were the simplest, most beautiful machines in the world. You didn't burn anything, like in a Saturn. You just heated up high-pressure liquid hydrogen in a reactor core, and let hot gas squirt out of the rear of your ship.

A nuclear upper stage would uprate a Saturn V by a factor of two: Moon payloads could be increased by more than half.

But there were major technical challenges.

The working fluid was liquid hydrogen at twenty-five degrees above absolute zero. Once it was pumped to the reactor the hydrogen had to be flashed to above two thousand degrees.

Cooling systems were Mike Conlig's specialty.

There were other difficulties. Like, if you were looking at space applications, there was the need to shield the crew from radiation. And the fact that you couldn't cluster too many of these babies in a given stack, because their neutron emissions interfere with each other, and, and . . .

Still, the project was making progress. In the short term they were aiming for a RIFT, a Reactor-in-Flight Test. But there was a hell of a lot of work to do before then. You couldn't cut corners with nuclear technology: nobody wanted a live nuclear pile to be smeared over Florida thanks to some fuck-up at Kennedy.

But, Conlig thought, they'd fly one day. They had problems to solve. But they'd solve them. Just as soon as Nixon gave his go-ahead to the Space Task Group's proposals.

The Space Task Group was a committee, headed by Vice President Agnew, which Nixon had set up to formulate post-Apollo goals for the space program. The STG had been due to report in September. The rumors were they'd endorsed a manned Mars landing program. When a manned Mars landing program happened, this project would get some serious money to spend.

Ben Priest was still talking Natalie through the details of the XE-Prime. They looked good together, Conlig thought suddenly. Relaxed. He felt a remote stab of unease.

But Natalie was giving Priest a hard time. She was talking about politics, as usual.

Natalie York laughed, uncomfortable; a shiver of awe – or maybe disgust – swept over her, as she studied the slim XE-Prime.

'You said there have been nuclear rocket developments here for ten years?'

'Yes,' Priest said.

'Why? We've not been considering Mars missions that long, have we?'

Priest scratched his ear. 'Well, the original objectives of the site didn't have much to do with spaceflight, Natalie. Back in the late 1950s, big chemical rockets were still a thing of the future. And the nuclear weapons were bulky, heavy –'

'Oh. They were building ICBMs here. *Nuclear* ICBMs.'

'Just engineering experiments,' Priest said evenly. 'In case of need. And remember, the USSR was well ahead of us then, with their big, heavy-lift chemical ICBMs. But our chemical rockets got bigger, and the bombs got lighter, and the need went away. Later NASA thought they might need the nukes for Apollo Moon missions. But then the Saturn rockets came along . . .'

'And now, we still need to build nuke rockets because we're going to Mars.'

'Hey, Ben,' Mike said now. 'Maybe you'll be the first man on Mars. In the nuclear rocket ship *Spiro Agnew*.'

Ben snorted. He cupped his hand over his mouth, and intoned Cronkite-style, 'And now we take you live to the aptly-named Jackass Flats, where the good ship *Agnew* is ready to lift Man In Space to his new destiny . . . over to you, Dan.'

'Thanks, Walter, and here as I stand under the painted sky of Nevada, I cannot but help recall . . .'

On they clowned, like two kids, laughing and bumping against each other. Petey came away from the fence, drawn by their laughter, and pulled at his father, punching his back playfully.

York, indulgently, let them walk ahead of her.

She looked around more carefully now, trying to figure the layout of the place. When the laughter had faded, she said to Priest, 'Tell me how they operate here.'

'Well, the rail track is the key to everything.' He pointed. 'The track runs out of that building, the Radioactive Material Storage Facility. The test articles aren't too radioactive, you know, until they've been fired. They are delivered on their flatwagon trucks to the test cells, and go through their firing. Afterwards they are taken to a dump over there, at the eastern end of the track.'

'Because they are too radioactive to recover?'

'Yeah.' Priest shrugged. 'Mike talks about restart capabilities, but it looks more likely now that an interplanetary ship is going to have a whole host of big NERVA rockets clustered together. After you've fired one, you'd dump it, to save the crew from the radioactivity. And you'd use them all up at Earth departure; you'd stick to chemical rockets for mid-course corrections.'

'Good grief. And this strikes you as a *rational* way to fly?'

He grinned at her, his teeth pale in the gathering darkness. 'If it's what it takes to get me to Mars, hell, yes.'

'Have they had any accidents here?'

'Sure. It's a development site. What do you expect?'

'What kind of accidents?'

'Ruptured cores. Ozone production in trapped air bubbles. Loss of moderator –'

'And injuries?'

'Ruptured ear drums. A few burns.' Priest looked uncomfortable. 'Natalie, what do you want me to tell you? The NRDS was born in a different age. You have to see things through the eyes of the times.'

'Oh, sure.' A different age. *But we're still using this hideous place now. And Mike works here, for God's sake.* She shivered, as if she could feel old Cold War radioactive particles sleeting through her flesh.

She looked around. 'How do they do their containment? When the test rockets fire. All that radioactive hydrogen, pluming into the air –'

Ben said, 'What containment?'

They all piled into Ben's Corvette and roared off down the Interstate toward Vegas, where they were going to spend the night, and Sunday. Petey quickly drifted off to sleep, his head lolling against the seat cushions.

Ben turned on the radio. A news program was broadcasting; York, sitting up in front with Ben, listened desultorily to dreary statistics from Vietnam.

Outside, light leaked from the sky, and hard starlight poked through the desert blue.

Ben leaned forward and turned up the volume. 'Hey, Mike, listen to this. It's Agnew.'

... the three options identified by our Space Task Group represent a balanced program ... a wide range of manned flights, unmanned planetary expeditions and applications satellites – serving people on Earth and increasing international cooperation in space ...

Wernher von Braun's cultured voice came on, testifying to the Senate. *I say let's do it quickly and establish a foothold on a new planet while we still have one left to take off from ...*

'So they are still talking about going to Mars,' York said.

'Sure they are,' Ben said. 'Agnew's three options are all about going to Mars; the only difference between them is, the more you spend per year, the faster you get there. Although –'

'What?'

'Although he did put in a fourth option, where we give up manned spaceflight altogether.' Priest stared at the road ahead. 'We're just going to have to see, I guess.'

'Agnew is an asshole,' York said mildly.

'Maybe, but he's an asshole who likes spaceships and astronauts,' Mike said, leaning forward from the back. 'And that makes him my kind of asshole.'

'Going to Mars is a beautiful idea,' York said. 'But it's science fiction. Isn't it?'

Mike squeezed her shoulder. 'You've seen the XE-Prime. We can build this bird. All we need is the money.'

'How much money?'

'It's not outrageous,' Ben said. 'Probably not as much as Apollo, in real terms. The whole program is going to be modular. A few basic components, used in different combinations for different missions. You'd have a Space Shuttle to get to orbit cheaply, a nuclear rocket for long-haul missions to the Moon and beyond, and cans – space station modules – you could assemble in different configurations. You'd put together your Mars ships using space station cans as habitation modules, and nuclear boosters –'

York felt like arguing, trying to get the unease out of her system – she had been shaken by what she'd seen at the test station. 'But what's it all for? More footprints and flags, like Apollo?'

'No,' Mike snapped.

There had been an edge of impatience in his voice since they'd left the Flats. She sensed her response there hadn't been what he'd hoped for.

He said now, 'Haven't you been listening, Natalie? Agnew's presented a great vision. We could be on Mars by 1982. And by 1990 we'll have a hundred men in Earth orbit, forty-eight on the Moon, and forty-eight in a base on Mars –'

'Oh, sure,' she said, bristling. 'Yes, actually, I have been listening. And I hear that Agnew gets booed when he talks in public about going to Mars. People don't want this, Mike; the war is fucking up the economy too comprehensively.'

Ben, gratifyingly, looked startled to hear her swear.

'Well, I doubt Nixon's going to buy it all anyhow,' Ben said.

'The word is he's leaning a little toward the Space Shuttle, as the one element in the STG proposals to preserve over all the rest. Because it promises low-cost access to space. On the other hand, Nixon likes heroes . . .'

'But he's backed into a corner, by what Kennedy said to Armstrong and Muldoon in July,' Mike said. 'And by the pro-Mars statements he's been issuing ever since.'

York grunted. 'Nixon hates Kennedy. Besides, Kennedy's just another opportunist. Do you really think *he* would have continued pumping funds into Apollo the way Johnson did, if he'd not been invalided out of the White House back in '63? If he'd actually had to *pay* for any of the things he was able to call for, from his wheelchair?'

'Johnson was a genuine space enthusiast,' Mike said. 'You're too cynical, Natalie.'

'Johnson was interested in his own advantage. Why else have you got so many NASA centers in the south?'

'Does make you think, though,' Ben said. 'What if Kennedy hadn't taken those bullets in Dallas? Or – what if they'd killed him, instead of his wife? Without him as a cheerleader on the sidelines, maybe the whole program *would* have got itself canceled.'

'Anyway,' York said, 'I just hope that whatever happens this time around they make room for a few scientists among all you *av-i-at-ors*.'

'Don't listen to her, Ben,' Conlig said. 'She's playing it cool. Guess what she keeps on the wall of her bedroom in her mom's house.'

'Shut up, Mike –'

'Pictures of Mars.'

Priest looked at her, evidently intrigued.

'Hell, I was just sixteen. For a while I got caught up in all that showbiz about Mariner 4 . . .'

Mariner 4 was a NASA space probe which reached Mars in July, 1964. Mariner hadn't carried the fuel to put itself into orbit around Mars; it made one sweep past the planet, firing off pictures as it went. Mariner sent back twenty-one pictures, in all. They covered maybe one per cent of Mars's surface.

Natalie York had never even thought about Mars, other worlds, before Mariner. She wasn't even *interested* in astronomy, or space travel, or other worlds, or any of that. Astronomy was a subject for the handful of old men who controlled access to the big telescopes, and used them to pursue their obscure, decade-spanning projects. Even back in 1964, geology – the study of the Earth – was what captured *her* imagination. Stuff you could walk around in, and pick up, and examine with your eyes and hands.

Mariner made everything different. For a while, anyhow.

She remembered a teacher at school, trying to put over the basics of astronomy.

In July 1964, when Mariner reached Mars, the planet had been in opposition. Mars was a planet that circled the sun, like Earth; but its orbit was outside the Earth's, and its year was twice as long. That meant its distance from Earth was constantly changing, as Earth scooted by on the inside track. But when sun, Earth and Mars were lined up, in that order, Mars would come closest to Earth. *Opposition. That's what it means. So at opposition, Mars is almost opposite the sun, seen from Earth. At its closest point.*

She remembered, as she'd learned of this, a sudden sense of herself as a passenger on the Earth – as if it was a giant spinning spaceship, steaming past this great red liner called Mars.

To do their jobs, astronomers have to be able to figure out where they are, in relation to the rest of the universe. They have to be able to imagine, really and truly, that they aren't living on a flat Earth.

She'd gotten copies of the pictures radioed back by Mariner 4, and had indeed taped them to her bedroom wall.

The first photo showed the limb of the planet, seen from close to; the horizon curved, and surface markings were vaguely, frustratingly visible. Still, the image was a hell of a contrast to the misty, unreal disk you could see through a telescope.

Mariner's photos showed how Mars would look to an orbiting astronaut.

The next few pictures showed views of the surface, as if looking down from directly overhead. The monochrome images looked like aerial pictures of a desert, Arizona maybe . . .

Ben Priest said now, 'You know, Mariner was a big shock to us all. Before Mariner, we thought we understood Mars pretty well. You could walk around on the surface with nothing more than a facemask. We thought we saw seasonal changes in dark patches on the surface, that were maybe down to some kind of spreading vegetation.

'But now, everything looks different. We had it wrong – *all* of it. Earth-like Mars certainly isn't.'

It was Mariner's seventh picture that was the real surprise.

The seventh picture showed craters. Nobody was expecting to find *those*.

Not Arizona, then. Mars looked more like the Moon.

Priest said, 'We know now the atmosphere is impossibly thin. It's mostly carbon dioxide, and there's no oxygen, and hardly any water vapor. Not even nitrogen . . . Mariner didn't find any canals, incidentally. Even though it flew over an area where a lot of the most prominent canals were expected.

'All our ideas were turned upside down by this. With such a thin atmosphere, any life must be very hardy. Nothing like terrestrial life at all. But, of course, the question of life won't be settled until humans land there. It was one hell of a disappointment, the NASA guys tell me. Suddenly, Mars became a place it wasn't worth traveling to. If we don't make it to Mars, if the funding and resources aren't assembled, then for me, that shock of Mariner 4 will have been the turning point.'

York shrugged. 'But NASA oversold Mars for years. It was a kind of holiday resort in the sky, teeming with life, justifying all the billions they wanted to pour into rockets and spaceships . . .'

Priest laughed. 'A holiday resort. I like that.'

To York, Mars was much more than that. After Mariner she'd become interested in Mars, and its history in the human imagination. She got books from the library. *Mars as the Abode of Life* by Percival Lowell, New York, 1909; *Mars and its Canals* by Lowell, New York, 1906 . . . She remembered fantastic, gaudy pictures of huge irrigation canals dug across the face of a dying, drying Mars, long descriptions of the waves of vegetation and the herds of animals which must sweep across the red Martian plains. *The Mars Project*: Wernher von Braun, University of Illinois, 1953. It had a big rocket ship on the cover, like a kid's book. Von Braun wanted to build ten spaceships in Earth orbit, each weighing three and a half thousand tons, and carrying seven men. It would take nine hundred flights to orbit to assemble the fleet. There would be two-hundred-ton landing boats, to take fifty people down to the surface for a year-long stay . . . These visions, she'd thought, were a boy's dreams of power, dressed up as serious engineering plans.

York had put this stuff aside. Even at the age of sixteen, York was hot on science, on the strictness and logic of it; she found herself getting unreasonably impatient at illogic, and wishful thinking, and the emotional coloration of rational processes of all sorts.

(Actually she was much too severe for most of the boys her mother tried to match her with. You'd think that someone who'd

31

suffered as messy a divorce as Maisie York would learn not to meddle in other people's relationships . . .)

The fact was, to her, the *real* Mars was a hell of a lot more interesting than Lowell's anthropocentric dreams.

Because of Mariner, Mars had turned into a place you could do some geology.

How would the geology of Mars differ from Earth's? What would that tell you about Earth, that you couldn't have learned from staying at home? A hell of a lot, probably.

Mariner's thirteenth frame had electrified her.

The thirteenth picture showed craters with frost inside them.

My God. Not the Moon, not Arizona. Mars is something else. Something unique.

Ben eyed York, interested, speculative. 'So you're a closet Mars nut. I ought to take you out to JPL sometime. That's where they run the planetary probes from . . . Hey, Natalie. Maybe you ought to apply.'

'What for?'

'The astronaut corps.'

'Me? Are you joking?'

'Why not? You're qualified. And we need people like you. Even Spiro says so; he thinks people were turned off by Apollo because it was too engineering-oriented.'

'Well, so it was.'

Priest eyed her. 'I'm serious, actually, Natalie. It's a genuine opportunity for you. You could go work for Jorge Romero's geology boys in Flagstaff, and train the moonwalkers. That's how Jack Schmitt got into the program, and they say he'll make it to the Moon.'

'You worry me, Ben. How can a crazy man like you be allowed to drive a car at night?'

'Here.' Driving with one hand, he reached up, turned back his lapel, and unclipped a silver pin, in the shape of a shooting star trailing a comet's tail.

'What is it?'

'My rookie's pin. Some day soon I'm going to get a flight. So you need this more than I do. Take it. And when you're the first human on Mars, when the *Spiro Agnew* lands in 1982, drop it into the deepest damn crater you see, and think of me.'

'You're crazy,' she said again. 'You should give it to Petey.'

They fell silent.

Her thoughts turned back to Jackass Flats.

They don't even contain the vented hydrogen. And Mike never thought to tell me about any of this. Why? Because he thought I couldn't stand to hear it? Or because he can't even see what's wrong, here?

What does that say about us? And – do we really have to do this shit, to get to Mars?

She closed her fingers around the little pin Ben had given her.

Ahead of them, the Interstate was a band shining in the starlight and stretching toward the glow of Vegas.

Monday, October 27, 1969
Edwards Air Force Base, California

Major Philip Stone joined the USAF in 1953, at the age of twenty.

He arrived in Korea in time to make a series of hazardous sorties. Well, Korea had been a turkey shoot. But Stone hadn't enjoyed combat. His buddies called him too serious – a straight arrow. But for Stone, the important thing was what he could learn in each flight, either about his machines, or about himself.

After the war, his disciplined curiosity found a new focus.

In the early 1960s the most promising route to space, if you were inside the USAF, had looked like the experimental high-altitude rocket aircraft program. The X-15s could even give their pilots astronaut wings, by flying through the officially recognized lower limit of 'space,' at fifty miles high. The X-15s were to lead on to the advanced X-20 – the Dyna-Soar – in which a guy would have been boosted into orbit, and then he would have *flown* back down, landing like an airplane.

But with men routinely being hurled into space in ballistic capsules like Mercury and Gemini, the X-20 looked too advanced for its time, and it soon ran up a bill as large as that for the entire Mercury program without delivering a single flight article. And it was canned.

Now, the only way for a pilot to reach space was to transfer to NASA. Neil Armstrong was another X-15 pilot who had gone that way before. And so that was what Stone had determined to do.

But first he had some unfinished business.

In 1969, Stone was thirty-seven years old.

'Drop minus one minute.'

'One minute,' Stone said. 'Rog. Data on. Emergency battery on.

33

I'm ready when you are, buddy. Master arm is on, system arm light is on . . .'

The B-52 reached its launch station over Delamar Dry Lake in Nevada. The rocket plane was suspended from the bomber's wing pylon like a slim, black, stub-winged missile, crammed full of liquid oxygen and anhydrous ammonia, ready for its mid-air launch.

Stone was sealed up inside the X-15. The B-52's engine was just feet away from his head, but Stone, cocooned inside the pressurized cockpit, could barely hear its noise. From the corner of his eye he could see the chase planes clustered close to the B-52. *At last, this damn flight is going to be over and done with.*

After fifteen years, the X-15 program was winding up. There was only one serviceable X-15 left: this one, X-15-1, the first to fly back in 1960, a veteran of seventy-nine previous missions. The Edwards people wanted to finish up the program with one last flight, the two hundredth overall; and they had asked Phil Stone to stay around long enough for that. But then there was a series of delays and technical hitches, and the winter weather had closed in; until by now the flight was all but a *year* later than it had originally been planned for.

For Stone that was a year wasted out of his life. But he'd spent the time preparing for his move to NASA, trying to be sure he started off his new career as well placed as he could be.

'Fifteen second mark to separation. Chase planes on target. Ten seconds.'

He felt his heart, somewhere under the silver surface of his pressure suit, pumping a little harder. As it was supposed to at such moments.

'Three. Two. One. Sep.'

With a solid crack the B-52's shackle released the X-15, and the plane dropped away from its mother, and Stone was jolted up out of his seat.

Stone emerged from the shadow of the bomber's wing, at forty-five thousand feet, into a shock of brilliant sunshine. He was already so high that the morning light was electric blue, more like dusk. The chase planes were little points of silver light around him, with their contrails looping through the air.

The land curved below the plane's nose, as if the Mojave was some huge, smooth dome. He could see the worn hump of Soledad, the Lonely Mountain, brooding over Rogers Dry Lake, half a mile above sea level. Everywhere the dried-up salt lakes glistened like glass, speckled with gray-green sagebrush and the twisted forms of Joshua trees. It was a flat, desolate, forbidding place. But every summer the desert sun baked the damp lake beds to a flat and smooth surface. The whole place was like one huge runway, and you could land anywhere in reasonable safety.

It was a little after ten thirty in the morning.

Stone pushed the button to ignite the X-15's rocket engine.

He was kicked in the back, hard. The plane's nose was tipped up into the sky as ammonia and oxygen burned behind him, and he rode higher into the deepening blue. He could hear his own breathing inside his helmet; otherwise, there was barely a sound – he was outpacing the noise and exhaust plumes behind him.

Far ahead he saw a speck of light, like a low star. It was a high chase plane. It grew out of nowhere in a flash, and plummeted backwards past Stone, as if it was standing still.

At forty thousand feet he reached point nine Mach, and he could feel a bumping, like a light airplane flying in turbulence. He was moving so quickly now that the air molecules couldn't get out of the way of his craft in time.

The turbulence smoothed out as he went supersonic.

Eighty thousand feet.

He moved the rocket's throttle to maximum thrust, and he was pushed back into his seat by four and a half G. X-15-1 climbed almost vertically. The sky turned from pearl blue to a rich navy. He was already so high he could see stars ahead of him, in the middle of the day; so high there were only a few wisps of atmosphere, barely sufficient for his plane's aerodynamic control surfaces to grip.

The sensations of power, of speed, of control, were exhilarating.

Ninety thousand feet; thirty two hundred feet per second. The Mojave spread out beneath him, over two thousand feet above sea level, was like the dried-out roof of the world.

Less than a minute into the flight, the problems started.

He got a message from the ground. It sounded like they were losing telemetry from the bird. The trouble was, the voice link had suddenly got so bad that he couldn't tell for sure *what* they were saying.

A warning light showed up on his panel. Another glitch. For some reason his automatic reaction control rockets had deactivated. It wasn't too serious for now; he was still deep enough in the atmosphere that he was able to maintain control with the aerodynamics.

The X-15 flew like an airplane in the lower atmosphere. It had conventional aerodynamic surfaces – a rudder and tail planes – which Stone could work electronically, or with his pitch control stick and rudder pedals. But above the atmosphere X-15 was a spacecraft. The automatic RCS (reaction control system) – little rocket nozzles, like a spaceship's – was controlled by an electronic system called the MH96. And there was a separate manual RCS system Stone could control with a left-hand stick.

Quickly he was able to trace through the fault. The automatic RCS had shut itself off because the gains of his MH96, his control system, had fallen to less than fifty per cent. The gains were supposed to drop when the plane was in dense air; then the MH96 was designed to shut itself off, to conserve hydrogen peroxide rocket fuel. But this time the gains had dropped because the hydraulics which controlled his aerodynamic surfaces were stuttering. So the automatic control system couldn't rely on the data it was getting, and it had shut down the automatic RCS.

It looked as if the electrical disturbance that had started with the radio was spreading. *Looks as if we might be snake-bit, old buddy.*

Well, he was close to the exhaustion of his rocket fuel anyhow. He pressed a switch, and the engine shut down with a bang.

He was thrust forward against his straps, and then floated back.

He had gone ballistic, like a hurled stone; now X-15-1 would coast to the roof of its trajectory, unpowered. He lost all sensation of speed, of motion. He was weightless inside the cabin, and he felt as if his gut was climbing up out of his neck.

He tried to put the problems aside. He was still flying, still in shape. And, no matter what was happening to the MH96, he had a program to work through, a whole series of experiments for NASA and the USAF.

One minute forty-one.

He activated the solar spectrum measurement gadget, and the micrometeorite collector in his left wing pod.

Suddenly, the MH96 control system's gains shot up to ninety per cent, for no apparent reason, and the automatic RCS cut back in.

He checked his instruments. Like most experimental aircraft, the X-15's cockpit had a primitive, handmade feel, with rivets and wires showing. Well, it seemed he had full control ability for the first time since entering his ballistic flight path. He welcomed the return, but he was unnerved, all over again. What next?

He had very little confidence left in this battered old bird. *Maybe she knows it's her last flight; maybe she'd prefer a blaze of glory to a few decades rusting in some museum.*

He would soon be going over the top, the peak of his trajectory, at two hundred sixty thousand feet.

It was time to begin the precision attitude tracking work required for the solar spectrum measurement. He needed a nose down pitch, and a yaw to the left. He was already flying at almost a zero degree angle of attack, but was yawing a little to the right, and rolling off to the right as well. So he fired his wing-mounted roll control thruster for two seconds to bring his wings level, and his yaw control thruster to bring the X-15's nose around to the left. The X-15 was like a gimbaled platform, hanging in the air, twisting this way and that in response to his commands. To stop the left roll he fired another rocket –

He was still rolling, too far to the left. *Christ. What now?*

The MH96 had failed again, and had cut out the automatic RCS, just as he was completing his maneuver.

He continued to rotate. To compensate he held his right roll control for eight more seconds. But the air was so thin up here that his aerodynamic controls were degraded, and the response was sluggish. He fired his manual RCS yaw rockets.

He could feel sweat pooling under his eyes; one problem after another was hitting him, *blam blam blam.*

Suddenly the MH96 cut back in with its automatic RCS. That stopped his yaw, short of the correct heading. Stone fired his manual yaw again; this time as he approached the reference heading the yaw was countered by the automatics, apparently correctly – but now the damn thing cut *out* again, and he yawed past the reference.

And now, on top of that, his roll attitude indicator ball was rotating. He had started rolling to the left again. He tried to wrestle that back with three short pulses on the manual roll RCS, but he overshot, and started a roll to the right . . .

Fifty miles high. The sky outside his tiny cabin was a deep blue-black, and the control lights gleamed brightly, like something off a Christmas tree. At the horizon's rim he saw the thick layer of air out of which he'd climbed. He could see the western seaboard of the USA, all the way from San Francisco to Mexico; the air was clear, and it was all laid out under him like a relief map.

Three minutes twenty-three seconds. His yaw deviation was increasing, five or six degrees a second. And his heading had deviated from the B-52's, maybe as much as fifty degrees. His angle was becoming extreme, and the air started to pluck at his aircraft, rolling it over to the right. He was in danger of rolling off completely. He might even reenter at the wrong attitude.

And if *that* happened, he'd finish up spread over the welcoming desert in a smoking ellipse one mile wide and ten miles long.

To stop the roll he applied left roll RCS, full left rudder and full left aileron. Everything he had. But the roll seemed to be accelerating. And now the nose was starting to pitch down too.

The starry sky, and the glowing desert below, started to wheel, slowly, around his cockpit, while he continued to work his controls.

At two hundred forty thousand feet above the ground – still supersonic – the X-15 went into a spin, tumbling around two axes at once.

He reported his spin to the ground.

They sounded incredulous. 'Say again, Phil.'

'I said, I'm in a goddamn spin.' He wasn't surprised at their disbelief; there was no way of monitoring the X-15's heading from the ground, and they would only see pronounced and slow pitching and rolling motions.

And besides, nothing was known about supersonic spin. Nothing. There had been some wind tunnel tests on X-15 spin modes, which had proved inconclusive.

There was no spin recovery technique in the pilot's handbook.

Stone tried everything he knew, using his manual RCS and his aerodynamic controls. *Full rudder; full ailerons. What else is there?*

The plane began to shudder around him; he was slammed from side to side; it was hard to breathe, to think. It had all fallen apart so quickly. *I lost my tail. I've had it.*

Suddenly the MH96 armed the automatic RCS again, and the little rockets started firing in a series of long bursts, opposing the spin. Stone worked with it, reinforcing the RCS with his aerodynamics.

The X-15 broke out of the spin and leveled off. The buffeting faded away.

Stone felt a brief burst of elation. He was at a hundred twenty thousand feet, and Mach five. *Now all I got to do is reenter the goddamn atmosphere.*

He pulled up the nose; he muttered a short, obscene prayer as the controls responded to him. He reached the correct twenty-degree nose-up angle of attack, and opened the air-brakes, flaps on the plane's rear vertical stabilizer. A sensation of speed returned as deceleration started to bite, and shoved him forward against his restraint. The leading edges of his wings were glowing a dark, threatening red.

The sky brightened quickly. He could see Edwards, a grid laid out over the desert below, two hundred and sixty miles from his takeoff point.

At eighteen thousand feet he pulled in his air-brakes, and hauled on the aerodynamic controls to initiate a corkscrew dive. The idea was to shed more speed, and energy, as fast as possible.

At a thousand feet above the dry lake bed he pulled out of his dive and, with the slipstream roaring past his canopy, jettisoned his ventral fin. He extended the landing flaps and pulled up the scorched nose, blistered from the reentry. Chase aircraft settled in alongside him.

The X-15 hit the dirt. The skids at the rear sent a cloud of dust up into the still desert air; Stone was jolted as the crude skids scraped across the lake bed. The nose wheel stayed up for a few seconds, before thumping down to add to the dust clouds.

A mile from touchdown the X-15 came to a halt. The chase planes roared overhead.

As the dust settled over his canopy, Stone switched off his instruments, closed his eyes, and slumped back in his seat.

The ring of his pressure suit dug into the back of his neck.

Stone had proved himself as a pilot today. But a flight like today's wouldn't do him a damn bit of good, with NASA. *I got out of a supersonic spin! I got my hide back down, and if I can figure out how I did it, I'll be in the manual. But I screwed up. I didn't finish the science; I didn't make it through the checklist.* And for NASA, that was what it was all about.

A fist banged on his canopy. The ground crews had reached him; through the dusty glass he could see a wide, grinning face. He raised a gloved hand and joined thumb and forefinger in a 'perfect' symbol.

All in a day's work, in the space program.

Monday, April 13, 1970
Fish Hook, Cambodia

In 1970, Ralph Gershon was twenty-five years old.

He had grown up on a farm in Iowa, surrounded by near-poverty and toil, dreaming of flight. As a kid he'd gone to Mars with Weinbaum and Clarke and Rice Burroughs and Bradbury; later, he'd followed the emergent space program with fascination. He'd got himself some flight experience, had crammed his head at school, and – in the face of a lot of prejudice – had finally made it into the Academy, and the Air Force.

He'd been following a dream.

But it hadn't worked out so wonderfully.

As soon as he had climbed away from the base, Gershon was over jungle. It was just a sea of darkness under him, blacker than the sky, rolling to the horizon.

His wingman had pushed in his power and was invisible; he would already be somewhere over the four thousand feet mark.

As the Spad climbed, the noise of its turbine rose in pitch, and the prop dragged at smoky air. Now Gershon could see flashes of light, pinpricks of crimson embedded in the masked ground. The pinpricks were muzzle flashes from the bigger guns down there.

The air was dingy with the smoke: it was about twice as bad as the average Los Angeles smog. The smoke struck Gershon's imagination. Down there hundreds, thousands of little farmers were patiently tending smoky fires in their own soggy fields, each doing his bit to thwart him, Gershon, and his fellows. If you thought too hard about it, it was awesome; it gave you a sense of the size of this land, of how it was capable of absorbing a hell of a lot of punishment.

So Gershon resolutely tried not to think about it.

Now he leveled off. 'Back to cruise power,' he told his wingman.

The Combat Skyspot radar controller came on the line. He'd been expecting this. He snapped on his flashlight and prepared to mark his map.

Gershon had been briefed for a target inside South Vietnam. But now, in terse sentences, the Skyspot gave him a new target.

Gershon changed his heading; more miles of anonymous, complex jungle rolled beneath his prow.

After the raid was over, ground controllers would destroy all evidence of the diversion, shredding documents and reporting that the attack had taken place, as planned, inside South Vietnam.

And not inside neutral Cambodia.

And, as on previous flights, Gershon was going to have to file a false report.

He glanced into the sky. Somewhere up there, Apollo 13 was heading for the Moon.

Gershon found it hard to reconcile the terrific adventure going

40

on in the sky, three guys hanging their hides out over the edge, with the mindless, lying bullshit of this war.

After an hour the Spad started trembling – pogoing, vibrating longitudinally, so that he was juddered back and forth in his seat. Night flying seemed to magnify everything, every little problem, until you could damn near scare yourself out of the sky. It was hard to know if vibrations like this were a real problem or something that he'd just dismiss during daylight.

He tried to ride it out, and after a while the juddering let up. Production of the Spads – single-seater Douglas A-1 Skyraiders – had been stopped in 1957. Thirteen years ago. They shouldn't be flying any more. Operational ships had to be nursed along with components cannibalized from wrecks.

In the dark Gershon had to fly time-and-distance: a kind of dead reckoning, based on nothing but his heading, his airspeed, and the time he flew. It wasn't exactly accurate. Still, soon Gershon figured he was over the FAG's reported location. The FAG was his Forward Air Guide, the friendly Cambodian spotter who had been assigned to guide his bombs home.

He twisted the knobs of his VHF radio. 'Hello Topdog, this is Pilgrim. How you hear? Topdog. Pilgrim. How you hear?'

He heard the barking of a thirty-seven-mil airburst, miles away.

Gershon tried to keep his patience. After all, the poor guy was down there in the night, surrounded by mortar-firing hostiles.

There was a crackling of radio static, a distant voice. 'Pilgrim. Topdog. You come help Topdog?'

'Yes, Topdog. Pilgrim come help you. You have bad guys?'

'Rager, rager, Pilgrim.' *Rager* for *roger*. The FAG was talking the abbreviated lingo the pilots had worked out with the locals they had to deal with. 'Have many, many bad guys. They all around. They shoot big gun at me.'

Big gun? Gershon peered down at the dark. Maybe it was so. He couldn't see any muzzle flashes, so maybe the fight was just a small-arms affair.

Small-arms fire was okay with Gershon. It was even kind of interesting. It sounded like rain on tin, and put little holes in the airplane.

But 'big gun' could mean a mortar.

It was hard to be sure. Things would be looking kind of different to Topdog, helpless in his blacked-out hell-hole on the inky ground.

41

'Okay, Topdog, you give us coordinates where you are. We come help you.' Gershon flicked on his flashlight and wrote out the numbers, then checked them against the map.

The coordinates didn't tie up with where the FAG was supposed to be.

Gershon called his wingman. 'Hey. You copy that?'

'Copy.'

'Either he doesn't know where he is or he's a hundred miles from here.'

'Your call, Pilgrim.'

Gershon hesitated, trying to figure what to do. Sometimes this kind of hide-and-seek was normal with an FAG.

Then again, sometimes voices would come floating up out of the dark to the bombers, confidently calling out positions to hit. On checking, the flyers would find the locations to be the designated areas of friendly troops.

'Topdog, this is Pilgrim. You hear my airplane?'

'Pilgrim, Topdog. I hear your airplane. You come north maybe two mile.'

Gershon pushed north.

Gershon looked down. The mountains here were high, and his cruising altitude of ten and a half thousand feet didn't put him all that far above them.

'Hey, Topdog. You hear my airplane now?'

'Rager, rager, Pilgrim. You over my position now.'

There was a valley below him, a black wound in the landscape, coated with the fur of jungle.

'Topdog. Pilgrim see big valley. Where are you?'

'Rager, Pilgrim. Bad guy in valley. You put bomb in middle of valley.'

It was a pinpoint target. 'Look, Topdog, I want to know where *you* are.' Gershon didn't want to bomb out the FAG himself.

'Pilgrim, Topdog on top of mountain. You bomb bad guy.'

'All right, Topdog, Pilgrim drop bomb in valley.'

Gershon set his wing selector to the left stub, where a five-hundred-pound napalm bomb nestled. He peered down, into oceanic invisibility. He put on a single fuselage light, so the wing-man would be able to see where he was going.

He rolled over, relying on his instruments in the darkness, and stabilized into a forty-degree dive.

He descended below the tops of the mountains and closed rapidly.

Through his gunsight he could see glimmers outlining the valley below.

The altimeter unwound, and Gershon's breath was ragged and hot. He wasn't worried about anti-aircraft fire; right now he was more concerned about not hitting the ground.

He hit the release button.

Five hundred pounds dropped away from the ship with a jolt. He pulled up, and grunted as three G settled on his chest.

The nape splashed over the landscape. It was like an immense flashbulb, exploding from the valley floor, and it lit up the smoky sky, turning it into a milky dome above him. It was eerie, alien, almost beautiful.

'Pilgrim! You have number one bomb. Very good. You do same again.'

'Okay, Topdog, we'll put it right there.'

Gershon swapped altitudes with his wingman, and let the wingman dive in. The valley wasn't dark any longer; it was a mass of fires and splotches of twenty-mil hits, which sparkled like little fire jewels. Gershon caught glimpses of his wingman's Spad, rolling down and leveling off, silhouetted against the blaze below.

'Very good bomb, Pilgrim.'

'Okay, Topdog.'

'Hey, Pilgrim. You got radio?'

Gershon couldn't figure what the FAG was talking about; the raid was over. 'Say again, Topdog. Say again.'

'Topdog listen to radio. Voice of America. You brave boys in trouble.'

'What?'

'Apollo. Brave boys. Spaceship in terrible danger, say Voice of America. You understand?'

Jesus. He felt electrified. *I wonder what the hell has happened, if they can get home . . .*

But what a way to find out, from some poor little guy, lost in a shit-hole in the mountains of Cambodia.

'Rager, Topdog. I copy. Thank you.'

'And to you, Pilgrim, a good night.'

Yeah. A good night faking my records.

Somewhere in the sky above him – for all the peril those guys were in – Americans were undertaking vast, wonderful adventures. And here he was, flying this bucket of bolts, splashing liquid fire over peasants. Doing something so shitty that even his own Government wouldn't admit it was happening.

I got to get out of this. Of course, despite a lot of pressure from the White House, NASA had yet to fly a black man into space. It would be a long haul for Ralph Gershon . . .

But it couldn't be worse than this.

Gershon and his wingman climbed back to altitude, and Gershon turned his nose for home.

Mission Elapsed Time [Day/Hr:Min:Sec] Plus 000/00:12:22

Earth was a wall of blue light, as bright as a slice of tropical sky; it dazzled her, dilating her eyes, making the sky pitch black when she looked away. The Command Module's windows were tiny, already scuffed, but even so they let in shafts of startling blue, and the cabin was bright, cheerful, light-filled.

'Houston, we have a hot cabin.' Stone tapped a gloved forefinger against a temperature gauge. 'Running at seventy-seven.'

'Copy, Ares,' Young said. 'We recommend you put coolant fluid through the secondary coolant loop.'

'Rager,' said Gershon. 'Ah, okay, Houston, now I'm seeing a fluctuation of my water quantity gauge. It's oscillating between, I'd say, sixty and eighty per cent.'

'Copy, Ralph, working on that one . . .'

And Stone said he suspected there was a helium bubble in an attitude thruster propellant tank. Young recommended that he perform a couple of purge burns of the attitude thrusters to burn out the bubble. So Stone began to work that out. Meanwhile, Young came back with an answer to the water gauge problem; it looked as if it was traced to a faulty transducer . . .

And on, and on, a hail of small checks and detailed, trivial problems.

York had her own checklist to follow. She worked her way through the pale pages quickly, opening and closing circuit breakers, throwing switches, calling out instructions for Stone and Gershon. She was immersed in the hiss of the air in her closed helmet, the humming of the Command Module's instruments and pumps, the rustle of paper, the crackle of Young's voice calling up from the ground, the soft voices of Gershon and Stone as they worked through their post-orbit checklists.

This was a mundane procedure they'd followed together dozens of times before in the sims.

But, she realized, it was a profound shock to go through this

44

routine – not in some stuffy ground-based trainer – but *here*.

If she looked ahead of the craft she could see the planet's curve. It was a blue and white arc with black space above it. But when she looked straight down, the skin of the Earth filled her window, scrolling steadily past as if she were viewing some colorful map on a computer screen.

She was amazed by the transparency of the air. There was a sense of depth to the atmosphere, a three-dimensional appearance that surprised her. There were shadows under the clouds as they slid across the face of the seas. The clouds thickened toward the equator, and when she looked ahead, tangential to the Earth's surface, she could see them climbing up into the atmosphere, as if Ares was heading for a wall of vapor. On the land she could easily make out cities – a gray, angular patchwork – and the lines of major roads. The orange-brown of deserts was vivid, but the jungles and temperate zones were harder to spot; their color did not penetrate the atmosphere so well, and they showed up as a gray-blue, with the barest hint of green.

She found the lack of green disappointing.

She saw the wake of a ship, feathering out like a brush stroke on the sea's calm surface.

Gershon, in his center seat, leaned toward her. 'Quite a view, huh.'

She turned her head – and quickly regretted it; her head felt like a tank of fluid, sloshing when she moved. She held her head steady for a few seconds, and let the sloshing settle down again. Resolutely, she tried not to think about her stomach.

Space adaptation syndrome. She understood what was happening to her. Without gravity, little particles of calcium on sensitive hairs in the inner ear took up random positions, and the body couldn't work out which way was up. It generally went away after a few days.

But right now it was a huge embarrassment to York.

More carefully, she turned back to the window. They were passing over storm clouds now, thunderheads which piled up on top of each other as if solid, cliffs and ravines of cloud miles deep. She could see lightning, sparking in the clouds like living things, propagating across storm systems thousands of miles across. The clouds, illuminated from within, glowed purple-pink, like neon sculptures. 'Look at that. It looks as if the thunderheads are reaching up toward us.'

'Only about a tenth of the way,' Gershon said mildly.

'Pressure's okay,' Stone said now. He began to take off his gloves and helmet.

York unlatched her gloves and pulled them off, and shoved them into a pocket on her couch. She grasped the sides of her helmet, which came loose with a click; she pushed it up over her head.

She moved too quickly. Suddenly her head was full of sloshing fluid again, and saliva flooded her mouth.

Her helmet, rolling loose, clattered against a bank of switches. Gershon grabbed it easily, laughing. 'Interception!' In his pressure suit he looked small, compact, comfortable. He threw the helmet up in the air again with a twist; the helmet revolved, oscillating about two spin axes.

York felt embarrassed, clumsy. And, watching the helmet, suddenly she was retching.

'Oh, man,' Stone said in disgust. He handed her a plastic bag, and York fumbled it open, and pushed her face into it.

As she heaved, a greenish sphere, about the size of a tennis ball, came floating up out of the bag. It was shimmering, and complex pulsations crossed its surface.

York watched in awe. *Maybe I ought to film this.* It was a demonstration of fluid mechanics in the absence of gravity; she wondered if the wave patterns, dominated by surface tension, could be predicted by computer.

Now the glob of vomit split in two. One half headed toward the wall, and the other made straight for Gershon.

'Ah, shit,' Gershon said, and he tried to squirm out of the way.

The glob hit him in the chest, with a soft impact; it immediately collapsed and spread out over his suit, as flat as a fried egg. *Surface tension again,* York thought absently.

'Oh, Jesus,' Gershon said. 'Oh, shit.'

Stone reached for wet wipes, and passed some to Gershon. 'Come on, man. It might have been any of us. We got to get this place cleaned up.'

So they began chasing around the cabin, hunting down bits of vomit with paper towels and plastic bags.

Now that her stomach awareness had receded a little, York found, oddly, that it wasn't actually so unpleasant. It was a little like chasing butterflies.

'NC One phasing burn,' Stone said. He held down the thrust control, watching his instruments.

The burn felt tight and rattly to York. She was shoved into her couch again; the acceleration was low, but crisp.

Through her window she could see vapor venting from attitude control thruster nozzles; the vents looked like fountains of ice crystals, the particles receding from the walls of the craft in precise straight lines.

The burn was taking place over the night side of Earth. The planet pulled away; it was as if she was rising above a floor of dark, frosted glass. The continents were outlined by chains of brilliant dots, like streetlights seen from the air. But those dots weren't streetlights; they were *towns*.

She twisted in her seat and looked ahead, toward the limb of the planet.

She could see the airglow layer, the bright layer of ionized oxygen at the top of the atmosphere, a fine line that was like a false sunrise. And then, as she watched, a sliver of sky turned blue and spread along the horizon. More colors came up, coalescing around a bright patch that was the rising sun, a spectrum that washed around the curve of Earth. The light of the dawn reached her *through* the layer of atmosphere; for a brief moment she saw the shadows of the clouds streaming across the orange surface of the sea.

Then the sun rose high enough to illuminate the tops of the clouds. The sea turned to crimson, and a wash of pale blue and white spread from the horizon toward her.

On a whim, she dug into a pocket of her pressure garment, and pulled out the handful of grass which Vladimir Viktorenko had given her. She held it in her palm and rubbed it gently; it gave off a sweet aroma, like a herb. It was *polin*, a kind of wormwood, common all over the Kazakhstan steppe.

Stone finished the burn. His push-button control, released, popped back out of the panel on its spring. 'Two hundred seven feet per second,' he said.

'Right on the wire,' Gershon murmured. 'One hundred ninety-five times two hundred zero one.'

Young called up, 'Copy your burn, Ares. You are two hundred fifty miles from the stack, and closing.'

'Copy, John. Preparing for NC Two . . .'

The crew had arrived in orbit with half the Ares cluster: their Apollo Command and Service Modules, the Mars Excursion Module – the MEM – and the Mission Module, their habitat for the journey. The rest of the cluster – the main injection booster and its huge fuel tanks – had already been placed in orbit and assembled, ready for them to dock with it.

The Mission Module was a squat cylinder, with the Apollo a slim, silvery cylinder-cone attached to its front, and the MEM – a fatter, truncated cone – stuck on the back. Fixed to the base of the MEM's shroud was an Orbital Maneuvering Module, a fat dough-nut fitted with a modified Apollo Service Module propulsion system. The OMM would be discarded before they docked with the booster cluster. But first Stone had to use the OMM in a series of four burns, to chase the booster cluster around the sky.

Stone announced: 'Ready for NCC.'

'Copy,' Young said. 'Ninety miles and closing.'

The corrective burn was crisp and short, a brief hiss.

Stone murmured, 'Natalie, you ought to be able to see the booster by now. Right out front.'

York pressed her face to the window. The brief burns were plac-ing Ares on segments of successively wider orbits; following the new orbits, Ares would eventually overtake the booster stack.

The craft was noticeably higher than when they had first been injected into orbit; the curvature of the Earth was much more pro-nounced, and she was able to see complete landmasses, speckled with cloud.

Suddenly it was there: a pencil, gleaming silver, hanging over the dipping horizon.

'I have it.'

'That's a relief,' said Stone dryly. 'Okay, Houston, I'm going for the twenty-eight feet per second coelliptic combination burn.'

'Copy, Phil.'

Another sharp rattle.

Young said, 'Slight underburn that time, Ares. One point six feet per second.'

'Copy that,' said Gershon, and he clucked at Stone in mock disapproval.

Young said, 'Your orbit is now ten miles under the booster's. Range sixty-three miles and closing.'

'Rog,' Stone said. 'Going for terminal phase initiation.' York could hear solenoids clatter as Stone worked the pushbutton con-trols of the reaction control clusters. 'How about that. Right down Route One.'

'Good burn, Ares,' Young said. 'You're closing at one hundred thirty-one feet per second.'

Stone went through two more corrections, and five sharp braking maneuvers. Then, maybe half a mile from the booster, he took the Apollo on a short, angular inspection sweep. The reaction control systems bit sharply, rattling York against her restraint.

York watched the cluster roll with silent grace past her window.

The booster cluster was squat, pregnant with fuel. Its heart was a fat MS-II booster, a Saturn second stage, modified to serve as an orbital injector. Fixed to the front of the MS-II was an MS-IVB, a modified Saturn third stage, a narrower cylinder. To either side of the MS-II were fixed the two External Tanks, fat, silvery cylinders as long and as wide as the MS-II stage itself. These supplementary tanks carried more than two million pounds of liquid oxygen and hydrogen, propellant Ares would need to break clear of Earth orbit.

The MS-II and its tanks looked like three fat sausages side by side, with the slimmer pencil shape of the MS-IVB protruding from the center. The rest of the Ares stack – the Mission Module, MEM and Apollo – would be docked onto the front of the MS-IVB, to complete the assembly of the first Mars ship, a needle well over three hundred feet long.

The cluster was oriented so that it was pointing toward the sun; that way, boiloff of the cryogenic propellants inside the tanks was reduced. Shadows of struts and attitude thrusters lay long against the sunlit white and silver bellies of the fuel tanks. The booster's underside was illuminated only by the soft blue and green of Earth-light. She could see the great flaps of the cluster's solar panels, folded up against the sides of the MS-IVB stage like wings; the panels would be unfurled when Ares was safely launched on its trajectory to Mars. There was the bold red UNITED STATES stenciled against the side of the MS-II, and the finer lettering along the long thin protective flaps masking the solar panels, and the NASA logo; and she could make out the support struts and attachment pins which held the External Tanks in place against the flanks of the MS-II, and the gold-gleaming mouths of the MS-II's four J-2S engines, upgrades of the engines which had pushed Apollo to the Moon.

To assemble this much mass in Earth orbit had taken all of nine Saturn VB flights over the last five years – half of them manned. The booster stages and their tanks had been flown up here and assembled more or less empty, and then pumped full of gas from tanker modules. The cluster was an exercise in enhanced Apollo-Saturn technology, of course, and the essence of its design went all the way back to the 1960s. But NASA had had to develop a raft of new techniques to achieve this: the assembly in orbit of heavy components, the long-term storage of supercold fuels, in-orbit fueling.

Sailing over the Earth, brilliantly lit by the unimpeded sunlight, the booster stack was complex, massive, new-looking, perfect, like a huge, jeweled model. Once they'd docked, she wouldn't see the cluster from outside again like this for a year. Not until, she realized with a jolt, she receded from it in the MEM, in orbit around Mars.

Stone stretched, raising his arms above his head and reverse-arching his back, so that he floated up out of his frame couch. His long limbs unfolded with evident relief; he really did look too tall to be an astronaut, York thought.

He said, 'It's been a long day already. What say we have ourselves some lunch before we proceed with the docking? If you can take it, Natalie.'

Food? Now? 'Sure,' she said. 'I'm fine.'

'Rager,' said Gershon. He climbed out of his couch. He moved in microgravity as if he'd been born to it; he just floated up out of his couch, pushed at the instrument panel in front of him, and went swimming around like an eel.

He rooted in the equipment bay beneath the couches. He got to the food locker and lifted the lid; it was full to bursting with little cellophane packets of food, all Velcroed in place.

Once they got into the Mission Module, the standard of cuisine would improve, York knew. But while they were stuck inside this Apollo they had to make do with squirting water into color-coded plastic bags of dehydrated food. Still, she wasn't about to complain. The Command Module was like a cute little mobile home, with its warm water for food and coffee, and toothpaste, even a system for the guys to shave.

Gershon came floating up with a handful of gold-painted bags. 'Hey. I found these at the front. None of us is coded gold, are we?'

Stone smiled. 'Nope. I had those put there for you to find.'

York studied the bags. 'Beef and potatoes. Butterscotch pudding. Brownies. Grape punch.' She looked at Stone. 'What's this? None of this was in my personal preference. In fact, I hate butterscotch pudding.'

'I thought it was kind of appropriate. This was the first meal the Apollo 11 crew ate in space. Straight after trans-lunar injection, after they left Earth orbit for the Moon.'

'All *right*,' Ralph Gershon said, and he pulled a hose out of the potable water tank and squirted the spigot into his bags with enthusiasm.

York looked at the bags again. *Butterscotch pudding, in memoriam.* Bizarre.

But maybe, after all, it was appropriate.

Monday, April 13, 1970
Manned Spacecraft Center, Houston

Chuck Jones snapped closed his visor and tugged at the umbilicals on his pressure suit, testing their fittings.

He stepped to the edge of the tank. It was a big blue rectangle, like a swimming pool. T-shirted divers were already moving through the water, playing around the sim like dolphins; cables trailed through the water, around the blocky white shape of the sim itself.

It's like a fucking kid's game, Jones thought. *Sims. How I hate sims.*

He turned to see his partner, Adam Bleeker. Because his suit was so stiff, Jones had to hop around like a rabbit. 'You okay, kid?'

Bleeker seemed to start. 'Sure. Yeah, sure, Chuck.'

Jones snickered to himself. He knew he could put a bug up the ass of a raw kid like Bleeker, just by smiling at him. 'Good boy. Welcome to the Weightless Environment Training Facility, here in sunny Texas. Beautiful sight, isn't it?'

Bleeker turned to the water. 'I think I've got a kind of Monday morning feeling about this, Chuck.'

'So do I, Adam; so do I. I hate this fucking fish tank. But we gotta go through with crap like this, or they won't let us fly their beautiful birds. You all set?'

'Let's do it.'

His breath loud in his ears, Jones stepped onto the white platform before him. Now he was suspended over the pool. With a whine of hydraulics, the platform lowered his clumsy, umbilicalled bulk into the water.

The divers loaded him up with weights that would neutralize his buoyancy, and so simulate weightlessness. Then they got hold of Jones's suited arms, and began to drag him through the water toward the sim. The water was hot, for the benefit of the divers.

The WET-F, pronounced 'wet-eff,' was one of the largest simulator facilities here at MSC. The pool was set at the center of

Building 29, a big circular building that had once served as a centri-fuge. Now, a sleek ambulance stood beside the pool, and there was a decompression chamber nearby. Big clunky white pieces of kit, simulators for other exercises, stood beside the water; cranes run-ning along the roof would lower them in when required.

Jones hated the WET-F. He could never forget the presence of the water around him: the resistance to every movement, the clammy light, the glopping of bubbles, the shadowy forms of the divers.

Conditions more different from the ice-cold stillness of space it was hard to dream up.

Looming ahead in the water he could see the sixty-feet-long hulk of a mocked-up S-IVB, a Saturn third stage, with the mouth of its single engine bell gaping at him. The Multiple Docking Adapter was a squat cylinder fixed to the front of the S-IVB, and a crude, open-ended mockup of a docked Apollo Command Module was fixed to the front of *that*.

The idea was that the empty S-IVB would be used as a space station shell, a Skylab, once it had reached orbit. The S-IVB and the Apollo carrying its crew would be launched separately, by Saturn IB boosters, the smaller, cheaper cousins of Saturn Vs. The astronauts would dock with the booster by nuzzling the nose of their Apollo against the Docking Adapter, and then enter through specially fitted airlocks. The crew would clean out the shell, and settle down to live inside the big liquid hydrogen tank.

This sim wasn't painted, or finished in any way. It all looked ungainly, ugly, evidently lashed up in haste.

The simulation supervisor's voice sounded in his headset. 'Good morning, Chuck, Adam.'

Good morning to you, asshole.

Bleeker turned and waved at one of the ubiquitous TV cameras.

The SimSup said, 'I just want to review the basic parameters of the sim with you, before you start. Now, you know this isn't an integrated sim.' Meaning they weren't hooked up to Mission Control. 'This is just a preliminary trial of the checklist we're going to have to use, when we fit out the workshop in orbit. Okay, let's proceed.'

The divers nodded to Jones, and they guided him closer to the Apollo mockup. It was just an open cone, fitted to the Docking Adapter. The simulation was supposed to start at the moment at which the crew were moving into the workshop to configure it for habitation.

Their first job was to dismantle the docking assembly in Apollo's nose and open up the tunnel to the workshop. This part, at least, should go smoothly, because this sort of docking was standard operating practice on the Moon missions.

Jones heard Bleeker's breath scratching as he hauled at the heavy docking probe assembly. 'Take it easy, kid. We're being paid by the hour.'

Bleeker laughed, and his posture relaxed a little.

When they had the probe assembly loose, Bleeker passed it to a diver.

Bleeker moved ahead of Jones into the Multiple Docking Adapter. The Adapter was a tight tunnel, lined with lockers. All the equipment for living quarters, clothes, food, experiments and the rest was stored in these lockers during the launch; when they'd fitted out the hydrogen tank for habitation, Jones and Bleeker would have to come back here, unpack the lockers, and move this equipment into the tank.

Bleeker passed on, into the hydrogen tank itself.

The metal walls of the tank opened out around him. It was pitch dark, and Jones had the feeling that he was following Bleeker into a huge, forbidding metal cave. 'Hold up, Adam; let's throw a little light on the situation here.' Jones unclipped a portable light from his belt and fixed it to the fireman's pole that passed along the axis of the tank.

The lamp sent glimmering light through the water along the length of the tank, to a wall at the far end that bulged inward toward him. This was the bulkhead between the hydrogen tank and the booster's lox tank beyond. Helium pressurization spheres clung to the walls like big silver warts. Handrails and poles looped across the metal cave, and folded-up partitions and other bits of kit were stowed neatly against the walls of the tank. *Too neatly. I wonder what those poor schmuckos will find when they meet this bird in real life, in orbit.*

The Skylabs were just lash-ups, really, improvisation. But they would give NASA experience it needed of orbital operations and long-duration flights, before the real space station cans started flying later.

'Okay, guys,' the SimSup said. 'As you know, in orbit the first job would be to check that the propellant lines are properly blocked. Today, we want you to skip over that and proceed straight to the assembly of the floor.'

'We've read the checklist,' Jones growled. 'Come on, pal.' He shimmied along the fireman's pole, deeper into the tank.

Bleeker and Jones manhandled packs of floor panels away from their stowage against the tank walls. Their job was to fit a floor of aluminum grid across the width of the tank, maybe two-thirds of the way along its length. Putting the panels together would be like assembling a jigsaw puzzle, working their way in to the tank's axis.

The two men worked their way around the perimeter of the tank. It was simple work, but slow, clumsy and tiring; Jones found it hard to grip tools with his suited hands, and the water resisted every motion.

Divers had followed them into the tank. One of them had brought in an underwater TV camera, and was filming them.

The SimSup tried to cheer them up. 'We appreciate your help here, guys. We're well aware that you two are slated for other missions, and probably won't even be the ones to carry this out for real anyway . . .'

I sure as hell hope not, Jones thought.

Chuck Jones was supposed to be going to the Moon. He was backup commander on Apollo 15, which, according to the basic framework of crew rotation, would give him his own mission three shots later, on Apollo 18.

But Congress had cut NASA's budget for Fiscal 1971, making it the leanest budget for nine years. And Nixon still hadn't responded to the Space Task Group's proposals for the future shape of the space program, although the word was he was now leaning toward a Mars program of some kind, under Kennedy's relentless public pressure.

Anyhow, NASA was going to need Saturn Vs to launch its Skylabs and space station modules and NERVA test flights. So, NASA was going to have to conserve Saturn V launches. The remaining lunar expeditions, Apollos 14 through to 20, were going to be stretched out to six-monthly intervals . . .

There were rumors in the Office that the later flights might be cut altogether.

Jones had flown in space. Once.

He'd finished three orbits of Earth on the second orbital Mercury flight, following John Glenn. It had been a picnic. He'd enjoyed the feeling of microgravity, being able to yaw the little capsule about so that the glowing Earth sailed every which way past his tiny window.

But he used up too much of his hydrogen peroxide maneuvering fuel, playing around in orbit.

By the time he got to the retro-sequence, nobody was sure if he had enough fuel to set the capsule at the right angle to reenter. He might have burned up, having wasted all his fuel playing around in orbit. Well, he hadn't; he'd overshot his splashdown point by two hundred fifty miles, but he was picked up within a couple of hours by choppers from the carrier.

Jones had been content with his adventure. But the NASA hierarchy were less than pleased with him. He might have augured in: killed himself by playing around.

Officially Jones stayed on the roster, for assignment to a later flight. But there was a certain distance, now, between Jones and the rest of the Astronaut Office. Deke Slayton, the chief astronaut, had dropped heavy hints that he might want to drop out of the program altogether.

But Jones, mad as hell, had flatly refused. He'd wanted to prove the astronauts really were aviators. *He* knew he'd done well; he knew he'd done better than Glenn, even, as far as he was concerned.

So he was going to stay on as an astronaut, and he was going to go to the goddamn Moon. In the meantime, to keep in the program, he accepted a job with Slayton and Alan Shepard – another of the original astronauts, also grounded, in his case for an ear condition – in the Astronaut Office.

Jones had served in there for eight whole years: scheduling and training, working on sims and mission profiles. *Eight years.*

Now enough bigwigs had moved out of NASA, it seemed, for his indiscretion to be forgotten, and he was back on flight status.

But if the Moon flights got cut, so did he. He'd probably be too damn old for Mars.

Jones didn't want to go to the Moon for the thrill of exploration. For him it wasn't the destination that counted but the journey: a mission that offered the most challenging flying test anyone could devise.

The Skylabs just weren't going to offer that. He had no wish for his career to climax in a low-Earth-orbiting trash can, where the job would be to endure, just logging days, boring a hole in the sky.

He really would hate to miss out on the Moon.

Jones hauled at floor bolts with a vigor that alarmed the surgeons who were monitoring his vital signs.

When the floor was completed, the SimSup congratulated them. 'Okay, boys; we'll take a break and refurbish before the next session. Come out through the Docking Adapter.'

Preceded by the divers, Bleeker made his way through the cramped Adapter and toward the brightly lit water beyond.

'Now you, Chuck,' the SimSup said.

Jones made his way into the shadowy Adapter; the lockers clustered about, restricting his movement. He was illuminated by the tank lights behind him, and the free blue water of the facility ahead of him.

When he was well inside the Adapter, the exit to the Apollo mockup slammed shut.

Jones pulled up short. He wrapped his gloved palms around the hatch lever. It wouldn't give.

'What's going on?'

'Jones.' The SimSup voice was terse now. 'You've suffered a multiple failure. Your Command Module is disabled; you can't return to it; you can't get it loose of the docking port. The power in the workshop cluster is about to fail. What do you do? Go.'

Now the lights failed. He was left floating in pitch darkness. Even the tank lights had gone out.

'What kind of asshole game is this? . . .'

He took a breath, and calmed himself down. SimSups were famous for throwing crap like this at you. He had to find an answer to this, and fast; he could yell at them later.

He knew the theory. If Skylab astronauts couldn't get home, a new Apollo would be sent up from the Cape. But if the disabled Apollo was jammed to the docking port, what use would that be?

In the pitch darkness, he was starting to forget which way up he was.

These fucking sims.

He tried to concentrate; he pictured the Adapter as he'd seen it just before the 'failure': the useless docking port before him; the access tunnel back to the workshop behind him.

He suffered a surge of panic. He reached out at random; his gloved hands clattered against lockers and handholds. The space here was *too big*, he realized suddenly; that was what was disorienting him. If he were safely tucked up in Mercury –

Take it easy. You're not in any danger. You can always back out into the tank. The divers are still there.

Yeah, he thought sourly. *But if I do that I'll have fucked up. The Grand Old Man of the Astronaut Office. Put him in a swimming bath for two minutes, and he screws the pooch.*

In fact, he thought, *I'm already screwing up by taking so long.*

How many seconds? Half a minute? There must be something obvious I'm meant to do; something I'm missing. Think, damn it. If the docking port is blocked, then how –

Then it came to him. The Docking Adapter had *two* docking ports. Bleeker had got out through the axial port; but there was also a radial port, stuck to the side of the Adapter for just such a purpose as this.

He reached down, and found the port on his first try; it was jammed, but it gave after a couple of tugs.

Bleeker clapped Jones on the shoulder; the impact was deadened by layers of suit fabric. 'What were you doing in there, pops, having a shave? Next time, make sure you've studied the manual.'

'Asshole,' Jones growled. 'You were in on that, weren't you?'

'Just another Monday, Chuck. Don't take it personal.'

Fucking engineers. Fucking smart-ass rookies.

With the help of the divers, they swam clumsily to the side of the facility.

Tuesday, April 14, 1970
Manned Spacecraft Center, Houston

According to Fred Michaels's antique vest-pocket watch, it was a little after a quarter to two. He'd been watching the time compulsively, he realized.

Tim Josephson oiled up to him. 'Mr Agronski is here to see you, sir. He's waiting in your office.'

'That's *Doctor* Agronski, damn it.'

'Sorry. Shall I tell him you'll meet him over there?'

Michaels, resenting the intrusion, turned away rather than answer. He looked through the glass, at the three rows of flight controllers.

Seen from the Viewing Room here at the back of the MOCR – Mission Operations Control Room, pronounced to rhyme with 'poker,' and known as 'Mission Control' to the world – there was no obvious drama. But the controllers looked pretty crumpled, with ties loosened or discarded, shirts creased, and the operations desks were strewn with coffee cups, manuals and scribbled notes.

He could see Joe Muldoon wandering about at the back of the MOCR. Nine months after his own lunar flight, Muldoon had just finished a six-hour stint as capcom to Jim Lovell and his Apollo 13 crew, but he showed no desire to leave; in fact, he knew that Muldoon was intending to head on over now to Building 5, where other off-duty astronauts were running continual simulations of the improvised procedures the Apollo 13 crew would have to adopt to get home.

Already seventeen hours had passed since 13 had started to fall apart; Michaels wondered how many of the controllers had got a minute's sleep since.

Josephson coughed. The aide was a slim, prematurely balding young man, with a PhD in some discipline or other. You needed a PhD to make the coffee, here at MSC. 'Sir, Dr Agronski –'

'Yeah, yeah.'

Leon Agronski worked on President Nixon's Science Advisory Committee, with special responsibility for the space program, and all its expensive evils. Michaels knew why Agronski was here: to thrash out 'options' for NASA's budget for FY1971 and beyond, before any formal submission by the White House.

More cuts.

Michaels was an Associate Administrator with responsibility for Manned Spaceflight, a direct report of Thomas Paine, NASA's Administrator. It had broken Michaels's heart when Paine had gone public back in February to announce the cuts to Skylab, even some terminations at NASA.

'You know,' he mused, 'maybe, if we can pull this off, this Apollo 13 thing, it will bring us back together, just a little. If we can remember how it feels to have worked like this, today, then maybe we'll be able to achieve great things again . . .'

Josephson had been avoiding his eyes; now he confronted Michaels, a little more boldly. 'Fred, I know you're upset. But the wheels don't stop turning. And Dr Agronski has flown out from Washington to catch you.'

Michaels grunted. Josephson was right, of course. The wheels never stopped turning.

And maybe, just maybe, he could use this mess to his advantage. He felt his mood lighten a little.

'All right, let's go see him,' he said. 'But not in some goddamn bureaucratic office block. Call him over here – ask him to come to the lunar surface back room.' Another thought struck him. 'Oh – and, Tim –'

'Sir?'

'Ask Joe Muldoon to join us, would you?'

*   *   *

The back room would have been used as the center of operations for the moonwalks. Its walls were covered with crew checklists, and with Orbiter and Apollo photographs of the landing area – called Fra Mauro, a place in the lunar uplands: the first ambitious, scientifically interesting site they'd planned to land. Now, it was deserted.

When Michaels arrived, Muldoon and Agronski were sitting at a large walnut desk in the center of the room. Agronski, thin to the point of sharpness, was leafing through some notes from his briefcase; Muldoon was hollow-eyed with fatigue, and he had folded his big, powerful hands on the desk top. He glared impatiently at Michaels. Josephson fussed around, pouring coffees.

Michaels pulled out a chair, and accepted a coffee. Then Josephson withdrew, leaving the three of them alone.

Michaels introduced Muldoon to Agronski. 'Leon, Joe here is on the backup crew for Apollo 14, and then should command his own mission, on 17. Joe, you're here at my invitation. To help remind us what this damn thing is all about.'

Here is the second American on the Moon, Agronski, you thin-lipped asshole, Michaels thought. *Here he is! Large as life, and twice as brave! A living symbol! Show a little respect!*

In the dazzle of the room's strip lights, Michaels couldn't see Agronski's eyes behind his thin-rimmed glasses.

Joe Muldoon was glaring back at Michaels. Muldoon's look, those blue eyes hard under that balding prow of a skull, said it all; he was thinking that Michaels was a paper-pushing prick who shouldn't be wasting Muldoon's time on a day like this. Not when he – Muldoon – could be in Building 5 or the MOCR with the other guys; not when he might be able to come up with something to save the crew out there –

Christ, Michaels thought suddenly. *Maybe I've miscalculated. If Muldoon blows his stack here, this could turn into a hundred-kilowatt disaster.* He shot an imploring look at Muldoon.

Agronski handed Michaels a document from his case. 'I'm sorry, Colonel Muldoon; I wasn't expecting you to be here. I brought only two copies.'

Muldoon turned that bald-eagle glare on the science adviser, who seemed oblivious.

The document was a photostat, stapled together, covered in pencil notes, and with the Presidential seal on the first page.

'This is the statement President Nixon was drafting, to make in March,' Agronski said. 'A formal response to the Space Task Group report. But he withdrew it. I want you to see this draft, Fred, to understand the way the thoughts of the Administration are heading.'

Michaels scanned the statement.

. . . Over the last decade, the principal goal of our nation's space program has been the Moon . . . I believe these accomplishments should help us gain a new perspective of our space program . . . We must define new goals which make sense for the seventies. We must build on the successes of the past, always reaching out for new achievements. But we must also recognize that many critical problems here on this planet make high priority demands on our attention and our resources. By no means should we allow our space program to stagnate. But – with the entire future and the entire universe before us – we should not try to do everything at once. Our approach to space must continue to be bold, but it must also be balanced . . .

Christ, Michaels thought. *We're in trouble.*

He read on. Economies everywhere. One rationalization after another. No money for more lunar flights beyond Apollo 20. The space station projects cut back to little more than Skylab. All decisions on later stuff, beyond Apollo and Skylab, deferred: that is, *canned.*

The feasibility studies on the Space Shuttle seemed spared, but even that was only because Nixon perceived the Shuttle as saving the bottom line: *We should work to reduce substantially the cost of space operations . . . As we build for the longer range future, we must devise less costly and less complicated ways of transporting payloads into space . . .*

Michaels put the paper down. *So Nixon thinks we can cost-cut our way to Mars.*

It wouldn't have been like this with LBJ.

But Johnson was gone. Now there was this new breed of shifty Republicans in the White House. And suddenly Michaels, at sixty-one, found the political levers he was used to pulling weren't connected to anything any more. Even his links with the Kennedys didn't seem as useful as they once had.

Sitting here, he felt old, tired, used up.

Maybe I should retire back to Dallas, he thought. *Go work on my golf swing.*

He noticed Agronski glancing around at the walls at the moon-walk maps. 'Poignant, isn't it?' Michaels said sharply.

Agronski didn't react.

60

'Leon, why did the President withdraw this draft?'

'Because, frankly, nobody in the White House is sure about the impact Kennedy's remarks about the Mars option are having on public opinion. And now –' Agronski waved a hand at the curling photographs of Fra Mauro '– now you people have served us up with all *this*. The public mood is a fragile thing, Fred; after Apollo 13 America may want to go to Mars as fast as it can – or it may want to close down the space program altogether.'

Muldoon's nostrils went white. 'You're talking about the lives of three men, damn it.'

Agronski studied him, analytically. 'You know, you people at NASA have been the same whenever I've dealt with you. So emotive, so unrealistic. Even you, Fred. Every time we ask for proposals, back you come wanting everything: look at this Space Task Group report with its "balanced programs," its "wide range of technologies." You ask for Mars, but that brings everything else in its wake, it seems: nuclear boosters, a Space Shuttle, huge space stations. The same old vision von Braun has peddled since the 1950s – even though you didn't need a space station to get to the Moon. Your hidden agendas are not, frankly, very well hidden. Why can't you learn to prioritize?'

Muldoon said angrily, 'The Task Group is asking for a mandate to begin the colonization of the Solar System. And to secure the future of the human race, just as Kennedy is saying. What could be higher priority than that?'

'Oh, for God's sake,' Agronski snapped. 'We're a country at war, Colonel Muldoon. And the war is a hemorrhage of money, resources, national morale.'

'Sure,' Muldoon said. 'And Apollo is going to end up having cost as much as it takes to keep the war going for another twelve months. What a price to pay.'

Agronski ignored that. 'The budget just isn't big enough to do everything you want. You don't have to be a White House insider to see that. And the public mood is against you too. I don't suppose you fly boys have heard of a thing called Earth Day, planned by the environmentalists in a couple of weeks' time –'

'Yes, I've heard of it, damn it.'

'Clean-ups. Marches. Teach-ins. *That's* where the public is going to focus in the coming decade, Colonel Muldoon: on our problems here on Earth, not more of your stunts in space.'

'Maybe so. But Agnew chaired the Space Task Group, not NASA,' Michaels growled.

61

Agronski ploughed on. 'It's time you people dropped the idea that you're some kind of heroic super-agency. During Apollo you thought you were the Manhattan Project. Well, now you're a service agency with a limited budget. And that's what you have to learn to live with . . .'

Michaels knew Agronski had a point.

In Michaels's humble opinion, the current NASA Administrator, Thomas O. Paine, was an idiot: a naive dreamer who was pumping Agnew full of grandiose visions, without a thought about how acceptable they would be to the decision makers inside the White House. Paine was a real contrast to his predecessor, Jim Webb, whom Michaels had greatly admired. Webb was a real political operator – he had known where the bodies were buried, up on the Hill – and he had actively avoided long-term planning. NASA was bad at it anyhow – long-range plans always got bogged down in infighting between the centers – and Webb believed that long-term plans were just hostages to fortune, a distraction for budget authorizers and NASA managers.

Paine couldn't seem to see that the real problem right now lay in holding NASA together, in the tough times to come, not starting up new programs.

It just wasn't the way Michaels would run things.

Agronski said, 'Fred, forget your huge space stations, your fifty men on the Moon in 1980. The President wants what he's calling, in private, a "Kennedy option."' He tapped the document again. 'In this statement he was going to pick out one element from the Task Group's report, the Space Shuttle, on which to focus. But what if he were to choose something else – a more visible, major goal – to achieve as quickly and as cheaply as possible?'

Muldoon was staring at Agronski, evidently baffled.

But Michaels understood. *He's speaking obliquely. In code. He has to. But Kennedy is evidently making his point. Nixon wants to save money. But he doesn't want to be the President who killed the space program, not with Kennedy bleating in the background.*

'You're thinking about Mars,' he said to Agronski. 'After all that bullshit about the Manhattan Project and Earth Day, you're here to talk about going to Mars. Aren't you?'

Muldoon looked startled.

'What does Paine say about this?'

Agronski looked at him carefully. 'Let's think about Doctor Paine later,' he said.

I knew it. They're forcing Paine out. He'd heard the rumors from within the White House. Not only was Paine not cooperating, he was being seen as undermining the President. *We need an new Administrator who will work with us and not against us, and will reflect credit on the President, not embarrass him* . . . Paine was a dead duck. And now – from the way Agronski was studying him – Michaels understood that he, Fred Michaels, was being offered the chance to succeed, in preference to George Low, Jim Fletcher.

Mars, and the post of Administrator, all in one day. Games within games. But I'll have to give Agronski something to take home with him, the bones of a cheap Mars option. And there is sure as hell going to be a price to pay, and I need to find out what it is.

The talk was affecting the astronaut differently. There was a look of *hope* on Muldoon's face, Michaels recognized; a delicate, fragile hope, as if Muldoon thought this magical possibility – *we might go to Mars* – might melt away if he longed for it too warmly.

He wondered how much, if anything, Muldoon was aware of what was really going on here, under the surface. Looking at Muldoon's angry, open face, Michaels felt vaguely ashamed of his calculation. In fact, Muldoon's presence seemed to be working on *him* the way he'd hoped it would work on Agronski.

Joe Muldoon felt scared to say anything, to disturb this difficult, mysterious process of negotiation. In case he made it all somehow go away.

Mars. They're still talking about Mars. If Fred Michaels says and does the right things now, the road to Mars might actually be opening up, for us.

For me.

And Joe Muldoon would have something to do with his life again.

The months since his return from the Moon had been as bad as Muldoon had expected.

His most recent PR jaunt had been to some place called Morang, in Nepal. He'd given his standard-issue schoolkids' talk. *When I was on the Moon* . . .

'When I was on the Moon, I couldn't see Earth so well. Tranquillity Base was close to the Moon's equator, and right at the center of the face of the Moon as you look at it. So Earth was directly above my head, and it was difficult to tip back in my spacesuit to see it.

'The sunlight was very bright, and, under a black sky, the ground was a kind of gentle brown. It looked like a beach, actually. I remember looking at Neil bounding around up there, and I thought he looked like a beach ball, human-shaped, bouncing across the sand. But the colors of the Moon aren't strong, and the most colorful thing there was the *Eagle,* which looked like a small, fragile house, done out in brilliant black, silver, orange and yellow . . .'

His attention had kept drifting from his words, to the hiss of warm rain on the school's wooden roof, the coin-like faces of the children sitting cross-legged on the floor before him, the teacher's odd, suspicious frown.

Once, his brief couple of hours' walking on the Moon were the most vivid thing in his mind, colorful as an *Eagle* on the flat, tan expanse of his memory. But in the endless goodwill tours which had followed the splashdown, he'd given all his little speeches so often, already, that he felt the phrases, the underlying memories, had gotten polished smooth, like pebbles. Eventually the tale would be rendered trivial by the retelling.

Hell, but I'm a long way from the Moon now. And with all these damn cuts I'm never going back. All I can do is talk about it. Damn, damn.

When he'd done, the Nepalese schoolkids had started to ask questions. The questions seemed strange to Muldoon.

'Who did you see?'

'Where?'

'On the Moon. Who did you see?'

'Nobody. There's no one there.'

'But *what* did you see?'

Muldoon started to understand, he thought. Maybe his American-flavored images of beach balls and sand were too foreign for these kids, their level of education not what he'd been prepared for. He needed to be more basic. 'There's nothing there. No people, no plants or trees, no animals. Not even air, no wind. Nothing.'

The children looked at each other, apparently confused.

The rest of the talk, the questions, rambled into nothing.

At the prompting of the teacher – a slim girl – there was some polite applause for him, and he gave out little American flags and copies of the mission patch.

As he left the little school house, he heard the teacher say, 'Now, you mustn't listen to him. He's wrong . . .'

Back in his hotel room, he'd started working his way through the mini bar.

It turned out that the Nepalese believed that when you died, you went to the Moon. Those kids had thought the spirits of their ancestors, their grandparents, lived up on the Moon, and Muldoon should have seen them when he was there. He'd been telling them there was no heaven. No wonder they had been confused.

He'd walked on the Moon. And now, in that corner of his own Earth, he'd been confronted by rows of kids in a wooden shack who were still being taught – despite his actual presence, despite his eye-witness account from the Moon itself – superstitious fairy tales.

It made the whole damn enterprise seem futile.

Just before coming over to JSC to do his capcom shift today, he'd gotten a package in the post. It was a script for a credit card commercial. *Do you know me? Last year I walked on the Moon. That doesn't help me though when I want to reserve an airline seat* . . . Goddamn garbage.

It was for more money than he'd make in five years. He could only do it if he retired from the Agency.

Jill would surely welcome it. Jill wasn't like some of the other wives. She didn't have a military background; Jill had never gotten used to the flights, the dangers, the dilute bullshit that NASA doled out during a mission . . .

And the fact was, NASA was never going to let him go back to the Moon.

What if he did retire?

Maybe the moonwalker tag wouldn't endure; maybe he wouldn't be seen as a hero for much longer. The mood seemed to have turned even more against the program. There had even been criticism, in the press, about his and Armstrong's conduct on the Moon. They'd spent too long on the ceremonials. They'd collected fewer rocks than hoped for. Most of the samples weren't properly documented. They'd used the wrong camera to photograph their footprints, so they'd lost time and come home with less interesting photographs. They'd had to cut short the 3-D photography. Even the shots they'd taken in orbit were criticized, as being tourist shots of Earthrise, while the unexplored Moon whipped by beneath them.

Hell, it was hardly our fault. Nixon called us, not the other way around. And what the hell can you do with all that science stuff? It was hardly idiot-proof: too damn easy to make mistakes, when you only have a couple of hours, out of your entire life, to walk on the Moon . . .

He was already drinking too much, fighting off the depression, the deflation, with alcohol. He'd been just the same after his Gemini flight. A few years of this and he'd turn into some sad, paunchy

65

slob telling war stories to anyone who'd listen, to increasingly blank faces.

He remembered, that day in Nepal, that he'd taken a nap. When he woke up, he needed the bathroom. He tried to float out of bed, and his torso went crashing to the floor, his legs wrapped up in a sheet. And then, when he'd shaved, he tried to leave the after-shave bottle floating in the air. It fell into the sink, smashing into big sharp chunks.

That evening in Nepal, he was to be guest of honor at a dinner at a swank, Western-standard restaurant a mile off. He elected to walk, to clear his head of beer fumes. The road was rocky, badly made, and steep; he was, after all, in the foothills of the Himalayas here. He soon tired.

All along the side of the road as he walked, there were children, kneeling down. They all held candles and looked up at him, their round faces shining in the dusk light like images of the Moon.

It was an act of veneration.

They think I'm a god. A god, come to visit them.

They shouldn't do this to people, damn it. They'd made him into a stranded moonwalker. He just wanted to walk on another glowing beach.

He tried to focus on what Michaels and Agronski were saying.

Michaels hauled his bulk out of his chair, and let his impressive, waist-coated gut hang over the polished table for a minute. 'Gentlemen, let's see if we can't cut to the chase.'

He pulled a flip-chart away from the wall. The first few sheets were covered with barely comprehensible notes relating to the Apollo 13 astronauts' abandoned moonwalk checklists: 'DOCUMENTED SAMPLE: select sample/ place gnomon upsun of sample/ sample & gnomon [8,5,2] x sun/ retrieve sample . . .' There was a peculiar poetry in the way these technical people communicated with each other, he reflected.

On a clean page, he began to scribble. 'Let's see what we got here. How would we do this? What's the minimum we have to do to get to Mars? I can see three strands of work for the short term. First, we'll need flight tests of the nuclear rocketry. Second, we'll have to man-rate the modules of the Mars ship itself, such as a lander. Finally, we're going to have to get some experience of long-duration missions in space.' He listed the items quickly. 'But, whether we go for the Space Shuttle, or for an uprated Saturn program, or both, you're looking at maybe five years before a new launch system comes on stream. So for the time being we're going to need to use the Saturn V to get by.' He eyed Agronski. 'You know we've already announced the suspension of the Saturn V production line.'

'Of course.'

'Now, in addition to the moonshots, we have our Skylab program, which might have needed a couple of Vs. But a couple of months back we redirected the program; we're going to revert to the Wet Workshop concept, which can be launched by a Saturn IB. So as of now our remaining Saturn Vs – seven of them built or in production, SA-509 through SA-515 – are dedicated to Apollo Moon missions.'

'How many launches will you need for a Mars program?' Agronski asked.

Michaels blew out his cheeks. 'Let's say, in the next half-decade, six Saturn V flights, and perhaps ten Saturn IBs. That should get Skylab well underway, and perhaps take us as far as the first Earth-orbit manned flights of the NERVA, before we get the new launcher. Joe, does that sound reasonable?'

Muldoon grunted. 'Yeah. I guess. If you want to cut it to the bone; if you want to run the risk of another Apollo 1 fire.'

'Now, Joe . . .'

'Six Saturn Vs,' Agronski said. 'And there are seven Moon flights left, Apollos 14 through 20.' His lips pulled tight into a thin grin.

So that's it. Now I know the price, for Mars, for Paine's job. It was as if Agronski was taking a much-delayed revenge. Agronski had always despised the manned Moon program, opposed it when-ever he could. *Agronski knows that this is the end of Apollo. Right here and now; right in this room.*

Agronski said smugly, 'Well. Of course I'm aware that there's a lot of opposition to further Moon flights, even within NASA. The whole system's too complex. "One of these days Apollo will kill somebody, if it hasn't already killed Lovell and his crew" – that's what is being said, isn't it? I imagine a curtailment wouldn't be impossibly difficult to sell, even within NASA, now that the first landings have been achieved. And –'

Muldoon kicked back his chair and stood up. 'So we're cutting the Moon flights,' he said. He was tall, intimidating, his disgust majestic. 'Just when we've got there. Jesus Christ, Fred. The later flights would have been the crown of the program,' Muldoon said. 'J-class missions, with advanced LMs, three-day stays on the surface, long-duration backpacks that would extend each

67

moonwalk to up to seven hours, and electric cars. We'd have gone to sites of terrific wonder, and beauty, and scientific interest. We've even got a tentative plan to go to the far side of the Moon.'

Michaels stared at Muldoon. He prided himself on being a great off-the-ballot politician, but he found words deserting him, at this moment of all moments.

'I know, Joe. I know.'

Michaels could imagine the attacks he'd suffer from the scientists. It was even possible he wouldn't be able to sell a deal like this to Paine, and to others in the Agency, such as George Mueller, the great space station proponent. And, looking further ahead, he supposed there was a danger that a Mars program would keep NASA a single-issue Agency, everything subordinated to one goal, just like in the days of Apollo.

He tried to focus on Muldoon, to handle the situation in front of him.

'It may not be a case of canceling the flights, Joe. Maybe we could stretch out the schedule. Defer some of the flights until later –'

Muldoon faced Michaels; the knotty muscles bunched around his shoulders, under his shirt. 'Don't do this, Fred. Don't kill the missions.'

From the corner of his eye Michaels could see Agronski's face, his revulsion at this outburst of monomania.

He knows he's won. He knows I'm going to have to do more than just defer; that I'm going to agree to make these sacrifices, to sell them within the Agency and then manage them through as Administrator, in order to give us all a future. And there is more pain, much more, to come.

Michaels felt as if all of history, past and present, were flowing through him, in this room, right now; and that whatever he decided might shape the destiny of worlds.

Sunday, June 21, 1970
Hampton, Virginia

When Jim Dana passed Richmond he turned the Corvette off Highway 1 and onto the narrower State Highway 60, heading southeast. The towns were fewer now, and smaller. And, at last, after Williamsburg, there seemed to be nothing but forests and marshland, and the occasional farmhouse.

It was a fresh June day, and soon Dana could taste salt and ozone from the coast; the sunlight was sharp on the bare arm he propped in the window frame. The landscape around him seemed to expand, to assume the huge, hollow dimensions of his childhood, echoing with seagull cries.

A little after noon he reached Hampton: his home town, right at the tip of the Peninsula. It was a fishing town, a backwater. He drove down streets so familiar it seemed his memories had reached out to reconstruct an external world. Here were the same shabby boatyards, the crab boats lolling in the brackish tidal flow, the gulls: all the symbols of his childhood, still in place. It was as if twelve years had rolled off him, taking away all his achievements – Mary and the kids, the Academy, his USAF service – leaving him a scraped-raw ten-year-old again.

Men had walked on the Moon. And the thinkers of the Langley Research Center, just a few miles to the north, had played a key role in putting them there, Dana's father Gregory included. But it all seemed to have made damn little difference to Hampton.

Both his parents came out onto the porch to greet him. The house's windows gleamed, the porch was swept until it shone, and the wind-chimes glittered in the fresh blue daylight. But the little wooden-framed house had an air of shabbiness about it, and the downtown neighborhood seemed to have got rougher than ever. Dana felt a certain claustrophobia settling over him, like an old, ill-fitting coat.

His mother, Sylvia, was rounder, older, her face more tired and slack than he remembered, but she was lit up by a smile of such intensity that Dana felt obscurely guilty. And here came his father, Gregory Dana, in an old cardigan and with tie loosely knotted, wiping his hands on an oily rag. It was hard to see Gregory's eyes through his dusty wire-rimmed spectacles – *John Lennon glasses,* Dana realized suddenly, and he suppressed a grin.

Gregory shook Dana's hand. 'So how's the great astronaut coming along?'

Gregory had asked that question as long as Dana could remember. The difference now was it looked as if the question might soon have some bearing on the truth.

Lunch was a stiff affair. His parents had always been a little awkward with him, undemonstrative in their affections. So he talked about Mary, the children, how much they'd appreciated the presents they'd been sent for their recent birthdays: the Revell Saturn V rocket kit which had been much too advanced for two-year-old Jake, the hand-knitted sweater for Maria.

When lunch was done, Gregory Dana tucked his tobacco pouch into the pocket of his shabby gray cardigan. 'Well, Jimmy. How's about a little Brain-Busting, back in the shop?'

Dana's mother gave him a glistening nod. It was okay, she'd be fine.

'Sure, Dad.'

The workshop, so called, was actually a small unused bedroom at the back of the house, filled with tools and books and bits of unfinished models, a blackboard coated with obscure, unreadable equations.

Dana cleared some loose sketches from a stool. His slacks were already coated with a patina of fine dust. Every surface was covered with scraps of paper, chewed-off pencils, shreds of tobacco, bits of discarded models. Gregory had always banned Sylvia from doing any cleaning in here. As Dana had grown a little older he'd done a certain amount to keep down the level of detritus and mire; but since he'd left home it looked as if the shop hadn't been cleaned out once.

His father began to bustle about the workshop, pulling together obscure bits and pieces from the clutter, sorting haphazardly. Gregory puffed at his pipe as he worked, quite content, and the rich, seductive scent of burning tobacco filled the room, evoking sharp memories in Dana.

On Sunday afternoons, Gregory had often taken Dana out to the meadows alongside Langley's airfield, and there they would join other Langley engineers in flying their model airplanes and rockets – made not from kits, but in ramshackle home workshops just like Gregory's, here. It had been terrific for Dana to be out there on a wind-blown afternoon, with these gangling, noisy eccentrics – the Brain Busters, they called themselves, isolated from the Hampton locals, who scorned them.

To Dana as a boy of eight or nine, to be able to work at Langley on airplanes and spaceships had seemed the best possible future in the world.

'So,' Gregory said without looking at him, 'where's the next assignment?'

'I'm not sure. It's most likely going to be Edwards.' Down in the Mojave Desert, the USAF's premium flight test station.

'Will you fly there?'

'Maybe. Well, probably. But not the most advanced planes.'

70

'And,' Gregory said levely, 'is that likely to be your long-term posting?'

'Nothing is long-term, Dad. You know that.' It was a question he was asked every time he came home.

Gregory's face was soft, round, a little jowly; his thin hair was plastered over a dome of skull. 'It's your mother. She gets concerned. I –'

'Dad,' Dana said, 'I'm not a combat pilot. You shouldn't worry about such things. I'm not going to Nam. I'm aiming for the space program, not Nam. I don't know how many times I have to –'

'Can you get to be an astronaut, out of Edwards?'

Dana took a breath. 'Sure. In fact, Edwards's day might be coming,' he said. 'The studies are coming in for the Space Shuttle. That will lean heavily on the old lifting-body research that was performed at Edwards. And there is talk of having the Shuttle land at Edwards. Gliding down from space, to land right on the old salt flats.'

Gregory grunted. '*If* the Shuttle goes ahead. The studies are also going ahead for Martian landing missions. And *there* we are looking at more big dumb rockets. More V-2s.'

Dana grinned. 'Those Germans, Dad?'

'It's the crudity of their approach that galls me. Von Braun's designs have always looked the same. For thirty years! Immense, overpowered machines! Leaping to the stars, by the most direct route possible!'

'The Germans got a man on the Moon,' Dana said gently.

'Of course. But it's not *elegant.*'

Not elegant. And that's not the Langley Way.

Gregory was saying, 'Even the basic thinking about interplanetary travel has hardly advanced since Jules Verne.'

Dana guffawed. 'Oh, come on, Dad; that's hardly fair.' The lunar voyagers of Jules Verne's nineteenth-century science fiction had been fired at the Moon out of a huge cannon, situated in Florida. 'Even Verne could have worked out that the gun's acceleration would have creamed his travelers against the walls of their projectile.'

Gregory waved his pipe. 'Oh, of course. But that's just a detail. Look – Verne launched his travelers with an impulse: a shock, a blow, imparted by his cannon. After that brief moment, the spacecraft followed an elongated orbit about the Earth, without any means of directing itself.

'And just so with Apollo. Our great rockets, the Saturns of von

71

Braun, work for only minutes, in a flight lasting days. Effectively they apply an impulse to the craft. Even the Mars studies follow the same principles. Here – look here.'

Gregory walked to the blackboard and wiped it clean with the sleeve of his sweater. He rummaged in his cardigan pocket until he dug out a fluffy piece of chalk, and he drew two concentric circles on the board. 'Here are the orbits of Earth and Mars. Every object in the Solar System follows an orbit around the sun: ellipses, flattened circles, of one eccentricity or another.

'How are we to travel from Earth, on this inner track, to Mars, on the outer? We do not have the technology to fire our rockets for extended periods. We can only apply impulses, hopping from one elliptical path to another, as if jumping between moving street-cars. And so we must patch together our trajectory, to Mars and back, from fragments of ellipse. We kick and we coast; kick and coast. Like so . . .'

Dana watched as his father sketched, and thought about Langley.

The Samuel P. Langley Memorial Laboratory was the oldest aero-nautical research center in the US, and it was father to all the rest. It had been founded during the First World War, conceived out of a fear that the land of the Wright brothers might start to fall behind the European belligerents in aviation. It had been a different world, a world in which the individualistic traditions of old America were still strong, and there was a great suspicion of falling into the emerging technocratic ways of the totalitarian powers of Europe.

Langley stayed poor, humble and obscure, but it succeeded in keeping abreast of the latest technology. And back then – Gregory had told Jim – Hampton was a place where people still referred to the Civil War as 'the late war.'

Gregory had often taken Jim around Langley. The Research Center was a cluster of dignified old buildings, with precise brick-work and extensive porches, that looked almost like a college cam-pus. But, set amongst the neatly trimmed lawns and tree-shaded streets, there were exotic shapes: huge spheres, buildings from which protruded pipes twenty or thirty feet wide. These were Lang-ley's famous wind tunnels.

Jim Dana had come to identify the layout of Langley – the odd mixture of the neatly mundane with the exotic – with the geography of his father's complex, secretive mind.

Hampton was so isolated that a lot of bright young aeronautical engineers didn't want to come within a hundred miles of the place.

Those that did come to Langley tended to be highly motivated, and not a little odd – like Gregory himself, Jim had come to realize ruefully. And the local Virginians hadn't thought much of the 'Nacka Nuts' arriving in their midst – as they still called them even now. So the Langley engineers had kept themselves to themselves most of the time, on and off the job, and Langley had evolved into its own peculiar little world.

As Dana had grown and moved away, he'd become aware of the bigger world beyond Virginia.

'I don't know why you stay here,' he'd once told his father. 'All the real action in NASA is at other sites. Why don't you ever think about moving away?' He couldn't figure his father's lack of ambition.

'Because things don't get any better for people like me than they are here,' Gregory had replied. 'The press don't care much about Langley. Even the rest of NASA doesn't care much. To the outsider, the place is just a set of gray buildings with gray people working slide rules and writing out long equations on blackboards. But if you're in love with aeronautical research, it's a kind of heaven – a unique and wonderful place.'

Jim knew that Langley had made immense contributions to the US's prowess in aeronautics and astronautics. It had got involved with the development of military aircraft during the Second World War and then in the programs which led to the first supersonic airplane, the Bell X-1. Langley staff had formed the task force which had been responsible for the Mercury program, and later it got involved with studies for the optimal shapes for the Gemini and Apollo ships . . .

Gregory never talked about his past. Dana knew he'd suffered during the war. Maybe, he thought, Langley was kind of a refuge, after all that. It buffered him from the pressures of the competitive aircraft industry, and on the other hand from NASA politics. It was as if the men of Langley – and they *were* men, almost exclusively – had made a kind of unconscious decision that their site and budgets and scope should remain small, even as the space program Langley had spawned had grown like Topsy.

Gregory was still only forty-one. But Dana could see, now he'd grown a little more, that Gregory had found a place that suited him; and here he was going to stay, getting older and slower, charming everyone with his lingering traces of French accent, working at his own pace inside this peaceful, isolated cocoon.

Staying at Langley meant, though, that Gregory and Sylvia were more or less stuck, here in downtown Hampton, on Gregory's plateaued-out salary; and here they'd probably have to stay, despite the inexorable decay of the neighborhood . . .

Gregory had drawn a half-ellipse which touched Earth's orbit at one extreme, and reached out to kiss Mars's orbit at the other. 'Here we have a minimum-energy transfer orbit. It is called a Hohmann ellipse. Any other trajectory requires a greater expenditure of energy than this . . . To return to Earth, we must follow a similar half-ellipse.' He moved Mars around perhaps two-thirds of its orbital path, and drew another kissing ellipse, this one out of Mars and inwards toward the Earth. 'The flight home takes just as long as the flight out, around two hundred and sixty days. And in addition, we must wait all this time at Mars, until Earth and Mars have moved into the right configuration for us to return: for no less than four hundred and eighty days. And so our mission time is a remarkable nine hundred and ninety-seven days: more than two and a half years. Our longest spaceflight to date has been around two *weeks*; we surely can't contemplate a mission of such magnitude.'

'And yet, Rockwell are studying just such a mission profile, for NASA,' Dana said. 'Chemical technology only. And at Marshall they are looking at nuclear options.' Nuclear rockets, more powerful, could put ships into shallower, more direct ellipses. 'The Marshall study is showing journey times of no more than four hundred and fifty days, total . . .'

'More big rockets! Huh!'

Dana grinned. 'Still not *elegant* enough for you, Dad? But where's the room for elegance in all this? It seems we're kind of constrained by the laws of celestial mechanics. It's either Hohmann, or brute force.'

'Exactly. So the elegant thing to do is wait: wait until we've developed a smart engine, like an ion drive, which can *really* cut down the transit times. But that won't come in my lifetime, and maybe not yours.'

'Humm.' Dana took the chalk from his father, and drew more concentric circles. 'Of course, you didn't show the full picture here. There are other planets in the system: Venus inside Earth, Jupiter beyond Mars. And the others.'

Gregory scowled. 'What difference does that make?'

'I don't know.' Dana dropped the fragment of chalk back into his father's pocket. 'You're the specialist.'

74

'No, no, this is not my field.'

'Maybe there is some way to use the other planets, to get to Mars. There are NASA studies going on of a Grand Tour: using the gravity field of Jupiter and the other giant planets to accelerate a probe out to Neptune . . .'

'So what are you suggesting? That we fly to Mars via Jupiter? That's ridiculous. Jupiter is three times as far from the sun as Mars is.'

This tone – hectoring, impatient – was all too familiar to Dana. He held his hands up, irritated. 'I'm not suggesting anything, Dad. I'm just chewing the fat. The hell with it.'

But Gregory continued to stare at the board, his eyes invisible behind the layer of chalk dust on his glasses. Some remark of Dana's had sent him off, like a Jules Verne impulse, on some new speculative trajectory of his own; Jim Dana might as well not have been there.

The hell with it, he thought. *I have my own life now, my own concerns. I don't have time for this any more.*

Maybe I never did.

Dana withdrew from the workshop, brushing the dust off his jacket, leaving his father to his thoughts.

He spent the rest of the afternoon with his mother. They sat on the swing seat back of the house, drinking home-made lemonade and talking in the warmth of the sun. In the distance, seagulls cried.

Gregory Dana carefully sketched interplanetary trajectories.

. . . At age fifteen, in the year 1944, Gregory Dana was no rocket engineer. In fact he was no more than garbage, just one of the thirty thousand French, Russians, Czechs and Poles who toiled inside a carved-out mountain in Thuringia.

Everything was slow – even dressing was slow – and Dana was already hungry by the start of his work at five a.m. And yet he would receive nothing until his soup, at two in the afternoon.

And then would come the rush into the smoking mouth of the tunnel into the mountain, with the SS guards lashing out with their sticks and fists at the heads and shoulders of the worker herd which passed them. The tunnel was like Hell itself, with prisoners made white with dust and laden with rubble, cement bags, girders and boxes, and the corpses of the night being dragged by their feet from the sleep galleries.

Gregory Dana was prized by the supervisors for the capacity of his small hands for skilled work. So he was assigned to lighter, more complex tasks. Gradually he picked up something of the nature of the great machines on which he toiled, and learned of the visions of the Reich's military planners.

It was well known among the workers within the *Mittelwerk* that Hitler had ordered the production of no less than twelve thousand of von Braun's A-2 rockets – or rather, what the Germans now called their V-2: V for *Vergeltungswaffe,* revenge weapon.

There was a plan to construct an immense dome at the Pas de Calais – sixty thousand tons of concrete – from which rockets would be fired off at England in batches of fourteen at once. And then there were the further schemes: of hurling rockets from submarine craft, of greater rockets which might bombard targets thousands of miles distant, and – the greatest dream of all! – of a huge station orbiting five thousand miles above the Earth and bearing a huge mirror capable of reflecting sunlight, so that cities would flash to smoke and oceans might boil.

Such visions!

. . . But the V-2 was the daily, extraordinary reality. That great, finned bullet-shape – no less than forty-seven feet long – was capable of carrying a warhead of more than two thousand pounds across two hundred miles! Its four tons of metal contained no less than twenty-two thousand components!

Dana came to love the V-2. It was magnificent, a machine from another world, from a bright future – and the true dream inherent in its lines, the dream of its designers, was obvious to Dana.

Even as it slowly killed him.

One morning, so early that the stars still shone and frost coated the ground, he saw the engineers from the research facility at Peenemunde – Wernher von Braun, Hans Udet, Walter Riedel and the rest, smartly uniformed young men, some not much older than Dana – looking up at the stars, and pointing, and talking softly.

Dana had glanced up, to see where they were looking. There was a star, bright, glowing steadily, with the faintest glimmer of red, like a ruby.

The 'star' was, of course, the planet Mars, burning brightly.

Of course: *that* was the dream which motivated and sustained these young, clever Germans: that one day the disc of Mars would be lit up with cities built by men – men carried there by some unimaginable descendant of the V-2.

At fifteen, Gregory Dana had been able to understand how these young men from Peenemunde were blinded by the dazzling beauty of their V-2 and what it represented. It was not simple callousness:

yes, he could understand the duality of it, and he would comfort himself with plans for after the war. Perhaps, he would dream, he himself would pursue a career in building still greater rocket machines, and even father a son who would be the first to travel beyond the air to Mars or Venus.

How he envied the young engineers from Peenemunde, who walked about the *Mittelwerk* in their smart uniforms; *they* seemed to find it an easy thing to brush past the stacks of corpses piled up for daily collection, the people gaunt as skeletons toiling around the great metal spaceships! The duality of it crushed Dana. Was such squalor and agony the inevitable price to be paid for the dream of spaceflight?

He tried to imagine how it would have been had *he* been born to become one of these smart young Germans in their SS uniforms.

When he immersed himself in such dreams, something of his own, daily pain would fall from him.

But then the morning would come again.

In his workshop, in the sunny June of 1970, Gregory Dana labored at his blackboard, immersed in memories, and the resolving dream of spaceflight.

As Dana's car was pulling away, his father came running from the house. He rested his hands on the Corvette's window frame. There was chalk smeared across his forehead.

'Where are you going?'

'I've got to get away, Dad,' Dana said apologetically. 'I have to be at –'

'I think it works,' Gregory said breathlessly. 'Of course it's too early to be sure yet, but –'

'What works?'

'Venus. Not Jupiter – *Venus*. Kiss good-bye to Verne – we don't need those immense nuclear rockets after all!'

'Dad, I –'

Sylvia linked Gregory's arm. 'Good-bye, dear. Drive safely.'

'I'll call when I'm home, Mom.'

Dana looked back once, at the end of the block. Sylvia was waving, but his father had already gone back to his shop.

Thursday, July 9, 1970
San Gabriel Mountains, California

It was nearly noon; from a burned-blue sky the sunlight bore down on York's bare head and shoulders.

Jorge Romero had led them all into a little valley that afforded a good view of the hills. Now he went bounding up to a twisted old ironwood tree. 'This tree is your LM. You've just landed on the Moon. Now I want each of you to come stand over here and describe what you see.'

The three astronauts – Jones, Priest, Bleeker – stared back, all but anonymous in their baseball caps, T-shirts and chromed sunglasses.

Romero's question wasn't hard, York knew. This was an interesting area: non-lunar, but with easily visible geologic relations among colorful rock units. But the stances and expressions of the astronauts betrayed a mixture of bafflement, embarrassment and resentment.

Christ, York thought. *This trip is going to be a disaster.*

But Romero was windmilling his arms at them. 'Come on! The one thing you're always short of on the Moon is time. You – Charles. Come over here, and start us off.'

With a kind of lazy grin at Bleeker, Chuck Jones went strolling over to Romero. He leaned against the tree, beside Romero, and began to summarize what he could see.

Romero was maybe fifty now, York supposed, but he was vigorous and supple, apparently still full of energy; his sunburned nose stuck out from under his sunglasses, and a few strands of graying hair licked out from under his floppy hat. York had taken in a graduate lecture of Romero's some years back. Working out of Flagstaff, Romero was a great field geologist as well as a geochemical analyst. He had immediately struck her as someone who could not fail to inspire the most reluctant of students – such as your average beer-swilling, wise-cracking, pilot-astronaut hero, for instance.

So when Ben Priest had told her that Romero had agreed to give the Apollo 14 crews, prime and backup, some geologic training, and Ben had invited her along to help out, she'd been pleased.

'. . . No, no, no! What about the layers in that mountainside over there?'

'Look, Professor –'

'And you have missed the most important feature of the landscape altogether!'

78

Jones looked baffled; he was squat, solid, dark, and the thick primate hair on his hands and arms seemed to bristle with anger. 'What "important feature," for Christ's sake?'

'Look here.' Romero knelt and picked up a handful of fragments, of a white rock, from the floor of the valley. 'Can you see? Such rocks are everywhere – are they not? – now that you *observe*.'

Jones had had enough. 'This is a goddamn boot camp.' He kicked at one of Romero's white rocks. 'Ben, this is a *fucking* waste of time. Our program is compressed enough without this crap.'

'Come on, Chuck,' Adam Bleeker said easily. 'You haven't given it much of a chance.'

'Fuck it, and fuck you,' Jones said. 'Listen up: we're only the goddamn backup crew for Apollo 14. That's the first thing; we probably won't even make it to the Moon. Two. The target is the lunar Apennines, not goddamn California. So why am I here tripping myself up on a pile of Californian rocks? Three. I'm an aviator. I don't see why I need to know a fucking thing about the geology of the goddamn Moon to do my job.'

'Look, Chuck –' York stepped forward.

The look he gave her then – of sheer, undiluted contempt – made her hesitate, just long enough for Romero to raise his hand.

'Now, now. Of course Mr Jones here is absolutely right.'

Jones looked startled.

'It doesn't matter how much you know about the San Gabriel mountains. Of course not. It doesn't really matter what you know about the Moon. What does matter to me, though, is that for you to make your mission into a full-up success, you're going to have to learn how to *observe*.'

A full-up success. Ben Priest was suppressing a grin; York wondered if he had coached Romero to throw dumb-fighter-jock slang at Jones.

It caught Jones off balance, anyhow. He bent and picked up a piece of the white rock. 'Just tell me what the hell the relevance of this is.'

'It is called anorthosite,' Romero said evenly. 'And it is our best guess that this was the primary component of the Moon's primordial crust.'

'Really?' Adam Bleeker stepped forward now, and took the piece of rock from Jones – as if it was the only sample of anorthosite in the valley, York reflected wryly. 'How so?'

Jones still glowered, but for now he was sidelined from the conversation, and Romero was back in control.

'When it first formed, the Moon was probably entirely molten. Then the outer hundred miles or so cooled to form a crust of anorthositic rocks – bright rocks, just like these. The main components of anorthosites, you see, like plagioclase, are light; heavier minerals, including those rich in iron and magnesium, sank into the body of the Moon. Now, the anorthosite – we think – dominates the brighter, older areas we see on the Moon's face, while the dark maria are cooled seas of lava.'

Bleeker was grinning at the idea. 'So the maria really were seas, once.'

York nodded. 'It must have been a hell of a sight, back then: oceans the size of the Mediterranean brimming with red-hot, molten lava . . .'

She tailed off. Jones, his eyes hidden by his sunglasses, was watching her as she spoke, and cracking some joke to Ben Priest. Something crass, about the way she moved her eyebrows up and down when she was talking.

Ben looked uncomfortable, caught between a grin with his crew commander and embarrassment for his friend.

And York was silenced, just like that. She felt as if she was sixteen again, gawky, clumsy, infuriated.

With a fling of the arms, a grand actor's gesture, Jorge Romero walked a few yards away. 'Listen to me. I want you to leave this place as better observers, after today. But I also want you to leave with something else: a sense of the great *drama* of geology.' He glanced around. 'When you look at a valley like this, you see a few dusty old rocks, perhaps. But *I* see immense processes which churn the surfaces of worlds, frozen in time as if by a flashbulb. I am sure Natalie has the same perception. It is only our mayfly life spans which restrict us all from seeing this.

'And now you may be going to the Moon! You must grasp this opportunity, and go there with open hearts and minds. Believe me when I say that I would give anything to exchange places with you.'

Chuck Jones stepped forward and spat a piece of gum onto the dusty ground. 'Yeah, well, we won't be going either unless Dave Scott and Jim Irwin drive their Lunar Roving Vehicle over a god-damn cliff on one of these dumb jaunts. They'll be taking the last Apollo to the Moon, and not us. So I think you should cut the speeches, Prof, and let's get on with the checklist, and get this over.'

He kicked a piece of ancient anorthosite out of his way, and stalked out of the valley.

There should have been at least four astronauts on this field trip.

But the good old guys seemed to have lost heart in what they saw as pointless training exercises, after the program cancelations Fred Michaels had announced earlier in the month. At least these three had turned up, but Jones's attitude was turning the whole thing into a walk through Purgatory.

York was pretty uniformly appalled by the astronauts she'd met so far. Ben was clearly atypical. And she couldn't believe guys like Jones; they were like relics from some grisly Flintstones version of the 1950s. The whole bunch of them seemed utterly self-obsessed, to her.

Well, screw them.

She and her friends at Berkeley had done little, over the last couple of months, but follow the fall-out from the events at Kent State, in May. Some of them were preparing their own demonstrations in support and sympathy. She was prepared to bet Chuck Jones – probably Bleeker too, even Ben – hadn't even heard of the Kent State trouble, the way it was tearing the country apart. They were so cocooned inside their precious programs.

She felt blind, unreasoning anger, almost a hatred of these astronauts, and the system that had produced them.

As he stumped over the landscape, Chuck Jones could barely see the rocks around him. He just kept on going over and over the events of the last few days.

Fred Michaels, Associate Administrator, had come to the Astronaut Office in Building 4 personally, to wield the axe. He'd stood there in his waistcoat, plump as a seal, in front of a room full of sports shirts and crew cuts.

Michaels's personal presence wasn't much consolation, for Chuck Jones.

Michaels was here to announce, tersely, that the bean counters were cutting *all* the remaining Moon flights – save only for one more, Apollo 14, which was due to fly early in 1971.

Jones couldn't believe it; in a few words, Michaels was shredding his, Jones's, one-and-only chance of a Moon flight.

There was some argument from the floor, but Michaels slapped down their questions. 'It's for the good of the program, damn it, the longer-term good of the Agency. We've done what we've had to do. And Tom Paine –' the NASA Administrator – 'doesn't like this any more than I do. Less, even. But we've had to accept this, to give us all a future. I'm sure most of you men understand that.'

Sure, Jones thought, you might understand it in your head. But, when you've just had the flight you've trained for over years taken away, you can't take it in your fucking *gut*.

And the anguish in the Office had gotten all the greater when Deke Slayton stood up, his face like granite, to announce that it had been decided that this last mission, 14, should be upgraded to a J-class, a sophisticated scientific expedition. So 14 would get the advanced LM with the Lunar Rover, and the Service Module with orbital instrument pallet, which had been assigned to Apollo 15. And with 15's equipment had come its landing site: a place called Hadley, in the foothills of the lunar Apennines.

But 15's original crew – Dave Scott, Jim Irwin and Al Worden – were already in intensive training for the Hadley site.

So, Deke said, he was standing down Alan Shepard and his crew, who had been the prime assignment for Apollo 14. Scott and his crew had been promoted to 14 instead, and they'd take their back-up crew of Jones, Bleeker and Priest with them. The date of the flight would be put back a few months, to give Boeing a chance to get the Rover ready, and let Grumman finish their LM upgrades. Deke said he'd expect Shepard's crew to pitch in and support Scott's training from here on in.

Jones saw Al Shepard walk out of that meeting, his face like a tombstone. You didn't want to cross Al at the best of times, and it was obvious that despite his seniority he hadn't been taken into confidence about the rearranged schedules before the meeting. Slayton was a good old buddy of Al's, too, all the way back to the Mercury days. *A hell of a way to handle things, Deke.* Well, Jones expected Slayton would be getting a few choice words of advice from Shepard after this.

Jones had his own points to make, though.

He left it a couple of hours, then he went storming into Slayton's office.

'Damn it, Deke, I shouldn't be backup. You ought to be making me commander of the prime crew for 14, in place of Scott.' After all he – Jones – had been one of the original batch of Mercury astronauts, *and* the fourth American in space. And he'd already started his training for his own later J-class mission besides.

He'd waited a hell of a long time for this, the crown of his career, and he wasn't giving up his mission – to be busted down to hole-in-the-sky trash-can Skylab flights – without a fight.

But Deke had just waved him away. 'You don't have a case, Chuck. Listen: Al Shepard is also one of the original batch, in case you forgot that, *and* he's been waiting for a lot of years for a second flight after that damn ear illness. And he was the *first* American in space; Al outranks you, Chuck. But I'm still standing him down in favor of Dave Scott. You've got to face it, Chuck. I don't like this any more than you do, but Scott's is the best prepared crew I have, for the one mission we've got left.'

'Yeah.' Of course Jones understood that. The mission was the thing; nobody within NASA wanted to do anything that carried the slightest risk of a foul-up.

Nobody, that is, save the astronauts who weren't aboard the last Apollo Moon ship.

Understanding it didn't stop him trying, though; and he had stayed in Slayton's office for a long time, arguing hard . . .

There was another piece of the old rock, anorthosite or whatever shit it was, in his way. Jones kicked it aside and stalked on.

The afternoon was to be a simulated three-hour moonwalk. York had to make up the numbers, in the absence of enough astronauts. Jones teamed with Priest, and Bleeker paired off with York. Jorge Romero would stay behind in the truck, and act as a capcom. The astronauts wore backpacks, radios and cameras, and they followed traverses laid out on coarse maps designed to match the quality of low-resolution orbital photographs.

York and Bleeker stopped at the first sample point. There was a large, fractured boulder here, shot through with anorthosite. Bleeker set up a gnomon and took a photograph of the rock face. The gnomon was a device for calibration, a little tripod with a color scale for the photography, and a free-hanging central rod to give local vertical. Bleeker hit the rock with his hammer, and broke off a piece the size of his fist. He placed the sample in a small Teflon bag and dropped it into the pack on York's back. He'd donned lunar gloves to do the work; York could see how stiff and clumsy the gloves were.

'How was that?'

She grinned back at him. 'Standard operating procedures, Adam; Jorge will be proud of you.'

They walked on.

Bleeker raised his face to the sun, a vague half-smile on his face. Bleeker was pale, freckled – a northern boy – and he wore plenty of sun-block on his exposed skin, here in the Californian heat. York hadn't spent any time alone with him before today. He seemed bland, unimaginative, rather empty. *Ideal profile for a moonwalker,* she thought wryly.

'I guess this training is very different from what you've been used to,' she said.

'Oh, you bet. Especially compared to my assignment before joining the Astronaut Office.'

'What was that?'

'510 Squadron. That's a fighter-bomber squadron, based in Virginia. Beautiful part of the country. Do you know it?'

'No . . . What kind of bombs?'

He glanced at her, professional reserve coming down behind his eyes. 'Special weapons.'

Oh. Nuclear.

'We were trained to deploy out of West Germany. We'd have flown low, a hundred feet, under the enemy's radar.' He mimed the maneuver with a dusty hand. Now he pulled his hand so it soared straight upwards. 'The idea was to let go of the payload at just the right moment. The package would follow a two-mile arc to the target.' He grinned again, almost shyly. 'While it was falling I'd be high-tailing it out of there, as fast as I could go, before the detonation.'

'I'll bet. It sounds risky.'

'All flying is risky,' he said levelly. 'But the F100s we flew were beautiful ships . . .'

He waxed lyrical about the F100 for a while: the 'Super Saber,' the world's first fighter capable of sustained supersonic speed.

York tuned out.

The F100 had been produced by Rockwell: the company who had built Apollo, and who were now bidding to go to Mars. Given where the bulk of the money went, it was as if the space work of companies like Rockwell was a thin, glamorous patina on the surface of their real mother lode, military development.

'The part I didn't enjoy so much was ejecting.'

'Ejecting?'

'It was a one-shot mission. The planes didn't carry enough fuel to make it to their targets and back. We had to eject hundreds of miles short of home, let the planes crash, and then survive as best we could.'

'Christ,' York said. 'Walking home, through a nuclear battlefield?'

'I was trained for it,' he said. 'I was part of a global strategy. The weapons are new, so you need new strategies to use them. It's all about mutual deterrence. "Safety will be the sturdy child of terror, and survival the twin brother of annihilation . . ."'

84

She was startled by the quote. 'That's well expressed.'

'Winston Churchill.' His eyes were like blue windows.

He wasn't unintelligent, she realized. Just – different from her, and the people she mixed with. A Cold Warrior. She shivered.

He glanced at his checklist. 'Hey, look; we've missed our last stop.'

They turned and retraced their footsteps, reaching for fresh sample bags.

At the end of the afternoon, they met up back at the truck. Romero was still grinning, even joking with Jones, but York thought she could see a strain around Romero's eyes, under the dust and sunblock.

On the truck radio, a commentator was quoting a speech by Walter Mondale in Congress, where NASA's budget submission was being debated. . . . *I believe it would be unconscionable to embark on a project of such staggering cost as this Mars proposal when many of our citizens are malnourished, when our rivers and lakes are polluted, and when our cities and rural areas are dying. What are our values? What do we think is more important? . . .*

York and Ben Priest got cups of coffee from a communal flask, and walked off a little way. The sun was low, now, and blasted directly into their eyes; it had lost little of its heat.

'I guess Romero is soaking up a lot of Chuck's frustration at losing his flight,' York said.

'Naw. Chuck is always like this, when it comes to the "science,"' Priest said. He took a pull of his coffee. 'It's damaging.'

'Damaging is right. Can't you exert some influence on him?'

He grinned at her. 'I'm afraid you don't know astronaut psychology, Natalie. Where these guys are concerned, the commander's word is *everything*. He sets the tone for the crew, the whole mission. If the commander is somber and quiet, like Armstrong, then that's the way the crew must be; if he wants to wear a beanie hat with a Teflon propeller on it, and sing all the way to the Moon, like Pete Conrad, then we all have to wear our beanie hats and like it. That's the way it is. Thank God Dave Scott is taking the science seriously. I think if Chuck was the prime commander, 14 might be the nadir of Apollo's science program, not the zenith.'

Now, she heard, voices were raised again. Romero was telling Jones how important it was to take samples from large boulders, if they could, because large rocks wouldn't have moved far from where they were formed. And the *context* of a sample was just as important, to the good geologist, as the *content* of the rock –

Jones was telling Romero where he could stick his geological hammer.

This isn't good enough, York fumed. *We can't keep sending these clowns to the Moon. Beanie hats, and kids' jokes –*

We can't go on like this. If we're really going to Mars we need a new class of astronaut. A better breed.

Ben had continued to encourage her to apply, to join the program. *Maybe I should. I know I could do a better job than a moron like Chuck Jones.*

She went back to the truck, and got more coffee.

Mission Elapsed Time [Day/Hr:Min:Sec] Plus 001/13:45:57

'You are go for TOI,' capcom Bob Crippen said. 'One minute thirty.'

'Thank you,' Gershon replied.

York pulled on her helmet and locked it to the neck of her pressure suit. She fumbled slightly, her fingers clumsy inside her stiff gloves. She buckled her canvas restraints around her.

Once more she felt cool, stale air wash over her face.

Ares, assembled, was a slim, fragile pencil of metal. It was a big, bright object, and it would be easily visible from Earth, as a naked-eye star passing over Cape Canaveral.

Stone said, 'Go for ET H-two pressurization.'

'Confirm.'

York began closing switches that would raise the temperature inside the booster's two great External Tanks. Liquid hydrogen would boil and evaporate, and the resulting gas would force liquid propellant through the feed pipes and into the combustion chambers of the MS-II.

York was a geologist, and that was why she was going to Mars. But a crew was only three people. So, if you expected to fly in space, you had to expect to study up on a lot of mundane crap that was necessary just to keep the spacecraft and booster working.

And Natalie York's specialty was the External Tanks.

She knew enough to give expert papers on External Tanks to the industry. In fact, she *had* given a paper on them, God help her.

'One minute,' Gershon said.

York glanced at the window to her right. She was over the west

Atlantic, and it was early morning down there; she could see boats on the Gulf, ribbons of land laid out like a cartoon map.

TOI was Transfer Orbit Injection: it meant departure from Earth orbit, the start of the long transit to Mars. This was a key moment in the mission – in her life, in fact.

But a day and a half here, orbiting Earth, wasn't enough.

She had tried to fix some of the more memorable scenes of Earth in her head. *Night over Africa:* the fires of nomad encampments, spread across the desert. *Thunderstorms over New Zealand:* lightning like flashbulbs, exploding under cottony layers of cloud, discharges sparking each other in great chain reactions covering the country.

November 6, 1986. That was the day when Ares was due to return to Earth orbit. Mission day five hundred and ninety-five. *Then I'll be back; I'll be seeing you again. A bright Sunday morning, with my crates full of bits of Mars.*

'Ares, you are go for the burn,' Crippen said.

Stone set the 'master arm' switch to ON, and York could see him checking over the rest of the instrument panel. Guidance control was set to primary; thrust control was on automatic; the craft was in the correct attitude; the engine gimbals were enabled, so that the nozzles could swivel, like eyeballs in their sockets, to direct the craft.

Eight seconds before ignition, York felt a push at her back. Ullage: small rockets firing around the base of the stack, settling the propellants before the main burn.

'99:40,' the commit code, started flashing up on the small computer screen before Stone. *Are you sure you want to do this?*

There was a small button marked PROCEED under the screen. Stone reached out a gloved finger, and pressed the button.

Gershon counted down: 'Five. Four . . .'

York braced herself.

There was a distant rumble, carried through the stack, as the MS-II's four huge engines ignited, three hundred feet away from her. The acceleration was low, almost gentle, pushing her into her couch with a soft pressure across her chest and limbs.

After thirty-seven hours of microgravity, she felt enormously heavy. But at least it was smooth: this time, the ride really did feel like the simulator. Later in the mission – when Ares had burned off its fuel, reducing its mass – the acceleration of the MS-II would be a lot tougher.

Gershon read out velocity increments. York could hear how his voice was masked, slightly, by the gum he chewed. *Juicy Fruit.* How can you eat gum in a spacesuit? Gershon wasn't above sticking a wad to the inside of his faceplate, with his tongue, for retrieval later. The guy was gross.

'Ares, Houston, you're looking good here,' Crippen said. 'Right down the old center line.'

'Thank you,' Stone said. 'Things look fine up here too. Rates looking good.'

She looked out her window. The Earth was falling away, visibly; it was a remarkable sight, as if the Earth was a special-effects prop, being hauled away from her window.

The sense of motion, of speed, was remarkable.

'How's it going, York?' Stone asked dryly.

She started. He'd caught her rubber-necking again. 'Fine. Fine, Phil.'

She turned back to her station. She had her job to do, and she should get to it. *It won't fail because of me.* The mantra of everyone involved with the Ares program.

She stole a glance at Stone. He was watching his own readouts, eyes fixed on the goal, apparently oblivious to her again. Stone was in utter control of himself. He always was.

She began to watch the status of the External Tanks in earnest, their brief biographies spelled out by the displays in front of her.

Floods of liquid oxygen and hydrogen, sixty-four thousand gallons a minute, pumped out of the Tanks to be consumed in the engines of the MS-II. Already the pressure in the Tanks was dropping away, she read; to keep the pressure up, there was a complicated backfeed system which took vaporized gases back from the engines into the Tanks. The fuel system was surprisingly complicated, elaborate, a system of huge pipes, fountains of supercold liquid propellants cascading into combustion chambers as hot as the sun . . .

In the middle of the burn, Crippen said, 'Okay, Ares, Houston, we'd like to try for the TV request.'

Stone and Gershon both stifled groans. York glanced up self-consciously, at the little Westinghouse TV camera fixed to its bracket above her head.

Crippen said, 'We would like five minutes' worth of TV, and we would like an exterior shot, with a narrative if you can give us one.'

'Copy,' Stone said.

NASA was following a policy of televising the most dramatic moments of the mission. It was all to drum up interest and enthusiasm for Ares, to allow the great American public to see what they were paying for. A feed from the Command Module to the TV companies had been provided during the launch itself, for example. But York wasn't so sure that had been a good idea. The launch probably looked too damn comfortable, to a generation that had been brought up on the glamorous pyrotechnics of *Star Wars*.

Stone nodded to York, and she pushed a button on her console to start the camera.

'Okay,' said Stone. 'Welcome to Ares. You're looking at us in our Command Module here. We're in the middle of our TOI maneuver. We see through our windows the sun going by, and, of course, the Earth. We can give you the time of day in our system of mission elapsed time: thirty-seven hours, and fifty-one minutes, and umpteen seconds. Now maybe Ralph can show you the view.'

Stone nodded to York. She reached up to pull the TV camera off its mount. Because of the thrust she couldn't just float it; she had to pass the camera to Gershon. It felt massy, awkward, in the gentle acceleration of the MS-II.

'Okay, Houston, here you go,' Gershon said. 'Here you see the Earth, falling away beneath us.'

'Copy, Ares. Fine images.'

'It really is a fantastic sight,' Gershon said. 'We're somewhere over the Atlantic right now, and I can see the eastern seaboard, from Florida all the way up to Newfoundland, as clear as crystal. I don't know if that's visible in your images.'

'We see it.'

'And as I look to my right, I can see, just toward the limb of the planet, what must be Western Europe and Africa. I can see Spain, and the British Isles, all kind of foreshortened. The British Isles are definitely a greener color than the brownish-green that we have in Spain. There's a little haze over Spain, and what looks like cumulus clouds piled up over the south of England.'

'Copy. That matches the weather reports we have today.'

'Good to know I'm looking at the right planet, Houston . . .'

Stone said now, 'I got a comment about the point on the Earth where the sun's rays reflect back toward us. In general the color of the ocean is uniform, a rich blue, except for that region – a circle, maybe an eighth of the Earth's radius. In this circular area, the blue of the water turns to a grayish color and I'm sure that's where the sun's rays are being reflected back on up toward us.'

'Roger, Phil,' Crippen said. 'That's been observed before. It's similar to a light shining on a bowling ball. You get this bright spot and the blue of the water then turns into a grayish color.'

'A bowling ball, yeah. Or maybe the top of Phil's head.' Gershon laughed at his own joke.

It was true, York saw, twisting her head; there was a huge highlight on the blue surface of the ocean. *Damn. The thing really is a sphere. Like a ball of steel.*

'Thank you, Ares. How about an internal position now, please? Maybe you'd like to talk us through what the TOI is all about, today.'

Gershon passed the camera back along the cabin, and York fitted it to its pedestal, so it had a panoramic view of the three of them. She caught Stone's face; he rolled his eyes, and pointed to her, and to the camera.

York was on.

She turned back to her displays, and tried not to look up too often at the camera. Her throat felt tight, her face flushed inside her helmet; suddenly she could feel every hot crumple of her pressure suit. She keyed the press-to-talk switch on her headset cable. 'Okay, Houston. This is our TOI maneuver: TOI, for Transfer Orbit Injection. Right now, the big engines on our main booster stage, the MS-II, are firing to push us out of Earth orbit. The MS-II is just a version of the second stage of the old Saturn V, modified to serve as an orbital injection vehicle. The S-IIs which took Apollo to the Moon had five J-2 engines. Well, we've got just four engines, upgrades called J-2S; the central one was removed to accommodate a lox tanker docking port. The MS-II has got more insulation, to stop boiloff, and its own small maneuvering engines, and more docking ports at the front.

'I guess you can say we're all pretty much relieved that the MS-II is working as well as it is; we're going to rely on the MS-II not just to leave Earth but to slow us when we get to Mars, and to bring us out of Martian orbit when we're ready to come home . . .'

She dried up. She was speaking too fast, waffling. 'Stand by,' capcom Crippen said. 'Okay, we've cut the live feed. Ares, you've got a pretty big audience: it was live in the US, it went live to Japan, Western Europe and much of South America. Everybody reports good color, they appreciate the great show.'

Gershon said, 'Keep those cards and letters coming, folks.'

'Missing you already,' said Crippen.

Christ, what rubbish. No wonder they cut the feed.

She hadn't meant to say any of that; she'd wanted to say something personal.

To say how it felt, to see the Earth fall away.

She'd always criticized earlier generations of astronauts, for their lack of eloquence. Maybe it wasn't so easy, after all.

'ETs depleted,' York reported. 'Ready for sep.'

'Roger,' Stone said.

More than two million pounds of fuel, a treasure that had taken five years to haul up to Earth orbit, had burned off in sixteen minutes.

'Three, two, one. Fire.'

Right now, pyrotechnics would be severing the securing bolts and frames at top and bottom of each Tank, and guillotines should be slicing across the wide feed pipes which had carried fuel from the Tanks into the MS-II's belly. York half-expected to hear a rattle of bolts, muffled clangs, like the staging during the Saturn VB launch; but she heard and felt nothing.

'ET sep is good,' she said.

'Confirm ET sep,' said Crippen.

'Hey, how about that.' Gershon was looking out his window. 'I can see a Tank.'

York twisted in her couch, and turned to look. Silhouetted against the gray-blue of Earth, the discarded ET was a fat, cone-tipped cigar case, colored muddy brown and silver. On its flank she could see bits of lettering, and small patches of orange insulation amidst the silver. Propellant dribbled from one of the severed feed pipes, a stream of crystals which glittered against the skin of Earth. The dribble made it look as if the ET had been wounded, like a great harpooned whale.

The Tank rapidly receded from Ares, falling away and tumbling slowly.

Both Tanks were moving quickly enough to have escaped Earth's gravity field, with Ares. The Tanks would become independent satellites of the sun, lasting maybe for billions of years before falling into a planet's gravity well.

She waved the Tank good-bye, with a little flourish of her gloved fingers. *Good luck, baby.*

The engines finally died. She felt it as an easing away of acceleration; a gentle reduction of the subliminal noise and vibration from the remote engines.

'That's it,' Stone said. 'Shutdown. Everything looks nominal.'

Crippen called up: 'You got a whole room of people down here who say you are looking good, Ares.'

Gershon whooped in reply. 'It was one hell of a ride, Bob.'

Stone said dryly, 'From up here the burn was copacetic, Houston. Thank you.' He began to uncouple his helmet and gloves.

York watched the receding Earth fold over on itself, becoming a tight, compact ball in space, with the Atlantic Ocean thrust outwards toward her, wrinkled, glistening.

The Ares cluster was only a couple of hundred miles further from the Earth than in its low orbit. But now, it was traveling so fast that Earth's gravity could no longer hold it. *Four hundred miles a minute*, York thought: so fast that she would cross the orbit of the Moon in just twelve hours.

Crippen said, 'Is that music I hear in the background?'

'No,' Stone said. 'Ralph is singing.'

Saturday, August 7, 1971
Manned Spacecraft Center, Houston

Bert Seger had some paperwork to finish up before he got to go home today. But when news of the splashdown came in he walked out of his office, into the Control Center's high corridor. He pulled a cigar out of the breast pocket of his jacket, his hand brushing the pink carnation that his wife had placed there for him, as always.

After a twelve-day flight, Apollo 14 had splashed down in the Pacific, four miles from the carrier *Okinawa*. NASA was going to be on a high for a while, Seger realized. Scott and Irwin had spent nineteen hours outside the LM, compared to under three hours for Armstrong and Muldoon, and they had traversed seventeen miles around the terrain at the base of a fifteen-thousand-foot mountain. The flight controllers and astronauts had become pretty good at coordinating with the scientists in the back rooms about where and how they should proceed. Almost every one of the J-class mission's innovations – the upgraded LM, the Rover, the orbiting Service Module's instrument pallet – had worked without a hitch.

14 had been the biggest success since the first landing: even skeptics among the scientists were applauding the mission.

But now it was done.

Seger's footsteps echoed in the quiet. It was just two years since Apollo 11, he thought, and yet the first age of lunar exploration was already over. *Damn it*, Seger thought. *We just got good at this stuff, and now we have to stop.*

He stopped at the door of the MOCR, Mission Control, and stepped in. The MOCR was deserted; everybody had already left for the splashdown party, some almighty gumbo affair the Mission Evaluation guys were holding over in Building 45.

He climbed the steps to the Flight Director's console: the heart of a mission, even more so than the couch of the spacecraft commander himself. The big twenty-by-ten-feet screen at the front of the room was black, cold. The controllers' consoles were littered with books, logs, checklists, headsets, and ashtrays filled with cigarette butts and half-smoked cigars. Some of the controllers had left behind the little Stars and Stripes they'd waved when the spacecraft splashed down.

Maybe, he thought, some day these consoles would be full of data streaming in from a manned spacecraft in orbit around Mars.

Standing here, thinking of it in those terms, it didn't seem possible; but then, the lunar landing must have seemed just as impossible back in 1959, when NASA didn't yet exist, and technicians had taken Mercury boiler-plate capsules to the Cape on the backs of flatbed trucks, cushioned by mattresses.

It was Bert Seger's job to make Mars happen.

Seger had been appointed, just a month ago, as a deputy director of the Office of Manned Spaceflight, one of NASA's four big divisions. His job was running the embryonic Mars Program Office, here in Houston.

Fred Michaels had become the new Administrator, after Tom Paine's resignation, and he seemed determined to pull the Agency out of the mess his predecessor had left behind. And he had appointed Bert Seger himself.

'Bert, the damn Mars thing is already coming apart at the seams, and we haven't even got back the final Phase A definition reports yet. Look – I need someone to do for Mars what Joe Shea did for the Moon program, back in the early days. To pull the thing together. Or we're never going to get it past Nixon.'

Seger understood. 'You need a foreman,' he'd said. 'And an enforcer.'

'Damn right I do. Will you do it?'

'Damn right I will.'

'Then here's your first job,' Michaels had said. 'Sort out the goddamn mission mode . . .'

The competing industry contractors, preparing their Phase A

preliminary studies, were all working on different ways of getting to Mars, but the routes they were planning were all direct: Earth to Mars, and back to Earth. Now there was some guy in Langley who was kicking up a fuss about another mode. Something to do with flying by Venus on the way.

'Some little jerk called Dana,' Michaels said. 'Gregory Dana. He wrote direct to me. Can you believe it?' Dana had bypassed all the bureaucratic channels, and had got right up a lot of asses.

'Is he right? About Venus?'

'How in hell do I know? Could I care less, at this point? This Dana has got them all – the Marshall guys, the rest of Langley, the contractors, the Budget Office, the damn Science Advisory Council – buzzing like wasps in a jar. The Requests for Proposal for Phase B detailed definition studies are about to go out. This Dana is putting all of that under threat. Bert, I want you to sort it out for me . . .'

Seger didn't doubt his own ability to resolve this mode issue. Nor did he doubt that he'd be able to fulfill his greater commission: to pull together the Mars program. If that was what the country decided it wanted to do.

Seger always prayed, intensely, for a few minutes at the start of the working day, or before tackling a major task. He felt that showed his character had deep roots, strength, conviction. Standing there in the MOCR, he offered up a brief prayer now.

He thought of that fragile little world two hundred and forty thousand miles away, where three LM descent stages still sat, surrounded by footprints and scuffed-up lunar soil. But the footprints, and the flags, even the science – none of that was really the point, as far as Seger was concerned. Not even getting there ahead of the Russians. To his mind, what Apollo had proved was that men could indeed travel to places beyond the Earth, and live and work there.

The Moon hadn't been as exotic as some had suspected. Some had predicted that the astronauts would sink into miles of dust. Or that the mountains of the Moon might be fragile, like huge gray meringues maybe, and would collapse in puffs of dust when the astronauts tried to walk there. Or maybe the moondust would catch fire, or explode, when the astronauts brought it into the LM. Or the astronauts would be afflicted by terrible diseases . . .

In the end, those hard-headed engineers who had stubbornly insisted that the Moon would be just like Arizona – and had designed the LM's landing gear that way – had turned out to be

94

right. *That's what I gotta bear in mind,* he thought. *Mars will be just like Arizona, too.*

To Seger, that was a magical thought, as if Earth and Moon and Mars were somehow unified, physically, as they were bridged by the exploits of Americans.

He walked carefully down the steps, away from the Flight Director's console, and latched the door behind him.

Monday, August 16, 1971
George C. Marshall Space Center, Huntsville, Alabama

Gregory Dana arrived late, his Vu-graph foils and reports bundled under his arm; by the time he reached the conference room – right next to the office of von Braun himself – it was already full, and he had to creep to the back to find a space.

The room was on the tenth floor of Marshall's headquarters building, colloquially known as the von Braun Hilton. Just about everybody who counted seemed to be here: senior staff from Marshall and Houston, a few managers from NASA Headquarters in Washington, and a lot of people from the contractors whose studies were being presented today.

At the front of the room, so remote from Dana that it was difficult to see his face, Bert Seger, head of the nascent Mars Program Office, was making his opening remarks.

They were all here to listen to the final presentations of the Mars mission mode Phase A studies. Their purpose today, Seger said, was to settle on a recommended mode for the development program. This group had to regard itself as in competition for resources and endorsement with the parallel studies going on into the reusable Space Shuttle; a similar heavyweight meeting had recently been held in Williamsburg to thrash out some of the conceptual issues involved in that program.

In his rapid Bronx delivery Seger gave them a little pep talk: about the need for open discussion, for receptivity, and for a willingness for all here to walk out of this room with a consensus behind whatever mode was favored. Dana could see a little crucifix glinting on Seger's lapel, under a wilting pink carnation.

Dana doubted that anyone missed the subtext of what Seger was saying. Congress was approving the requested funding for NASA's FY1972, but the big expenditure for whatever program was settled on was going to start in FY1973. And President Nixon still hadn't

95

made up his mind about the future of the space program. It was said he might even can manned spaceflight altogether, and look for some superscience stunt on Earth that might prove a better fit with the mood of the times.

Meanwhile there was open warfare going on between two of NASA's centers, Houston and Marshall, over their preferred Mars modes.

It was just what NASA didn't need right now, and all the old hands at NASA had been here before, too many times. Dana knew that Seger had already been trying to get around the conflict by encouraging informal contacts and discussions, and by having the Houston people help with the devising of Marshall's presentation, and so forth. And it was obvious that Seger's intention today was to lance that boil before sending the recommendations further up the chain of command.

Now Seger flashed up a draft agenda. The meeting was going to run for the whole day. The two major modes – chemical and nuclear – would be presented first, followed by the other studies . . .

Dana found with dismay that his would be the last of the five major presentations. *I'm coming at the nutty end,* he realized. *Even after the guys from General Dynamics with their ludicrous atomic-bomb motor. I'm being wheeled on as light relief.* In the midst of this organizational in-fighting, he was going to be squeezed out; he had probably upset too many people by circumventing the hierarchy. He felt his stomach knot up with frustration and anxiety. *Damn it, I know I'm right, that I have the way we should be going to Mars, right here in this folder.* He pushed his spectacles up onto his nose, agitated.

First up was the nuclear rocket option.

Dana thought the timing was significant; this option, heavily pushed by Marshall, was, he had heard, the preferred option amongst the NASA brass.

The presentation was opened by a hairy young man called Mike Conlig. Conlig reported into Marshall now, but he had worked for several years at the nuclear rocket development station in Nevada. 'We've achieved twenty-eight starts of our XE-Prime liquid hydrogen prototype, running up in excess of fifty-five thousand pounds of thrust.' Conlig showed a photograph of an ungainly test rig, framed by dismal mountains. 'Next we will proceed to the development of NERVA 1, which will develop seventy-five thousand pounds of thrust. Then the full NERVA 2 module will be developed, to support the Mars mission itself. NERVA 2 will be flight tested in the mid 1970s, in fact launched into orbit as a new Saturn V third stage . . .'

Conlig spoke well and enthusiastically; Dana let the data rattle through his head.

Now a slim, cold-looking man, his blond hair speckled with gray, walked to the stage. 'To achieve the necessary performance for interplanetary travel, we have evolved a "building block" technology, in which separate NERVA propulsion modules will be launched into Earth orbit, and clustered to achieve different requirements . . .' The voice was shallow, a little clipped – overlaid by a disconcerting Alabama drawl, after all these years at Huntsville – but still underpinned by sharp Teutonic consonants.

This was Hans Udet: Udet, who had worked at Peenemunde with von Braun, and now one of von Braun's senior people at Marshall.

Dana showed no reaction.

Dana had dealt with the Huntsville Germans many times, over his years at NASA. And even now he recognized many faces from those ancient days in the Harz Mountains, here in the halls and offices of NASA.

But he had never been recognized, in his turn – why should he be? – and he had never volunteered his identity. He had mentioned this antique link to no one. The *Mittelwerk* was buried deep in the past, and they had all moved on to new concerns.

He'd never even discussed that part of his past with Jim.

But he had never lost his sense of inferiority, before these confident, clever Germans.

Udet put up foils showing *two* identical ships, to be assembled in Earth orbit. There would be four or six crew in each ship. The ships would be boosted out of orbit by disposable NERVA modules, and then docked nose-to-nose for the flight to Mars. Udet flashed up summaries of mission weights, flight durations, development costs and other key parameters. 'Our baseline study,' Udet said, 'will allow us to launch to Mars in November 1981 . . .'

It was a huge, grandiose scenario. Typical von Braun, Dana thought: unimaginative, brute force, over-engineered.

Bert Seger opened the presentation up for questions. The hostile Houston contingent put in a lot of detailed probing about the untried nuclear technology: the difficulties of clustering the nuclear modules, progress on the advanced cooling techniques needed. There were also questions about the significance of the treaties banning atmospheric testing of nuclear technology; it seemed to Dana that these issues were still unresolved.

Seger let the questions run on for some time – well over the option's allotted slot – and then orchestrated a round of applause. All this reinforced Dana's view that this was the mode preferred within NASA, unofficially, and Seger had a brief to make sure that it was fully understood and accepted.

The second major presentation was of an all-chemical-engine mode. It was prepared by Rockwell, and championed by Houston staff. Rockwell were, incidentally, the favorites to be selected as lead contractor for the Space Shuttle.

The mission profile, Dana soon saw, was close to the classic minimum-energy Hohmann transfer profile he'd sketched out to Jim, that day in the shop at the back of his house in Hampton.

The chemical mode had some advantages. The development program would be comparatively cheap, since the hardware would be based on incremental upgrades of Saturn technology, for example the use of an enhanced Saturn second stage to serve as an orbital injection booster.

But the nuclear camp from Marshall, led by Udet and Conlig, didn't find it hard to pick holes in the case. Compared to the NERVA profile, twice as much mass would have to be hurled into Earth orbit, for a mission twice the length. Chemical technology couldn't manage much better than that. *Not without imagination, anyway*, Dana thought; *not if you stick to direct transfer . . .*

Dana knew that most of the points raised in the discussion were a repeat of the sterile arguments which had plagued NASA for some months.

At the end of the question session Seger didn't call for any applause.

Lunch turned out to be steak and chicken served buffet style. The debate continued during the meal, with delegates making points by jabbing bits of steak or fried potato at each other.

Dana spotted the sleek, handsome figure of Wernher von Braun himself. He was talking to an astronaut: Joe Muldoon, a moonwalker, tall, erect, his thinning, gray-blond hair clipped to military neatness.

Few people spoke to the obscure little man from Langley with his peculiar presentation. *Venus swingby modes? What the hell is that about?* That suited Dana. He left the lunch early and returned to his seat in the hall; he didn't much like steak anyway.

*　　*　　*

The conference looked at two more options, before Dana's pitch. Both of these were more ambitious, technically, than either the main chemical or nuclear options reviewed earlier; Dana suspected they had been explored just to make sure nothing obvious was missed before the primary mode was selected.

A representative of McDonnell presented a so-called nuclear-electric option, together with representatives of NASA and ARPA, the Government's Advanced Research Projects Agency. Plasma – a charged gas – would be accelerated electrodynamically out of a rocket nozzle. A plasma rocket's thrust was tiny, but would last for months; plasma rockets would move spaceflight techniques away, at last, from the antique Jules Verne kick-and-coast model. The technology was unproven, but there had been some trials; an electric rocket had been operated at high altitude as long ago as 1964.

The McDonnell man flashed up a conceptual design for a manned nuclear-electric ship. It was a staggering arrangement, like a three-armed windmill. Two of the arms – each fifty yards long – contained reactors, and the third the habitable section. The rockets were mounted at the hub of the rotor, and the whole thing was designed to spin about the hub, to provide artificial gravity. It would be, Dana thought, like a great metal snowflake, spinning toward Mars. It was a terrific concept, and utterly impractical.

Next up was a project manager from General Dynamics. He got to his feet with a broad grin gleaming from out of a Californian tan. 'I got to tell you,' he told the audience deadpan, 'that I can beat you NERVA folks hands-down. With two million pounds in Earth orbit I can get to Mars and back in just two hundred and fifty days – not much more than half your time – and taking no fewer than twenty guys. Gentlemen, I give you Project Put-Put.'

The idea was to throw one-kiloton nuclear bombs out of the back of the spacecraft – thirty devices every second – and let them off, a thousand feet behind the ship. The shocks would be absorbed through water-cooled springs, and the ship would be driven forward. 'Like setting off firecrackers behind a tin can. Am I right?'

The concept seemed ridiculous, but General Dynamics had done some preliminary studies, called 'Project Orion,' in the early 1960s, and the presenter was able to show photographs of a small flight-test model which had used high explosives to hurl itself a few hundred feet into the air.

The technical problems were all around the high temperature flux on the rocket's back end structure, which would have to radiate

99

away excess heat between explosions. And of course the system had one major drawback, the General Dynamics man said, and that was the radioactive exhaust. But that hadn't seemed such an obstacle back in 1960 when the first Orion studies had been initiated. Then, it was thought that the unscrupulous Soviets might use this quick-and-dirty method to short-cut to space, so we had to look at it too.

The General Dynamics man joshed and wisecracked his way through his talk. When he sat down he got the biggest hand of the day.

Dana felt himself shrink into his seat. *How the hell do I follow that?*

When he got to the podium Dana shuffled with his notes and foils, trying to avoid looking out over the sea of sleek suits before him. There was a spotlight on him; it seemed to impale him. It was already four thirty, and after the General Dynamics pitch the delegates had lost concentration; they were still laughing, talking.

Dana began to read from his notes. 'Manned Mars stopover missions of duration twelve to twenty-four months are characterized by Earth return velocities of up to seventy thousand feet per second, over the cycle of mission opportunities. A promising mode for reducing Earth entry velocities to forty to fifty thousand feet per second, without increasing spacecraft gross weight, is the swingby through the gravitational field of Venus. Studies indicate that this technique can be applied to all Mars mission opportunities, and in one-third of them, the propulsion requirements actually can be reduced below minimum direct mode requirements . . .'

There was a ripple of reaction in the audience, a restless shifting. Dana ploughed on. He felt sweat start over his brow, around his collar.

He hurried through the idea of gravity assist. He tried to emphasize the history and intellectual weight of the idea, showing that his own computations had built on the work of others. 'The concept within NASA of using a Venus swingby to reach Mars dates back to Hollister and Sohn, working independently, who published in 1963 and 1964. This was further elaborated by Sohn, and by Deerwester, who presented exhaustive results graphically in a format compatible with the direct flight curves in the *NASA Planetary Flight Handbook* . . .'

It was a little like a game of interplanetary pool, he said. A spacecraft would dive in so close to a planet that its path would be altered by that world's gravitational field. In the swingby – the bounce off the planet – the spacecraft would extract energy from the planet's revolution around the sun, and so speed up; in exchange, the planet's year would be minutely changed.

In practical terms, bouncing off a planet's gravity well was like enjoying the benefit of an additional rocket stage at no extra cost, if your navigation was good enough.

'We have already studied the Mariner Mercury mission, which would have swung by Venus en route to Mercury. A direct journey would have been possible, using for example a Titan IIIC booster; but the gravity assist would have allowed the use of the cheaper Atlas-Centaur launch system . . .'

'Yeah,' a voice called from the audience, 'but Mariner Mercury got canned. And there were no men on it anyhow!'

Laughter.

Dana pressed on, brushing the sweat from his eyes. There were two ways Venus could be used to get to Mars, he said. The spacecraft could swing by Venus outbound, and use Venus's gravity to accelerate it toward Mars. Or Venus could be used to decelerate the craft, on its way back to Earth.

'First estimates show a mass in Earth orbit of two million pounds would be required for a mission duration of six hundred and forty days.' Same weight as nuclear; two-thirds the trip time of chemical. 'Thus a mission profile close to optimal is delivered, without the need for ambitious new technologies, and hence significantly reduced development costs compared to other candidate modes . . .'

And it's elegant. Don't you see that? No brute force here: no huge nuclear V-2s. Just proven technology, and elegance, and style. A little thought, gentlemen.

'In conclusion, it has been shown that the Venus swingby mode is generally applicable to all of the Mars flyby and stopover round trip launch opportunities, with very favorable benefits.'

Dana stepped back from the podium, retreating from the glare of the light. He was numbed, a little giddy, unable to feel his hands or face.

Seger thanked him, then opened up for questions; with a glance at his watch he signaled that these should be brief. '. . . What about guidance and navigation? Don't you realize that you're now talking about devising a mission profile with possibly *four* planetary encounters? – Mars, Venus maybe twice, and Earth on return? And at each encounter the accuracy of positioning will have to be of the

101

order of a few hundred miles, after traveling tens of *millions*. How can we navigate so accurately? Why, we haven't yet proved we can manage a single swingby on such a scale.'

'But we will,' Dana insisted. 'Remember, NASA committed to the lunar-orbit rendezvous mode for Apollo – which required a rendezvous a quarter of a million miles from home – before a single space rendezvous had been demonstrated.'

There was some muttering at this. *Hardly a valid comparison.*

'What about the design constraints? Near Venus the sunlight is four times hotter than at Mars, so you'll be sacrificing payload space for a cooling system that will be dead weight at Mars. And there'll be problems with the increased level of radiation coming from the sun . . .'

Dana tried to answer – *I've incorporated spacecraft design modifications into my weights analysis, and* . . . But he was all but drowned out by the noise of an audience which had little interest in him.

Now Hans Udet stood up, and a hush gathered. Udet said precisely, 'On what basis have you arrived at your figures? I am aware of the preliminary analyses of the complicated mission classes you describe. I am aware of no detailed analyses which show the savings you claim.'

Dana began to stammer out a reply. *But our understanding of spacecraft systems has advanced since those early studies, and with the figures I have compiled, we can now show that –*

'These results are false.' Udet glanced around at the audience, tall, aristocratic, in control, charming even now. 'This is obvious. The figures we are shown are based on unstated suppositions. The speaker doesn't know what he's talking about. It may be incompetence, or malice, whatever. We should not expend further energy on this red herring.' He sat down, his back ramrod-straight.

There was an uncomfortable stirring in the audience, some nervous laughter.

Bert Seger got to his feet, quickly thanked Dana, and turned away from him.

Udet's words were incredible to Dana. *Such accusations should not be made, in such fora as these, or beyond. It is – uncivilized.* Somehow, though, now that it had happened, there seemed a certain inevitability about it all. *Of course, I have been rejected. But this isn't about logic, or engineering, or science.* It was because he'd gone outside the hierarchy, the formal channels. *This really is about power. In-fighting. It's possible Udet is even sincere. Maybe he really does think I've cooked up these numbers, that I'm just in-fighting for Langley.*

Dana gathered together his foils, clumsily, and got off the stage.

The lights went up, and the conference room was quiet. Bert Seger got to his feet and began stalking along the stage, eyeballing the delegates as if challenging them, his hands on his hips.

'I've heard a lot of good things today about the nuclear mode,' he said. 'And I've heard nothing else today, frankly, that makes a hell of a lot of sense to me in comparison.' He glared at the audience. 'Now, I have to say that I think we can do this. I think we do indeed have a "Kennedy option" to present to the President. And I'd like to hear now what sonofabitch thinks nuclear isn't the right thing to do.'

There was a little more to and fro. Wernher von Braun got to his feet to make a brief statement commending the nuclear option. Then one of the chemical option presenters from Houston got up, and graciously conceded defeat to the guys from Marshall.

Seger closed the meeting. 'Gentlemen, I want to thank you here for all the work you've done. I think we've found a way we can work together and do this thing. I think we've worked out how we're going to Mars.'

He started to clap, then; and the hall joined in, applauding themselves for their achievement.

All but Dana. At least he could resist that much.

The Germans had won again.

Seger might be right. Perhaps we've made a historic decision that will, indeed, take men to Mars within my lifetime. But it's wrong. I know it's wrong.

Anyhow, he thought, it's still possible this huge mission will never be funded. Perhaps Nixon will choose to build the Shuttle. Or nothing at all.

Nothing at all.

The applause went on, until the delegates started to cheer themselves.

FUTURE OF NASA

Present tentative plans call for major reductions or change in NASA by sharply reducing the balance of the manned space program and many remaining NASA programs.

I believe this would be a mistake.

103

1) The real reason for reductions in the NASA budget is that NASA is entirely in the 28% of the budget that is controllable. In short we cut because it is cuttable, not because it is doing a bad job or an unnecessary one.

2) We are being driven, by the uncontrollable items, to spend more and more on programs that offer no real hope for the future: welfare, interest on National Debt, Medicare, etc. Essentially they are programs not of our choice, designed to repair mistakes of the past.

3) There is real merit to the future of NASA and to its proposed programs. Skylab and NERVA particularly offer the opportunity, among other things, to secure substantial scientific fall-out for the civilian economy at the same time that large numbers of valuable (and hard to employ elsewhere) scientists and technicians are kept at work on projects that increase our knowledge of space. It is very difficult to reassemble the NASA teams should it be decided later, after major stoppages, to restart some of the long-range programs.

4) In response to our pressure NASA has reduced its requested development budget for the next several fiscals by *half*.

5) Apollo 14 was very successful from all points of view. Most important is the fact that it gave the American people a much needed lift in spirit (and the people of the world an equally needed look at American superiority). Announcement now that we were canceling or severely diminishing the US manned space program would have a very bad effect. It would be confirming in some respects a belief that I fear is gaining credence at home and abroad, that our best years are behind us, that we are turning inward, reducing our defense commitments, and voluntarily starting to give up our superpower status, and our desire to maintain world superiority.

America should be able to afford something besides increased welfare . . .

Handwritten addendum: I agree with Cap. RMN.

Caspar W. Weinberger, Deputy Director of the Office of Management and Budget, Memorandum to the President, August 27, 1971. White House, Richard M. Nixon, President, 1968–1971 File, NASA Historical Reference Collection, NASA Headquarters, Washington DC

Wednesday, December 1, 1971
Jet Propulsion Laboratory, Pasadena

Ben Priest swung through Glendale and then turned north on Linda Vista, heading past the Rose Bowl. His hired car was an antique Dodge, and its heating was malfunctioning; outside it was a cold December day, and York alternately baked and shivered.

'This seems a long way out of Pasadena,' she remarked.

He grinned. 'Yeah. Well, they used to test rocket engines here. Everyone thought the place would be dangerous, so they built it way the hell out there, in the arroyo. And then they built a sprawling, expensive suburb all around it.'

York saw that office buildings filled the arroyo; some of them were drab boxes, but there was also an imposing tower of steel and glass.

There were cars parked for a quarter mile along the road leading to JPL, and the street outside the press center was nearly blocked by TV vans.

There was a guard at the JPL entrance; he waved them into a parking lot. It seemed to York that pretty much every space was taken.

They got inside quickly; the cold seemed to be deepening. Priest guided her through corridors littered with computer cards and print-outs. Close-up photographs of the Moon's surface were casually framed and stuck on the walls. JPL seemed a strange hybrid; this might have been any office complex anywhere, York supposed, except that people were younger than the average – and not one of them wore a suit, or a tie – and there was a *lot* of hair about, bristling above yellow Smile buttons. Some of the women even wore hot pants. But at the same time the place didn't have the ragged, laid-back feel of a college; there was too much urgency for that. There was a sense that things *happened* here.

She remarked on how full the car park had been.

Priest said, 'You should have been here a week ago, when the first pictures began coming through from Mars. You couldn't move for press guys, and VIPs, and politicos, and science fiction writers – anybody and everybody who could scrounge a pass.' He laughed. 'You should have seen their faces, when all we got back was a picture of the dust-storm.'

It was odd to be with Priest again. *A blast from the past.* She hadn't seen him for more than a year, and she'd been surprised

105

when he'd come through on his old promise to bring her here to see the results from Mars come in. He hadn't changed, as far as she could see: slim, dedicated to his job, easy-going, intelligent.

Fun to be with. Comfortable. Married.

She felt vaguely restless.

Right now, she admitted, she was basically drifting, doing some post-doc work here and there. She was looking for a focus, a topic, trying to figure out what she wanted to do with her life.

And she was still in her mess of a relationship with Mike Conlig, who was so immersed in his NERVA work he barely seemed aware she was there, when she got any time out of him at all. NERVA was the center of Mike's life; a kind of monomaniacal obsessive seemed to be emerging from inside the gentler, more intellectual outer shell that had first attracted her.

She got the impression that the space program was full of people like that.

The question for York was, did she really want to be a bit-part player in the story of someone else's goals?

They reached the communications center. The walls were coated with TV screens, all filled with grainy, obscure black and white images. Hard copies littered tables, and ribbons of computer print-out trailed across the tables and floor and along the walls. The workers here – mostly men, mostly shirt-sleeved, uniformly hairy – pored over the images and print-outs, their security badges dangling from their top pockets. There were cups of stale coffee all over the tables, some perched close to precious print-out, and in one corner she spotted a half-eaten doughnut, the jelly still oozing from its center.

There was a smell, faint but distinctive, of body odor.

Priest shrugged, looking a little sheepish. 'It's always pretty much like this, Natalie. Kind of slow chaos. This is the heart of the SFOF, what they call the Space Flight Operations Facility. The results from Mariner are coming in all the time; the guys work in shifts here. And it's adaptive; the results from one orbit may be used to influence what they do on the next. There isn't a lot of time for housekeeping.'

'You don't need to apologize. You ought to see the average geology field site after a couple of days.'

There was a model of the Mariner 9 spacecraft itself, a couple of feet across, hanging in one corner of the room. She slowed, looking up at it. Four silvery solar panels unfolded like sails from a central octagonal box. A rocket engine with propellant tanks was mounted on top of the box, and underneath sprouted a cluster of instruments. York could recognize the tiny lenses of TV cameras, glinting in the fluorescent light. The craft was comparatively crude, compared to the heavy Viking landers which were already under development for the 1975 launch opportunity. But still, Mariner 9 was quite beautiful, like a fine watch.

York retained lingering suspicions about the value of spaceflight in terms of its science. As a kid she'd been intrigued, even startled by the Mariner 4 pictures. But that had worn off, and she hadn't followed the progress of later probes closely. But still, this beautiful, delicate thing had been assembled by humans – made by hands like hers – and then thrown across interplanetary distances, to orbit Mars itself: it had become the first man-made object to orbit another planet.

It was quite a thought.

Priest was talking about the dust storm. 'It covered the whole damn planet, Natalie. When we arrived we couldn't see a thing. They did some measurements at the limb of the planet, and found the dust reaching an altitude of fifty miles. It seems impossible, but it's true. Anyhow, the storm did us one favor.'

'How's that?'

'All of a sudden, funnily enough, everybody got *very* excited about looking at the moons. Listen, you want me to get you a coffee? A doughnut, maybe?'

'No thanks, Ben.'

He led her through more corridors, to a smaller laboratory. More shirt-sleeves, working at terminals and screens.

'Image Processing,' Priest said. He took her to an unoccupied monitor, and they sat on rickety fold-up chairs. He began tapping at the key-pad. 'They got the first reasonably clear image of Phobos on revolution thirty-one – just last night. I stayed up until the small hours watching them process the data . . .' An image began to build up on the video monitor now, line by line, working from top to bottom. 'Mariner records its pictures on magnetic tape, and sends them back to Earth in pretty much the way a newsprint wire-photo is transmitted. This is exactly how the first image emerged, for the team last night.'

She smiled. 'What's this, Ben? Why not just show me the finished picture? More NASA showmanship?'

He raised his eyebrows. 'You're too cynical. Or would be, if I thought you meant it.'

Impulsively she touched his hand. 'I'm sorry, Ben.' His skin was warm and leathery.

He grinned at her easily.

Today she was finding Ben, with his intelligence and enthusiasm for this wonderful Mars project, unreasonably attractive. *Damn it. I'm not supposed to feel like this.*

She concentrated on the pictures.

The upper few lines of the image had been black – just empty space. But now she saw some detail, a curve of gray and white, building up line by line. At first she thought she was seeing the limb of a sphere, but the shape soon looked much too irregular for that.

Phobos turned out to be a rough ellipse, half in shadow, with a battered, irregular edge. It looked much more like York's preconception of an asteroid than any moon. There were craters everywhere, huge and ancient, some so deep that the impacts that caused them must have come close to splitting the battered little moon in half.

'Natalie, this is more or less the face of Phobos, about half the size of our full Moon, that you would see if you were standing on Mars right now.'

Phobos looked like a diseased potato. Priest was staring at the picture, and its gray and black reflected in his eyes. 'This is history, Natalie. Think about it: mine were among the first human eyes ever to see Phobos and Deimos, the moons of Mars. I wanted to show you this, kind of share it with you, the way I saw it.'

She was moved to touch him again, but she resisted the impulse.

'Show me Mars, Ben.'

'Sure.'

After a few more minutes Priest had retrieved images of the surface of the planet itself. But the dust storm was still continuing. There was only one place away from the poles where any detail was visible: an area called Tharsis, close to the Martian equator. Here the pictures showed four dark, irregular spots, roughly circular, three in a line running at an angle to the equator, and the fourth a little way away to the west.

She asked, 'What the hell can these be?'

'Who knows? I guess we'll figure it out when the storm clears. The lab staffers are calling them "Carl's Marks." After Sagan, see –'

The shapes in the images intrigued her; they were familiar, somehow. If only she could see just a little more . . . 'You say this region's called Tharsis. Do we know anything else about it?'

'Actually, yes. You're the geologist, Natalie. You ought to know.'

'Just tell me, asshole.'

'There have been radar studies of Mars since the mid-sixties. This

Tharsis region – which is just a bright splotch seen from Earth – looks as if it's the highest plateau on the planet.'

'Really? How high?'

He shrugged. 'Ten or twenty miles above the mean datum. We can't say for sure. *Mean datum* – you understand there's no ocean on Mars, so no convenient sea level to –'

'You must have some better resolution images than these. It's the only visible spot on the planet, for Christ's sake. Somebody must have pointed the cameras again.'

Priest began to work the keyboard. He found a couple of images which showed her some more detail. She stared at the screen, pressing close to the glass.

'You're telling me these features are stable? That they aren't, uh, whirlwinds in the dust storm or somesuch?'

'No way. They've lasted since Mariner got to Mars, a couple of weeks ago. We're undoubtedly looking at some kind of surface feature, here.'

She could see circular markings within each spot. And there was some kind of scalloping. *They almost look like volcanic caldera. The mouths of volcanoes.*

But why should these features, of all of Mars, be showing up at all? *Because they're in Tharsis. And Tharsis is the highest region on Mars.* And why these particular features? *Because they are the highest points in Tharsis – therefore the highest points on the planet . . .*

'My God,' she whispered.

'Natalie? What is it?'

These spots had to be volcanoes, sitting on top of some kind of vast shield system. Big enough to dwarf anything on Earth. Everest was only five miles high; those babies must be fifteen miles at least. So high they were poking above the dust storms; so high they were above the bulk of the atmosphere itself.

'Natalie? Are you okay?'

York couldn't believe her eyes. She had Priest call up image after image.

At least, she reflected later, the mystery of the Martian geology had taken her mind off Priest.

Saturday, December 11, 1971
NASA Headquarters, Washington DC

After Fred Michaels hung up, Tim Josephson sat in his office, a glass of whiskey in his hand.

The decision was made.

He supposed he ought to be feeling triumph. Exultation. *We've got what we wanted, by God. Another huge boondoggle, a program that ought to keep thousands of us NASA employees gainfully employed for a decade or more.*

But the truth was, he felt too tired and beat-up to care. He was having a little trouble focusing his eyes. He'd been chained to his desk and phone all day, working in support of Fred Michaels's machinations. And there were still a hundred and one things to be finished up. But, he told himself, there was nothing that wouldn't keep until the next day.

So he took his shoes off and got his feet up on his desk, and he started dictating into a pocket tape recorder.

The last few months had given Josephson, working as a close aide of Fred Michaels's, a startling insight into the way major national decisions were made: at the highest level in the land, with at stake national prestige, tens of billions of dollars spread across many years, and hundreds of high-profile careers in politics, industry, the military. Some day he was going to write a book about all this. *Management in the Space Age*, maybe.

The decision about America's future in space had turned out to be extraordinarily painful.

It had been clear to Josephson from the beginning that Nixon wanted to spend as little as possible on space.

The fact was, Nixon – belying his image – had brought a pretty liberal domestic agenda to the White House; in the midst of a debilitating war, he wanted to free up money to pay for expanded social entitlement programs, and wage and price controls.

Space was one place that money could come from. But space was a tough lobby to fight.

So, soon after coming into office, Nixon had allowed Congress to reorganize the standing space committees out of existence, so that now space was the purview of the Senate Commerce and House Science and Technology subcommittees. Losing its special interface to Congress, NASA was in danger of being emasculated, losing its heroic status, becoming just another spending department fighting for funds.

110

To most people involved in the space program, even within NASA, such changes were all but invisible; but to an insider like Josephson – and Michaels – they were dramatic, a potent signifier of Nixon's real determination to downgrade the profile of space.

But then the White House had come up against the aerospace industry.

Aerospace was ailing, as ever. In fact technological progress was making life even tougher. New systems were either not deployed at all or had short production runs: *if it works, it's obsolete.* Aerospace firms had to bet the farm every time they accepted a contract.

But obviously the government needed a healthy aerospace industry. So ways had to be found to feed the industry in slack times: to spread wealth, and to subsidize research. The civilian space program was perfect for this purpose. It always had been.

So, from the start of 1971, Fred Michaels had started to put it about that the aerospace industry might not be able to survive another year of diminished space work; he spoke particularly to Congressmen from states like California, Texas and Florida, where aerospace depression was an acute electoral issue. And he quietly encouraged the contractors contributing to the various program studies to talk up their estimates of the employment the various options would stimulate. It was all designed to keep the pressure on the White House. *1972 is an election year. We need a space program to keep the aerospace guys in work . . . But what's that program going to be?*

Josephson was mildly shocked how quickly the scientific and exploratory aspects of spaceflight were discarded as factors in shaping the new program. Nobody with any clout cared about going to Mars, or anywhere else, for the *science.* And nobody argued – he was more surprised to observe – on the basis of the benefits of space spin-offs. After all, if you wanted the spin-offs, why go into space at all? Why not turn the R&D money and NASA's fabled management skills directly to other, more worthy programs?

These were hard questions to answer. So Michaels, bluntly, avoided them.

In public, Michaels played up space as an adventure – something a nation like the US ought to be able to afford, damn it. Astronauts from the heroic days, including Joe Muldoon, were wheeled out to serve as living reminders of good moments gone. After Michaels's skillful PR hoopla, Mars came to seem a little more acceptable. There was a snowball effect, and some support for the option started to appear on the Hill.

And, slowly, the opinion polls showed public opposition to a Mars option dropping.

But NASA's budget was still far too high. In July, members of Congress had moved twice to delete manned spaceflight altogether from the FY1972 budget.

It was a dangerous moment in history, and the hard bargaining continued.

What can we drop?

At one point Josephson had believed Nixon was coming close to approving the Space Shuttle system – just that one item, out of all the options his Task Group had presented. At least the goal of the Shuttle was to do with reducing costs, and the Shuttle would actually have been the favored option of the aerospace lobby because of all the new development it would have entailed.

But the Shuttle program had quickly become a mess. It was obvious, Josephson thought, that the final, low-cost Shuttle design was a bastardized compromise, put together by committee to satisfy conflicting interests. And Michaels wasn't above drafting in his predecessor, Paine – a great lover of the Mars option whom Michaels had replaced in September – to point out the Shuttle's strong military flavor: it was no accident that the low, hundred-mile orbits which were all the Space Shuttle was capable of, and its wide-ranging flyback capabilities, were ideally suited to Air Force missions.

The Space Shuttle would be cute technology, with nowhere to go except low Earth orbit reconnaissance missions. In an era in which detente was becoming the fashion, the military taint of the Shuttle was unpalatable. And besides, Kennedy and others never ceased to remind the public, there was nothing *heroic* about it.

So Josephson had watched, not unhappily, as the Shuttle quietly faded from Nixon's thinking. The next generation of launch vehicles for manned flight, instead, would probably be a series of upgraded Saturns.

It looked as if there would be no elaborate space station modules, either, as the Space Task Group had proposed; just an extended series of Skylabs, improvised from Saturn fuel tanks. The engineers inside NASA screamed like hell at this, especially Mueller and his space station lobby. But it all brought the cost profile closer to something the White House might be able to endorse.

Of course, contained in the final program there would be trade-offs. Rockwell had been hot favorites as lead contractors for the

112

canned Shuttle. And now it looked as if their big rivals Boeing were going to get the largest piece of the new space booster pie, because Boeing, manufacturers of the huge Saturn S-IC first stage, were going to be lead contractors in the new enhanced Saturn project. Boeing had all sorts of ideas for reducing the costs of the Saturn V system, for instance by adding strap-on reusable rockets to it, and even making the S-IC itself recoverable, including wings, parachutes, hydrogen-filled balloons, drag brakes, paragliders, and rotary systems of spinning parachutes.

So Rockwell – manufacturers of Apollo – looked, to everyone's surprise, like being left with very little out of all this. They were offered a consolation: they would be allowed to proceed with a program to turn the S-II, their hydrogen-fueled Saturn second stage, into a heavyweight interplanetary injection engine. But this, of course, was the job that NERVA would perform, so strictly speaking the S-II program was redundant before it started, and questions were already being asked about its requirement and viability.

Still, Josephson thought wryly, Rockwell were bound to pick up other compensations along the way. Already they were hot favorites for the one big new start-up spacecraft program to emerge from today's decision, even before it had been announced . . .

Meanwhile the military had been bought off, to Josephson's way of thinking, with a promise of a presence on the new long-duration Skylabs, a restoration of their old Manned Orbital Laboratory mission objectives.

The new space program, then, was going to be a balance of forces, a compromise among the warring factions lobbying the White House and Capitol Hill. Thus, Josephson thought, as it always was.

But it wouldn't have come together without Michaels's string-pulling and favor-calling, exploiting the web of political alliances he'd built up over the years. A less astute Administrator – Thomas Paine, for instance – wouldn't have had a prayer of delivering this. And yet Josephson knew that Michaels's work was only just beginning. Michaels had worked to obtain the initial commitment to a new program; the challenge now would be to keep that commitment in the long, wearying years ahead.

Fred Michaels had known Nixon all the way back to the Sputnik days, when he'd been Eisenhower's veep. Michaels believed that Nixon was a man who grasped the symbolism of the space age, right from the beginning. 'Politics is frankly more important than science,' Michaels had told Josephson, and Josephson repeated it now into his tape recorder. 'The real motive for space is prestige. Nixon understands that. He's the right clay to be shaped. I tell you, Tim; I'm not so surprised at the way all this has turned out. All he needed was the right argument . . .'

Maybe, Josephson thought. But Nixon was also pragmatic, highly intelligent, a man who saw space as fairly low down his priority list.

He might have chosen to shut down the manned program altogether.

And yet, and yet . . .

And yet there was dear old Jack Kennedy, speaking like a ghost from his study in New England, quietly telling Americans that they were better than their pessimistic visions of themselves: that they had, after all, succeeded in landing men on the Moon, and in the full view of the world; that they should not pause now, but should go on, endlessly reinventing themselves in the light of the fiery dream that was space travel, a dream of which Kennedy had become the living embodiment . . .

It had come to a head, at last, today. Michaels had been asked to a meeting with Agronski, other Presidential aides, and representatives of the Office of Management and Budget.

Agronski, Michaels told Josephson, had opened the meeting briskly. 'You're going to get your Mars boondoggle, Fred. Against my better judgment.'

'The President's approving the program.'

'Yes.' Agronski shuffled papers. 'There are still some decisions to be made about size and cost . . .'

Michaels grunted. 'What decided him?'

'A number of factors. The point that we can't afford to forgo manned spaceflight altogether, for our prestige at home and abroad.' He sounded rueful. 'We're stuck with you, Fred. That the Mars mission is the only option we have that is meaningful and could be accomplished on a modest budget. That we were only thinking of cutting NASA anyway because we could. That not starting the program would be damaging to the aerospace industry . . .'

Michaels had understood, and Josephson wasn't surprised. Kennedy's lobbying, and his own machinations, had swung public opinion just enough. And 1972 was going to be an election year; unemployment queues in states heavily dependent on aerospace – California, Texas, Florida – wouldn't look good for Nixon. *But we were damn lucky to find an ally in Cap Weinberger.* Without Cap's lobbying inside the Administration, Josephson knew, the manned program could have been lost.

The meeting had started haggling over details, the wording of a Presidential announcement. But the decision was made.

Mars.

Josephson, through his weariness, felt a deep satisfaction growing inside him. It was like the feeling of having enjoyed a fine meal, brandy and cigars.

It was actually unfortunate for Nixon, Josephson thought. Nixon's thinking had been sensible, really; he'd wanted an affordable program with more than just one goal, a program which would lay a more solid foundation for the future. But it looked like he was going to end up with another footprints-and-flags extravaganza. And Jack Kennedy – or maybe Ted, drawing on the credit of one assassinated and one crippled brother, now making his own way to the White House – was going to get the credit.

Anyhow, thus, in a crucible of social, political, economic and technical forces, wielded by men like Michaels and Nixon and Kennedy, the decision had emerged. And, incremental and contingent though it might be, it was – against all the odds – a decision to send Americans to Mars.

A cleaning woman knocked and entered, towing a heavy vacuum cleaner. Josephson turned off his tape recorder. Millie Jacks grinned at Josephson; she was used to seeing him work as late as this.

'I hear we're going to Mars, Dr Josephson?'

'Looks like it, Millie.'

'Hoo!' Millie chortled her disbelief. But then, she'd been shaking her head over everything NASA had done since 1966; Josephson sometimes wondered if she actually believed that men had been to the Moon, that it wasn't all some kind of stunt.

Of course, what would be unbelievable – what would really make Millie shake her head – would be if we got a few black faces, even female ones, among the Mars crews.

Maybe it will change. Maybe it will be a different world, when we fly to Mars in 1982.

Wednesday, January 5, 1972

... I have decided today that the United States should proceed at once with the development of systems and technologies designed to take American astronauts on landing missions to Mars. This system will center on a new generation of rockets, exploiting nuclear power, which will revolutionize and routinize long-haul interplanetary flights.

The new year 1971 was a year of conclusion for America's current series of manned flights to the Moon. Much was achieved in the three successful landing missions – in fact, the scientific results of the third mission have been shown to greatly outweigh the return from all earlier manned spaceflights, to Earth orbit or the Moon. But it also brought us to an important decision point – a point of assessing what our space horizons are as Apollo ends, and of determining where we go from here.

In the scientific arena, the past decade of experience has taught us that spacecraft are an irreplaceable tool for learning about our near-space environment, the Moon, and the planets, besides being an important aid to our studies of the sun and stars. In utilizing space to successfully meet needs on Earth, we have seen the tremendous potential of satellites for international communications and world-wide forecasting, and global resource monitoring.

However, all these possibilities, and countless others with direct and dramatic bearing on human betterment, will not be achieved without a continuation of the dream which has carried us so far and so fast: I mean the dream of exploration, of American and human expansion into space, the greatest frontier of all. In my decision today, I have taken account of the need to fully encourage and sustain that dream.

NASA and many aerospace companies have carried out extensive design studies for the Mars mission. Congress has reviewed and approved this effort. Preparation is now sufficient for us to confidently commence a new development program. In order to completely minimize technical and economic risks, the Space Agency will continue to cautiously take an evolutionary approach in the development of this new system. Even so, by moving ahead at this time, we can have the first components of the Mars spacecraft in manned flight test by the end of the decade, and operational a short time later. But we will not set arbitrary deadlines, as some have called for; we will make decisions as to the pace of our program in the fullness of time and with the wisdom of experience.

It is for the reason of technological robustness that I have decided against the development of the reusable Space Shuttle at this time; despite the manifest economic benefits of such a launch system if available, I am not convinced that our technology is so mature that we are ready yet to confidently tackle the huge problems posed by the project without cost overruns and delays, and many of its economic benefits should in any case be realizable from enhancements to our existing 'throwaway' platforms.

It is also significant that this major new national enterprise will engage the best efforts of thousands of highly skilled workers and hundreds of contractor firms over the next several years. The continued preeminence of America and American industry in the aerospace field will be an important part of the Mars mission's payload.

We will go to Mars because it is the one place other than our Earth where we expect human life to be sustainable, and where our colonies could flourish. We will go to Mars because an examination of its geology and history will reflect back a greatly deepened understanding of our own precious Earth.

Above all, we will go to Mars because it will inspire us to clearly look beyond the difficulties and divisions of today, to a better future tomorrow.

'We must sail sometimes with the wind and sometimes against it,' said Oliver Wendell Holmes, 'but we must sail, and not drift, nor lie at anchor.' So with man's epic voyage into space – a voyage the United States of America has led and still shall lead. Apollo has returned to harbor. Now it is time to swiftly build new ships, and to purposefully sail further than our ancestors could ever have dreamed possible . . .

Public Papers of the Presidents of the United States: Richard M. Nixon, 1972 (Washington DC: Government Printing Office, 1972)

Wednesday, January 5, 1972

. . . As indicated in the President's statement, the studies by NASA and the aerospace industry of the Mars mission have now reached the point where the decision can be made to proceed into actual development of mission components. The decision to proceed, which the President has now approved, is consistent with the plans presented to and approved by Congress in NASA's FY1972 budget. The Mars mission will consist of a pair of ships assembled in

Earth orbit. The ships will be clusters of several nuclear-rocket propulsion modules, launched by chemical vehicles based on our proven Saturn V technology. The spacecraft will be designed in this modular form to enable different configurations to be assembled speedily: for example, to complete missions to other planets or to the asteroids. The crew will inhabit modules developed from the first 'dry fuel tank' Skylab space stations we intend to fly from next year. The crew will ride a new landing craft to the Martian surface.

As the President indicated we are not going to work to a set timetable. However we hope to fly our first mission to take advantage of Mars's opposition with Earth in 1982. This first mission will be preceded by an intensive development program including flight phases in Earth orbit. The program will include the full development of the new nuclear technology, of life support for long-duration missions, of interplanetary communications and navigation techniques, of the increased reusability and reliability of systems, and of Mars entry and landing systems. Calls for recruitment of astronauts for the new program will shortly be issued.

To survey landing sites for the eventual manned mission a new series of Mariner unmanned photographic orbiters will be sent to Mars. These flights will replace the previously proposed Viking science platforms, which are now canceled, and so will take place within the envelope of current funding levels.

The decision by the President is a historic step in the nation's space program. It will transform man's reach in space. In another decade the nation will have the means to transfer men and equipment across interplanetary space; shortly thereafter we expect such missions to be mounted as routinely as we now have sent men to the Moon and returned them safely to Earth. Not just Mars, but our sister planet Venus, the resources of the asteroid belt, and the moons of Jupiter and the outer planets will come within our compass. This will be done within the framework of a useful total space program of science, exploration, and applications at approximately the present overall level of the space budget.

Thank you . . .

Frederick W. Michaels Chronological File, 1972, NASA Historical Reference Collection, NASA Headquarters, Washington DC

Wednesday, January 5, 1972
NASA Headquarters, Washington DC

Gregory Dana had spent the day at a meeting on rendezvous techniques for the upcoming Skylab missions. He came across a number of Houston people gathered in the hallway, before a notice board.

'What's going on?'

'Don't you know? We're going to Mars. Nixon has confirmed it at last. Look at this.' They made way for him at the board. At first Dana could see nothing of interest to him on the board: an offer of tickets for the Cowboys vs Dolphins Superbowl, classes in TM and acupuncture (posted here, in NASA HQ!), and a bright orange sticker saying simply JESUS HEALS. But there, crowded out by the trivia, was a closely-printed piece of headed paper. It was a statement from Nixon, and a subsidiary statement from Michaels, the new NASA Administrator. Some supporting press briefing material was pinned up too: a 'Mars mission digest,' with simple question-and-answer chunks of information about the mission, and a few spectacular artist's impressions of the mission's various phases. There were even a few outlines of the modes which had been evaluated and discarded.

There was no mention of Dana's Venus swingby mode.

Since that apocalyptic Phase A meeting in Huntsville back in July, Dana had heard almost nothing of the development of the Mars options. And this was the first he'd learned of the final decision – along with the Headquarters cleaning staff, and the rest of the nation. It was clear, now, that he'd been excluded from the decision-making process since July.

What could he do about it? Write another letter to Fred Michaels?

He felt the injustice, the stupidity of it, burn a hole in his stomach.

Well, it was nothing to do with him any more. Maybe, at least, Jim would be able to realize some of his own dreams, in the slow unwinding of this decision.

Dana tucked his briefcase under his arm and walked away.

Book 2

TRAJECTORIES

York floated in her sleeping bag. She was dog tired, but sleep just wouldn't come. Her lower back was sore, and she had a stuffy headache, as if she was developing a cold. Her heart was suddenly too strong; blood seemed to boom through her ears. She missed the pressure of a pillow under her head, the security of a blanket tucked in close around her. The bag was too big, for one thing; she found herself bouncing around inside it. And every time she moved, the layer of warm air which she'd built up around her body, and which stuck there in microgravity, tended to squirt away, out of the bag, leaving her chilled.

When she managed to relax, she had a feeling of falling. Once she almost drifted off, but then her arms came floating up, *and a hand touched her face* . . .

She let her eyes slide open.

She was inside her sleep locker, at the base of the Mission Module. The locker was little bigger than a cupboard, with a foldaround screen drawn across it. On the surface above her head was her overhead light, and a little comms station, and a fan. There were little drawers for personal things, like underwear; when she opened them the drawers had blue plastic nets stretched over them, to stop everything from floating away.

A lot of light and noise leaked around the foldaround screen. She could hear the hum and whir of the Mission Module's equipment, and the occasional automatic burn of the attitude clusters as they kept Ares pointing sunwards. With the bright, antiseptic light of the wardroom beyond her screen, and the new smell of metal and plastic, it was like trying to sleep inside an immense refrigerator.

Apparently there had been plans to provide solid doors on the sleep lockers. She even remembered seeing a memo which talked about the need to provide privacy for astronauts 'significantly relating,' in the typically obscure, euphemistic doubletalk NASA employed when talking about the functions of the warm bodies they were shipping into space at such expense. But the doors had been skipped, for reasons of saving weight. *So much for significantly relating.*

And now – on top of everything else – she needed a pee.

She tried to ignore it, but the pressure on her bladder built up steadily. *Christ.* Well, it was her own fault; the relief tube – the Mission Module's toilet, the Waste Management Station – was so uncomfortable she'd put off using it. Besides, she seemed to be peeing more than usual, since coming up into microgravity.

She succumbed to the inevitable. She squirmed her way out of the bag, turned on her overhead light, and folded back the screen. When she moved, her back hurt like hell.

After the TOI burn, the Ares modules had undergone the first of the cumbersome waltzes the crew would have to endure before the mission was done. Under the command of Stone, Apollo, containing the crew, had separated from the nose of the stack, turned around and docked nose-to-nose with the Mission Module.

When she'd first been talked through the mission profile, waiting until *after* the TOI burn to do this separation and docking had seemed bizarre to York. Why wait until you were already on your way to Mars to cut loose of your main ship? But it made a kind of sense, in the convoluted, abort-options-conscious way the mission planners figured these things. If the MS-II had blown up during the TOI burn, the crew, in Apollo, could have got out and done an abort burn to get home. And if the injection burn was successful but the docking hadn't been, the crew could use the Service Module's big engine to blast back toward Earth.

Anyway, after the successful docking, the crew had been able to crawl through a docking tunnel and started moving into the Mission Module, their interplanetary home-from-home.

As long as she didn't think about the wisdom of taking apart the spacecraft in deep interplanetary space, it didn't trouble York.

York let herself drift across the wardroom. She was light as a feather, and invulnerable; it was like moving through a dream. The Mission Module was a lot roomier than the Apollo Command Module had been, of course. But she was learning to move around, to operate in this environment. She'd found she couldn't move too quickly. If she did she'd collide with the equipment, dislodging switches and maybe damaging gear. It just wasn't a professional way to behave. She was learning to move slowly, with a kind of underwater grace.

It wasn't a big deal. Microgravity was just a different environment; she'd learn to work within its constraints.

The wardroom, with its little plastic table and three belted chairs, was clean and empty, bright in the light of strip floods. The walls and floors weren't solid; they were a gray mosaic of labeled storage drawers and feet restraints – loops of blue plastic – and there were handy little blue rectangles of Velcro everywhere. There were up-down visual cues, signs and lighting and color codes. Everything was obviously designed for zero G.

The whole thing had the feel of an airliner's crew station, she thought; it was all kind of pleasing, compact, well-designed, everything tucked away. Like a mobile home in space. Of course right now everything was still bright and new, every surface unmarked; it would be different after a few months' occupancy. Much of the Mission Module's equipment was still in stowage; the crew would spend the next few days hauling ass around the Module, configuring it for its long flight.

The Waste Management Station was a little cubicle containing a commode, a military thing of steel and bolts and terse metal labels. She pulled across the screen, swiveled in the air, dropped her shorts and pants, and pulled herself down. Thigh bars, cushioned and heavy, swung across her legs to clamp her ass to the seat.

She pulled a hose out of the front of the commode; the hose would take her pee to a tank, for dumping in space later. The hose justified the Apollo-era nickname, 'relief tube,' that the crews still used for the waste station. In a cupboard beside her there was a set of funnels, all color-coded to ensure they weren't mixed up by the crew; hers, anyway, were of the distinctive female variety. The cupboard was already starting to stink a little, and the clear plastic of the funnels was turning yellow. *Eighteen months of this.*

She fitted the funnel to the hose, clamped it over her private parts, and opened the valve to the urine store.

There was a certain strategy to this, which involved aiming for the minimum of pain when using the device. If she opened the valve too soon, the suction would grab at her. And when it resealed itself it was liable to trap a little piece of her inside it. The way round that was to start pissing a split-second *before* opening the valve. But there was a danger that the funnel would just slip off, and off would float her piss in little golden globules.

It took her a few seconds to be able to let go.

Now she'd got set up here, she considered whether to try taking a dump. That was actually easier, mechanically, than peeing. She'd have to start up the slinger, a spinning drum under the commode. The shit would stick to the walls of the drum, and later she would turn a switch to expose the drum to vacuum, and the shit would be frozen and dried out.

But, though she felt a pressure in her lower gut, there was nothing doing for now; she suspected it was going to take her a few days to relax enough to unclench. And besides, there was no gravity here

125

to help her, as the guys had informed her with glee; she wasn't looking forward to the experience.

She took a couple of wet wipes and cleaned out the inside of the funnel. The wipes might have come out of any drug store back home, except for the strong stink of disinfectant about them.

She unlocked herself from the john seat. She pushed her hands into the wash-basin, a plastic globe which sprayed water across her skin and out into a waste tank. One or two droplets escaped the basin and went oscillating around the john, but she swatted them out of the air easily. There was a row of towel holders on the wall, little color-coded rubber diaphragms: towels, their corners shoved into the holders, hung out in the air like flags. She dried her hands.

She heard a noise; she turned.

Ralph Gershon was in the wardroom, wearing a T-shirt and shorts. He was just floating, with a plastic can of Coke in one hand and a silver-gray lithium hydroxide canister in the other. The lith canisters were used to scrub carbon dioxide out of the recycled air, and they had to be checked and changed regularly. The familiar red and white Coke can was pretty much the normal size and shape, expect for a baby-style microgravity dispenser at the top.

Gershon held a finger up to his lips – evidently Stone was still asleep – and he held the can out toward her.

She shook her head. 'Too gassy.'

'Yeah,' he whispered back. 'Coke paid a million bucks to get these cans on the Mission Module, but they just can't get the damn mix right.' He started to juggle with the lith and Coke cans, sending them spinning and oscillating from hand to hand. York had already observed that microgravity was like a three-dimensional playground for the guys; as soon as they'd got into the Mission Module's big workshop area Stone and Gershon had started doing cartwheels and loops and spins, throwing bits of gear to each other like frisbees.

Gershon's eyes kept straying to her chest.

She resisted the temptation to fold her arms across her T-shirt. *Well, that's it.* She had a stock of sports bras, and in future she'd be wearing one *every* time she left her sleep cubicle. *No significant relating on this damn mission.*

Gershon looked away and sipped at his Coke.

'What's with the lith cylinders?'

He shrugged. 'You know me. I catnap. I'm not sleepy now; I figured I might as well get ahead of myself.' He cackled. 'You know, I even got a little shut-eye during the docking.'

That was true. And now, with York still unable to rest, here he was, drinking Coke and ogling her chest and getting ahead of his chores.

'You're an asshole, Ralph,' she said with passion.

He grinned at her. 'I know how you're feeling, by the way.'

'You do?'

'Sure. Stuffy head, right?'

'I know what it is. Zero G. Blood gathering in my chest and my head –'

'Look, if it's really bad you should take a scop/Dex.'

'I'll be okay.'

'Suit yourself. What else? You got a sore back, right?'

'Yeah.' She rubbed at her lower spine. 'How did you know?'

'You want to know where that comes from? I'll tell you. In your bag, you're never perfectly stable. There's always a little bit of movement. You drift this way and that. And you know what your body does in response?'

'Tell me.'

'Your toes clench. Right up, into tiny little balls.'

'Why?'

'Because here we are flying to Mars, but we're still goddamn apes who think we're going to fall out of a tree any minute. Anyhow, that's where the back pains come from.'

'So what do I do?'

'Just unclench.' He grinned. 'Chill out and unclench. And, Natalie. Use eye masks and ear plugs if you have to. What the hell. I won't tell.'

She went back to her closet. *Maybe I'll give up on trying to sleep, and follow Gershon's example. Get ahead of the day.* But she climbed back into her sleeping bag, and it felt warm, and she turned off her overhead light and stretched out again.

She made a deliberate effort to uncurl her toes. Immediately, her back felt easier. *Hey, what do you know? The asshole was right.*

She closed her eyes.

Wednesday, May 24, 1972
Moscow

The United States of America and the Union of Soviet Socialist Republics:

Considering the role which the USA and the USSR play in the

Exploration and Use of Outer Space for Peaceful Purposes;

Striving for a further expansion of cooperation between the USA and USSR in the Exploration and Use of Outer Space for Peaceful Purposes;

Noting the positive cooperation which the parties have already agreed in this area;

Desiring to make the results of scientific research gained from the Exploration and Use of Outer Space for Peaceful Purposes available for the benefit of the peoples of the two countries and of all the peoples of the world;

Taking into consideration the provisions of the Treaty on Principles Governing the Activities in the Exploration and Use of Outer Space, including the Moon and other Celestial Bodies, as well as the Agreement on the Rescue of Astronauts, the Return of Astronauts, and the Return of Objects Launched into Outer Space;

In accordance with the agreement between the United States of America and the Union of Soviet Socialist Republics on Exchanges and Cooperation in Scientific, Technical, Educational, Cultural and other fields, signed 11 April 1972, and in order to develop further the principles of mutually beneficial cooperation between the two countries;

Have agreed as follows . . .

ARTICLE 3 (of 6)

The parties have agreed to carry out projects for developing compatible rendezvous and docking systems of United States and Soviet manned spacecraft and stations in order to enhance the safety of manned flights in space and to provide the opportunity for conducting joint scientific experiments in the future. It is planned that the first experimental flight to test these systems be conducted during the second half of the decade, envisaging the docking of a United States Apollo-type spacecraft with a Soviet Salyut-type space station, and/or a Soviet Soyuz-type spacecraft with a United States Skylab-type space station, with visits of astronauts in each other's spacecraft and stations. The implementation of these projects will be carried out on the basis of principles and procedures which will be developed in accordance with the summary of results of the meeting between representatives of the US National Aeronautics and Space Administration and the USSR Academy of Sciences on the question of developing compatible systems for rendezvous and docking of manned spacecraft

128

and space stations of the USA and the USSR, dated 6 April
1972 . . .

Extract from Understanding Signed by President Richard M. Nixon and Chairman of the Soviet Council of Ministers A. N. Kosygin. Public Papers of the Presidents of the United States: Richard M. Nixon, 1972 (Washington DC: Government Printing Office, 1972)

Saturday, October 28, 1972
University of California at Berkeley

Ben Priest called her after midnight.

'It's over, Natalie. I thought you'd like to know. We lost Mariner.'

She sat up in bed. 'Oh? How come?'

'They'd just taken more images of Tharsis and Syrtis Major, and the pictures were on the tape; but then Mariner had to position itself to point its high-gain antenna at Earth to play back the pictures, and – zippo. Nothing. Out of attitude gas. So we lost fifteen pictures.

'But what *really* pisses me,' he growled into the phone, 'is that Mariner still has fuel on board; it's just in the wrong place – in the retro-rocket tanks, not the attitude control tanks. We could have run tubes to carry the retro stuff to the attitude control jets. If we'd done that we might have another year of useful life out of Mariner.'

'But . . .'

'But it would have cost another thirty thousand bucks. Out of a hundred million dollar mission. So we didn't do it.'

'Oh, well, Ben. I guess nobody figured that Mariner would last so long anyhow. The basic mission plan was only ninety days.'

'Maybe. But if I'd known, I'd have paid up the thirty grand myself. And then the fuckers axed Viking!'

She had to laugh. 'Come on, Ben. This isn't like you. You're the great Man-In-Space hero. That thirty thousand bucks has probably gone to pay your salary anyhow.' That was basically true; the unmanned scientific exploration of Mars had been scaled right back, with the savings being pulled into the manned effort.

'Well, I sometimes get my sense of priority back, Natalie. It's not the lost year that bugs me, you know; it's just those fifteen pictures. There they are, sitting on that tape, even now . . .

'We had to send up a last command. To make Mariner turn off its radio transmitter.'

Oh, God. The poor, brave little probe. She pushed her pillow

129

against her face until she was sure she wouldn't guffaw. After all, it was only a couple of days since she'd called Ben in a similar mood herself, after an evening spent poring over the latest polls showing Nixon heading for a landslide over McGovern. 'How long before Mariner's orbit decays?'

'Oh, fifty years.'

'Well, maybe we'll have a manned mission by then. You'll get there yourself, Ben. Maybe you'll be able to retrieve your pictures. And maybe pick up the old spacecraft itself; who knows?'

She heard him laugh. 'Sure. Why, we'll bring it back and hang it up in the Smithsonian where it belongs.'

'What next for you, Ben?'

She heard him sigh. 'Apollo-N. The test flights for the NERVA. Some time in Tomorrowland.'

'At least you and Mike might get to see more of each other. Maybe I'll see more of the two of you, in fact.'

'Perhaps. But the flights are looking a long way off, Natalie.'

'Now I think I ought to get some sleep, Ben.'

'Okay. Goodnight, Natalie.'

'Yeah. You too, Ben.'

She lay in the darkness, wide awake.

Mike wasn't here, of course, or anywhere within five hundred miles of her. He was losing himself in the NERVA developments. As Ben had hinted, that damned project was slipping again.

Anyway, she realized, things hadn't been quite the same between the two of them since that day in 1969 when she'd gone out to Jackass Flats with Mike and Ben.

She'd tried to talk this through with Mike. It had gone beyond a simple argument for her, beyond the kind of sparky debating exercise they'd enjoyed so many times in the past. NERVA seemed to symbolize, to her, a lot of her unease about the way her country was being run. And eventually that seemed to get through to Mike. Impatiently, he'd shown her schemes to trap the hydrogen venting, to bury the expended cores more deeply . . .

Somehow that didn't help. Obviously Mike was smart enough to understand the issues that concerned her, but it was pretty clear he didn't *care*; not as much as he cared about a successful project, anyhow.

She loved Mike. She believed. And he loved her. But, she thought, their disparate lives, their different perspectives over the value of projects like NERVA, all of it was steadily pulling them apart.

130

They'd gone out to Jackass Flats, she recalled, just six months after they'd met. And that was all of three years ago. Maybe she should start regarding those first happy six months as the anomaly, not the norm.

Meanwhile, in March – four months into Mariner's orbital survey – the first detailed maps of Mars had begun to appear from the US Geological Survey people, at Flagstaff. York had got hold of copies of these, and pored over them.

Mars was very different from what anyone had expected.

Mars was asymmetrical. The whole of the southern hemisphere was swollen, the land lifted well above the datum level, and heavily cratered. The northern hemisphere was mostly below the datum, and was a lot smoother than the south . . . but the north had Tharsis.

Tharsis was a bulge in the planet the size of southern Africa. It was as if a quarter of the whole surface of Mars had been lifted up by some colossal event. The bulge was surrounded by an array of cracks and grooves: to the east of Tharsis, in the Coprates region, a huge canyon system stretched nearly a quarter of the way around the circumference of the planet.

The ancient cratered terrain in the south was cut by gullies and channels which seemed to have been incised by running water. York was entranced by images of Moon-like craters, eroded by flash floods. But there was no sign of water on the surface now, in the quantities needed to cut the gullies; maybe the water had escaped from the atmosphere, or was trapped under the surface.

It was this that intrigued her about Mars, she'd decided, this mix of exposed, lunar terrain and Earth-like weathering, a combination that made up an extraordinary world: neither Earthlike nor lunar, but uniquely Martian.

But it had nothing to do with her.

The work she was doing, she'd long realized, was building up into an unspectacular, if solid, career. She was becoming just another rock hound: her future was probably in commercial geology, and would be spent in messy oil fields, or mines. She could expect a life of heat, cold, rattlesnakes, cow pies, poison oak . . .

The prospect left her pole-axed with boredom.

She never got to see Mike. She wasn't interested in her work. And, meanwhile, she spent her spare time imagining geologic traverses across the ancient, battered surface of Mars.

What it amounted to, she told herself with brutal frankness, was that her personal life had been on hold for, hell, years. Just like her professional life.

131

She felt a germ of a new resolution somewhere inside her, like a dust mote around which a new future might crystalize.

I got to get closer to this Mars stuff. And not for Mike, not even for Ben Priest. For me.

There might be a way. Maybe she could transfer into the Space Sciences Laboratory, right here at Berkeley, that big white building on top of Grizzly Peak.

She got out of bed, dug out her loose-leaf folder of Mars photos, and began to study the eroded craters again.

Thursday, June 7, 1973
Lyndon B. Johnson Space Center, Houston
(formerly Manned Spacecraft Center)

Phil Stone was the first to understand Seger's suggestion.

'My God,' he said. 'You're going to send us to the Moon. Aren't you?'

'Yes. Yes, that's right. That's what I'm considering. I want to reassign your mission a Saturn V, and send you to lunar orbit.'

Chuck Jones stared at Seger, astonishment crinkling up his squat face. 'Like hell you will.'

For long seconds, the three of them sat in silence.

Stone felt stunned; here in this sterile, mundane office, on an ordinary Thursday morning, it was impossible to absorb such news.

Skylab B, the second Earth-orbital Saturn Wet Workshop, was to have been Stone's first flight into space. He'd already been training on the science and operational aspects of the mission for months. And now Seger was thinking of changing it all around, and sending him to the Moon? Jesus.

Seger played with the carnation in his lapel. 'You got to look at the bigger picture. The NERVA is slipping again, so its program of test flights is being cut. And that's freed up a Saturn V. And we need to use it, or we'll lose it. And I want to use it to send you boys to lunar orbit.'

Stone frowned. 'It's a man-rated Saturn V, for God's sake. It's already built. How can we lose it?'

Seger shrugged. 'We may have built the thing, but we haven't yet spent the money to make it fly.'

'We can't go to the fucking Moon,' Chuck Jones said. 'We're still waiting on the J-2S.' Lunar orbital workshops were planned, but a few years down the road, following extensive modifications

132

to the S-IVB: the upgraded J-2S main engine, additional payload capacity, a self-ullaging system, electrical heating blankets and mylar insulation, additional batteries, upgraded electronics . . . 'The fucking S-IVB doesn't have the power to inject itself into lunar orbit.'

'No, it doesn't. But it doesn't need to. Look at this.' Seger had a glossy presentation on his desk; he handed them copies.

Stone looked quickly. It was a summary of an old McDonnell-Douglas study called LASSO – *Lunar Applications on a Spent S-IVB Stage (Orbital)*. It showed how Saturn components could be used to establish lunar orbit workshops of varying complexity and weight. It was full of cutaway isometric diagrams and color pictures and big bold bullet-point blocks of text, and – naturally, as it came from the manufacturers of the S-IVB – it was relentlessly optimistic: some of the projected dates were already in the past.

'Look at Baseline 1.' Seger pointed to sections of the presentation. 'That shows how we can take a workshop to lunar orbit *without* the J-2S upgrade, or any of the rest of it . . .'

A Saturn V would be launched looking superficially like those for the Apollo landing flights. But instead of a Lunar Module, the booster would carry an airlock module, fixed to the front of the third stage.

The S-IVB would send the spacecraft toward the Moon. Just like the landing missions. But, once exhausted, the third stage wouldn't be discarded. The Apollo would decouple and dock with the empty stage via the airlock adapter. The stack would follow a long, lower-energy trajectory to the Moon: a day and a half more than the three-day landing flights. Then the Apollo Service Module's main engine would be used to brake the whole stack into lunar orbit.

The empty stage would have the same weight and dynamic characteristics, roughly, as a loaded LM. So an Apollo would indeed be able to deliver it to lunar orbit. The only modifications needed for the S-IVB would be the usual passivation and neutralization kit – equipment to turn the stage from a dry fuel can into a working station – and equipment brackets and pallets. Enough supplies could be carried for a four-week stay in lunar orbit, and the station would be refurbished for later crews.

As he read, Stone began to see the feasibility of it. It could, he realized, be done. *But . . .*

'Why?'

Jones looked up from his own reading; Seger fixed Stone with a glare.

'Why what?'

'Why are we doing this, Bert? It's just a stunt. We'll have to cut out so much to save weight we'll be compromising a lot of our science objectives for Skylab B.'

'I know about the science, Phil. But we can send all that stuff up on the second crew flight, can't we? And your flight will simply turn into a more limited engineering trip, with less emphasis on the science.' Seger was a thin, intense man, with black, slicked-back hair and an Irish darkness; Stone found him unnerving. 'If you're in my chair, Phil, you have to look at the benefits for the program *as a whole*. Beyond your one mission alone. Yes, it will be a stunt. But a hell of a stunt. It will put us right back on top of everything . . .'

Jones talked now about the training they'd already completed toward their Earth-orbital mission. 'And what about the Russians?' The Soviets were proposing to dock a Soyuz ship with Skylab B in Earth orbit. 'Changing that stunt around to a lunar-orbit rendezvous mission is a hell of a trick,' Jones said. 'I mean, the Russkies haven't lifted a single cosmonaut out of Earth orbit yet.'

'The Soviets still say they'll have at least a circumlunar capability in a couple of years – within the life of the station,' Seger said. 'So we can get around that. And even if we can't, maybe we could downgrade the Russian thing into a simple dock with an Apollo in Earth orbit. Anyhow, never mind the damn Russians. Chuck, you'll be hanging out over the edge. Fitting out a station in lunar orbit. Nobody's done anything remotely like that before. I thought a challenge might appeal.'

Jones looked thoughtful.

Stone knew Seger was pressing the right buttons, as far as Jones was concerned. The thought depressed him.

Stone could see Seger's point, to some extent. Morale in NASA had been low, paradoxically, since the Mars decision. A lot of staff had been geared up to the abandoned Space Shuttle program, which they'd seen as new and exciting, technically; by comparison, the Skylabs looked like an extension of 1963 state-of-the-art. And the continuing budget cuts had put endless pressure on the Agency's ambitions.

If you counted contract staff, only a hundred thousand people were still working on space programs, compared to a peak of half a million during Apollo. There had even been a program of terminations, at Houston, Marshall and the other main centers.

Meanwhile NASA had run into a lot of flak over the first orbital workshop, Skylab A. Pete Conrad had led the first set-up mission

134

to open up Skylab. But then the second crew had been military, a consolation for the DoD after the Shuttle cancelation. Ken Mattingly, an Apollo veteran, had led a crew of military astronauts – Manned Spaceflight Engineers – through a secretive program testing 'Terra Scout' and 'Battleview' surveillance equipment, radiation monitoring gear, encrypted communications beams. Every previous NASA flight had been completely open; it had been a deliberate and popular policy going back to Kennedy.

And, meanwhile, US intelligence had learned that Soviet cosmonauts in Salyuts had overseen military exercises in Eastern Siberia, sending down real-time tactical information to battlefield commanders.

A lot of people thought this militarization of space was a deeply shitty development, a fall away from the dream of Apollo. And Jack Kennedy had attacked it, publicly.

So maybe Seger was right that a morale-raising stunt was a good idea at this point. But it *would* be a stunt.

Stone had a military background himself. But he hadn't come into the space program to play spies in space, or to fly stunts. For him, this proposal was a sour compromise. Screw the science, for the sake of the politics. *Just like the old days.*

And, to him, it didn't say a lot for Seger's sound judgment.

Now Seger cut the discussion short. 'Chuck, Phil, every so often you've got to take a chance like this. To go back to the Moon so soon would be a hell of a thing for us. A hell of a thing. The nation needs a boost right now: why, you've got two White House aides testifying in the Senate against the President right this minute. And as for the risks, remember, they flew Apollo 8 to the Moon and back on only the *second* manned Apollo, the *first* manned Saturn V, and the *first* V to fly after the unmanned Apollo 6, which was a shambles . . .'

Stone understood now. Seger had been reading his history. *This is Bert's Apollo 8. Back to the Moon! A grandiose stunt: a way to make his mark. And Skylab B is to be sacrificed for it.*

Seger was saying, 'Just think what a hell of a lift it will give us when you're successful . . .'

'If, Bert,' Jones said. '*If.*'

When he'd thought it over, Stone still wasn't happy.

But he wanted to fly in space. If he was going to have to swallow this ill-thought-out, gung ho crap to do it, then that was the price he would pay.

135

And anyhow – Stone reflected, in the midst of the revised, hectic training schedule – he kind of liked the idea of going to the Moon . . .

Friday, July 20, 1973
Mason City, Iowa

The piece was splashed over the front page of yesterday's *Washington Post*. Ralph Gershon sat in the public library of his home town, reading it over and over.

. . . American B-52 bombers dropped about 104,000 tons of explosives on Communist sanctuaries in neutralist Cambodia during a series of raids in 1969 and 1970 . . . The secret bombing was acknowledged by the Pentagon the Monday after a former Air Force major described how he falsified reports on Cambodia air operations and destroyed records on the bombing missions actually flown . . .

Ralph Gershon felt a deep satisfaction. At last it was coming out.

He was convinced all that covert crap had worked against his career progression in the years since. Maybe it had also killed off the tentative feelers he'd put out about getting into the space program. That and the color of his goddamn skin. Maybe there were people afraid of what he might say, if he got to be a public figure, right? Well, now at last it was all going to be out in the open, and there was nothing anybody could do about it.

He made his decision, sitting there in the musty heat of the library's reference section, with some old guy opposite him drooling in his sleep. As soon as he got back to his squadron he'd start progressing a new application to NASA.

Before he got up he read some more about how Ehrlichman and Haldeman were going to have to testify in front of the Senate. At last, he thought: at last that asshole Nixon was getting his.

Erosion by Catastrophic Floods on Mars and Earth

Ronald R. Victor (Department of Geological Sciences, University of Texas at Austin), Natalie B. York (Space Sciences Laboratory, University of California at Berkeley)

Received March 18, 1974; revised October 6, 1974.

ABSTRACT:

*The large Martian channels, especially Kasei, Ares, Tiu, Simud and Man-
gala Valles, show morphological features strikingly similar to those of
'Channeled Scabland.' Features in the overall pattern include the great
size, regional anastomosis, and low sinuosity of the channels. Erosional
features are streamlined hills, longitudinal grooves, inner channel cataracts, scour upstream of flow obstacles, and perhaps marginal cataracts
and butte and basin topography. Depositional features are bar complexes in expanding reaches and perhaps pendant bars and alcove bars.*

*Scabland erosion takes place in exceedingly deep, swift floodwater
acting on closely jointed bedrock as a hydrodynamic consequence of
secondary flow phenomena, including various forms of macro-turbulent
vortices and flow separations. If the analogy to the Channeled Scablands
is correct, floods involving water discharges of millions of cubic meters
per second and peak flow velocities of tens of meters per second, but
lasting perhaps no more than a few days, have occurred on Mars . . .*

From The Bulletin of Geophysical Research, *vol. 23, pp. 27–41 (1974).*
Copyright 1974 by Academia Press, Inc.; all rights reserved.

July, 1976
Jet Propulsion Laboratory, Pasadena

Later, York would pinpoint the divergence in the trajectory of her
life to a couple of days in the middle of 1976.

After that point, things just seemed to unravel, for her, as she
fell toward a new destiny.

York wished she had something to drink. Even with all the windows
open, the sun beating down on the roof made the car as hot as hell.
Her sunglasses kept slipping down her nose, and every time she
rested her arm on the sill of the window frame she burned her skin.

She rattled her nails on the steering wheel, waiting for Ben Priest.

In the middle of the aimless mess of her life, she seemed to be
regressing, to some kind of childhood.

She'd had a huge image of Mars taped to her bedroom wall, a
black and white photomosaic compiled from fifteen hundred
Mariner 9 photographs, with the scar of Olympus Mons square at
the center. At least, she'd had it there until Mike had made her
take it down. He said Olympus Mons looked like a huge nipple.

And now here she was hanging around at the gates of JPL –
without a security pass – like a goddamn groupie, hoping to get an

137

early look at the Soviets' new pictures from the Martian surface.

At last, here came Ben Priest. With his graying crew cut he looked every inch the military man. He was carrying a fat cardboard folder with a blue NASA logo stenciled on the front. He was moving at a half-trot, despite the heat, but he showed no signs of sweat; his crisp short-sleeved shirt glowed white in the brilliant noon light.

This time he hadn't been able to get her into the lab itself. Nobody was supposed to see the stuff the Soviets were sending back from Mars.

Ben clambered into the car beside her. 'Got it.'

She reached over. 'Give.'

'Hell, no. Is that any way to greet an old friend? Let's get out of this heat first. Mars can wait a few more minutes.'

She suppressed her eagerness. *Be polite, Natalie.* And, after all, this was Ben. She started the car. 'Let's find a bar. Do you know anywhere?'

'Only the waterholes where the JPL hairies hang out, and I'd rather take a break from them.'

'I'm staying at the Holiday Inn. It's only a few minutes from here.'

'Go for it.'

She pulled out.

'I was expecting to see Mike too,' Ben said.

'Oh, in the end he couldn't get away. He has his head shoved much too firmly up a NERVA 2 exhaust pipe.' *Or up his own ass, maybe,* she thought sourly.

'You know the NERVA thing still isn't going too well. My flight on Apollo-N has been delayed again, and –'

'Mike doesn't tell me anything. Half of it's classified, any-how.'

'Well, that's the word in the Astronaut Office. So how's life for my favorite girl-geologist?'

She grunted, and pushed her slippery sunglasses back up her nose. 'Shitty, if you want the truth. My professor at Berkeley – Cattermole – is a jackass.'

Priest laughed out loud. 'I wish you'd say what you mean.'

'Cattermole's smart at departmental infighting, and putting together grant applications. But that's it. The rest of his head shut down long ago. His projects are lousy, as are his methods. He sees Berkeley's Space Sciences Lab as just a way to chisel money out of NASA. If I was smart enough to have seen that before I signed up, I wouldn't have gone within ten miles of the man.'

'But your contract is only short-term.'

'Yeah, and then I have to find another.'

'Which you will. If you want it. You're a bright girl, Natalie.'

'Don't patronize me, asshole.'

He laughed again.

'Yes, I'll find another job. Maybe I'll even get an assistant professorship somewhere. But . . .'

'But you don't think life as a rock hound is going to work out for you.'

'I don't know, Ben. Maybe not.' Not even working on Mars data was satisfying her.

'So what's your alternative?'

'Well, there are plenty of jobs for geologists with the oil companies. Good pay; lots of travel.'

Ben said nothing. When she glanced sideways, he was pulling a face.

She felt infuriated. 'So what else do I do, smartypants?'

He grinned, and patted the folder on his lap. 'It's obvious. Your trouble is, thousands of geologists have been to Alaska before.'

'So?'

'So, I know a place where there are no geologists at all. Your problem is you're working on the wrong planet.'

The bar at the Holiday Inn was pretty full. It was July 5, the day after the Bicentennial. Bunting drooped around the walls, and there was other Bicentennial debris: a couple of newspaper pictures of Operation Sail, the big regatta in New York Harbor, and yellowing, handwritten, out-of-date signs for local pie-eating, baton-twirling and greased-pole-climbing contests.

York found them a table in the corner. When Ben went to get drinks, she grabbed the folder out of his hands and spread the Soviet material over the veneer table top.

The first couple of images were Soviet publicity shots, of a Mars 9 lander mockup on a simulated Martian surface. The craft landed hard, closed up into a ball, and then four petals unfolded to reveal instrumentation and antennae; in place, the lander was a splayed-open sphere, four feet across.

Ben returned with drinks: Buds, in bottles that glistened with dew.

She pushed the publicity shots across the table. 'Look at these damn things. Red sand, and blue sky.'

He laughed. 'Well, you can't blame the Soviets. That's what we

139

expected to find down there too. The trouble is, we want Mars to be just like Earth.' He took one of the pictures. 'Still, isn't their Mars lander pretty?'

'Oh, sure,' York growled. 'But Viking would have been a hell of a lot prettier. Viking would have had stereoscopic cameras and a full meteorology station and *four* biology experiments. And Voyager would have had a *surface rover*.' Voyager, a heavy Mars probe to be launched by Saturn V, had been killed by budget cuts in 1967, and the Viking landers in 1972. 'Think of it. After traveling hundreds of millions of miles, if we want this Soviet probe to see behind some rock twelve feet away, we can't do it. Pathetic.'

He held his hands up. 'Don't ask me to argue. Anyhow, the Soviets haven't done so badly.'

'We'd have done better, Ben. You know it.'

All NASA had to show for this Mars opportunity was another Mariner orbiter, taking high-resolution photos of equatorial landing sites, plus one hard-impact probe which had sampled the atmosphere before crashing into the surface. It was just like the lunar program of the 1960s; the unmanned science program had been completely subordinated to the operational needs of the manned mission to come. The new Mariner, laden with imaging equipment, wasn't a scientific probe but an advance scout for the manned missions. *And we could at least have sent a couple of Vikings.*

Meanwhile the Soviets were sending up their own clumsy probes, evidently intent on genuine science. In fact the Soviets had sent probes to Mars in every launch opportunity since 1960. And of this year's pair of probes, Mars 8 had failed, but Mars 9 had started transmitting surface images the day before – on America's Independence Day. Humanity's first Martian lander had probably provided all the propaganda benefit the Soviets could have wished for.

Priest dug more pictures out of the folder. 'Here. This is what you want to see . . .'

She grabbed the photographs and started leafing through them eagerly. The pictures were grainy, and the resolution wasn't great. But they were in color. Soon the bar table was covered with images of crusty, rust-brown Martian regolith, a rocky horizon, a pink sky.

Ben said, 'These are strictly for JPL consumption only. The Soviets passed them over because we gave them Mariner images of their landing site, in Hellas. So you're not seeing them now. Okay?'

'Sure.' Her heart pumped harder. 'Oh, God, Ben, I can't tell you how much I appreciate this. It would have taken me months to get my hands on this stuff otherwise.'

He touched her hand, briefly; his palm was cool and dry, the feel of his skin somehow startling. 'You know, it means a lot to me to see you like this.'

She looked at her hand inside his. She felt confused, conflicting emotions surging. So her dubious relationship with Ben Priest was still dubious.

She pulled back her hand, unwilling to think about this right now. Not when she had *Mars* on the table top.

The Soviet lander was sitting in the middle of a flat, undulating landscape of ochre-colored material, with boulders scattered between small dunes. It was, she thought, like the stony deserts of North Africa, North America or Asia. Some shots showed pieces of the lander itself: an unfolded petal here, resting on the regolith, there a jumble of clunky Soviet equipment on the upper surface, a series of white-painted boxes contrasted with the pink sky. Another photo showed a sampling arm upraised, as if in triumph, over the surface; she could clearly see trenches, scooped out of the sandy regolith by the arm.

It looked very real, the rocks so sharply pictured it was almost as if she could reach into the frames and pick them up . . .

'Natalie? Are you okay?'

She looked up at him. He looked blurred; she found some kind of hot liquid rolling down her left cheek.

'Natalie?'

'Yeah.' She wiped her eyes, quickly, with a napkin. 'I'm sorry.'

'You don't have to apologize.'

'It's just that it's as if I'm *there*. Sitting on top of the lander, on Mars itself . . .'

I know where I am, precisely.

I am in Hellas. One of the deepest impact basins on the planet.

It is a little before the solstice: deep midwinter, here in the southern hemisphere of Mars.

The surface is reddish, boulder-strewn. Over there I can see what look like impact craters, between the dunes. Those dunes are obviously of windborne material. And I see other wind effects, such as those trails of fine grains lying between the boulders. That tells me that the prevailing winds here are in quite consistent directions.

But it's obvious that the landscape doesn't owe its morphology just to erosion and deposition by winds. Over there, I see stretches

141

of a hardened vitrified surface. Vitrified: a crust of mineral salts,
left behind by evaporation.
There has been water here, shaping the surface . . .

He ordered them both more beers; she drank, and felt the cool
glow of the alcohol suffusing her.

'Now. Look at this stuff.' Ben dug out a photostatted report.
'This is the real pay dirt.'

She scanned it quickly. It was a statement of preliminary conclusions by Academician Boris N. Petrov, of the Soviets' life sciences
team. The report seemed very guarded. It was couched in the language of a discipline with which she had only a nodding acquaint-
ance, and further masked by cautious Soviet official-speak.

She dropped the paper back on the table. 'It's so damn circum-
spect. It's hard to make out anything at all.'

'Yeah.' He cradled his glass. 'Well, the results are ambiguous.
The life experiment is a gas chromatography mass spectrometer.'

'We'd have done better. Viking would have carried –'

'Yeah, I know. Anyway, the GCMS looked for organic molecules
in the regolith.'

'And?'

'The GCMS found nothing, Natalie.'

'Nothing? But that's impossible . . .'

Organic molecules didn't necessarily imply the existence of life.
'Organic' just meant 'carbon-based.' But organic molecules were a
necessary precursor to Earth-type life, and they had been expected
on the Martian surface; organic materials had even been found in
meteorites from outer space.

Ben said, 'The JPL guys figure there must be some process on
Mars that actively *destroys* organics. Ultraviolet flux from the sun,
maybe.'

'So the surface is actually sterilized.' She felt a crushing disappointment. She had, she realized, been hoping, unreasonably,
that some kind of life might turn up after all. Maybe a hardy lichen
clinging to the lee side of a rock . . . 'Mars is dead.'

'Should you be jumping to conclusions like that, a true scientist
like you?' He found another piece of paper. 'Hey, listen to this. It's
from their meteorology team. *Winds in the late afternoon were
again out of a generally easterly direction. Once again the winds
went to the southwesterly after midnight and oscillated about that
direction through what appears to be two cycles. The maximum
wind speed was twenty-four feet per second but gusts were detected*

reaching forty-five feet per second. The minimum temperature attained, just before dawn, was almost the same as on the previous day, minus ninety-six degrees centigrade. The maximum, measured at two sixteen p.m. local time, was minus forty-three degrees. This was two degrees colder than at the same time on the previous day. The mean pressure . . . Natalie, my God, this is a weather report from Mars.'

She looked up at him. His blue eyes were on her, his face gentle; she felt as if he were looking right into her.

For years, she thought, she had been heading toward Ben Priest, maybe toward this moment, like some dumb spacecraft on its blind trajectory to a target planet.

She pushed close to him, leaning across the photographs of Mars. Their lips touched, gently, almost timidly. His skin felt cool, a little rough. She pressed again, and this time the kiss was deep.

This has been coming for a hell of a long time. Ben Priest, and Mars. It was a potent combination.

Eventually they broke.

He touched her cheek. 'Now, where the hell did that come from?'

'The Soviets have sent pictures from the surface of Mars,' she said. 'It's a hell of a day for all of us, for all of humanity. Maybe a new step in our evolutionary history. What else do you want to do to celebrate?' She reached into the pocket of her shirt, and dug out her room key. 'Come on.'

Long after Ben had fallen asleep, York remained awake. It had turned into a hell of a night, the darkness laden with heat and humidity; the sheets lay loosely over her, faintly damp against her skin. She heard the ticking of the small clock beside the bed, the creak of the window shutters as they cooled. Mars 9 pictures and print-outs were scattered over the floor at the end of the bed, with clothes piled loosely on top.

She could feel the tousled warmth of Ben beside her. Ben had flown around the Moon, and now here he was, in her bed.

She remembered Ben's question. *Where the hell did that come from?* Where, indeed. And where were they going now?

She wondered if she should ask him about Karen, and Peter.

He hadn't mentioned them; York didn't even know where Karen was right now. He had told her they were having difficulties with their boy: young, enthusiastic Petey had metamorphosed into Peter, a difficult seventeen-year-old, who had painted the walls of his room black – covering up the stars and astronaut pictures he'd pasted there – and spent more time listening to Alice Cooper than his father.

But Ben didn't say much about that, even though she could see it caused him distress. Ben rarely did talk about his family, in fact.

And York was being a hypocritical asshole. A couple of hours ago, she couldn't have given a damn about Karen.

Would Ben ever leave Karen? They went back a long time, obviously. And theirs was a Navy marriage. When Karen married Ben, she took on a lot of separation, of anxiety. Perhaps Ben thought he owed her.

Anyhow, if he did leave her – what then? Would York want him? What about Mike?

It was all, she thought, just one hell of a mess. It was hard to understand how come, for a person who had advanced so far on her rationality and logic, she could work out so little about a small affair of a handful of people, and their unexceptional relationships to each other.

She stopped thinking about it.

She picked the folder off the floor and, as quietly as she could, she dug further through the contents of the Soviet file.

She found XRF results. The X-ray fluorescence device had sent back to Earth a preliminary assay of the composition of Martian regolith. She scanned it quickly. Silicon dioxide, forty five per cent; ferrous oxide, eighteen per cent . . . There was a lot of silicon, iron, magnesium, aluminum, calcium and sodium. But the proportions weren't like any terrestrial rock. There was a lot of iron there. And not much potassium. That was probably significant; it meant that Martian rock hadn't suffered as much differentiation by internal heating as had the Earth. Maybe Mars hadn't got a large core of nickel and iron, as Earth had . . .

She swore under her breath. She was speculating. This data was so limited. That Soviet lander had set down in just one spot, on a planet with a land area the same as the Earth's. And she could see the limitations of the sampling scoop just by looking at the photos of it. It was only going to be able to sample loose, friable material; what geologists called fines. It just wasn't enough to give a complete picture.

What we need is someone out there, climbing off the lander, with a spade and a hammer.

Now she'd got over her initial disappointment, she didn't much care about the life results. It was geology that fascinated her; life was a just second-order consequence of geology, after all. A positive

144

biology result would have been convenient, though. *If only we had seen a silicon-based gorilla jumping up and down on the damn Russian camera, we'd be going to Mars tomorrow. Even a fossilized trilobite would do.*

She remembered those scratchy Mariner 4 pictures. And later, those astonishing images of Phobos, and the Olympus Mons, from Mariner 9. Humanity had learned more about Mars from the probes in the last decade or so than in the whole of previous human history. She was lucky to live at such a time, when so many ancient mysteries were being resolved.

Lucky. Maybe.

But it was as if Mars was somehow teasing her. Enticing her.

She put down the reports. It was time she was honest with herself. This dribble of data wasn't enough. She didn't want to spend the next thirty years as she had the last two or three, poring over grainy Mariner images, constructing hypotheses she could never confirm. *I want to go to Mars, damn it. I want to get down on my hands and knees on that rocky ground, and dig a trench, and bury my gloved fingers in the surface. I want to see the pink sky, and the twin moons, and drive to the peak of Olympus Mons, and stand on the lip of the Valles Marineris . . .*

Mars, with its slow, teasing unveiling, was seducing her. She realized now that Ben saw this more clearly than she did. And certainly more clearly than Mike, who could barely see anything beyond his own concerns.

But the dream, the ambition itself, wasn't the problem. The problem was, she had an outside chance of getting there. As Ben kept telling her, York was the right age, with the right qualifications, to compete for a place in NASA.

The problem was, she might actually try to do this. But joining NASA, trying to get to Mars, meant throwing away her whole life. It meant she'd have to go back to school, and she'd have to go through endless, meaningless training with those assholes at NASA, and she might spend years in low Earth orbit working on crap outside her specialty.

It probably meant, too – it occurred to her suddenly – that she wouldn't have any kids.

Did she really want to sacrifice all that, to go through so much shit, just for an outside chance of walking on the slopes of Tharsis?

But her fingers itched to get into that dirt, to dig around, to get beyond the loose surface crust of Mars.

*   *   *

145

The very next day, she was supposed to meet Mike. She'd booked them into a hotel in downtown LA, so they could spend some time together.

After last night she felt truly shitty about going ahead with the meeting, or date, or whatever the hell she was supposed to call it at this point in her relationship with Mike. But she decided to go anyhow; she didn't see she had much choice.

Before they parted, Ben dug a leaflet out of his jacket pocket. 'Here,' he said. 'For you.'

Eighteen hours later, in their LA motel room, York rubbed the tension out of Mike's shoulders, and at last he slept.

After that it was York who seemed to be stuck awake.

She was stiff and a little cold, and the sheets beneath her were crumpled, digging into her back as she lay there. The mellow feeling from the mini-bar brandies had worn off, leaving her feeling stale, her heart over-stimulated.

And besides, she had something she needed to talk over with Mike.

She opened the drawer of the bedside table and pulled out Ben's leaflet.

In the soft glow of the splinters of light on the ceiling she couldn't read any of it, but she could make out some of the images: the famous photograph of Joe Muldoon standing on the Moon with his gloved hand across his chest, little schematic diagrams of spacecraft flying around the Solar System. At the back there was a tear-off application form; she ran her finger-tip along the perforation.

Issued by the National Academy of Sciences on behalf of NASA, the leaflet was titled 'Opportunities for Scientists as Astronauts.' It set out a glowing future in space: expanded laboratories in Earth orbit, more stations around the Moon, even semi-permanent scientific colonies on the surface to follow the preliminary toe-dips of Apollo. And then there were NASA's goals beyond cislunar space: the first manned Mars mission, orbital surveys of Venus – and manned flights to the asteroids and the Jovian system. All within the lifetimes of scientists working now.

It was an application form to be an astronaut.

She'd been tempted to throw the leaflet into the trash. She was immensely disappointed by this garbage: typical NASA dreaming, predicated on an unwavering expansion of funding, and an unrelenting political will. For this, she should sacrifice her career, throw

146

away a decade of her life? After all, none of this astounding program was *real* . . .

None of it. Except, maybe, Mars.

Everyone knew about the problems: Mike's NERVA program was years behind schedule, there were delays in the enhanced Saturn booster development, and the Mars lander base technology project was underfunded and lacking focus . . . And so forth. In the end, if it succeeded at all, NASA would probably reach Mars much as it had reached the Moon: not as part of any long-term integrated strategy of expansion into the Solar System, as set out in this glossy little pamphlet, but as a precarious one-of-a-kind stunt. NASA seemed organizationally equipped for no other mode of working.

But, for all that, progress was being made, and funding seemed secured for the near future. Jimmy Carter's attitude to space remained to be demonstrated, but Ben told her that Fred Michaels, the NASA Administrator, had thrown his weight behind Ted Kennedy as Vice President, and helped him secure the nomination against Walter Mondale – who was well known as a critic of the space program, all the way back to the 1960s. Carter/Kennedy were now clear favorites to win the November election. And after that, things would look better for Michaels, with his links to the Democrats, and allies among the Kennedys both inside and outside the White House . . .

NASA, it seemed, was still headed for Mars.

She'd intended to talk to Mike about it tonight. Somehow, though, the subject hadn't come up.

She put the leaflet back in the drawer.

Beside her, Mike shifted a little, but he didn't wake up. He was turned toward her, and his hair lay in a dark halo about his head. He slept like a child, she thought: face down, with his arms up around his head, and his face turned sideways. In sleep the tension had drained out of his face, and he looked years younger than his age of thirty-four.

She'd hardly seen Mike in the last few months. His schedule was grueling. NERVA 2 was now only seven months away from the Critical Design Review at the scheduled end of its Phase A development. After that Phase B, production and operations, should be starting up in earnest, with the first unmanned flight tests scheduled for 1978, and the Preliminary Flight Certificate – issued after the first manned flight – to be obtained by mid 1979.

But Mike's people still hadn't been able to demonstrate a sustained burn of their huge new engine for more than a couple of seconds.

Mike seemed to be taking it particularly hard. He'd clearly been working fifteen or eighteen hours a day for weeks now. He'd become gaunt, his eyes sunk deep in shadows, his clothes and hair rumpled and ill-maintained. She wasn't sure if that reflected the way he was coping personally, or the fact that a lot of the problems seemed to be in the cooling systems for which he was responsible.

Still sleepless, she turned on the TV.

An old *Star Trek* re-run was flickering through its paces. The warp engines were in trouble again, and Mr Scott was crawling through some kind of glass tube with a spanner.

'If only it was as easy as that,' Mike mumbled.

His head was lifted off the pillow, and, bleary, he was squinting at the TV.

'I didn't mean to wake you, Scotty.'

He reached for a cigarette. 'You want something else to drink?'

'No. The brandy is keeping me awake, I think.' The comforting smell of stale smoke reached her; it reminded her of her mother. 'It's times like this I wish I smoked.'

He grunted. 'Don't even think about it.'

She debated telling him about the form in the bedside drawer.

But he was checking the clock. 'I think I'd have woken up anyhow. They should be running the latest burn about now. Something inside me, some dumb kind of timer, wakes me up at moments like this, even when I'm twenty miles away from the Facility.'

'The burns. The tests. Always the fucking tests. Mike, unless you can figure out a way to relax, you'll make yourself crazy.'

He blew out smoke. 'I think we're all a little crazy already.'

The trouble was, driving people like this had become part of NASA culture. *We all worked eighteen hours a day for eight years to get a man on the Moon with Apollo, and if we have to do it all over again to get to Mars, well, by gosh, that's what we're going to do . . .* But mistakes *had* been made on Apollo, and those mistakes had claimed lives.

She put her hand over his; she could feel how it was bunched up, almost into a fist. She stroked his knuckles. 'Listen. I've been thinking. We don't see enough of each other.'

'Hell, I know that. But what can we do about it? We've always known what the deal would be.'

She sought for words. 'But I think our lives are kind of hollow, Mike; we've been neglecting ourselves too much. Too many other things to distract us.' She waved a hand at the motel room. 'We

148

need something more than patches of neutral territory like this. We need something solid. I think we should get a place to live –'

He snorted out a billow of smoke. 'Where? We're lucky if we're both in the same state for more than twenty-four hours.'

She was irritated at his dismissiveness. 'I know that. "Where" doesn't matter. Anywhere. Here, or Berkeley maybe. And it wouldn't even matter if the damn place was empty for three-quarters of the year. *It would be ours,* Mike; that's the point. It would be a kind of base for us. At the moment, all we have is this. Holiday Inn. I don't think it's enough.' *I'm twenty-eight years old, for God's sake.*

He stubbed out his cigarette and watched her; on the TV screen, ignored, Captain Kirk was facing another crisis. 'You're a crazy woman, Natalie York.'

'Maybe so. What do you say?'

'Why now? I mean, it's not going to make a damn piece of difference to the way we live our lives, the extent to which we see each other. You're not going to give up your career.'

'Of course not, and neither are you.' She pulled at his fingers. 'But that's not the point.'

Then what is, Natalie? What primeval instinct has dragged this up, after all this time? And right at this moment, when you're thinking of getting on a road that could take you off the Earth altogether . . .

She surely hadn't come to terms with what had happened last night, yet.

Maybe this – tonight, with Mike – was all just some kind of way of dealing with Ben, she thought bleakly.

But if that was true, where did it leave her and Mike? . . .

Christ. What a mess.

The phone rang, its sharp tone startling her.

'Jesus.' He reached out and took the receiver. 'Hello? . . . All right, I'll be there.' He put the phone down.

'Mike –'

He was already half-way out of bed; he scrabbled over the floor, looking for his pants. 'The burn was another failure. Sustained for less than half a second. *Shit.*' He touched her hair. 'I've got to be there, Natalie. You go back to sleep.'

'I haven't been asleep.' She kicked away the sheets and stood up; the air in the room was distinctly cold now. 'I'll come too.'

'You don't have to.'

'I'd prefer it. Anyway we have a conversation to finish.' Mike had already pulled on his shirt; he was muttering to himself, as his mind started to whirl around the problems of the engine.

He's probably already forgotten what we were talking about.

They set off for the Test Facility a little after three a.m. It was going to take half an hour to drive out to Santa Susana from downtown LA.

Mike drove out of the San Fernando Valley, and York could see streetlights glowing down there, neat rectangular blocks of light plastered over the Valley floor and walls.

Mike drove anxiously, too quickly, without speaking to her.

The Test Facility nestled in a rough, boulder-strewn depression in the Santa Susana Mountains. When Mike stopped the car, York was struck by the chill of the air.

She walked with Mike to the center of the Facility.

The stars were out overhead, though the young Moon had long set.

Santa Susana was operated on behalf of NASA by Rockwell International. It had been built as part of the development program for the old S-II, the Saturn V second stage. There was still some S-II development work going on here, in fact. The whole site was a swarm of activity, with technicians – some of them in flame-proof or radiation-proof gear – crawling all over the rig. To York, they looked like ungainly insects.

The NERVA 2 engine stood upended at the heart of the Facility, surrounded by a wire-mesh safety fence. Glowing in powerful floodlights, the broad engine bell flared toward the sky.

When they got close to the rig, technicians came up to Conlig. Mike managed one last, apologetic glance back at York, and then he was lost.

Alone, she began to walk slowly around the rig.

'Hi. You look like you need this.'

She turned. A man was at her elbow, grinning; he was tall, pale, with blond hair; he wore grimy coveralls. He looked as if he had been up all night. He bore two plastic cups of a brownish liquid. 'It's from a dispenser. It's supposed to be coffee,' he said, 'but I wouldn't bank on it without a full chemical analysis.'

'I know you. Don't I?'

'Yup. Adam Bleeker. We took a field trip together a few years back, in the San Gabriel Mountains.'

'Oh.' The Cold Warrior astronaut. 'With Ben, and Charles Jones. What a disaster that was.'

150

'Oh, I wouldn't say that. You did your job well. And everyone calls him Chuck, by the way.'

'Whatever.'

She took the coffee gratefully and sipped it. It was warm, but almost flavorless.

Bleeker told her he was the Astronaut Office representative on the project here. Ben Priest had covered the same assignment some years before.

'It's kind of an odd time of day to run an engine test,' York observed.

'Well, we're so far behind schedule. Every hour counts.'

'Tell me about it. I came out with Mike. Do you know him? – Mike Conlig –'

'Sure.'

'Nothing was going to keep him away from here, once the call came.'

They started to walk around the test rig, slowly. Technicians were everywhere, arguing desultorily. There was an almost tangible air of tension, of depression; it was Mike's mood writ large.

The contrast to Jackass Flats – to the raw enthusiasm Mike had represented to her there – was marked.

In the middle of it all, the huge NERVA 2 engine stood erect and silent, aloof, remote behind its safety cordon. This motor, Mike had told her, was the 'Integrated Subsystems Test Bed Engine'; it was a complete, more or less operational machine, but it was trapped in this ungainly test rig, and when it fired, it could only drive itself into the solid Earth.

Just looking at the rig, York could tell that NERVA was still years away from flight status, from delivering its promised two hundred thousand pounds of interplanetary thrust.

The upturned nozzle sat atop a short, fat cylinder, and two smaller bells protruded from the cylinder's sides. The cylinder was the pressure shell which contained the radioactive core, and the smaller nozzles, gimbaled, were attitude control rockets. She saw the ring of cone-shaped actuators at the base of the engine; the actuators operated the control drum which moderated the reactor. A huge spherical hydrogen tank sat close to the engine, and pipes snaked from it to swaddle the pressure shell and nozzle. Plumes of vapor vented from the tank, and sheets of ice encrusted its sleek metal walls.

Adam Bleeker helped her trace out the engine's operation.

'Liquid hydrogen works as both propellant and coolant – it's called regenerative cooling. A pump pushes the hydrogen through that cooling jacket surrounding the pressure shell and the bell. Then the hydrogen is forced through the radioactive core, where it flashes to vapor, and drives its way out through the bell . . .'

There was still no trap for the vented hydrogen, York noted absently.

Bleeker showed her how an efflux pipe from the reactor carried a proportion of the hot hydrogen gas to a turbine, to power the engine's pumps in flight. The turbopump exhaust was used as attitude control gas, vented off through the small supplementary nozzles.

'What's the problem tonight?'

'Cavitation. Gas bubbles in the liquid hydrogen flow. We raised the core temperature to its working regime, and we'd started the hydrogen flow. We reached nominal thrust, for about half a second. But then the core temperature started to climb. We were cavitating, somewhere below the pump: hydrogen bubbles, stopping the circulation of coolant. And that was why the core temperature was climbing. We had to shut down.' He sounded tired. 'You can imagine the safety restrictions we're under here. If the pressure shell had been breached, we'd have had radioactive products reaching the atmosphere, and there would have been hell to pay. So as soon as we saw the problem, we had to obey the rule book, which said to shut off the hydrogen, and flood the whole damn core with water to ensure the temperature comes down. Now we're going to have to siphon off all that radioactive water, and take the core apart by remotes, and make sure the propellant flow cylinders haven't been damaged in the heat . . . It will be days before we're set for the next test.'

'Christ. What a mess.'

York studied his profile; picked out by the powerful floods, Bleeker's skin looked thin, almost translucent. She found it hard to read Bleeker's own reaction to all this. Was he impatient at the restrictive rules, the need for safety? Did he have any qualms about handling lethal substances in such an unstable, unproven rig? She couldn't tell. Just as when she'd first met him, Bleeker struck her as utterly calm, cool. Or, perhaps, completely without a soul.

'You're all under a lot of pressure,' she said. 'I know a lot of questions are being asked about the ability of NASA to deliver NERVA 2.'

'By who?'

She shrugged. 'The press. Congress.'

'Yeah,' he said evenly, showing no resentment. 'Well, hell, maybe there are questions to ask. You know, the program's led by the Germans, from Huntsville. And they didn't pick the design goal – which is two hundred thousand pounds of thrust for thirty minutes – because they *knew* they could build it; they chose the goal because that's what we *need* for the Mars mission profile. They didn't go through a lot of analysis to try to figure it out; they just started building toward it. It's the way they've always worked. And it's kind of hard to argue against their kind of record. But . . .'

'But you're not so sure.'

He hesitated. 'The truth is, the development schedule we're working to was modeled on experience of chemical technology. Nuke stuff is *different*. I think they're only just figuring out how different. And that's even after we've eliminated a lot of nice-to-haves, like a deep throttling capability . . . I think maybe we've underestimated the schedule, here. We're pushing too hard.'

Now a crew, in white protective gear, was moving into the cordoned-off zone, converging on the NERVA. York wondered vaguely if one of them was Mike. There was no way of knowing.

She stared at the inert NERVA 2, resentful. *Thanks to that broken-down thing, I'm not going to see a trace of Mike for weeks now.*

Bleeker had to leave her, to get on with his own work.

She watched the slow, painstaking demolition job for a few minutes, then she went back to the car, and managed to fall asleep in the passenger seat.

When she awoke, the sun was well above the horizon, and the car was stuffy and hot. There was no sign of Mike. She found a bathroom, and left a note for Mike.

She drove herself back to LA.

Mission Elapsed Time [Day/Hr:Min:Sec] Plus 004/21:38:11

Daily execute packages were uploaded from Mission Control overnight, as twenty feet of teleprinter output. The packages contained suggested timelines, and a few personal messages. York split up her portion of the list and put it into her ring binder, throwing away yesterday's draft, and began to figure out how to follow the day through.

She looked down the list, searching first for time-critical items.

153

Then she looked for stuff that would need advance setup and preparation, and items that weren't solo, where she'd have to work with the others.

The execute package wasn't so much a detailed timeline, as the first generations of astronauts had had to follow, but a 'shopping list' of objectives. Mission planning was a lot more laid back now, compared to the days when moonwalks had been choreographed down to the minute. The shopping list approach had evolved during the long-duration Skylab flights of the 1970s. York was relieved; she was a senior professional, after all – they all were – and she didn't need her activities hand-held by some remote roomful of experts down in Houston.

In her pocket, to help her with the timing, she carried a small personal alarm clock, a cute clockwork thing she'd picked up from a five-and-dime in a mall in Nassau Bay. Its crudity and lack of accuracy appealed to her, in the midst of all this high technology.

Her main objective for the day was going to be powering up the Ares Transfer-Orbit Science Platform. She drifted upwards, along the cylindrical length of the Mission Module.

The Mission Module was based on the design of the Skylabs which had been in use for more than a decade now. Such was the lifting capacity of the Saturn VB, the Mission Module had been delivered to Earth orbit 'dry' – carrying no fuel, and with interior partitions and equipment already fitted. The crew occupied what had been the hydrogen tank, all forty-eight feet of it, with its domed ceiling and floor. Hidden under the floor was the lox tank, much smaller, a cramped, squashed sphere. The lox tank was used to hold stores, and with its thicker walls it would serve as the crew's storm shelter – shielding them from solar flares, if any blew up in the course of the mission.

The hydrogen tank was split into three levels by partitions of triangular metal mesh. York was wearing Dutch shoes, with v-flanges in the sole, to enable her to cling to either side of the floors. There was a fireman's pole running down the middle of the workshop, and there were straps and guide ropes and harnesses everywhere.

The tank's bottom level was 'home' – the wardroom, sleep and waste compartments. The middle belt doubled as a command and control area, covering all of the spacecraft's subsystems, environmental processes and flight operations, and as an experiment and exercise area, with a running strip around the tank's circular wall. The exercise machines, still in their launch configuration, were strapped against the pressure hull. And the top level, closest to the prow of the Ares cluster, was the Science Platform.

The whole Module was something like a big engine room, York thought, with clunky tanks and storage boxes stuck to the curved walls, and cables and pipes running everywhere, under smooth covers of yellow plastic.

When she floated up into the Science Platform, it was like entering an octagonal cave. Bulky equipment racks and storage bays were fixed all around the curved hull. One side of the octagon served as a ceiling, broken by a couple of high-quality viewing ports – disks of darkness – and by small science-experiment airlocks, sturdy wheeled hatches like the doors of little safes. Everything was still in its place, stowed neatly away, still in the wrapper.

She pulled herself to the right-hand wall, and locked her feet into a couple of stirrups. This was the display and control console: a long rack of switches, cathode ray displays, and numeric and qwerty keypads. She closed switches and began booting up the Science Platform's computers, and started to power up and check out the rest of the equipment.

As it started to come to life, the cramped little science station reminded her of some bespectacled kid's bedroom laboratory; it was compact, miniature, kind of sweet.

Some of the experiments carried by Ares were part of long-term microgravity research programs. There were experiments in protein crystal growth, and the diffusion of bacteria in microgravity conditions, and a chunky arrangement called the Heat Pipe Performance experiment, a dry engineering test of the diffusion of heat from hot-spots on pipes and ducts in microgravity.

But Ares offered some special opportunities. There was a scheme to observe major solar events like spots and flares from the two widely separating vantage points of Ares and Earth, and so there was a whole bunch of instruments which would be directed at the sun: a coronagraph, a spectroheliograph, a spectrographic telescope. Since in flight the Ares cluster would keep itself aligned to point at the sun, to save boiloff, all this equipment was mounted in a pallet which would be unfolded and held out from the body of the Mission Module, like a rear-view mirror.

The setting up took longer than she expected. The computers, Hewlett-Packard minis, were slow. The models Ares was carrying were out of date: the design of the Platform, already nearly a decade old, had become frozen around these customized, low-weight, low-power machines years before. Hewlett-Packard and the other computer suppliers had made a commitment to keep supporting NASA's in-flight equipment as long as was necessary. But it was ironic that here York was – in deep space, en route to Mars – having to make do and mend with technology which no self-respecting middle-sized savings and loan in Gary, Indiana, would put up with any more.

And besides, microgravity was turning out to be a pain in the butt to work in. Anything that wasn't tied down just floated away. It was easy enough to remember that for major pieces of equipment, but it also applied to her notebook, pens, pencils, handkerchief. She wasted a lot of time chasing down elusive items of equipment. And she had to make a conscious effort to anchor herself – with foot stirrups, or by holding on to a rack surface, or by wrapping her legs around a strut – before she tried to move anything. Otherwise, every time she turned a switch on the control panel, the switch would just turn her back.

It was like working on an ice-rink: a huge, invisible, three-dimensional ice-rink, across whose surface items kept escaping from her, slithering away along perfectly straight lines, and on which she felt she was constantly losing her balance.

When York came floating back down into the wardroom, Phil Stone was already in the little galley area, working on the lunch. Food packages and trays floated in the air beside him.

A TV camera, fixed to the wall of the wardroom, was fixed on him; York vaguely remembered that they were scheduled for another public broadcast about now. She wondered how many people were still watching.

Stone glanced up at York. 'You're starting to look like an astronaut, Natalie.'

'How so?'

'Take a look in the mirror.'

The nearest mirror was fixed over the wash basin. York floated over and inspected herself. Stray wisps of hair floated up around her head in a kind of halo, and the skin under her eyes looked puffy, as if she had been crying. This was another effect of microgravity: the accumulation of fluids under the skin of the face. She prodded at the fleshy pads under her eyes; the skin was tender, as if stretched.

Gershon came soaring down the fireman's pole, upside down. 'Hello, Japan-ee lady,' he said, pulling his eyes slantways.

There was a hiss of static from the comms panel fixed to the wall. 'Ares, Houston. We see a box of goodies there, Phil.' Capcom today was Bob Crippen.

York sensed the others stiffening, subtly. Crippen's forced banter signalled they were going out to the public. *We're on stage again, guys.*

Stone held up an anonymous brown bag. 'Good day, Bob. Would you believe you're looking at chicken stew? All I have to do is push the pack inside this little sliding drawer here like so, and that injects the bag with three ounces of hot water, and I pull it out and mush it up a little. And there you go; beautiful chicken stew.' He stuck the stew onto a tray floating beside him; now the tray held four bags, a can of nuts, and a sachet of tropical punch, all fixed with Velcro. Stone floated the tray to Gershon. 'Come and get it.'

'Yum.' Gershon snipped the top off his chicken stew bag and began to spoon it into his mouth. He waved at the camera and grinned; he was eating his meal upside down relative to Stone.

Stone said smoothly, 'We've been flying in space now for more than twenty years, and I guess we've figured out how to provide decent food. We're basically having much the same kind of food that the workshop crews are eating right now, in lunar and Earth orbits. We have a menu that repeats, every six days or so. Most of our food is rehydratable. Like my noodles and chicken here.' He pointed at his tray. 'That's because rehydratable gives the best food value per pound of weight. But we do have some foods which are thermostabilized – cooked before launch, and then stored in a cold box. I've got here stewed tomatoes, and ground beef with pickle sauce, for instance. And some foods we can carry in their natural form, like my almonds here. And then I have these freeze-dried pears, and this strawberry drink ... We don't have a refrigerator or a food freezer, as the Skylabs have, but we do have something new: an oven. It's fan-forced, of course, not convection. Because hot air doesn't rise anywhere, in zero G. And we've even got hot and cold running water, here in this little galley of ours.'

Gershon said sotto voce, 'Tell him about the farts, Phil.'

Oh, sure. Hot mike, asshole.

Actually the farts were a real problem. There was a device in the spigots that was supposed to scrape excess hydrogen out of their water supply, which was a by-product of the Mission Module's power cells. But the gizmo didn't work too well, and a lot of gas got into the crew's stomachs. And out again almost as quickly.

'Ares, Houston.' Ares was already so far from Earth that it took a full six seconds for their signal to reach Houston, and for

Crippen's reply to come back. 'Phil, we're told we have a pretty good audience here.'

'We're gratified to hear that.'

'Phil, would you say you actually enjoy the in-flight catering?'

Stone hesitated. 'It's hard to say. Even stuff in its natural form tends to taste different, somehow, up here; I guess there's some subtle physiological change – a response to microgravity – we don't understand yet. Then there's the packaging. I know this form of food has a lot of advantages. There's little chance of food particles getting into the equipment. But the Russians have been sending their cosmonauts up with cakes and bread since 1965 . . .'

Six seconds.

'Copy all that, Phil,' Crippen said, 'but it wasn't quite the question I asked.'

Stone said firmly, 'It's the answer you're going to get, Bob.'

After the delay, York heard laughter in the background, in the MOCR.

'Ares, Houston, thank you. Ah, Ralph, Phil, Natalie, could we get you all in shot for a moment, please?'

Stone looked puzzled. 'Say again, Houston.'

'If we can have you all in the camera's field of view for a couple of minutes.'

Stone drifted close to York, who stayed by the table; and Gershon floated down behind them, facing the camera.

'Ares, Houston,' Crippen said. 'Just about now, ah, at five plus one plus forty-two –' one hour into the mission's fifth day '– you are passing a significant boundary. Although you may not feel it. It's something you might like to think about as you eat your meal today.'

'We look forward to hearing about it, Bob.'

'. . . Maybe one of you could tell us what you can see out of your picture window right now.'

York turned. The 'picture window' was a two-feet-wide viewport set in the wall of the wardroom, big enough to have to curve to follow the concavity of the pressure hull; it was triple-paned, with the thick, tough feel about it of an airplane window.

'I see Earth and Moon,' she reported. 'They're both pretty much full, although I can see a thin slice of shadow down the right-hand limb of each of them.' Earth was now so distant its sphericity wasn't obvious; it was reduced to a flat blue bowl of light, with its pale, shrunken companion close by its limb. 'The Earthlight is still bright,' she said. 'Strong enough to read a book by, I'd say. But . . .'

158

'Go ahead, Natalie.'

'Something is different.' She peered into the window to see better. 'The sky is just like a clear night on Earth. And – my God – it's *full* of stars. Earlier in the flight the glare of Earth was so bright it blacked out everything else. Now, I can see the stars. I can recognize the constellations again, for the first time on the trip.'

'Ares, I guess you've really gone up into night.'

'Yes, we have. A huge, empty, cold night at that.'

'Ares, Houston. Thank you, Natalie. Ares, here's the significance. You're now almost exactly five hundred and sixty-two thousand statute miles from the Earth. That's twice as far as any human has traveled before. And you're now passing out of the Earth's sphere of influence.'

Sphere of influence – an imaginary bubble in space centered on Earth, an almost perfect sphere where the gravitational potential of Earth and sun were in balance. Inside the sphere of influence, Ares had essentially been in an orbit dominated by Earth; beyond this point, however, the craft had escaped from Earth, and was in solar orbit, a new planet.

Stone said, 'Thank you, Bob. We understand, and we're impressed, almost humbled, with the thought . . .' Stone seemed dissatisfied with his own trite words. He was looking at York thoughtfully. 'Natalie, you want to add anything to that?'

She stared back, frozen, her mind suddenly empty. *Well, you've griped often enough about the inarticulate grunts they send into space. Now's your chance to do better.*

For some reason she thought of Ben Priest. What would he advise her?

Just say what you feel, Natalie. Don't hide behind technicalities. And don't let it embarrass you.

'Houston, Ares. I guess what strikes me now is that we humans have spawned at the bottom of a hole. A deep gravitational hole dug into space-time by Earth's mass. And of all the humans who have ever lived, all the billions of them, only the three of us – Phil, Ralph and myself – have ever climbed to the lip of that hole . . .'

She was aware of Gershon and Stone exchanging doubtful glances; Stone waved Gershon to be still.

York stared back at the receding Earth. She held up her hand, and covered the Earth-Moon system with her palm. 'I'm holding up my hand now, and the whole of human history – including even the voyages to the Moon – is hidden from my view by my palm. We'll spend another year in space before we see Mars loom close,

159

just as Earth is falling away now. A year in this collection of tin cans, with nothing but the stars and the sun beyond the windows. We know it's going to be difficult, despite all the training and the preparation. But what's important is that we've come out, over the edge of the gravity hole, and now we're going to see what lies beyond. We have indeed gone up into night, Houston.'

Stone nodded. He was still looking at her, thinking.

York shivered. Suddenly the Mission Module – drifting through space with its ticks and whirs and smells of food and stale farts – seemed like a little home to her, impossibly fragile, the only island of warmth and light in all that dark night.

Sunday, August 15, 1976
Between Earth and Moon

After a couple of days of floating around inside the Command Module in their longjohns and jump suits, Jones, Dana and Stone started to help each other back into their pressure suits. To go through the Lunar Orbit Insertion burn they were going to have to return to their couches and strap on their canvas harnesses.

They finished up a meal: soup and cheese and spreads on crackers, with a grapefruit-orange mixture to drink. Dana had a plastic bag of pea soup. He would take a spoonful of the soup, tap the handle, and the glob of soup would float off, still holding the shape of the spoon. But when he poked the liquid with a finger-tip, surface tension hauled it quickly into a perfect, oscillating sphere. Dana leaned over to suck it into his mouth, a little green marble of pea soup.

Jim Dana found life in microgravity startling, the endless unexpected details enchanting.

Most of it, anyhow.

Before suiting up, Chuck Jones decided to take a dump.

This involved stripping stark naked, and climbing into the storage bay under the three metal-frame couches. Apollo's Waste Management system consisted of a collection of plastic bags, with adhesive coatings on the brim, and finger-shaped tubes built into the side. Jones had to dig into the bag with his finger – nothing would *fall*, after all – and hook his turds down into the bag. And afterwards he had to break open a capsule of germicide, drop it into the bag, and knead it all together.

In a moment the sounds and smells of it were filling the cabin.

Dana just sat and endured it. The lousy design of the system was hardly Jones's fault.

The irony was, the Apollo system had been heavily upgraded in the last few years. Rockwell had stretched the original lunar flight design, making it more robust and reliable, and increasing its capacity; Apollo was mostly used as an orbital ferry craft for taking crews to and from the Skylabs, but even flying solo it was capable of supporting as many as four men for eight days in orbit. Rockwell were even trying to make the Command Module reusable, by providing salt water protection and modularizing its components – so a Command Module could be cannibalized after splashdown, even if the whole thing couldn't be flown again.

But some things they hadn't got around to fixing, like the plumbing arrangements.

Dana was finding his first flight in space, with its long string of hassles and discomforts, a surprisingly depressing experience. The contrast between the Zen-like emptiness of cislunar space, and these scrambled human attempts to survive in it, struck him powerfully. And the immaturity of the technology compared to his aviation background was striking.

But we really are at the edge of our capabilities out here. Dad's right. We're not really up to this. Not yet. We just aren't smart enough. Clever monkeys, improvising, making it up as we go along, riding our luck, hauling along our plumbing . . .

Still, it was one hell of an adventure to tell his son Jake about.

Dana took his turn on trash detail. He collected up the food bags, spiked them with pills to dissolve the residue, and rolled them up tightly and stuffed them into a plastic garbage bag. He stashed the garbage in a storage compartment. The compartments had been almost full within a few hours of leaving Earth orbit, and the garbage was dumped regularly into space; *Enterprise* was heading for the Moon surrounded by a little orbiting cloud of food bags and other trash.

The crew settled down to their pre-LOI checklists. It was all done in an uncharacteristic silence, Dana observed. It wasn't hard to figure out why. Arguably Lunar Orbit Insertion was the key moment of the mission; on it depended the success of their flight – and, of lesser importance to the career astronaut, the success of Moonlab itself.

And they'd have to perform the burn during the loss-of-signal period, while the craft was round the back of the Moon and shielded from the Earth. So there would be no way the men in Mission Control could help them out.

Since his decision to initiate it, Bert Seger had built up this mission, orchestrating the media coverage carefully. Apollo/Moonlab was going to be a feel-good extravaganza, a return to the Moon, a demonstration of competence: a distraction from the collapse of Saigon, the rocketing cost of fuel, the stagnant economy, inflation ... He'd even given way to a write-in campaign by *Star Trek* fans who wanted *Enterprise* as the call-sign for the ship, the first Apollo to the Moon in four years. It didn't do any good for the Astronaut Office to protest that they didn't *need* a call-sign for this mission.

It was all fine PR. But the high profile meant that a failure – and a failure due to some dumb programming fault – would be *very* embarrassing.

Apollo shuddered slightly, and solenoids rattled. That was the firing of the reaction control clusters, halting the spacecraft's slow roll. The stack had been rotating since leaving Earth orbit, to even out the sun's heat; the crew called it 'barbecue mode.'

Stone, in the center of the three frame couches, said suddenly, 'Hey. I got the Moon. Right below us.'

Dana looked up from his checklist.

It looked as if streams of oil were descending across the glass of the window to Dana's right. Dana felt a stab of fear; he couldn't figure what malfunction could have caused this. Then his eyes refocused, and he realized he was looking at mountains. They slid slowly past the window, lit by the slanting rays of the sun, trailing long black shadows.

The mountains of the Moon. 'Oh, Jesus. Look out there.'

'It's only the fucking Moon,' Jones said. 'You're going to be staring at it for a long time. Come on, get back to your lists. Thousand miles out. Six and a half thousand feet per second ... We've fifteen minutes until LOS, twenty-three minutes from the LOI burn ...'

The sun was hidden behind the orb of the Moon, Dana saw, and the Moon was back-lit by the corona, the sun's outer atmosphere. So there was light all around the Moon, as if the far side was on fire. But Dana could see the shadowed side quite clearly; it swam past the window, illuminated by Earthlight, ghost-pale.

The Moon looked like a ball of glass, its surface cracked and complex, as if starred by buckshot. Tinged pale white, the Moon's

162

center loomed out at Dana, given substance by the Earthlight's shading: the Moon was surprisingly three-dimensional, no longer the flat yellow disk he had known from Earth.

He picked out a large, deep crater; perhaps it was Tycho. There was an elusive quality to the Moon's features, an uncertainty about the shading. Sometimes the craters looked like domes, the mountains like pits. The dead surface of the Moon was like a mask, reversing itself in his vision.

In Earth orbit, Dana had been able to see the curve of the horizon, but the Earth was so huge that most of it was out of his view. But the Moon was a small world. The curvature was so tight he could extrapolate the rest of the sphere; he could *see* that he really was flying around a ball of rock, suspended in space, with darkness stretching to infinity in all directions.

It looks so alien. This isn't our world. And yet three Stars-and-Stripes, three abandoned LM descent stages, already stood on those silent hills.

'Thirty seconds to LOS,' Jones said.

'*Enterprise*, Houston.' Ralph Gershon was the rookie astronaut serving as capcom today. 'Coming up on LOS. Going around the corner, all your systems are looking good. We'll see you on the other side.'

'Roger, Ralph, thank you. Everything looks okay up here.' The hiss of static from the comms units faded suddenly, to be replaced by a low-volume hiss.

'Going around the corner,' Phil Stone said quietly. 'Loss of signal.'

Dana stared at the little loudspeaker grille closest to his position. He was startled by his own reaction: he felt abandoned, bewildered. Apollo was out of the line of sight of Earth, for the first time since launch; for the first time, Mission Control couldn't get in touch with the crew, and it was as if a rope had been cut.

Dana quietly suspected that a kind of dependency culture had grown up among the astronauts over the years. Whether it was healthy or not, the knowledge that Mission Control was always there, always staffed up with the best and the brightest, took a lot of the responsibility away from the pilots. It was as if Houston was flying your ship for you. By contrast, these few moments when you and your bird would have to function entirely independently of the ground – well, these times brought fear. Not of the inherent danger, but of failure. *Don't let me be the one who screws up.*

Now the stack was barreling toward the Moon. They were falling steeply into the satellite's gravity well, and the Moon was growing

– getting visibly larger by the minute, its features sliding past the windows.

'Look at that old Moon,' Jones said. 'Rougher than the surface of my butt. Well, I guess I'm never going to get to land down there, but I'm glad I came along after all. That smartass kid Gershon should be here now. Make him feel right at home. It's just like Cambodia.' He cackled.

Dana tried to grin along with his commander, but he failed. To his left, Phil Stone looked uncomfortable too.

This jock banter crap just wasn't appropriate any more, Dana thought. Maybe it never had been.

The craft fell into lunar shadow, and entered total darkness: no sunlight, no Earthlight touched the hidden landscape rushing below.

The radio remained silent.

We're alone, the three of us. All of humanity, imprisoned on the Earth, is hidden by the bulk of the Moon.

Dana felt a sudden surge of conviction. *However it was arrived at, we made the right decision, to continue the space program. How could we have turned our backs on adventures like this? We have to keep on going out. Experiences like this will change us. We'll become something more: something beyond the human.*

The broken, complex lands scrolled beneath his window.

'Okay, you assholes, enough rubber-necking,' Jones said. 'Let's get in shape for this fucking burn.'

Enterprise sailed around the limb of the Moon.

Wednesday, May 25, 1977
NASA Headquarters, Washington

Mike Conlig hated Washington.

As soon as he got off the plane the steamy, oppressive heat closed in around him, and he felt a kind of psychic pressure, from all the people crowded into this shabby corner of the Earth.

Now, along with Hans Udet and Bert Seger, he sat in Tim Josephson's immense, plush office. Conlig felt awkward, out of place, lost in the huge room, in this great, soft armchair. And he wasn't so keen on wearing a suit either; the knot of his tie seemed to be compressing his throat.

Tim Josephson came bustling into the room, a file under his arm. He slid behind his modest, polished desk. 'I'll come straight to the point,' Josephson said. 'I've read your status reports. You know the question you have to answer here today. NERVA is a hell of a long way behind schedule. The Critical Design Review is scheduled in three months. And from what I hear you're not going to be ready.'

Seger shrugged. 'You won't hear any argument about that, Tim.'

Josephson steepled his fingers. 'All right. We're under a lot of pressure on this; we're having to defend your work against attack in Congress, and elsewhere. People are saying that we've put our shirts on the wrong horse here. Nuke rockets are a new development; maybe we should be following an incremental process of change, by enhancing our chemical technology. And on top of that you have the nuclear safety lobby, who say we shouldn't be throwing up tons of radioactive fuel on top of Saturn rockets.' He looked at them, one by one. 'I suppose you have read about the Seabrook protest, up in New Hampshire: two thousand people demonstrating, trying to stop the construction of the fission plant there. By using nuclear technology we're swimming against the tide, gentlemen.

'But it's clear to me that we can't let the problems on this one development stop the whole goddamn program. You know that since 1972 Rockwell have been carrying through a parallel chemical-technology development, based on an S-II enhancement. Fred Michaels is thinking of going to Congress to ask for funding to be switched away from NERVA to that development stream . . .'

Hans Udet shook his head; his blond-gray hair shone in the fluorescents. 'No. You must understand –'

Josephson leaned forward. 'No. Today, *you* must listen, and understand, Hans. This isn't a game we're playing, here. It takes a hell of a lot of effort to build and sustain a political coalition behind a program like ours. Jim Webb did it for NASA in the 1960s; we're lucky to have Fred Michaels in the same role now. But he can't work miracles . . .'

This was the first time Conlig had met Josephson in the flesh. The Assistant Administrator gave off the aura of sleek, bureaucratic competence which came over on TV. *Every inch the organization man.* In his early forties, and with that small face perched on a long neck, that prematurely high forehead, the thick spectacles, and those rapid, decisive movements, Josephson was like some tall, flightless bird.

But his dry words connected with Conlig; suddenly it was an intense, electric moment for him. *My God. He's serious. We're in real trouble here; it's genuinely possible that these bastards could*

165

close us down. And you can bet your life if that happens, none of us working on NERVA would be allowed within a thousand miles of whatever new program they turn to. Conlig's whole career – everything, all his self-belief – funneled through this one moment in time, this decision point. *If I say the wrong thing now, my professional life will be over. Because there will never be another NERVA project; not for me.*

'Now.' Josephson had finished his preamble. He swiveled his head and stared at each of them. 'Sum up. I want you to tell me where you are, and what your prospects for success are. I want the truth as you see it; this isn't the moment for false pride. The whole program depends on us making the right decision.' He glared at Udet. 'How about you first, Hans?'

The old German sat up straight in his chair. 'The truth, Tim? The truth, as you can tell from the reports, is that NERVA, at this stage of its development, is in trouble. We haven't been able to sustain a single worthwhile burn yet . . .' In his clipped, accented, slightly imprecise English, with its bizarre overlay of Alabaman drawl, Udet began to go through NERVA's myriad problems – pump stresses, nozzle hot spots – and the steps the teams were taking to resolve them.

'So you see,' Udet finished up, 'the NERVA is indeed not worth a snap, today. *But* –' And now he leaned forward, fixing Josephson with a glare. 'But neither was the F-1, the Saturn's great first-stage engine, at a similar stage in its development, back in '62 or '63. If anything, the prospects were worse. *There* we had combustion instability problems; *there* the damn things kept exploding on us. But we were allowed to stay on the case, Tim. We got on with our work. And we solved the problems, so much so that the Saturn V has never suffered a single significant engine failure.

'It is the same now. We do not need an alternative program. With NERVA we face problems: yes, of course we do. But they are only engineering issues. We have never let such issues intimidate us before, and we will not now.' As he spoke, Conlig thought, a kind of subliminal message was radiating out of him at Josephson. *When you look at me you are looking at von Braun himself. My engines are heroes. We got you to the Moon; we can get you to Mars. Trust my judgment, and allow me to proceed with my work . . .*

Conlig longed to be in Santa Susana – or better still, back in Nevada, at Jackass Flats, in the still emptiness of the desert. He longed to get away from all this politicking, and back to the engineering.

166

He thought of Natalie.

His relationship with Natalie was a kind of nagging ache, on the fringe of his awareness. He knew she wasn't happy. Damn it, neither was he. But right now there just wasn't room in his head to think about it. Maybe in a couple of years, when NERVA had dug itself out of this hole, he –

Josephson was looking at him. His cue to perform.

Slowly, haltingly, with none of Udet's Prussian-aristocrat fluency, Conlig began to speak.

He described the steps being taken to reduce the latest cavitation and hydrogen-graphite corrosion problems, and the difficulties they were having with the way the intense radiation was making capacitance gauges produce erroneous hydrogen tank measurements. And so forth. But, he told Josephson, the team was hopeful nevertheless of getting to the first extended burn and full system test soon, and the rigs were demonstrating that the design would hold up under the vibration and shock to be expected during a flight . . .

As he spoke, he couldn't tell how well he was doing.

Josephson listened without comment. Then he turned to Bert Seger.

The program director had been sitting in with the NERVA people over the last week, poking around Santa Susana and the other sites, evidently figuring out for himself what the prospects were. Now he sat facing Josephson, whiplash-thin, with his trademark carnation glowing in his buttonhole, just above the Crucifix pin there.

Briskly, Seger summarized his own view of the various problems. 'Tim, I don't know what the hell shape our schedule for NERVA is going to be in when we get through the current replan. What's hamstringing us are the safety precautions; we have to drown and dismantle each damn rig after every bitty problem. I'm not saying we should skip the safety stuff; of course not. But we're going to have to plan realistically for every milestone in the program from now on. More realistically than we have up to now. But –' A pause.

'Yes, Bert?'

'You've got some good people out there, Tim. Both ours and the contractor's; some of our best. And they're doing their damnedest to make this thing fly. I recommend we stay with this horse, Tim; don't think about backing another.'

Josephson listened in glassy silence. 'All right. Thank you, Bert, gentlemen. You've said pretty much what I expected you to say. I think I have to back your judgment, your faith in that balky machine of yours, this NERVA. I'll keep on going in to bat for you. But I

167

hope you've heard what I've told you today. Bert, I want you to pull together a coherent status summary I can pass up the line. And I want to see a new schedule out of your people, Hans: a credible schedule. And I want to see you adhering to it, from now on.'

These tough words, delivered in a flat monotone, seemed at odds with Josephson's dry, file-clerk appearance. Conlig felt restless, eager to get out of here.

As they were walking out of the door, Josephson called Bert Seger back. Conlig could hear Josephson distinctly. 'I want you to ride herd on these assholes, Bert. Don't take any more bullshit. Ride herd, and make them fix this nuclear skyrocket of theirs . . .'

We don't need to be told, Conlig thought, as he followed the others through the carpeted corridors.

When he got out of the building, despite the humid heat outside, Conlig felt a surge of relief; prickles of sweat broke out over his forehead. It was like being let out of school. *Fucking bureaucrats.*

Now, at any rate, he could get back to work: start expending energy once more, and relieve the huge anxiety that was knotted up inside him.

January 1977–January 1978

Her application to NASA took a full year to resolve itself. And yet, once started, the process had a kind of inevitability about it, a grinding logic.

A couple of weeks after her first application, she got a telegram from the National Academy of Sciences. They wanted more information: a fuller resume, reprints of published papers, a five hundred word essay on experiments she would like to conduct on the surface of Mars.

She complied. She wrote about her ideas on outflow channels, and on searching for water under the Martian regolith, and what that would mean for the future colonization of the planet.

She shaved her essay to exactly five hundred words; she'd had previous dealings with government agencies, and she knew that breaking the smallest rule might cost her her chance.

She wasn't taking this application too seriously, in the privacy of her own mind. But she wanted to get as far as she could: maybe put herself in a position where she could give herself a choice of pursuing this crazy option – a career in the space program – or not.

168

York read in *Science* that less than a thousand scientists sent their names in response to the National Academy of Sciences flyer: far fewer – according to the press – than NASA had been hoping for.

York could understand that. A scientist's career was brief, in terms of productive years: the peak time was late twenties to early thirties. Right where York was now. Losing that time could be very damaging, in terms of a long-term career.

And scientist recruits had been given a rough enough ride by NASA in the past. Not *one* of the first batch of scientist-astronauts, who'd signed up in 1965, had made it to the Moon with Apollo.

You'd have to be crazy to risk your career, your reputation, on the slim chance of a flight into space someday, with an organization of engineers and pilot jocks like NASA.

Of course you would.

A few weeks after submitting her essay she got a letter from the Academy.

She wasn't rejected yet.

She had passed their preliminary screening, as regards age, height and health, and she was scientifically qualified for the program, with proven expertise in a relevant field. She was sent more forms to complete: an Application for Federal Employment, an Aeromedical Survey form designed for Air Force pilots, several others.

And she was invited to go for medical examinations at Brooks Air Force Base in Texas.

To the lair of the hero test pilots! Jesus. I'm getting close.

Texas, as she descended toward it, struck her as a pancake-flat plain. It was a hot June day; stepping out of the plane to walk the few yards to the terminal building was like walking through a furnace.

She met the other candidates at the Best Western where they'd been lodged. They intimidated the hell out of her. There was a chemistry department chair from Caltech; a Princeton MD who was also a PhD candidate in physiology; a physics professor from Cornell; a PhD physiologist who was also a jet pilot; an MD who was also a jet pilot. And so on. It was obvious that the 'scientists' whom NASA was considering largely had 'operational' bents too; they were mostly pilot-scientist hybrids.

York was the only woman.

Jesus. White male pilots with professorships. What chance do I have?

The candidates congregated at lunch, and over dinner. The men organized trips to the Alamo, in downtown San Antonio. York kept away from these macho gatherings, and tried not to let herself get depressed.

On the first morning of the tests, she had to start at six o'clock Texas time, which was four a.m. Berkeley time. So that was the first of her handicaps. She couldn't even get a coffee; she was supposed to fast until lunch for the purposes of the tests.

The tests were going to last all week.

The first test was for glucose tolerance. Blood was drained from her arms while she forced down incredibly sweet glucose liquid.

Then she was subjected to eye tests: there was an Ishihara color-blindness test, and a photograph of her retina taken by a flash blazing into her eye. She had to drink a liter of lukewarm water, after which a weight was placed *on* her eyeball, to measure the fluid excreted.

There were internal medicine tests. She had to lie for an hour inside a Faraday cage, a metal box that excluded electric fields, while a cardiogram was taken. York felt like a chimpanzee in a zoo. Then she was strapped into a device fitted with a parachute harness, designed to hang her while the blood pooled to her feet. She had to hyperventilate until black-out symptoms began to show, little dots darting around her vision.

Then – brutally quickly – she was given a Master heart test, where she climbed and descended stairs while holding electrodes to her chest. At the end of the test she had to fit her mouth around a mouthpiece so her exhaled carbon dioxide could be collected for volume measurements.

There were tests of her vestibular system, the balance apparatus of her middle ear. Hot and cold water was poured into her ears to confuse her vestibular canals, making her dizzy. Doctors peered into her eyes, watching how long it took her eyelids to stop flickering.

Later, she was told to walk in a straight line through a darkened room. The idea was to test for vestibular imbalances. When the lights came up she found she'd drifted maybe a yard to the left of the room's center line.

The tilt chair was another vestibular test. It looked a little like an electric chair, mounted on a rotating platform in the middle of a pitch-dark room. She was strapped into the chair, and electrodes were fixed to track her eye motion. The chair was spun around, once every three seconds, and tipped back and forth. Every so often they would reverse the direction of tilt and rotation. It was like a

170

carousel ride, run by lunatics; every tilt made York feel as if she wanted to upchuck, but she was determined she wasn't going to give these assholes that satisfaction.

She had to give urine samples at half-hour intervals, for three hours; she had to drink quarts of water to generate the raw material. She had to give blood six times. In the end the veins in both her arms collapsed from repeated pricking.

In the midst of the physicals, she went through psychological tests: playing with blocks, drawing self-portraits, completing a five-hundred-question multiple choice personality test. There were IQ tests, Rorschach ink-blot tests, memory tests, vocabulary tests, tests of math and reading.

She went through a written paper on her 'personal values,' which sought to examine the motives she had for going into space. She labored over the fifty questions, covering possible motives like money and fame, the good of mankind, and the thrill of it all, as well as the possibility of scientific discovery.

On her first pass through this, York tried to answer honestly. *Of course, it's the scientific discovery. They're selecting mission specialists here! What the hell else do they expect?* But then she wondered if she ought to try to be smarter. It would be a bad thing to seem unbalanced, obsessed about the science over all else. Any astronaut, even a specialist, was going to have to help out with the chores. And besides, the Mars crew was going to have to be presentable to the press, projecting the right all-American, NASA-tradition, John Glenn-wholesome image.

She went through her scores again, trying to anticipate what the selectors might be looking for.

Then she figured that all the other candidates would have worked this out as well and would similarly be doctoring their answers.

She went through a third time, trying to take that into account . . .

An earnest young man took her through a scatter chart rendered by a computer. He sounded puzzled by the results: *here* she showed herself to be dedicated to a single goal, *there* flexible and capable of balancing multiple objectives; over *here* the results said she was strongly self-motivated, but *there* she was coming up as happiest working with a team . . . and so forth. It was a complex, meaningless dance.

She gritted her teeth and tried not to say anything to make it worse. She wondered how much all this was costing.

* * *

171

One morning she was given barium sulphate for breakfast, to provide contrast in x-rays of her gall bladder. Another time she was provided with a tritium solution, so her percentage of body fat could be measured. She took pills which gave her diarrhoea, and which caused her piss to come out green. In the EEG test, eleven needles were poked half an inch into her scalp.

Even her teeth were checked over. A cheerful, inane dentist tutted over her mouth's state of disrepair, and he seemed to take a lot of comfort in telling her in great detail how much preventative dental work she'd have to endure. *You don't want toothache or an abscess half way across the Solar System, ho ho!*

York had had hardly any experience of hospital, in the course of a healthy life. The doctors here were Air Force, specialists in aerospace medicine. In her ignorance, she had expected the tests to be tough. In fact what they hit her with here was so far beyond her experience that it scared the hell out of her. The tests struck her as ordeals: barbaric, brutal, often ridiculous, barely scientific.

The final test, on the Friday, was a sigmoidoscopy. She had to give herself an enema. Then she lay on a bench while a woman doctor shoved a rod up her rear, straightening out the intestines, probing further and further.

York, by now, was exhausted, angry, humiliated, frightened. It took a powerful effort of will to submit herself to this last invasion.

Before San Antonio, she'd treated the whole thing casually. An indulgence for Ben, maybe. An adventure. An amusing battle of wits between herself and NASA, in which she would see how far she could get before they found her out.

Now, all that had changed. She didn't want this investment in pain and humiliation to be wasted.

Withdrawing her application became unthinkable.

Her test results, when they came, showed her medical history to be 'unremarkable.' She was 'in no apparent medical or psychological distress.'

Comforting, she thought. Well worth a week in medical hell.

Then she was called for interview to Houston itself.

The plane landed at Houston Intercontinental. York made her way into the terminal, and as she'd been instructed found the Continental Airline Presidents' Club. She faced a plain glass door with a one-way mirror. When she knocked, the door was opened by a NASA protocol officer, a short, dapper man in a blazer. She identified herself, and he hurried her inside – *out of sight of the press?* – and offered her a diet soda.

When all the candidates had arrived – it was the San Antonio group – they were to be taken in a limousine to the Nassau Bay Hilton.

When she stepped out of the air-conditioned airport building the August heat hit her in the face, moist and enclosing, as if the ground was steaming. Although the afternoon was well advanced, the sun seemed to be directly overhead.

The limousine worked its way south, toward downtown, on the I-59, and then east and south around the 610, the Loop. The Nassau Bay Hilton was close to JSC, more than twenty miles from the city center, out on the I-45.

Houston was hot and flat, sprawling, evidently very new. The roads were well-maintained and modern. Huge, colorful billboards battered at her eyes, lining the Interstate. Many of the signs and ads were in Spanish; after all, Texas had nearly been part of Mexico.

There were few signals of the presence of the space program here: inflatable rockets in the used car lots, a 'Tranquillity Plaza' shopping mall, the basketball team called the Rockets.

Beyond the heat haze of the freeway, the downtown skyscrapers thrust out of the plain like a collection of launch gantries, isolated, crowded. There were water towers, big oval tanks, like the Martian fighting machines from *The War of the Worlds*. They passed roadside neon thermometers, which read high nineties or low hundreds, even this late in the day.

Houston was going to be very different from the older cities she'd grown used to. *Do I really want to live here?*

All the other candidates were talking about the death of Elvis, a few days earlier. She had nothing to say on that – in fact the endless, obsessive coverage bored her – and she was glad when they got to the hotel.

The Nassau Bay Hilton was a tower block by the shore of Clear Lake, a few minutes from JSC. The receptionist's voice contained a strong Texan twang, and there was a gift store in the lobby, with ten-gallon hats and cowboy boots. Her room, a single, was plush. It had a view of a marina, and a bright blue swimming pool, which she wouldn't have time to use.

In the morning she was up at five thirty. *Three thirty, Berkeley time.* The sun was already high.

*　　*　　*

173

Her interview was directly after breakfast. And so there she was, with the time not yet seven thirty, being driven in a limousine west along NASA Road One.

The cow pasture to her right, along the north side of the Interstate, had been fenced off. Blocky black and white buildings were scattered across the plain, each numbered with big black round figures, like toys from some giant nursery.

The driver – a beefy, sweating man called Dave – took a right into a broad entrance. On the right was a granite sign saying 'Lyndon B. Johnson Space Center.' And on the left a Saturn V lay on its side, its stages separated and mounted on wheeled trailers.

Dave grinned when he caught her gawping at the Saturn. 'That's just a test article,' he said. 'The first one built. The story is that when it looked as if we might be canning Apollo altogether, there was talk of taking one of the flight articles and putting it on display here, or maybe at the Cape. A man-rated moon rocket as a lawn ornament.' He chuckled and shook his head. 'Can you believe it?'

It seemed to take forever for the limousine to drive past the grounded Saturn. The booster was aging. York could see corrosion around its big rivets, cobwebs on the big A-frames which supported it, and some of the fabric parts around the engine bells were stained with lichen. The Stars and Stripes painted on the flank of the fat second stage was washed out, the red of the stripes running down toward the ground.

Beyond the Saturn there was a small rocket garden. York recognized a Redstone, the slim black and white pencil which had thrown the first Mercury capsules on their sub-orbital hops. The Redstone was upright, but held to the ground by wires, like Gulliver. And she saw a Space Shuttle, a wind-tunnel test article, a scale model of a ship which had never been built; it was an airplane shape, upright against the gleaming white of a big external fuel tank.

The Shuttle's body looked chunky, clumsy. But York was entranced by the curve of the wings, set against the crude cylinders of the throwaway rockets around it; the spaceplane looked elegant, a stranded relic of a lost future.

She was checked into security, in Building 110, and given a photocopied map and directed toward Building 4. She set off on foot.

The buildings were black and white blocks. Many of them were clustered around a kind of courtyard, where thick-bladed grass shone in the sunlight, bright green. There were cherry trees, and a duck pond with an attractive stone margin. But no ducks: Ben Priest had told her how they left too much mess, and had been chased away. *We're not here for ducks.* There was a flat tropical heat, the air still, suffused by the chirp of crickets. It was hard to move around; she could feel the heat drain energy out of her.

She tried to imagine working here.

Bicycles leaned up against every building, and there were big sand-filled ashtrays by the doorways, with stubs sticking out of them.

There was an air of calm here. The blocky buildings didn't have the feel of most Government establishments. It was more like a university, she thought. In fact, Dave, her driver, had called this the 'campus.'

JSC had its own Martian water towers. There was an 'antenna farm,' a fenced-off field of big white dishes, turned up like flowers. And, here and there, huge tanks of liquid nitrogen gleamed.

Inside Building 4, the air-conditioning was ferocious; it must have been thirty degrees cooler than outside. The building was actually quite gloomy, even cramped; it had small ceiling and floor tiles, and the walls were painted a 1960s corporate yellow-brown. She felt her spirits dip a little. It was like an aging welfare office.

She took the elevator. The interview was in the 'astronaut library.'

When she knocked, the door opened, and a man greeted her: tall, wire-slim, with gray-blond hair and blue eyes, he wore jeans and a Ban-Lon shirt. He smiled at her, easily, and shook her hand.

She recognized him. He was Joe Muldoon. A moonwalker was shaking her hand.

It hit her suddenly, a change of perspective, in a surge. This really was the Space Center. There were *astronauts* here, for Christ's sake. *Veterans.*

She tried to look at Muldoon, but found it impossible to face him directly; her vision seemed to moisten up, and it was as if he was glistening, shining.

But now I'm applying to become one of these people. My God. Will people look at me the same way? How the hell will I cope with that?

Joe Muldoon guided her to her seat, a chair stuck in the middle of the room.

There were hardly any books here, in this 'library.' On the wall behind her chair was a row of photographs: portraits of dead astronauts, Russian and American. *Jesus. Put me at my ease, why don't you.* There was a big TV running in the corner, the sound turned down low. It ran a continuous feed from the crew up in orbit in Skylab A, right now; the split screen showed a shot of the Earth, taken from Skylab, and Mission Control ground track displays. Occasionally she heard the controlled murmur of the air-to-ground loop.

The panel was seven people: seven white males, behind a long oaken desk. Many of the faces were familiar to her, from TV and newspaper coverage of the space program: astronauts, senior NASA science managers, administrators.

And there at the center of the table – she recognized with a sinking heart – was Chuck Jones. He nodded at her, dark and squat, his graying black hair a fine bristle.

Christ. Chuck Jones. She hadn't seen him since Jorge Romero's ghastly field trip in the San Gabriel Mountains, all those years ago. She wondered if Jones remembered her.

Jones rapped on the table and called the group to order. 'Thanks for coming in, Natalie. We've all seen your application and it's very impressive.'

'Thank you.'

'So we can skip all of the stuff you've covered before. Now we want you to tell us about your scientific studies, and how they are going to help us get to Mars. In your own time.'

Suddenly, her mouth was dry as the sands of Jackass Flats. *What a question.* It was so loaded.

Slowly, she began her answer.

She summarized the main thrust of her work, the geological surveys based on Mariner data, and how she'd helped formulate a hypothesis that maybe Mars had once had surface water, in liquid form, and maybe that water was still there, under the oxidized soil. And how, if the first crew could find incontrovertible evidence of that water, it would all but assure the continuation of the exploration of Mars. *Find water, and there will be lots more flights, guys. Seats for you all. But you need me to find the water.*

Chuck Jones was staring at her. She was sure he remembered her from that field trip.

She tried to seem relaxed, to smile, to meet their eyes. All she got back was cold stares. But as she spoke about her work, she grew in confidence; some of her awe rubbed away. These men were just that: men. Even Joe Muldoon. And, now she looked at them that way, she became aware that three of them, at least, were discreetly checking her out, glancing at her chest, and following the line of her legs.

She was asked follow-up questions. Then Jones asked what criteria she would use to select a Mars landing site. Another loaded question, but she was getting more confident now. She smiled at the panel, from one end of the long table to the other.

'My goal, obviously, will be a successful science program on the first mission,' she said. 'And the scientific worth of a site will be a key criterion. But it's also obvious that the first landing is going to be extremely difficult. So we must primarily choose a site which will enable the crew to land in safety.' She rattled through a brief checklist: the site ought to be on a smooth, unbroken plain, with no highlands nearby to interfere with the final landing approach, and the winds should be low, and the season should be chosen to minimize the prospect of dust storms, and so forth.

'We need to get a scientist on Mars. But a dead scientist on Mars wouldn't do anybody any good.'

That actually got a smile. As well it might; it was a deliberate echo of Deke Slayton's famous justification of his policy of keeping scientists off the early Apollo missions. It was all part of the message she was accumulating for them, in word, gesture and subtext. *I'm a scientist, and a good one, with very relevant experience. But I'm prepared to help you guys achieve your own dreams. More than that – you need me, in order to achieve those dreams.*

Now, tougher questions started to hit her.

'Doctor York, would you submit to a two-year journey to Mars?'

'I . . . Sure. I'd want a reasonable chance of success. But I would love to go, for scientific reasons. And I feel I could maybe articulate the experience better than –'

'Is that a yes or a no, Doctor?'

'Huh?'

'I asked you a question. Would you take the trip to Mars?'

'I guess so. Yes.'

'Doctor York. Suppose I tell you that the chances of surviving the trip are one in two. Do you go?'

'You can't know that. The statistics are so uncertain, the analyses –'

'Assume I know it. Do you go?'

'One in two?' *Tell the truth, Natalie.* 'Absolutely not. I might accept, say, one in twenty, if it could be demonstrated.'

'One in ten?'

177

'If it could be demonstrated.'

'How are you going to balance your two careers, as an astronaut and a scientist? Won't there be incompatibilities?'

'Sure. But the opportunities are so great.' *On Mars, you would only have to look around to make discoveries. You'd be Darwin in the Galapagos . . .* 'But I need to keep some momentum in my career. I'd be looking for some kind of split.'

'What kind of split?'

'Maybe one third to one half of my time should be spent on my own research.'

Chuck Jones leaned forward. He had black eyes that seemed to peer right into her. 'Doctor York. You aren't married.'

What the hell now? 'No, I'm not.'

'What is your view of the forthcoming National Women's Conference?'

'. . . What about it? I'm sorry, I don't follow –'

'You must know it's coming here to Houston, in November. I understand there's going to be a parade through Houston – the First Lady, Billie Jean King . . . If you're here then, working with NASA, will you be attending?'

'Perhaps. I doubt it. I'm a little passive about such things, I'm afraid.'

'Will you be supporting it – *passively* or not, Doctor York?'

Are you one of these new-fangled feminists? Jesus Christ. Do I have to answer this? She let her anger show in her voice. 'I support the Equal Credit Act of 1974, and I'd like to see it enforced. I support full employment, flexible child care, other basic provisions. Hell, yes, I'll support the Conference, if you want to know.' She glared at them, challenging. *And if that counts against me, to hell with you, you assholes.*

'Would you like to tell us about your relationship with Michael Conlig?'

She felt a cold sweat break out across her palms. *My God. It gets worse.* This was just outrageous. For a half minute, she considered walking right out of there.

Then, slowly, she gave them a brief, factual account of her on-off relationship with Mike.

'And you're together now?' Jones asked.

She thought of bluffing through. What would be a better answer? Yes or no? She could probably get Mike to back her up later . . .

Ah, the hell with it. 'I don't know, sir. It's complicated.'

Jones held her stare for a few seconds. Then he leaned back in his chair. 'Okay, Doctor. Michael Conlig works for one of our main contractors, on the NERVA 2 project. As you know. You could well find yourself working together.'

'I guess.'

'Do you feel your *complicated* relationship would cause you any problems?'

Her anger flared, and she let them see it. 'No, I don't. Frankly I resent the implication, sir. Mike is dedicated to his work. In fact he has tunnel vision about it. As I do about mine.'

Jones's eyebrows went up. 'Is that the source of the complications?'

Screw you. 'We both have goals to pursue. We would both do our jobs, to the best of our ability, whether we worked together or not.' She glared around at the panel defiantly, as if daring them to ask more follow-ups.

But that seemed to be an end of it. The next question was for more detail about water on Mars.

When they were done, she felt a cold satisfaction.

She had no idea whether she'd won through or not. There were too many factors here beyond her control, including the culture and politics of NASA; too many things over which she, with all her qualifications and experience and persuasiveness, could exert not the slightest influence. But she felt, at least, that she'd done her best.

She felt kind of soiled, though. Those damn questions about Mike. She wished she'd found some way of not answering.

But the only choice had been, answer or quit right out. She'd chosen to answer. Now, as the adrenaline rush faded, she felt as if she'd somehow let herself down. She'd made the first of many compromises she'd have to accept, she suspected, if she got into NASA, and she was to survive here.

As she got up to leave, the moonwalker winked at her, long and slow.

The response from NASA arrived – at last – just after Christmas.

She stood in the hall of her Berkeley apartment, looking at the crisp white envelope, with its blue NASA logo.

This, suddenly, was one hell of a moment in her life. A real branch, a fork in her destiny. One way lay the space program. Maybe even Mars. The other –

Somehow she couldn't visualize what might lie down the other

179

track, what might follow if this letter, this slim, high-quality white envelope, turned out to contain a rejection.

She put it down on her desk, unopened.

She went to make coffee, to open her other mail. Somehow it didn't seem right to open The Letter just like that.

Mike was out at Santa Susana, buried in the latest test runs. York hadn't even heard from him for a couple of weeks.

His absences seemed to matter less and less to her. They'd never finished the conversation they'd started, that night in the LA motel. *Christ, it was January. Nearly a year ago.* She didn't know where her life was going. York hadn't even told Mike about this application to join the corps, her visit to Houston, her ordeal at the Air Force Base. Ben Priest knew, of course, but she'd asked him not to mention it to Mike. Ben had been puzzled – in fact, she was a little puzzled at herself – but she'd insisted.

She didn't expect her application to succeed. Not really. But she wanted to see how far she could get. And in the meantime she wanted this to be something she achieved for herself, without the approval, or otherwise, of Mike or anyone else.

She'd tell Mike all about it, when she failed.

If she failed.

And if she succeeded? How would she raise the subject with him then?

Oh, hi, honey, it's me. Oh, nothing special. Uh huh. Uh huh. Yeah. I miss you too. Oh, by the way. I've had a complete career reversal, I've joined NASA, and I'm going to Mars, and my ovaries will be zapped by cosmic rays in outer space. Why didn't I tell you about it? Oh, you know how it is. We're both so busy busy busy! . . . Mike? Mike? . . .

She opened the envelope.

She'd failed. She wasn't going to be selected. In the end, she'd failed the damn NASA physical.

She groped her way to a chair, and sat down. Something melted inside her, softening and guttering and flowing away.

It's not going to happen. Maybe I'll get to look at a couple of pounds of samples, under glass, in some sterile receiving laboratory in Houston. But someone else is going to walk on Mars, to run their hands through the rusty dirt. Not me.

Now that it had happened, it was remarkable how much she *cared.* Looking back, she saw that the dream of Mars had been

180

like a beam of ruby-red laser light lancing through her life, linking everything she'd done. She'd clung to her cynicism about the space program: its culture, its impact on the society of her country. Well, hell, she *did* disapprove of it. The whole thing was crass and wrong and a waste of money, and there were much more effective ways of achieving the scientific goals without sending up ill-trained human beings, in overweight craft riddled with leaky plumbing . . .

But as long as it existed, this precarious ladder off the Earth, she'd wanted to climb it. *Yes! I admit it! I wanted this! I wanted it more than anything!*

She crumpled up the letter and threw it to the floor.

She was glad Mike wasn't here.

Ben Priest phoned a couple of times, leaving messages on the answering machine. He was sympathetic.

She didn't return his calls.

Jorge Romero called. He was boiling mad.

'Do you realize that not one geologist made it through the final cut? Can you believe that? Jesus Christ. How can you go to Mars and not take a single geologist? I'm telling you, Natalie, I'm going to fight this.'

York didn't really want to hear this.

It had been a week now, and she'd been trying to put the whole thing behind her. Mostly she preferred her own company, but this was one time she'd have kind of liked someone to talk to. Even her mother might have served.

Well, maybe not.

She suspected she was in a mild state of shock: it was as if she had gambled everything, invested all her emotional energy, in planning for a future which contained Mars.

But the dream of Mars was a kind of adolescent fantasy, she was starting to tell herself, something she was going to have to grow out of at last. She felt vaguely ashamed of playing the crass games of the selection panel. And it was surely true that she could achieve far more – even in terms of Mars studies – right here on Earth, rather than waste a decade of her life on the vain hope of getting a spaceflight.

It was time to be mature.

The last thing she needed was a siren voice like Romero, now.

But he was still talking. 'Of the geologists, you came closest to passing, Natalie. There were no women in the final cut either. My

181

God, what do those guys in Houston think they're doing? It isn't a boys' flying club. I don't want to give up. I want to appeal this decision, challenge them.'

'I don't know, Jorge . . .'

On and on. But she didn't hang up.

And, eventually, she agreed that Jorge could put her name forward again.

Romero pulled in a lot of favors. She suspected he'd even spoken to Ben Priest.

She had to fly back to San Antonio, and undergo some of the tests again. Romero brought in senior aerospace physicians, the best in the country, to look over her case. This time the tests were even harder to bear, so tense did she feel about the whole situation.

She went along with it all. She went through the motions of the tests and reviews, as if numb; she figured she must be in some kind of state of denial.

In the meantime she tried to make plans for the rest of her life, here on Earth. And she tried, unsuccessfully, to figure out some way to talk to Mike.

A month after the revised medical reviews, the phone rang. When York picked it up, she recognized Chuck Jones's voice.

'Natalie?'

Her breath caught in her throat.

It had been an ordinary day, one among thousands, soon to recede from her short-term memory and become lost in the blur of time; now, she realized, whatever Jones said, she would remember this day as long as she lived.

'Yes. York.'

Jones said bluntly: 'The new medico stuff is fine. How would you like to come fly for us?'

My God.

'Natalie? Are you there?'

'Uh, yes, I'm here.'

'Are you going to accept?'

. . . Is that it? But what about all the normal things that come with a job offer? Salary, reporting date, duties? What about the pension plan, for Christ's sake? Am I just supposed to leap in gratefully, blindfolded?

'Well, I guess there's a ninety-nine per cent chance I'll accept.'

There was a long silence. When Jones came back his voice was stern. 'We need a yes or no, Natalie. What's with these shades of gray?'

She took a breath. *What the hell. Geronimo.* 'You got a yes.'

Mission Elapsed Time [Day] Plus 066
[Hr:Min:Sec] 06:34:51

Phil Stone hadn't slept well. It was almost a relief when his intercom started piping out some kind of music, gentle elevator stuff with guitars.

He closed his eyes and buried his head in his sleeping bag; perhaps he could grab a couple more minutes.

He heard thumps, bangs and suppressed curses from the sleep locker next to his. A fist slammed into an intercom control panel. *Shut the fuck up.*

Ralph was awake, then.

He could hear Natalie sneezing. That would be the dust. It was a problem; dust didn't settle under microgravity, and, despite the circulation and filtering of the air, there was a lot of it in the atmosphere: from the food, from hair and whiskers being shaved off, from epidermal flaking.

The music cut off.

Now Fred Haise, working as capcom, came on the line. 'When you're ready, Ares, I've got a couple of flight plan updates and an update on your consumables, and the morning news, I guess.'

'Give us the news, Houston,' Gershon growled.

'Surely. What have we got . . . The Lakers have beaten the Boston Celtics four to two for the NBA title. Natalie might be glad to hear that. Or she might not. The TWA hijack continues. It looks as if the passengers have been moved out and dispersed around the Beirut slums . . . Here's something for you, Ralph; I know you're a sci-fi buff. Gene Roddenberry has said he's scrapping the treatment he'd prepared for a new *Star Trek* series. It was going to be like the first, with the huge space cruiser *Enterprise* with massive phaser banks, bigger and more powerful than anything they're likely to encounter. But he's changed his mind; he's been inspired by you guys, apparently. Now, Roddenberry says he's aiming for something called *Star Trek: Explorer*, about a small, pioneering band of humans and aliens in their fragile craft, going much further than anyone has gone before . . . How about that, guys. Science fact changing the face of science fiction. It says here.'

183

Gershon laughed. 'Who's playing me? And which one of us is the alien?'

Haise, good-hearted but no public speaker, read on. After a couple of minutes, Stone found he was able to tune out the halting voice from his awareness.

The news from home was important, though, he figured. It reminded them all that there was still a whole world back home, something more to go back to than the confines of these cans they were stuck inside.

Stone took a leak, washed, and pulled on a T-shirt and shorts. He suspended a pair of reading glasses around his neck on a string.

Actually today should be a good day. The mission plan said that Stone was due to do some optical tracking work to complete in advance of the TCM-2, tomorrow's course correction maneuver. It was a mission highlight he'd been looking forward to since the flight plan had been drawn up.

But he had a lot of crap to get through first.

[Hr:Min:Sec] 08:15:31

After the usual slow, messy breakfast, the crew's first task of the day was to swab down the walls of the Mission Module with disinfected wipes.

This had to be done every couple of weeks – more often sometimes, if the boffins on the ground told them that bacterial activity in the Mission Module was becoming unacceptably high. It was a microgravity problem. Microorganisms tended to flourish on free-floating water droplets, and they collected in odd corners of the Module. On top of that, microgravity lowered the crew's immunity response: something to do with reduced numbers of lymphocytes in the blood.

After that, the three crew drifted to the Space Ark.

The Ark was a collection of cute-animal experiments, some suggested by high school kids. There were plastic cages of varying sizes, bearing minnows, six mice, a few hundred fly pupae, and a spider called Arabella. There was even a box of worms. Stone tapped a perspex wall; he could see that the minnows were swimming about in tight circles, evidently disoriented by the lack of gravity.

During mission planning York had been earnestly skeptical about the validity of the Ark's science, and Gershon had flatly refused to have anything to do with such crap. But now, Stone noticed, both of them were drawn to the little kit.

Stone found the worms interesting. They were called palolo, from Samoa. They lived in tunnels gnawed deep into coral reefs, and they timed their emergence, to mate, by the last quarter of the October Moon. Every year. But nobody knew *how* the worms did this. At Samoa, the tides, linked to the Moon, were too small to be noticeable by the worms. And moonlight could hardly penetrate more than an inch or two into the worms' rocky burrows.

So this experiment was to find out what would happen to the worms when they were no longer in Earth's gravity field.

Meanwhile, the spider was contained in a shallow box, labeled *Araneus Diadematus*. A healthy web, at least a foot across, spanned the box, with the spider plucking at its heart.

'Okay, Arabella,' Stone murmured, 'so you're an astronaut now, eh? Let's see how smart you really are.' He moved the front of the box, and the web's longerons were ripped; the web rapidly imploded, leaving the spider drifting. He felt obscurely cruel in wrecking the web. But the point of the experiment was to record fresh web-building. There were acoustic transducers which set up a high frequency sound field in the cage; any movement of the spider would disturb the sound, and trigger lights and a still camera.

The three crew clustered around the little box, making wisecracks about the spider and poking at the cage and its equipment.

Now Stone moved over to a little experimental garden. It was more like a window-box, a tray of soil the size of a suitcase. There were peas, wheat, cucumbers, parsley, onions, dill, fennel and garlic. Some of the plants were growing in pure microgravity and some in a small botanic centrifuge, simulating lunar and Martian conditions.

Stone tended the rows of little plants. The peas had grown well for the first four or five weeks, but now they looked as if they were dying, and he fed them water and nutrient carefully. The plants wouldn't consistently go to seed, but tests had shown that the food value of the plants was high; microgravity didn't impair protein synthesis. Their roots straggled, though, unable to orient themselves without gravity.

Stone was struck by the contrast of the warm, green, fertile little plants, and the cold blackness a few inches away, beyond the wall of the Mission Module. He breathed on the little pea plants, hoping to provide a richer mix of carbon dioxide for them.

185

Stone hauled at the isokinetic exerciser. The machine was bolted
to a bracket in the middle of the Mission Module, and it had a
two-handled lever, with shoulder pads and handgrips, linked by a
sprocket chain to an air turbine. The exerciser was a new-fangled
gadget, to replace the treadmills and rowers that had been carried
on earlier flights. By bracing himself on a foot platform, Stone could
do squats, toe raises, shoulder presses, high pulls, bench presses,
tricep presses.

Every so often he would glance at the machine's timer, and get
newly depressed at how much more time he had to spend at this.
He was uncomfortable, his vest soaked, pools of sweat clinging to
his chest and between his shoulder blades. His only distraction was
a small round observation port, set in the pressure hull near him,
and he stared into its darkness.

After a couple of months – the way Stone understood it – the
various functions of the body adapted to microgravity, settling
down to a new equilibrium, different from that on Earth. The
neurovestibular system, the balance mechanism within the ear, was
the first to fall apart – hence, space sickness – but also the first to
recover, after a few days. The body's fluid balance would adjust
then, and next the cardiovascular system, the heart and blood
vessels.

But things didn't go back to Earth-normal.

Stone's brain, which didn't know about microgravity, thought
that all that extra blood was pooling in his head because there was
too much fluid in his body, and it told his kidneys to release more
urine. And that way lay dehydration. So Stone had to drink an
extra five pints of fluid a day, laced with water-salt imbalance
counteragents. That was something NASA had learned from the
Russians.

But all this extra pissing flushed the calcium and potassium out
of his bones. The calcium deficit could make his bones brittle, or
give him kidney stones, and the potassium could leave him prone
to heart problems; so he had to take diet supplements, and there
were anabolic steroids in case any of them suffered severe bone
loss.

His muscles didn't do any work they didn't have to, and – if he
left them alone – they would atrophy. So he had to go through all
this exercise on the isokinetic device. There were other measures,
too, like the penguin suit – so called because it made you waddle
around on the ground during training – a set of elastic straps that

tried to pull you into a foetal position all the time, so your muscles were constantly working, as if against gravity. And there was the *chibis*, a Russian word for lapwing bird, another idea loaned from the Soviets: reinforced leggings that reduced the air pressure over the legs, to make the heart work harder to pull blood up from the lower body.

The isokinetic exercises ought to help with reducing bone mineral loss, too; bones always kept themselves just strong enough to resist the maximum loads imposed by the muscles.

The crew had to submit, every two or three days, to electrocardio-grams, seismocardiograms, measurements of their breathing rates and volume. All of this was fed back to the surgeons on Earth. All the biomed stuff added up to a *whole day* lost out of every week.

None of it was popular. Stone realized, though, that it was up to him to set an example to the others. If he skimped, so would they. So he made sure he did at least his regulation hour's exercise, every day.

Despite all the precautions, though, Stone was developing a classic case of chicken legs, as astronauts called them, as his leg muscles atrophied. The soles of his feet were as soft as an infant's. And the parts of his body which got most tired, every day, were his hands. His hands worked constantly, in ways they didn't have to on Earth, hauling him around the Module, braking his mass.

[Hr:Min:Sec] 11:43:24
Today was Stone's shower day. Each of them was allowed one shower a week.

He stripped off his vest and shorts, and swung his legs over into the collapsible shower. It was a cylinder of white cloth, like a big concertina. He pulled the curtain up around him and hooked it to a metal lid fixed to the ceiling. He soaped up and rinsed himself with a spray; airflow, rather than gravity, drained away the water.

He felt as if layers of skin were coming off as he worked; the sponge baths that were all that was possible between showers just weren't sufficient. And the shower seemed to be getting some of the stiffness out of his muscles.

Actually, with the way the water hung suspended in the air, it was more like a sauna than a shower.

He thought about his crew.

They had all been trained up by NASA psychologists in how people behave during long periods of isolation. Stone saw himself, after his several flights, as pretty level-headed and robust. But he could recognize, at one time or another, most of the signs of isolation in his crew: sleep disturbance, boredom, restlessness, anxiety, anger, depression, headaches, irritability, lowering concentration, a loss of the sense of time and space.

Ares was bombarded daily with messages from well-wishers, families and friends, but the time lag was so great that it was impossible to conduct a meaningful conversation. And, somehow, hearing those familiar voices calling from behind a lightspeed barrier made the crew's isolation that much more poignant.

All of this was telling on the crew.

Gershon seemed the less affected, on the surface. He was still the bullshitting jock, always there with the jokes. But there was an increasingly jagged edge. Gershon was basically a pilot, used to short, sharp bursts of adrenaline-pumping action.

Still, in Stone's judgment Ralph would be fine. Gershon knew he would get his chance when he took the lander down to the surface. Stone saw his job as being to keep the guy together until they reached Mars.

York was different, though.

York was uptight, a stickler, a little reclusive. A *lot* arrogant and patronizing. And a civilian at that. Gershon's jokes and gotchas irritated the hell out of her, clearly, but she wouldn't say a word about it; instead she kept it to herself, and just kind of smouldered. Which didn't do anyone any good.

York was like a lot of professional women Stone had met before, he thought. That is, she had one hell of a chip on her shoulder.

But he envied, and admired, her inner resources.

To him, Stone was ready to admit, the mission was everything: flying the craft, doing his job when they eventually hit the Martian dirt, getting home again.

York, by contrast, had an awareness of the grandeur of it all: this remarkable experience, the interplanetary flight. These were depths inside herself which York was able to tap, and – as she'd come out of her shell during the mission – to articulate to others.

She was almost poetic, at times.

Stone felt he understood how important that was. He'd hoped it would work out that way. And according to Houston, even the ratings for their weekly TV briefings – which had dipped pretty fast after the excitement of the launch – were reviving again, mainly thanks to York.

He dried himself off with a towel, and then he had to suck up

188

stray drops inside the shower with a vacuum hose. It was fiddly and time-consuming.

In the end, as usual, by the time he was able to dismantle the shower and fold it away he felt frustrated and tense once more, the benefits of the shower lost.

[Hr:Min:Sec] 13:12:51
Stone set himself at the Mission Module's control station. He ran quickly through the parameters of the cluster's operation: consumables usage, attitude control propellant usage, cryogenic store boiloff . . .

Most of it looked nominal.

But the big solar panels, sticking out like wings from the sides of the S-IVB booster, were getting too hot. The panels could tilt through twenty-five degrees, so that the sun's radiation would come in on them at a slant, reducing their temperature. Stone put together a recommendation that Mission Control should think about performing the tilt a few days ahead of schedule; minutes later, Houston replied that they would evaluate the proposal.

Then there was a problem with the feed system of one of the steerable dish antennae, which was targeted back at Earth. There was a three decibel loss in downlink signal strength: maybe some part of the system had cracked under thermal stress. That was a potentially serious problem; it would reduce the bit rate at which high-quality images could be sent back to Earth. The ground said they wouldn't take any action on that one at this time, but would do some simulations and analysis first.

And now he found a problem with some of the Module's seventeen chargeable battery regulator modules. One of them, number fifteen, had malfunctioned days before, and now number three was off-line. All this cut the power available in the Module by around two hundred watts. Houston thought there might be a low-voltage trip occurring somewhere, which was switching out the regulators too often, and Stone had to go around the Module firing up systems and calling out power consumption numbers to the specialists in the back rooms behind the MOCR.

It was slow, dull, almost mindless work. The routine stuff really ground you down; it was a hazard of long-duration missions. But all of it was essential to keep this hand-crafted bucket of bolts flying.

189

At last he could get to his interplanetary navigation.

He headed down to the wardroom, to the picture window there, and dug out his optical kit.

The kit contained a one-power telescope and a twenty-eight-power sextant. The sextant was a chunky little gadget with an eyepiece and a calibrated semicircular dial, to measure angles between stars. These were nice devices, compact, heavy things of brass, which Stone enjoyed handling. If he was going to take away any one souvenir of this flight, then to hell with a Mars rock; it would be this little kit.

Stone set to work by the picture window.

First he measured the apparent size of the sun's disk, which would give him a good measure of how far the craft was from the sun, and then he measured the angles between Venus and a fixed star, and the Earth and a fixed star. Those three basic measurements would fix him in three-dimensional space. He would finish up with a couple more redundant measurements.

He'd found he couldn't hold the optical equipment steady in the microgravity. But the way round that was to set the gadgets floating in the air, as well aligned as possible; then he could bring his eye up to the eyepiece and make an accurate reading.

The first TCM – Trajectory Correction Maneuver – had taken place ten days after leaving Earth. At that time the flight path had been pretty badly misaligned. The trajectory planners back in Houston had sent corrective burn parameters chattering up the line to Ares, and the MS-II stage's maneuvering propulsion system – two modified Lunar Module engines – had applied a hefty velocity change of twenty-five feet per second. But, according to the latest data, the craft was still on a slightly divergent trajectory. Today Stone would check the craft's position and velocity, and the track would be recomputed; and tomorrow, if they could get it right, the second TCM burn would fix the trajectory's small remaining anomaly.

There was a whole slew of ways for the ground to keep track of a spacecraft. The faster the craft was receding from Earth, the more its radio carrier frequency was shifted, like a whistle on a speeding train. Or, to fix distance, an uplink modulation pattern – a brief digital code – could be transmitted to the spacecraft, and sent straight back. The delay in receiving the copied signal would tell the specialists how far away the craft was from Earth. And on Ares another radio method was being run, an experiment involving the change in angle between Ares and a quasar, a radio source in the background sky.

But even all these techniques in combination weren't accurate enough to position Ares; the combined accuracy was only maybe half that required.

The answer was to use equipment on board the spacecraft itself.

In fact Ares had its own automated optical sensors. There were two sun sensors – little cadmium sulphide photoresistors – placed on the solar cell array. And there was a star tracker, a lens with an image dissector tube. But the automatic system just wasn't too smart. Every few days, the star tracker got fooled by bright particles, bits of junk floating along with the spacecraft in its orbit around the sun.

So – just as had sailors on Earth's oceans for millennia – Phil Stone had to navigate his ship by the stars.

He found himself humming as he worked. He knew he was good at this. He'd practiced the techniques in planetariums on the ground, and in Moonlab; he could get a measurement true within a few thousandths of a degree, and he took a lot of satisfaction from the basic craft of it.

When he'd finished he packed away the instruments, and drifted back up to his control station. He ran the numbers through the computer, to figure out the position for himself. He would feed the raw data down to Houston, of course, but it kind of satisfied him to know that he could do this independently.

Stone liked to visualize the mission trajectory, to figure out where he was.

The energy expended by the injection booster – although monumental in human terms, the result of five years' fuel haulage to orbit – was so low on the cosmic scale that the craft's trajectory barely diverged from Earth's. The Ares stack, having pushed itself away from Earth, was now scooting alongside the home planet in its orbit like a dog beside its master.

The first results looked good; the spacecraft was pretty much where it was supposed to be, and he figured that the TCM-2 burn would only have to be a few feet per second.

When he was done he indulged himself. He doused the wardroom's lights, and sat in the warm darkness close to the picture window, surrounded by the hum of fans.

Ares was alone in space now: Earth and Moon were reduced to

191

star-like points of light, side by side. In all the universe, only the sun showed a disk.

The sense of isolation was extraordinary: far deeper than he'd known in space before, even during his time in Moonlab. Unless you were around the back of the Moon, Earth was always in view. And in Skylab A, the Earth itself dominated every waking moment, and you took your reference from that huge quilt of light, from the continents and oceans sliding under you.

Out here, it was different. There was no 'up' or 'down': there were just little islands of rock, floating around in the sky. For interplanetary flight humans would need to develop a new kind of perception, he thought, a three-dimensional awareness.

As his eyes dark-adapted, the stars came out: millions of them, far more than were visible through Earth's murky atmosphere. He could see the galaxy, a great speckled river of stars; he made out the edge of the disk in the direction of the galactic core, in Sagittarius, with its ragged edge caused by black swirls of obscuring dust clouds, and the nearby stars sparkling in the dark scars. And he could see the moons of Jupiter, four of them, in a line alongside the planet's bright spark.

Ralph came floating out of the brightness of the wardroom area to bring him a meal, a couple of packets of warmed-up rehydrated stew. With a pencil light in his mouth Stone mashed in the water, until the food was moist through.

[Hr:Min:Sec] 19:37:20

After thirteen hours awake, the crew had finished up their duties for the day. York was feeling queasy again, so she took a scopolamine and went to bed. Stone wanted to spend some time alone, maybe writing letters.

But Gershon, still full of nervous energy, wanted to play darts.

The dartboard was the Mission Module's great recreation, along with magnetic cards. The darts were tipped with Velcro, and they flew straight and level.

It was quite different from playing under gravity. To get accuracy, the best technique was rather to push the dart comparatively slowly through the air, maybe with a little spin for stability. But if the dart was too slow, currents in the air would knock it off track.

Gershon set up the dartboard in the Science Platform, and he and Stone threw the darts so that they arced easily the length of the workshop.

[Hr:Min:Sec] 21:01:32
Gershon called him out of his sleep locker, and over to the Space Ark.

Arabella's cage hadn't been closed properly, and the spider had got out. Gershon pointed out a huge, sweeping web, which spanned yards of space, crossing from side to side of the Mission Module.

Stone just hoped enough insects of some sort had survived the various sterilization checks to make it into the Module to sustain Arabella. Gershon was all for shaking out the fruit fly pupae for her.

Flying to Mars, bound up in spider-web. It was a beautiful image, Stone thought.

[Hr:Min:Sec] 23:32:37
When he slept, Stone had his usual space dream.

Oddly, he was vaguely aware of the causes of the dream, even while he slept: the breeze from the wall fan, the falling sensations of microgravity, maybe a subconscious realization of the speed with which he was traveling.

All of it merged into a dream of flying.

He was surrounded by woods and rivers and blue skies, and he was flying, low like a bird of prey.

June, 1978
University of California at Berkeley

Sometimes the prospect of starting at Houston seemed attractive to York, compared to the clique-ridden, insulated world of the universities. She was moving to a place where people were doing great things: working on stuff of more substance than the next grant application, a place where achievement was measured by more than just the number of journal citations per year.

At other times, though, she couldn't believe she was doing this.

She was offered plenty of advice against NASA, from senior staff on down. For example, she was told, the center of gravity of space science was not at Houston, but at the universities: like Cornell, where Sagan was based. Would her own work on Martian outflow channels have been improved if she'd upped sticks and moved to Texas?

In fact NASA seemed to be actively anti-science. In the wake of the Apollo 11 landing a shoal of scientists had abruptly quit: Bill

193

Hess, Houston chief scientist, Elbert King, lunar samples curator, Eugene Shoemaker, Apollo field geology principal investigator. Shoemaker talked about his concern for the direction of the space program, and what a poor system Apollo was for exploring the Moon: nothing but a rope and pulley, for instance, to haul surface samples into the LM's cabin! And what evidence was there that things had gotten any better? Was the Mars program going to be any different?

It was depressing. If these eminent men couldn't cut it inside NASA, what chance did *she* have?

Earnest friends shoved newspaper stories under her nose. The *Tennessee Valley vs Hill* case had just concluded, with the Supreme Court ruling that the new Tellico Dam couldn't be built, because it would drown the only known habitat of a three-inch fish called a snail darter . . . People nowadays were dead against big, mindless technological stunts – hell, she was herself – and what could be bigger, more mindless, than NASA?

Then, it was said, she'd end up serving as a non-scientific grunt on training trips. Making sandwiches for astronauts. And if she came back into the mainstream of academic science later, she'd have a hell of a gap in her bibliography. She could be blowing a promising career.

Besides, you only have to watch Dallas *to see what kind of a cultural desert you're walking into. And the climate down there in Texas, my dear. Oh, my!*

She got stubborn. She even started defending the space program. As an application of government technology, space was somewhere between true science and the opposite. At least it didn't actively *kill* people. By contrast she cited Ben Priest as an example of an intelligent, thoughtful adult who was able to survive, precariously maybe, in the dumb-fighter-jock snakepit of NASA.

Anyway, the only way she was going to get to Mars was via Houston. So that settled the argument, as far as she was concerned.

She didn't see Mike Conlig.

When she'd finally got up the nerve to tell him about her application, he didn't seem surprised. He didn't even seem to take it seriously, she thought.

He called a few times, from Marshall or Santa Susana. But he wouldn't come to Berkeley, to talk, or help her close out her life.

Maybe he was being patronizing – maybe he thought she was following a whim, that she wasn't serious, she wouldn't see this

194

through. If that was true, he didn't know her too well after all.

Or – she wondered – perhaps he suspected something about her and Ben Priest. She'd fallen into bed with Ben only once more, since that time at Pasadena, all of two years ago. But she was no actress; she knew she couldn't help showing what had happened, in her voice, her eyes, her body language . . . that is, if Mike was perceptive enough to see, caring enough to devote the attention.

Which, she figured sadly, he wasn't.

But their conversation was too stiff, too many things left unspoken, for her to tell for sure.

There were a *lot* of details.

She got another letter. It said she was to report to Houston to start her ground training in just six weeks, which was a ludicrously short period of time for any working scientist to disengage herself from her commitments. She entered into a regime of eighteen-hour days. She tried to close out her research work with final papers and draft contributions to joint work, and she reassigned the graduate students who were working with her, and she disengaged herself from her teaching commitments.

Her salary offer was on a Government grade equivalent to what she would have got as a civil service scientist. She hadn't expected riches as an astronaut, but the pay seemed lousy, actually, considering the dislocation to her life, the hours she would have to put in, the *risks,* for Christ's sake.

She was concerned enough to call Ben Priest about it.

'Am I being picked on?'

'It's nothing personal. You got to remember you're at the bottom of an immense pecking order, Natalie. You can't make more money than the senior military astronauts. I guess you can see that. And their salaries are rigid, because they are locked into a military pay scale.'

'Yeah, but civil service salary scales are rigid, too, once you're inside. Promotion is slow, and –'

He cut her off. 'You have to ask yourself, Natalie. Is this really an issue for you? Is the salary a genuine factor in your decision to join NASA? If it isn't, quit beefing and move on.'

She thought about that.

She signed the forms.

She had to sort out her pension contributions. She sold her car, and gave up her rented apartment. She made out a new will: her mother was the main beneficiary, and, after some thought, she made

195

Ben Priest her executor. She bought herself a new wardrobe: slacks and light shirts, suitable for Houston. She spoke to her Savings and Loan and her bank, and made arrangements for her mail to be forwarded.

She even got chased by the press, local paper and radio crews looking to run comic pieces on the new lady astronaut. After the first embarrassing result appeared – *Space Beauty Is Over the Moon* – she chased the reporters away, and they soon seemed to forget about her.

There was a round of farewells, which she hated.

She took a final drive around Berkeley. She headed up Dwight Way and across Telegraph Street, passing the little shingle houses there, and then into and above Strawberry Canyon. The hills were a lush summer green. Further off, beyond the flats of Berkeley, she could see the misty blur of San Francisco and Marin County, linked together by the rust-colored Golden Gate Bridge. The air was fine, laced with eucalyptus.

How the hell could she give up all this for the humid smog of Houston?

She hadn't anticipated how difficult this aspect of her odyssey would be. Her workplace, the apartment she'd rented for years, Berkeley itself: all of it, she realized, maybe belatedly, made up the fabric of her life. Pursuing Martian geology, flying into space, was one thing – but she hadn't bargained for how hard it would be to clean out her apartment, and to accept the cards and small presents and exchanged addresses, and continually, constantly, say *goodbye.*

Wednesday, July 5, 1978
Headquarters, Rockwell International, Los Angeles

Gershon walked around the car park, working the stiffness out of his legs after his drive out from the city. It was colder than he'd come to expect for California.

The LA division of Rockwell was strung out around the southern border of Los Angeles International Airport. Beyond the fence, the airport was a plain of concrete, with aircraft rolling between distant buildings like little painted toys. There was a distant rumble of jets ramping up, and a remote, evocative whiff of kerosene. If he squinted, he could see a line of big airliners stacked up in the sky.

The Rockwell headquarters building was an uncompromising

cube of brick, four stories high, without a single window. Ralph Gershon had never seen anything like it; it was like the kind of dumb, baffling modern sculptures that earned their creators thousands of dollars. *No natural daylight at all. Christ.* He was here for a regular meeting of the MEM Technical Liaison Group, and Liaison Group meetings were meetings from hell anyway. The thought of spending all day inside this goddamn box of bricks was depressing.

Beyond the clutter of Rockwell buildings, he could see all the way down Imperial Boulevard to Santa Monica Bay. He liked the way the morning light was coming off the water, steely gray and flat.

'Here.'

There was a small, wiry man at his side, with a balding head and rimless glasses and big, ugly freckles; he was holding up a cigarette packet.

'Thanks,' Gershon said. 'I don't.'

'Uh huh.' The guy took a cigarette himself, tamped it against the box, and lit up. His arms were disproportionately long and bony, and they stuck out of his sleeves. Just behind him in the parking lot, there was a T-bird, gleaming black. 'You looked like it was a good moment for a smoke.' He had a broad, bold New York accent. He was maybe fifty, and he looked familiar to Gershon.

'You here for the MEM thing?' Gershon asked.

'Yeah. And you? You from NASA? A pilot, maybe?'

'How do you know?'

The guy tapped his own small paunch. 'Because you look fit.'

'I'm the Astronaut Office rep.' Gershon hesitated when he used the word 'astronaut.' As he always did. *Look at me, the great astronaut. When I haven't flown anything for NASA except a T-38 trainer.* But then this little guy had used the word 'pilot.' Maybe he understood.

The stranger stuck out his hand. 'My name's Lee. John K. My friends call me JK.'

The handshake was firm, the palms callused. It wasn't the grip of a pen-pusher.

'You from one of the MEM bidders?'

'Nope,' Lee said. 'I'm from CA. Columbia Aviation. Tell me you've heard of us.'

Gershon grinned.

Lee shrugged. 'We do a lot of subcontracting work for Rockwell, and others, and we're doing some experimental stuff for NASA.

197

Lifting body shapes and such. We're small, but we're growing, and we're smarter than the rest. When it comes to Request For Proposals time, we'll throw in our lot with one of the big guys and hustle for a piece of the pie.' He stared up at the HQ building, the big brick cube. 'You know, I worked here, for a while. Under Dutch Kindelberger.'

Gershon looked at Lee with new interest. He knew that name, of course. Any kid like Gershon, who had grown up steeped in planes and the men who built them, would know about Dutch Kindelberger. Dutch had built up Rockwell – then called North American Aviation – in the war years by delivering perhaps the finest American flying machine of that conflict, the P-51 Mustang.

'Dutch designed this building himself,' Lee said. 'We used to call it the Brickyard.'

'I didn't know Kindelberger was an architect.'

'He wasn't.' Lee grinned. 'You don't think it shows?' He looked around, at the airport, the Boulevard, the sprawl of Rockwell buildings. 'There used to be a sign, on top of the main building over there –' He pointed. 'You could see it from miles away. "Home of the X-15." '

Something clicked in Gershon's mind. 'I thought I knew your face.' He had a vague memory of an old photograph, from the scrapbooks and cutting files he'd kept as a kid: an experimental airplane, up at Edwards, with a line of grinning young engineers, all spectacles and buck teeth and uncontrolled hair. 'You worked on the X-15?'

Lee said, 'No. But I bet I know what you're thinking of.'

'The B-70. You worked on the B-70, didn't you? With Harrison Storms.'

'Yeah. With Stormy.'

Harrison Storms was the man who had built the Apollo spacecraft for Rockwell. And before that, there had been the B-70, a supersonic bomber. Gershon remembered old photographs: that stainless steel surface painted white to reflect Mach 3 heat, the huge delta wing two stories off the ground . . .

'Congress canceled the project on us,' Lee said. 'We only ever made two of the damn things. And I know one of them crashed with an F-104. I guess the other was scrapped.'

'No. It survived. It's in a museum.'

Lee eyed Gershon and smiled. 'How about that? I never knew.'

Gershon glanced at his watch. 'Come on. It's gone nine. We have to go in.'

198

'Sure. We don't want to miss the read-through of the minutes, do we?'

Side by side, they walked into the Brickyard.

Two portly, shirt-sleeved aerospace executives were struggling with a balky Vu-graph machine. One said, 'You sure you know how to fly this thing, Al?'

Al laughed.

Gershon tried to settle himself in the small, hard-framed chair, with his briefcase tucked under the table. It was already hot, airless, and his collar chafed at his throat.

That word, 'fly,' tugged at him. Flying a projector. Flying a desk. Jesus. Words misused by people who knew no more about *flying* than how to order a drink from a stewardess.

The chairman called them to order. He was Tim Josephson, a NASA Assistant Administrator, a tall, thin, bookish man. He sat on a swivel chair behind a desk at the head of the table, and rattled through the minutes and agenda.

Lee leaned over to Gershon. 'How do you like that? This is Dutch's old office. That's Dutch's chair, for God's sake. Rockwell must really, really, want this contract.'

Behind Josephson the whole wall was covered with a mural. It showed a P-51 Mustang coming right out at you.

Gershon wanted to be out of here, *doing* something.

But life in the Astronaut Office wasn't like that. You had to pay your dues.

'Listen to me,' Chuck Jones had said, in his role as chief astronaut. 'We gotta have someone from the Office assigned to the Mars Excursion Module.'

Gershon had thought he was being dumped on. 'But there is no MEM.'

'Even better.' And Jones had spun Gershon a story about how Pete Conrad had helped to design the controls and instrument displays for the Lunar Module. 'Conrad spent fucking *months* in plywood mockups of that lander, surrounded by painted switches and dials, trying to imagine himself coming down onto the Moon.' Jones held his thumb and forefinger up, a hair's breadth apart. 'And he came *that* close to being the first man to land there. Now. You want to tell me you know more about how things work around here than old Pete Conrad?'

So maybe this wasn't such a bad assignment after all, Gershon had concluded.

The trouble was, though, it still didn't look as if the MEM was ever going to fly, except in the glossy promotional brochures of the aerospace companies.

Landing a spacecraft on Mars wasn't an easy thing to do. And that was just about the only thing everybody was agreed on. Even after you'd hauled ass all the way out there, you found yourself facing a planet that was an awkward combination of Earth and Moon: the worst features of each, Gershon supposed. That smear of air was thick enough that you couldn't fly a tin-foil buggy on rockets right down to the surface, like the Lunar Module landing on the Moon; you were going to have to take a heatshield along. On the other hand, the air was too thin to allow you simply to fly your way down to the surface in a glider with wings, the way the Space Shuttle would have flown to Earth. You had to have some compromise, a bastard cross between a flying machine and a rocket ship.

So disagreement was inevitable. After all nobody had done this before, tried to build a machine to land people on Mars.

But there was a lot of money and politics involved, so, of course, the arguments went far beyond the technical.

This Liaison Group was a relatively new initiative, and it came from Fred Michaels himself, as an attempt to cut through the mess of arguments holding up the MEM design. The Group got all the warring factions together – the aerospace people from Rockwell and McDonnell and Grumman and Boeing, and the NASA groups from Marshall and Ames and Langley and Houston – to thrash out the issues.

The formal presentations started.

First up was a delegation from Grumman, to present their current thinking.

The Grumman MEM would come in from Martian orbit as a half-cone, like an Apollo Command Module split down the center. With the aid of a lot of electronics, the crew could actually steer the thing. Then, inside the atmosphere, the MEM would tip downwards, so that it was falling to the ground nose first. The heatshield shell would fall away, revealing something that looked like a fat Lunar Module, with landing legs that would spring out. The whole thing would come down on rockets mounted in the nose. On the ground, the MEM would unfold, with crew quarters swiveling out from the sides toward the ground.

Grumman had built the Apollo Lunar Module. Gershon

happened to know that Grumman had the tacit backing of Marshall, with Hans Udet and all the other old Germans. And so what you got was a kind of beefed-up Lunar Module, coupled with some typical brute-force heavy engineering from the Germans.

The Grumman people had a model, a little Revell-kit version of the thing, which was all unfolding legs and rotating compartments and bits of plastic heatshield. Parts of it kept falling off in the hands of the nervous presenter. The thing looked ludicrously overcomplicated. When that upside down cone came apart, revealing all the plumbing inside, Gershon was reminded of an ice cream cornet.

JK Lee leaned over and laughed quietly. 'Christ, that thing is ugly. And you'd waste a lot of development effort.'

'How so?'

'The thing's a bastard. Too many smart-ass ideas. You'd have to develop a new heatshield material, to cover that huge flat surface. *And* you'd have to figure out how to build a lifting body to fly in the Martian atmosphere. *And* you've got a whole new Lunar Module to build as well. And for what?'

'So what would you do?'

'Me? If I was Grumman? I'd tell my designers to cut out the ice cream and focus on the meat and potatoes. Pick one approach and stick to it. If you're building a lifting body, fine. Don't give me damn Moon-bug legs as well.'

The delegation led by Boeing weren't too specific about the details of their landing craft itself; instead they concentrated on how it would get down through the atmosphere. Their MEM would descend from orbit and go through reentry, and then, about six miles up and still traveling faster than sound, it would sprout a ballute – a cross between a balloon and a parachute, a huge, inflatable sail that would grab at the thin air. Then, a complex sequence of parachutes would bring the craft close enough to the surface for hover rockets to take over for the landing.

The problem was that nobody had yet made a ballute, or even tested one in a wind tunnel. And it would be all but impossible to test in the thicker atmosphere of Earth.

A lot of the Boeing presentation was to do with the technicalities of packing parachutes. It was deadly dull. Gershon made himself take notes on his jotting pad; but sometimes, when he glanced down at the pad, he didn't recognize what he'd written.

The third presentation was from Rockwell themselves, backed by a combination of Langley and JPL. And this was the most advanced option of all. It was another lifting-body shape, but more advanced than Grumman's crude half-cone: it was a biconic, a segment of a fat cone topped by a thin nose. This MEM would be able to enter the Martian atmosphere direct from Earth, without the need to stop over in a parking orbit around Mars first. The biconic would be controlled one hundred per cent by the pilot, with a joystick and rudder pedals. The ship would follow a complicated entry path, dipping and swooping and swirling, losing heat gradually and bleeding off speed. And then, approaching the surface, the biconic would tip up and land on its tail, ready for an ascent back to orbit.

But there were drawbacks. The electronics would be so complex there was no way an astronaut could land the thing in the case of computer failure. And all those curved surfaces would take a lot of buffeting from the air; the biconic would need heavy heatshielding over most of its surface.

The biconic looked to Gershon like a hybrid of Langley's traditional love of aircraft, and JPL's expertise in robotics and computer control, all mixed up together with Rockwell's immense appetite for fat and ambitious development budgets.

Looking at the presentation, Gershon felt an odd itch in the palm of his hands and his feet.

Lee was grinning at him. 'I can see that look in your eye. You'd like to fly that thing down through the Martian air, maybe do a couple of banks over Olympus Mons.'

'Yeah, yeah.'

Lee waved his hand. 'I'm not mocking you. But you need to understand that you're looking at a twenty-year development effort there, minimum, in my judgment. Christ, nobody's flown a biconic *ever*. Not even a fucking wooden mockup. Unless the Russians are up to something, which I doubt.

'And then you're talking about building a biconic to land on *Mars*. What do we know about the atmosphere of Mars? Boy, if you want to see your grandson flying down onto all that red dust, then you put your money on a biconic. But you and I sure ain't going to see it . . .'

The three presentations took them right through the day and on into the evening. Then, in a long final session, the meeting argued out the merits of the comparative designs: possible crew sizes, surface stay capabilities, gross weight in Earth orbit, required delta-vee, aerodynamic characteristics like lift-to-drag ratio. It all got bogged down in picky detail, and it became clear to Gershon after a while that all sides were more intent on filibustering than reaching any kind of decision.

Gershon stared at Dutch Kindelberger's mural of the Mustang, and wondered what it had been like to fly.

As the meeting broke up, around nine p.m., the delegates began to make plans to rendezvous in various bars.

JK Lee approached Gershon. 'You're looking kind of strained.'

Gershon grinned at him. 'I like the idea of a couple of pitchers of cold beer. But not in some shitty bar with these corporate suits, frankly.'

'Yeah. Listen. You want to get out of here? It's a clear night. We could take a drive, maybe up toward Edwards.'

Edwards Air Force Base. Up on the high desert. 'Let's go.'

They got out of the Brickyard. Lee pulled his little black T-bird out of the parking lot, and they stopped to pick up a couple of six-packs, and then Lee headed north, out of the city.

The night was crisp and cool and cloudless, but the horizon was ringed with the conurbation's sulphur-orange glow. Gershon had to tilt his head back and stare straight up to see any stars, in a little clear circle of sky directly above him. He thought he recognized the big square of Pegasus up there, the winged horse.

He had a sense of confinement, as if the city and all its smog was a great big box he was stuck inside.

Lee drove one-handed, hanging onto the T-bird's wheel with one finger. 'I remember coming up here. I mean, 1955 or earlier. The days of the B-70. The road out of the city was just a two-lane blacktop, winding up out of the Newhall Pass and through Mint Canyon, until it gave onto the high desert. And Palmdale was just a gas station, with a whole bunch of Joshua trees . . . All changed now, huh.'

'I guess.'

'So. You had a good day?'

Gershon grunted. 'Not one of my best.'

'You're not a lover of engineering debate.'

'That wasn't a debate about engineering. And most of those guys sure weren't engineers.'

Lee hooted. 'You're right there. But you got to understand the politics, my friend. Look at it this way. When Nixon canned the Space Shuttle, back in 1972 – well, that wasn't the most popular decision with the big aerospace boys. They would have loved the Shuttle because the whole damn thing would have been *new*. They would have been able to throw away all their old Saturn tooling facilities and start afresh, at great public expense. But with the incremental program we've got now, everything is a derivative of something else. And it's all pretty much owned by the companies who designed those pieces.

'So you got Boeing working on the new MS-IC, for example, the enhanced Saturn first stage, which was what they'd originally built. And McDonnell Douglas, over at Huntingdon Beach, have built the Skylabs and Moonlabs – space stations lashed up from disused Saturn third stages – which McDonnell built in the first place. And so on.

'But the plum contract – the most advanced technology, the real glamor work for the next decade – is going to be the MEM. A whole new spacecraft, to take a few guys to the surface of Mars. Making a lot of other guys very rich in the process . . .'

'But NASA hasn't even issued a Request For Proposals yet.'

'Of course not. What do you expect? NASA's taking too much heat from its contractors. And then on top of that you got all the usual bullshit infighting between the NASA centers.'

'Maybe so,' Gershon said gloomily. 'But we've already pissed away six years, since '72.'

'You want to fly something before you retire.'

'You got it.'

'Hell, I understand that. Listen, you want to break open that six-pack?'

'You want one?'

'Sure.'

Gershon's can was still dewed from the store's refrigerator. The beer was crisp in his mouth; he felt some of the tension of the day unwind.

The San Gabriel Mountains were behind them now, and Lee pushed the T-bird hard through the blackness. The road was vacant, laser-straight, fore and back, in the lights of the T-bird.

Now, there were stars all the way down to the horizon. JK Lee propped the wheel between his bony knees, and, holding his beer in one hand, extracted a cigarette and lit it up with the other. The light of the tip combined with the dashboard's glow to cast soft, diffuse light over his face.

Gershon asked, 'So what would you do?'

'Huh?'

'If you were going to build a MEM.'

'Me? Oh, we aren't going to bid. We'd ruffle too many feathers. And the big boys would crowd us out anyhow. Rockwell is going to get the contract. Everybody knows that. They'll pull strings, just like they did to get Apollo. I understand the MEM was part of the deal, kind of, when Nixon canceled the Shuttle. That and their Saturn second stage injection-booster project. You got to balance your constituencies.' His Bronx accent came out comically on that last word.

Gershon grunted and pulled at his beer. 'But if you were bidding,' he pressed.

'If we were?' Lee thought for a moment, balancing his beer on his lap. 'Well, you got to adjust your philosophy to accommodate the situation. You might get just one shot at this, a trip to Mars. So you want something that you know you can build quickly, and cheaply, that's gonna work first time. And we don't know if lifting bodies and biconics are going to work, and we could spend a lot of time and money finding out they don't.'

'So what?'

'So you use what's worked before. Start with a low L-over-D shape, say of zero point five.'

L-over-D: lift over drag, the key aerodynamic measure of shape. 'Point five. That's an Apollo Command Module shape.'

'Exactly. Build a big, fat Command Module. All you'd need to figure is how to build a wider heatshield. We know it's a design that works. Apollos flew eight manned Moon program flights, and since then three missions a year to Skylab, and one a year to the Moonlab since '75 . . . what's that, twenty-five flights? And the Apollo 13 CM even survived its Service Module exploding under it.'

'You'd have no maneuverability in the Martian atmosphere.'

'Not as much as a biconic, but you'd have some. Just like with Apollo. If you offset the center of gravity you get a certain amount of control, with lift coming from the shape. And here's the thing. The aerodynamics would be simple enough for you to fly the fucking thing down by hand if you had to, even if the electronics failed. You couldn't do that with a biconic.'

'What about after the atmosphere entry? Parachutes?'

Lee thought about it. 'Nope. Air's too thin. You'd have to have some system of busting out of the heatshield and landing on a descent engine, like the Lunar Module. Like the Grumman bid, I guess. And then you'd have an ascent stage, the top half of the cone, to get you back to orbit. You'd leave behind the heavy heat-shield, and all the surface gear.'

It all made sense to Gershon. It would be low cost, low development risk, low operational risk. *It's all I need, to land on Mars. And you could have the thing flying in a few years.*

'JK, you ought to put in a bid. I'm serious.'

Lee just laughed.

He waved ahead, gesturing with his can. 'Look out there.'

Gershon saw that the desert here was a flat, pale white crust in the starlight. Salt flats. And, on the horizon, a row of lights appeared out of nowhere, like a city in the desert.

'Edwards,' Lee said. 'Where I came with Stormy Storms to watch the X-15 fly. Christ, they were the good days.' He took another pull of his beer, then threw the can out of the car.

Gershon handed him another can, and the T-bird sped on, as the giant hangars of the Air Force Base loomed out of the darkness around them.

Monday, August 7, 1978
Lyndon B. Johnson Space Center, Houston

She was held up for an hour at Building 110, the security office of the JSC campus.

How are you supposed to present yourself, if you're a rookie astronaut reporting for your first morning's work? You have no identification badge on your shirt pocket, because on that first day, you have to enter the Space Center grounds to have the badge issued . . .

Strictly speaking, of course, York thought, it was an infinite regress, a paradox. It was logically impossible ever to enter JSC. She tried to explain this to the receptionist.

The receptionist, her broad, fleshy face a puddle of sweat, just looked at her, and turned to deal with the press people queuing behind her. After a while York shut up and sat in the poky little building, trying to stop her hands folding over themselves.

Finally a secretary, tottering on heels, came out to collect her.

The secretary led her across the spiky grass of the campus. The woman was around thirty. She trailed a cloud of cosmetic fumes – perfumes and face powder and hairspray – that made York's eyes sting. She looked oddly at York, and York could see the woman considering giving her girl-to-girl tips about where to get *something* done about that hair.

York clutched her empty briefcase and wondered what the hell she was doing here.

The secretary took her to Building 4, and told her she was expected to attend the regular pilots' meeting straight away. Every second Monday morning, at eight: she was already late.

She slipped into the meeting room, at the back.

There were maybe fifty people sitting around in the room: all men, clean-cut, close-shaven, crew-cut, wearing sports shirts and slacks. There was a lot of wisecracking, and deep, throaty laughter that rumbled around the room.

Chuck Jones, chief astronaut, stood at the front of the room, hands on hips. Jones was talking about some technical detail of the T-38 training aircraft.

York spotted an empty seat, not far from the door, and with muttered apologies she squeezed past a few sets of knees toward it. The astronauts made way for her politely enough, but she was aware of their gaze on her, curious, speculative, checking out her figure, studying her un-made-up face. *What the hell's this? Is it female? Are you here to take notes, baby? Make mine decaffeinated* ...

She spotted Ben Priest, sitting up front with his arms folded, looking the part.

'Now,' Jones said from the front of the room, 'I've had reports from Ellington that some of you guys aren't checking out your equipment before flying the T-38.'

There were groans. 'Christ, Chuck, do we have to go through all this again?'

'We want to keep the privilege of flying the T-38s. But it's a privilege that can be rescinded any time. You may be astronauts, but you aren't free from the routine responsibilities of checking out what you fly. All I'm asking for is a little more effort, to keep those guys at Ellington sweet ...'

Jones started going through assignments for the next two weeks. 'Okay, we have Bleeker, Dana and Stone to the Cape Tuesday to Friday. Gershon to Downey, all week. Curval and Priest to Los Angeles.'

Someone spoke up from the floor. 'Hey, Chuck. I thought you were coming with us to LA.'

'No, I changed my mind. I'm going to the Cape. I want to go through the new CM sim they're building out there.'

'Don't you like us any more, Chuck?'

'You guys go west and I'll go east any time ...'

This kind of bullshit went on for half an hour. By the end of it, York was feeling restless, baffled by the barrage of jargon, bemused by the slowness and apparent waste of time. It was like, she imagined, being inside an unusually clean men's locker room.

She felt intimidated and out of place. *How can I make a mark in an environment like this?*

She met the rest of the cadre she'd been recruited into: eight others, all men, mostly with flying experience. They looked bright, eager, young, alert. Christ, three of them were already wearing astronaut-issue sports shirts! How had they *known?*

Chuck Jones took the new rookies on a tour of the Center.

York peered through doorways into the empty offices of senior astronauts. All the rooms looked the same, neat and spruce and barely lived-in, with pictures of spacecraft and airplanes on the walls. On the desks were boys' toys: aircraft and lunar modules, and models of the new Saturn VB, with solid rocket boosters you could snap on and off.

She half-expected to see spare sports shirts hanging behind the veneered doors.

Everywhere they walked, people deferred to Jones, as if he was some kind of king. He didn't seem to notice. *My God,* York thought. *There are going to be some monumental egos, around here.*

Jones led the nine of them into his big office in Building 30, and gave them coffee. He walked them through their induction program. For her first year York would be an 'ascan' – an astronaut candidate. She'd go through six months of classroom lectures on astronomy, aerodynamics, physiology, spacecraft systems, interplanetary navigation, upper atmosphere physics . . . Back to school. There would be visits to Kennedy, Marshall, Langley and other NASA centers.

They'd be 'smoothed,' as Jones put it; the instructors would try to ensure that they all emerged with a certain base level of skills in every discipline, regardless of their background. That was partly for PR purposes, York gathered, so they could talk intelligently on every aspect of their future missions.

There would be some physical training, in simulators and centrifuges and the like. There would be some compulsory flight experience, in the back of a T-38, but, unlike previous cadres of scientist-astronauts, this group would not have to attend flight school.

It was a break from tradition. *They're letting in astronauts who aren't pilots!* Chuck Jones looked as if he was chewing nails as he forced this news out, and some of the more bushy-tailed guys looked disappointed; one even asked if he could *volunteer* for flight school.

208

After their ascan year, the candidates would be put on the active roster, and would be considered for assignment to flights. Then, maybe two years before a flight, mission-specific training would begin . . .

'In theory,' Jones said.

Someone spoke up. '*In theory*, sir?'

Jones said bluntly, 'I might as well just tell you guys straight out. You're not going to be seeing any action for a while. None of you is dumb, so you know what the funding situation is like up on the Hill.

'Even if we get to Mars, and even if – *if* – a scientist is selected,' and Jones's tone of voice made his feelings about that clear enough, 'there are too many people in line ahead of you new guys. Including previous batches of scientists, some of whom have been here for years and haven't got to fly yet. It's even worse than with Apollo. At least with Apollo several Moon flights were planned. For Mars only a single flight has been inked in, and competition for places on that flight is going to be ferocious.'

Jones swiveled his cold black eyes, and York found it difficult to withstand the pressure of that gaze, as if his vision had contained some sizzling, hostile radar energy. 'You're looking at long delays, and maybe no flights, ever. *We don't need you around here.* I'm saying this just so you'll understand.'

Ben Priest took her out to lunch at the Nassau Bay Hilton.

She surveyed the menu. 'Steak. Seafood. Salad. Potato. More steak. Jesus, Ben.'

He grinned as he sipped at a Coke. 'Welcome to Houston.'

'How does a civilized man like you stand it here, Ben?'

'Now, don't be a snob, Natalie.'

York ordered chicken-fried steak. When it arrived, it was a great plate-sized disk of meat, heavily fried and coated in batter. The first few mouthfuls tasted good, but the meat was tough, and her jaws soon started to ache.

Oh, how I am going to love Houston. A home away from home.

'So tell me,' Priest said. 'What do you think of the astronauts, now you've seen them en masse?'

'Football captains and class presidents. Straight out of Smallville.'

He laughed. 'Maybe. Well, that describes me too. Round here I'm just a "bug-eye" from Ohio.'

'Look, I'm serious, Ben. Maybe this is what's wrong with NASA. These guys have had it easy.'

'Easy?'

'Sure. For all their great achievements. Every day of their lives the astronauts are handed single, easily visualized objectives; all they have to do is go ahead and achieve. Unlike the rest of mankind.'

He grunted and cut into his steak, a big T-bone. 'Well, one thing's for sure,' he said.

'What?'

'Whether you're right about this colony of Eagle Scouts, or whether it's just your perception we're talking about here, you're going to have one hell of a job trying to find a niche.'

He was right, she felt. Flying to Mars could turn out to be the easy part.

After lunch, Priest took her sightseeing, and apartment hunting. Sitting in the familiar comfort of Ben's Corvette, she felt a great relief when they got away from the JSC area. And it was a relief to be with Ben.

She turned to him. He drove steadily, not speaking. If he reached out to her now –

But he didn't. He sat stiffly, as if unaware of her. *Hell, he probably doesn't know how to handle this any better than I do.*

Her relationship with Ben was an odd thing, she thought. Almost as odd as her long-running relationship with Mike Conlig. *Sure. So what's the common factor, York?*

When she and Ben came closer, physically, they talked a lot less. And when they did it was about superficialities. Ben didn't seem able even to contemplate leaving Karen, and as for York, her on-off relationship with Mike Conlig continued its stuttering course, accreting a kind of emotional mass the longer it lasted. *Are Ben and I having an affair, then? Just the occasional jump in the sack?*

It was as if their two bipolar relationships drew the two of them, Ben and York, apart every time they got close.

She was sure of one thing, though. If her first morning at JSC was anything to go by, she was going to need Ben's patient company just to keep her sane.

Houston dismayed her. The place sweltered under a layer of air that was hot, laden with humidity and thick with smog. The land was flat and at sea level, without a hill for a hundred miles, and criss-crossed by muddy rivers and swamps. Out of town, the soil was a gluey mixture the locals called 'gumbo,' a mess of mud, clay and oyster shells; pines and snarled oaks thrust reluctantly out of fields of stiff, bristly grass.

Ben drove her out to the San Jacinto monument, a grandiose 1930s obelisk topped by a Texas star, celebrating the victory of General Sam Houston over the Mexicans. They rode to the observation deck at the top. Around the monument's landscaped park, square miles of oil refineries stretched away. From here, JSC might not have existed; the oil-price fluctuations of the 1970s had been good to Houston, and to York, looking down at the great spaghetti-bowl of pipelines below, it was obvious that Houston was built on oil money, and the space program was no more than just another local employer.

Around the base of the monument, there was a faint reek of petrochemicals.

To find an apartment, Ben drove her back to the NASA-Clear Lake area, south-east of downtown. Clear Lake, as Ben pointed out in what was evidently a standard JSC joke, was neither clear nor a lake, but actually a sluggish inlet of Galveston Bay. NASA Road One, the road from JSC, ran parallel to the coast of the Lake, and there were big communities of modern housing developments – Nassau Bay, El Lago – set between aging coastal resorts. The resort areas were old-fashioned, strange to find so close to the Space Center: faded, shabby, a little sinister, eroded by the sea and sun. York thought it must have been a hell of a shock to the locals when NASA had landed here, by Presidential decree, twenty years earlier.

The developments were all ranch houses, cute little bungalows with tiny private docks. Everything was green, prosperous, well-maintained.

York grunted. 'My God. The American dream, vintage 1962. The little home, the mom and two kids, the barbecues and the sailing. We're in *The Dick van Dyke Show*.'

'No.' Priest smiled behind his sunglasses. 'This is astronaut country, remember. You're thinking of *I Dream of Jeannie*. Anyhow, you're not giving the place much of a chance, Natalie.'

'No?'

'No. Clear Lake is a kind of academic community. That's because of JSC, and also the chemical industry in the area. It's got more PhDs per square yard than most places outside of the university towns. I figure you might feel at home here.'

'Stop trying to cheer me up, damn it, Ben.'

'I'm not! Believe me. Anyhow things could be a hell of a lot worse. Starry Town in Moscow, where the cosmonauts have to live, is more like a military barracks . . .'

The apartment complexes Ben showed her were called The Cove and El Dorado and Lakeshire Place and The Leeward. A lot of them looked good, and the more expensive had access to the water.

211

But they were all depressingly similar within: boxy, with inefficient air-conditioning, plainly furnished, and with unimaginative prints hanging on the walls.

She settled on a place called Portofino. The architecture was as dull as everywhere else, but it did have a large, clean-looking swimming pool which she was anxious to try out.

When she'd settled terms, the landlady – a compact, knowing woman with an incomprehensibly thick Texas accent, and wearing a T-shirt saying '*Kiss Me, I Don't Smoke*' – left the two of them alone in the apartment.

York sensed Ben move away from her, subtly.

She went to the window. The air was so thick it was hard to breathe. There were thick gray clouds overhead now, threatening rain and trapping even more of the heat.

She felt a dumb misery envelop her, as dense as the air. *What am I doing here, in this lousy apartment, working in this goddamn Boys' Town?*

Out back of the apartment building, she spotted a car that had gotten mildewed from the moisture in the air.

Friday, December 8, 1978
Wasatch, Utah

As he flew into Salt Lake City Gregory Dana got a spectacular view of the Lake. Feeder streams glistened like snail tracks, and human settlements were misty gray patches spread along ribbons of road. The morning was bright and clear, the sky huge and transparent and appearing to reach all the way down to the desert surface far below the plane.

Dana allowed himself briefly to imagine that he was landing on some foreign planet, a world of parched desert and high, isolated inland seas.

To most people, he reflected, the complex world of human society was the entire universe, somehow disengaged from the physical underpinning of things. Most people never formed any sense of *perspective*: the understanding that the whole of their lives was contained in a thin slice of air coating a small, spinning ball of rock, that their awareness was confined to a thin flashbulb slice of geological time, that they inhabited a universe which had emerged from, and was inexorably descending into, conditions unimaginably different from those with which they were familiar.

Even the view of the air traveler gave a perspective that hadn't been available to any of the generations who went before. *If spaceflight gives us nothing else than an awareness of our true nature*, he thought, *then that alone will justify its cost.*

He glanced back into the cabin. Most of his fellow passengers – even those attached to NASA and the space program, as he was – had their faces buried in documents, or books, or newspapers.

Morton Thiokol sent a car to meet him at the airport. The driver – young, breezy, anonymous behind mirrored sunglasses – introduced himself as Jack, and loaded Dana's bags into the trunk, although Dana kept his briefcase with him.

Jack drove onto the freeway heading north, toward Brigham City. The driver told him that he was to be taken straight to the first test firing of the SRB, the new Saturn VB-class Solid Rocket Booster.

Dana grumbled at this, but saw no option but to submit.

Dana had been asked by Bert Seger to participate in the Critical Design Review of the new SRB, the formal checkpoint that marked the end of this phase of the rocket's development. The use of solid rockets in a man-rated booster stack was one of the most controversial elements of the whole Saturn upgrade program, and it was one on which NASA was determined to be seen to be absolutely clean.

But Dana had been uncertain about working with Udet, about his own ability to get the Marshall people to listen to him. And anyway, such an assignment was well outside his own area of competence.

Seger had insisted: 'You can inspect what you like, and recommend what you like, and I'll make sure you get a hearing. We have to get this right, Doctor Dana . . .'

But what was he to learn from viewing a test firing? This was a stunt, obviously, designed to impress and overwhelm him. It was typical of Hans Udet; Dana felt immediately irritated at the waste of time.

He opened up his briefcase with a snap; as if in revenge he turned away from the landscape unrolling beyond the car windows, and buried his attention in technical documentation.

The car delivered him to the Wasatch Division of Morton Thiokol, a few miles outside Brigham City. With a touch of Dana's elbow, Jack led the way to a small prefabricated office module, set on trestles a little way from the dusty road.

The test site was a bleak, isolated clutter of buildings, cupped by

213

a broad crater-shaped depression in the desert. Low hills peppered with green-black vegetation rimmed the site. To the east, blue mountains shouldered over the horizon.

Jack pointed to a test rig, a couple of miles away. Dana squinted to see in the brilliant light; he made out a slim white cylinder laid flat against the ground.

The office module, surprisingly enough, was air-conditioned, equipped with a refrigerator and some coffee-making equipment, and Dana breathed in its warm, moist air with relief. Inside, Hans Udet was waiting for him.

'Doctor Dana. I'm delighted to see you here today.'

Really? Quite a contrast to the last time we were up against each other, Hans, at the Mars mission mode presentations in Huntsville . . .

Dana shook the German's hand, warily, and glanced around the office module. There was a cutaway model of the SRB, and artists' impressions executed in the compelling, visionary style which had, Dana thought, become so much of a cliche from NASA in recent years. A loudspeaker taped high on one wall carried muted commentary on the progress of the test.

Obviously this office was a honeytrap, designed to impress visiting decision makers. *Like me. I suppose I should be flattered.*

'We're alone here?'

'Doctor Dana, this is a big day for us – the first integrated test firing – and I particularly wanted you to be here to see it. As my guest. Come; sit down. Let me take your briefcase. Would you like some coffee? – or perhaps cold beer –'

Dana accepted a glass of orange juice – chilled, it felt like, almost to freezing – and he sat on a stackable chair.

Udet was already moving into what appeared to be a standard sales pitch. 'I want you to be aware of the full background of our SRB project,' Udet said smoothly. He pointed to a chart showing the intended launch profile. 'The Solid Rocket Boosters will stand one hundred and fifty feet tall from engine bell to nose, and will be twelve feet in diameter; in the Saturn VB's launch configuration four of them will be strapped to the core MS-IC first stage. The SRBs will supplement the MS-IC's thrust with more than five million pounds of thrust combined, making the VB capable of raising more than four hundred thousand pounds of payload to low Earth orbit: that is, *twice* as much as the base Saturn V. The MS-IC itself features many upgraded features, including the new F-1A main engines, manufactured with new techniques and materials. The SRBs will be the largest solid-fueled rockets in the world – and, for economy, the first designed for reuse . . .'

'And the first used on a manned booster.'

'Yes, that is so.'

Dana opened his briefcase and spread a briefing document across his lap. 'Doctor Udet, our time is limited. Can we get to specifics? It is the launch sequence which particularly concerns me.'

Udet's eyes were pale blue behind his glasses. The German studied Dana, analytically, as if computing the way forward. Then, every movement evidently calculated, he sat down beside Dana; he sat easily, with his arms open, in a friendly and welcoming posture. 'I understand your concerns, Doctor Dana; I have read the memoranda you have prepared for Bert Seger. My purpose today is to alleviate those concerns – to assure you that they are groundless.'

Despite himself, Dana felt disoriented by Udet's control, his Prussian-aristocratic command. Dana's glasses had slipped; he pushed them back, and tried to speak forcefully. 'And my concern is that no compromise in safety is being made, for the sake of subsidiary goals such as reusability, or schedule, or economy.'

'Of course. And if I –'

'Can we return to the question of the launch?' Fumbling in his case, he extracted a brief, handwritten note. 'I have completed a preliminary analysis of some failure modes during launch. I will of course document this formally.'

'I'm sure we have considered every failure mode, Doctor Dana.'

'I'm sure you have too,' Dana murmured. 'But perhaps we could review this. As an example: it appears that just before launch the Solid Rocket Boosters, and the rest of the stack, will be subject to what my son calls a "stretch" – when the MS-IC's engines fire up a few seconds before the release of the stack's hold-down posts.'

Udet's smile was thin. 'I am familiar with the astronauts' term.'

'The structural loads stored in the assembly by this "stretch" will cause the whole stack to vibrate on release, shivering back and forth for the first few moments of flight, with a period of three or four seconds.' Dana prodded at a part of the page he had underlined heavily. 'According to this rough outline, you will see that the greatest stresses on the joints of your segmented rockets are likely to occur during the "stretch" and the subsequent bounce; I believe the stresses at that time might even exceed those of the period of maximum dynamic pressure during the flight.'

'The joints are designed to resist such pressures. All of this is under consideration,' Udet said, sounding a little testy.

215

'I'm sure it is. But I will want to see documentary evidence of tests before I could consider signing off the Critical Design Review. I have further recommendations.' He dug out more pieces of paper. 'I would like to see the rubber of the segment seals replaced with a composite, temperature-resistant material. The field joints should be redesigned. All of this will reduce the possible flexing of the joints during the "stretch" by many orders of magnitude. In addition, viewing ports for launch-site testing and electrical heating for the joints should be installed . . .'

As he went through his points, Udet listened politely, imperturbable.

A new announcement, incomprehensible to Dana, came over the sound system, and Udet turned his head to listen. When he turned back to Dana his smile was restored, creasing his papery cheeks. 'We will talk further,' Udet said. 'But the test fire will begin in a few minutes. If you will accompany me – you may bring your drink if you wish . . .'

Dana followed. Oddly, he felt as if he had acted without manners – as if it had been crass to raise all these niggling objections, on a day of such visionary significance.

Udet drove Dana out to the test range, in an open cart like a golf buggy.

They stopped perhaps a mile from the booster. Udet, with an outstretched hand, helped Dana from the cart, and then to climb down a short metal ladder into an open trench. The trench was maybe four feet deep, a crude affair lined with rough-finished concrete. A technician handed Dana a set of goggles and a white hard-hat.

The test booster was a cylinder of slim white, lying flat against the orange ground. The booster was strapped to the Earth by huge rectangular frames, and its nose was capped by an immense, open half-sphere. *As if it is a fallen god, pinned down, lest it escape.* The field joints between the casing segments gleamed gold in the sun, which was now climbing toward noon. The big engine bell flared toward a low hill.

Men walked around the booster, dwarfed by its white flanks; instruments and cameras, mounted on delicate-looking tripods, clustered about the rig, and there were probes inserted into the black mouth of the engine bell itself.

Udet tapped Dana's shoulder and leaned toward him. 'We still have a couple of minutes. Let us speak freely, you and I.'

Dana studied him suspiciously.

Udet said, 'I want to talk about *risk*. I think this lies at the heart of the debate we are engaged in. We have accumulated, in this country, the best part of two decades' experience in designing and operating manned spacecraft systems. And in that time, the concept of risk has –' Uncharacteristically Udet hesitated, evidently searching for the right word.

' "Evolved?" ' Dana suggested dryly.

Udet arched an eyebrow. 'Very well. "Evolved." We have found it necessary to develop principles more sophisticated than simple admonitions to "protect the crew at all costs," and so forth.'

' "We?" '

'Yes,' Udet snapped. '*We* who are responsible, ultimately, for the safety of the young men we loft into orbit, as opposed to those – with all respect – who merely stand to one side. Such as yourself.

'The evaluation of "risk" itself evolves during the progress of a mission. Consider this. The Apollo 12 booster was hit by lightning during launch. The spacecraft reached orbit safely, but Apollo's electrical systems had been severely battered, and it was impossible to check if the parachutes in the Command Module would function correctly. On balance, it was decided to continue the mission; once we have survived a launch, however problematic, if we do not proceed we must subject another crew to the greater risks of a *further* launch to reach the same point. And as for the parachutes, if a return to Earth would kill Conrad and his crew, it may as well be after a lunar landing as before.'

'I know the story, Doctor Udet. What is your point?'

'Simply that this whole business –' Udet waved a hand ' – is just the realization, the fabrication in metal and rubber and cryogenic liquids, of a *dream*. A dream which you and I share. But it is not a dream which can be achieved without risk. Our mission, therefore, is not to eliminate risk but to *manage* it. And it is this perspective which must inform your review of the project . . .'

Dana felt uncertain, once more, in the face of Udet's calm competence and assurance. Could he really oppose this man's powerful conviction?

Over a remote PA, a countdown began. Udet stood upright in the trench, his silver hair shining in the sunlight. *It is for moments like this that Udet is alive*, Dana thought.

'Later,' Udet murmured to Dana, 'I would like you show you the manufacture of the propellant, here at Wasatch; the compound is mixed in great bowls and then poured straight into the casing

217

segments. It has the look and feel of rubber . . .' *Thirteen. Twelve.*
The rocket was clear of personnel now; it lay, alone and shining, on the desert floor.

'. . . The final compound will ignite only under extreme heat, and is not sensitive to static, friction or impact. It is very safe, you see.'
Six. Five.

'Indeed, a small rocket motor is required to fire *inside* the casing to ignite the propellant. And once ignited there is no need for pumps, or cryogenic storage; a solid rocket simply burns . . .'
Yes. And, once lit, it can't be doused.
Two. One.

White flame lanced from the engine bell, in an instant of eerie silence. The flame reached out toward the bland hillside behind the tethered rocket, and to Dana, dazzled, it was as if the desert sunlight had been dimmed, the blue and orange of the landscape leached to gray by comparison with this fire – rocket light, hotter than the surface of stars – which humans had brought to Earth.

And now the noise reached him.

At first there was a deep rumbling which seemed to emerge from the depths of the Earth. And then came a fierce crackling, a pulse of high-frequency sound that was like the tearing of an immense sheet of canvas, a sound that flapped his clothes and blew at his hair. He felt the ground shake, as if suffering repeated blows from a great invisible hammer.

Udet leaned over toward him and shouted. 'This is the dream, Doctor Dana.' He stared at Dana, his hair mussed and coated with orange dust. 'Zero to twenty million horse power, in less than a second! *This* is what I wanted you to see; *this* is what we are working for, you and I; *this* is what you must always bear in mind, as you make your studies, and file your reports.'

Dana felt overwhelmed by the man's intensity. Of course, Udet was right. It was indeed a dream, a dream of rocket light, made real in the deserts of the western United States, before the eyes of two battered old men from Europe. The dream of the *Mittelwerk*.

The flames from the captive rocket continued to plume, and smoke billowed against the hillside, stained orange and gray by desert dust.

February, 1979
Lyndon B. Johnson Space Center, Houston

The room was dark and warm. Several of the trainees around York had their feet up on their desks. One – Bob Gold, a big-eared Texan, a few feet ahead of York – had his head resting on the fold of fat at the back of his shaven neck, and he was snoring in a thin, bird-like cackle.

The instructor at the front fumbled another Vu-graph slide onto the projector. The focus of the projector was out, so the image was blurred at the center. The instructor, an astronaut called Ralph Gershon, picked up his extensible pointer and tapped at the projection screen, making it oscillate and blurring the image further.

Gershon didn't fumble like this because he was nervous, York perceived wearily, but because he didn't care enough to concentrate hard on what he was doing.

'This here is the ECLSS of your basic MEM configuration,' Gershon said. 'Take a good look at it. Maybe your life is going to depend on knowing your way around this baby some day.'

The new slide was a block diagram of bewildering complexity, covered with spidery arrows and puzzling acronyms. This new picture showed no resemblance, as far as York could see, to anything she'd been shown before.

The snoozer ahead of York gulped, and chewed on a loose piece of phlegm.

'Now,' said Gershon, tapping the diagram again, 'here you got your basic ECLSS concept, which is likely to fly whatever choices we make about the rest of the MEM's engineering. You got your standard two-bed molecular sieve here for cee-oh-two scrubbing. And the aitch-two-oh management is by means of this multi-filtration unit here.' He pronounced the prefix *mult-eye*. 'That supplements the output of your fuel cells. And your atmospheric gases are cryogenically stored, of course. As opposed to being stored under pressure.' Gershon blinked around the room. 'Anybody figure out why that is? Because it's a better weight-to-volume ratio. And we don't operate any kind of oh-two recovery system here. We take all our breathing air along with us, and just vent the waste. You want to tell me why? Because the MEM is a short-duration craft, and the weight of the recovery systems wouldn't be justified . . .'

York realized that this trick of Gershon's – of asking a question of his class and carelessly answering it before anyone got a chance to speak – was slowly driving her crazy.

219

Gershon told the class they should complete the copy of the diagram in their books, and he wandered out of the room in the direction of the coffee machine.

Although Gershon clearly knew his way around MEM designs, he was not a trained educator. He was a short, wiry, black man in his mid-thirties. Apparently he hailed from Iowa, but he'd been hanging around Houston long enough for a Texan drawl to color the way he pronounced his vowels, making the acronyms even tougher to cut through; ECLSS came out like '*Aye she ale esh esh* ...' And after so many years here Ralph Gershon was just another rookie astronaut, still waiting for his first flight, ploughing through another lousy assignment, lecturing to a new class of bright-eyed hopefuls.

Gershon was a depressing role model, for York.

She flicked desultorily through her coloring book. That was what the students called the volumes that were passed out at the start of each lecture; they were fat books containing diagrams, no text. The diagrams on the Vu-graph charts were supposed to be identical to the diagrams in the books, except for the colors, and the rookies – all of them highly qualified specialists – had to work like grade school students, coloring in their copies of the diagrams with pens. They were supposed to memorize every transistor and valve and duct and pipe and wiring conduit in every goddamn spaceship, planned or actual.

Coloring books were a fantastically dumb way to teach anybody anything, she'd quickly decided. And besides, all the systems knowledge in the world wouldn't have helped Jim Lovell's Apollo 13 crew when that oxygen tank blew.

And you also had the problem that the MEM design in particular was a moving target. The MEM was being built in a different, more leisurely manner from previous generations of spacecraft, with the basic research – into biconic shapes, ballutes, plug-nozzle rocket engines – being proven *before* the first ships were assembled. It was all a marked contrast to Apollo, and, she supposed, a lot more logical; but because of that the ECLSS diagram in her book didn't match in all its detail the diagram on the screen, which in turn, probably, didn't match the reality of what anybody would build, one day. So why did she need to fill her head with all this crap?

It was all part of their ascan syllabus, a document that was, incredibly, set out like a flowchart. You followed the flow, doing a one-hour module on subsystems here, a couple of hours of reading on space medicine there, until you passed barriers in the flowchart

220

which *proved* you'd reached another level of skill. It was formulaic, an education system designed by an engineer, not a teacher.

It was typical NASA, really. Not that she could get anyone to listen to that kind of complaint.

The rookies got to bring in their own pens, though, and York derived some ignoble pleasure in producing books full of Day-Glo orange engine bells, puce oxygen tanks, and electric blue reaction control solenoids.

After the class broke up she ran into Ben Priest. Ben was heavily caught up in the training for his own first flight: Apollo-N, the NERVA 2 orbital proving mission, planned for the end of next year.

Today he was frustrated too, hot as hell and irritated after spending all day in a niggling integrated sim.

For some reason, the usual silent barrier between the two of them wasn't working today. They just stood in the corridor, close together, facing each other, Ben's shirt crumpled and open at the neck. Maybe it was their shared frustration. Anyhow, today she just *knew*.

They got in Ben's car and went back to her apartment.

It was their third time, in as many years.

'Those damn coloring books. It's like learning to drive a car in a classroom,' she growled. She took another mouthful of Coke and rested the chilled, dew-coated can against her chest.

Ben, lying back in her bed, laughed and lifted his own drink, a Budweiser. 'Well, if you're sick of the classroom, grab time in the simulators.'

'Christ, Ben, we can't get near the sims. That's another problem. They're too damn full of astronauts. I mean *real* astronauts,' she said bitterly. 'Dumb fighter jocks like you, who are really getting to fly.'

'Never mind that. Find time anyway.'

'The sims are booked until three a.m.!'

He looked impatient. He pulled a sheet up over his flat stomach. 'Then come in at three a.m. What do you want, Natalie? Nobody said it was going to be easy. You got to get ahead by getting ahead around here. Put yourself out. Make them notice you. Bang on Chuck Jones's door, demanding assignments.'

She grunted. 'It's a damn stupid way to run a space program.'

'Maybe so, but it's our way.'

Lying there he looked oddly restless, though she wasn't sure how she could tell. She knew he was going to have to go back to JSC later this evening. But she felt a need to keep him here, to keep talking. She was imposing on him, but Ben was the only intimate York had out here.

In fact, since the Three Mile Island thing a few weeks ago, she'd even lost touch with some of her friends back at Berkeley; they'd decided it was immoral of her to keep on working in a Big Technology program that was going to fly nuclear materials into *orbit*, for God's sake.

Without Ben to beat up about all the problems she was having inside the program, she suspected she'd go quickly crazy.

'Anyway,' he said now, 'how's Mike?'

She looked away. 'I don't know. Busy. Wound up like a watch spring.' She hesitated. 'Now you tell me how Karen is.'

He winced. 'I didn't deserve that.'

'. . . I guess not. I'm sorry.'

He grunted. 'Me too.'

She gripped her Coke can, trying to force herself to focus on the issue. *We can talk about Mars, and culture clashes at NASA, but we always skirt around us.* 'I don't know whether Mike wants me to follow my career here or not.'

'Would it make a difference?'

No. Not any more. She couldn't bring herself to say it.

Priest drained his beer. 'I think you're kind of making your choice, Natalie. And maybe Mike is too. It's a pity. I love you both. But I guess we're not all cut out to bake bread and raise kids.'

'Probably not. You neither, huh.'

He looked defensive. 'What the hell's that supposed to mean?'

'Nothing. I'm sorry, Ben.'

He cradled his beer can, avoiding her eyes. 'I've thought of leaving home.'

'What for?'

He looked irritated. 'What do you think? To come here, for Christ's sake. To be with you.'

'Oh.' That took her aback. 'So,' she said gently. 'What's stopping you?'

'. . . I don't think I can leave Karen.'

'Why not? Do you still love her?'

He turned to her and ruffled her hair. 'Come on, Natalie, you're a scientist. What kind of question is that? What does "love" mean when you've been married to someone for more years than you can

222

count, when you've raised a son ... You go beyond love. Love's for teenagers.'

'So, why don't you leave?'

'Because I owe her.' He shook his head, irritated. 'No, that's not right. Because we have a kind of deal, going right back to the start. Karen has had to – invest in me. Every time I fly –'

'Oh, I get it,' she said. 'She's a Navy wife.'

'Don't you dismiss it, Natalie. It might seem odd to you, but it's a stable system. Karen has bought all my risk, over the years, and I'm asking her to buy even more when I go up on Apollo-N. I owe her. Maybe we'll split up; but if we do, it ought to be her decision.'

She grunted. 'Well, that's as clear as gumbo.'

He laughed. 'So what are you telling me? That if I turned up here with a suitcase, you'd have me?'

She thought about it. 'I don't know,' she said honestly. 'I could never be a Navy wife.'

'I know it.' He cupped her cheek. 'You're something new, Natalie.'

She sipped her Coke. Her thoughts drifted back to NASA. 'You know, in the Office, the Old Heads don't even want us around ...'

'*Old Heads?*'

'Ben, don't pretend you haven't heard that before. *Old Heads.* It's what we call you guys, the senior cadres.'

'Even me?'

'Even you, asshole. And the worst of the Old Heads are the oldest. Chuck Jones and the rest of the Mercury generation.'

'Oh, come on,' Ben said. 'Those guys are straight enough. I mean, these are the good guys. The ones who've stuck with the program, trying to get another flight; the ones who didn't take early retirement to make Amex commercials or take worthless corporate directorships, or appear on talk shows, or sell off bits of their spacesuits. Guys like Joe Muldoon and John Young and Fred Haise and Chuck Jones ...'

'Maybe so.' It was hard for her to remember, even now, the reverence she'd brought here for those guys. But it was remarkable what a deep change of attitude could be induced by a couple of months of being snubbed by a person. 'All they talk about is *flying,*' she said, peevish. 'And goose hunting, and racing their Corvettes in from their cute little houses in El Lago.'

'Well, how do you expect them to behave? Those guys are basically test pilots.'

'But I'm not going to be taught how to fly! Anyway, it's more than that. Even the science activities we want to do are frowned on.'

'By Chuck Jones too?'

'By Jones especially. Like, do you know Bob Gold, in my group?'

'Sure.'

'Bob wanted a leave-of-absence faculty appointment at the University of Texas, to start next year. Ben, when we were inducted we were all promised the chance of appointments like that – back at our home universities, keeping our careers alive. Well, Jones wouldn't do it. He said he needed Bob here! For what, for Christ's sake? To make up the numbers in the Crew Compartment Fit and Function tests? Ben, for some of this work all they need is a warm body. You don't even have to be *conscious*. Anyhow, now Bob is thinking of quitting.'

'Then let him.' That restlessness she'd perceived in him seemed to be getting closer to the surface. 'Look, I hear what you say. But you got to work this out for yourself, Natalie –'

York wasn't done yet. 'And there's more. Maybe you're sitting in the Office trying to catch up with your reading. Then some grinning asshole walks in and says, "Hey, Natalie, there's a meeting over in Building 4 on EVA overshoes, or S-band antenna mounts, or some other damn thing, that I think you ought to attend." So what do you do?'

'You attend,' said Priest firmly. He set his beer can on the bedside table with a kind of finality. 'Listen to me, now, Natalie, for once in your life. You need to come to a decision. All this damn griping . . . If you want to go back to academic life, back to your old work, then just pick up and go.'

'Plenty have.'

'Sure. And plenty more will. But if you want to stick around, you got to play the game. By *their* rules, the Old Heads, or whatever you want to call them. Jack Schmitt was the most successful scientist-astronaut in the '60s. How come?'

'Because he was the best geologist?'

'He was a fine geologist. But there were plenty of fine geologists who left the program, leaving Schmitt standing there. Schmitt made himself useful, and in ways the other guys – the decision makers – could recognize. He was asked to be the astronaut representative on the Apollo lunar surface gear, and he did it. And without waiting around to be asked he went on to cover the whole of the Lunar Module's descent stage. He worked on lunar exploration strategies.

224

He helped to get the other guys to take the geology seriously.'

'But, Ben – *Schmitt never walked on the Moon.*'

Priest shook his head. 'You aren't listening. Because Schmitt was around at the time, the geology we did on the Moon was a hell of a lot better than it might otherwise have been. You ought to think about that. The late landings got canceled under him, and that was that. But if any scientist was ever going to walk on the Moon, it would have been Schmitt. He gave himself the best possible chance.' He eyed her. 'Anyhow, Schmitt has had a tour in Moonlab. He's got as close to the Moon as sixty miles, at least. And you know Ralph Gershon, don't you?'

'Sure. One Grade A asshole.'

'No,' Ben snapped now. 'You're being the asshole, Natalie. I'm sorry, but that's the truth. Listen: Gershon is having just as hard a time as you, but from a different angle. He's the best pilot in the Agency, and most of us know it. But he doesn't fit in. He's a different generation from these other guys. He's fought in a dirtier war, and maybe they think that's left him a little dirty.

'But,' Priest went on, 'Ralph hasn't given up. He's doing his damnedest to get a seat. Here he is, for instance, making himself useful by nursemaiding you guys.'

'But he's a lousy instructor!'

Priest shook his head. 'Wise up. That's not the measure. Taking the assignment, completing it, being a team player: *that's* what counts. And on top of that Ralph spends half his life out at Langley, and Rockwell, wherever the hell they are trying out bits of MEM concepts. And you know why? Because he figures that when push comes to shove, he doesn't want there to be anybody around here who knows more about flying the MEM than he does. Just like Schmitt, he's giving himself the best shot he can.'

'And that's what I should do?'

'That's what you should do. More. Stop griping, for Christ's sake. You got a great opportunity here. Get on the sims. Grab all the training you can, no matter how obscure and irrelevant it seems. Go to the meetings about the damn EVA gloves, or whatever. And try to find ways to leverage your own skills. Get on the Mars landing site selection board, for instance . . .'

'I didn't know there was one.'

'Well, there you are,' he said heavily.

'Goddamn it, Ben, I hate it when you give me advice.'

He laughed. 'Only because I'm right.' He checked the time on his Rolex watch, which he'd put on her bedside table. 'Shit. I'll have to go. Classroom work for me too, now. The latest modifications to the NERVA control systems.'

'So,' she said. She stroked his back. 'We've still got unfinished business, huh?'

'Yeah. Unfinished business. We'll talk.'

He swung his legs out of the bed.

A couple of weeks later, life got more interesting.

York's cadre was moved on to systems training. York worked her way up through the hierarchy of training systems, at first paper-based, later electronic and computer-driven, heading toward a more complete representation of the spacecraft she would fly.

There were single-systems trainers – fragments of Apollo control consoles – set up in offices scattered through Building 5, with computers running simple simulations behind them; and there were integrated trainers for each of the three crew stations in an Apollo Command Module.

Finally she was taken into Building 9, the Mockup and Integration Lab. Full-sized training mockups of spacecraft littered the floor of the hangar-sized building. The equipment here was for generic training, to develop skills applicable to any flight; the more elaborate simulators were assigned to specific missions.

This was a low-tech place, the trainers scuffed and scarred, visibly aged. There were chalked graffiti on the wall, and the work benches scattered around the place were littered with mundane items: paper towels, a big pail full of empty Coke cans. No astronaut on the active roster came down here. If she came in on a weekend, the place was generally deserted; after so many years of routine, long-duration missions, there was pretty much a nine-to-five atmosphere about much of JSC.

Building 9 made her feel her place, she thought; as an ascan she was a long way down the food chain.

She tried out the air bearing facility, an office chair suspended by a hovercraft-like cushion of downwards air jets. She floated over the epoxy-resin floor like an ice-hockey puck, pulling her way around a mocked-up Skylab workstation, learning about action and reaction in an environment that simulated zero G, if only in two dimensions.

At last she clambered into the Crew Compartment Trainer, a full-scale mockup of an Apollo Command Module, which sat like a metal teepee in the middle of the floor of Building 9. The hatch was incredibly small, and she had to swing herself in feet first.

The three couches were just metal frames slung with canvas slings, constricting, jammed against each other. Under the couches, in the fat base of the cone, was a storage area called the lower equipment bay.

York sat in the center couch, the Command Module Pilot's. She was looking up toward the apex of the cone. The windows seemed small and far away; even though the hatch was open she felt enclosed in here. Directly in front of her there was a big, battleship-gray, one-hundred-and-eighty-degree instrument panel. There were five hundred controls: toggle switches, thumb wheels, pushbuttons, and rotary switches with click stops. The readouts were mainly meters, lights and little rectangular windows containing either 'gray flags' or 'barber poles'; the barber pole was a stripy piece of metal that would fill the window when the setting had to be changed. There was a tiny computer key-pad, a small cathode ray tube, and 8-balls – artificial horizons. There were small joysticks and pushbuttons: translational controllers, to work the Command Module's clusters of attitude rockets.

The panel seemed complex, almost ludicrously so. How the hell was she going to find her way around all this?

She experimented with the switches. They were mostly of two types: little silver three-way tabs, or – for more critical functions – cylindrical levers, two-way, that you had to pull out before they would move. These would be awkward in pressure-suit gloves, she thought. The switches were protected by little metal gates on either side, to save them being kicked by a free-fall boot. She worked her way across the panel, practicing flipping the dead switches, getting used to the feel of them.

There were little diagrams etched into the panel, she saw, circuit and flowcharts. She consulted her manuals. Here, for example, was one diagram which connected a set of switches that controlled water output from the fuel cells. The little gray lines mirrored the way the water flowed, either to controls for the storage tanks, or for the dumps.

All the switches were contained by one diagram or another. Once she started to see the system behind the diagrams, she began to figure the logic in the panel, how the switches clustered and related to each other.

Sitting alone inside the quiet Apollo, she worked her way through her manuals, learning how the spaceship was flown.

Monday, June 11, 1979
Starry Town, Moscow

The convoy of buses skirted around Moscow, following the freeways. They were heading northeast, toward Kaliningrad. There was a lot of traffic, most of it freight, and the road was lined with apartment blocks, huge, drab monoliths.

Joe Muldoon stared out of a grimy window. It was the most depressing sight he had ever seen.

Here they were, hauling ass direct from the airport, straight out of the city to Starry Town. This was Muldoon's second visit here. Their first trip out had been better. Then, the American crew – Muldoon, Bleeker and Stone, with the NASA technical people and program managers – had stayed in an Intourist Hotel. It was no palace, but it was right in the middle of downtown Moscow, with Red Square and the Kremlin a walk away. Every morning the Soviets had arrived with buses to take the Americans out to Starry Town, and every evening they'd brought them back.

And the hotel had had a bar, in the basement.

That bar had proved to be a magnet for foreign nationals, one of the few congenial places in the city. There were other Americans to be found there, and Germans, Cubans, Czechs. Muldoon and the NASA guys had made that bar their own.

There'd been no harm done, save for a few late nights and bleary mornings. But in retrospect, he could see the problem for the program managers. Not to mention the Soviets. *In that bar, they are out of control, those Americanskis!*

So this time out, things were arranged differently.

At Kaliningrad the convoy turned east toward Shchelkovo. The architecture changed. Now there were wooden houses, along both sides of the road; unlike the Soviet-style apartments closer to Moscow, these were painted brightly, and they were decorated with ornate wood carvings. Muldoon could smell wood smoke. And every few hundred yards there were hand-pumps.

It was all kind of cute and rural, but desperately primitive. Wooden houses and hand-pumps, next door to a cosmonaut training center.

The convoy turned right on an unmarked road, into a pine forest. Just around the bend there was a guard post. After a couple of minutes' checking with the drivers, the convoy went on into a large clearing in the forest. There were several tall apartment buildings

228

here, a few low office buildings, some stores. At one end of the clearing there were small lakes, at the other a dozen large, blocky structures.

Shawled babushkas pushed baby carriages along the sidewalks, while the noise of jet aircraft ripped down constantly from the air.

This was Starry Town, purpose-built to house and train the cosmonaut corps. It struck Muldoon as a cross between a university campus and a military training camp.

The driver pointed out the hydro pool, a neutral buoyancy trainer, the Cosmonaut Museum. At the center of the clearing, facing the convoy, was a statue of Gagarin: larger than life, heroic, inspirational.

Muldoon grimaced. There were no statues to *him*, anywhere, even though he'd gone so much further than Gagarin. But then, he wasn't safely dead.

His apartment was huge. More like a suite. He wandered through the rooms. The place was crammed with furniture, all of it heavy and old-fashioned: sofas, overstuffed chairs, heavy tables. There was a thick shag pile on the floor, and flock paper on every inch of wall. He found the bathroom, and there he had to laugh. There was no soap, and there were no plugs for the bath or sink, and only one towel.

And probably a bug in every damn light fitting.

He glanced out of the window. He saw white pines, barbed wire. A black limousine cruised along one of the central access roads: probably KGB, Muldoon thought. *Home from home. Like a fucking prison camp.*

He jammed a facecloth in the plug hole and ran a bath.

He dressed in his dinner suit and went down to the bar.

It wasn't much like the Intourist place in Moscow. But there was a barman, polishing glasses; he had a thin, Asiatic face. Muldoon asked for a beer. It proved to be cold; it was a Czech brand, and it tasted good. There was nobody else here. Some kind of god-awful piano music tinkled over a PA.

There was going to be a reception tonight, before a dinner in the place's dining room, all to celebrate the progress of Moonlab-Soyuz. Fred Michaels himself was supposed to be here, and God alone knew how many Soviet big fish. *You'll have to take it easy, Muldoon. Watch what you say. No more hostages to fortune.* He knew

229

what to expect at the dinner, though: meat, lots of it, with piles of cream and butter. Deliciously bad for him.

He was clapped on the back. 'My friend Joe. I thought I might find you the first here. Welcome back to *Zvezdnoy Gorodok*, to Starry Town. You are still drinking that warmed-over piss you prefer, I see. Barman!' Vladimir Viktorenko snapped his fingers.

The barman delivered a bottle of vodka, two glasses, and a small bowl of salt. 'Here. Drink. Mother's milk,' Viktorenko ordered. He poured out a glass for Muldoon.

Muldoon took a lick of salt, then threw back the liquid; it was tasteless, harsh, clawing at his throat. 'Thank you, my friend,' he said in his hesitant Russian. 'Immediately you appear a much more handsome fellow.' The idea was that in lunar orbit, the Americans would speak Russian and the Soviets English. Muldoon was finding the language training the hardest part of the whole damn program.

Viktorenko bellowed out a laugh. He took a drink himself. 'Tonight, all five of us will drink from this bottle, and we will sign the label. When we have returned from the Moon we will meet again, and toast our success from the very same bottle.' He poured Muldoon another glass.

'To the mission,' Muldoon said.

'Oh, no.' Viktorenko threw up his hands in mock horror. 'One must not say such things. In Russia, this is bad luck. Seven hundred hours of Russian lessons, and they did not teach you this? *Tsk*. We should toast our preparations. That is enough.'

'Our preparations, then.' Muldoon drank again.

Vladimir Pavlovich Viktorenko was something of a legend among the cosmonauts – among the astronauts too, come to that. He was stocky, jovial, full of energy; his broad head with its graying crew-cut looked as if it had been bolted to his shoulders, and his ruddy cheeks were puffed up. All that borscht and potatoes. He was of the same vintage as Muldoon, roughly: he had applied to join the cosmonaut program in its first recruitment sweep, in 1960. He had co-piloted the Voskhod 3 mission in 1966, a flight in which an adapted one-man Vostok capsule had taken two men, precariously, into orbit, and Viktorenko had watched as his co-pilot had taken a space walk out of a flimsy blow-up airlock.

There had been a rumor that Viktorenko had been the Soviets' prime candidate for their abandoned lunar landing program. Muldoon had tried probing about that, but Viktorenko wouldn't open up.

And now here was Viktorenko as Muldoon's counterpart, the commander of the Soviet crew for Moonlab-Soyuz.

Viktorenko asked after Jill, Muldoon's wife, whom he'd met, and charmed the pants off, in Houston.

Muldoon just shrugged.

Jill hadn't been too ecstatic about him being back on the active roster, and returning to the *Moon*, for God's sake. Now, truth to tell, he wasn't sure if she'd even be there for him, when he got back from this jaunt.

There wasn't anything he could do about it. He had to fly; for him that was a parameter, a fact he had to live with. Even to the exclusion of Jill. He didn't express any of this, but he sensed Viktorenko understood, and the cosmonaut didn't press him.

Muldoon felt himself mellowing as the vodka went to work; he washed it down with a little more Czech beer.

Now the bar was beginning to fill up, mostly with NASA engineering staff, and a few Soviets. Adam Bleeker walked in, nodded to Muldoon, and made toward the bar.

It was encouraging to see the American and Soviet teams working together properly, Muldoon thought. It had taken a long time. The idea of joint flights had been opposed by the Soviets because of a distrust of Americans – and from within the US, for suspicion that the Soviets' true motives for cooperating were all about getting their hands on American technology.

But that was a lot of crap, Muldoon thought. After all both Soyuz and Moonlab/Apollo technologies were ten years old now; what the hell was there to steal? Besides, Carter and Ted Kennedy were putting a lot of muscle behind this trip now; for Carter, the Moonlab stunt – originally a scheme of Nixon's – had become a way of symbolizing his achievement in getting the Soviets to sign up to the SALT II treaty.

Sometimes, Muldoon felt bewildered by the pace of change; it seemed to accelerate as he got older.

'You know, Vladimir, we've been working on this program for a couple of years now, but it still seems odd to me sometimes that here we are, you and I, drinking vodka together in a Moscow bar. Even one run by the KGB.'

'How so?'

'If things had turned out differently, I might have found myself flying solo into Moscow with two nukes strapped under my wings, instead of my pajamas and toothbrush.'

'Nukes,' Viktorenko said. 'Indeed. And now we are comrades

231

again. But that is what makes us unique, men like you and I, Joe. We are aviators. We rise to our mission, whatever it may be. To the edge of the envelope, and beyond. Once our mission was to ferry nukes. And now our mission is to shake hands in space. And that we will do, as well as we can. These others – the paper-pushers, even the engineers: these others can never understand such things. It has always been so.

'Why, I remember my induction into the Vostok program,' he said. 'I was put into an isolation chamber. A box. For several weeks. And then a thermal chamber, and then a decompression chamber. And then, straight away, I was taken to the airport, put on a plane, and ordered to parachute back to Earth. The doctors, the quacks, justified such treatment by saying they needed to know how I would react on the abrupt change from an enclosed cabin to the boundlessness of infinite space. *Ha.*'

'Colonel Muldoon. Lieutenant-Colonel Viktorenko. Good to see you here . . .'

It was Fred Michaels. The NASA Administrator stood not two feet away from Muldoon, his jowls peppered lightly with sweat; behind him Muldoon recognized the Assistant Administrator, Josephson, the quintessential paper-pusher.

Viktorenko made Michaels effusively welcome, and insisted on pouring him and Josephson slugs of vodka.

Tim Josephson drew Muldoon away from the others. 'I'm sorry to bother you with this now, Joe. But we need a decision from your crew tonight.'

'On what?'

Josephson opened up a folder. 'The call-sign for your Apollo on the Moonlab–Soyuz flight. As you know, at the instigation of Congress, we've been holding a competition for elementary and high school students to come up with a name.' He began shuffling pieces of paper in the folder. 'We had seven thousand entries, submitted by teams totalling seventy-one thousand schoolchildren. Each name had to be backed up by a classroom project. The judging criteria were: eighty per cent for the quality and creativity of the project, and twenty per cent on the name's clarity during transmission, and its ability to convey the American spirit. And –'

'Oh, give me a break, Josephson. For Christ's sake.'

'I have a shortlist of the twenty-nine finalists here. We're behind schedule with this already. I thought if you and the crew could get together tonight on this, and –'

Muldoon threw back another vodka. 'Fuck off,' he said.

232

Josephson, behind his glasses, looked shocked. He opened his mouth, then closed it again. He looked down for a minute, as if composing himself.

Then, when he looked up, his face was hard.

'Colonel Muldoon. Perhaps we could discuss this elsewhere. Your room?'

Michaels looked furious, thunderous. Vladimir Viktorenko winked at him.

Ah, hell. 'Sure. Let's go.'

Muldoon drained his vodka.

'Listen, Josephson. I –'

'You listen to me.'

Josephson was still just a skinny streak of piss, but he was in absolute control of himself, Muldoon realized; and, in the confines of Muldoon's room, he had suddenly become genuinely intimidating. 'I'm tired of your drama queen incompetence, Colonel, the way you're prepared to embarrass yourself, the Agency and the government, even here. You and those other space cadets of yours are damn lucky to have got this flight at all. We've heard your public pronouncements. We know you were pissed at the cancelation of the last Moon landings. We know you think the joint flight is just a PR stunt. We know you think you're stuck here working on creaky Soviet technology.'

Muldoon had a deepening sense of danger. 'Look –'

'I had to go in front of Congress because of the way you mouthed off against the Agency. *You*, Muldoon. The astronauts go in there and they're treated like heroes. I went in and I was totally humiliated. That is never going to happen to me again. Is that clear? Now take this list.'

Staring into Josephson's narrow, calculating eyes, Muldoon saw everything – his whole life, all his aspirations – narrow into this one moment. *The road to Mars lies through this bottleneck, this piece of paper, the seventy thousand high school kids and their seven thousand fucking names, in this shitty room on the wrong side of the planet. I really have to do this.*

And the lightness of the Moon was, after all, a long time ago.

He took the list from Josephson. He looked at the names on it. *Adventure. Blake. Eagle. Endurance . . .*

Josephson said, 'Do you want me to go find Phil and –'

'No. I'm the commander. Here.' He stabbed at a name. 'This one.'

Josephson looked at the paper. '*Grissom.*'

'The commander of Apollo 1.'

Josephson studied Muldoon's face for a moment; then he nodded. He turned, and left the room.

Muldoon splashed water in his face. Then he went back to the bar, and started working on getting seriously drunk.

Thursday, April 10, 1980
Ellington Air Force Base, Houston

It took her an hour to get suited up, in the personal gear room.

The safety instructions alone were intimidating enough. Hundreds of facts were thrown at her, about D-rings and lanyards and oxygen bottles and hypoxia and survival procedures . . . *My God. And I'm only going to be a passenger in the damn thing.*

But now here she was, trussed up in a flight suit, with an oxygen mask, straps everywhere, a parachute, emergency oxygen, intercoms, survival kits for several unlikely environments tucked into her pockets. There was a sick bag in a pouch on her leg. She even had her own flight helmet, a World War One-style Snoopy hat. *Look at me, the newest fighter jock hero.*

She walked out to the field. There was Phil Stone, the senior astronaut who was going to take her up today. Stone was tall, proudly bald, the best part of fifty. He grinned and shook her hand with a big gloved mitt. 'Welcome to the carnie ride,' he said.

She smiled back uncertainly.

Beyond him, a gleaming toy on the tarmac, was the T-38 itself. The trainer was an intimidating white dart. The wings were just little stubs, incredibly short, and the sleek white shape had more of the feel of a rocket about it. It seemed incredible, against intuition, that such a small, compact machine could support itself in the air and fly.

You're getting down to the wire, Natalie. You say you want to be an astronaut. You mock the hero pilot tendency. That's fine.

But it means you have to cope with experiences like this.

Two techs helped her climb up and lower herself into the cockpit. The T-38's white-painted walls were only just wide enough for her to squeeze in. She would actually be in a separate cockpit behind Stone's, under her own little bubble of glass.

Stone clambered aboard, in front of her, and spoke over the intercom. 'Natalie, can you hear me?'

'Sure, Phil. Loud and clear. And I –'

He cut her off. 'Final safety instructions,' he said. 'I'll tell you when to close your canopy bubble. Do it slowly, Natalie. Now, your parachute is set to open as soon as you eject. That's appropriate for low altitude. Later I'll tell you when to change the setting to high altitude, when you need to have a delay between ejection and the chute opening; you do that by fastening the hook to that ring on your 'chute, and . . .'

And the noise of the jets rose to a roar, drowning out his words.

The plane started to taxi.

Stone, sitting in his bubble ahead of her, looked out calmly, his motions deft and precise. The controls before her moved in sympathy with Stone's, working themselves like a high-tech pianola.

She felt her pulse rate rising, her breathing deepening, and the rubber stink of her oxygen mask grew sharper; she felt sweat pool under her goggles, on her squeezed-up cheeks.

She consoled herself that she was going on a ride which few people would experience: high, fast, probably extraordinarily beautiful. Even if she left the corps tomorrow, she would have this to take away from here.

Yes, but I'm pretty sure I could get by without it . . .

Without warning, the plane threw itself down the runway, pressing her back into her seat. Within a few seconds she could feel the wheels leaving the ground.

The plane pitched upwards steeply, and she lost sight of the ground.

There was a layer of cloud above, lumpy cumulus. The clouds seemed to explode at her, and she shot into white mist. She was through it in a second, emerging into bright, clear sunshine.

She glanced down: the land was already lost, remote, a patchwork of faded brown with the gray shadows of clouds scattered over it.

The T-38 rose almost vertically, like a rocket. In a few seconds, the sky faded down to a deep purple.

The surface of Earth was remote, small, the works of humanity already reduced to two-dimensional splashes of color. It astonished her to think, given the facility with which she had leapt from the ground, that just a century ago no human on the planet had undergone such an experience.

Scientist-astronauts no longer had to slog through the hell of flight school. But they still needed to go through dynamic situations:

to gain experience of microgravity and acceleration, to recognize the symptoms of airsickness and hypoxia. So, the price the scientist-astronauts had to pay was regular hours of flying backseat in a Northrup T-38, the most advanced jet trainer.

Experienced astronauts were encouraged to take up the rookie scientists. And once you were up there, they could do whatever the hell they liked with you.

But she trusted Stone. She appreciated the fact that he was taking time out of his own Moonlab–Soyuz training for this piece of nursemaiding.

'How about that,' Stone said now. 'Forty-eight thousand feet. Higher than you've ever flown before, Natalie.'

So high she was already in the stratosphere, higher than the tallest mountain, so high she couldn't breathe unaided. *The edge of space, right? Welcome to your new home, space girl.*

'Okay,' Stone said now. 'Let's start gently. We'll slow her down. Can you read the airspeed?'

'Sure.'

'Follow what I do.'

When the jet got to under two hundred miles an hour, it bucked and juddered, as if the air had become a medium of invisible lumps.

'She doesn't like being reined in,' Stone said. 'So –'

He opened up the throttle and the plane surged forward. Sunlight gleamed from the carapace around York, and the Earth curved away beneath her, brilliantly lit.

'Slow roll,' Stone said now.

The Earth started to tilt, sideways. It wasn't as if she was rolling at all; York felt only a slight increase in the acceleration pushing her into her seat.

The horizon arced around her, tipping up, and the bruised purple of the stratosphere slid beneath the belly of the plane.

Then the plane righted itself, sharply. The roll had taken maybe fifteen seconds.

'Snap roll,' Stone said.

This time the plane twisted over in a second, land and sky and sun rolling around, the light strobing across her lap and hands. Her stomach resisted the roll as if she was suddenly filled with mercury.

After one and a half turns the plane finished upside down. When she looked up, she could see the Gulf of Mexico, set out like a huge map painted across a misty ceiling. Gravity plucked at her – *one negative G* – and her shoulders strained against the seat harnesses, and her helmeted head bumped against the canopy. The blood pooled in her head, making her feel stuffy, as if she were developing a cold.

'Just like the tilt table, huh, Natalie,' Stone said dryly.

He snapped the plane through a fast half-roll, righting it; the plane settled onto the level, rocking slightly in the air.

For a second they were still. Stone's precision and control were remarkable, York thought –

And then Stone threw the plane down on a dipping curve, diving down toward the remote ground; the noise of the jets increased.

'Parabolic curve,' Stone called over the jet noise.

So I should be weightless. She relaxed her arm, and watched her hand drift upwards. 'My God.' She felt the weightlessness in her gut; it was as if her organs were climbing upwards, inside her chest cavity.

'You feeling queasy?'

'A little.' She reached down, checking she could reach the bag in the pocket on her flight suit leg.

Stone made no signs of taking the plane out of its dive. 'Ah, you'll be fine. If it gets too bad, just watch the instrument panel; don't look out of the window.'

'Okay, but –'

Her sentence fell apart as Stone threw the plane into a ferocious S-shaped curve. She was turned every which way, and the glowing landscape wheeled around the canopy.

And then he took the plane into a straight dive, accelerating at the Gulf of Mexico. The ocean shone like a steel plate, far in front of her face.

At twenty thousand feet Stone hauled the nose of the plane upwards. The jets howled, and the Gs shoved her hard into her seat; her head was pushed into her shoulders, and her vision tunneled, walled by darkness.

The T-38 leapt back up to the sky, and the light reverted to its deep purple.

She tasted saliva at the back of her throat, sharp, like rusty iron. 'Phil, I don't feel so good.'

'If you have to barf, take off your oxygen mask.'

I would if I knew how.

'And turn the mix in your mask to a hundred per cent oh-two,' he said. 'Turn on your cold air blower.'

When she tried that, taking deep breaths of the oxygen, the pressure on her throat lessened.

'Anyhow,' he said, 'you wouldn't want to miss this next part.'

'Huh?'

At forty-five thousand feet, Stone lit the afterburner. Over her shoulder York could see white condensate blossoming behind the T-38. She watched the airspeed climb up toward six hundred miles an hour, higher, higher.

And through Mach 1. *Jesus.*

There was the mildest of vibrations, and then the ride got a lot smoother. The noise of the jets died to a whisper; the plane was now traveling so fast, York realized, it was outrunning its own sound.

The cockpit was a little bubble of serenity, of cool, easy flying; meanwhile, she knew, sonic thunder was washing down on the ground below. A few feet ahead of her there was Stone inside his own canopy, the only living thing within miles of her, and around them the plane was a little isolated island of reality, gleaming paint and warm air and hard surfaces, up here in the mouth of the sky. She felt somehow closer to Stone, as if bonded to him.

'How you doing now?' Stone asked, his intercom voice loud in the stillness.

'Oh, good, Phil,' she said. 'I'm good. This is –'

'I know.' He glanced over his shoulder at her, his eyes concealed by his sunglasses. 'And in orbit, you'll fly twenty times as fast, many times higher. Maybe now you'll understand better why some of us get so hooked on this stuff.'

She grimaced. 'Is my disapproval that obvious?'

'To me it is. I don't blame you. But you got to learn to understand the other guy's point of view.'

Suddenly she felt defensive. 'What do you care?'

He laughed, evidently not taking offence. 'More than you think, maybe. Natalie, I've seen you work around the Office. I think you got potential. I think we need people like you in the program. But you have to learn to work in a team.'

He threw the plane suddenly into a new series of dives and barrel rolls.

York pulled out her bag and sat in misery, staring at her knees, while the world wheeled around her.

The T-38 approached the runway like a falling rock. The landing, when it came, was soft and quick.

The techs helped York out of the cockpit. Her queasiness had gone already, but she felt disoriented, as if she had grown smaller, lighter; she felt oppressed by the heavy sky above her, the hot, moisture-laden air.

Stone slapped her on the shoulder. 'You did good,' he said.

'I nearly threw up.'

'But you didn't. I told you you got potential, York.'

'Yeah. Maybe.'

Standing there on the mundane tarmac of Ellington, she looked up at the lidded clouds, remembered how it had been, in those few seconds, to be weightless. She let her hands drift up from her sides.

Stone was watching her, observing, evaluating.

Embarrassed, she tucked her helmet under her arm, nodded curtly to Stone, and headed for the personal gear room.

Thursday, November 27, 1980
Tyuratam Cosmodrome, Kazakhstan

The sky was empty, a harsh blue. Beyond the launch facilities, the wind whipped sand across the nude, flat steppe. Bert Seger was glad he was safely tucked away behind the glass of this observation room, three miles from the pad.

Behind him there was a murmur of conversation from the other guests – program managers, minor politicians, academicians, celebrities – who seemed more intent on the food and drink, which was lavish enough, and on pursuing whatever low-level political and diplomatic gains were still to be wrung out of this joint mission.

Seger had binoculars around his neck; now he raised them and fixed them on the launch complex itself.

The N-1 booster stood tall on its pad. N for *Nosityel* – the Carrier. It sat on a porch-like structure at the lip of a flame pit. The mobile service structure had already been lowered; at three-quarters of an hour before lift-off the towers had been swung down through ninety degrees to the ground, leaving the booster exposed. Now the booster was a vertical line, out of place in this huge, horizontal landscape.

Seger saw propellants vent from the N-1's multiple stages, and flags of vapor smeared across the still, layered air. The lower three stages made up a slim, truncated cone, flaring at the base, and the upper stages and the spacecraft itself were an upright cylinder stacked on top of that. The upper stages alone were about the size and shape of a Saturn IB. And somewhere inside that complex, Seger knew, the Soyuz T-3 spacecraft was buried; and somewhere

239

within *that* were two cosmonauts, sitting out the final minutes of their countdown.

The whole thing looked like a piece of the Kremlin. Nobody could mistake an N-1 for an American design. But the N-1 was nevertheless the step-brother of the Saturn, fathered by a group of post-war German exiles who'd built on the same Nazi technology taken to White Sands by von Braun and his people. Another child of the V-2.

'Here.' Fred Michaels stood at his elbow; he held out a glass of vodka. 'You look like you could use this.'

Seger eyed the drink doubtfully. 'Thanks, but I don't encourage drinking on launch days, Fred.'

'Drink. That's an order. Bert, it's their launch, not ours.'

Seger forced himself to laugh, and took the drink. 'You're right. I suppose I'm a control nut.'

'I know the feeling. But you have to learn to relax, when there really isn't a damn thing you can do to change the course of events.'

Michaels was right, of course. The Soviets and Americans had exchanged mission control staff for this flight, with some American controllers being stationed at Kalinin. And here at Tyuratam the Americans had been let into the cosmodrome as far as this observation bunker. But that was the extent of it. There was no way Seger, or any of the American staff, could exert any influence over the way this launch developed. 'I'm just glad they aren't two of *our* boys up there,' he said. 'I wouldn't let this damn thing fly. Fred, we wouldn't even man-rate the N-1.'

Michaels, sleek, in control, dug his antique watch out of his vest pocket and checked the time. 'So the Soviet space program is all hat and no horse, eh, Bert?'

Seger sipped his drink. It was sour vodka, but the alcohol seemed to have no effect on him. 'It's not so funny when you know as much as we do, now, about the Soviets' preparations for launch. They do a lot of check-out in their assembly building. But then there's very little check-out once the thing gets to the pad. Hell, there's hardly even any electronic monitoring gear there, and only a limited computer interface. It lets them get to a launch point faster, but at the cost of a hell of a lot of reliability. No wonder they suffered so many failures with this booster.

'And did you know they've got a roll axis with pitch and yaw control only? That damn thing can't control its own flight azimuth, and they have to swivel the whole support structure to align –'

'Give me that in English, Bert.'

240

'The Saturn V can steer itself into orbit, with its on-board computer. The N-1 can't. Depending on where they want to head, they have to *point* the thing . . .'

This was the Soviets' main cosmodrome, their nearest equivalent to Kennedy. It was lost in Soviet Central Asia, a couple of hundred miles east of the Aral Sea: where the Americans used the Atlantic as their firing range, the Soviets used the huge, empty heart of their country. The nearest town was Tyuratam, a small railway junction fifteen miles away, which had remained poor, shabby and backward, despite the spectacular cosmonaut hotel planted in the middle of it.

The launch facility in use today was isolated even from the rest of the cosmodrome, situated maybe twenty miles further to the east. *They're taking no chances. And I don't blame them.*

Seger felt cut off here, isolated, impotent. *I'm nearer to the Chinese border than I am to Moscow, even.*

Well, he'd done what he could to make this joint mission work. He'd pushed through a lot of steps to try to make sure his American charges and their Soviet counterparts could work together effectively, and safely. For instance he'd soon realized that the language barrier went far beyond just the Russian–English gap, and he'd assigned 'Russian Interface Officers,' to translate NASA jargon into plain English, which could then be translated by the Russian interpreters. And then there was the daily schedule. His mission planning guy had come along to Russia last year loaded down with documents. His Soviet counterpart had shown up with a pencil. There just wasn't any *paper* in these offices; for instance, even now there was only one copy of the Soyuz mission plan for this joint project, handwritten on long rolls of paper and taped up on the walls of the Soviet Mission Control in Kaliningrad. Seger couldn't figure if it was some sinister Soviet thing about controlling information, or just a dearth of photocopiers.

Now, showing on a TV monitor, there was a film of the two cosmonauts – Vladimir Viktorenko and Aleksandr Solovyov – taken earlier in the day. In their pressure suits, they were leaving their quarters and climbing aboard a bus. The bus looked like a tourist coach.

Seger felt a pull inside him, a protective urge. He offered up a brief prayer for the safety of the cosmonauts, and he touched his crucifix lapel pin.

Michaels observed this and raised an eyebrow.

'You do need to take it easy, Bert. I figure you're just going through – what do they call it? – culture shock. Hell, Bert, these aren't our boys. We're just going to have to accept the Soviets know what they're doing, in their own sweet way. After all the N-1 seems to be getting there as a launch system. They've fired off two unmanned circumlunar Soyuz shots and brought them back to Earth. And we've got Muldoon, Bleeker and Stone up there in lunar orbit waiting for their bird; the Soviets really, really don't want to screw up with this shot.'

'Maybe. I just wish they'd let some of our guys redesign their launch facilities a little bit.'

Michaels guffawed. 'That would have gone down *very* well. Anyway, we need some success too, Bert. As you know well enough.'

That was true, Seger realized.

The TV played a snatch of music; it was bland, slow stuff, and a PR announcer said in clipped English that this was being played simultaneously to the Soyuz, as a relaxant for the cosmonauts. *Good grief*, Seger thought. *It must be like being stuck in an elevator.*

And now, Seger saw from the timers, there was just a minute to go. He raised his binoculars.

The electrical and propellant umbilicals fell away from the walls of the ship, and the N-1 stood alone: huge, clumsy, fragile. *My God. It looks like boiler-plate.*

Ignition came at four seconds.

Smoke and light flooded from the broad base of the N-1, across the steppe, and fire billowed into the trenches beneath the ship.

Seger watched as the glare built up. That broad first stage contained no less than thirty rocket engines, compared to five on a Saturn.

The first few moments of launch were critical. Unlike Saturn, the N-1 was not held back for a controlled release while its thrust built up. Rather, it simply lifted from the pad once its thrust exceeded its weight. And there was no provision for engine shutdown.

The huge stack lifted, impossibly, on its pillar of fire. It was like watching a cathedral raise itself off the ground.

Once the stack was more than its own length from the ground, the N-1 accelerated quickly. Following its flight path it tipped over, its base an explosion of light.

Now the sound reached the observation bunker, and the window before Seger rattled; the light blazed into the room, as if a small

242

sun had arisen from the steppe. He felt the throb of the rockets deep in his gut.

Michaels leaned over to Seger. 'It seems to be going okay.'

'Max-Q,' Seger shouted back over the noise. 'It has to get through max-Q.' The point of maximum aerodynamic pressure was the point at which problems had occurred on previous flights. It was the early failure of the N-1 which had, essentially, lost the race to the Moon for the Soviets. For example the last N-1 trial before Apollo 11, in 1969, had suffered such violent vibration that an internal line had come loose. Liquid oxygen had sprayed through the body of the rocket. Engines exploded; turbo-pumps tore themselves apart . . . The explosion was equivalent to a tactical atomic bomb, so powerful it had been detected by American reconnaissance satellites.

The timers on the wall said sixty-six seconds.

'I think that's it,' Seger breathed. 'The engines will be throttling back up to full power.'

'So they're through the worst of it?'

'Oh, no. No, with this bird it isn't over until the fat lady sings, Fred.'

Michaels clapped him on the shoulder, and went to talk to the other guests.

Seger stayed at the window long after the others had moved away, and the rattling of the launch had dispersed. He watched the dwindling light in the sky, and counted through the launch events in his head.

Mission Elapsed Time [Day/Hr:Min:Sec] Plus 121/12:23:34

Gershon floated out of the Docking Adapter and into the Command Module's forward access tunnel. He emerged head-first at the top of Apollo's conical cabin. He did a neat somersault in the air, translating from the 'up' of the Mission Module to the 'down' of the Apollo.

To Gershon, this inversion was one of the strangest aspects of the whole trip.

He closed the hatch behind him, dogging it loosely.

He settled into Stone's seat, at the left-hand side of the cabin, and stuck his checklist to a Velcro square on the control panel in front of him. He had a little foil tube of orange juice in the top pocket of his Beta-cloth coveralls, and he dug that out now, pulled out the straw, and took a sip. He adjusted his headset and made sure he had a working comms link to the rest of the Ares cluster – both York and Stone responded from intercoms in the Mission Module – and he fired off a call to Fred Haise, who was the capcom on the ground right now. He didn't wait for his signal to crawl across the Solar System to bring him a reply before beginning work, however.

He began to power up Apollo's systems.

During the transfer to Mars and back, all but essential systems were quiescent on Apollo. There were umbilical connections through the docking system which hooked up Apollo to the main solar panel arrays, so Apollo didn't have to run on its own power. Every fifty days or so, Gershon was supposed to go through this routine of checking Apollo's systems. He was making sure they would be working when it came time for the crew to ride Apollo home, back down through the air of Earth.

The chore took maybe forty per cent of his attention.

He dug a cassette tape out of his pocket, and slid it into the deck forward of Stone's flight station. The sound of violins – a light, delicate phrase – came drifting out into the cabin's thin air. Gershon closed his eyes, and let the music wash over him. Mozart: the fortieth symphony. *Exquisite.* He felt himself relax, and even the cabin around him started to feel bigger.

Nam vets were supposed to live up to the image of spaced-out Jimi Hendrix fans. And in Houston, image was an important thing: when you had ten guys, with equally good qualifications, competing for one seat, intangibles like image could win you a flight, or lose you one.

So Gershon kept his Mozart to himself.

He was alone in the cabin as he worked through his checklist. Closing the hatch was strictly against regs, and he had to clear it with Stone every time he came in here. But Apollo was one of the few places in the whole cluster where you could get a little genuine privacy. Stone understood. You had to have a little *space*, a little time to yourself.

It was strange to think that there were only three human beings within tens of millions of miles of this point, and yet here they were cooped up together, for months on end, in this collection of tin cans. The only solid interior partitions in the Mission Module were those around the crapper.

And the truth was, the three of them didn't really get along. York never said much to anyone, Stone was too much the USAF goddamn straight arrow commander to get involved, and Gershon himself said far too much, all the time.

But it didn't bother Gershon. Or his crewmates, he suspected. All the psychiatric team-building stuff was so much horseshit, to Gershon. They weren't on this mission to make friends with each other; they were here to fly to Mars. And to achieve that they would overcome a little interpersonal friction.

As long as a man got a little time to himself, it was no big deal.

He worked steadily through the gauges and dials and computer screens in front of him, and compared them with the expected readings printed out on his teletyped checklist. His headset was voice-activated; he'd fixed it so that the Mozart stopped playing when he spoke.

Gershon liked working with Apollo hardware.

The basic design was antiquated, but it was fifteen years since its last major failure, on Apollo 13. Anyway, there wasn't necessarily anything wrong with 'antiquated.' To a pilot, it was the difference between a development vehicle and an operational bird; for 'antiquated' read 'proven.' In Gershon's view it would have been a crying shame to have abandoned the Apollo line back in the early 1970s and try to build a new-fangled spaceplane. Nice as the Shuttle would have been to fly.

The enhancements Rockwell had applied over the years had turned the basic configuration into a flexible, robust space truck. Outwardly the ship stuck nose-first to the front of the Mission Module Docking Adapter looked much the same as every other Apollo which had ever flown: it was made up of the classic configuration, the cylindrical Service Module, with its big propulsion system engine bell stuck on the back, and the squat cone of the Command Module on top. But this Apollo – called a 'Block V' design by the Rockwell engineers who had built her – was put together very differently from the early models, the old Block IIs, which had flown to the moon in the 1960s, and even from the later Block III and IV Earth-orbital ferries.

The first lunar missions had been only two weeks in length. But the Ares Apollo was going to have to survive eighteen months of soak in deep space. And the temperature extremes Apollo would endure, as Ares flew across the System, were much greater than on any lunar flight. So most of Apollo's main systems had been redesigned from the floor up.

The Service Module had more reaction control gas and less main engine propellant. The old Service Modules had vented excess water, produced by the onboard batteries; the Ares model stored its water in tanks, to avoid having frozen ice particles drifting around near the cluster. The whole configuration had more batteries, and there was more stowage area and locker space in the Command Module. There was an atmosphere interchange duct in the upper docking assembly, to cycle air from the Mission Module into the Command Module. And so on.

Reliability was essential, on long-duration missions. Many of Apollo's systems had redundant backups – straightforward copies, to be substituted in case of a failure – but the old triple-redundancy design paradigm they'd used to get to the Moon wouldn't work, it had been found, on long-duration missions. Enough redundancy to achieve an acceptably low level of risk over such a span of time would have resulted in a spacecraft of immense weight and complexity.

So the designers had got smarter. In addition to simple redundancy, some functions could be performed by dissimilar components, or by components from different subsystems, to reduce the chance of a single failure mode knocking out many functions altogether – as had happened in Apollo 13. And the maintenance capabilities of the crew weren't ignored, either. The whole ship was more modular and accessible than in its first design, so that components could be reached, repaired or replaced comparatively easily, and there were isolation valves, switches, test equipment and fault diagnosis tools. Some of the components contained their own BITEs, microelectronic built-in self-test units.

Hauling an Apollo all the way to Mars also provided some abort options. On return to Earth the Apollo, with the Mission Module, was due to be inserted into a highly elliptical orbit around the planet: two hundred by a hundred thousand miles, a swooping curve that would take the stack half-way out to the Moon and back, an orbit accessible to Ares at relatively low expenditure of fuel. The Command Module would be able to take them down to the surface of Earth from such a trajectory; the reentry heating would be less than a return from the Moon. And if Apollo were to fail, the crew could survive in their high orbit until rescue came, in the form of another five-man stretched Apollo.

If they couldn't make Earth orbit at all – for instance if the J-2S, the single engine of the final MS-IVB booster stage, were to fail – they could attempt a direct entry from the interplanetary coast. The heatshield on the Command Module's underside had been thickened and toughened up, so that it would at least give them a fighting chance of surviving a direct reentry into Earth's atmosphere. The velocity would only be around fifteen percent faster than a lunar return.

And, if the Mission Module's life support were to fail inflight, it would even be possible for the crew to retreat to the Command Module and use it as a shelter. A lifeboat. Right now, with Gershon alone in here, the Command Module seemed pretty roomy; it wasn't like that with three of them aboard, and things would be pretty tough if they had to spend weeks, or even months, cooped up in here.

But it was better than dying.

Every aspect of the mission had been designed with failures in mind, to give options at every point, to leave no 'dead zones' where there was no abort capability. The designers had almost succeeded.

Gershon hummed along with Mozart as he worked.

This fifty-day checkup was a chore, of course, but *everything* on this fucking flight was a chore for Gershon. And it was the same on every long-duration spaceflight.

Gershon's moment was going to come, when he took that MEM down through the thin air of Mars itself. But he'd basically be working at peak effectiveness for, what? – forty, fifty minutes? – out of a flight that was going to last a year and a half. *Not much of a payload ratio, Ralph.* But that was okay. It was a bargain that Gershon was prepared to accept. Because here he was, on an odyssey to Mars.

The first time he'd come across the name 'Ares' had been in a battered old book he'd picked up from a dime store in Mason. It was a collection of science fiction stories, by someone called Stanley Weinbaum. The title story was 'A Martian Odyssey,' and it featured a ship called Ares, and four men exploring the surface of an exotic, mysterious Mars. Weinbaum's magical words were alive in his memory, still, after all these years; it was as if he could feel the stiff, yellowing pages of that battered old paperback in his hands now.

When he'd heard they were going to use Weinbaum's name for the mission, Gershon had whooped.

He'd worked his way through the science fiction canon as he grew older, and he'd ridden many other ships to Mars. Bradbury had been elusive, with his hinting descriptions of silver locusts – pulsing with fire, swarming with men – falling to the surface of a beautiful, inhabited planet. Clarke's Ares, on the other hand, had been described in great detail. It was a dumbbell shape of two huge spheres, separated by a hundred yards of tube-way. The rear contained atomic motors – serviced by AEC robots – and the leading sphere was living quarters, with cabins and a huge dining room and an observation gallery . . .

Sitting in the canvas frame couch, Gershon sucked some more juice out of his tube, and ran his hand over the surface of the grimy instrument panel before him. He grinned. *Dining rooms, huh.*

Gershon thought of Apollo technology the way, he supposed, other guys might think of classic cars. Like a Corvette, maybe. Apollo was a beautiful machine, and it worked, and it had achieved great things. And even after all these years it was still better than anything the Russians could put up . . .

And it seemed entirely appropriate to him that the first mission to Mars – for real – should be conducted not in some lost von Braun-type dream of the 1950s, but in a handful of strung-together Apollo-application cans.

Still, he knew that this voyage was a fulfillment of more dreams than just his own. As Ares followed its long, spiralling trajectory to Mars, he felt that it wasn't alone: it was accompanied by a fleet of ghostly ships, huge silver forms, from the pages of Clarke and Heinlein and Asimov and Bradbury and Burroughs . . .

The Mozart floated around the cabin, and Gershon worked patiently through his checklist.

Book 3

APOLLO-N

Rolf Donnelly swung his car into his space outside Building 30, the Mission Control Center. He got out, whistling.

There was a new sign up, in a car park space close to the building: MCC M&O EMPLOYEE OF THE MONTH. Donnelly laughed. Welcome to government work! You're in Mission Control, and your prize for a good job well done is a loan of a parking space!

He took a breath of the muggy autumn air. It would be his last fresh air for a while; one of the few things he didn't like about working in Building 30 was that it was completely enclosed. He walked slowly by the big air-conditioning grilles on the outside of the building; in the spring, birds nested in there, but he couldn't see any activity now.

Donnelly was still whistling as he turned into the building. He was a Flight Director, and now he was going to be lead Flight for the Apollo-N mission.

The big display screens at the front of the room bore spectacular images from Kennedy, of climbing metal, billowing smoke, flames as bright as the sun.

The Saturn VN lifted smoothly off the pad.

A few seconds into the Apollo-N flight, the Mission Operations Control Room was an amphitheater of calm, of control, of patient work. From his position in the command and control row of the MOCR, third from the front, Donnelly could see everything: the rows of blocky benches, the workstations with their clumsy old CRTs and keyboards bolted into place, manned by the controllers that made up his flight team. *Indigo Team.* The workstations were littered with ring binders of mission rules, polystyrene coffee cups, yellow notepads.

'Roll and pitch program,' Chuck Jones's voice called down on the air-to-ground loop. His voice was shaking, barely audible to Donnelly. 'Everything's looking good. The sky is getting lighter.'

On the brown-painted walls there were mission patches, dating all the way back to Gemini 4; and there were plaques, framed in the team colors of retired Flight Directors. There was a big Stars-and-Stripes at the front of the room. The light was low, the colors gloomy; but the CRTs glowed brightly.

The booster passed the launch tower. And, smoothly, Indigo Team took control of the mission from the Kennedy Firing Room.

Donnelly could feel adrenaline surge in his system.

The Saturn VN pitched itself over, arcing east over the Atlantic. The booster was flying itself, gimballing its engines so that it neatly followed its preprogrammed trajectory; for now the crew, Jones, Priest and Dana, were passengers, their nuclear rocket just payload.

Natalie York, capcom for the shift, called up to the spacecraft. 'Apollo, Houston . . . You're right smack dab on the trajectory.'

'Roger, Houston. This baby is really going.'

'Roger, that.'

Numbers scrolled across CRT screens, and Donnelly's controllers talked quietly to each other on their comms loops.

It was York's first assignment as capcom. She sounded calm, controlled; Donnelly was pleased.

The flight was going well. Rolf Donnelly could feel it. Right now he didn't have to do a thing.

There were a lot of unique features about this mission. It was the first time the US had tried to maintain *two* ambitious flights at once, with no less than six astronauts above the atmosphere: Jones, Dana and Priest climbing to orbit for their NERVA test flight on top of the Saturn VN, and Muldoon, Bleeker and Stone already out in lunar orbit in Moonlab, waiting for their rendezvous with the Russians. It was also the first time NASA had operated both its MOCRs at once.

And this was, of course, the first manned flight of the S-NB, the new Saturn booster third stage with its NERVA 2 nuclear engine.

Management Row, behind Donnelly in the MOCR, was full today. For instance, there was Bert Seger, just over Donnelly's shoulder, his trademark carnation a glare of white. And in the Viewing Room behind the glass wall at the back of the MOCR, Donnelly had spotted Fred Michaels himself, puffing on one of his cigars, watching the numbers unroll with baffled anxiety. This was a very important, and very public, flight.

But Donnelly wasn't concerned; not right now. He had a lot of faith in his people. The controllers in this room were actually leaders of the teams, three or five strong, who worked in the back rooms clustered around the MOCR; to get as far as this room, the controllers had had to work in the back rooms on a good number of missions. That was the way Donnelly had come up, himself. The controllers would often get poached away by the higher salaries offered by the aerospace companies: a spell in Mission Control looked good on your resume. But that was all right; it kept down the average age in here.

252

Anyway, Donnelly had no such ambitions. The MOCR was much closer to the center of gravity of decision making, on any flight they'd launched to date, even than being in the cabin of the actual spacecraft. This was where things were run; in this room, Donnelly was in control. As far as he was concerned, it was better than flying.

One minute into the flight.

The vibrations of the launch smoothed out

Jones shouted, 'This goddamn bird doesn't ring right . . .'

Jim Dana couldn't see Jones's face inside his helmet.

There wasn't time to think about it. Gs were piling on Dana, as the five heavy engines of the S-IC stage continued to blast. *Two, three, four G* . . . he could feel his chest flattening.

But this was about as bad as it would get. In fact, the Gs were oddly reassuring. They were coming right on schedule. Maybe Jones was wrong. So far this was just like the sims. *Almost . . .*

Suddenly he was thrown forward against his seat restraints. *What the . . . ?* The smooth build-up was gone. Could an engine have failed? But now he was hurled back, deeper into his couch; and then forward again, so hard he could feel his straps bruise his stomach and chest through the suit's layers. Then back again –

'Pogoing!' Jones shouted. 'Hang onto your hats, guys.'

Now the vibrations, forward and back, were coming at the rate of five or six a second, and their violence was astonishing. How many Gs? And oscillating all the time –

Dana could no longer see; the craft was a blur around him, and he felt as if he was being pummeled about the chest, head and legs. *We'll have to abort. We can't survive this. It'll shake us to pieces.* He tried to turn his head, to see if Jones was reaching for his abort handle.

The pogoing didn't show up in the MOCR.

To the controllers there, the first-stage burn looked nominal. It was only apparent in the Marshall engineers' equivalent of Mission Control, called the Huntsville Operations Support Center.

On a closed loop from Marshall, a warning was whispered to Mike Conlig in Houston. 'The S-IC is pogoing. The accelerometers are showing plus or minus eight G.'

Conlig was sitting at the left-hand end of the Trench – the front row of the MOCR at Houston – working as the Booster controller for this launch, with special responsibility for the new NERVA stage. The pogo had to be occurring because the natural vibration of the thrust chambers of the F-1 engines was close, somehow, to the structural vibration of the stack as a whole. *Christ*, he thought. *But we put in absorbers to de-tune the vehicle; this shouldn't be happening.* Evidently those assholes at Marshall hadn't done enough resonance testing on the new Saturn VN stack, with its nuclear third stage. *We could lose the mission because of this.*

He prepared to report to Flight.

But now the whisper from Huntsville came through again. 'Amplitude diminishing.'

Conlig held his breath, and waited.

The pogoing faded, as suddenly as it had begun.

By comparison, the steady pressure of three or four Gs on Dana's chest was a welcome relief.

He saw the mission clock, hovering before him. *Ten seconds. That's all it was. Ten seconds.*

He turned his head to see the others; there was a zone of blackness around his vision. He focused on Chuck Jones's face. 'Chuck? Ben? Are you okay?'

Jones's hand was closed tight around the abort handle; Dana wondered what effort of will it had taken to keep from turning it. Jones said, 'Houston, we've been a-pogoing. But we is still here, like three dried peas in a tin can.'

'Roger.' Natalie York sounded puzzled. It was possible the Houston people didn't know, yet, what the crew had gone through. They didn't see the accelerometer readouts. Dana just hoped they were watching the rest of the telemetry.

But now the events of the launch sequence came rushing on them. 'Three minutes,' Jones called. 'Get set for staging, boys.'

Dana shook his head, and the darkness at the edge of his vision began to disperse. He thought uneasily of the additional stress the staging would place on the pogo-rattled S-NB.

Rolf Donnelly had *not* enjoyed the pogoing. He had also not enjoyed not knowing about it until the crew's verbal report came through.

At this stage of the flight, the Marshall people were more or less in control; they had the best understanding of the status of their bird. *But I don't know why we didn't abort during that damn pogo. They must be really keen to get their nuclear stage into orbit.*

Ascent to orbit was always the most difficult and dangerous phase of a mission: the phase when a hell of a lot of energy was being expended, to get those tons of metal up to an orbital speed of five miles per second. Reentry was infinitely easier, when you could dissipate all that energy at your leisure. Ascent was the phase when you were buying the most risk, the phase when Donnelly always braced himself for problems.

He felt he needed more control than he'd had on this flight so far.

The trouble was, the Marshall Germans had developed their skills in an era of automated, unmanned vehicles. You couldn't send a command to a V-2 once it was off the pad. And even now, the thought of trying to control a bird in flight was alien to them. So the Germans had done their best to turn their controllers, the people involved, into robots – extensions of the machine. *Don't improvise. Be disciplined. Follow the book: you're paid to react, not to think.*

Donnelly made a silent vow that he would campaign to have procedures changed. He didn't want to be put in the position of having to trust the judgment of the Marshall people again.

Still – although the Saturn was riding a little above its planned path, on the big trajectory plot at the front of the room – the crew seemed to have ridden out the pogo, and the booster's telemetry looked nominal. The stack had survived its first staging, the discarding of the spent S-IC, and the second-stage burn looked smooth.

Maybe we'll get away with this . . .

Donnelly could feel a pressure on his back. There were men in that Viewing Room, among the VIPs and celebrities and headquarters people and politicians and crew families, who would know things were going wrong. There was Fred Michaels himself, with his nose practically pressed up against the glass. And beside Michaels was Gregory Dana, Jim's father. Donnelly didn't know Dana Senior personally, but he understood he was some kind of mission specialist from Langley. The pressure exerted by the man was worse even than anything induced by the presence of Michaels. *Goddamn it, that's my son up there.*

Donnelly was a man on the climb. He looked forward to a bright future – a few more years here in the arena, then maybe a move up into program management. And when he'd pulled off this complex and difficult mission, it would be one *hell* of a feather in his cap.

He loved his job. He wanted to go a lot further; he wanted to run the flight to Mars. He did *not* want this mission to fail.

But now it was time to light the nuke.

*   *   *

Apollo-N shuddered as explosive bolts severed the spent S-II second stage. Dana drifted, weightless, waiting for the next kick.

'Here we go again,' Jones said. His Tennessee twang was calm and relaxed – *as if he does this every day.*

Well, Chuck Jones could play-act his calmness all he liked; but even he had to be wound up tight as a watch spring now, Dana thought, because the most important moment in the flight was approaching. The third stage of this stack was not the old reliable S-IVB which had carried the Moon missions to Earth orbit and beyond; it was an S-NB, with the first operational NERVA engine. And the damn thing was going to have to work now to get them to orbit, Dana knew, or they were going to be flying across the Atlantic to a hard landing in the goddamn Sahara.

York called up: 'Apollo, Houston, you are go for orbit. You are go for orbit.'

For long seconds the spacecraft soared, without acceleration; and then, at last, Dana was kicked in the back.

'She's lit,' Chuck Jones breathed. 'How about that. We're flying a goddamn nuke.'

The NERVA burn was nothing like so jarring as the second-stage ignition six minutes earlier; the ride now was crisp and rattly, with just two hundred thousand pounds of thrust pressing a full G into his back.

And then Earthlight strobed past Dana's window. The Apollo had dipped toward the ground.

He was thrown forward against his restraints, the breath knocked out of him. *My God. What now?*

The nose of the craft pitched up again. Metal groaned, and Earth's brilliant face swooped past his window. His helmet thumped against the sparse metal frame of his couch. Blue light flashed over his visor.

Chuck Jones's voice was dry. 'We're riding a bronco here, Houston. Please advise.'

'Booster, Flight. Tell me what you got.'

To Donnelly, it looked as if the little Saturn icon on the plot board was drunk, as it wandered crazily around its programmed trajectory. A dozen voices jabbered in Donnelly's ear at once; he listened to them all, somehow simultaneously, trying to piece together what was happening.

But the most important voice wasn't there. Mike Conlig wasn't speaking to him.

'Booster, Flight,' he repeated. 'You got anything you want to say?'

Even without Conlig he could follow the bones of what was happening. The S-NB seemed to be working nominally, in fact. This pitching must be due to left-over problems from the pogoing. The vehicle had been tipped up too high when staging came. So when the S-NB cut in, it found itself pointing too far into space. It had gimballed its nuclear engine, and tried to point its way toward the center of the Earth. For long seconds the guidance system battled with the limits of gimbal on the engine. And then the S-NB seemed to figure that its path had gotten too low, so it pitched itself up again . . .

And on, and on, in a wild feedback process, as the S-NB's instrument unit strove to bring the ship back to an unreachable flight path.

Where the hell was Conlig?

'Booster, Flight. *Booster.*'

Christ, Fred Michaels thought, watching from the Viewing Room at the back of the MOCR. *I do not want this bird aborted.*

This would be a very bad time to foul up.

The new Reagan Administration was shaping itself up after its landslide, and Michaels was already gloomy about the future. He figured it was Ted Kennedy's defection from Carter during the primaries that had done for the peanut farmer, although Michaels suspected Carter's time might have been up anyhow. And here came Reagan, rattling his saber at the Russians over Poland and Afghanistan, and promising to get the hostages out of Iran . . . Maybe Reagan would be gung-ho about space; nobody knew.

Meanwhile Michaels had lost a close political buddy in the White House, and his Kennedy card was looking a little worn.

Anyhow, the Apollo-N flight had so far gotten NASA some extensive coverage – some of it even favorable, as it showed the elaborate precautions the Agency was taking over its nuclear materials. It had even crowded out the 'Who Shot JR?' hoopla that was so fascinating everybody. Michaels did not want to turn those front pages into damning coverage of another Apollo disaster; not now, not ever . . .

Bert Seger, a few rows back from Michaels in the Viewing Room, knew this was NASA's most controversial flight since the military crews of Skylab A. There had been a march and protest rally by campaigners at Kennedy today, people with kids, and banners

257

saying REMEMBER THREE MILE ISLAND. The Cape security people had kept them well away from the launch site, and from the main public viewing areas. But Seger, hot-footing it back from Tyuratam for this launch, had had to work his way past it all.

Seger had been cocooned in the project for years now. He'd found the anger he'd witnessed in those massed faces, on the news programs and on NASA's closed-circuit loops, startling, deeply troubling.

Of even more concern to him was the grumbling he'd heard from inside the Agency. Some of the astronauts, that loudmouth Joe Muldoon for instance, had been getting a little too vocal about the flight-readiness, or lack of it, of NERVA. Fortunately, however, Muldoon was safely out of the way right now, on the other side of the Moon.

But Muldoon, and the others, had planted seeds of doubt in Seger. Had he been pushing too hard? If anything went badly wrong today, then after bulling through the protests, NASA might after all smear nuclear fuel all over the eastern seaboard.

Yesterday, in the Operations Building at Kennedy, the Apollo-N crew had given Seger a small, informal photo, in a brass frame. It showed the three of them in their spacesuits, smiling, and was signed by them all. The inscription was: *To Bert – In Your Hands.*

'Booster, Flight. Booster, damn it.'

Donnelly's voice was persistent in Conlig's headset, like a buzzing insect. It made it hard to think.

The mission rules were clear enough. In the event of a failure like this at such a point in the launch, Conlig, as Booster, should push his abort switch. The little icon representing the Saturn continued to deviate from its path. *But . . .*

But the deviation wasn't as bad as it had looked at first. And there clearly wasn't any tumbling.

The S-NB was a smart bird. It could exert a lot of control over its trajectory by gimballing its engine bells. It looked as if the booster was doing all it could to keep to its target path. The trajectory was still under control.

Conlig forced himself to reply to Donnelly. 'Uh, Flight, Booster.'

'Jesus Christ, Booster. Go.'

Conlig took a deep breath. 'Flight, Booster. We seem to have good control at this time.'

Now calls began to come in from the other controllers: guidance, flight dynamics, the systems guys in the row behind Conlig. Apart from this oscillation around the trajectory, everything was performing nominally.

Donnelly said: 'You sure, Booster?'

Are you really sure you have this bird under control? Are you sure you shouldn't ask for an abort?

Are you sure you know what you're doing, Conlig?

Conlig felt as if the room, the world, was closing in around him; the headset seemed to burn on his ears, and the little Saturn icon on the plot board was like an image of his own wavering determination.

I should abort. But the thing is flying.

'You sure, Booster?' Donnelly pressed.

'Data indicates it, Flight.'

'Roger.' *I'll trust you, Conlig.*

Conlig stared at the icon, willing it to keep on climbing, up toward orbit.

He knew it was in nobody's interests to abort, if they didn't have to.

The burn lasted two and a half minutes. Apollo-N was boosted five miles higher and another two hundred and fifty miles downrange.

Then the S-NB stage shut down its NERVA engine.

Jones read off the DSKY display before him. 'Natalie, you can tell the boys at Marshall that their rascally bird performed beautifully. Except that we've ended up in orbit ass-backward.'

'Roger,' York replied laconically. 'I'll relay that, Chuck; thanks.'

Mike Conlig was aware of Natalie sitting, as capcom, just a few yards away from him.

I should have aborted. But I didn't. I got away with it.

He didn't turn; he didn't want to meet Natalie's eyes.

Donnelly felt some of the tension drain out of him.

He went round the horn, polling his controllers; they all reported a ship that was, in spite of everything, reasonably close to nominal. *We got through it. How, I'll never know.*

Bert Seger knew they had been lucky. He determined to poke a hot stick up the asses of those guys from Marshall over this. The S-IC had pogoed. The Saturn first stage should not be letting them down, not after more than a decade of experience, not after so many flights.

Seger walked into the MOCR and leaned over Donnelly's station. 'I want you to make damn sure you're confident about that NERVA engine of Marshall's. Otherwise, bring those guys straight back down.'

Friday, November 28, 1980
Apollo-N; Lyndon B. Johnson Space Center, Houston

They shoved their pressure suits into net bags and crammed them under their couches; now Jim Dana was wearing only a pair of Beta-cloth coveralls over his long johns.

He was a hundred miles up, a thousand miles downrange from the Cape, and covering five miles every second. Here in his center couch, his feet pointed up at the stars, he was peering at his home planet through the Command Module's window.

He couldn't get over how beautiful the sunlit Earth was. It was a wall of color and light, gently curving, which divided the universe in two; cloud lay across land and ocean in brilliant white plumes, like feathers.

Ben Priest, to Dana's right, was grinning at him. 'How do you feel?'

'Like I was born to be up here.'

Chuck Jones unbuckled his seat belt, and pushed himself out of the left-hand couch. He floated up toward the instrument panel. 'Hot *dawg*,' he said. 'We is in orbit, gentlemen. Welcome to the astronaut corps. Now all we've got to do is figure out if we can stay here.'

Priest and Jones set to work on checking out the craft's flight path and velocity estimates with the ground stations and instrumentation aircraft. Dana could hear Jones humming as he worked. Meanwhile, Dana's job was to make sure the guidance platform was aligned.

He floated up into the air and folded back his couch, the center of the three. In microgravity, the cramped cabin seemed roomy. Dana pushed a finger-tip against an instrument panel; it was enough to launch him slowly down past the others into the equipment bay under the couches.

He drifted among coolant pipes and storage compartments. There was room to stretch out here, for the first time since the launch, with his feet by the hatch and his head pointing at the floor. As he stretched he felt twinges at his stomach, chest and knees: the

260

aftermath of the pogoing. It was actually less painful than he'd expected; his pressure suit had evidently protected him.

Dana floated down to the Inertial Measuring Unit. The guidance device was a metal sphere the size of a beach ball. Inside the casing a platform was maintained in position by three nested spheres. The whole thing was like a table on a boat, gimballed to remain level regardless of the boat's heeling. The system was the spacecraft's way of being able to sense where it was relative to a reference trajectory. Checking the alignment was a routine chore; it was a checklist item on every flight. But there was a big fear, now, that the pogoing and wild gyrations Apollo-N had suffered during the launch might have thrown the platform out of line.

To align the platform Dana had to take sightings on various stars through a small optical telescope and sextant. The idea was to pick a couple of stars from a standard list, and then tell the spacecraft to find them. If the star wasn't exactly centered in the cross hairs of the telescope, Dana would make an adjustment to correct it, and the computer would enter the adjustment into the platform, which would then reset itself.

He selected the constellation of Orion, with its distinctive three-star belt across the middle. He shielded his eyes more carefully from the glare of the Earth and the cabin lights, and he pointed the 'scope where he knew Orion ought to be. At last he made out the three faint dots, and bright Sirius nearby, right where they were supposed to be . . .

He grinned. The alignment was fine. Maybe the worst was over, and the rest of the flight was going to work out.

After all, the first objective of the flight test had already been achieved: to prove that the S-NB could loft itself, and a crewed spacecraft, into orbit. Now the mission was to show that NERVA could safely be restarted several times. During the week-long flight Apollo-N would be sent on thin, elliptical orbits, looping a hundred thousand miles into space – half-way to the Moon.

There would be plenty of science to do, with an extreme ultra-violet telescope, helium observations, high-altitude atmospheric studies, and Earth observation and photography; there was equipment inside the Command Module, and various external experiments and sensors stored in an instrument bay in the Service Module. But the science was nominal, Dana knew. The real purpose of this mission was simple: *make sure the damn NERVA works, and can be controlled from the spacecraft, without smearing nuclear waste all over everything.*

When he'd taken his star readings, he used the sextant to measure the angle between two fixed stars. This was a check of the platform's memory; Dana had to get his calculations to agree to within a ten-thousandth of a percentage point: the goal, in fact, was to get five balls, a perfect reading of .00000 on the star angle comparison.

Dana scored .00003: four balls and change.

Meanwhile he was getting used to microgravity. When he put his hands out he found he could make himself spin in the air, like a sycamore seed.

The feeling was wonderful. He felt like laughing.

Rolf Donnelly was at the center of a web of information, argument and extrapolation, a web that swept across the country: from the Marshall people in Alabama, to Rockwell at Downey with their intimate understanding of Apollo, to Boeing who were doing some hard analysis of the telemetry data from their balky S-IC first stage, to a dozen or more groups here in the MOCR, and the back rooms, and in Building 45. He imagined phone lines singing, as the ground controllers and the crew worked through comprehensive checklists covering the propulsion systems, gimbal systems, gyros, computers, life support, spreading their findings out across the country.

Slowly the answers were coming in, filtered and assembled by Indigo Team.

The S-IC pogo was, it seemed, down to an unexpected resonance mode of the Saturn VN, the new Saturn/NERVA stack. It should have been anticipated by somebody, long before the stack was assembled for launch.

What the hell happened to quality control on this program? Donnelly understood how everyone involved was under great time pressure. But still: *It won't fail because of me.* It sounded like some assholes at Boeing or Marshall had kind of forgotten that motto; and there couldn't have been a worse mission to forget it on.

Anyhow, what now?

The logical thing to do was just to abort, to bring the crew home. After all, the spacecraft hadn't been designed for the treatment it had received during launch.

But Donnelly had started out as a physicist, and he remained, at heart, a scientist. *Never mind the mission rules, or the politics: what does the data tell you?*

The failure had been Saturn's, not NERVA's. And now Saturn

262

had been discarded, and the Booster people were assuring him that everything was fine, that the pogoing hadn't hurt the S-NB nearly as badly as it might have. Besides, the S-NB had already worked – and well, given the situation it had found itself in when it had tried to find its flight path. Meanwhile, the other subsystem teams were continuing to click off the items in their checklists as sweet as honey.

Behind him, in Management Row and the Viewing Room, there were more little clusters of senior management, worrying themselves to death. There was Bert Seger, with the directors of Flight Operations and Crew Operations; and behind Seger, beyond the Viewing Room glass, Donnelly recognized Tim Josephson.

The strategic importance of the flight was obvious to everyone: NERVA's nuclear technology had to succeed – it had to be demonstrably safe – because if public hostility wasn't assuaged, and if the nuclear program was cut back or even terminated altogether, well, hell, you could kiss good-bye to Mars.

Donnelly had to make the right call. By tradition only Flight, or Surgeon, the mission doctor, could call an abort. NASA senior management had never before overridden a Flight Director's decision during a mission.

It was a first Donnelly didn't want to happen on his watch.

Natalie York, as capcom, was sitting in the workstation row in front of Rolf Donnelly. She watched the faces of the controllers around her. She'd got to know them all, during the intensive training for this mission, the long, complex integrated sims, the frenetic drinking sessions later. They were all men, all very young. They shared a brand of intense, fragile intelligence which made them socially awkward, maybe temperamental, ultimately unstable.

They'd all had a tough time during the flight to orbit, and they faced equally tough decisions now.

Mike sat in the Trench, the row in front of her, a little to her left. He was hunched over his console now, his posture redolent of tension, his hair loose and greasy at his neck. He was bent in some huddled discussion with a colleague from Marshall.

She remembered all her old doubts about Mike's temperament – whether he was suited to high-pressure situations like this, involving erratic boosters and manned spacecraft and rapidly unraveling missions . . .

She had an impulse to reach out and touch him, to try to reassure or calm him. But she knew that her intrusion wouldn't be welcomed. Mike was off on some trajectory of his own, now, as out of her control as had been the Saturn/NERVA stack, guiding itself into space.

Anyhow, she ought to be concentrating on herself. This assignment was a big moment for her. York was an ascan no more. She was now officially on the flight roster, and this capcom posting was her first operational duty: quite a vote of confidence.

It was much more difficult than she'd expected. The capcom was the only person allowed to speak to the crew. She was the funnel for inputs from all around the MOCR, and beyond; she had to be alert, to think constantly, to filter and integrate all the information she received. Nobody was writing her a script; she had to figure it for herself, in real time.

So far, she reckoned, she was doing fine. But nobody was noticing her, one way or the other. They wouldn't until she screwed up.

I just hope you make the right choices today, Mike. For Christ's sake, it's Ben up there . . .

Jones and Priest drifted down to sleeping compartments in the equipment bay. Each of these was actually just a six-foot-long shelf with a foot of clearance, big enough to take a body-sized mesh hammock.

Dana strapped himself into the left couch, in front of the control panel. He knew that being in the couch he'd drawn the most comfortable sleeping berth. But as Command Module Pilot Dana had to keep his headset on during the night, in case the crew had to be woken by Houston. And even if Houston restricted their chatter, there was always a dull roar of static, which wasn't going to help him sleep.

None of this mattered.

My first night in space. All around him the cabin of the Command Module hummed and glowed, gray and green and warm, a small boy's dream of the perfect den. A loose page from a checklist came drifting over his head, on some random air current; when he blew toward it, the page crumpled a little and drifted away.

He turned to the window. Apollo-N was flying over a mountain range. He could see the wrinkles in the land, as if the world were some huge, sculptured toy beneath him; thick clouds lapped against one side of the range, like a turbulent fluid.

He felt detached from the frustrations and complexities of his life below: the routine, the time-eating training, the press stuff he hated so much, the endless waiting he'd had to endure for this, his first flight. All of the problems seemed flattened, two-dimensional, like the surface of the Earth, and he felt a warm love reach out from him to envelop Mary and the kids, his parents, the whole of the glowing planet of his birth.

Christ, it's true. I was born to be up here. None of the rest of it – the engineering, the science, even the prospect of going to Mars – none of it counts, compared to this moment. I never want to go back down.

They'd checked out everything they could, and all the telemetry looked good, and the inertial table was lined up, and the subsystems checked out, and all the back-room guys and the engineers and the contractors with their test rigs were saying, yes, we know what went wrong; and no, we're confident this mission is going to throw you no more curved balls.

I'll tell you how we can achieve zero risk, Donnelly thought. *We won't fly.*

Donnelly stood up and turned to face Bert Seger, who stood behind him in Management Row.

'Bert, I'm going to recommend we proceed with the mission. All the parameters have fallen into line.'

Seger, hollow-eyed with jet lag, just nodded.

It was 4 a.m. The decision was obvious.

Donnelly sat down. He'd been resting his hands on sheets of his flight plans; when he lifted his hands now he found he'd left behind two perfect, wet images of his palms.

Monday, December 1, 1980
Moonlab

Adam Bleeker was the first of the Moonlab crew to eyeball the approaching Soyuz. 'Hey, Phil, Joe. Come see.'

Stone drifted down to the wardroom's big picture window.

Soyuz T-3 was silhouetted sideways-on against the pale brown Moon, which slid liquidly past.

Soyuz was shaped, Stone supposed, something like a green pepper pot, a cylinder topped by a squat dome. The cylindrical body was the Instrument-Assembly Module, containing electrical, environmental, propulsion systems. Two matte-black solar panels jutted from the flanks of the Instrument Module, like unfolded wings. A parabolic antenna was held away from the ship, on a light gantry. Stone was able to make out the flat base of the craft; there was a toroidal propellant tank fixed there, surrounding small engine bells. The dome at the top of the pepper pot was the Descent Module: living quarters for the cosmonauts, and the cabin that would carry them through reentry into Earth's atmosphere. For Earth-orbit missions the Descent Module would have been capped, Stone knew, by a large, egg-shaped Orbital Module, a work and living area.

The body of the ship was a light blue-green, an oddly Earthlike color set against the bleak uniformity of the Moon. Soyuz looked, frankly, like a piece of shit to Stone. The solar cells were big black squares, crudely tiled onto the panels, and thick wires ran along the edges of the panels; Stone could see fist-sized big blobs of solder where some greasy technician had finished his job crudely.

The engineering was agricultural. The approaching Soyuz was like something out of a parallel universe, he thought.

The crew pulled away from the window; there was still work to do before the Soviets arrived.

Stone went up through the hole in the open mesh floor, and climbed the fireman's pole to the Multiple Docking Adapter at the far end of the hydrogen tank, the main experiment chamber. The Adapter had three clusters hanging from its ports. There was the Apollo which had brought the crew up from Earth, known as *Grissom* to thousands of school kids. *Grissom* had actually been adapted to carry five men home if need be, with two additional couches stowed in the Command Module's lower equipment bay. Then there was the Telescope Mount, a small lab module with four wide solar arrays and a battery of science experiments and sensors. The Mount had been adapted by Grumman engineers from a left-over LM ascent stage; in a different reality, that LM would have carried the astronauts of Apollo 16 up from the lunar surface.

The third component fixed to the Adapter was a short, squat cylinder called the Soyuz Docking Module, an interface between the incompatible atmospheres and docking kits of Soyuz and Apollo. Viktorenko and Solovyov were going to have to dock with this Module, and use it as a kind of airlock to get into Moonlab.

Now Stone began putting the Docking Module through a final check-out. As such assignments went, it wasn't too frustrating. At least the Module was a new piece of kit. People had lived and worked in the rest of Moonlab for five years now, and it showed.

When he'd done, Stone drifted back down to the wardroom. His next job was to run a visual sextant check of the Soviets' position.

As he made his observations, Soyuz maneuvered away from the backdrop of the Moon, and floated against the stars.

'Moonlab, this is *Komarov*. Moonlab –'

Muldoon replied for Moonlab. 'We hear you, *Komarov*. The VHF link is working fine.' Viktorenko, on Soyuz, had used English; Muldoon replied in halting Russian.

Now Muldoon went through a four-way conversation between Moonlab, Soyuz, and the two ground control stations at Houston and Kalinin, testing out links and confirming system status.

Soyuz wheeled around so that it faced Moonlab. 'Moonlab, *Komarov*. We are ready for the final docking maneuver. I will turn on my beacon.'

A light began to flash on the spine of Soyuz, easily visible through the picture window.

'I see you, *Komarov*.'

'And I you, Joe. Your elegant Moonlab is difficult to miss. We have our spacesuits on, all ready for docking. And our bow ties on top, for we are ready for a fine dinner with you.'

Houston and Kalinin both called up 'go' for the docking. Soyuz spun slowly on its long axis, rolling through sixty degrees to align correctly with the Docking Module. The solar arrays made Soyuz look almost bird-like, swooping around the Moon like some unlikely metal swallow.

Soyuz came in slowly and hesitantly, with many small attitude and angle corrections. At one point the ship even backed off from Moonlab. The Moonlab crew and Houston kept quiet; Stone listened to the soft, tense, dialogue in Russian between *Komarov* and Kalinin.

Komarov was evidently a pig to fly. Soyuz was a flexible ferry craft, but it was essentially a contemporary of the American Gemini, lacking much of the sophistication and power of Apollo. There was a real lack of precise attitude control and translation instruments, with most of the operations conducted by pre-programmed mission event sequencers.

In fact, the poor maneuverability of Soyuz had caused some friction during the planning stages of this joint flight. Some on the US side had suggested, half-seriously, that Soyuz should be the 'passive' partner – that Apollo should haul the bulk of Moonlab into the docking with the tiny Soyuz ...

Anyhow it looked now as if Soyuz was coming in on its final approach. As it neared, bristling with detail, *Komarov* arced up and out of Stone's view, and he heard Muldoon calling out in Russian.

'Five yards ... three yards ... one ...'

267

There was a soft clang, a rattle of docking latches.

'Well done, Vlad,' Muldoon called. 'Good show, *tovarich*. You came in at just a foot per second.'

'Indeed. Now Apollo and Soyuz are shaking hands, here in the shadow of the Moon. Yes?'

The cosmonauts moved into the small Docking Module and sealed it up. They had to sit out three hours as the pressure was reduced to match Moonlab's.

Stone pulled himself into the tunnel at the core of the Multiple Docking Adapter, close to the entrance to the Soyuz Module. Muldoon and Bleeker were already there, and the little tunnel, packed with instrument boxes and oxygen bottles, was crowded. Stone's job now was to work the small hand-held TV camera, and relay handshake pictures back to Earth.

There was a soft tapping. Muldoon opened the hatch.

Vladimir Viktorenko, beaming broadly, reached out and shook Muldoon's hand. 'My friend. I am very happy to see you.' He came tumbling out of the hatch, squat and exuberant, and gave Muldoon a bear-hug. He gave Muldoon a little packet of bread and salt, a traditional Russian greeting. Solovyov followed his commander out. And there were the five of them crowded into the Docking Adapter's tunnel, grinning and hugging, always with one eye on the camera.

Muldoon led them through the clutter of Moonlab toward the wardroom. Viktorenko and Solovyov made the obligatory polite remarks about the bird, but, Stone thought, they were being kind.

The first task of each new crew up here was to use their Apollo Service Module to tweak Moonlab's orbit. The Moon's gravity field was so lumpy that anything left in low lunar orbit would soon fall to the surface. And when he'd first approached 'Lab in *Grissom*, Stone might have been tempted to let the thing just fall.

After five years Moonlab's outside hull was pretty much dinged up, with big fist-sized meteorite holes knocked in the shield. The solar cells, also dented by meteorites, had degraded, and so the power was down to half its peak. Inside, the lights were dim, and jerry-built air ducts ran everywhere to make up for the broken fans. Stone was already sick of half-heated meals, lukewarm coffee, and tepid bathing water.

And the interior was like someone's utility room – more like a survival shelter than a laboratory, Stone thought – with every surface scuffed and scarred, every piece of equipment patched up, every wall encrusted with junk. Moonlab was an improvised lash-up anyhow, and the place really hadn't been designed for growth; and every time a crew had come up here with some new experiment or a replacement article they had just bolted the kit to whatever free hydrogen-tank wall space there was, and left it there forever. Now, after five years, the walls were growing inwards, as if coated with a metallic coral. Sometimes you couldn't even find the pieces of kit you needed, and you had to radio down to previous crews to find out where they'd left stuff.

The place was kept hygienic – it had to be – but you wouldn't call it *clean*. Hell, you had highly trained pilots and scientists up here. They didn't want to spend their lives on maintenance, for God's sake; they had work to do. And the result was unpleasant, sometimes.

Like the black algae that had finally put paid to the shower.

Even the toilets never seemed to vent properly. And the old bird was a chorus of bangs, wheezes and rattles when they tried to sleep at night. Some long-duration Moonlab crews had gone home with permanent hearing loss, he'd been told.

It was much worse than his first flight out here. It was all a kind of hideous, long-drawn-out consequence of Bert Seger's original decision to redirect this 'Lab from Earth orbit, back in 1973.

Maybe I shouldn't be so sniffy about that big tractor out there, the Soyuz. At least the Soviets must feel at home, here; 'Lab's no worse than a Moscow hotel.

Still, you could see Moonlab as a kind of huge experiment in space endurance. Moonlab was a Type II spacecraft. Type I you'd never repair; you'd use it once and bring it home to discard, or fix on the ground, like Apollo. Type II, like the 'Labs, were supposed to be repairable, but with logistic support from nearby Earth. Type III, the ultimate goal, would be able to survive for years *without* logistic support. Any Mars mission would have to be aboard a Type III spacecraft, a level of maturity beyond Moonlab.

Without the long-duration experience of Moonlab and Skylab, the Mars mission would not be conceivable.

They reached the wardroom, where the plastic table was fixed to the mesh floor, and the crew had rigged up five T-cross seats. They sat at the table, hooking their legs under the bars of the seats, and Stone fixed the TV camera to a strut.

Now the performance really began.

There were flags to swap, including a UN flag which had been carried up by Soyuz and would be returned home by Apollo. Each crew had brought along halves of commemorative aluminum and steel medallions, which Muldoon and Viktorenko joined together. They traded boxes of seeds from their countries: the Americans handed over a hybrid white spruce, and the Soviets Scotch pine, Siberian larch and Nordmann's fir.

Now it was time for the ritual meal. The Americans were hosts today, so, from the customary plastic bags, the cosmonauts were treated to potato soup, bread, strawberries and grilled steak. There was much forced bonhomie and laughter in all this. Tomorrow it would be the Russians' turn, and – as Stone knew, because they'd practiced even this – the menu would be tins containing fish, meat and potatoes, tubes of soft cheese, dried soup, vegetable puree and oats; there would be nuts, black bread, dried fruit.

As he ate, Stone looked dubiously at the TV camera staring at him from above. As space PR stunts went, this one was turning out to be a stinker. *Jesus*, he thought. *I hope nobody I know is tuned in to this.*

Now Viktorenko said, 'Of course, as the philosophers say, the best part of a good dinner is not what you eat, but with whom you eat.' He dug out five metal tubes from a pocket of his coverall. The tubes were labeled: 'vodka.' The astronauts made dutiful noises of pleasure, and when they opened the tubes up, they found borscht, which they displayed to the camera. *A Soviet joke. Ha ha.*

With the meal cleared away, the telecast should have been finished, so the crews could relax. But Bob Crippen, capcom for the day, called up from Houston. 'Moonlab, we have a surprise for you. Go ahead, Mr President; you're linked up to Moonlab.'

Familiar Georgian tones crackled over the air. 'Good evening, gentlemen. Or is it morning where you are? I'm speaking to you from the Oval Office at the White House, and this must be the most remarkable telephone call since John Kennedy spoke to you, Joe, and Neil Armstrong on the surface of the Moon, eleven years ago . . .'

The crews sat around the table, staring into the camera, smiles bolted in place.

Carter made a speech of stunning banality, a ramble that seemed to last forever. Solovyov and Viktorenko looked pole-axed. Carter was duller than Brezhnev.

Stone thought, *It wouldn't be so bad if we didn't know that Carter was on his way out. And that he has always been dead-set against the space program.*

Carter went around the table, speaking to each astronaut and cosmonaut in turn. 'So, Joe, I believe this is your first flight in eleven years.'

'Yes, sir, that's so, my first since the Moon landing. And it's wonderful to be back.'

'Do you have any advice for young people who hope to fly on future space missions?'

Muldoon's face might have been carved from wood. Stone knew exactly what he was thinking. *Yeah. Don't fuck yourself over by mouthing off against the Agency.* 'Well, sir, I'd say that the best advice is to decide what you want to do and then never give up until you've done it . . .'

As long as Carter doesn't ask if he's missing his wife, Stone thought, Muldoon will be home clear; everybody in Houston knew that Jill had walked out a couple of months before the launch, but somehow it had been kept out of the press.

Across the table from Stone, Viktorenko dug out five more 'vodka' tubes; wordlessly he passed them around. Stone opened his and sniffed at it. Viktorenko nodded to him, holding his gaze. *Yes, this really is vodka. But they will think it is borscht. A double joke!*

Stone drained his tube in one pull and crushed the metal in his fist.

As the banal speeches and ceremonies went on, the mountains of the Moon, ignored, cast complex shadows over the table top.

Wednesday, December 3, 1980
Apollo-N; Lyndon B. Johnson Space Center, Houston

Rolf Donnelly went round the horn, one last time.

'Got us locked up there, INCO?'

'That's affirm, Flight.'

'How about you, Control?'

'We look good.'

'Guidance, you happy?'

'Go with systems.'

'FIDO, how about you?'

'We're go. The trajectory's a little low, Flight, but no problem.'

'Booster?'

'Everything's nominal for the burn, Flight,' Mike Conlig said.

'Rog. Capcom, how's the crew?'

Natalie York was on capcom duty again. 'Apollo-N, Houston, are you go?'

'That's affirmative, Houston,' Chuck Jones replied briskly on the air-to-ground loop.

'Rog,' Donnelly said. 'Okay, all controllers, we are go. Thirty seconds to ignition.'

York said, 'Apollo-N, you are go for the burn.'

Apollo-N was drifting over the darkened Pacific; Ben Priest could see a bowl of white light in the waters below – the reflection of the Moon – and, all but lost in that milky vastness, the lights of a ship.

The crew lay side by side in their couches, cocooned in their pressure suits once more. Priest felt his heart pumping harder. *We've done everything we can to check this damn bird out; now we have to go full bore on it, and that's all there is to it.*

At ten seconds the DSKY threw up a flashing '99.' Chuck Jones reached out and pushed PROCEED.

Through the changing numbers on his console, Mike Conlig watched as NERVA's nuclear core was brought back up to its working temperature. Liquid hydrogen was already gushing out of the big S-NB tank and pumping into the cladding of pressure shell and engine bell, and, Conlig knew, would be reaching the radioactive core about *now*, where it would be flashed to vapor as hot as the surface of a star.

The core temperature began to climb, following the curve laid out in the manuals –

No, it didn't. The rise was too fast.

Conlig watched with dismay as his numbers drifted away from nominal.

As NERVA lit, the spacecraft shuddered.

Priest was pushed back into his seat with a long, gentle pressure. *Perfect. Just like the sims.*

Natalie York called up, 'You're looking good here. We're hawk-eyeing your trajectory. You're right down the center line.'

Priest's job was to watch the pressure and temperature readouts from the S-NB stage, the NERVA engine and its big hydrogen tank. Jones was monitoring the attitude indicator with its artificial horizon, ready to take over the steering if the automated systems failed. Dana was calling out their increasing velocity from the DSKY readout. 'Thirty thousand feet per second . . . thirty-three . . .'

*　　*　　*

Mike Conlig was aware of a deadly dryness in his mouth. On the loop from the back room, someone was screaming in his ear.

The numbers, white on a green screen, filled his world.

The computers worked constantly to update the numbers, and making sense of them wasn't easy. He had to check the data-source slots at the top right-hand corner of the screen, to make sure that the sources of his numbers were all still updating him properly, and he had to be sure that he wasn't diagnosing some problem incorrectly because of a mismatch in numbers of different vintages, fifteen or thirty seconds old.

But he discounted all that. He understood exactly what the silent parade of numbers was telling him. The NERVA core was still overheating.

He tried to increase the flow of hydrogen through the core. That would take away some of the excess heat.

He got no response. In fact, one readout told him that the volume throughput of the hydrogen was actually *falling*.

Maybe there was a problem with a hydrogen feed line. Or maybe a pump had failed. Or maybe it was his old enemy, cavitation, somewhere in the propellant flow cylinders.

The core's temperature continued to rise. More screaming in his ear.

Damn, damn. He'd have to abort the burn. And this was probably the end of the mission; he doubted they'd be allowed to go ahead with another engine restart after this.

He sent a command to the engine's moderator control. He would slow the reaction in the NERVA core, reduce the temperature that way.

He got no response.

If the temperature had gotten high enough, the fuel elements could have distorted, even melted, and it would be impossible to insert the control elements into the core. Was that happening already?

If it was true, there wasn't *anything* he could do to retrieve the situation. As he watched his numbers evolve, Conlig felt the first touches of panic.

Priest could clearly see the cones of the volcanoes of Hawaii, upthrusting, broken blisters. Earth receded visibly, as if he was rising in an elevator. The ride was exhilarating.

He felt a surge of elation. *The damn nuke works.*

*   *   *

273

It unraveled with astonishing speed.

Conlig watched power surge through the overheating core. After that, the resistance to hydrogen flow through the core sharply increased. Bubbles built up everywhere. The nuclear fuel assemblies were starting to break up. Pressure rose abruptly in the propellant channels, which were also beginning to disintegrate.

The whole structure of the core was collapsing.

The pressure in the reactor began to rise, at more than fifteen atmospheres a second. And, because of the massive temperatures, chemical and exothermic reactions were starting in the core.

And now the increased pressure inside the reactor backed up to the pumps, and the pumps' feedback valves burst. With the pumps disabled the flow of hydrogen through the core stopped altogether.

The reactor's main relief valves triggered, venting hydrogen to space. That offered some respite. But the discharge was brief; unable to cope with the enormous pressures and flow rate, the valves themselves were soon destroyed.

And now the massive pressure was working on the structure of the pressure shell itself.

I've lost it. I've lost the reactor. It had taken seconds, for his life to fall apart. He tried to react, to think of something to do, to make a report to Flight. But his mouth was dry, the muscles of his jaw locked.

There was a loud, dull bang, and the Command Module shook: bang, whump, shudder.

Dana, strapped into his center seat, could feel the spacecraft quake under him. Hollow rattles and creaks sounded from around the cabin, a groan of metal as the can around him was stressed; it was a noise oddly like a deep-throated whale song.

The master alarm shrilled in Dana's headset, a shrill of staccato beeps. Yellow warning lights lit up all over the control panels.

He turned to look at his companions. Jones was staring at the instrument panel, and Priest's eyes were round. *That sure as hell wasn't routine, whatever it was.*

Jones cleared the master alarm.

The feeling of thrust died abruptly. It was like a slow collision in a car; Dana was thrown forward, gently, against his straps.

Jones said, 'Jim. The Main A light is on. Check it out.'

Dana looked at his console. A red undervolt light was glowing. *Damn. I should have been the first to see it.* The Command Module's systems were Dana's responsibility.

'Confirm that,' he said. 'We've got a Main A undervolt.' He was surprised his voice was level. He began to check voltage and current levels; they were showing erratic, inconsistent readings.

He heard pinging and popping noises. It was the sound of metal flexing. The spacecraft was still shuddering. *Some damn thing has blown up on us.*

Earth was wheeling past the windows. The Service Module thrusters ought to be firing, as the spacecraft tried to maintain its orientation. But he couldn't hear any solenoids thumping.

Jones was talking to Houston. 'Natalie, we be a sorry bird up here. We've got a problem.' He unbuckled his restraints and floated up to the left-hand window. Dana knew he was following an old pilot's instinct: at a moment like this, regardless of the telemetry, you needed to take a walk around the bird, to look for leaks and kick the tires, see for himself what was wrong.

Dana glanced out of the window to his right, past Ben Priest.

He saw sparks, chunks of some material, flying up past the Command Module. The material was glowing, red hot.

Now he could smell something, inside his helmet. It reminded him, oddly, of Hampton: his childhood, the ocean.

Ozone.

Donnelly didn't even need to hear the specific words. He could *feel* the event, see it in the changed postures of controllers all over the room, hear it in the sudden urgency of their voices.

Something had fouled up. But at first the cause wasn't clear; all Donnelly got was a rash of symptoms, monitored by his controllers.

'We got more than a problem.' That was EECOM, in charge of electrical and environmental systems: life support in Apollo-N. He was shouting. 'I got CSM EPS high density. Listen up, you guys. Fuel Cell 1 and 2 pressure has gone away.' Controller jargon, for *fallen to zero.* 'And I'm losing oxygen tank 1 pressure, and temperature.'

Natalie York was talking to the crew. 'This is Houston. Repeat that, please.'

'. . . We've got a problem,' Jones said over the air-to-ground. 'The NERVA is out, and we're seeing a Main Bus A undervolt.'

'Roger. Main Bus A. Stand by, Apollo-N; we're looking at it.'

Now Guidance said, 'We've had a hardware restart. We don't know what it was.'

A hardware restart meant some unusual event had caused the

275

computer to shut itself down and reboot. Donnelly called for confirmation from another controller.

The crew kept reporting their Bus A undervolt.

The electrical power for Apollo-N came from three fuel cells in the Service Module. The current from the cells flowed through the A and B Buses, conduits which fed the rest of the spacecraft's components. An undervolt alarm meant the spacecraft was losing its electrical power.

Donnelly tried to get confirmation of the problem from EECOM. 'You see a Bus undervolt, EECOM?'

'. . . Negative, Flight.'

But EECOM had hesitated.

He knows more than he's telling me. He's still trying to figure it through. What the hell was happening here? The mission seemed to be falling apart before his eyes.

Donnelly pressed EECOM again; he needed more data. 'The crew are still reporting the undervolt, EECOM.'

'Okay, Flight. I got some instrumentation problems. Let me add them up.'

Instrumentation problems. *EECOM sees the undervolt, all right. But he doesn't believe what the instruments are telling him. He's looking at a lot of ratty data; he thinks some kind of major telemetry failure is underway. He wants to be sure before he reports it to me.*

Donnelly said, 'I assume you've called in your backup EECOM to see if we can get more intelligence applied here.'

'We have him here.'

'Roger.'

Now INCO, the instrumentation and communications controller, called in. 'Flight, INCO. The high-gain antenna has switched to high beam.'

What in hell did that mean? 'INCO, can you confirm the time when that change occurred?' If he could, it might be a clue in pinning down what was happening . . .

Before INCO could reply there was another call. 'Flight, Guidance. We have attitude changes.'

'What do you mean, attitude changes?'

'The RCS valves appear to be closed. They should be open.'

Reaction control problems. Antenna problems. Problems with the oxygen tanks, and the fuel cells.

He'd never seen a systems signature like this before, not in any of the sims he'd gone through. But then, even after twelve years of

276

flights, Apollo-Saturn was still an experimental system. You'd test-fly an airplane far more times than any spacecraft had ever flown, before declaring it operational.

So what was hitting him? It *could* be instrumentation problems, flaky readouts, as EECOM seemed to suspect. Or it could be that the Service Module had blown out, knocking the whole stack sideways. Or something else might have blown, and damaged the Service Module.

INCO's timing came in. His antenna problems dated from a few seconds after they'd lit the NERVA.

For the first time in several seconds Donnelly glanced at the trajectory plot board. The spacecraft was diverging, markedly, from the path it should have followed, had the NERVA been burning smoothly.

The S-NB looked to have shut down.

'Guidance, you want to confirm that deviation?'

'Rog, Flight.' Guidance was the ground navigator. Guidance must be looking at multiple problems too, as the spacecraft drifted from its trajectory, and tumbled away from its intended attitude.

'Booster, you got anything to report?'

Mike Conlig did not reply. Donnelly could see how he was hunched over his console. 'Booster?'

York said, 'The crew is reporting a smell of ozone, inside their helmets.'

'Flight, this is Surgeon. I have a contrary indication.' The flight doctor on this flight was a crop-headed Oklahoman sitting in the row in front of Donnelly, with the systems guys, at the left-hand end next to Natalie York. He was wearing a button badge which read FUCK IRAN. His voice was taut, urgent.

Donnelly switched him onto a closed loop. 'Go, Surgeon.'

'Flight, I'm monitoring a surge of radiation flux through the spacecraft cabin. And some changes in the crew's vital readings.'

Donnelly was thinking through York's brief report. *They can smell ozone. Oxygen, ionized by radiation. Radiation from the NERVA. Jesus Christ almighty.*

It was real, then. Not just flaky instrumentation. *And the Russians orbited a goddamn Vietnamese in Salyut this year. The press will crucify us.*

Because of the two simultaneous missions in progress Bert Seger had been away from the office for three days, and he was taking a chance to work through his mail. He'd only been at it for a few

277

minutes when he got a call on the squawk box, the line that linked up the senior staff in Building 2.

There had been some kind of problem with the Apollo-N flight, and Seger had better get on over to the MOCR.

Angrily Seger folded up his mail. With the NERVA, it was one damn thing after another.

The voltage needle on Bus A sank past the bottom of its scale. More warning lights came on.

Dana checked the Service Module's fuel cell 1, which was supposed to feed Bus A. It was dead. His gloved fingers clumsy with the switches, Dana began to reconnect the Command Module's systems from Bus A onto Bus B.

Now another red light came on. Bus B was losing voltage as well. He checked fuel cell 3, the feed for Bus B; it was dead too.

Jesus. We've lost the Service Module. It's Apollo 13 over again.

He made his report, trying to keep his voice level. Mary would be listening, probably the kids. 'Okay, Houston, I tried to reset, and fuel cells 1 and 3 are both showing gray flags. I've got zip on the flows.'

'Acknowledged, Apollo-N. EECOM has copied.'

Earth, beautiful, unperturbed, drifted past the windows.

The spacecraft and booster had been set rotating by that mysterious bang. Dana knew the ship's attitude control systems should have been trying to steady their slow tumble, but there was no sign of any correction.

'Chuck, I think the Service Module's RCS must be out.'

'Rog,' Jones said. 'Houston, we don't have reaction control, either from the Service Module or from S-NB.'

If the Service Module *had* blown, it was the end of the mission. But still, the crew ought to be able to get home, from this low Earth orbit.

As the spacecraft rolled, a cloud of ice crystals, sparkling, dispersing, drifted past the window to his right. It seemed to be venting from somewhere in the stack. It was quite beautiful, coalescing above the shining face of Earth.

More alarms lit up, as the problems multiplied and spread.

Donnelly had Surgeon feeding radiation dosimeter readings into his ear on the closed loop.

EECOM said, 'Flight, I want to throw a battery on Bus A and Bus

278

B until we psyche out the anomalies. We're confirming undervolts.'

Donnelly tried to shut out Surgeon's voice so he could figure out EECOM's suggestion.

EECOM wanted to run the Command Module off battery power. It was a reasonable short-term suggestion. But, looking ahead, the Command Module's batteries would have to be conserved to allow the crew to reenter the Earth's atmosphere. 'What about limiting that to a single Bus, rather than both?'

'Hold on that, Flight.' EECOM would now be conferring with his team of experts in the back rooms.

It was obvious from multiple indications, not least the crew's report, that the NERVA had indeed shut itself down after only a few seconds of the planned burn. 'Booster, you have anything you want to say to me?'

Conlig didn't reply. The guy seemed to have frozen out.

'The crew's health is going to be severely impacted,' Surgeon said on the closed loop. 'Though they probably don't know it yet. In fact, Flight, you can't expect them to function normally for much beyond a few more minutes.'

Guidance came on line. 'The bird's attitude is still changing. They got to stop it. We're heading for gimbal lock.'

'I hear you, Guidance.'

Gimbal lock meant the spacecraft tumbling beyond the tolerance of the inertial guidance system. The platform could be reset by eye again. But if Donnelly was forced to go for an emergency reentry, he needed alignment control now.

Somehow, though, he felt that alignment loss, even a gimbal lock, was the least of the spacecraft's problems right now.

'Houston, Apollo-N.' It was Jim Dana; to Natalie York, Jim's voice sounded thin, frail, but controlled. 'We're seeing some kind of gas, venting from the stack.'

York's skin prickled with a sudden chill.

'Rog, Apollo-N,' she said. 'Can you tell if it's coming from the S-NB tank, or the Service Module?'

'We can't tell. Both, possibly.'

She'd been following the controllers' terse dialogue. The controllers were still working to the assumption that there was some kind of instrumentation or telemetry problem here, to explain the multiple anomalies.

But if the ship was venting gas, that couldn't be it. The problem *couldn't* be just instrumentation or an electrical screw-up. And

279

besides, she could see that Surgeon, next to her, had switched onto a closed loop.

Something, some violent and destructive event, had happened to Apollo-N, up there in low Earth orbit, to a spacecraft with a nuclear pile attached to its tail.

She glanced across at Mike. He was still hunched over his console and whispering into his headset. *Why doesn't he say something to Flight?*

She became aware that her right hand was clutching the thin metal maintenance handle of her console; her hand was closed into a fist, painfully.

Her throat was dry, and she had to force herself to swallow before she could speak again.

Ben's up there. What in hell is going on?

Gregory Dana, in the Viewing Room, could see the spacecraft icon drifting from its programmed trajectory on the big plot board, and he could follow enough of the controllers' terse exchanges to figure out that something catastrophic had happened to Jim's ship.

Now the Viewing Room was steadily filling up – as was the MOCR amphitheater itself – as off-duty personnel came hurrying in, responding to the deepening atmosphere of crisis.

Dana was joined at the window by one of the astronaut corps, Ralph Gershon, whom Dana had met a couple of times through Jim.

Gershon stared out at the frantic huddles in the MOCR and snorted contempt. 'Jesus. Look at them huddling up. They always go through the same thing. *What happened? Where are we? What are we going to do about it?* They're so damned slow, and restricted in the way they think. And meanwhile the bird drifts around the sky, broken-winged.'

Broken-winged.

The problems must be with the nuclear engine. Everything, every anomaly, had flowed from that moment.

They have to get the crew away from that damn booster. Dana couldn't understand why that hadn't been done already.

He glanced around. He couldn't tell if any of this was being broadcast on the public networks. What if Mary, and Jake and Maria, were seeing this on TV? What about Sylvia?

Silently, his lips moving, Gregory Dana began to pray.

*   *   *

280

The NERVA has blown. That's got to be it.

Jim Dana, lying in his couch, thought he could *feel* the tingle of radioactive particles within his body. It was a thin wind, working its way into his bones. His face and chest felt as if they were on fire. He felt a burning sensation and a tightness about his temples, and his eyelids were smarting, as if they had been doused with acid.

With every breath, he must be filling his lungs with radionuclides. His throat hurt, and he began to cough.

Wednesday, December 3, 1980
International Club, Washington

The Executives Group were about to take dinner at the International Club on 19th Street. Vice President-elect Bush attended, along with members of the Senate and House who held key positions on the Space and Appropriations Committees; and now they were standing around with drinks in their hands.

Under the surface of talk and networking, Fred Michaels was running over the events of the day.

Michaels had inherited the idea of the Executives Group from his predecessors at NASA. The Group consisted of the space program's top people: Michaels and his NASA senior managers, and the prime contractors' senior executives, from Rockwell, Grumman, Boeing, McDonnell Douglas, IBM. It was an elite club that Michaels liked to bring together four or five times a year.

Today had been a good day, he decided. The Executives Group session had gone well, and Bush's closing address had been encouraging. Michaels had worried about losing outgoing veep Ted Kennedy, who, with his brother, continued to support the space program. Today, though, Bush seemed to be positioning himself as – if not an advocate – then at least as an ally.

Yes, a good day. But Michaels was tensed up, his big stomach growling. He always found it impossible to relax in the middle of a mission. Any one of a hundred thousand malfunctions could, he knew, spell the end of the flight, and maybe cost the lives of the crew, and conceivably put a bullet to the head of the whole Mars initiative – and, incidentally, Michaels's own career. How the hell could anyone relax through that? And tonight there were not one but *two* American crews beyond the atmosphere, one floating around the Earth with a nuke on their tail, and the others bouncing off the Moon with those Russians. What a situation.

Still, the S-NB seemed to be functioning well, so much so that Hans Udet – the most senior of Marshall's Germans on the project – had felt able to take time out to be here with the Executives tonight. Michaels could see him now, glad-handing a brace of Congressmen with all the Prussian charisma and charm at his disposal. *Udet looks confident enough. Why the hell shouldn't I be?*

That was when the phone calls started coming in. Afterwards, Michaels would never be sure who got the first call.

He saw the president of Rockwell in excited conversation with another man. Then all the Rockwell executives left the Club's main room, and returned a few minutes later, visibly distressed. They began to go through the room, seeking out others; Michaels could see the news – whatever it was – spreading through the Executives Group like a contagion of dismay.

Then Michaels himself was paged to take a call from Tim Josephson, who was still at NASA Headquarters a few blocks away.

'Fred, the crew has lost the NERVA. The technical parameters got out of their nominal boundaries. Ah – in fact, the thing might have exploded.'

'Jesus Christ. And the crew?' Michaels snapped. 'What about the damn crew, Josephson?'

Josephson's voice was even, analytical. 'It's hard to say from here, Fred. The updates are patchy. I'd say we're looking at a potential crew loss situation.'

A waiter paged Michaels with another urgent call. This time it was Bert Seger from Houston. Seger, his voice high and clipped, gave him more details: some kind of runaway in the NERVA reactor, extensive damage to the Service Module, damage unknown to the Command Module –

Michaels cut him short. No American astronauts had been killed in space before. No previous Administrator had lost a crew. 'Bring them home, Bert.'

Michaels felt someone grabbing at his arm. It was Udet; the tall German was smiling, a little flushed with the drink. Udet wanted to introduce Michaels to a portly Senator.

Michaels drew Udet to one side, and told him the news.

Udet's smile evaporated. He seemed to withdraw into himself; he held himself straight and erect, his face a mask. With precision, he put his glass down on a waiter's tray.

'What must we do?'

'Hans, I want you to call the White House and tell them what's happened. Tell them I'll be in contact as soon as I can. And then I

282

want you to get the hell out of here and back to Marshall.'

The German nodded his head, and walked stiffly from the room. Michaels watched him go.

He thought back. Seger's telephoned voice had been distant, light, oddly false; Michaels felt a stab of worry. *But the guy is under incredible pressure. Of course he's going to sound strange. As long as he stays in one piece long enough to get the bird down.* Seger's mental state was something Michaels could deal with later. *Christ. I'm going to have a few crazies on my hands before we're done with this damn business.*

Michaels walked back to his guests in the reception room. Obviously word was continuing to spread amongst them. *Hell, they only need to look at my face to see that.* He even saw one man crying.

In the dining room the waiters were laying out dinner; nobody was paying any attention to them.

Michaels found Bush, and spoke briefly with him. Then he called for quiet, and broke the news officially to the rest of the guests.

After that the Group broke up quickly. The contractors who had hardware involved in the accident left to find planes to take them to Houston.

Michaels made his apologies to Bush, left the Club, and ordered his driver to take him to NASA Headquarters.

Wednesday, December 3, 1980
Apollo-N; Lyndon B. Johnson Space Center, Houston

The Astronaut Office was quiet that night. Ralph Gershon was here, though, in the Office. As a MEM specialist he didn't have any specific assignments to do with the current shots. Most of the pilots were wrapped up in work in support of the flights in the simulators, or working at contractors' plants around the country.

But Gershon had heard something about the problems on the NERVA flight today. He'd gone over to the MOCR, but there wasn't a damn thing he could do there. He was just in the way, radiating anxiety all over everybody else. So he made sure his location was known, in case he was needed, and now here he sat in the office he shared, quietly going through his in-tray.

The phone rang. He picked it up on the first ring.

'Ralph? I'm glad I caught you.'

'Natalie? Are you still on shift?'

283

'Yeah. Rolf Donnelly asked me to call you. I –'

'Yes?'

'We think we might lose the crew.'

Gershon could hear voices in the MOCR behind her, taut, shouting.

York wanted Gershon to arrange for astronauts and wives to go to the homes of the crew.

Gershon agreed straight away, and York hung up.

It was a tradition, dating back to Mercury, that if you had to receive bad news like this, you'd get it from an astronaut, or his wife – someone close enough to the risks and pressures to understand how you'd be feeling.

Gershon dug out his phone book. He'd start with people he knew lived close to the families.

The assignment was going to be as hard a mission as he'd performed in his life.

He began to dial.

Venting gas.

Donnelly understood the implications of that observation as well as anyone.

On the loop he said, 'Okay, now, Indigo Team, let's everyone keep cool. We're going to stick to the mission rules, and remember the priorities.

'Let's go back to basics. EECOM tells me that right now we still have a sealed can.' An airtight ship, a place to keep the astronauts alive. 'We've faced situations like this many times in the sims' – *but never for real, damn it* – 'and you know that having a sealed can is always the number one requirement; as long as we have that, at least, we have some time to figure things out. We're going to solve this problem, but we don't need to make things worse by guessing. Now, let's get to it.'

It seemed to do some good; the atmosphere in the MOCR, the angle of hunch of the white-shirted shoulders, seemed to ease a little. Donnelly nodded to himself, pleased; maybe he'd lanced the boil of panic that had been building up.

Donnelly knew he had to work systematically. He was going to 'down-mode,' in the jargon, move from one set of options to another, more restricted set. He had to preserve as many of the mission objectives as he could without further endangering the lives of the astronauts. *If you can't land on the Moon, can you at least orbit it?* And he didn't want to close out any options he didn't have to, because he didn't know what else was likely to be thrown at him, and he needed to keep contingencies open. For example, it was conceivable they might have to use the S-NB engine to direct a reentry, if the problems turned out to be with the Service Module after all.

Tread lightly, lest ye step in shit. That was the motto. The trouble was, Donnelly was quickly running out of options altogether.

In the background, her heard Natalie York talking to the crew. 'Apollo-N, we've got everyone working on this. We'll get you some dope as soon as we have it, and you'll be the first to know.'

Good girl.

Chuck Jones replied. 'Thank you, Houston.' On the air-to-ground, Jones's voice sounded dry, weak.

In response to the sound of Jones's voice there was a brief, distressed silence in the MOCR, despite the array of amber lights before Donnelly.

He scanned the MOCR. Each of his controllers was staring into his own screen, digging deeper and deeper into the problems he saw in his own area. As if his own problems were somehow separate from the rest.

Donnelly had a pang of doubt, suddenly. *Am I handling this the wrong way?* The controllers were getting isolated from each other and from the real spacecraft up there; some of them were probably still convincing themselves that there was nothing worse here than a booster shutdown and some funny instrumentation glitches.

But we know that isn't true. The crew heard a bang. And they can see gas venting.

He needed to start talking to his controllers again, to try to keep them thinking as a team.

'Okay,' he said, 'I want to get everybody on the loop. Retro, Guidance, Control, Booster, GNC, EECOM, INCO, FAO. Give me an amber, please.'

An amber light on the Flight's console indicated talk-and-listen; it meant that controller wanted attention. One by one, the lights turned from listen-only green to amber.

Except Booster.

'Goddamn it,' Donnelly snapped. 'Booster, Flight. Give me an amber, please.'

'Acknowledge,' Mike Conlig said quickly. The last amber lit.

'All right, people, tell me where we stand. What's your most urgent item? Who wants to start?'

'Flight, Guidance. That attitude drift –'

285

'Rog. Capcom, please inform the crew that they need to maneuver out of a threat of gimbal lock.'

'Acknowledge,' said York.

Now Bert Seger came stalking down from Management Row, gaunt, intense, every gesture stiff with nervous energy. He stopped at Donnelly's elbow. He plugged into a console and listened in to the controllers' loops.

'Flight.' Now it was EECOM. 'I think the best thing we can do right now is start a power-down. Maybe we can look at the telemetry, and then come back up.'

That sounded damned optimistic to Donnelly. 'Hold on that, EECOM.' He wanted to keep the Command Module's systems powered up for now, so he had available the option of bringing the crew down quickly. 'Okay, who's next?'

That asshole at Booster, Mike Conlig, still wasn't speaking to him.

'It's the NERVA,' Seger said in his ear.

'Yes. I –'

'The fucking nuke has blown on us. And it looks like it's disrupted the Service Module as well. That's obvious even to me. Rolf, you're moving too slowly. You got to get them away from that thing, and get them home.'

'But –'

'Do it, Rolf, or I'm going to override you.'

Donnelly closed his eyes, for one second. *Jesus. There goes my career.*

'Capcom, please relay new instructions to the crew.'

Apollo-N continued to pitch and yaw. Metal groaned, and Priest could feel the motion, as a wrench at his stomach.

'We got to ditch the NERVA,' Chuck Jones said. His voice was a rasp. 'These rates are killing us. Do it, Jim.'

Dana didn't respond.

Priest looked to his left.

Jim Dana, in the center couch, seemed to have lost consciousness. His face, under his helmet, was severely blistered; in some places strips of flesh were hanging loose, drifting in the air. He looked as if he had vomited; globs of thin, brownish liquid clung to the inside of his faceplate.

Priest reached across to Dana's station. Separating Apollo-N from the S-NB booster stage was a routine maneuver, something any of them could handle. But Priest's thinking seemed to be cloudy, and

286

he was having trouble seeing the panel before him. He couldn't feel the switches through his pressure-suit glove. He fumbled at the glove, but his hand seemed to have swollen up, and the glove was tight. Finally he got the glove off, and let it drift away.

He looked at his bare hand, puzzled. The skin had turned a deep, uniform brown. *A nuclear tan. How about that.*

He snapped switches.

There was a series of sharp bangs, a shudder.

'Houston, we've got separation,' Jones said.

The Earth slid more rapidly past the windows, as the freed Apollo-N tumbled away from the S-NB. With separation, the tumbling seemed to ease; maybe, Priest thought, gas venting from the S-NB had been causing some of the pitching.

Jones worked at hand controllers which should have operated the RCS clusters on the Service Module. He was trying to kill the residual rates, the unwanted tumbling. 'Zippo,' he said. 'Still nothing, Houston; we don't have any attitude control.'

'Acknowledged, Apollo-N,' Natalie York said. 'We're working on it. Watch out for gimbal lock.'

Priest could see the red warning disk painted on the 8-ball, drifting into the ball's little window, the warning for incipient gimbal lock.

'Well, hell,' Jones groused, 'I don't see I can do much about that, Natalie.'

Now the tumble brought the discarded nuclear booster into Priest's view. The slim black and white cylinder looked almost beautiful as it drifted away from him, silhouetted against the Earth's shining skin, highlighted by sunlight. But he could see that a panel had blown out of the pressure shell surrounding the reactor core, at the base of the hydrogen tank. Inside the shell, Priest could see a tangle of pipes and Mylar insulation. And the hydrogen tank itself had been ripped open; a thin wisp of gas still vented from it.

Priest wondered vaguely if they ought to be focusing a TV camera on the booster.

Jones began to describe the S-NB to Houston. 'There's one whole side of the damn thing missing. I can see wires dangling, and the base of that hydrogen tank is just a mass of ripped metal. It's really a mess...'

Now, as the S-NB rolled, Priest could see through the base of the ripped-open tank, all the way through to the NERVA reactor itself. And in there, he saw a point of light, white-hot. *That's the goddamn core. The reactor's blown itself apart, and exposed the core*. There was no sign of the biological shield, which must have been blown away. Perhaps that was what they had seen, in red-hot fragments, founting past the Command Module's windows.

As he stared into the wreckage he thought he could actually feel heat on his face: heat radiating from the core itself, as if it were a tiny, captive sun.

He glanced at the radiation dosimeter number on his DSKY. Thirty thousand roentgens an hour were now spewing out of the core, and through the spacecraft, in an invisible hail of gamma and neutron radiation.

Thirty thousand. It was a hard number to believe. The safe limit, according to the mission rules, was one *thousandth* of a roentgen per *day*.

'I guess we're kind of privileged,' Priest said. 'Nobody in the history of mankind has ever got up so close to an exposed nuclear reaction before. The victims of Hiroshima were killed by heat and the shock wave rather than by radiation . . .'

Jones cackled, and he closed his eyes. 'Another first for the space program. Oh, thank you, Lord.'

Wednesday, December 3, 1980
Timber Cove, El Lago, Houston

Gregory Dana found it a scramble to get out of JSC. Dozens of TV, radio and print reporters were turning up at the security blockhouse, requesting clearance and asking for access to whatever briefings NASA was planning. The car park opposite Building 2, the Public Affairs Office, was one of the busiest on the campus.

It was pitch dark by the time Dana arrived at the ranch house in Lazywood Lane.

Jim and Mary lived in a pretty place. Timber Cove was a development that had sprung up in the 1960s, a couple of miles from JSC. Around the tidy, manicured streets the ranch houses were sprinkled in the greenery like huge wooden toys, individually styled, encrusted with stone cladding. The grass was rich and cool-damp, and the cultivated pine trees on the lawns were a dark green, almost black in the low lamp light.

The area was soaked with NASA connections. Once, Jim liked to boast, no less than Jim Lovell had lived next door, with his family. Here, on happier days, Dana had come to throw baseballs with Jake, and to make paper airplanes for little Mary, and to

argue the politics and engineering of spaceflight with his son . . .

For a few minutes Dana sat in the car. He felt as if the strength had been drawn out of him. He rolled down the window and let the cooler air waft over his face.

He could hear water lapping at the back of the house, the clink of the chain that tied up Jim's little dinghy.

He took off his glasses, and wiped them on his crumpled tie.

Later tonight Gregory was going to have to fly up to Virginia to be with Sylvia, and bring her back here. He'd spoken to her on the phone several times already – the Mission Control people had given him a line – and she'd sounded calm enough. But Dana couldn't begin to imagine how she was going to react to this.

Well, how am I reacting? Do I even understand that? My son, my only son, is in orbit right now – perhaps trapped up there – with his poor, fragile body irradiated by Marshall's hellish abortion of a nuclear rocket. It was a situation, he thought, which the human heart simply wasn't programmed to cope with.

And, under all his grief, he felt the dull, painful glow of anger that none of this need have been so – that it wasn't, never had been, necessary to build nuclear rockets to get to Mars.

He pushed his glasses back on his face, shoved open the car door, and got out.

There was a Christmas wreath on Jim's front door.

It was physically hard for him to walk up the drive, he observed, bemused. He watched his feet, his shoes of brown leather, as they lifted and settled on the gravel path, as if they belonged to some robot.

He reached the door.

He felt exhausted, as if the path had been a steep climb. *It won't be so bad*, he told himself feverishly. *Just ring the doorbell; that's all you have to do.* Seger had said someone from the Astronaut Office would have been here by now. *So you won't have to give her the news, at least.* And besides, Walter Cronkite was probably already intoning gloomy predictions on CBS.

You won't even have to break the news. So ring the bell, damn you.

His hands hung at his sides, heavy, weak, useless.

Wednesday, December 3, 1980
Apollo-N; Lyndon B. Johnson Space Center, Houston

'Apollo-N, Houston. We're going to bring you home. Just take it easy, and we'll bring you down. The Command Module systems are looking good at this time. You might want to dig out the medical kit –'

Natalie's voice remained calm and controlled, and Priest, through the mounting pain in his chest and eyes, felt a surge of pride. *Good for you, rookie.*

'I think we'll have to pass on that,' he said. 'I doubt if any of us could reach the kit, Natalie.'

'Just hang tight, Apollo-N.'

'Hey, bug-eyes,' Jones said to Priest. 'I got Jim's pin in my pocket.'

'What pin?'

'His flight pin. The gold one. He's no rookie now. I was going to give it to him after the burn. You want to reach over? He might like to see it.'

'Maybe later, Chuck. I think he's sleeping.'

'Sure. Maybe later.'

Donnelly, listening to the clamor of voices on the loops, felt numb, unreal, as if all that radiation had gone sleeting through his own body.

The reentry was going to be a mess. The systems guys were hurrying through an improvised checklist, designed to get the Command Module configured to bring itself home. At the same time, the trajectory guys were figuring out where they could bring the bird down; it had to be near enough to a Navy vessel that could effect an emergency recovery and offer medical facilities . . .

He became aware that he'd said nothing, even in response to direct questions from the controllers, for – how long? A minute, maybe.

Christ, what a mess.

At the end of her shift York turned and looked for Mike, but his seat at the Booster console was already occupied by somebody else, some Marshall technician she didn't know. He'd left and she hadn't realized – and nor, she thought, had he chosen to seek her out.

She considered asking where Mike had gone, but the new Booster guy was already immersed in his work.

Some of the controllers coming off shift were going to the Singing Wheel, a roadhouse near JSC that was a traditional hangout. They invited York, but she refused.

When she got out of JSC she drove quickly to the Portofino. Mike wasn't there.

She prowled around the place, restless; she felt caged in by her few possessions, depressed by the images of Mars taped to the walls.

She took a bath, and lay down on the double bed to try to sleep. It was past eleven p.m. But sleep wouldn't come; she seemed to feel the pressure of the headset around her skull, see the numbers glowing on the screen before her, hear the voices whispering on loops in her head.

She tried the TV news; every channel was full of Apollo-N, of course, but there was no substantive information.

Ben's up there.

Mike still hadn't showed up.

She got dressed again, picked up her purse, and drove out to the Singing Wheel.

Some of the Indigo Team controllers were still there. The Wheel was usually a venue for bright, noisy conversations; it was a red-brick saloon crowded with dubious antiques, and the Mission Control staff went along to wind down after simulations or to celebrate milestones, like splashdowns. But tonight nobody was rowdy. They just sat around a cluster of tables, drinking and talking quietly. In this regard, York knew, the controllers had a lot in common with flight jocks, when they lost one of their number: their reaction was just to sit and talk about how and why it happened, and get drunk while doing so.

York stayed with them until the small hours.

When he finally got away from his desk Donnelly pulled his flight log toward him. He checked the clock on the wall to fill in the Mission Elapsed Time column, and signed himself out. His hands were trembling, and the signature was shaky.

He flipped back through the log. The last few pages were all but illegible.

Thursday, December 4, 1980
Lyndon B. Johnson Space Center, Houston

It was already after midnight when Bert Seger called Fay from his office.

He asked Fay to send him some fresh clothes. He made a mental note to arrange a security pass for her; JSC, and the Cape, had been sealed off as soon as news of the accident's severity had started to break.

He asked after the kids, and failed to hear the answers. Then he told Fay he loved her. He hung up.

It was evident he was going to be working out of Houston for a while, or maybe the Cape, if and when the Command Module was retrieved after reentry. Fred Michaels had already told him that Carter was ordering a Presidential Commission to look into the accident, to which he'd expect NASA to respond fully, and for which response he'd be holding Seger accountable.

Seger expected nothing else.

Sooner or later, he'd always known, an astronaut was going to die on him.

The systems they were building simply weren't reliable enough to guarantee safety. Most of the astronaut corps, even now, were test pilots; they knew the odds better than anyone else, and they accepted them. But the people on the ground were Seger's greater concern. His ground crews would have to live with the knowledge that they might have done something differently. *It won't fail because of me.* What happened when that transmuted to: *It failed because of me?*

The phone rang. It was Tim Josephson, who wanted to talk about nominees for NASA's internal investigative panel, that would be set up to anticipate and assist the Presidential Commission.

Seger forced himself to focus on what Josephson was saying.

He and Josephson soon agreed on a core list, save for the astronaut representative.

'What about Natalie York?' Seger said. 'She was capcom when the stack blew; she showed herself to be cool and analytical under pressure. And she's a personal friend of Priest's.'

Josephson vetoed that. 'York is still a rookie. And besides, she's attached to Mike Conlig. Had you forgotten that? How can she assess a case, maybe involving defective designs or suspect management practices, involving her boyfriend?'

292

They went through some more names, without success.

Josephson cut him off. 'Bert, I'll tell you who Fred wants. Joe Muldoon.'

'Muldoon? Are you crazy? Muldoon is a loose cannon.'

'Yeah. He's been a loud-mouth, but that maybe gives him a reputation for independence, which wouldn't harm right now. And he was a moonwalker. Fred has a lot of time for him.'

'Muldoon's not available anyway. He's in lunar orbit.'

'But he's due to return in a week. That's time enough . . .'

They argued around it for a while, but eventually Seger gave in.

He was uneasy about having someone as crass and loud as Muldoon in a role as high-profile as this. There was bound to be a lot of dirt to be dug out over this incident, particularly from Marshall; he shuddered when he imagined what kind of stuff Muldoon, hero astronaut, might start feeding the press.

He would have to keep a lid on all of that.

When Josephson hung up, it was three a.m.

Seger knew he needed sleep. He kept a fold-up bed in a closet for times like this.

He slipped off his shoes, and got to his knees and tried to pray. But he couldn't concentrate; his mind kept on making up lists of things he had to do, prioritizing.

Strangely, the doubts he had felt earlier in the mission – doubts induced by the hostility of the anti-nuke protesters – had melted away, now that the worst had come to pass. He felt confident about his ability to cope with all of this. NASA's ability, in fact. It was only some damned hardware fault, after all. A fault they could fix, now it had identified itself.

And NASA had survived problems like this before: he remembered that just two years after the Apollo 1 fire, Armstrong and Muldoon had landed on the Moon. And after Apollo 13 had blown up on the way to the Moon, not only had they got the astronauts back, but they'd gone on to fly, on 14, the most successful damned mission of them all.

He touched the gold crucifix at his lapel. He felt oddly light, almost giddy. They'd get through this; he had no doubt about it now. With God's help.

But it was difficult to pray. Somehow, he felt God was far away from him, that night.

Finally, at around four a.m., he slept. But he was up again and making his first calls of the day by seven.

Thursday, December 4, 1980
Apollo-N; Lyndon B. Johnson Space Center, Houston

The pain was everywhere now, unbelievably intense, a huge cellular agony that went on and on until he couldn't bear it, and then on some more. It felt as if every soft surface of Priest's body, inside and out, had been coated with acid, as if he was rotting away from the outside in.

He still wore his pressure suit, and that was maybe just as well, because the pain was like one immense itch; he'd probably have rubbed himself raw if he could get to his skin. But the suit had its disadvantages. His bowels had been loose for hours, and he'd thrown up inside the helmet, which was every aviator's nightmare. But by now at least the floating globs of vomit had stopped drifting about in front of his face, and had stuck to something: the helmet's visor, or maybe his hair and skin; he didn't really care, as long as he could forget about the damn stuff.

He couldn't seem to smell anything now, and that was probably just as well.

He tried to turn his head to the left, to see Chuck and Jim. But he couldn't move. Anyhow, they hadn't answered the last time he'd spoken to them. They'd looked surprisingly composed, sealed up inside their pressure suits, as no doubt he did himself; all the vomit and shit and human pain was neatly confined to the inside of the suits, leaving the Command Module cabin antiseptic and efficient, save for the banks of glowing warning lights on the instrument panel.

Anyway, he didn't really want to turn away from his window. That window was very, very important to him, because it framed the night side of Earth. He could see the auroras: colored waves surging down from the poles, high layers of air glistening red and green under the impact of the particle wind from the sun. And he could see flashes, high in the atmosphere, and sometimes straight streaks of light that lingered in his retina for long seconds – meteors, specks of extraterrestrial dust plunging into the atmosphere . . .

Priest used to sit with Petey, when he was small, gazing up at the meteor showers caroming into the roof of the air. And now, he was watching meteors burning up *beneath* him. *This is one hell of a trip, Petey.*

There were other lights in the night.

At the heart of South America, he saw a huge, dispersed glow:

a fire, devouring trees at the center of the Amazon rainforest. And as Apollo-N sailed over deserts, he would spy oil and gas wells sparkling brightly, captive stars in all that darkness.

Cities stunned him with their night brightness. If there was cloud it would soak up and diffuse the illumination, and he would see the shape of the city as a huge, amorphous bowl of light. And if the sky was clear he seemed to be able to make out every detail as clearly as if he were taking a T-38 on a buzz just over the roof-tops. He saw streets and highways like ribbons of light, yellow and orange, and tall buildings ablaze like boxes of diamonds. He saw bridges and out-of-town highways shining with the headlamps of queues of cars. It was as if he could feel all that light, and heat, pouring up out of the atmosphere to him . . .

'We need you to help us, Ben. You're the only one talking to us up there. Stay with it, now.'

'Yeah.' *But it hurts, Natalie . . .*

'I know it's hard, Ben. Come on. Work with me. Can you reach the pre-burn checklist? It's Velcroed over the –'

'Walk me through it, would you, Natalie.'

'Yes. Yes, sure. You just follow me. We'll be fine. Okay. Thrust switches to normal.'

'Thrust switches normal.'

'Inject prevalves on.'

He had to reach for that one; the pain lay in great sheets across his back and arms. 'Okay. Inject prevalves on.'

'One minute to the burn, Ben. Arm the translational controller.'

Priest pulled the handle over until the label ARMED showed clearly. 'Armed.'

'Okay, now. Ullage.'

Priest pushed the translational controller; the Apollo-N shifted forward, the small kick of its reaction jets settling the propellants in the big Service Module SPS engine, in preparation for the main deorbit burn.

'Good. Very good, Ben. Thirty seconds,' York said. 'Thrust-on enable, Ben.'

Priest unlocked the control and gave it a half-turn. 'Enabled.'

'Say again, Ben.'

'Enabled.' Even his throat hurt, damn it.

'Fifteen seconds. You've done it, Ben. Sit tight, now.'

Sure. And what if the SPS doesn't fire? Christ knows what condition the Service Module is in after the goddamn NERVA blew

295

up under it; we've been losing power and telemetry since the explosion . . . And they had to assume that the Command Module's systems – the guidance electronics and the computers for instance – hadn't been too badly damaged by NERVA; he didn't think all those roentgens passing through could have done the ship's brains a lot of good.

He braced himself for the kick in the back.

'Two, one. Fire.'

Nothing.

He shuddered, the tension in his aching muscles releasing in spasms.

'Okay,' York said calmly. 'Direct delta-vee switch, Ben.'

'Direct delta-vee.' He reached for the manual fire switch and jerked it out and up, ignoring the pain in his arm.

Now there was a hiss, a rattly thrust which pushed him into his couch.

There was a green light before him. 'Retrofire,' he whispered.

The pressure over his wounded back increased, and he longed for microgravity to return. But it didn't, and he just had to lie there immersed in pain, enduring it.

'Copy the retrofire, Ben.' York's voice was trembling. 'We copy that. We'll do the rest. Stay with me, now.'

The pain overwhelmed him, turning his thoughts to mud.

Beyond his window, Earth slid away from him. The big SPS was working, changing the ship's trajectory.

'Be advised that old SPS is a damn fine engine, Houston,' he whispered. Even after having a nuke go off under it, the thing had still worked, faithfully bringing him home. How about that.

Now someone was talking to him. Maybe it was Natalie. He couldn't even recognize her voice now, through the fog of pain. That last checklist had just about used him up. Either this bird was going to fly him home or it wasn't; there wasn't a damn thing he could do about it any more.

He could see Natalie's face before him now: serious, bony, a little too long, with those big heavy eyebrows creased in concentration; he remembered her face above his, in the dark, that night after the Mars 9 landing.

He couldn't visualize Karen at all.

What a mess he'd made of his life – the warm heart of it anyhow – by his negligence, his focus on his career, his indecision. And all for these few hours in space.

He'd change things when he got back down, and back to health. *By God, I will.*

Now the thrust sighed to silence, and he had a couple of minutes of blessed relief in the smooth balm of microgravity.

There was a muffled rattle, all around the base of the cabin. That would be the ring of pyrotechnic bolts at the base of the conical Command Module, firing under command from Houston, and casting off the messed-up Service Module.

He might be able to see the Service Module as it drifted away. His duty, probably, was to find a camera and photograph the damn thing. *Sure.* He couldn't even close a fist; every time he tried, the pain in his hand was like an explosion of light.

There was something rising above the Earth's atmosphere now; it was golden-brown, serene. *The Moon.* Right slap in the middle of his window. He thought of Joe Muldoon and his crew up there with the Soviets; probably Muldoon would be following the progress of this reentry.

The couch kicked him, gently; fresh pain washed over his skin. That was the Command Module's own small attitude controllers: Houston, or the onboard computer, was trying to keep the Command Module in its forty-mile-wide reentry corridor.

Through the pain, Priest felt a kind of security settle over him. As best he could tell, this was about the point in the reentry sequence when the automatics were supposed to kick in anyway. Apollo-N was back on its flight plan, for the first time since the NERVA core had blown.

'You got that Pre-Advisory Data ready yet, Retro?'

'Not yet, Flight.'

It was getting damned late. *Something is wrong. What isn't he telling me?*

Rolf Donnelly had thought that the most dangerous moment in this reentry would be when the Command Module dug deep into the atmosphere, when it would be totally reliant on its heatshield. And if that shield had been cracked during the explosion, the craft was going to split open and burn like a meteor. He couldn't do anything about that; it was a question of waiting and hoping.

As yet they'd barely grazed the top of the atmosphere. But, right now, totally out of the blue, he feared already he was about to lose the Command Module.

The controller called Retro, down in the Trench, was in charge of controlling the Command Module's reentry angle. Just before the Service Module separation, Retro had been telling Donnelly that Apollo-N's angle of attack was right in the middle of the entry corridor. It could hardly have been better, in fact. And that meant that the Pre-Advisory Data Retro had prepared earlier was still valid. The Pre-Advisory Data contained the final vector that would control the spacecraft's degree of lift while it fought the atmosphere.

But Retro still had to feed the final Pre-Advisory to the Command Module's onboard computers. And now, minutes before the atmosphere started to bite, Donnelly could hear Retro arguing with FIDO, the flight dynamics controller, who was passing Retro updated predictions on the spacecraft's trajectory.

Retro blurted: 'I don't believe you, FIDO!'

Donnelly felt acid spurt into his stomach. 'Clarify, Retro. You want to tell me what's going on over there?'

'The trajectory is shallowing, Flight. We're up by point three one degrees.'

Still within the corridor. But that was a heck of a lot of shallowing at this point. And if the shallowing continued, Retro was going to have to revise the Pre-Advisory Data. 'You have any idea what's happening up there, Retro?'

'No idea, Flight.' Now there was tension in the voice, and Donnelly could see Retro peering over the shoulder of FIDO, next to him, trying to get the latest trajectory updates.

Was the trajectory going to shallow any more? That depended on the cause. If, say, one of the attitude thrusters was stuck open, the shallowing would continue. But if propellant or coolant was boiling off from some flaw in the hull, then the cause might dwindle and the shallowing stop.

The trouble was, nobody knew. None of them was sure about the extent of the damage the Command Module had suffered in the core rupture.

Donnelly, if he had to lose the crew, would prefer an undershoot, a burn-up. If the Command Module skipped off the atmosphere and was left in orbit, circling for months or years up there with a cargo of three radioactive corpses, the space program would be dead.

He took another poll of his controllers. None of them had any data to feed him on the trajectory. And besides, the telemetry was starting to get uncertain, as ionization built up around the Command Module.

It's a gamble. I just have to leave it to Retro. Does he change his figures, or not?

298

Now Retro spoke again. 'The rate of shallowing is slowing, Flight.'

'I need that Pre-Advisory Data, Retro.'

'Yeah.' Again Donnelly could hear the tension in Retro's voice. That controller was a very young man approaching the key moment in his life, a decision which would live with him forever.

Donnelly breathed a silent prayer; the only thing he couldn't accept right now was indecision, freezing. Like that fucking asshole, Conlig.

'We're still shallowing. I'll stick with the Pre-Advisory Data figures.'

'Say again, Retro.'

'I'll stick with the original Pre-Advisory Data. If the shallowing continues, we won't tip up by more than another tenth of a degree.'

Suddenly Donnelly became aware that he'd been holding his breath; he let it out in one huge explosion of stale air. 'Rog, Retro.'

Now there was a haze beyond his window, a soft, pink glow, like a sunrise. At first he thought it might be something to do with the thrusters. But then he realized the glow was ionized gas, atoms from the top layer of Earth's atmosphere, broken apart by their impact with Apollo-N's heatshield.

There was a soft pressure over his lower body – subtle, but enough to make his pain blaze anew. He thought he cried out. The cabin vibrated. Earth's atmosphere was snatching at the Command Module, and Apollo-N was beginning to decelerate, hard.

Suddenly the pressure mounted, climbing fast, crushing him into the couch. He could feel his skin crumple and break open inside the pressure suit. He felt as if he was deliquescing, as if his body had no more substance than a piece of lousy fruit.

A cold white light flooded his window now; misty, it glared into the cabin, drowning out the instrument lights.

The last moments before radio blackout seemed almost routine. As if this had been just another nominal mission, instead of the most dangerous and uncertain reentry since Apollo 13. The silence was broken only by occasional updates on the Command Module's trajectory and attitude, and the disposition of the emergency recovery forces, and by the steady voice of capcom York as she tried to reach the crew.

You'd never know, Donnelly thought.

Then telemetry from Apollo-N was lost.

The MOCR fell silent. Now there was nothing to do but wait.

It was possible that any small crack in the heatshield would heal itself as the heatshield ablated in the heat of reentry. *Possible*. But it was another unknown. If, alternatively, the shield was damaged and failed, they would lose the bird anyway.

Priest, suffused by pain, lay on his back, buffeted, compressed, while the cabin rattled around him and fire lapped up from the base of the Command Module behind him.

The glowing chunks of heatshield falling upwards past his window were *big*. Maybe something was wrong. Maybe the shield was failing.

If we're really reentering. If I'm not hallucinating; if we're not dead already.

Anyway, he couldn't do a damn thing about it.

Ben Priest, falling to Earth butt-first, waited for sun heat to sear through the base of Apollo-N and engulf him. It would be a relief.

'Network, no instrumentation aircraft contact yet?'

'Not at this time, Flight.'

Four minutes passed. Five. That should have been enough time to reacquire after the blackout.

On the loops there was nothing but a hiss of static – 'ARIA 4 has acquisition of signal, Flight.'

'Rog,' Donnelly said, barely recognizing his own voice.

There was a stir around the MOCR, a shifting of tired shoulders, weary, tentative grins.

It was an odd feeling, a kind of half-relief. Acquisition didn't mean the crew was alive – and it was still possible that the electronics of the parachute system might be shot – but at least the Command Module wasn't a cinder.

He heard York calling the crew, over and over, patient and plaintive.

The glow had died, fading out to an ordinary sky blue, and the G meter read 1.0, and he was falling toward the ocean at a thousand feet per second. The events of the splashdown ticked by, clear in his sharp, fragile thoughts.

There was a crack: that was the parachute cover coming off from the tip of the conical Command Module. And now another sharp snap, as the three small drogue chutes were released. He saw bright streams of fabric beyond the window.

300

He took a kick in the back as the drogues plucked at the air, stabilizing the fall of the Command Module.

There was a loud hiss; that would be the vent opening to let the cabin's pressure equalize with the air outside. Any second now and –

There. Another bang. That had to be the mains, the three eighty-footers which would lower Apollo-N gently to the ocean surface.

As the mains filled with air, the cabin was jolted. Priest was rocked in his couch, and the pain climbed off the scale.

Through his window he could see a slab of blue sky, wisps of cloud.

There was a distant voice in his head, brisk, friendly, competent. 'Apollo-N, Apollo-N, Air Boss 1, you have been reported on radar as south-east of your recovery ship at thirty miles. Apollo-N, Apollo-N. Welcome home, gentlemen; we'll have you aboard in no time.'

Priest wanted to reply. But he was too far away now, too sunk into the shell of his body.

The big screen at right front of the MOCR lit up with a TV picture of Apollo-N. Its three ringsail mains were safely deployed, three great, perfect canopies of red and white.

The cheering was so loud it drowned out Donnelly's headset, and he had to call for quiet.

There was a lot of radio traffic, chattering remotely in his headset. 'This is Recovery 2. I see the chutes. Level with me at precisely four thousand feet.' 'Affirmative, we do have a capsule in sight . . .'

There was a checklist the crew were supposed to follow now, Priest recalled vaguely. They should be closing that pressure relief valve, for instance, and setting the floodlights to post-landing, and getting set to cast off the mains after splashdown, so that the Command Module didn't get dragged through the water.

But there was nobody to do it.

Priest tried to relax, to submit to the pain.

Now there was a huge impact, an astonishing eruption of agony throughout his battered body.

Water poured in through an open vent above him, showering Priest, so much of it that he thought the Command Module's hull must have cracked open.

And now the Command Module tipped. He could feel the roll, see the ocean wheel past his window.

301

When the windows dipped into the sea water, the cabin went dark. Priest found himself hanging there in his straps, with cabin trash raining down around him: bits of paper, urine bags, discarded washcloths. *Stable 2*, he thought. *Upside down. Chuck will be furious. We screwed up. Nobody cut loose the mains.*

He hung there like a bat in the inverted cabin, and the darkness, broken by just the Christmas-tree lights of the instrument panel, was kind of peaceful. In a moment the flotation bags would flip the Command Module upright, to the Stable 1 position.

He closed his eyes.

Sunday, December 7, 1980
NASA Headquarters, Washington

The first image showed the five crew in their Snoopy flight helmets, sitting on their T-cross chairs around the small table in Moonlab's wardroom. Joe Muldoon sat at the center of the group, holding a piece of onion-skin paper.

This is the crew of Moonlab, coming to you live from lunar orbit. The five of us – our guests Vladimir Viktorenko and Aleksandr Solovyov, and Phil Stone, Adam Bleeker and myself – have spent the day following our flight program, and taking pictures, and maintaining the systems of our spacecraft . . .

Tim Josephson, sitting in his Washington office and watching the small TV on his desk, found he needed a conscious effort to keep breathing. *Keep it bland, calm, unexceptionable. This will do, Muldoon.*

In turn, the five astronauts spoke briefly about the work of the day – in the Telescope Mount, on the biomed machines, working on troublesome Moonlab equipment.

Interest in the previous telecasts from this mission – save for the original 'handshake' – had been minimal. None of the major channels had carried live coverage, and the astronauts' families had been forced to come into JSC to follow what was happening up there.

But all that changed as soon as the NERVA blew, and people grew morbidly fascinated anew by the spectacle of humans risking their lives, out there in space. *It's our biggest TV audience since Apollo 13,* Josephson thought now. *Don't foul it up, Joe.*

. . . We're a long way from home, and it's hard not to be aware of it. If the Earth was the size of a basketball, say, then the Skylabs would be little toys orbiting an inch or two from the surface. But

the Moon would be the size of a baseball, all of twenty feet away, and that's where we are right now.

Our purpose is to do science out here. You may know we're on an inclined orbit, so we're seeing a lot more of the Moon than was possible during the old Apollo landing days. We're carrying a whole range of cameras, both high-resolution and synoptic, and we have a laser altimeter and other non-imaging sensors, all of which has allowed us to map the whole surface of the Moon at a variety of scales.

And we've made some neat discoveries. For instance we've found a huge new impact crater on the far side of the Moon, fifteen hundred miles across – that's nearly a quarter of the Moon's circumference. I'm told that the Moon is turning out to be a much more interesting place than it was thought to be, even when Neil and I first walked on the surface.

In fact, just at the moment we're sailing over the Sea of Tranquillity itself. If you look at the disk of the Moon from the Earth, that's just to the right of center. So you can look up at us and see where we are, right now. And in our big telescopes, I can sometimes make out the glint of our abandoned LM descent stage.

Now, for all the people back on Earth at this difficult time, the crew of Moonlab has a message we would like to send to you.

Oh, Christ, Josephson thought. *That sounds bad. What now?*

Adam Bleeker drifted out of his seat toward the camera. He took the camera, his outstretched hand foreshortened to grotesque proportions, and swiveled it so that it was pointing out of the wardroom's window. The image settled down; it was low quality and a little blurred, but Josephson could clearly see the blue crescent Earth, rising above the unraveling, monochrome desolation of the Moon.

The next voice was Phil Stone's.

> *Abide with me; fast falls the eventide;*
> *The darkness deepens; Lord, with me abide.*
> *When other helpers fail and comforts flee,*
> *Help of the helpless, O abide with me . . .*

Stone's voice, made harsh by the radio link, was clipped, brisk, almost efficient. Next came the heavily accented tones of Solovyov, high and nervous.

Swift to its close ebbs out life's little day;
Earth's joys grow dim, its glories pass away;
Change and decay in all around I see;
O thou who changest not, abide with me . . .

What in hell is Muldoon doing? When the Apollo 8 astronauts had done a Bible reading from lunar orbit, NASA had actually been sued by an atheist, for violating constitutional prohibitions against the establishment of religion. *The Soviets have banned religion altogether! – and now here's a cosmonaut reading out some old hymn from an American space station. My God. What a mess.*

And yet – and yet . . .

Adam Bleeker read, simply and confidently.

I need thy presence every passing hour;
What but thy grace can foil the tempter's power?
Who like thyself my guide and stay can be?
Through cloud and sunshine, O abide with me . . .

And yet there was something beyond Josephson's calculation here. The old, simple words seemed electric, alive with meaning; it was impossible to forget who these men were, what they had achieved, where they were.

Vladimir Viktorenko's gruff, heavy English took over.

I fear no foe with thee at hand to bless;
Ills have no weight, and tears no bitterness.
Where is death's sting? where, grave, thy victory?
I triumph still, if thou abide with me . . .

Joe Muldoon read the last verse.

Hold thou thy Cross before my closing eyes;
Shine through the gloom, and point me to the skies;
Heaven's morning breaks, and Earth's vain shadows flee;
In life, in death, O Lord, abide with me.

And from the crews of Apollo and Soyuz, we close with goodnight, good luck, and God bless all of you.

The image of Earth faded out.

Tim Josephson found his eyes welling over with tears. He bent over his paperwork, embarrassed, glad he was alone.

304

Monday, December 15, 1980
Cape Canaveral

Bert Seger set up camp at Hangar 'O' at the Cape Canaveral Air Force Station.

The hangar had been loaned to NASA by the USAF as a site to run the checking-out of the Apollo-N Command Module, now that it had been recovered and brought to the Cape.

The Command Module itself was a victim, rather than a cause, of the accident, of course. But nevertheless the CM was the only portion of the Apollo-N stack that the investigators were going to be able to get their hands on, and it was expected that it would contain a lot of clues about how the accident had come about. So the spacecraft was going to have to be disassembled piece by piece.

When he first got to Hangar 'O' Seger found things moving slowly. Nobody had touched anything in the interior of Apollo – except for the medical team on the recovery ship, who, in their radiation-proof protective clothing, had removed the suited bodies of the astronauts – and the investigating teams at Canaveral now were in a paralysis of indecision on how to proceed, for fear of fouling up this highly public operation.

So Seger made some calls, and looked out some old records, and radioed up to Muldoon a recommendation on how to proceed. Muldoon, still on his way home from the Moon, agreed.

The first task was to put together a cantilevered Lucite platform, hinged so that it could fit inside the hatch of the Command Module and then be unfolded to cover the interior of the craft. That way the investigators, hampered by radiation-proof gear, could crawl on hands and knees around the interior, looking and photographing and disassembling, but without touching anything they didn't need to.

Next Seger initiated the disciplines he wanted in the disassembly process itself.

For example he watched as a crew checklist – doused by sea water, pathetic and battered – was lifted out of the spacecraft. The disassembly team had prepared a TPS, a Test Preparation Sheet, for this, and every other action in the disassembly. The TPS detailed the physical action required, the part number of the checklist, its location. Before the checklist was touched the presiding engineer read out an instruction from the TPS. A Rockwell quality inspector

305

moved into place to see, and a NASA inspector got ready. A photographer was called over. A Rockwell technician got carefully into the craft and then, using the specified procedure, took the checklist from its Velcro holder. The technician had to record the effort it took to get the checklist free, and any other anomalous observations he made.

The technician handed the checklist to the Rockwell quality inspector, who made sure that it was the right part and the right part number, recording his results on his copy of the TPS. The NASA inspector took the list, and he recorded his independent observations. The photographer took a picture of the part. The engineer put the list into a plastic bag, sealed it up, labeled it, and took it off to the appropriate repository.

If the engineer hadn't been able to get the checklist out, because of some unanticipated obstacle, everything would have come to a halt while a revised TPS was sent to a review panel for approval of the modification.

. . . And on, and on.

And, meanwhile, everybody working on the hot Command Module was in a white radiation suit, and they had to shower and get tested for dosage every few hours.

It was painstaking, agonizing, intense work, made all the more difficult by the fact that only two or three workers could get into the Command Module at any one time. But Seger insisted on adhering to the procedure, and Muldoon supported him. It was the way they had done it on Apollo 1, after the fire, and it was the way they were going to do it on Apollo-N. It was just the kind of detailed, meticulous job Seger enjoyed getting his teeth into.

Sometimes he thought back over the incidents surrounding the flight. He recalled the hostile faces of the protesters on launch day. That still returned to haunt him. And he was worried by the way the internal communication of his organization had fallen apart, even within Mission Control, on the day. Seger as Program Office head had been keeping up the pressure, of budgets and timescales, on his people for years now, and they'd seemed to be responding well; but he wondered now if there were greater problems under the surface than he'd been perceiving. Hell, maybe he hadn't *wanted* to perceive them.

Well, if there were such issues, he would address them. You had to be rational, to overcome doubt, in order to go forward, to achieve things. The crew had known the risks, when they climbed aboard the NERVA ship in the first place. They'd paid the ultimate price.

Now Seger owed it to their sacrifice to ensure that their lives hadn't been wasted, that NASA learned from this and moved forward.

Away from the hangar, Seger spent a lot of time on the phone lines arguing with Fred Michaels and Tim Josephson and others about the future shape of the program.

It couldn't be denied that the incident was going to set the program back. But Seger wanted to make up time by putting the all-up testing approach to work. The next flight, Seger argued, should be another manned Saturn/NERVA launch. Maybe they should even be more ambitious, such as by taking an S-NB out of Earth orbit and sending it around the Moon.

But he found Michaels opposing him. Michaels said if they weren't forced to discontinue the nuclear program altogether, they should run a couple more unmanned tests and then repeat the Apollo-N mission profile. If Apollo-N had been a useful mission (and if it wasn't, why had they lost three men to it?) they owed it to the program and to the memory of the crew to do the mission.

Seger thought that was just an emotional argument.

They chewed it over for hours. Sometimes it bothered Seger that his personal position was so different from that of Michaels and Josephson. He had to take care not to get himself isolated. But, now that the first shock of the accident had passed, he felt confident once more, in command; the accident was a finite thing, within the ability of human beings to comprehend and resolve, and they shouldn't let this tragedy get in the way of their greater ambitions.

He tried to catnap in his office, but he couldn't sleep.

By seven each morning he would be back in 'O,' or on the phone to the people at the Cape and Houston and Marshall who were working around the clock on the various facets of the investigation.

At the end of the first week he flew out to Houston, and spent the evening with his family. And then the next day he drove with Fay around Timber Cove and El Lago, visiting the wives and families of Jones, Priest and Dana.

Then it was back to the Cape on Sunday, where he threw himself into the investigation once more.

He was working with an intensity that eclipsed any effort he had made in his life. It was the only way he knew to deal with the way he felt about the incident: to burn it out of his system with work, to make damn sure nothing like this happened again. And he spent a lot of his spare time in church, alone, praying and contemplating. Coming to terms with it all.

In a way he was enjoying it. As he got to grips with the issues

307

he felt suffused with strength, courage, certainty. He prayed every day, and he felt that God was helping him.

Sometimes he needed a little help to get to sleep. A couple of pills or a drink or two. He allowed himself that. He was on high blower, he told his wife; he was like a T-38 on afterburner.

Thursday, January 8, 1981

... On admission, Colonel Priest was nauseated, chilled, and agitated, with glassy eyes. His temperature was a hundred and four degrees. He had been cut from his pressure suit. He suffered repeated vomiting, and swelling of the face, neck and upper extremities. His arms were so swollen, in fact, that his blood pressure could not be taken with the normal cuff, and the nurses had to enlarge it.

He was periodically conscious, and sometimes coherent and logical, but I judged he was not strong enough to contribute to any debriefings concerning the accident.

Priest's difficulty in speaking and lapses into incoherence made his relatives in attendance, and some of my staff, feel uncomfortable.

Twenty-four hours after admission I ordered four samples of bone marrow to be taken from Priest's sternum and iliac bones (both front and rear). Priest was very patient during the proceedings. The samples were used to determine the whole body dose.

During the fourth and fifth days after admission, Priest was in great pain from injuries to the mucous membranes of the mouth, oesophagus and stomach. The mucous membranes were coming off in layers. Priest lost both sleep and appetite. Starting on the sixth day his right shin, on which the skin was now disintegrating, began to swell and feel as if it was bursting; it then became rigid and painful.

On the seventh day, on account of a profound agranulocytosis – that is, a drop in the number of granular forms of leucocytes, responsible for immunity – I ordered an administration of seven hundred and fifty milliliters of bone marrow with blood.

Priest was then moved to a room sterilized with ultraviolet light. A period of intestinal syndrome began: bowel movements occurred between twenty-five and thirty times every twenty-four hours, containing blood and mucus; there was tenesmus, rumbling, and movement of fluids in the region of the caecum.

Owing to the severe lesions in the mouth and oesophagus, Priest did not eat for several days. We provided nutrient fluids intravenously. In the meantime, soft blisters appeared on the perineum and buttocks, and the right shin was bluish-purple, swollen, shiny and smooth to the touch.

On the fourteenth day Colonel Priest began to lose his hair, in a curious manner: all the hair on the back of his head and body fell out. He grew weaker, and his lapses into unconsciousness or incoherence grew more prolonged.

On Friday January 2, the thirtieth day after the accident, Priest's blood pressure suddenly dropped.

Fifty-seven hours later, Colonel Priest died; I recorded the immediate cause of death as acute myocardial dystrophy.

Under the microscope, it was quite impossible to see Priest's heart tissue. The cell nuclei were a mass of torn fibers. It is accurate to say that Priest died directly from the radiation itself, and not from secondary biological changes. Gentlemen, it is impossible to save such patients, once the heart tissue has been destroyed.

Of the three crew of Apollo-N, only Colonel Priest was found to be alive when the capsule was recovered after reentry. The radiation from the ruptured NERVA core had hit Colonel Priest from behind, doing most harm to his back, his calves, his perineum and buttocks.

His mother, wife and son were in attendance at his death.

Report of the Presidential Commission on the Apollo-N Malfunction, Vol I: Testimony of Dr I. S. Kirby to the Medical Analysis Panel (extract) (Washington, DC: Government Printing Office, 1981)

January, 1981
Lyndon B. Johnson Space Center; Clear Lake, Houston

One of the back rooms behind the MOCR had been turned into the primary site for investigating the telemetry data received from Apollo-N in the moments leading up to the accident. The walls were papered with strips displaying the readouts from every sensor they'd had the crew and craft wired up to.

And it was here that Natalie York had to sit and listen to voice tapes from the Command Module cabin, and read through and annotate typed transcripts.

Everyone was clinical, of course. Even scientific. The point was to gather data. Had the astronauts had any earlier indication that some problem was developing with the NERVA? Perhaps a close enough analysis of the tapes could tease that out, provide further clues about the cause.

And York, as capcom on the day, was the best placed to interpret their words.

She had to listen to the tapes over and over.

Every time York went through the tapes it was like reliving the whole incident. *Did it fail because of me?* If only Mike hadn't frozen. If only she'd had a little more intuition about what was going on – if she could have warned Ben that the core was getting out of control, he might have overridden the automatics from the Command Module and shut the damn thing down . . .

Eventually York got to a point where she felt that if she had to listen to Ben's weakening voice one more time her heart was going to burst.

I guess our business will stay unfinished, Ben. Oh, God.

They hadn't even let her see him, before he died.

'Mom?'

'I'm coming out there, Natalie.'

'No, Mom.'

'Now, don't try to stop me. I know you need me right now.'

'For what?'

'I know how much Ben meant to you.'

York was silent, for long moments; she even considered hanging up. 'What do you know, exactly?'

'You aren't very experienced in this stuff, are you, dear? When I saw you at that party, when you first moved into Portofino . . . It was obvious, Natalie. Even if I hadn't been your mother I would have known. I only had to see the way you two behaved toward each other. The way you were careful not to pay each other atten-tion. And the way, when you *did* come together somehow, it was as if you knew each other so well you could anticipate the other's needs . . .'

Jesus. Well, I guess I'm not so much of an actress. So does every-body know?

There was a rattle of keys at the door.

'I'll have to go, Mom.'

'I'll come out there.'

'No.'

'Ben Priest was married, wasn't he? I read in –'

'Good-bye, Mom.' She put the phone down.

Mike Conlig stood in the middle of the room, looking at her. He carried a bag, with airline stickers that betrayed he'd been out to Marshall.

It was the first time she'd seen him since the accident. More than a month.

'You froze,' York said without hesitation. '*You froze.* What the hell were you thinking of, Mike?'

Mike put his bag down, and started to pace about the apartment, his coat heavy. His hair straggled out of an unkempt pony-tail, and his beard had grown down over his neck. 'I didn't freeze,' Conlig said.

'If you knew you were going to choke up like that you should have just got out of that goddamn chair,' York said. She felt her throat tighten up, a pressure behind her eyes; but, by God, she was going to see this through without falling apart. 'You had a responsibility! Those men in orbit were relying on you . . .'

He stood over her, his face twisted in disgust. 'First time I see you in a month and it's straight on the attack. Happy fucking New Year to you, Natalie. So I killed them. Is that what you're telling me?'

'But the damn NERVA wasn't ready to fly. Was it?'

'Natalie, you don't know what you're talking about.'

'*Was it?* You worked on the cooling systems for years, and in the end, with three men on board, the damn thing overheated and exploded –'

'I knew what I was doing, Natalie.'

'You knew you were letting the NERVA melt down?'

'No.' He shook his head. 'No, damn it. Natalie, it's the easiest thing in the world to abort. If I'd aborted, we'd have lost the mission –'

'But not three men.'

'– and maybe,' he went on doggedly, 'we'd never have known what went wrong. And we'd have had to risk throwing three more men up there to try all over again.' He pulled at his beard in quick, nervous gestures. 'At the time – it happened so fast – I just wasn't sure. I thought the situation might stabilize, that we might be able to salvage control of the NERVA. It might have happened that way, Natalie, and saved us risking more lives. As we'll have to now. It's a question of cost and benefit.'

311

She was appalled. 'God, you callous asshole, you did kill them.'

'But it isn't like that.' He sounded querulous, hurt, misunderstood. 'Look: NASA is too cautious. Every safety precaution increases the complexity and cost of the mission. With fewer safety precautions we could have reached the Moon a little sooner, done a lot more exploring, learned more, and' – defiantly – 'yes, and created a martyr or two –'

'How can you talk about martyrs? If you hadn't screwed up, Ben might be alive now. And the others, damn it.'

'Oh, sure. Precious Ben. That's what this is all about, isn't it?' He was angry now.

'What are you saying?'

He snorted. 'I know all about you and Ben fucking Priest, Natalie. Come on. I've known for years.'

You, too? She considered protesting, telling him he was mistaken. But Ben was dead. It would be beneath her.

He shook his head. 'I don't want to hear when, or how, or why. I don't give a damn. And you know what? Right now, I don't know if I ever did.'

She watched him pace around the room. He was like a stranger, an alien, here in her apartment. 'No. You never did give a damn, did you? I can't believe –'

'What?'

'I can't believe I ever thought I loved you.'

That took him aback for a moment, and he looked at her; but then his face resumed its mask of anger. 'Yeah, well, you can believe what you like.'

'How can you rake up all of this now? Ben's *dead*, for God's sake.'

'I know he's dead!' he shouted. 'As dead as my fucking career!'

'Is that all you care about?'

His anger was consuming him now. 'Yeah. Yeah, maybe it is. That and the fact that this will probably kill off the nuke program.'

'Get out,' York said.

'Omelets and eggs, Natalie! You don't get anywhere without taking a few risks! And with what we learned from this flight – if we're allowed to fly again – we'll get it right next time.' Under the anger in his voice, she thought she heard vulnerability, still, a plea for understanding. 'Christ, Natalie, we could be on Mars *by now*. But fucking NASA –'

She turned away from him. 'Get out. Go, Mike.'

She didn't watch him leave.

*   *   *

Mike was right, in a way. He spoke a truth, as perceived by many within NASA. If only public sentiment would get out of the way, and let us move as fast as we know we can . . .

Lower reliability would mean lower development costs, and a faster schedule.

It was an insidious, strangely seductive argument.

The machine is everything! Oh, we have to put men inside those machines, and we have a few problems with that, and some of them are driven crazy by their experiences, and some of them die, in squalid, painful, unheroic ways – as dear Ben had died, decaying in a hospital bed, a month after his flight – *but it's worth it for the goal.*

And besides, we're never short of volunteers.

What made it worse was that NASA – a child of the Cold War – never told the truth about a situation if it didn't have to. And certainly not if the truth damaged PR. So much was hidden behind the glamor: the dangers, the awful shitty deaths, the almost psychotic desire by some, engineers and crew, to keep on flying.

It isn't just Mike. There isn't even a 'them' to blame for this.

All the astronauts were implicated: all of those who would volunteer for the most dangerous mission, and go along with the cover-ups. Even Ben himself. He'd worked on NERVA; he must have had a good idea of its lack of flight-readiness.

Even me, she admitted at last. *Even I am guilty. I agonize about compromising my scientific principles by being here. But it's more than that.*

By being in the program, by giving it my tacit support, I killed Ben, as surely as that failed NERVA.

She sat in a chair and curled over on herself, tucking her arms into her belly, letting her head drop to her knees.

And now I have to decide. Do I get out? Maybe start shrieking the truth to the world?

Or will it make Ben's death mean something, if I stay?

Something inside her, cold and hard and selfish, pointed out that it was Ben who had died, not her. And Mars was still there, waiting for her.

Maybe she was just rationalizing; maybe she was just trying to find a way to justify staying in the program.

And maybe she'd thrown out Mike and his talk of martyrs so angrily because – somewhere inside her – there was a part of her own soul that agreed with his brutal analysis.

*   *   *

313

The next day she had the locks changed, and packed up Mike's stuff and sent it to Huntsville. And she put the Portofino apartment up for sale.

Tuesday, January 20, 1981
NASA Headquarters, Washington

When the first draft report of NASA's internal report landed on his desk, Michaels called a meeting of Seger, Muldoon and Udet, in his office in Washington.

The three of them sat in a row on the other side of his desk. Muldoon was tense, angry, uncomfortable; Seger seemed eager, energetic, somehow too bright; and Udet was reserved, watching Michaels and the others through his pale blue eyes.

Michaels picked up the draft report and dropped it on his desk. 'I've tried to read this. I know I'm going to have to answer for it line by line. Gentlemen, I want you to walk me through this fucking blow-out. Step by step, over and again, until I understand. You got that? Hans, you want to lead?'

Udet nodded crisply. 'Of course, Fred. The malfunction occurred at the time at which we were preparing the S-NB for its restart burn. I will remind you that the rocket had functioned flawlessly during its first burn –'

'I remember.'

'The moderators were adjusted to lift the temperature of the core to its working range of three thousand degrees. The turbopumps were started, and hydrogen began to flow through the cooling jackets and the core. We registered thrust rising to its nominal levels; the cabin transcript indicates the crew were aware of this. Then –'

'And then,' Joe Muldoon said dryly, 'we hit a glitch.'

The flow of liquid hydrogen into the coolant jackets became intermittent, Udet said. It turned out later that a flaw was developing in the piping carrying the hydrogen to the engine.

Michaels asked, 'Shouldn't you have shut down the core, as soon as that happened?'

'Yeah, that's standard procedure,' Muldoon put in. 'Without coolant, the core is going to overheat.'

'We had a split-second to make the decision,' Udet said. 'That is all. If we had allowed emergency shutdown immediately, we might have lost the engine altogether, and the mission would have been

314

scrubbed. And perhaps for nothing, if the flow problems had recti-
fied themselves. We were trying to keep options open. The report
describes all this.'

'All right, Hans. Go on.'

'We adjusted the moderators to reduce the temperature in the
core, short of shutting it down. But we could not reach the target
temperature –'

Muldoon said, 'And there you got your first basic design flaw,
Fred.'

Both Udet and Seger leaned forward to protest at this, but
Michaels waved them silent.

'We only had one control system – the reactor moderator – and
so only one shutdown option. When that failed, we had no way to
stop the runaway temperature climb.'

Michaels nodded. 'Hans?'

Udet spread his hands. 'We must balance reliability against
weight, Fred. This has been the dilemma of all spaceflight: to carry
an additional redundant system, or to add value elsewhere? In our
opinion, in this case, the moderator system was sufficiently reliable
to justify flying without the weight penalty of a backup.'

'Bert? You want to comment?'

Seger, his eyes brilliant, shrugged his narrow shoulders. 'We made
the best call we could; we did all the tests. We got it wrong. Next
time we fly a NERVA, we'll fix it.'

These things happen. Not an answer to satisfy the White House
Commission, Michaels thought sourly.

'Go on, Hans.'

'By now,' Udet said, 'the crew were aware that the thrust had
died, after that first shove. We were only a few seconds after the
f..st glitch in the flow. Now the hydrogen flow increased, markedly,'
Udet said. 'It was like a spurt, from the faulty piping. The hydrogen
passed its nominal flow rate and effectively flooded the core. We
withdrew the moderator further –'

'And this is another point at which the standard procedure said
shutdown,' Muldoon said harshly. 'The moderators' control margin
was too low now; we didn't have full control of the core. But again,
we overrode the automatics.'

'We tried to save the mission,' Udet said.

'All right. Let's stick to the facts for now; we can justify ourselves
later. What next?'

'Now the flow of coolant into the core stopped altogether,' Udet
said. 'Perhaps at this point the piping failed completely.'

315

'This is the key moment, Fred,' Muldoon said. 'You have a reactor that's already unstable. The hydrogen flood has made the core isothermal – that is, at the same temperature throughout – so any changes happen all over the core, simultaneously. And the coolant flow has stopped; the core's main heat sink, the flow of hydrogen through the jackets, has gone.'

'So it starts to heat up.'

'So it starts to heat up. Uniformly. And a lot faster than before.'

Udet said, 'We tried to shut down. But the moderator was too far out of the core to have any immediate effect. The hydrogen in the core and the jacket boiled quickly, and started to expand . . .'

'And now you got a runaway,' Muldoon said. 'Because the reactor was designed with a positive temperature coefficient.'

Michaels sighed and locked his hands behind his head. 'Just pretend I don't know what you're talking about.'

Muldoon grinned tightly. 'I know. It took me a while to figure this stuff out. Look: suppose the temperature of your core rises. And suppose that the core is designed so that when it heats up, the reactivity drops – that is, the reaction rate automatically falls. That's what's meant by a "negative temperature coefficient." In that case you have a negative feedback loop, and your reaction falls off, and the temperature is damped down.'

'Okay. It's kind of self-correcting.'

'That's right; the whole thing is stable. That's how they design civilian reactors. But in the case of NERVA, that coefficient was *positive*, at least for some of the temperature range. So when the temperature went up, the reactivity went up too –'

'And the rate of fission increased, leading to a further temperature rise.'

'And so on. Yes.'

Michaels glared at Udet. 'I can see the fucking headlines now, Hans. Why the hell did we fly an unstable reactor?'

Udet sat forward, his face pale, a muscle in his neck rope-taut with anger. 'You must understand that we are not building a reactor to supply domestic electricity, here. We are not boiling kettles. NERVA 2 is a high-performance booster, a semi-experimental flight model. Stability is not always the condition we require.'

Michaels frowned. *And you just hate having to answer these asshole questions, don't you, Hans?* 'Why do we need instability? What do you mean?'

Seger put in, 'It's like a high-performance aircraft, Fred. A ship that's too stable will wallow like a sow. So you might *design* for

316

instability. If a bird's unstable, it can flip quickly from one mode to another; if you can control that, you've gained a lot of maneuverability.'

'But that's a big if, Bert. And evidently, when it got to the wire, we couldn't control it. Hans, why didn't you beef up the control system to cover for this?'

Udet punctuated his words by thumping the edge of his hand on Michaels's desk. 'Because – of – unacceptable – weight – penalties.'

Michaels dreaded having to put this man in front of the Commission. 'Let's move on. What next?'

Udet said, 'Events unfolded rapidly. The power output began to rise exponentially, doubling in a fraction of a second. The fuel pellets – which are uranium carbide coated with pyrolytic carbon – shattered due to the thermal shock of the sudden power rise. The flow passages within the core melted. The moderator systems became inoperative. There was a hydrogen explosion, which ruptured the pressure shell and the biological shield –'

'All right.' Michaels found himself shuddering. 'We know the rest.' *Jesus. What a mess.* 'So the whole damn thing was caused by faulty hydrogen pipelines.'

Bert Seger nodded, and then he startled Michaels by saying: 'It's actually not as bad a scenario as you might have feared.'

'Not as bad? What the hell are you talking about, Bert?'

'The glitches in the hydrogen flow came from a simple component failure. What you had was ruptures in a six-foot length of stainless-steel fuel line, five-eighths of an inch in diameter, carrying liquid hydrogen from the tank into the nuclear engine. That's all. So it's easy to fix.'

'Why did the damn pipe rupture?'

'Well, we were flying with a new innovation,' Seger said, 'that was supposed to guard against the effects of vibration. Each length of the pipe line had two vibration-absorbing "bellows" sections in it, with wire braid shielding on the outside. When the new line was put through vibration tests on the ground, it worked perfectly.'

'So how come –'

Udet said, 'It turned out that in the atmosphere, the liquid hydrogen running through the pipe caused ice to gather on the braided shield. And that altered the characteristics of the pipe, enough to enable it to dampen out the most severe vibrations in the bellows during our testing.'

'Oh,' Michaels said. 'But in the vacuum, no ice could form.'

'And those little bellows sang like a rattlesnake,' Joe Muldoon said. 'When the Saturn first stage started its pogoing, the bellows couldn't handle it. They just fell apart.'

Michaels asked Udet, 'But how come you didn't pick up the ice thing when you ran vacuum ground tests on the bellows?'

Udet faced Michaels squarely; he looked calm, somehow confident. 'We did not run vacuum tests on this component. We did not anticipate the necessity.'

Michaels held his gaze for long seconds, but nothing more was forthcoming: no more data, no justification, no apology. 'Well, I will be dipped in shit. Joe?'

Muldoon leaned over the desk and tapped the report. 'This is where we show ourselves as culpable, Fred. Those goddamn bellows were Criticality One components: that is, their failure was liable to cause the loss of the spacecraft. But we didn't test them out under true flight conditions. And, what's worse, we've now dug out evidence of bellows problems on the S-NB's previous unmanned test flight, although in that case we didn't lose the mission.'

I'm dead meat, Michaels thought.

They could have anticipated the fault, and that was always deadly. And, it was always the way, some obscure little asshole technician somewhere at Marshall or the Cape would have written a report predicting precisely the failure they'd suffered, a report which no doubt had been laughed off and suppressed by NASA senior management, a report which was no doubt falling into the hands of some Congressman even now . . .

'Culpable. Jesus. How I hate that word.'

Michaels got to his feet. He crossed to his window, and folded his hands behind his back as he stared out over Washington. The light was fading from the sky, softened and stained by smog.

'I don't want to minimize the impact of this, gentlemen. Quite apart from losing the crew, this is a genuine catastrophe. I have the ecology lobby around the world jumping up and down on my back. We've even been criticized for bringing a radioactive Command Module back into the atmosphere. There was strong opposition to flying nuclear materials into space even before the flight. And now the Russians have got a fucking Soyuz up there taking pictures of the out-of-control glowing radioactive core we've abandoned in orbit.

'You're right, Joe; there's no doubt in my mind – and there won't be in the minds of public, Congress and White House – that we're culpable. And now we've got to put our house in order, and be seen to be doing it.

'All right, gentlemen. Your recommendations as to what we do next?'

Seger was the first to speak. 'The main recommendation is not to panic here, Fred. I hear what you say; this accident we've suffered is unacceptable. There's no doubt about that. But the problems are straightforward and limited in scope. We have to get S-NB flying again, as soon as possible, *with men aboard,* and push on for Mars. We can't lose our nerve. That's the message you have to take back to the Hill, Fred.'

More bland generalities, Michaels thought, delivered in Seger's weird, intense, gung-ho style.

'Hans?'

Udet sighed. 'Bert is right. We must repair our NERVA program and move on. We have no other option, if we are to reach Mars. It is as simple, and as dramatic, as that.'

'Well, hell, I disagree,' Muldoon said harshly. 'With both of you. I think that if they let us keep on flying at all after this fuck-up, we're going to have to do a sweeping review of the whole system, spacecraft, booster stages, management procedures. Everything.'

'And if you do that,' Seger said hotly, 'you risk throwing away everything. You'll come out of that process with an immature system, overdesigned and carrying too many changes, which will hit us with a host of problems we've not even thought of yet.' He turned his glassy stare on Michaels again. 'Look, Fred, this is a lousy business, and I wish it hadn't happened, and I'll spend the rest of my life trying to come to terms with this: what I did wrong, what I could have done differently to avoid this, and all the rest of it. And I'll do all in my power to avert such an accident in future. But at the end of the day, we're flying experimental craft here. Pilots die flying experimental craft; they always have. *You lose crew.* And that's a truth we've got to learn to live with.'

Michaels grunted. *The trouble is, I don't think we're going to be allowed to live with it.*

When Udet, Seger and Muldoon had gone, he stood by his window for a long time.

He couldn't imagine that the manned program would be shut down altogether. That would have such a devastating impact on the American aerospace industry that it was surely politically unthinkable.

But it seemed highly likely to him, almost certain in fact, that the NERVA was going to be grounded.

319

And without NERVA, how the hell were they going to get to Mars, in this decade or any other? Were they going to be reduced to pottering around in low Earth orbit?

. . . Maybe he had more immediate problems.

Seger had sounded like he was fraying at the edges. That disturbed Michaels. Both Houses of Congress were going to convene their own hearings on the accident, just as soon as the Presidential Commission reported. Michaels had already had a few clues as to the tone of those hearings; they would be intent on charging NASA's engineers – meaning Seger, primarily – with criminal negligence.

But Michaels had heard, from Tim Josephson and others, that Seger was working a sixteen-hour day, sleeping for three or four hours, and spending his spare time on his knees in some church. It was as if Seger was using physical exhaustion, and an immersion in his religion, like a drug. But even that wasn't always enough, and – so Michaels had heard – Seger was using Seconals and scotches to knock himself out.

Michaels was worried that Seger might be under too much stress to testify. And besides, if Seger started to come out with his line about limited damage and everything's under control, they'd all sound like such complacent bastards that the Congressmen would cut out their livers.

He poured himself a drink. *Hell. Were we, after all, going too far, too fast?*

He couldn't get the glassy, feverish look in Bert Seger's eyes out of his mind.

He knew he had a decision to make.

Wednesday, January 21, 1981
Lyndon B. Johnson Space Center, Houston

The day after the meeting in Washington, Fred Michaels called up Seger in Houston.

He leaned on Seger to take some leave.

Seger was reluctant; he felt fit and energetic, and he was getting on top of the issues coming out of the accident.

They finished the call without resolving the issue.

Later that day, Tim Josephson, who'd been working out of Houston since the disaster, came to see Seger in his office.

'Look, Bert, we want you to take an extended leave.'

'But I've discussed this with Fred.'

'So have I. And I've already drafted an announcement, to go out tomorrow.'

Seger was furious. 'In that case, you can announce my resignation instead.'

Josephson met his stare, steadily, analytical. 'Bert, you're over-stressed. You're not thinking straight.'

'Oh, is that so? How the hell do you know that? What are you, a doctor that you can diagnose me?' He stared into Josephson's thin, intelligent face. 'What's going on here, Tim? Overstressed, what the hell is that? I think you're acting on rumors, and half-truths, and things you don't understand.'

'Really?' Josephson asked dryly.

'Really. Listen, me and my guys down here are doing fine. We're working through the issues with the guys in Huntsville. With the grace of God, we're going to get through this. In spite of whatever you're hearing I'm not going into shock.'

'It's not like that, Bert. Nobody wants –'

'Listen, Tim. If you want to fix up some kind of psychiatric hearing, then you do it; I'll abide by the decision of any competent psychiatrist. If he thinks I need R&R, then I'll discuss it with you. But I'm not having you, or Fred Michaels, or any other amateur, diagnosing my psyche. Now, you got that?'

Josephson seemed to think that over. Then he nodded, his face expressionless, and got out of the office.

Seger got on with his work; he hoped he'd heard the end of *that*.

But a little later Josephson called back and said that he'd arranged a hearing with two psychiatrists in the Houston Medical Center, for that very evening.

Seger spent three hours with the psychiatrists, talking things over. They fed back their conclusions to him quickly.

He was obviously under a strain, they said, but he didn't have a psychosis. There was no danger that Seger was going to fall apart under further pressure.

Seger went back to his office, elated. He called Tim Josephson, and told him he should cancel his press release. Then he got to his knees, in his darkened office, and prayed his thanks.

He felt like laughing; if he was truthful, he felt as if he had fooled the psychiatrists.

*   *   *

321

The next day Fred Michaels phoned again. Michaels began to describe a new job to him, a more senior position in the Office of Manned Spaceflight.

'You've spent long enough at the detail level, Bert, and you've done a damned fine job. But now we're going to need help steering NASA through the next few years, which will be as hard as any we've faced before. I want you to move up to the policy level. I want you to get to know the Cabinet people; I can arrange the introductions for you. It's a job on the mountaintop, Bert.'

Yeah. The mountaintop, in Washington.

Seger hesitated. 'You're making it sound good, Fred.' *But I know what this is all about.* 'Fred, I'll say what I believe, one more time: whether you get me out of your way or not it's going to be a mistake to go back into our systems now and make sweeping changes. We have to make fixes, obviously, but they should be straightforward and limited; if we go beyond that, we risk coming out with a less mature system, with new problems hiding from us . . .'

'Look, Seger, I'm tired of hearing that. I can't agree with you. I just don't see it that way, and I don't think that's the prevailing view inside NASA. And I know for sure that's not how they see it up on the Hill.'

'What are you saying, Fred? I've seen your tame shrinks, and –'

'I know.'

'I'm no psychotic, Fred.'

'I know that,' Michaels said gruffly. 'And I'm glad for you. But that isn't really the question.'

'Then what is?'

'Whether you're the right man to continue leading the program, right now.'

Seger picked up a paperclip from his desk, and began to fold and unfold it with his free hand.

Friday, January 30, 1981
Arlington National Cemetery

Michaels found himself shivering, despite his topcoat. The sky was overcast, the clouds impossibly low. *Thank Christ this is the last.*

The mourners stood in rows: there was Jim Dana's grieving family, with poor, beat-up old Gregory Dana, the dreamer from Langley, standing in the front row with his arms around his wife and his widowed daughter-in-law; there were the usual ranks of NASA managers and engineers, of Congressmen and senators; and there was the Vice President of the United States himself. And right at the front there was a row of astronauts, standing straight and tall, saluting their fallen comrade: Muldoon, York, Gershon, Stone, Bleeker, others – men who had flown the first Mercurys, men who had once walked on the Moon, men – and women – who might walk on Mars. And there was Vladimir Viktorenko, who had flown with Joe Muldoon to lunar orbit, and who Muldoon had insisted should be here – the Afghanistan situation or not – to represent that other astronaut corps, from the other side of the world.

There was a volley of rifle shots, a slow litany from a bugler. The ceremony dragged on, poignant and exquisitely painful.

There was a roar that seemed to shake the ground. Michaels looked up into the sky, startled.

Four Air Force T-38s were coming in from the southwest, in a close diamond formation, no more than five hundred feet from the ground. The planes gleamed white against the lead-gray sky. As the formation roared overhead, their jets screaming, the wingman veered out of the diamond and climbed vertically, disappearing into the clouds in a couple of seconds.

The other three T-38s carried on toward the north, their afterburners glowing.

Michaels recognized the formation. The missing man. He could see the astronauts at the graveside, the row of them, rookies and veterans alike, all with their heads turned up to the jets.

As the ceremony broke up, Michaels worked his way through the milling, black-coated throng, toward Joe Muldoon.

'Joe, I need to speak to you. I have an assignment for you.'

Muldoon just glared back at him. He towered over Michaels, rigid, intimidating. His muscles were visible under his uniform, his face a scowling mask. Michaels could see a righteous, terrible anger burning in there.

Michaels drew a deep breath. It was that anger he wanted to tap into now. 'I want you to keep this to yourself for now. I'm transferring Bert Seger. I'm bumping him further up in the Program Office. I've found him a job here in Washington.'

'He won't accept it.'

'Well, he's going to have to accept it. Hell, man, you saw how he was, in that meeting with Udet. I've had to take him out of the line.'

323

Muldoon shook his head. 'Bert worked damned hard. And none of it was his fault –'

'I'm not interested in allocating blame,' Michaels said firmly. 'Let them do that up on the Hill. All I'm concerned about is taking the program forward, from here on in to the end zone. And I don't think Bert Seger is the right man to do that any more.'

'So who is?'

'You.'

Muldoon looked at him with his mouth open and his eyes round blue disks, a caricature of amazement. 'Me? You're kidding. I'm no manager. I'm the asshole with the big mouth you nearly grounded, remember.'

'Yes, you are an asshole sometimes,' Michaels said testily. 'But I trust your judgment, over the things that matter. You're a moon-walker, for God's sake. And you handled the Moonlab mission well. That broadcast –'

'That was a stunt.'

'Don't decry yourself. Down here, that broadcast was like a cath-arsis. I think it helped a lot of people, in NASA and beyond, come to terms with what happened. And you've done a good job with the post-accident review.' He sighed. 'Look, Joe, I need you because we're in a damned hole. I still don't know which way Reagan is going to swing. But I know the accident looks bad, very bad, up on the Hill. I think it's highly likely we won't be allowed to proceed with the nuclear rocket program. And the MEM isn't even a bucket of bolts yet; it was months behind schedule even before this mess . . . What I need is someone impatient, tough, charismatic – *you*, Joe – to get hold of the program and pull the damned thing out of Marshall, and the contractors, and all the rest, and make it happen.'

Muldoon looked across the cemetery. 'Let me get something clear,' he said quietly. 'If I take this job, I won't be able to remain on the active roster.'

Michaels took a breath. 'No. There's no way you could maintain both schedules.'

'So if I take this job, to get your ass out of a sling, I pass up on my chance of going to Mars.'

'I'm not going to pretend that's not true, Joe. But if you *don't* take the job, I think the chances are *nobody* will be going to Mars, not in my lifetime or yours.'

Muldoon's mouth worked. 'It's one hell of a price you're asking me to pay.'

'I know it.'

324

'And it's not exactly *orderly*, Fred,' Muldoon said. 'How are all those engineers and managers and space cadets going to feel when you put a dumb jock like me at the top of the structure chart?'

Michaels smiled. 'Well, back in the Apollo days managers used to bounce around the organigram without paying too much attention to that kind of thing. Maybe we need that spirit back again. I don't think you ought to worry about the color of the carpet on the floor, Joe. And if anyone does start bothering you about ranks and status – well, you just come to me.'

'Hell, no,' Muldoon said. 'If any paper-pusher with his thumbs up his ass tries to fuck *me* over –'

'Does that mean you're taking the job?'

'It means I'll think about it. You're a bastard, Michaels.'

They began to walk toward their waiting cars.

Tuesday, February 3, 1981
Ozero Tengiz, Kazakhstan

The wind across the steppe pierced the layers of York's pressure suit. She tried walking around, to keep warm. But the Soviet-design suit, wired for internal strength, resisted her motion, and she soon felt herself tiring; and the 'appendix,' the bunched-up opening at the front of the suit, irritated her chest.

Beside her Ralph Gershon was huddled over on himself. His head tucked into the collar of his suit, his helmet was under his arm. Gershon's eyes were glazed. He had a knack, York had observed, of retreating into some private cosmos when the outside world got sufficiently shitty. Well, right now that was a knack she envied.

The mockup of the Soyuz Command Module sat squat on the Kazakh plain. A handful of trucks – battered, unpainted – stood around the capsule. Beside the Soyuz was the flatbed truck which had carried the capsule dummy out here. Fifty yards beyond that stood a Soviet Army helicopter, its rotors turning slowly. Cables trailed from the Command Module, coiling across the dust of the steppe, leading to winches attached to the chopper.

There was a smell of wormwood grass: thin, almost lost on the cold air. The ground was baked to a yellowish, brick-hard glaze, with just a few tufts of grass. In some places patches of snow lingered. Vladimir Viktorenko had told her that in the early spring, the steppe would be covered in flowers. York found it hard to believe.

She didn't know what had caused the latest delay. Technicians stood around, showing no apparent concern for timetables or schedules. That seemed to be the way in the Soviet Union, even around the space program.

York tried to be tolerant, but she found it hard. She didn't feel she had the time to hang around on a steppe with a bunch of ragged-assed Soviets. *Let's get on with this. Get it over.*

Now Vladimir Viktorenko came stalking up to her, compact and purposeful, his flight helmet fixed over his head. 'So,' he said, and he clapped her on the shoulder. She was braced for the blow, and managed not to stumble. 'You are ready for your ride? And you, Ralph?'

Gershon lifted his head out of his suit neck, like a turtle poking out of its shell.

York stared up at the wall of the Command Module, her apprehension growing. 'We've had no preparation for this. Where's the hatch? At the top of the Soyuz?'

'Yes, it is at the top. I will climb in first.' He tapped her shoulder, then Gershon's. 'Then you, then you. You will see. It will be easy.'

The technicians were snickering. York felt her resentment build. 'So, Vladimir, why are these guys of yours laughing at me?'

He raised his eyebrows. 'Vlad-*im*-ir,' he said, accenting the second syllable. 'Oh, it is nothing.'

'Like hell it is.' She felt anger surge in her. She'd been burning up with it since Apollo-N, lashing out at anything that came in her way. She suspected it was one reason she'd been sent over here, right now, despite her involvement in the post-accident investigations. To keep her out of the way. To cool her off, on the steppe.

Well, it wasn't working.

She stalked over to one of the techs, a burly guy in a shirt, grease-stained, that strained at his ample belly. 'What's so funny? Huh?'

Viktorenko came to her side and took her elbow. 'You must be calm, my dear.'

She shook his hand off. 'Oh, sure. Just as soon as these ill-mannered assholes –'

'No,' he said, and there was some steel in his voice.

'Why the hell not?'

'*Soy-uz.*' He pronounced the word the way she had, as an American-eared best guess, with the syllables rhyming with 'boy' and 'fuzz.' Even to York's ears it sounded clumsy. 'That is what is so amusing. I suspect your English transliterations are at fault,' he said

326

smoothly. 'That "y" is perhaps deceptive. You see, in the standard orthography, "yu" stands for a specific Cyrillic letter, and so the "y" and "u" should not be split. The syllables are *So-yuz*, you see. Now. Since the stress is on the second syllable, we would allow the unstressed "o" of "So" to soften into a weaker "ah." And then "yuz" has a long "u," like "shoe." *Sah-yooz*. But, of course, in speaking, final consonants tend to drift to the unvoiced. One must soften the "z" to "s." So: *Sah-yooss. Sah-yooss*.'

She tried it a couple of times, and drew an ironic hand-clap from the big, burly tech.

'Better,' Viktorenko said. 'Now, you see, you have taken the trouble, here in my country, to pronounce correctly one of the three or four words of Russian with which one could reasonably expect an American astronaut to be familiar.'

She was aware of the tech watching her, a leer in his eyes. She glared back. These Russians were even more full of macho bull than their American counterparts.

But then, some of that might be to do with the lousy international situation. She tried to imagine what these men must feel about their countrymen fighting and dying in Afghanistan – and what went through their heads when they looked at her, a vulnerable, isolated American, and remembered the aggressive anti-Soviet rhetoric that had been emanating from the White House from the day Reagan had walked in. They'd be entitled to despise her, she supposed.

Her anger dissipated. *Hell. Maybe I deserve it.*

She shivered, and tried not to think about it.

A rope ladder came snaking down out of the Soyuz toward the ground.

She knelt at the summit of the Command Module, with the heavy hand of a tech on her shoulder to steady her. The Command Module was like the headlight of some huge car, upended on this plain, its green paint a striking contrast with the washed-out brown of the soil. From up here the steppe looked immense, intimidating, deserted save for the small group around the capsule; the sky was iron gray, a lid clamped tight over the land.

In the remote distance she spotted a silvery glint that might have been water. Some godforsaken landlocked salt lake.

Viktorenko clambered into the capsule first. He told York to give him a couple of minutes before following; he said he had to check the bolts holding the seats in place. As far as she could tell he was serious.

At last Viktorenko poked his head out of the hatch and waved her in. The technician pulled off her outer boots, and the anti-scratch cover she had worn over her helmet.

The cabin was laid out superficially like an Apollo Command Module – which, after all, was of the same vintage as this Soyuz technology – with three lumpy-looking moulded couches set out in a fan formation, their lower halves touching. Gingerly, feet first, she lowered herself down.

Vladimir Viktorenko was already in the commander's seat, over at the left of the cabin. He waved her toward the other side. 'Be my guest!'

She slid herself down, wriggling until she could feel the contours of the right-hand seat under her. The couch was too short for her, and compressed her at her shoulders and calves. The couches in a Soyuz were supposed to be moulded to the body of the cosmonaut; in this training rig the couches came in one size, to fit all, and were scuffed and battered from overuse.

The capsule was cramped even compared to the Apollo trainers she'd used, and was jammed full of bales of equipment for post-landing: parachutes, emergency rations, flotation gear, survival clothing. The main controls were set out in a panel in front of Viktorenko: a CRT screen, orientation controls on Viktorenko's right, and maneuvering controls to his left. There was an optical orientation view-finder set up on a small porthole to one side of the panel. York recognized few of the instruments, actually. But it didn't matter; she wouldn't be doing any flying. And besides, in this landing-drill mockup, most of the controls were obviously dummies.

The capsule layout struck her as truly clunky. It was all sharp corners; and some of the controls were so far from the cosmonauts' hands that they were provided with sticks to poke at the panels. It was low-tech, utilitarian.

There was a small, circular pane of glass at York's right elbow. She peered out of this now, trying to lose herself in the view of gray sky and flat steppe.

Ralph Gershon came clambering down from the hatch. His boots and knees were everywhere, clattering into the equipment banks and against York and Viktorenko. The Russian laughed hugely, and playfully batted away Gershon's clumsier movements.

Gershon twisted into the center seat and plumped down, compressing her against the wall; their lower legs were in contact, and there was no space for her to move away. 'Oh, Jesus Christ, Ralph.'

Gershon, chewing Juicy Fruit, seemed cheerful enough. 'Lighten up, York. This ain't so bad. At least we're out of the fucking wind.'

Viktorenko reached over Gershon and pushed closed the inner hatch, a fat plug of metal. Immediately the wind noise, the chattering of the technicians, was cut off, and York felt sealed in. Entombed.

She heard the techs slam shut the outer hatch.

The noise of the chopper increased to a muffled drone. She felt her heart pump harder. There was a pounding on the hull, and then a soft, slithering scraping, as, York guessed, cables slid over the surface of the craft.

Ralph Gershon picked his gum out of his mouth and stuck it under his seat, seemingly unconcerned.

The chopper's engine roared. There was a brief strobing of the light at her window – helicopter blades, passing over the Command Module – and then a yank upwards, as if the Soyuz had turned into a high-speed elevator.

York felt the air rush out of her lungs, and the pressure points of her couch dug into her back and hips.

Beyond her window the receding steppe rocked back and forth like a plaster-of-paris model in a sim. She saw a little circle of engineers, waving their caps, their faces turned up like dusty flowers.

Grit fled in concentric circles across the steppe, away from the capsule, and the technicians staggered back, shielding their eyes.

Then she could no longer see the ground: her window was a disk of clouded sky.

York's pressure suit was getting hot. She could feel perspiration pooling under her, in a little slick that gathered in the small of her back. But at the same time, thanks to some quirk of the Soviet suit's cooling system, her feet were cold. She tried to curl up her toes, inside the layers which constrained them.

Gershon, lying beside her, was all elbows.

There was a TV camera – a crude-looking thing, like something out of the 1950s – fixed to the cabin wall, just above Gershon's head. York didn't know if it was live or not. A small metal toy, a spaceman, dangled in front of the lens on a metal chain; as the cabin swung about under the chopper, the little toy rocked back and forth.

Viktorenko caught her eyeing the model. 'You are admiring my friend Boris.' He pronounced it *Bah-reess*. 'Boris has a major role to play, in the correct functioning of the Soyuz.' He pointed. 'You

329

see the TV camera. That is trained on Boris at all times. By watching his antics, the ground can determine the exact moment at which we become weightless. Ingenious, no? . . .'

Now the capsule lurched to the right. York felt the weight of the two men compressing her against the wall.

Viktorenko roared with approval. 'It is just like Disney World! Ha ha! Now, Ralph and Natalie. You must imagine that we are returning to Earth aboard a *real* Soyuz, perhaps after spending a hundred days or more aboard our wonderful space platform Salyut. We have endured the gentle buffeting of reentry – a mere three or four G, thanks to the cunning aerodynamic design of the Command Module – and soot has coated our window following the scorching friction of the air. But we discard our window shields, and we see bright sunlight, a Kazakhstan morning. Now here come the parachutes: the three drogues, *crack crack crack* in swift succession, and then the main chute, a great white sail above us.' Viktorenko mimed a slow, feather-like rocking. 'So we drift downwards, like a snowflake, all three tonnes of us . . .'

She closed her eyes. She was certain something was intended to go wrong, somewhere down the line. It was just a question of when, and how bad it would be, and whether she'd be able to cope when it came. It was like every sim: this was a sadistic game, in which Viktorenko was in complete control. And the bastard knew it.

'And now the moment approaches,' Viktorenko said. 'The reunion with the mother planet! But her embrace is hard. So compressed gases have been pumped into the base of your seats, to absorb the shock, you see. And, less than two meters from the ground, retrorockets will fire to cushion the impact. Of course we have no retrorockets, for this is only a training mockup . . . Perhaps we will be fortunate, and the wind will be low; otherwise, we may bounce –'

There was a crackle, a brief Russian message on the radio. Viktorenko acknowledged and checked a chronometer. 'Three, two, one.'

Loose cables clattered against the hull. The chopper had released the capsule.

The Command Module *fell,* dragging her down with it.

The Soyuz slammed against a hard surface, with a vast metallic slap.

The impact was more violent than York had expected. Her ill-fitting couch rammed into her back, all the pressure points gouging her body.

'Fuck,' Gershon gasped.

330

At least I'm down. She glanced around, quickly, at the still, almost silent cabin; she could hear the distant noise of the climbing chopper. *Is that it? Is it over? No bouncing, no dragging – are we down?*

Then the capsule tipped to her left, quite smoothly, so that her weight was pressed against Gershon's.

'Fuck,' Gershon said again.

York shouted, 'What the hell's this, Vladimir?'

The window beyond Viktorenko was briefly darkened, though York couldn't see by what. Viktorenko grinned. 'Evidently something has gone wrong.'

Now the capsule started to roll the other way, to York's right, and the weight of the two men came down on York again. Beyond her window, obscuring the glass, water, silvery-gray with murk, was bubbling up.

So that's it. This is the carefully designed screw-up. The Soyuz is supposed to come down on land . . .

'Fuck,' said Gershon.

'Welcome to Ozero Tengiz,' Viktorenko said. 'Tengiz Lake, a salt lake all of twenty miles wide, and less than a hundred miles from –'

York groaned. 'Do we really have to go through with this? I mean, rehearsing for an emergency water landing? *After* an emergency retrieval from orbit by a Soyuz?'

'Would you rather endure such an occurrence without preparation? All of your training has a context. You must understand that. Our cosmonauts are trained to handle all conceivable survivable emergencies.'

'Not the un-survivable ones,' York said.

'But few points in a mission are true dead zones; in most situations there are options. The present exercise covers just one contingency. Of course for this particular exercise you must thank my old friend, Joseph Muldoon.'

Gershon retrieved his wad of gum from the base of his chair, mashed it in his gloved hand to make it soft, and pushed it back into his mouth. 'Fuck Muldoon,' said Gershon. 'And fuck you.'

The Russian watched with appalled fascination.

York said, 'All right, Vladimir, we'll play ball. What's the drill?'

'Survival gear,' Viktorenko said. He unzipped his pressure suit.

York felt enormously weary. But she didn't have a choice.

She took off her helmet and jammed it behind her seat.

The outermost layer of her suit was a coverall of a tough artificial

331

fabric, with pockets and tool-loops and flaps. It opened up at the front, revealing the flaps of cloth called the 'appendix,' bound up with rubber bands; when York slipped off the bands the bunched material unfolded.

With the outer suit layer lolling around her like a deflated balloon, York went to work on the inner layer, of an airtight, elasticated material.

In the restricted space, with the ceiling of the cabin just inches from her nose, movement was virtually impossible, and she kept catching at controls and switches with her feet and hands. The interior of the cabin was becoming chaotic now, with the squirming bodies of the three of them and discarded bits of equipment sloshing back and forth in the confined, rocking space.

'It is easier if you help each other!' Viktorenko called cheerily.

'Fuck off,' Gershon said.

When her pressure garment was off, she was down to her long thermal underwear. She started to pull on her survival gear: a red sweater, a jumpsuit, a jacket, thickly padded trousers, an outer jacket . . .

'But this is poor,' growled Viktorenko. 'Poor! You must work as a team. On Mars, forty million miles from Earth, there are only your crewmates. You must turn to each other for aid as a child might turn to his mother, instinctively, without asking. Do you understand? And that aid must be offered without calculation or hesitation. It is the way you must adopt. Tomorrow we will do this better.'

'You must be kidding,' York snapped. 'We have to go through all this again?'

Viktorenko, pulling on his own gear, continued to lecture them. 'Listen to me. Our Soviet training is tougher than yours, and some within NASA have come to understand this. In some of our exercises, there is no chance of seeking help. There is no rescue team! For there will be none on Mars! It is all purposeful. For, when a man realizes a mistake might cost him his health or even his life, the situation is transformed. Suddenly there is an incentive to concentrate.

'In space, one needs the courage and resourcefulness to continue to work on a problem long after an average person, with hope of rescue, might have given in. And this is what I begin to instill in you now.'

York was tired, in pain, hugely irritated. The trouble was, there was a strand of thinking inside NASA that approved of the Soviets' tough approach: mostly the old military fly-boys, who seemed to think NASA astronauts were getting pampered. Joe Muldoon, for instance, Viktorenko's great Moon-orbiting buddy. *Yeah, pampered. Especially all these goddamn new-fangled hyphenated-astronauts who want to go to Mars . . .*

She said, 'All this macho training didn't help Ben Priest and the others, did it?'

Viktorenko studied her. More gently he said, 'No. It did not help Ben Priest.' He plucked at the cuffs of his thick sweater. 'Listen, Natalie. There is an old Russian folk tale. A young woman named Marushka was famous for being able to embroider fantastical designs. Her fame reached the attention of Kaschei the Immortal, an evil sorcerer, who fell in love with her and wished her to go away with him. She turned him down, despite his magic powers, for she was modest, and wished only to stay in the village where she was born.

'Enraged, Kaschei turned her into a fire-bird with brilliant plumage, and himself into a huge black bird of prey. The bird of prey seized the fire-bird in its talons and flew away with it.

'Marushka, realizing she was dying, willed that she should shed her plumage. Her feathers fell to the ground on the land she loved.

'Marushka died, but her feathers were magical. They remained alive, but only to those who appreciated beauty and chose to share it with others . . .

'So it is with death, among us. No *kosmonaut* dies in vain, Natalie York.'

The Command Module rocked harder, swinging back and forth through thirty, forty degrees. Water lapped, gurgling, against the hull. York had a nightmare vision of the capsule sinking, dragging them, padded trousers and all, down to the bottom of this lousy little salt lake.

It's so hot in here. Her head seemed full of blood; she could feel her pulse at her neck, and there was a yellow haze at the edge of her vision.

Christ. I'm going to faint.

But then the cabin tipped again, over to the right, and her stomach knotted up. Saliva pooled at the back of her throat. *No. No, that's not fainting.*

She turned away from the others, toward the wall; when it came, the vomit splashed against the port and wall and slid down under her seat.

There was a hand on her shoulder. 'York. You okay?'

It was Gershon; she waved him away. She tried to talk, but her throat was still closed up.

And then the stink hit Gershon. 'Oh, Jesus.' He lunged, sticking his head over the back of his couch, and began to throw up too, in huge, noisy spasms.

Viktorenko laughed. 'So, *Bah-reess*, only you and I are able-bodied seamen, eh?'

'Fuck,' Ralph Gershon groaned.

The water lapped against the hull of the Soyuz, and Boris the cosmonaut dangled from his silver chain above York's head.

She wondered what had happened to Gershon's gum.

Washington Post, *Monday, February 23, 1981*

... We have no hesitation in devoting this editorial exclusively to the report of the Presidential Commission into the Apollo-N space disaster, which has at last, after weeks of leaks, rumors and counter-rumors, been formally published. The report is 3,300 pages long and weighs in at nineteen pounds, and it does not mince words. The report makes it clear that the accident was not the result of a chance malfunction, in a statistical sense, but rather resulted from an unusual combination of mistakes, coupled with a deficient design.

The Apollo-N disaster has sparked a fresh national debate, led by a skeptical Congress, over whether the country should be spending tens of billions of dollars on a 'footprints-and-flags' program to send men to space, when it faces so many problems at home. Public opinion polls find many citizens asking if the program is costing too much, and feeling that any trip to Mars would be as much a political stunt as was the Apollo race to the Moon.

Meanwhile, many prominent scientists, such as Professor Leon Agronski, a former science adviser to President Nixon, are arguing in public fora that less expensive unmanned probes could teach us more about the composition of Mars and the other planets than astronauts.

On the other hand, supporters of the space program point out that the average American spends much more per year on cigarettes and alcohol than on sending fellow countrymen to other planets, and that untold scientific and technological benefits will flow from the continuing program.

This paper remains skeptical.

The most damaging part of the Commission report is a frank indictment of NASA and its senior contractors. The Commission's investigation revealed many deficiencies in design and engineering, in manufacturing and quality control. Numerous examples have been exposed, in addition to the simple and avoidable defect that led to the tragedy itself.

This newspaper is appalled at the incredible complacency of NASA engineers. Even a high school physics student would have known not to allow a nuclear core with instability built into its very design onto an operational space mission.

It seems likely that this nation will continue on to Mars, and beyond; successes in space travel have become essential to the image of the United States as the world's leading power in science and technology: an image projected to the Soviet Union, our allies around the world, the uncommitted nations of the Third World, and – perhaps most importantly – to our own citizenry. And we should not forget the cold, cynical political calculation that a cancelation of the space program would immediately cause a drastic oversupply in the aerospace industry, and inevitable job losses and shutdowns in that area.

But as we put Apollo-N behind us and strive to move forward, we should never forget how the dry technical prose of the Presidential Commission report convicts those in charge of NASA of gross incompetence and negligence . . .

Friday, February 27, 1981
NASA Headquarters, Washington

Joe Muldoon called on Fred Michaels in his office in Washington. He arrived a little after seven, having flown out from Houston.

Without getting up, Michaels waved Muldoon to a chair. 'Sit down, Joe. It's good to see you. You want a drink?'

'Sure.' Muldoon sat uncertainly, studying Michaels.

There was a decanter and glasses in a corner of Michaels's desk; Michaels poured Muldoon a careless couple of fingers and passed it over. It was good Kentucky bourbon. The place was darkened, somber, with the lights dimmed; the brightest source of light was the small TV set in one corner of the room, which was showing a news program, with the sound off.

Michaels rocked back in his chair, with his boots on the corner of his wide desk; his gold-braided vest hung open, and the dim light emphasized the deep grooves in his face as – in typical Michaels style – he waited for Muldoon to say what he wanted to say.

Muldoon began to tell the Administrator about the progress he was making in his new role as head of the Program Office. 'The NERVA contractors were running a fucking country club, Fred. And those bastards at Marshall have been letting them get away with it.'

Michaels, with one eye on the TV, shrugged. 'That's maybe a little harsh, Joe. We've been putting them all under a hell of a lot of schedule pressure. Maybe too much.'

'No, it's not that. In a lot of cases it's just sloppy practice. For instance, the first time I went up to the S-NB test installation at Michoud I found some of the technicians going for a few beers with their lunch. That's just outrageous, when you're working on man-rated hardware. And I saw some guy pumping lox out of a tank on the ground up into an umbilical tower. I asked him where the lox was going. "Beats the hell out of me," he said. Once it got out of the other end of his hose, that little guy didn't have a clue what happened to the lox. After that, I told them that I wanted every engineer to learn everything there is to know about every system he was running – where the stuff came from, where it was going, and all the things that might go wrong in between. Every one of those guys has got to know his system from womb to tomb.

'I made a list – I copied you on it – of thirty-odd things that got up my ass, in my first hour up there. Lousy materials handling, mixed-up demarcation of work spaces, wasted time . . .

'Sure, the schedule pressures are working against us, too. With the sloppy practices the manufacturers have got, there's no way they can keep to their development timetables. And then they cut corners on testing, to try to make the end date, which means you end up with a candle that's late *and* lousy quality.'

Michaels was nodding, rubbing the thick jowls under his chin. 'Yeah. I understand. You're doing a good job, Joe. You're doing just the job I hired you for.'

'Fred, we've gone wrong, somewhere. We scraped this kind of crap out of Apollo; back then we had an operation, right across the country, that was as slick as snot. But now we've slipped back.'

Michaels grunted and sipped his drink. 'Maybe. But we had many things working for us, back then. A goal you couldn't have defined more sharply, a lot of goodwill – even though Congress squeezed the budgets – and, hell, I don't know, a kind of romance about it all.

336

We were still moving outwards, Joe; it was still a great adventure, a time of firsts, every year. And we had one hell of a schedule pressure; we still thought the Russians might beat us to it.

'Now,' he ruminated, 'it's different. All the forces working on us have changed. Even though we've got the prospect of Mars, somewhere out there in the future, we've been mooching about in Earth orbit for a decade, and what the hell have we got to show for it but a couple of tin-can fuel-tank 'Labs, Apollo hardware still in orbit a decade after the Moon landings, a Saturn upgrade booster that hasn't flown once, and a lethal bucket of bolts called NERVA?'

'Yeah, but you have to take a positive view of it, Fred. Skylab A is still operational, nearly a decade after it was launched. What if we'd abandoned it? – let it fall back to Earth? What a hell of a waste that would have been; we'd have been a laughing stock. And Moonlab is still up there –'

'Okay, okay. But it's still just Apollo applications. Nothing we didn't design in the '60s. And meanwhile, the world is moving on, Joe. We don't have the lead that we had a decade ago. The Russians have kept on flying Soyuz and Salyut –'

'But our stuff is advanced over theirs.'

'Maybe, but their endurance records have been beating the pants off us. And the Soviets aren't the only ones. Even our buddies are moving into the gaps we're leaving. The Europeans have been flying their Ariane for a couple of years, so we're soon going to lose out in terms of commercial launches too, to our so-called allies.'

He rubbed the bridge of his nose with his fleshy fingers, and closed his eyes. 'Ah, hell. Another eight or nine years on, and here I am again trying to reshape the space program for another new president. And once again I'm trying to figure out the way the future is going to pull at us, and which way the new White House is likely to jump. Maybe it's not so obvious to you guys; I know what it's like when you're buried inside the program. But things are so different now, from 1971, and 1960; so different . . .'

Muldoon grunted. 'Oh, I look around, Fred. I can see the changes. In spite of the Afghanistan thing, the Cold War is done now. Or at least, people want to think so. And if space was all about fighting the War symbolically –'

'Then what use is it now?' Michaels smiled over his glass. 'You got that right. We were happy enough to play that card when it suited us, Joe; maybe we couldn't have flown without it. But now people have had enough, and we're being paid back. But on the other hand . . .'

337

Muldoon prompted, 'Yeah?'

'On the other hand, maybe there are still some angles we can use. You know Reagan is expanding his military spending.'

Muldoon grunted. 'Sure. Just as he's cutting taxes, and the rest of the budget.'

'And I don't think that's going to go away, not during Reagan's term.' Michaels was thoughtful, calculating. 'Haig is saying that all of Carter's human rights stuff was misguided; that what we've got to do now is counter the Soviets, who are still the main threat.'

'So what does that mean for us, Fred?'

Michaels smiled, tiredly. 'You got to see the angles. We have to position ourselves so we're in the part of the budget that gets expanded, not the part that gets cut. If all that money is going to flow into defense, then we've got to be in the way of that flow. Divert a little bit.' He sipped his drink. 'Then you got Reagan himself. That old ham. You know, I've been working with Reagan and his people since he was nominated. And I think it's possible he might want to emulate Kennedy. Or rather, finally put Kennedy in his box, after all these years. You know that in the Republican platform last year, Reagan attacked Carter/Kennedy for not keeping up NASA's funding the way they should have. Now, he has to deliver on that.

'And maybe, for Reagan, the state of flux we're in after the NERVA thing is an opportunity. A chance for him to shape events. The space program is like a litmus test for new Administrations, when they come in, a way for them to prove themselves. You had Kennedy and the Moon, and Nixon and his long-range Mars program . . . Joe, I think if we could come up with some program, some clear goal, that promised to restore our image, and put us back in the lead in space in a few years' time – say, in five or six years, within his possible term of office – Reagan might buy it.' His rheumy eyes gleamed. 'And now's the time to strike, while his Administration is settling in. But –'

'But what?'

'But Reagan's no Kennedy. And Bush sure as hell is no LBJ. An announcement isn't enough. I'm not sure if we're going to be able to assemble, and keep, a coalition of interests behind any such program. And besides, if NERVA's a busted flush, what the hell have we got to give Reagan anyhow, Joe?' He poured himself another drink. 'Ah, God. I tell you, I don't know if I can do it any more. I've used up a lot of credit on the Hill over the years, in the endless program delays and overspends. And now this NERVA thing. I don't know if I can go in there and start fighting again. I don't know if I should even be trying anymore.'

He's thinking of giving up, Muldoon realized. The sudden perception was painful to him, almost a physical shock. *Fuck. How come I haven't seen this before?*

Because, he thought, he hadn't wanted to admit it.

A NASA without Fred Michaels at the top was all but inconceivable to Muldoon, as it no doubt was to most Americans.

Muldoon knew enough about the workings of NASA to know what kind of man it needed as its Administrator. It shouldn't be a scientist, or an engineer. It had to be someone who understood the great issues of national and public policy. It had to be a manager, someone able to keep the multiple warring centers in effective and efficient operation. It had to be a man who knew his way around Congress, and the Pentagon, and the Budget Bureau.

Such a man was Fred Michaels.

Michaels, as had James Webb before him, had shown himself to have the ability to build up a political lobby behind a space program – and then, crucially, to sustain it across the years. Michaels's continuity, and his endless energy and commitment, had probably meant as much as Kennedy's advocacy in keeping the NASA show on the road, over all these long and seemingly fruitless years.

With lesser men in the Administrator's office, Muldoon realized, NASA might have fallen on bad times years before.

And now, at this lowest moment, he wants to give up, to slink back to fucking Dallas.

Muldoon sat there in the gloom of the office, listening to Michaels, watching the flickering of the TV screen.

He was reminded of the day, long ago, when his own father had admitted to him that he was terminally ill; he felt the same loss of foundations, of surety.

I guess I'm going to have to become one of the grown-ups now, he thought.

But what the hell am I supposed to do?

March–April, 1981
Lyndon B. Johnson Space Center, Houston

From Joe Muldoon's point of view, the arguments and decision-making about the future shape of the space program accelerated dramatically over the next few weeks.

Reagan asked his White House counsel to review options. A small meeting was pulled together in a room of the White House, overlooking the South Lawn. Tim Josephson briefed Muldoon on how the session had gone. Just a handful of men had been in there, talking and arguing for hours: the counsel, the budget director, Fred Michaels, Josephson and a couple of assistants, and Michaels's old adversary Leon Agronski.

'It was important to us, Joe. It could have been maybe the single most important meeting since the decision to go to the Moon. But we spent most of the time bitching about the lousy decisions that have landed us in this mess in the first place. And you had Agronski weighing in yet again about how manned spaceflight is a waste of time . . . I still feel Reagan is looking for something positive, and feasible, and real, that he can unite us all around; but so far we haven't come up with anything. We're in danger of being picked apart; Reagan will find his prestigious morale-boosters somewhere else, and we'll end up flying nothing but goddamn low-orbit spy missions.'

Muldoon wasn't sure why Josephson was getting into the habit of taking him into his confidence. Muldoon guessed Josephson spent a lot of time making tentative calls to a host of other contacts inside NASA and out, trying, in his own way, to help Fred Michaels through this difficult time.

Josephson had said: *We haven't come up with anything.* Muldoon knew that was true.

So Muldoon – already working all his waking hours on the Apollo-N investigations and organizational changes – started using the hours he should have been asleep to do his own research.

'What kind of program can we run?' he asked Phil Stone. He riffled a pile of photostats, journals and books on his desks. 'If I could eat proposals, I'd be a fat man; the one thing we're not short of is ideas. Should we go back to the Moon, and start mining it for minerals? Or maybe we should capture an asteroid, and push it toward the Earth, and mine that. Maybe we can build colonies at the libration points of the Earth-Moon system. Maybe we should have factories in space, making crystals, or drugs, or perfect, seam-less metal spheres. Maybe we could build huge hydroponic farms in space, where the sun always shines. Or maybe we ought to put up square miles of solar arrays, for clean power. Maybe we could mine the Earth's upper atmosphere for lox . . .'

NASA wasn't short of visionaries, and new ideas, and proposals of all sorts. But there was no unity. Historically, NASA as an organization was lousy at long-range planning; fragmentary ideas and plans came bubbling up from the bottom, from the centers, and almost all of them fell foul of turf wars.

Stone waved a hand. 'All this stuff is great, Joe. But I don't see what's distinctive about any of it.'

'What do you mean?'

'The Soviets are already ahead of us in putting together big structures in orbit, and they have more experience of long-duration spaceflight. So we're behind before we start. Whatever we try to do in this area, the Russians ought to be able to pass us easily. And there's something about all this, factories and power plants in orbit, that's kind of . . .'

'What?'

'Lacking inspiration. It's dour. Russian. Joe, with this stuff we're not *going* anywhere; and we haven't *been* anywhere since Apollo.'

'So what do we do? Some kind of stunt?'

'Go to Mars. That was the point of the last ten years anyhow, wasn't it?'

'But we never had a Mars program, in the way that we had a Moon program back in the '60s. The point was that we were going to develop the technology bit by bit – the nuke rocket, and new heatshields, and new navigation techniques, and long-duration experience, and so on. All of which could be put together into a Mars mission one day, if we chose to; but it would all be modular, and able to be configured into a lot of flexible mission requirements –'

Stone laughed. 'You'll have to get out from behind that desk, Joe. You're beginning to sound like you belong there.'

Muldoon grunted and rubbed his eyes. 'Well, anyhow, we sure as hell ain't going to Mars. Not any more; not in my lifetime or yours, Phil.'

'You're so sure? We've got most of the elements. We do know how to survive long-duration missions.'

'Sure I'm sure. The fucking nuke rocket blew up in orbit, remember. The Russians are still sending down pictures of the damn thing glowing blue in the dark. From what I hear there's no way we're going to be allowed to fly a NERVA again. And without NERVA –'

'There goes your Mars mission. Unless you fly chemical.'

'Yeah,' Muldoon growled. 'But how? Here – look at this thing.' He grubbed on his desk until he found a glossy report, full of spectacular color images. 'This is from Udet and his guys, at

341

Marshall. They've reworked some old papers that go all the way back to the early '60s. Have you heard of the EMPIRE studies?'

'Nope.'

'Marshall and a couple of contractors, back in '62 and '63. Back then, Apollo-Saturn had just about crystalized, and the engineers were asking, what the hell else can we do with this stuff? And they came up with EMPIRE – Early Manned Planetary-Interplanetary Roundtrip Expeditions. Look at this. Some of the options needed nuke stages, but others were chemical only. There were a lot of studies like that, from that period. Soon after, every aerospace engineer in the country had his head up Apollo's ass, and the flow dried up.'

Stone leafed through the report. 'So what is Udet doing with this now?'

'He wants to revive a chemical-only Mars flyby option. A couple of S-IVB third stages in orbit, ganged together and fired off on a minimum-energy trajectory, looping around Mars. You'd need two, maybe three Saturn launches to do it.'

'A flyby of Mars? What the hell kind of mission is that?'

Muldoon rubbed his face. 'Well, you're talking maybe a seven-hundred-day round trip, and about one day of useful work at Mars.'

'Whipping by at interplanetary speeds . . .'

'Oh, and by the way. You'd pass on the dark side.'

Stone laughed. 'You're kidding.'

'Well, that was the kind of mission they were proposing, back in 1963. The point was *to go* – just like Apollo, really – nobody cared what you did when you got there.'

Stone threw the report on Muldoon's desk. 'You can't approve this, Joe. We're beyond stunts like this now. Aren't we? In the long run, they come back to bite you. Damn it, Udet and his boys ought to know better than this. We'd probably get laughed out of Congress anyhow.'

Muldoon shrugged, cautious. 'Hell, it might get past Reagan, Phil.'

Stone looked reflective. 'Look at it this way. What would Natalie York think of this?'

Muldoon laughed; then the laugh tailed off, and he studied Stone. 'You know, you're right. York's a good touchstone.' Awkward pain in the ass as she is, if she wouldn't approve a mission, he thought, it's probably not worth flying. 'All right. So we need to find some way of devising an all-chemical mission that will deliver a crew into

Mars orbit for a respectable chunk of time – including a landing. But that brings us back where we started; it doesn't look as if we can do it with chemical.'

Stone shrugged. 'So find some smarter way of getting there.'

'Like what?'

'How should I know? Joe, you're head of the program now, for Christ's sake. There are a lot of smart guys around here. Use them.' He looked thoughtful. 'Natalie York, huh.'

'Yeah. Makes you think, doesn't it?'

Muldoon got back to his work on the investigation.

Except, as he tried to sleep that night in a small, stuffy room in JSC, with his head full of the conflicting demands of his new and complex job, Muldoon found himself thinking of a conference he'd sat in on long ago. It was in the von Braun Hilton over at Marshall, as he recalled: a seminar on Mars mission modes. And some little guy had stood up with a strange proposal – Muldoon had spent most of the conference sleeping off a hangover, and couldn't recall the details – some way to boost the lower delta-vee offered by chemical technology by using gravitational assists. Bouncing off Venus, en route to Mars. And the little guy had got laughed off the stage by Udet and those other assholes from Marshall.

Now, what the hell was that about?

At three a.m., he got out of bed and padded down to his old desk in the Astronaut Office, and began digging through his old notes and diaries, chasing down the elusive memory.

By five a.m. he'd found what he was looking for. *Gregory Dana. Jesus. It was Jim Dana's father.*

By seven a.m. he was on the phone, trying to find Dana.

So Muldoon started to dip his toes, tentatively, into the shark-pool of NASA politics.

He pulled strings and set up a short-term working group, of NASA people and contractors, which would be able to flesh out in detail the idea that was lodging in his head. While that was coming together he drafted a hasty report to Michaels, summarizing the research he'd been doing.

He had Tim Josephson polish up a final draft for him, thus further extending their unspoken, ambiguous alliance. And when Muldoon sent his report to Michaels, he sent a copy to Josephson, to make sure it got leaked to the White House.

*   *   *

343

Natalie York was the Astronaut Office representative on Joe Muldoon's task force. She was sent to NASA HQ for an initiation meeting.

Before arriving, she'd hardly thought much about this assignment. She was just grateful to have a break in Washington – to get away from the grind of training that had become meaningless in the context of a rudderless program, to get away from her empty, unsold apartment, and from all the holes in her life where Ben used to be.

But now she found herself in a meeting the likes of which she had only imagined a couple of months earlier – and which she'd thought would never take place again, after the disaster.

Muldoon had called in staff from all the major NASA centers, including Udet and his team from Marshall, and senior engineers and managers from all of NASA's major contract partners: Boeing, Rockwell, Grumman, McDonnell, IBM, others. Pulling out so many senior staff put a dent in a lot of other projects, including the post-Apollo-N inquiries and the rectification program, and really Muldoon was going far beyond his organizational authority.

But he evidently hadn't been shy of using his new position to pull strings.

Standing on a stage at the front of an overcrowded conference hall, Muldoon briefed the opening session.

'The meeting is scheduled for the next fourteen days,' Muldoon said. 'The objective is to come up with a new core space program, in that time. Nothing less than that. I'm expecting you to work all the hours it takes, including the weekends; I'm going to isolate this group from your other commitments by putting you up here in Washington, and I've arranged work rooms and computer facilities and phone lines . . .'

Despite Muldoon's vigorous presentation, York became aware of some muttering in the room around her as he spoke. *What the hell's he talking about? A plan to do what? Without the fucking nuke, we ain't going anywhere except low Earth orbit for a generation.*

But York had never seen Muldoon like this.

She'd come to know him as a difficult man: a moonwalker, obsessive about getting back into space again, forceful, foulmouthed, with maybe too much anger ready to spill out over the incompetence of anyone on the ground he saw getting in his way. Now, she watched as he dominated a room full of the toughest heavyweights in NASA, with passion and anger and a visible will to succeed. He'd grown, remarkably; for the first time she realized how perceptive Fred Michaels had been in selecting this man to run his spacecraft program after Bert Seger.

Muldoon sketched the guidelines for the meeting.

'I want you to focus on a baseline mission profile of a crew of four, with a thirty-day stopover, to be launched for the 1985 opportunity. It will be a very different mission from what we thought we were doing previously: all we have available now is chemical technology, and it is going to need some smart thinking from your trajectory planners.

'We need self-discipline. I can't emphasize that enough. The objective is to devise a bare-bones program based on what must be done, and what can be done based on the technology we have, not on what you'd *like* the program to do. The resultant plan, including the schedule, is going to have to be honest: no promises we can't keep, no wishful thinking . . .'

And slowly, through her vague numbness, York began to realize what Muldoon was talking about, what the subject of this task force actually was.

Going to Mars. Maybe it's still possible.

For the first time since Ben's death, York felt her interest quickening.

After a week, it seemed to Muldoon – amid the blizzard of computer printout, technical journals, Vu-graph foils, flipchart pages, half-eaten sandwiches and paper coffee cups – that something feasible was beginning to emerge.

His gut instinct was confirmed. *We really do have something here.*

He began to understand why Michaels had selected him for this job.

The Mars program had dominated the development of NASA since 1972 . . . No, Muldoon reflected, more than that: it had warped the Agency's post-Apollo growth, and that of all its programs. The Agency had become obsessed with one largely unspoken goal: *men on Mars.* Everything else was subordinated: the Earth-orbit programs were tailored to preparing for the long-haul flights to come, the unmanned programs were either canned or cut around to serve operational purposes.

So he could see why Michaels had put so much trust in him, Muldoon. Because he was a monomaniac too. His own obsessions were a kind of scale model of the Agency's.

He was the ideal champion.

*   *   *

345

After his couple of weeks, Muldoon had enough to put in front of the Administrator.

Muldoon had Josephson call a meeting in front of Michaels, with Udet, Gregory Dana, representatives of the contractors, and even a couple of tame Senators: all zealots for the new, embryonic program.

Muldoon summarized the proposed mission mode. 'We still need an orbital transfer booster to thrust the ship from Earth to Mars and back. That was the role that had been planned for the S-NB.' He looked at Michaels. 'But, even without the S-NB, we have an option, Fred. A chemical technology option. We can use an enhancement of the S-II second stage of the Saturn V. We have design studies by Rockwell dating back to 1972 showing how the S-II could be upgraded for such a role, by providing it with restartable engines, insulation, course adjustment verniers, docking facilities . . .'

Michaels grunted. 'Yeah. And those studies have been comprehensively rubbished by those bastards at Marshall since their inception.'

Udet kept his eyes fixed on Muldoon's foil, and did not react.

Dana said, 'I would need confirmation that development of the S-II is possible in the timescale.'

Michaels nodded seriously. 'You'll get it, Doctor.' He made a note to himself on a piece of paper.

Muldoon put up another foil. 'Fuel. If we assume that hydrogen/oxygen will be used, we've calculated that we will need a total of a thousand tons to depart from the Earth, three hundred tons to brake at Mars, and depart subsequently; and seventy tons to brake at Earth orbit. That's one thousand, three hundred and seventy tons in Earth orbit at the start of the mission. It would be a lot more if we didn't have Doctor Dana's gravity assist maneuver to save fuel. Now, the largest mass we can loft to orbit, with the Saturn VB, is of the order of four hundred thousand pounds – about one hundred and eighty tons . . .'

'The Saturn VB has yet to fly,' Dana pointed out.

'I realize that.' Muldoon changed his foil. 'But this is assumptive planning, Doctor; we do have time to remedy the problems in that area. Here's how the mission would proceed. We would deliver, first, an enhanced S-II to orbit, empty. The S-II would be docked to a new facility, which we will call the Orbital Assembly Facility. This would be a simple affair, just struts and attitude motors; it would be put into an orbit close to Skylab.

'Next, supplementary fuel tanks would be orbited, by unmanned VB launches. Each of these External Tanks will contain, when fully loaded, seven hundred tons of liquid hydrogen and oxygen, securely insulated. The Tanks would be docked with the Assembly Facility. Pods of fuel will be brought up by subsequent Saturn VB flights, and dumped into the Tanks and the S-II stage itself. In all we'll need a minimum of ten Saturn VB launches. Remember, the whole purpose of the Saturn VB configuration is its reusability – we can refurbish the four Solid Rocket Boosters and fly them again – which will reduce costs per launch. We are already devising operational facilities which will allow fast pad turnaround and rapid refurbishment of flight articles. And we can combine the fuel-delivery flights with other objectives, such as the flight tests of the Mars Excursion Module. The MEM is the main undefined article, by the way; we'll issue a Request For Proposals in a few weeks, if we get approval . . .'

Josephson orchestrated a series of follow-up presentations; there were tables and charts showing costings, development and testing timetables. The funding slides were based on the assumption that there would be an incremental program of test shots of the various components and configurations in cislunar space, leading up to an initial set of three operational missions. The presenters showed how the new technology could be extended beyond the first landings to be used for a return to the Moon, establishing a Mars base, orbital missions to Venus; the new program would serve as a base, not just for a one-shot Mars trip, but a new expansion into the solar system.

Michaels's jowly, politician's face was free of expression as he listened; some of the time he sat with his eyes closed, almost as if he was falling asleep.

As the presentations closed, Michaels massaged the bridge of his nose and the pads of fat under his rheumy eyes.

He asked Muldoon to stay behind.

'You've done a damn good job, Joe. What you've brought me is convincing. And I'm under pressure from the White House already to come up with some such proposal as this.'

Muldoon felt his heart pump a little harder at that.

Michaels reached into his desk and pulled out a bottle of Kentucky bourbon and two glasses; he poured them both a shot. 'Tell me what you think of NASA's long-term plans.'

Muldoon thought it over, and began to frame a complex, considered answer. Then he decide to short cut.

'*What* long-term plans?'

Michaels grunted. 'You got that right. You got all kinds of god-damn schemes coming out of the think tanks in the centers. Well, that's fine. But I've always resisted, hard, any demand for a firm long-term strategy for the Agency. In all my time here. You know why? Because there's so much damned opposition to the manned space program. Always has been, always will be. And every plan I produce – every damn statement – is a political fall guy, just a target for the opposition to shoot at. I learned all this from Jim Webb, back in the '60s. Webb defended Apollo at all costs – even at the expense of its own sequel. He knew what success with Apollo would mean: even more, its failure or cancelation. That's partly responsible for the mess we're in now. But, Joe, we've got to learn the lesson. Even if it means we're mortgaging the future . . .'

Michaels poured them more drinks and talked some more, about tactics, detailed aspects of the proposals, about obtaining support from the military, the aerospace industry, other lobbies.

Slowly, Muldoon began to figure out that Michaels was thinking aloud, groping for a way forward. *He's talking tactics. He may be tired, but he isn't played out yet; he's telling us what he's going to have to do to make this happen. He's buying it.*

After Michaels's meeting, Udet sought out Dana. 'Doctor Dana. We must speak. At heart we two are, I believe, at one in our ambition.'

Dana's voice was disconcertingly thin, his eyes unreadable behind his glasses. 'Once I would have said so, I think. But, I am now not so sure. Now, I am prepared to accept that I will *not* see humans travel to Mars in my lifetime – if the attempt incurs unacceptable risk.'

Yes, yes. But you did, nevertheless, accept Muldoon's invitation to participate in this task group. If the dream was so feeble in you as you protest, then you would not even be here.

Udet felt oddly exhilarated; he felt a surge of kinship, almost, with this odd, bitter little man. *But the battle is won, Hans. Do not endanger it with recklessness.*

Udet disregarded the prompting of caution.

'Doctor Dana. I think we must address what is unspoken between us. We have worked together, in our strange way, for many years now. And we have, despite personal difficulties, achieved great things. I will build this ship. And it will be a memorial to your son.'

348

Dana's head swiveled, like a gun turret. 'My son has no connection to you, Udet. Make no claim on him.'

'Of course not. I only meant –'

'And as for us, you and I – we have roots far deeper than you may believe.'

Udet felt a prickle of fear. 'Tell me what you mean.'

'That I was at the *Mittelwerk*.'

Dana picked up his briefcase, now, and, with a curt nod, walked away.

All Udet's exhilaration, his mood of triumph, drained away from him; he felt as if he had been toying, ignorantly, with a loaded pistol.

The *Mittelwerk*. He was there; one of those invisible thousands. *My God.*

There may be no limit to the power which this absurd little man can wield over me.

After Michaels's meeting, events began to move with a speed that stunned Muldoon.

There was predictable opposition to the new proposal from Leon Agronski of MIT. Agronski attacked NASA for continuing to give too much attention to manned spaceflight. And he raised economic objections. He had studies to show that whereas aerospace R&D attracted thirty-five per cent of the national effort into R&D, it accounted for only *four* per cent of the total value added by US manufacturers to their raw materials.

But Michaels was ready with other evidence which argued that two-thirds of all economic growth from the Crash of 1929 to Sputnik was traceable to new technology; and that the return on investment on NASA was, by 1980, around forty-three per cent.

Agronski, as Michaels expected, also attacked the new program as bad science. Michaels responded by saying that NASA was planning to deliver several astronaut-months on Mars, for a fraction of the cost of Apollo, which had delivered just a few man-weeks on the Moon . . .

Meanwhile, on another front, Michaels started negotiations with the Secretary of Defense, who suspected – rightly – that Michaels was trying to siphon off some of the billions Reagan had promised on military spending. So Michaels had to get the endorsement of the DoD for this new civilian space effort.

But it wasn't immediately obvious why such support should be forthcoming. Having seen the Soviets send up a whole series of low-orbit military Salyut flights, the DoD, and the USAF in particular, were fighting hard for a new program based on a restriction to low Earth orbit, for reconnaissance and other purposes, and maybe some accelerated experimentation with space-based weapons systems – such as anti-ICBM particle and projectile guns – that would fit in with Reagan's broader strategic thinking.

Michaels offered consolations to the military people. He showed how the Mars mission's technology – orbital refuelling techniques, for instance – could be adapted to military uses. And military personnel and experiments could fly on the Mars program test flights.

And there were larger considerations, to do with the health of the aerospace industry, which Michaels was able to point to. A new, big aerospace initiative would give the economy a massive – if inflationary – boost. And, for the benefit of the politicians, he played on a suspicion dating back to the 1950s that of all the services, the USAF was the most out of political control when it came to space. The service had campaigned from the beginning to be given its own space program, independently of whatever NASA got up to; and in recent years, it was felt, USAF insistence had damagingly distorted the goals of the Skylab project. Besides, a manned Mars mission *coupled* with the new military work could be attractive in PR terms: *the US is not afraid to defend itself, but it is still rich and strong enough to dream of other worlds . . .*

So a new, focused civilian space program – rich in new technology, but lying *outside* the reach of the DoD, in particular the USAF – could be presented as politically attractive.

And so the arguments went on, orchestrated by Michaels and Josephson, who gathered the forces of national policy around themselves to shape the program the way *they* wanted it; until, at last, it all spiraled into realms of economic theory and political infighting that left Joe Muldoon, a mere moonwalker, stranded on the ground.

Late in the process, Michaels and his staff, including Muldoon, were summoned to a meeting at the White House with DoD and Bureau of Budget delegations to discuss NASA's proposals. And then Reagan himself called a meeting of Cabinet members, and NASA, BoB, DoD and MIT officials.

Michaels was obviously exhausted, but Muldoon could see he did his best to bring his remaining energies to bear on the Cabinet

Room meeting. He knew he had almost won the argument, but this final hurdle still had to be crossed.

Reagan asked surprisingly sharp questions on wider aspects of the proposal. It seemed to Muldoon that he was seeking to pick out some element of it which he could deploy to his own advantage – just as had Kennedy two decades earlier. And Michaels was trying to work to Reagan's expectations; he implied that, just as with Kennedy, Reagan would find a big space initiative helpful with congressional power brokers, and he could use it to build up support for other plans . . .

But Reagan balked anew at the cost, and he and his staff began to scour through the program, picking away elements of it.

Muldoon was forced to watch, helpless, as in the rooms of the White House his careful test and development program was cut to the bone, all talk of Venus-orbit missions and Mars bases was dropped, and the three Mars flights were reduced – incredibly – to just a single shot.

And as the meeting developed, Muldoon became aware of another undercurrent. NASA had screwed up royally over the Apollo-N thing; well, here was Reagan offering to endorse a new, huge program. But there was going to be a price to pay. And the head of Bert Seger, and some internal reorganization at NASA, wasn't going to be enough.

Muldoon came to see, quite clearly, the act of repentance that would be expected, if NASA was to be cleansed.

Michaels compiled a final report for Reagan, setting the agenda for the new mission and laying out a program to obtain House and Senate approval.

When it was done, he refused to leave the document with aides. Instead, he walked the document himself into the Oval Office, and, shaking with fatigue, handed it to Reagan in person.

There was a note of resignation stapled to the cover.

Thursday, April 16, 1981
White House, Washington, DC

. . . Our great goal is to build on America's pioneer spirit, and to develop new frontiers. A sparkling economy spurs initiatives, sunrise industries, and makes older ones more competitive.

Nowhere is this more important than our next frontier, space.

Nowhere do we so effectively demonstrate our technological leadership and ability to make life better on Earth. The Space Age is barely a quarter of a century old. But we've already pushed civilization forward with our advances in science and technology. Opportunities and jobs will multiply as we cross new thresholds of knowledge and reach deeper into the unknown.

Our progress in space – taking giant steps for all mankind – is a tribute to American teamwork and excellence. Our finest minds in government, industry and academia have all pulled together. And we can be proud to say: we are first, we are the best, and we are so because we're free.

America has always been greatest when we dared to be great. We can reach for greatness again. We can follow our dreams to distant stars, living and working in space for peaceful, economic, and scientific gain.

My advisers are developing an overall National Space Policy which I will outline in full later in the year. This policy will establish basic goals for the US space program, which will include: to strengthen the security of the United States, maintain United States space leadership, expand United States private sector investment and involvement in civil space and space-related activities, and to promote international cooperative activities in the national interest. As we look to the future, we must begin to secure leadership in space through the end of the century and beyond. The way to do that is to set a fruitful new direction for the space program, one which will make the best use of our present capabilities, in chemical rocket technology and our ability to live and work for long periods in space. And the time to do it is now.

Tonight, against the background of the forthcoming Space Policy, I am directing NASA to proceed with the preparation of a manned mission to Mars, and to do it within five years. Such a mission will permit quantum leaps in our research in science and communications, and our understanding of the nature of our universe.

Just as the oceans opened up a new world for clipper ships and Yankee traders, space holds enormous potential for commerce today . . .

Public Papers of the Presidents of the United States: Ronald Reagan, 1981 (Washington, DC: Government Printing Office, 1981), p. 362.

Thursday, April 16, 1981
NASA Headquarters, Washington

Michaels called Tim Josephson into his office. He had loosened his tie, and broke open a fresh bottle of his favored Kentucky bourbon. But there was little mood of celebration, as the two of them sat there sipping their drinks in the half-light; Michaels seemed more exhausted than Josephson had ever seen him.

Josephson raised his glass. 'Here's to you, Fred. You've done one hell of a job, these last few weeks.'

Michaels drank. 'Yeah. Yeah, so I have. Well, we got our announcement out of Reagan. And when I go, I'll take most of the blame for Apollo-N with me, away from NASA.'

'Fred –'

'That's my job now, Tim,' Michaels said, his voice harder. 'My last assignment. It's the way these things work. But the biggest job lies ahead, still. Delivering this thing.' He eyed Josephson. 'And that's going to be a job you'll have to handle yourself, Tim. I've already made my recommendation to the White House.'

Josephson had been expecting this, but still, panic spurted briefly in him. 'I'm – delighted by your faith in me, Fred. But, am I the right guy? Hell, I'm a back-room boy. A functionary; a natural follower.'

'Jesus Christ, don't you think I know that?' Michaels snapped. 'But I also know there's no better candidate available. You're just going to have to overcome your weaknesses, Tim. You'll get there if you work at it.'

Josephson hid a smile behind his glass. 'Thanks, Fred. I'm going to miss you.'

'And I want you to lean on Muldoon. Use him. The two of you should make a hell of a team.'

'I'll remember that.'

Michaels stared into his drink. 'You know, sometimes I think we've lost something on the way in all this. I mean, the people furthest from the decision-making have been the guys whose idea it was in the first place – the engineers of Langley and Goddard and Marshall – people who have given their whole lives to dreams of spaceflight. People like Gregory Dana. We take their studies and reports and use them as ammunition for our games of politics. But all that visionary stuff about exploration and destiny, all their efforts to stretch our hearts and minds – it's gotten lost somewhere.'

Josephson sipped his drink. 'But could it be any other way, Fred? It was the same with Apollo. Once spaceflight becomes the religion of the empire, it becomes immensely powerful; but it can't stir us to dream in the same old way. And all of us involved – NASA, the White House, the DoD – just figure out ways in which the space program can serve our own interests. It's the way things are.'

'Maybe. And I *know* those guys at Langley are going to hate this one-shot business. Who the hell knows when we'll be back again? I remember LBJ saying to me once that Americans are a lot better at breaking new ground than caring for the ground already broken. He was sure right. Anyway, the hell with it. We can forget all the political crap now, Tim, and start dreaming about Mars.' He studied Josephson again. 'Tell you what I've been thinking,' he said. 'Now that we've got this nice tight goal, our new Apollo, this one-shot trip to Mars, we're going to need a new name. Something to sum the whole thing up.'

'I guess you're right,' Josephson said. 'In fact, maybe we should have done that before issuing the press briefings.'

'Well, you're in the hot seat now,' Michaels said. 'What are you going to choose, Tim?'

Josephson pulled his lip. 'Humm. How did the name "Apollo" come about? That was before my time –'

Michaels said, 'It was picked out by Abe Silverstein in 1960. Now Abe was the head of the Office of Manned Spaceflight at the time – or rather, its predecessor. Silverstein kind of dabbled in the classical myths. He'd picked the name "Mercury" a year earlier, because he liked the idea of a messenger in the sky. And then von Braun's people called their new launch vehicle "Saturn," and so another classical god seemed a natural choice to Silverstein.'

'Maybe so,' Josephson said with half-smile, 'but that's rather muddled. Isn't it true that von Braun was actually naming his rockets after planets? There was the "Jupiter," and then the "Saturn" –'

'Give me a break,' Michaels said good-humoredly. 'Silverstein was a research engineer; what did he know? Anyhow Silverstein remembered from his schooldays the story of the god who rode the chariot of the sun drawn by four winged horses: *Apollo*, the son of Zeus. So Silverstein did a bit of checking to make sure Apollo hadn't done anything that would be too inappropriate for the American public, such as screwing his mother, and found he hadn't – and so Apollo it was.'

Josephson studied his drink and thought about it. 'Well, maybe

354

we ought to follow the same tradition. I know a little mythology too. Apollo had a half-brother. Another great Olympian god. He had his own mythology; it was only later that he was identified with the Romans' war-god . . . Only battle and bloodshed gave him any pleasure; his twin children Phobos and Deimos – *Panic* and *Fear* – accompanied him onto the battlefield . . .'

Michaels grunted. '*Panic* and *Fear*. Sounds like the kind of guy who'd prosper up on the Hill.'

Josephson smiled. No other name was possible.

And the press would love it.

Book 4

APPROACHES

'Sixty minutes to pericenter,' Stone said.

All three of the crew were in the Mission Module's Science Platform. At the heart of this little octagonal chamber, lined with its banks of switches and displays, they were strapped into harnesses and had their feet hooked into stirrups.

Above York's head there was a small science viewport. A brilliant, shifting white light beat down over her face, flooding the fluorescents.

She could see the upper half of a fat, pale, gibbous disk.

My God. That's Venus.

To her naked eye, the day side of the planet was glaring white – much brighter than Earth, from a similar distance – and it washed out the stars. Of the thin slice of night side she could see nothing at all.

The trajectory of Ares had taken it arcing inside the orbit of Venus. So now, Ares was barreling out of the sun toward Venus, tumbling along a hyperbola into Venus's gravity well. Ares was already moving toward the planet at more than five miles a second, and as York watched, that gibbous disk was narrowing, and the reflected sunlight cast shifting shadows across her lap.

There was a Hasselblad Velcroed to the work surface near her; she ripped this loose now, jammed her face up against the port and began taking pictures.

Venus was about the size of the Earth, but this was nothing like her experience of Earth orbit. There was no detail: the surface of Venus was permanently hidden, baked under its huge layers of carbon dioxide cloud. From this close, the cloud tops looked utterly smooth, featureless, as if the planet was a huge pearl: perfect, entire . . .

Although, now she looked more closely, she thought she *could* see a little structure in the clouds, right at the limb: a fine shell, surrounding the main cloud decks, outlined against the darkness of the sky.

She snapped the camera furiously.

'You got a problem, Natalie?' Stone asked dryly.

'I think I see the haze layer,' she said. A shell of sulphuric acid clouds, swathing Venus, outlined against the darkness of the sky.

'Yeah. And that picture's not on the schedule,' Stone said.

Christ. 'Okay, damn it.' She slammed the Hasselblad back on its surface. 'I just saw something no other human being had even seen

359

before, that's all. I thought it was worth investing in a snapshot.'

'If we don't get through this encounter on the right trajectory,' Stone murmured, his eyes on the flickering CRT displays before him, 'you won't be going home to get that roll of film developed. Let's concentrate, guys.'

Yeah, yeah. We're in operational mode here. Stick to the god-damn mission plan.

York returned her attention to her displays.

Gershon was grinning over his shoulder at her.

The plan was for Ares to skim around behind the dark side of the planet. The slingshot would twist the ship's trajectory through thirty degrees, and Ares would be hugely accelerated. As Ares had crawled, unpowered, around the sun, it had drawn only a little way ahead of Earth; so now, Ares was passing between Venus and Earth. The cluster would pass into the shadow of Venus, but it would never be out of Earth's line of sight.

The crew all had their assignments for the Venus encounter phase: Stone was monitoring the cluster's trajectory, Gershon was to follow the atmospheric-entry subprobe Ares had released, and York was operating the Mission Module's sensor pallet.

In one of the video monitors she had an image of the cloud tops in ultraviolet light. It showed a wealth of blue-gray detail invisible to the naked eye: cloud structures that swept around the planet, complex bows and cells that distorted and stretched out along the planet's lines of latitude. The whole thing, in its computer-generated false colors, looked almost Earth-like.

The sensor pallet on its rear-view-mirror extensor arm was a collection of fat, awkward-looking tubes and antennae and lenses, all wrapped in foil. There was a TV camera to study the clouds, an airglow experiment to look for ultraviolet echoes of carbon, oxygen and hydrogen, an infrared radiometer studying cloud temperatures, a magnetometer, charged particle telescopes. Four horn-shaped radar antennae would be able to penetrate the cloud layer and map the strip of Venus over which Ares passed. The sensors were already working, peering forward from the rear-view mirror, the pallet which angled out from the Mission Module's pressure hull.

'Hey,' Gershon said. 'Here goes the probe. I'm passing through the ionosphere. Two hundred fifty miles above the ground. Progressing toward the main cloud layers, at hyperbolic speed . . . How about that.'

York unhooked herself from her stirrups and drifted over to

Gershon. There was a TV monitor at the center of Gershon's station; right now, the screen showed nothing but a snowstorm of static.

The subprobe had been ejected twenty-three days ago, from a compartment at the base of the Mission Module, and had been pushed onto a slowly diverging orbit. Ares was missing Venus by a few thousand miles; the probe, pushed ahead of Ares, was supposed to impact the planet directly, a few minutes before the closest approach of the main craft. The probe would hit in the middle of the day side, in an upland region called Ishtar Terra.

Right now, the probe was contained within its aeroshell deceleration module, a deep, streamlined pie dish. Its TV cameras couldn't see out of the aeroshell, but there was a radio-transparent window at the top, so the probe could talk to Ares.

Gershon said, 'I'm in the atmosphere now, but still above the main cloud banks. Fifty miles up. The temperature's low here; under a hundred below, in fact. But this is the minimum; it should soon start to rise as I enter the main cloud banks. Here we come to breakout . . . Three, two, one. Mark. Watch the screen, Natalie.'

Right now, somewhere in those clouds, York knew, that fat pie dish was falling apart. A pilot chute would pull away the lid, and the main chute should open above the probe.

There was a break in the monitor's snowstorm, a yellow, flickering blur.

Gershon whooped. 'How about that. We can see out, at last.'

On the TV the pale, jaundiced wash brightened and darkened periodically: the probe was rotating, slowly, under its chute, and that cyclical brightening must be the sun, a glare behind the diffuse haze of sulphuric acid particles.

'Visibility's dropping. Down to maybe four miles,' Gershon said. 'I've got a pressure of three-quarters of Earth's sea-level pressure, and the temperature is around fifty degrees. Yum. Balmy. And I'm still all of thirty-eight miles high.'

Thirty-eight miles. Two hundred thousand feet. On Earth, that would be the top of the stratosphere: pressure less than a hundredth of sea level.

The haze on the TV screen thinned out. 'Whoa,' Gershon said. 'Look at that. All of a sudden I can see for miles and miles.'

York found herself looking down on a layer of cloud, thick and unbroken, a pale, washed-out yellow. The clouds were fluffy, Earthlike. Almost friendly. Up above there was a featureless yellow sky; she could know longer tell where the sun was.

The probe dropped into the thick clouds.

'Coming up on twenty-eight miles. I'm through all that sulphuric acid shit. But temperature outside is all of four hundred degrees already. And pressure's higher than an atmosphere already. Three, two, one. Mark. Chute sep.'

The picture seemed to shudder, then it stabilized again.

The pressure vessel – the heart of the probe – had hatched out of its aeroshell, and cut itself loose from its parachute. The probe was still more than twenty-five miles high, but it had already cut away its last chute. The air of Venus was so thick that from here the probe could free-fall all the way to the surface.

The pressure vessel was a sphere of thick metal. There were vanes on the sphere to make it spin, so that it was stabilized during its fall, and there were tough little windows cut into the surface so that the probe's instruments could see out.

'. . . Hey,' Gershon said. 'Look at these numbers from the mass spectrometer.' He tapped a screen. 'I got me some heavy isotopes of hydrogen in the air.'

'So what?'

He narrowed his eyes. '*Water*, my dear. Oceans, maybe: once upon a time, anyhow. Long since boiled off by the greenhouse effect, caused by all this fucking cee-oh-two. But where there were oceans . . .'

Life, perhaps.

The probe was spinning slowly in the sluggish air. The light was dark, reddish, but the illumination was no worse than a cloudy day on Earth. She couldn't see the sun at all; there was only an ill-defined glare, almost baleful, spread across half of the cloud bank that covered the sky.

And now, suddenly, she could see the surface: the probe's fish-eye camera returned panoramic views of a landscape, dimly visible through the murky air. York made out what looked like a cleft in the land, running from side to side of the picture – no, not a cleft, she realized; it was a ridge, hundreds of miles long, leading up to a plateau.

'Wind speed down to zip,' Gershon said. 'Pressure and temperature still rising. Venus doesn't have air; that stuff is more like my momma's chicken soup.' He tapped the screen. 'That's Ishtar Terra,' he said. 'Or the edge of it; right where we're drifting. We're slap on course. Look at it, Natalie. Seven miles above the mean surface, and –'

'– and as big as the United States. I know.' Ishtar Terra was a

362

high, exposed plateau, already mapped by radar from Earth: Ishtar was how a continent might look if someone drained away Earth's oceans.

York felt excitement mount. At last, a chance to do some geology on this mission.

Venus and Earth were twins. So presumably Venus had a hot, radioactive core, just like Earth's, whose heat must escape to space. On Earth, that happened in two ways: plate tectonics and vulcanism. But, in the radar mapping and the crude Russian probes' results, nobody had observed any sign of plate tectonics on Venus: no rings of vulcanism, no rift valleys.

So York, along with every other geologist, believed that the dominant geological process for losing core heat had to be vulcanism: ongoing and continuing. There just had to be a whole bunch of live volcanic hot-spots, all round the planet, feeding the heat to the atmosphere, and thence to the ultimate heat-sink of space. Therefore, at Ishtar, she expected to see a young surface, heavily distorted by the upwelling of magma – liquid rock under the solid crust – and resurfaced by repeated lava flows. If there were any impact craters, they would be heavily distorted, maybe even buried, invisible under the fresh surface.

She pointed off to the right of the screen, to shadowy cones that loomed out of the murk. 'Look at that. That must be the Maxwell Montes.' The tallest mountain range on Venus. The probe was drifting toward the Montes, she saw, floating like a fat metal balloon in some sluggish current. The Montes were steeper, in places, than anything on Earth. The mountains were folds in the surface, illuminated by the diffuse, ruddy light and wreathed by thick air; it was like swimming over some undersea ridge.

Something showed up on the edge of the screen: a circular feature, on the flank of the mountain range.

'Hey. What's that?' The probe's slow rotation took the feature out of shot, almost immediately. 'Hot damn.'

Gershon grinned up at her. 'Sorry,' he said. 'No panning or zooming. This isn't *Wide World of Sports*.'

A circle? Could it be a crater? What the hell was that doing there?

Something was wrong; York could smell it. She waited, excited, impatient, as the camera panned around, agonizingly slowly, the image wobbling as the probe hit turbulence pockets in the soupy air.

The circular feature came back again, drifting in from the right.

363

York shoved her face right up to the screen. Almost a perfect circle, surrounded by a dark blanket of material: it had to be an impact crater, surrounded by a layer of ejecta. Like a bullet-hole centered in dried blood. And it was so large it was almost certainly several hundred million years old.

And it was pristine: no coverage by lava flows, no distortion by shifts in the landscape.

Which meant that Ishtar Terra had to have been geologically dead, too, for at least as long.

That's impossible. Her mind raced. *If that's characteristic of the whole surface, everything is turned on its head.* No plate tectonics, and no vulcanism either?

The enigmatic crater passed out of view as the probe descended.

'Ten minutes from pericenter,' Stone said. The mission commander was watching his instruments, York saw, not the images from the probe, the first pictures of the surface of Venus.

The probe was heading for a rough plain, broken up with large, jagged rocks. She saw some evidence of winds: dust streaks, scouring, a couple of flattened dunes. *The air isn't always so sluggish, then.*

'Coming on in,' Gershon said. 'Approach speed twenty-one feet per. Thirty seconds.'

Around fifteen miles per hour. Like a slow car crash: hard, but survivable.

'Nine. Eight . . .'

The ground rocked upwards, spinning toward the camera; York, trying to pick out features, felt oddly dizzy.

'Two. One.'

The picture fuzzed over briefly, then cleared.

She saw a steady image, a rocky plain, no longer rotating. The plain tipped a little, as the probe settled on its side.

Gershon whooped. 'Touchdown!' He pumped his arms, football-style. 'Welcome to a pleasant spring day on Venus. Air pressure is a soothing ninety-one atmospheres. Temperatures today will peak at a frisky eight hundred and eighty degrees Fahrenheit . . .'

Hot enough to melt lead.

York bent to stare into the screen. The image was distorted into a kind of bow by the fish-eye lens. She couldn't see the horizon; the visibility couldn't have been more than a few hundred yards. The sun was invisible, but the sky was bright. Like a smoggy day in LA.

Live, from the surface of Venus. York felt a surge of affection for the tough little superprobe.

The land was flattened, shattered into plates, littered with scattered rocks. The plates were reddish-brown, and looked vaguely shiny. The light was strong enough for some of the rocks to cast a sharp shadow. The surface looked like clay that had been baked, carelessly, in an oven that was set too high: cracked, fractured.

Could be basaltic. Volcanic. Probably highly alkaline. And those plates look almost sedimentary. But there's no water here! Laid down by deposition from the air, then? No. Maybe a volcanic origin is more likely. And where the hell did that surface rubble come from? What erosion mechanisms are available? The wind, the acidic atmosphere?

Without plate tectonics *or* vulcanism, how the hell did the interior heat escape?

Maybe it doesn't escape, she speculated wildly. *Maybe the heat gets trapped, under a stable surface, rather than leaking out steadily, like on Earth . . . building up until it reaches a point where the lithosphere can't contain it.*

She thought it through. Periodically the surface would *melt,* suddenly, dramatically, all over the planet, as all that trapped heat escaped. The whole damn planet would resurface itself at once. *Catastrophic vulcanism,* maybe once every half-billion years: hundreds of millions of years' worth of geology, crammed into a few millennia.

She felt breathless. The scenario seemed outrageous. *A hell of a hypothesis to spin out of one goddamn impact crater, Natalie.*

But what other explanation could there be, for that pristine wound on the Maxwell Montes?

She wondered if she should publish this. Maybe even radio home a paper, before they got to Mars.

Without corroborative proof, though? Peer reviews, to which she'd have to submit any formal write-up of the notion, weren't often kind. *I'd be laughed out of court. The dippy Space Lady from California . . .*

The distribution of impact craters would be significant, she thought quickly. Corroborative, in fact. On Mars and the Moon there was a clustering of craters, in certain regions. On Mars, you had one young hemisphere, smooth and unblemished, the other heavily cratered, ancient. The same on the Moon, with its separation into the younger seas and the ancient highlands.

365

Here – if I'm right – it would be different. The craters must be uniformly distributed, right across the planet's surface.

All we'd need is a reasonably detailed global map of the surface, and to do a simple crater count. Then we'd know.

But that map wasn't available, and it wasn't going to be. Not in her lifetime.

The radar mapping from this flyby would be the most detailed ever performed, but would be confined to a strip, wrapped around one side of the planet. Any crater counts based on that were going to be tentative, at best.

She slammed her fist into a working surface. Stone glanced at her, surprised; she kept her eyes averted from his face.

Damn. We shouldn't be here! A fifty-million-buck radar mapper in polar orbit would settle this. And they spent more than that on the backup john for this tin can of ours.

For fifteen years, most of NASA's budget had been sucked into manned spaceflight. Unmanned projects had been subordinated to the needs of the Mars mission or cut altogether. They had lost a gravity-assist flight to Venus and Mercury, asteroid and comet encounters, Grand Tour probes to the outer planets. The Large Space Telescope, a big Earth-orbital eye, had also been axed.

Sure, humans were on the way to Mars. But humanity knew nothing of the rest of the Solar System it hadn't known in 1957: the moons of Jupiter and Saturn remained points of light in the sky, the disks and rings of the giant worlds a telescopic blur.

And I'm cooperating with it, she thought sourly. *After all my great moral pronouncements, I've finished up as guilty as the rest. Maybe, because I know better, more so.*

The screen filled up with static.

The probe had imploded, crushed by the pressure.

York checked the time. It was just fifty-five seconds after landing.

Gershon pushed himself away from his console. 'Well, there you have it. Venus is, officially, a shit-hole.'

And now, suddenly, the cabin grew perceptibly darker. She glanced up. As Ares sailed into the shadow of Venus, the last crescent sliver thinned out into a hoop of light – it was suddenly multicolored *(I hope the cameras are getting this)* – and then it faded and died away.

Now there was a hole in space, above Ares: it was the blackness of the cloud decks of Venus, empty, scorching, lifeless.

York returned to her station. 'The TV mosaics have started,' she reported. 'And the planetary strip photography. Everything's nominal on the pallet.'

'Pericenter,' Stone said abruptly. 'How about that. Mission elapsed time one seventy-one days, fourteen hours, twenty-four minutes.' He checked his displays. 'It's September eighth, 1985, and here we are at Venus, guys. Distance to the surface three thousand, one hundred, fifty-five miles and change. We've come a hundred and seven million miles from Earth, and we're within fifty miles of the nominal trajectory. Damn fine shooting.'

York looked up, through the little science viewport above her. Her eyes seemed to have grown dark-adapted, and she thought she could see something of the cloud tops, presumably illuminated by starlight. The cloud-world looked like a huge, milky, pregnant belly, protruding toward her.

There was a flash, somewhere beneath the clouds, like a light bulb exploding under cotton wool.

She pushed up to the viewport and stared out. 'Jesus Christ.'

'What?' Stone asked.

I recognize that, from Earth orbit. 'I just saw lightning, under the clouds.'

Gershon looked at her. 'That's ridiculous. You get thunder and lightning on Earth from large particles, like ice crystals, being shipped around by updraughts. Venus has got a layer of stew for air. There's no evidence for updraughts or large particles. So how the hell can there be lightning?'

It happened again: a flash, roughly elliptical, that must have covered tens of square miles. For an instant she could see detailed structure in the gray clouds, layers and banks streaked out in the direction of rotation, illuminated from below.

'Don't argue about it now,' Stone said calmly. 'If it's there, the TV cameras will pick it up. Hell, Ralph, your fat little probe might even have goddamn *heard* it.'

Gershon was right, of course, York thought. There was no direct evidence on Venus of any of the mechanisms which generated thunder and lightning storms on Earth. *Then what? Vulcanism?*

She returned to her station, troubled. *A goddamn glimpse like this isn't enough. It's a whole planet out there. You need a year in orbit, a wider range of sensors, a hundred probes. With this swingby, we're going to come away with more questions than answers.*

'Makes you think,' Gershon said. 'We got a delta-vee of over thirteen thousand feet per second out of that. For free. That's more

367

than our two tanks of propellant gave us when we left Earth orbit! And now we're traveling at more than twenty-five miles per second, our greatest velocity . . .'

'How about that,' Stone said. 'Natalie, as of now you're riding the fastest man-made object in history. Quite a ride, for someone who didn't want to be a pilot anyhow.'

York wasn't listening.

We're only here to steal from you, she thought. Ares had no intrinsic interest in Venus itself. *We only want your energy.*

Light flooded the science station. She glanced up. A new crescent was forming, as Ares swept toward the day side of the planet.

She couldn't get that astonishing image out of her head: the single, pristine crater, punched in the top of a mountain range.

Wednesday, June 3, 1981
Headquarters, Columbia Aviation, Newport Beach

JK Lee thought the new Mars Excursion Module RFP was the roughest piece of crap he'd seen in many a long day.

An RFP, a Request For Proposals, was part of the standard procedure the federal government followed to award large contracts. This particular RFP had gone out to fourteen companies, including McDonnell, Boeing, Rockwell, Lockheed and Martin. Response was requested in ten weeks. NASA would then evaluate the proposals, using a scoring system based on a prearranged formula, to weight the technical approach, the personnel to be used by the bidder, the bidder's corporate expertise in areas relevant to the bid, and so on. For a large contract an RFP was a major piece of work in its own right.

The document JK Lee held in his hand – short, badly photocopied, some of it even completed by hand – was horse shit.

He called Jack Morgan into his office.

Lee threw the MEM RFP at Morgan. 'Look at this thing.'

Jack Morgan was compact, grizzled, with broad, strong hands. He sat down on the other side of Lee's big metal desk.

After skimming the RFP, Morgan dumped the paper back on Lee's desk.

Lee asked, 'So what do you think?'

'I wouldn't wipe my ass with it. I've never seen such a hasty, amateurish piece of work.'

'I know.' Morgan was right, of course. The weight limits on

the new MEM were fantastically tight, and the cost ceilings and timescales, to make a 1985 launch, were forbidding. The RFP had obviously been issued in a hell of a panic, as NASA, in the midst of its recovery from the Apollo-N thing, scrambled to put together a viable program for getting back on course to Mars.

Lee said, 'I agree. This RFP is a piece of shit. I'm surprised they put it out. But still . . .'

'But still, what? JK – you're not thinking of bidding.'

Lee sat back and put his feet up on his desk. 'Why not?'

'Because we wouldn't win. Because it would be a waste of money. I don't even know why we were sent this thing.'

Lee thought he knew.

He happened to know that Ralph Gershon was on NASA's evaluation panel for this bid. Since they'd met at that lousy Technical Liaison Group meeting over in Rockwell's Brickyard, and gone for that drive in the Mojave, and Lee had bullshitted a rookie astronaut about a MEM shaped like Apollo – making it up as he went along, really – he and Gershon had stayed in touch.

He had Gershon to thank for this RFP invitation, he figured.

'Anyhow,' Morgan said, 'Rockwell are going to get the MEM; everyone knows that.'

'Yeah, but suppose.'

'What?'

'I don't know. Just suppose.'

'One small detail,' said Morgan. 'We couldn't build the thing, even if we won.'

'Why not?'

'Because our specialty is airframes and avionics. That's what makes us a good subcontractor. If you're bidding for a complete *spacecraft*, for Christ's sake, you're looking at *everything*: the tanks, the engines, the navigation and flight and guidance stuff, the heat-shields, the life support –'

Lee had been waiting for that. 'We're okay on life support. We've got you.'

'Bullshit, JK,' Morgan said. 'If you think I'm going to hang my hide out for you in front of Art Cane over a goddamn hare-brained stunt like this, you've got another think coming.' He stood, picked up the RFP, and threw it at Lee's waste basket. 'If you've got any sense, you'll leave it there.'

'Yeah. I will. Thanks, Jack.'

When Morgan had gone, Lee settled back in his big swivel chair, propped up his heels more comfortably on his desk, and lit up a cigarette. The big gun-metal desk was a JK trademark; it was a gift from the crew he'd worked with on the old B-70 project, and it had followed him ever since.

He thought about Jack Morgan.

Morgan had been an Air Force flight physician during the Korean War, and he'd got into aerospace medicine by accident. After the war, working for Rockwell – North American as it was then – he'd been on hand when a pilot had been forced to bail out of an experimental F-100, a supersonic jet. The air at that speed was like a wall. Morgan had been on the team of surgeons who had helped to pull the pilot through. It was only the third time in history a pilot had left an airplane traveling faster than sound. So Morgan became, de facto, a leader in the new field of aerospace medicine.

Since then Morgan had become one of Lee's most trusted confidants – translate that as *drinking partner* – and he'd come along for the ride when Lee had busted out of Rockwell, back in 1967, disillusioned by the firing of Stormy Storms.

Lee valued Morgan's advice. That didn't mean he often took it, though.

After a quarter of an hour he leaned forward and pressed his intercom. 'Bella, I want you to set me up some meetings.'

'Yes, sir, JK.'

He got out of his chair and dug the RFP out of the trash.

Three days later JK Lee bustled into the office of his boss, Arthur Cane, with four of his top people. Including Jack Morgan. They had armfuls of charts and graphs, all making up a hastily assembled presentation called: 'Why We Should Bid For The MEM.'

Cane sat behind his big walnut desk, with his heavy English stone-cased fountain pen resting on top of the pile of paperwork before him.

Arthur Cane was now over seventy, and a huge Bakelite hearing aid clung to one fleshy ear, and he didn't have a hair on his head. But, after all these years, Lee could still see the look that came into the old man's eye when he walked around the company lot, past the big, gleaming walls of the wind tunnel. *Look at this. My very own wind tunnel.*

Cane was an old-timer who'd worked in the Hughes Corporation before the war, and had then spent a number of years with the boffins at Langley. Cane loved working on advanced aircraft concepts – the push of knowledge into new areas, the thrill of making materials and systems perform beyond the limits of what seemed possible – but he'd got frustrated at Langley, with its budget compromises and in-house politics.

So, when Langley was subsumed into NASA, Cane had got out, and formed his own company – Columbia Avionics – so that he could fund his own research and follow his nose, and sell the results back to NASA and the big players.

Which he'd done with success. But Cane had fiercely resisted growing Columbia too fast or too big, and he'd also defended his company astutely from the takeover bids that came along regularly from the big boys.

Well, today Lee was going to ask Cane for a couple of million bucks of company money, to bid for a contract so big it was bound to transform Columbia out of all recognition. *So I damn well need to understand how Art ticks.*

Lee opened the pitch. He kept his introduction flat, neutral and brief. Time enough for tub-thumping later.

First up after Lee was Julie Lye, a smart young MIT graduate. Lee had pulled her out of her regular research to give the proposal some academic weight. Lye gave a brief, concise talk on what was known, from the various spaceprobes, of Mars: the structure of the atmosphere, the properties of the surface. It was an introduction to the problems anyone would face in landing humans safely on Mars, keeping them alive, and bringing them home. Lye was trim, precise, reassuring.

Cane watched her with his face blank and his fingers steepled before him.

Next came Chaushui Xu, another smart kid, a Chinese American who was taking a doctorate in aerodynamics based on his work at Columbia. Xu's presentation was about the options for getting through the Martian atmosphere, and how Columbia's expertise could be leveraged to solve the problems.

Cane's eyes narrowed to slits, as if he was falling asleep.

Xu started to get nervous, and he fumbled a little. But Lee wasn't perturbed; he knew that Cane valued brains above everything else, and these were some of the brightest kids in the company. Cane was listening.

Xu got to the end of his presentation. He sat down, fumbling again.

Now Bob Rowen took the floor. A good bit older than the others, Rowen had worked with Lee on the old B-70 project, and with Lee and Storms on the later X-15 development. Rowen outlined how Columbia could handle the challenges of the spacecraft's avionics.

371

Soon, it was pretty clear that a Columbia MEM would be the smartest spacecraft that ever flew.

Half-way through Rowen's pitch, Cane very visibly turned off his hearing aid and started going through his paperwork.

Jack Morgan leaned over to Lee. 'Christ,' he whispered. 'What the hell do we do now?'

Lee grinned. 'We keep briefing. He's hooked, believe me. If he didn't like us we'd be out of here by now.'

The last pitch was Jack Morgan's, and he described how a Columbia MEM would keep four humans alive on Mars for a month. Clearly irritated by Cane's manner, Morgan rattled through his spiel as quickly as he could, and sat down with a clatter of showcards.

Lee got to his feet again. He summed up everything that had been said, and made a little speech about the future, and then just waited.

He was aware of his team getting restless behind him, but Lee had been here many times before. He stood before Cane's desk, unperturbed.

After a full two minutes, Cane put down his stone pen and leaned back in his chair. He turned his hearing aid back on. 'JK, you're a crazy man. I don't know why I keep you on the payroll.'

Lee leaned forward and rested his clenched knuckles on the table surface. 'Goddamn it, Art, we're in the aerospace business. And this is the finest opportunity to achieve something new in our field since Apollo.'

Cane rubbed his eyes. 'We're an experimental shop. One of life's subcontractors. Not a big player.'

'But it doesn't have to stay that way,' Lee insisted. 'And maybe it shouldn't.'

'And we wouldn't win anyway.' Cane picked up a piece of paper from the seemingly random pile on the desk top before him. 'Look at this, now. Look who we're up against. McDonnell, Martin, Convair, General Electric, Boeing. Not to mention Rockwell, who are going to win anyhow. Some of these guys have been involved in the MEM base-technology studies since '72. They've got a jump on us of years, damn it. *Years*. Look at this. Martin have spent three million bucks of their own money, and they've already got a detailed analysis that runs to *four thousand pages*. And we're starting from scratch.'

Lee waved his hand. 'Look, we can't get into a blueprint duel with these guys. But remember how Bell fumbled on its bid for the

X-15. Bell built the X-1 – the ship that Chuck Yaeger took through the sound barrier –'

'I know my aviation history, JK.'

'Sorry. Anyway, Bell *should* have won the X-15 contract. But what they proposed was an exotic spaceplane that was years ahead of its time. Rockwell won by giving NASA what it wanted, straight down the line, a simple brute force machine. And later, when the bidding for Apollo was going on, there were companies like Martin and Douglas who spent millions on all kinds of Buck Rogers stuff, lenticular shapes and lifting bodies and you name it. Rockwell won out by giving NASA precisely what it wanted and needed, which was a three-man Mercury capsule.'

'Yes, but, JK,' Cane said dryly, 'we're bidding *against* Rockwell this time. And you're saying you know better than Rockwell, and Martin with their team of three hundred engineers, and –'

'Yeah. Yeah, I do. Because those guys are going to be too busy defending the pet projects they've built up over the years to be able to see what the goddamn customer *wants,* Art.'

Cane thought about that. 'You're a smart guy, JK. Only you could turn the fact that we don't know what the hell we're doing into a strength. What's more, I have the feeling that you actually believe it when you say it.'

'Sure I do. Look, we have a real opportunity here; we could achieve something unique. *Columbia could go to Mars.* Now: are you going to back me or not?'

Art Cane studied him through small, sharp, watery eyes.

'I guess I got to allow you to bid. But if you spend more than two million bucks, I swear I'll have your ass in a sling. Now get out of my office.'

June, 1981
US Navy Acceleration Laboratory, Johnson, Pennsylvania; Lyndon B. Johnson Space Center, Houston

With a heavy whir, the Wheel started to rotate. It felt as if her chest was being pressed back to meet her backbone.

York, strapped into her couch, tried to comfort herself with the thought that according to pilots who'd actually made it into space, this fake experience was a lot worse than the real thing.

It was cold comfort.

She reached five Gs; she had to make a conscious effort to open up her ribs to suck in air. The cage rattled her back and forth, and from side to side – she felt like a pea in a cup, being whirled around on a rope – *a real flight's a lot smoother, Natalie . . .*

She had a checklist she was supposed to work through, and she conscientiously pressed her dummy switches with gloved fingers.

A gray curtain started closing in on her vision, as if sweeping in around her head. It was the first symptom of blacking out. There was an array of colored lights on a panel in front of her so she could tell how far gone she was. When she relaxed, the gray curtain was prominent; when she tensed herself up the curtain would disappear. She tried to ignore the pain in her chest; but every time she raised her arms or moved her head she felt giddy. That was the Coriolis force – the sideways force associated with fast rotation.

York was in the middle of a series of simulated reentries from Earth orbit. This particular exercise, the worst of the set, was modeling a high, steep trajectory, as if her Command Module were cutting into the layers of Earth's atmosphere too rapidly, and so undergoing terrific deceleration.

When she reached eight Gs, she found she couldn't raise her arms any more. She could only lie in the cage, and endure it.

Now the gray curtain around her eyes was thickening, and it wouldn't go away.

Of course it's worse than a real mission. The damn doctors design it that way.

Her vision started to blur. She found it hard to read her instruments. Twelve Gs; far higher than anticipated during a real mission. Enough to flatten her eyeballs. Her head was being battered against the inside of her pressure suit helmet. The lights of the lab beyond the cage whirled past the mockup cabin's small windows.

Fifteen Gs. Now she couldn't breathe at all. She became sure she was going to black out. *But I'm only half-way through the run.* And the doctors were watching her, every twitch of her flattened face, on closed-circuit television.

At last the load began to drop away; the pressure eased from her chest, and she sucked in great gulps of air.

Of course, nobody would complain about being subjected to high-tech torture in instruments like the Wheel, or query the relevance of all these exercises to actual spaceflight, or – still worse – admit that he or she had any problems with the routines. *Because if you complain, it's bound to get back to Muldoon, and a note will go into whatever damn system he uses to select his crews, and you'll*

374

never get off the ground. And that was the name of the game at the moment. Joe Muldoon, in his new role as head of the Mars program, had also assumed unto himself the old, separate function of director of Flight Crew Operations.

It was Muldoon who assigned crews to missions. And everyone knew that Muldoon was in the middle of drawing up his crew rota for the first flights in the new program, leading up to the Mars mission itself; the only thing that mattered in life right now – the *only* thing – was getting a berth in that rota.

So York was going to have to put on a front when she came out of the cage.

How'd it go? You didn't black out, did you?

Me? Come on. I felt like I was riding a little heavy on a T-38 afterburner, that's all . . .

Sure.

When the doctors helped her to limp out of the cage, she found her back covered with ruptured capillaries, where the blood had been forced through her flesh, and she had a headache like the worst hangover in the world.

Piece of cake. Problems? Me? Come on.

While she was soaking in a tub, recovering, she got Muldoon's message.

She – along with the rest of the astronaut pool – had to return to Houston by the next flight, for a meeting with Muldoon.

It was an unusual request, even unprecedented. But she knew what it had to signify.

She got out of her tub and began toweling herself off. She could feel her heart thumping a little faster, and it had nothing to do with acceleration.

Ares. It's beginning.

By the time York arrived, the small conference room on the third floor of Building 4 was crowded. Joe Muldoon sat isolated at a small desk on a stage at the front of the room; he was riffling through Vu-graph foils.

York pushed through a forest of sports-shirted male astronauts and found a seat near the back of the room. A man who had flown around the Moon sat down next to her.

Muldoon must know, York thought, that he had every person in the room by the metaphorical balls.

One of the many things she speculated about regarding the

mysterious crew selection process was whether men like Muldoon actually *enjoyed* wielding their power. Looking at Muldoon now, his foot tapping nervously on the stage, his shoulders knots of tensed-up muscles, she somehow doubted it.

Which, as far as she was concerned, was all to his credit.

All around her there was a babble of conversation, lively, deep-throated, maybe a little nervous. There was a kind of competitive cheerfulness in the air. Like none of this really mattered. *Oh, it's only the crew rota for the most significant new program of flights in years. Hey, you catch the ball game Monday?*

Now Muldoon got to his feet, and stood with his hands on his hips, facing the astronaut corps. Blue-eyed, his sharp crew cut graying blond, he looked like a caricature of a drill sergeant, York thought.

The remnants of conversation died off immediately, leaving Muldoon facing rows of silent faces.

Muldoon spoke without a mike, without preamble, and his words carried to every person in the room. He said: 'The guys who are going to be the first to fly to Mars are right here, in this room.'

'You've heard by now we've got a first cut of Ares mission profiles.'

He snapped on the Vu-graph projector, and an image was thrown up on a screen behind him; it was a simple list, typed and copied onto the foil. 'We've got eight flights here, both manned and unmanned. We've defined six preliminary classes of mission, designated here A to F. They are mostly Earth orbit tests of the system components. But they lead up to the final flight – mission class F – which will be the full Mars landing attempt.

'You can see from the foil that the two A-class missions will be unmanned shakedown tests of the new Saturn VB booster system, carrying boilerplate Apollos and MEMs. The B mission will be the first manned flight to Earth orbit – or maybe lunar orbit – to man-rate the Saturn VB. A live Apollo, obviously, but a boilerplate MEM again. The C mission is another unmanned shakedown, this time of a MEM test article in near-operational condition. The D mission will be the first manned MEM flight, to Earth orbit; this will be a long-duration mission to test for space soak.

'The two E-class missions will be further manned MEM tests; we're intending to trial the new descent systems with lunar and/or Earth landings. Also in this period we expect to confirm orbital assembly procedures. Finally, the F mission will be the Mars flight itself, and it's got to be ready to depart on March 21, 1985. Otherwise we wait two more years for the next opposition. The precise sequencing of the other missions, and their dates, is to be determined; we're intending to take advantage of success . . .'

York was hardly listening. Nor was anyone else, she suspected. *You've got just five manned flights up there.*

Just five flights.

Muldoon whipped away the foil; it showed for a moment as a gray curl in the light of the Vu-graph lamp. Then, without ceremony, he put up the next slide.

It was a list of names.

Muldoon said, 'It's not appropriate, at this stage, to assign crews all the way through to the F mission. I'm sure all of you understand that. You have here, instead, the assignments for classes B, D and the first E mission – that's the first three manned flights – plus backups . . .'

Like everyone else York was craning forward, squinting to make out the poorly-typed, badly-projected list, her lips working as she read the names.

It was a mix of three- and four-man flights. Phil Stone's crew – including Adam Bleeker and a senior astronaut called Ted Curval – would take up the B mission, she saw, the first, risky, shakedown of the enhanced booster, the Saturn VB. An all-USAF crew. York could see the logic behind sending up test pilots for what was basically a flight test, but it set a tone for the whole program, right from the start: the wrong tone, a military, test pilot tone. *More dumb fighter jock bullshit, just like it's always been.*

But then the D mission, the long space soak flight, would have a crew of four, including two mission specialists: *Ralph Gershon,* she read. And –

Natalie York.

She tried to read on. Phil Stone's B-mission crew made up the backup crew . . .

Natalie York.

She read her name over and over, unable to be sure if she was seeing it correctly, as if her eyeballs were still compressed by some invisible centrifuge. *Jesus. That really is me, up there, in a prime crew. I'm going into orbit.*

I'll be the first American woman in space.

She was one of just three female astronauts in the corps, and the only one who'd been named on Muldoon's chart.

All around the room there was an explosion of tension; there were whoops, a lot of handshakes, good-old-boy back-pats. York was even the recipient of a few of those herself.

There were a lot of forced grins around her. She knew what lay behind the grins; she'd be thinking the same. *I've got to smile, make like I'm really pleased for you. But it should have been me, you bastard, not you. Maybe it will be, if, pray God, you break your leg or otherwise fuck up somewhere down the line.*

Now Muldoon held up his hands for silence. 'I told you that beyond the first E mission I don't think it's appropriate yet to allocate crews. But I expect the selection to be made by the normal rotation system. Thanks for your attention; if you've no questions right now, you can come see me in my office . . .'

He'd said, *The normal rotation system.*

That hit York like an electric shock, burning away her brief euphoria.

She knew what that meant, and so did everybody else. She stared at the chart again, doing fast calculations. *It means I will make it to Earth orbit. But that's as far as I'll get. Phil Stone is going to Mars. I'm not.*

Nobody was going to get any more work out of the Astronaut Office that day; York guessed Joe Muldoon had planned the announcement around that.

She drove out to the Singing Wheel. The car park was packed with Corvettes, and inside she found Phil Stone, Adam Bleeker and a few of their ex-military cronies, already working methodically through pitchers of Bud. Stone pulled up a stool beside him, and gave her a dew-coated glass of beer.

'Congratulations,' he said warmly. 'So you're finally making it into space. America's first space woman. Here's to yah, Natalie. Come on, fellas –' He led a couple of toasts, in cold beer, which she endured. 'So,' he said. 'How are you feeling?'

'Mixed,' she said bluntly. 'I'm flying, at last –'

'Hey, you done well. What is it, three years since you joined the Agency? Hell, we got guys who've waited three, four times as long as that to get a seat. I'm looking forward to working with you on the D mission. I mean that, Natalie.'

'Yeah.' She tried to smile.

Stone was watching her carefully. 'Yeah, *but* –' he prompted.

'But, Phil, what I'm really thinking is that you're the asshole who's going to Mars, and I'm not.'

He laughed, mildly, and took another pull of his beer. 'Come on, Natalie. Nobody knows who's going to Mars. Not at this stage.

378

If the preliminary flights don't work out, maybe nobody will be going.'

'Give me a break. You heard what Muldoon said. "The normal rotation system."'

The 'rotation system' dated back to the earliest Mercury days, and it had been applied all the way through Apollo. Crews were assigned to missions in a leapfrog fashion. The rule was 'back one, skip two, fly one,' and then start over. Thus, Phil Stone and his crew were backups for the D mission, York's space soak flight. If the rotation worked out, they would skip two missions – the E missions – and fly the next, the F mission.

Which just happened to be the full Mars landing attempt.

Stone spread his hands on the table. 'Rotation's not a bad system, Natalie. At least it's orderly. I mean, Muldoon has got a pig of a job. Everyone wants to be on every crew –'

'Oh, bullshit, Phil. The rotation stuff isn't a goddamn machine. It's not hard to work it out so you get the crew patterns you want.'

'Look, Natalie, anything but a rotation system is an insult to the astronauts and destructive to morale. That's what I think, and I reckon it's what old Joe thinks too. Every crew should be able to fly every flight. It's like handling a squadron of fighter pilots. You've got a mission to do and so many flights to fly and so many pilots to fly them . . .'

'But this isn't a goddamn fighter squadron. We ought to be hand-picking crews for the needs of the mission.'

'And you think you should be handpicked for the F mission?'

She sipped her beer, her irritation increasing. 'It's foolish not to pick the very best for your key missions.'

He eyed her, amused. 'So now you're saying I'm not the best?'

'That is not the point, damn it, Phil, and stop patronizing me . . .'

But now Adam Bleeker came in – one of Phil's crew, another probable Mars-walker – and there was another round of general back-slapping and joshing.

For a while York joined in the wider conversation.

Her thoughts drifted back, ignobly, to her selection gripes.

She drank a little more beer; it was warming up, and tasted sour. She put the glass down and wiped her damp palm on a napkin.

She got out of the bar. She suspected half the guys were so far gone already they didn't even notice her leaving.

She was going to have to get this out of her system.

* * *

379

Without stopping to think about how smart it was, she drove straight back to JSC and stormed into Muldoon's office.

Muldoon was working through a pile of paper. 'Natalie. You want a coffee? I can send Mabel to –'

'No.' She realized, suddenly, she was trembling; it seemed to be coming from somewhere deep down inside her. *From three years of frustration inside NASA. From Ben's wasteful, needless death. From the fact that I'm thirty-three years old, and I've thrown away my academic career just so I can get to spend months in low Earth orbit, watching MEM components slowly degrade.*

Or, she thought, *maybe they're all correct. Maybe I'm just a goddamn hysterical woman after all.*

Muldoon was watching her sharply. 'I thought you'd be pleased at getting a seat in one of the prime crews.'

'I am.'

He sat back and sighed. 'But you want to go to Mars. And you can figure out the implications of the crew rotations as well as anyone else.'

'Damn it, Joe, I'm far and away the best mission specialist for Mars surface operations. You know that; I should be in line for the F mission, so I can get out there and *do* what I'm having to teach everyone else!'

He steepled his fingers. 'All I can tell you is, we're going to follow the rotation system. If it works out that Phil Stone takes his crew to Mars, then so be it; and if things get messed up or delayed for some reason, and your crew gets back in line – *through the normal rotation system* – then you'll have your chance. And maybe, if there's a second or third landing –'

'You know damn well there will be no second landing. We're putting everything we've got into this one shot. Square with me, Joe. I should be on the damn flight. And if I was a man, another Harrison Schmitt, I'd be inked in already as a no-brain choice. But I'm a woman, and that's why I'm not going.'

'Natalie, it's not like that.'

'Come on, Joe. Don't bullshit me, for once.'

He folded his fingers together. 'No bullshit?'

'No bullshit.'

'I'm not going to pretend that the gender thing doesn't cause us problems, Natalie.'

The gender thing. 'What problems, for Christ's sake? That I won't be able to fit my flight helmet over my bouffant hairstyle? Joe, it's 1981 –'

'Give me a break, Natalie. Look, it might have been different if we'd ever built the Shuttle, if we had big roomy ships to carry seven or eight to orbit, if access to space had ever become routine. Then we would be flying women every month. But we don't. So you work it out. If you have a mixed crew, you need extra facilities. Personal hygiene. Privacy. It's all avoidable payload weight. And that's not a good thing when you're planning an eighteen-month deep-space mission.'

'So take an all-female crew. No need for separate showers then; right? . . .'

Muldoon was starting to look exasperated. 'Look, Natalie, you know you're not going to win this argument. And I'm not even the right guy to be arguing with.'

'Then who is?'

He shrugged. 'American culture. The world. Hell, I don't know; I'm just the poor schmoe who recommended you for the D mission.' He studied her with, she thought, a little more sympathy. 'Natalie, take my advice. The main thing is to be in the rotation. That's all that matters; that, and doing your damnedest at the job. And I know you'll do that. We need you in the program, Natalie. You're an element we've missed before. We think a lot of you. You'd be surprised. And I noticed the work you did at capcom during Apollo-N.'

She shrugged. It wasn't an assignment from which she wanted to gain any credit. 'You need me in the program, but not necessarily on a ship to Mars.'

He shuffled the papers on his desk, the typed-out lists of crew assignments. 'Maybe that's true. Maybe you'd actually be more use to the program, overall – to the science goals – right here, in Houston, than stumbling around on Mars itself. Have you thought about that? Natalie, you're complaining about flying the space soak mission. Hell, I understand that; in your shoes, I'd be up here beefing too. But all *I* get to fly these days is this damn desk.' He looked wistful. Almost desperate. 'Two hours on the Moon just wasn't enough, for one lifetime.'

She couldn't help saying it. 'Two hours too many for your wife, maybe.'

He threw the papers down on the desk. 'Goddamn you, York, why do you have to be so abrasive?'

'I'm sorry, Joe.' She shook her head. 'I guess I'm just –'

'Listen to me,' he said bluntly. 'Who the hell knows what's going to happen? You just keep on doing what you're doing. Do whatever

381

that bunch of assholes out there do, but do it twice as often, and twice as good. And offer me things they *can't*; like your geology training. Keep yourself in the frame. Make yourself indispensable. Who knows where we'll all be, by 1986?'

For that brief moment she felt oddly cheered – almost confident. *He's right. I've got this far; maybe I can get through the final barriers. I can do this.*

But Muldoon's eyes started straying to the heaps of papers on his desk.

York was shut out again: she was out in the dark, with her mission prospects – her career, her life – reduced once more to being a matter of little more than guesswork and hope. Her brief warm stab of self-confidence faded as quickly as it had come.

She got out of Muldoon's office.

June, 1981
Headquarters, Columbia Aviation, Newport Beach

When he got up in the morning Lee liked to hit the ground rolling. Jennine fixed him two cups of coffee, both heavily sugared, so the second one had time to cool and he could down it in a gulp, on the run to the black T-bird in the yard.

His first task was to find somewhere to work on the proposal. He spent a day roaming around the plant.

Columbia's plant was a bunch of decrepit old factory buildings, with the big wind tunnel snaking through the complex. The site worked pretty well for the small-run experimental work that was the norm for CA's workload. But it was already bursting at the seams.

What Lee needed was office space.

Finally his eye settled on the canteen; it was the only open space big enough to take a hundred people or more.

'This is it. Bella, I want you to get rid of the serving hatches and the goddamn trestle tables. I've got drafting tables and desks coming in here.' He squinted upwards. 'Not enough light. Get some sky-lights knocked through. And check the power; we'll need a secured supply for the computers.'

'Yes, sir, JK. But –'

'What is it with you and these "buts"?'

'Where will we eat?'

Lee waved a hand. 'The whole of the goddamn US is full of McDonald's. Nobody will starve.'

'Yes, sir, JK.'

He looked around the canteen, with its battered serving bays and scuffed floor and stink of tomato sauce. It was the pits. And it was going to be a tough regime in here. He'd already issued a notice that for the duration of the proposal development he'd expect everybody to be at their desks by seven a.m. and to work through until at least nine p.m. And the work here would just be the center of a huge effort right across the company, with teams of engineers in laboratories and wind tunnels generating data to support the thesis that Columbia was going to be able to *do* this, to build this unprecedented machine . . .

But *this* was the focus: it was in this big, dirty room, he felt now with a growing excitement, that the final proposal for the Mars Excursion Module would be drawn up.

He started scouring the organization, taking out whoever he thought was going to be of use to him in constructing the bid. When anybody howled, he just waved Cane's name at them, and that was usually enough. That was Art Cane's culture, Lee reflected. He might have doubts about the wisdom of this bid, but now they had gotten into it, it was a corporate effort, all or nothing, and Cane would expect the whole organization to support Lee as best it could.

During that first week Art Cane spent some time trying to assemble corporate partners: potential subcontractors who would support Columbia's bid. A coalition of subcontractors was, by traditional wisdom, a major feature of any serious bid for a contract like this.

At Cane's recommendation, Lee and Bob Rowen flew out to Culver City, the headquarters of Hughes Aircraft. This was where Cane had cut his teeth, and he still had some contacts out there. Cane arranged an appointment for them with a vice president called Gene Tyson. As it happened Hughes hadn't been signed up by anybody else in the MEM bidding process yet. And Hughes were skilled in control and stabilization, so they would be good to have on Columbia's side.

But when Lee and Rowen got to Culver, Tyson kept them waiting for three hours, and when they'd given their pitch, Tyson and his aides laughed them out of the office.

Gene Tyson was a fat, soft-looking man who reeked of cologne and tobacco, and he irritated the hell out of Lee. He put a fatherly arm around Lee's shoulders as he walked him to the door. 'Take my advice,' Tyson said. 'Art Cane is a great old guy. But, JK, you're wasting your time. Not to mention mine. You have no chance of winning this contract, absolutely none. You're just a bunch of lab boys.'

Lee went back to Newport steaming – and worried. If Hughes wouldn't take their bid seriously, who the hell would? And not having a partner could leave a big hole right in the middle of the bid.

But the more he thought about it, the more he began to see that he might be able to turn this too from a weakness to a strength.

'Look at it this way,' he said to Art Cane. 'Fuck 'em. Fuck Hughes. And the rest. We'll go it alone. We'll go to NASA as a coach, not a team. That's what they need. Once you have Columbia as the coach, you can put anybody you like on the goddamn team. Let the customer make the choice when they're ready; we don't need to lock them in now.'

Art Cane shook his head. 'You're a crazy man, JK. Get out of my office.'

When the canteen had been converted, Lee set himself up at a desk on a stage. He appointed team leaders, his senior and smarter people like Bob Rowen and Julie Lye. But all the time he himself was going to hover over the whole thing like a hawk, looking out for trouble.

Rapidly, the concept of the Columbia MEM began to emerge.

Lee wanted something that would look, to the NASA evaluation panel, easy to build. So the MEM started out pretty much as Lee had outlined it, that night he'd driven out to the Mojave with Ralph Gershon. You had your basic Apollo Command Module shape, a squat cone thirty feet tall, with a heatshield all of thirty feet across at the base. And now his teams of engineers focused on that concept. Inside the conical, heat-resistant shell, the MEM would have two stages, like Apollo's Lunar Module: a descent stage for landing on Mars, which would later serve as a platform for an upper ascent stage, which would return to orbit.

Lee laid down rules about how he wanted as little innovation as possible. 'You can start being creative when we've won the goddamn bid, not before.' For instance, he didn't want to see any changes to the overall Command Module shape. The angle of that cone had been determined years back by wind-tunnel tests at NASA's own Ames Laboratory, and all the experience of Apollo had proven out that analysis since then, and he wasn't about to let anyone in his organization challenge it now.

In Lee's first sketch, the MEM would land on five fold-down landing legs. *Five* was chosen in case one of the legs broke off on landing; the MEM could stay stable even if that happened. The descent stage engine, the rocket which would carry the MEM down the last few miles to the surface of Mars, stuck out of the base of the MEM, with its fuel tanks clustered close by.

Inside the fat base of the descent stage there was a doughnut-shaped compartment. Some of this was taken up with fuel tanks, but the rest was given over to payload. Half of the doughnut was a surface shelter, a tightly curving chamber that would serve as crew quarters and laboratory for the crew while they were on the Martian surface. Then there were surface operations bays, with room for airlocks and equipment, and space for a small Martian rover.

Sitting on top of the descent stage was a smaller cone: the cabin of the ascent stage. This was a bubble of glass, to give all-round visibility. The crew would ride down to the surface and back to orbit again inside this cabin. It held room enough, just, for four guys, lying side by side in acceleration couches. But you could fold the couches out of the way, so the pilots could stand up to control the final descent.

The rest of the ascent stage was a cylinder, impaled down the spine of the MEM's descent stage. The ascent stage, rising from Mars, would look like a Kojak lollipop, Lee thought whimsically, a glass lollipop on a stick of propellant tanks and rocket engine, leaving behind a truncated half-cone: the descent stage, scorched and decapitated.

That was the skeleton of the thing, anyhow, and the teams soon began to put on some flesh, mapping out the subsystems.

ECLSS, the environment control and life support system: Jack Morgan's baby, with molecular sieves to scrub out carbon dioxide, and filtration for water recycling. *Electrical supply:* fuel cells for the descent stage, separate, smaller cells for the ascent. *Guidance and control:* there would be inertial guidance, and rendezvous and landing radar systems, and attitude rocket clusters, and gimballed main engines to allow thrust vector control. *Communications:* the engineering models of the ascent stage started to sprout antennae, S-band for TV links to the orbiter and voice to Earth, and VHF for voice links to the orbiter and EVA to MEM links . . .

Lee had his people borrow where they could. Details in the

subsystems, for example: they put in power cells that had already served in the Apollo Lunar Module, an L-band rendezvous radar from Gemini. As for a propellant, should they use the nitrogen tetroxide/Aerojet 50 Grumman had used on the LM? That was hypergolic – meaning it would ignite on contact with its oxidizer, with no need for an ignition system – but it was low-performance, corrosive, not to mention toxic. Not the stuff you'd want to have to store for a year or more as you hauled your MEM out to Mars. There had been some studies of fluorine-based compounds, but they hadn't been taken too far because fluorine was such difficult stuff to work with. What, then? . . .

As the teams worked, the design quickly evolved away from the first baseline sketched out by Lee.

That bubble of glass on top of the ascent stage, for instance. It would have given the crewmen an uninterrupted horizontal field of view, and a hundred and thirty-five degrees vertically: it would have been like riding some superb helicopter down to the surface of Mars. But if the bubble was made of laminated glass, it would be too heavy; and lighter alternatives like Plexiglas would discolor and weaken under the intense, ultraviolet-laden Martian sunlight. And, as Jack Morgan was quick to point out, all that glass would over-load the environment control system. So the beautiful bubble was discarded, in favor of small, LM-like, downward-slanting pilot's windows.

And the five-landing-leg geometry was soon upped to six, to provide the broad-based craft with better landing dynamics. To guard against excessive forces on landing, the legs incorporated a crushable aluminum honeycomb, so they would compress, absorbing the force of impact . . .

It was an exciting, invigorating time.

Lee didn't spare himself; he charged through the organization, checking, cross-fertilizing, collating, cutting through a lot of what he judged to be sterile crap.

Sometimes he'd realize he couldn't remember the last time he'd slept, or eaten. Sometimes, in fact, it was only a pressure in his bladder or bowels that made him attend to the human side of his needs at all.

Every day he went home in the dark and left in the dark.

It was incredible. He never even saw the apple blossom in his yard. He hardly saw his kids – two boys, Bert and Gerry, both high school age – for more than minutes at a time.

He had a little more time with Jennine, but most of that he spent eating, or – if he was lucky and could relax – sleeping lightly.

He worried a little about Jennine, when he thought about it. She'd grown used to the stupid hours he worked, over the years. Although she knew and cared nothing about airplanes, Jennine seemed to understand that these bursts of activity were like brush fires; they wouldn't last forever, and then she would have him back. For a while, anyhow.

But she seemed a little more strained, this time, although he couldn't quite figure out why.

They were both older, he supposed. That was one thing. And the boys were sure a handful.

But the MEM pressure would go away. She would get him back.

. . . *But what if we win?*

Then it isn't going to go away. Is it, JK? Not until 1986, and that ascent stage lifts off Mars, and it's all over.

But always, the *work* came crowding back in on him again, shutting out his consideration of anything else.

He kept two supreme goals in mind. One was meeting the proposal submission deadline, and the other was keeping the MEM's overall weight within the design limits specified in the RFP.

For the first, he had Bella print up a kind of calendar, which he pinned up around the plant and had checked off every day. *FORTY-SIX DAYS TO SUBMISSION DAY! AND ROCKWELL ARE STILL AHEAD OF US!* Lee was proud of this. 'It's kind of like the calendar they had in *When Worlds Collide*. Do you remember that, Bella? When they were building a rocket ship to get off the Earth? . . .'

'Yes, sir, JK.'

The weight problem was more difficult to crack.

Every design definition Lee had ever worked on was the same; each subsystem inevitably grew in scope and complexity as the engineers got into the detail. So Lee started to keep a list of best-guess weights for all the various components and subsystems.

Every morning Lee would call his senior people into his own office, into a progress meeting he called a hot griddle. It was something he knew they used at the Strategic Air Command. Seven forty-five smart and then the doors were locked; the chairs were pushed against the wall, and there was no coffee, so you couldn't sit down and take it easy. Then, everybody would talk through their top problem for the day and how they would resolve it.

At the griddle sessions Lee handed out weight summaries, show-ing how far the current aggregate design was over the limit. He was reluctant to start setting weight limits for subsystems – he wanted to find the best trade-off across the whole spacecraft – but he pushed his people every day to figure out what they could do to bring down their net weight, to give the rest a little slack.

Still, the daily totals weren't coming down fast enough, and the weight issue soon emerged as his major worry.

It wouldn't matter if, at submission time, they were a little heavy, a little above the target. If they won, there would be plenty of detailed design work to follow. But right now it seemed as if the Columbia MEM wouldn't even be in the right ball park.

The weight limits had been set by NASA to fit into their new all-chemical, gravity-assist system configuration. And the limits were thereby much tighter than they had been in previous nuclear-option baselines.

Lee started to worry, privately, that they might be too tight to be feasible.

The issue was brought to a head, at last, by Lee's closest ally.

Jack Morgan took Lee into a corner of the office, away from the hubbub. Morgan's face was long, uncharacteristically serious. 'JK, I think we're in trouble.'

Morgan took Lee through the figures he had been establishing for the MEM environment and life support systems. He had guideline figures, based on Apollo, for what it would take to support one human being for one day on Mars: food, clothing, air supply, waste disposal, living space, EVA consumables.

'Look at this. And this.' Morgan took Lee through a whole series of options, where he had tried to juggle elements of his ECLSS weight budget against each other. 'There's no way I can support four men for thirty days on the surface. That's one hundred and twenty man-days. It just doesn't fit. We're an order of magnitude out, here.'

Lee felt a bubble of panic swell up in his throat. It really looked as if they weren't going to be able to close the design.

Suddenly he was aware of the lack of sleep, all the meals he'd skipped, the adrenaline he'd been burning off; he felt ill, light-headed.

Come on, JK. Get a grip on yourself. If it's a problem for you, so it is for Rockwell, and McDonnell, and all those other assholes. Look for a way to turn this to our advantage.

Morgan was looking at him with concern. 'Are you okay, JK? You look kind of –'

'Don't turn into a doctor on me now, Jack.'

'Buddy, the way you eat yourself up, you're going to need a doctor some day. I mean it, JK.'

Lee railroaded on. 'You can't deliver a hundred and twenty man-days on Mars. Fine. What can you give me?'

Morgan thought about it. 'Maybe seventy-five per cent of that. Say ninety days.'

Shit. Worse than I thought. 'So we have our four guys down there for, what, twenty-three days?'

'You've just lost a quarter of your surface stay time, JK. I can't believe that's going to be acceptable.'

Lee shook his head. 'No, it isn't. But there has to be another way.' He thought about it. 'Ninety man-days, huh. Well, what if we only take three guys? Then we can still stay the full thirty.'

Morgan shook his head immediately. 'That's impossible. The RFP sets it out. Having spent all that money to get their guys onto Mars, NASA want to get twenty-four-hour EVA cycles going. They want two guys out on the Martian surface for as much of each day as possible. They want a "red" and "blue" team shift system –'

'Well, the "red" team can take a flying fuck at the "blue" team,' Lee snapped back. 'This won't be the only place where that shitty RFP is wrong.'

His mind was starting to race.

Three guys instead of four. If it could be done, he started to figure now, there would be knock-on savings throughout the rest of the program, beyond the MEM definition itself. For example, one quarter less life support would have to be hauled all the way out to Mars and back. And all at no, or minimal, cost to the value of the surface activities.

That's what he would have to demonstrate, anyhow.

If he could achieve this, he realized with growing excitement, it would be a hell of a strong plank in the bid.

All Lee's brief feelings of panic were gone now; he felt strong, fit, eager, pumping with adrenaline again. He grabbed Morgan's arm. 'So all we have to do is figure out some way of getting three guys to maintain a twenty-four-hour EVA shift pattern. Listen, Jack. This is what I want you to do.'

It was hardly a simulator: just a room within a room, fenced off from one of the Columbia site's larger lab areas. They fitted it out with a rudimentary life support system – food and water – but the room was left open to the outside air.

Morgan paid three students, from a paramedic class he taught at Caltech, to come and live in there for a month.

Every day the students went through a mocked-up EVA: they put on dummy spacesuits and backpacks loaded with lead weights, and they moved about simulating Mars surface experiments. And then the students would climb up a little ladder to simulate returning to the MEM, and vacuum each other clean of talcum-powder Mars dust.

The students experimented with work and sleep patterns, trying to find ways to optimize their surface shifts.

The whole set-up was crude, but effective; at the end of the month the students were a little bored, and definitely exhausted; but they were alert, functional, and actually fitter than when they had gone into the mockup. Exhaustion was fine, anyhow; the real crew were going to have the whole return leg of the trip, seven months of it, to sleep it off.

Morgan wrote this up for Lee, and Lee was delighted with the results. Not only was his three-man idea going to hit that Evaluation Board between the eyes, he was going to be able to throw at them detailed proposals about managing the Mars surface time: suggestions for shift rotas, the need to establish work and sleep patterns before arrival at Mars, how to schedule suitable rest periods, and all the rest.

Problems and opportunities. He had a mood of gathering momentum, of approaching triumph.

As the clock wound down to the deadline day, Lee started sitting in on the rehearsals as each group put together its own piece of the pitch.

He began to figure out how the final thing would come together. There would be him – and Xu, Rowen, Lye, Morgan, and a few others – on a stage in some kind of hotel or convention center, in front of a mass of NASA engineers, and they would have sixty minutes to make their case.

But the more he listened to the draft pieces of the pitch, the more he understood that it wasn't going to make sense to have five or six or seven presenters in that time. One man was going to have to do the whole show, from beginning to end, on every aspect of the proposal, every damned subsystem, with the others sitting there in support to help field questions.

So after that, he started taking material home – draft scripts, documents, notes – and set himself to memorize every piece of the system he was proposing. He even took the stuff to bed, and sat there propped up against his pillows, with his reading light and his glasses.

Jennine would wake up, and mumble something, and he'd be shocked to find it was four in the morning, or some such godforsaken time. An hour until he had to get out and start all over again.

But he was full of energy. He couldn't believe it. Day after day. He felt like he could fly.

Eventually he had a cot brought into his office. It seemed to him he saved a lot of time that way.

Lee got a call from Art Cane.

'I'm getting kind of worried about what you guys are costing me. If we don't win the bid I'm looking at one hell of a write-off. How's my two-million budget looking, by the way?'

'Fine, Art.'

Actually, that was a bare-faced lie. Lee was well aware that he had long since bust out of that two-million limit, and he was headed for three or four times as much.

One of Art's more endearing characteristics, from Lee's point of view, was his distrust of computerized accounting systems. He insisted on inspecting the figures every month, analyzed, summarized and interpreted more or less by hand. Just like when he'd started the company.

So Cane was always at least a month behind the action. And by a little manipulation, Lee could juggle his billings and payments to pick up another thirty days. So he had two months' grace in all.

That was all Lee needed. In two months, the bid would be in. He figured that if he won the bid, nobody would care how much it cost. And if he lost, Art would have his hide anyway. Either way the important thing was to have the resources he needed, at hand, now.

Cane said now, 'I just got a call from McDonnell Douglas.'

'Oh, yeah? And?'

'They want to throw in with us on a joint effort to bid on the MEM. How about that, JK? Now, I want you to think about this . . .'

Cane went on about the details.

Lee thought hard.

If you were objective about it, a call like this from McDonnell was second only in value to a similar call from Rockwell themselves. McDonnell had built Mercury and Gemini, the first two generations of manned American spacecraft, and the third stage of the Saturn V. So they would be good, credible partners. And Lee knew that there were plenty of muttering voices within NASA who had never been happy about Rockwell's work on Apollo, and had grumbled ever since. That community inside NASA, and Lee was sure there would be some of them on the evaluation board, would welcome a return to the good old days of partnership with McDonnell.

Every which way you looked at this, it made sense.

Lee cut through Cane. 'Not interested,' he said.

Art Cane was silent, for a long minute.

'Now, look here,' Cane said at last. 'You know I'm not going to jam this deal down your throat. That's not my style, JK.'

'I know that, sir. But this is our bid. Fuck McDonnell. Maybe we'll hire them as a subcontractor later. Who needs them?'

'JK –'

'I need you to back me, Art.'

There was a bass rumble on the phone line. 'Hell, Lee, you know I'll do that. Just don't let me down.'

'You know I won't, Art. Now get off the line, I got work to do.'

Monday, July 6, 1981
Flight Crew Training Building, Jacqueline
B. Kennedy Space Center

Natalie York and Ralph Gershon sat side by side in the Mars Excursion Module Biconic Simulator Number Three. York was hot and cramped in her closed pressure suit. Inside, the MEM cabin was realistically mocked up; from the outside, this motion-based simulator was a big, ungainly piece of engineering, with heavy white-painted hydraulics completely enclosing the cabin.

'Okay, Ralph, we'll give it to you at OMS burn plus one,' the SimSup said.

'Rog,' Gershon said tersely.

Around York, electroluminescent readouts and gauges and dials came to life, the needles flickering and the CRT tubes blinking awake, to register engine temperature and chamber pressure and fuel and oxidizer levels.

Gershon sat to the left, in the pilot's seat, and York to the right. The cabin's windows, at eye level around them, were big and square, so that it was like sitting in a small, cramped airliner cockpit. The instruments' soft green glow suffused the cabin; it was, York thought, like being immersed in water.

Now there was a smear of crimson beyond York's window. She saw a simulated Martian landscape, salmon-pink and softly curving, come rearing up beyond the glass. The landscape was a slice of painted plaster of paris over which, somewhere, a light television camera was panning under computer control. The sky was black, starless, probably just a backdrop. But there were splashes of orange light: representations of the tenuous upper atmosphere of Mars, reflecting the glow of the biconic's RCS thrusters.

'Take it that the burn was good,' the SimSup said now. 'Your residuals are three-tenths, and your pitch maneuver was successful.'

'Okay,' Gershon said.

Gauges flickered and acronyms scrolled across the CRTs before York.

'We've dumped our forward RCS propellants,' she told Gershon. 'OMS and RCS post-ignition reconfiguration complete. Auxiliary power unit start. We got two out of three APUs running, and that's nominal.'

Gershon flicked at a gauge. 'SimSup, I got a poor correlation with the attitude reading on the inertial ball. I'm going to center the readings manually. You got a problem with that?'

'No problem, Ralph. We agree with that.'

'Entry interface,' York said. 'We're in the atmosphere, Ralph. A hundred and fifty-eight thousand feet. Nose up at forty degrees.'

Gershon said, 'Let's see what they got to throw at us this time.'

'You're getting paranoid, Ralph.'

'Tell me about it.'

Now the plaster of paris was scrolling past the window more rapidly.

'Frictional heating,' York said. She watched sensors telling her how the temperature was climbing over the lower surface of the craft.

The biconic, based on Rockwell's current draft design, was the most advanced MEM configuration being studied by the various contractors. It would fall into the atmosphere belly-first, and then fly down like an airplane, so the whole of the underside was tiled with heat-resistant panels, forming a heat sink which absorbed the energy of the sparse Martian air molecules.

'Get ready for your comms blackout,' the SimSup said dryly. 'See you on the other side, guys.'

'I hope so,' Gershon said.

Beyond York's window a pinkish plasma glow built up.

Gershon grunted. 'What a fake.'

'I kind of like it,' York murmured.

York and Gershon began to monitor the systems displays before them, checking them against checklist cards taped to the consoles. Now the work of the sim became routine, almost dull . . .

Except that now, York knew, if this was for real, she would be feeling the first tug of deceleration in earnest, as the craft dug deeper into the Martian atmosphere. She could feel her pulse rising, beating at her throat. This simulation, designed more for engineers than astronauts, was crude: not even motion-based, it was a shadow play, mimicking life. But there was just enough in the sim, inside this static cabin, for it to catch at her imagination, to give her a taste of how it would be, really, to fly down from orbit to the surface of Mars.

She wished – suddenly, childishly – that this was for real. That she could somehow fast-forward through the years of training and uncertainty that lay ahead.

Oh, I want this. So badly.

Even if I have to get there with Ralph Gershon, she thought.

'A hundred and thirty thousand feet. Coming up to aerosurface control initiation.'

'Yo,' Gershon said. He began to work his stick and pedals.

The biconic was deep enough into the atmosphere, on this computer-generated dive, for the pressure to have rendered the forward attitude rockets useless. And the atmosphere would be almost thick enough for the biconic's control surfaces to start biting into the air.

Right now, York realized, the biconic was a peculiar, unprecedented mix of spacecraft and aircraft.

'Dynamic pressure twenty pounds per square foot,' York said. 'One hundred twenty thousand feet.'

'I got it,' Gershon said.

Now the last thrusters were switched off. The craft had become a glider, with only its aerodynamic control surfaces to maintain its attitude and trajectory.

The glow outside her window reached its peak now, racking up through pink and yellow and blue-white. Actually the colors changed in visible clunks, as the computer changed over its filters.

Gershon worked at his stick and pedals, the biconic's oddly

old-fashioned aerodynamic control system. 'The response seems sluggish to me.' He pushed the stick forward. 'I'm trying to descend. The elevons have gone down, the rear has come up. I don't feel a damn thing. Fucker. There we go. I overshot. Okay, bringing her up. Arresting my sink rate. Back on the stick. Elevons up, lift dumped, back end dropping down. Shit. Where's the response . . . Oh. Here it is. I'm wallowing like a hog in mud.'

The biconic would be slow, clumsy, heavy to handle by comparison with most Earth-bound aircraft, York knew. Flying the biconic was more like guiding a boat; you just had to rearrange your control surfaces and wait while the new configuration bit at the stream of thin air, and slowly changed your momentum.

'One hundred and three thousand feet,' she called now. 'Here we go,' Gershon said. 'First roll reversal coming up.'

In the electronic imagination of the computer, the biconic banked through eighty degrees to the right. York watched the tilting landscape; the plaster of paris appeared to quiver as some fault in the TV camera's control mechanism made the tracking shudder.

The biconic was designed to go through a series of S-shaped turns in the upper atmosphere of Mars. The flight path was a question of budgeting: the craft had to shed all of its orbital energy by the time it reached its landing site, but on the other hand, at any point in its trajectory, the craft needed to maintain enough energy to reach that landing point. So the craft had to manage the lift generated by its biconic shape, together with the kinetic energy of its descent, to shed heat and reach its target . . .

'Overshot,' Gershon muttered. 'Eighty-five degrees. Eighty-six. Banking left to compensate. Come on, SimSup. Is this where you hit us? Banking left. Okay. Here we go. Okay. First roll complete. Here we go. Second roll reversal.' Gershon's voice was tense, his movements fast, mechanical.

He takes these games too seriously, York thought.

At this point the biconic would be traveling at many times the local speed of sound. Still glowing, it would streak across the Martian sky, scrawling a wake of vapor across unmarked skies, shedding great crashing waves of acoustical energy across the dead, empty landscape, a land that had lain undisturbed for half a billion years.

This sure would be a spectacular phase of the mission, she conceded. A pilot's dream.

Maybe, York thought wistfully, the aborted Space Shuttle might have felt something like this. To fly down from orbit in huge graceful curves over the high desert would have been a hell of a difference

395

from falling into the sea ass-backwards in an Apollo. *We lost a lot of beauty, when we killed the Shuttle.*

'Sixty-one thousand feet,' she read off now.

'Rager. Reducing air brake to sixty-five per cent. Take air data.'

'Rog.' York flicked a dummy switch. On a real biconic a series of pitot-static probes would thrust out of the craft's surface now to confirm measurements of dynamic pressure and airspeed.

'Looking good,' Gershon said. 'Coming out of the third roll.' He grinned at York. 'Hey, maybe we're going to get through this fucker.'

'Maybe. Fifty thousand feet.'

'Banking for fourth roll.'

The plaster of paris plain, unobscured now by the fake plasma glow, tipped over again.

'Okay, coming out of the roll. Coming out . . . come on, baby . . . coming out of the roll . . . Shit.'

Here it comes, York thought. Every sim, they were out to get you somewhere. Her stomach contracted.

The attitude indicator was tumbling. Gershon worked his controls and snapped through emergency checklists. 'The aerosurfaces are biting. But just not enough. *Fuck.* What's going on?'

York glanced out of her window. Gershon couldn't get out of the roll, and the landscape had tilted up through more than ninety degrees, now; the biconic, in the imagination of the computer, had almost tipped over completely.

'Recommend you abort,' the SimSup said calmly, breaking his radio silence.

'Screw you,' Gershon said. He kept working through his lists, checking instruments, snapping switches.

This is what pilots do, at times like this, York realized. *Work through the book. Keep it logical, but move fast. Try A. If it doesn't work, try B. If it doesn't work, try C . . .*

But now the plaster landscape was upside down completely, the fake craters and canyons like a crimson roof above them.

York was shocked to find that only seconds had elapsed since the first sign of the problem. That was all you were granted: seconds, to figure out the underlying cause of what could be a complex, multiple failure.

There was virtually no chance of succeeding.

If anything went wrong, you had to get out of there, more or less immediately. Or you'd die. The equation was as simple, as finely balanced, as that.

'Ralph, we have to hit abort.'

Gershon didn't even bother to reply; he just kept working feverishly.

The landscape tilted further, visibly coming closer. The biconic was starting to go into a hypersonic spin.

'Hit abort,' she told Gershon again. 'Christ, Ralph, once we go into a spin we're through.'

The light in the cabin flickered as the fake Martian sky hurtled past the window. She had a sudden, comical image of a little TV camera on its robot arm spinning around over a plaster of paris floor.

If this were for real, my head would be shaking now, battering against the helmet, my inner ears coming apart from Coriolis forces. If this were for real the craft would start to break up, maybe before I lost consciousness.

'MEM, we recommend you abort. We recommend –'

'Ralph! Jesus Christ! Ralph!'

There was a shudder, a crunch, a puff of white powder.

The landscape froze in place.

'Welcome to Mars,' the SimSup said dryly. 'We're just figuring out the size of the crater you made.'

'Fuck,' Gershon said. He pulled off his helmet and threw it across the fake cabin.

The two of them clambered out of the back of the simulator. From outside it looked like the nose of a small light aircraft, a cockpit section roughly sheared off, with wires and umbilical cables dangling from the gaping rear.

The technicians were grinning at them. 'Hey, Ralph, you busted our camera. Flew it right on down into the plaster of paris. How about that.'

Gershon wasn't laughing. He confronted York. He pointed a gloved finger at her face. 'Don't you *ever* give me orders when we're flying.'

She was amused rather than disquieted; she'd seen such tantrums before. Most of the time she was able to cope with Gershon, and he seemed prepared, in his rough way, to accept her as an equal in exercises like this. Even though he'd lectured to her, back when she was an ascan. Then, every so often, he would blow his stack like this.

'Orders? Me? You're the pilot, Ralph.'

'Don't you fucking forget it.' And he went stalking off for the wake.

Phil Stone came strolling up to her, dressed in a light blue coverall, his hands in his pockets. 'Don't take it personally.'

'I don't.' York shrugged, and began to pull off her gloves. 'Pretty soon he'll be bawling out the techs. And then the SimSup. And then you, and . . . Bawling his way up the chain of command. I was just the first one to hand, the place to start. He hates to fail.'

'He didn't fail,' Stone said. 'That failure wasn't recoverable.'

'That hypersonic spin –'

'I wrote the book about hypersonic spins,' he said, and she suspected he had a war story behind that somewhere. 'I know about the spin. But even before that point, you couldn't have got out of it.'

'What happened?'

'You don't want to wait for the wake?' The wake was the long, harrowing official debrief.

'Just give me the headline.'

'Your nose RCS thrusters started firing. Just as you went into that fourth roll reversal. The aerosurface couldn't handle the additional torque.'

She thought about that. 'But that firing didn't show up in the instruments. And besides, it's impossible for the RCS to fire at that point. We'd dumped the fuel.'

'You thought you had.' He grinned. 'Just one damn thing after another, huh?'

'Christ.' She shoved her gloves into her helmet. 'Sometimes I think these guys want us to fail.'

'No. But you have to fail, a hundred times maybe, so you can succeed the one time when you need to. Besides, this is the place to do it. Nobody ever got killed in a sim. Anyhow, this was primarily a proving flight for the biconic design, not for the pilots.'

That was true, York reflected. The biconic sim was so unpopular, in fact, that only real sim hounds, people desperate to rack up some sim time, any sim time, in order to get a better seat in the crew rotation, would consider working on it.

People like Natalie York and Ralph Gershon.

Stone said now, 'And I don't think this thing is ever going to fly. There's too damn many things to go wrong. The percentage of biconic crashes we get in the sims is a joke . . .'

'It's just a shame Ralph doesn't have that perspective.'

'He may be the best we've got,' Stone said quietly.

She was surprised to hear Stone say that.

Stone went on, 'He kept on trying. Everything he had, trying to

398

pull her out of that spin. He came closer to saving the MEM than I thought anybody could get.

'By the way,' he said. 'You did pretty well in there yourself. Calling for abort when you did was the second best option.'

'What was the best?'

'What Ralph did. Come on.' He slapped her on the back, the pressure of his hand heavy through the layers of her pressure suit. 'I'll buy you a coffee before the wake.'

They walked out of the training building.

Wednesday, August 12, 1981
Headquarters, Columbia Aviation, Newport Beach

They flew into Newport News, the night before the presentations: Lee and Morgan and Xu and Rowen and Lye and all the others – even Art Cane, who had decided to top and tail Lee's presentation himself, to show that the corporation was committed to the bid.

They checked into the Chamberlain Hotel at Old Point Comfort, near Langley, where the presentations were to be held. Morgan beat a path to the bar, where he started drinking rum: Lemon Hart, a hundred and fifty proof.

But Lee went to his room with his boxes of slides.

He'd had a final run-through in front of Cane the day before and he was horrified to find that he still overran, by nearly twenty minutes. So he opened the boxes and began sorting the slides, trying to find something he could cut.

At about three thirty a.m. Jack Morgan came to the door, thoroughly oiled. He took a flash photo of Lee, with his slides spread out all over the hotel room's polished desk. 'For Christ's sake, JK, put that crap down and go to bed. If you don't know the pitch now you never will.'

Lee gave in. He cleared up the slides and got into bed. He even turned the light out, and lay there in the dark.

But he could see the slides more clearly than when they were physically in front of him.

After maybe thirty minutes of this he got out of bed, had a shower and a shave, and started working again.

His wake-up call came, and when he looked out of the window he found the planet had rotated again, and it had become light.

*   *   *

Thirty minutes before the Columbia pitch was due to start he went down to reception to meet the others. Bob Rowen was carrying a fat pc. The computer contained the whole Columbia case, split into little chunks and indexed so that in response to questions Lee could get at any point of it quickly.

Lee glad-handed the others, trying to radiate confidence and surety.

But suddenly his stomach clenched up, and he knew he was going to be ill.

Jack Morgan had been watching him, and he dragged Lee off to a bathroom, away from the others, where Lee threw up violently: a thin, brown, stinging liquid, nothing but coffee.

Morgan didn't say anything, but Lee knew what he was thinking. He'd been running on adrenaline and coffee and no sleep and little food for ten weeks now.

Morgan made him pull down his pants, and gave him a shot in the cheeks from a needle full of something, vitamin B-12 and other crap. But it worked; it got Lee back together again. And in a couple of minutes he was able to walk out of there, smart and spruce and neat and feeling just fine.

They arrived at the ballroom where the presentations were to be made.

The MEM Evaluation Board were sitting in rows before the stage: seventy-five of NASA's most senior people.

Lee knew many of the members by sight. There was Hans Udet from Marshall, and Gregory Dana from Langley – famous enemies, sitting stiffly side by side – and he spotted Ralph Gershon, skulking at the back of the room. Gershon nodded to Lee and grinned.

Joe Muldoon was sitting front and center, chairing the session; Muldoon might have become a power in the hierarchy, Lee thought, but he still didn't look like he fitted the blue pinstripe he had tucked himself into.

Tension hung in the room like ozone.

As the Columbia team set up, the team that preceded them was coming out. It was McDonnell, whose invitation for a joint pitch Lee had famously rejected. And among their subcontractor partners was Hughes, who had rejected Columbia's approach.

The contrast between the two groups struck Lee strongly. The McDonnell/Hughes cadre was sleek, weighty-looking, all middle-aged white men with slicked-back hair and comfortable guts. Here was Gene Tyson from Hughes, for instance, still stinking of cologne and tobacco, looking like he had stepped off the cover of *Fortune*. By contrast, Lee was carrying his own slide projector, for Christ's sake, and all he had to back him up was with this bunch of college kids and a hung-over doctor.

Lee had actually seen a copy of McDonnell's final report, the result of millions of dollars' worth of study. It called for a biconic approach, a variant of the theme Rockwell would be developing. The study was damned clever stuff, and so vast that nobody at Columbia had had time to read it.

Tyson came over to Lee. 'Well, JK. I'm surprised to see you here.'

'Oh, we were passing,' Lee said. 'So we thought we'd throw something together, and see how it hangs.'

Tyson laughed, quite good-natured, and he clapped Lee on the shoulder and walked off.

Now Art Cane walked up to the lectern, slow and dignified and very impressive, and he gave a short speech about the commitment of his company to the bid, and referred to their tradition and values.

Then Lee strolled to the front of the room, smiling and nodding, and exchanged a brief formal handshake with Cane. He stood at the lectern and called for his first slide.

The room lights dimmed and the slide came up, right on cue.

Thursday, September 24, 1981
Lyndon B. Johnson Space Center, Houston

Phil Stone and Adam Bleeker watched her steadily.

The three of them were in a small conference room that had been turned over to the Ares landing site selection committee. The walls were covered with images of Mars: Mariner orbiter photographs, US Geological Survey maps, false-color stratigraphic profiles, geological surveys. The long tables which ran in rows down the walls of the room were covered by more charts and pictures and ring-bound folders.

York unrolled a chart and pinned it up on a wall, covering maps and photos. It was a bright, simple, block-color map, with little flags scattered over it.

'Mars,' she said. 'In as much detail as you need to understand it for now. Know your enemy, right? This is a geological map of the planet, drawn from Mariner data.' Actually that wasn't true; the map was kiddie stuff, too simple to be anything but an operational guide. *Useful if you were planning to bomb Mars rather than study it.* 'Now. What's the first thing you notice?'

Stone grinned. 'I see seven little Stars-and-Stripes, and seven little Hammer-and-Sickles, all with labels beside them.'

'We'll come to the flags. Think about the geology first. Just describe what you see.'

Bleeker shrugged and said, willingly enough, 'North and south are different. The top half of your map is pink, the bottom yellow. More or less.'

'Right. The logical basis of geology is that no solid planet is either a homogeneous blob, or a disorganized jumble. They're all made up of pieces – called geologic units. Each unit was formed in a certain way at a certain time; each has depth as well as breadth and width, and when we do geology we're always trying to look beneath the surface, to reconstruct the three-dimensional structure that is hidden from direct view. The relations between the units show their age relations, something about the processes that formed them, and something about how far beneath the surface they extend . . .'

Stone, surreptitiously, was checking his watch.

'Have I got your full attention, gentlemen?'

Stone and Bleeker glanced at each other, like guilty children.

'I'm sure you're just doing your job, Natalie,' Bleeker said languidly, 'and we're glad you're running the site selection committee –'

'I'm not running it. I'm just on it.'

'Whatever. But we'd have a year en route to Mars with nothing much else to do but study this stuff. Can't this wait until then?' As usual, Bleeker sounded calm, rational, reasonable, colorless.

A year? Yes, but I won't be there to hold your hands, or make you think. I'll be light minutes away . . .

And this guy was likely to be designated the Ares mission specialist. *My God.*

Phil Stone waved Bleeker quiet. 'Go on, Natalie. We're committed to the science. You've got us.'

'All right. Now,' she ploughed on, 'the probes have shown us that in the case of Mars we have two main types of landscape. The yellow stuff in the south is heavily cratered, and looks ancient. And this pink stuff, to the north, is made up of smooth, young plains. The planet bulges out below the equator; most of the south is above the mean altitude, and most of the north is below.'

'You say "ancient" and "young," ' Stone said. 'Meaning?'

'"Young" is maybe half a billion years old. The plains are vol-canic – frozen lava fields. And the ancient cratered stuff is three to four billion years old. That's almost as old as the planet itself . . .'

Bleeker said, 'So let's get back to the flags. I guess those seven Hammer-and-Sickles are the sites the Soviets have identified as prime interest.'

'Yes. You can see –'

'So screw that,' Stone said easily. 'Let's look at the good old American selections. Those two white stripes at the top and bottom of your chart – I guess we're looking at the polar caps.'

'Yeah.'

'I see no flags up there.'

'No. We have to rule out high latitudes.' Spacecraft arriving from Earth would naturally settle into a parking orbit around Mars with not much inclination to the equator; changing the orbit to reach the poles would take a lot of extra energy. 'But it's a shame; the poles are interesting.'

'What are the caps? Water ice?'

'Maybe. The orbit of Mars is more elliptical than Earth's. And that distorts the seasons. In the south you get a short, hot summer, but a long, cool winter. And the make-up of the caps seems to differ as well. We think the cap in the north is water ice, yes. But the southern cap is probably carbon dioxide – dry ice.

'There are a lot of puzzles about the poles.' She walked across the room to a blow-up photograph; it showed a thick band of layering in brownish terrain.

'What the hell's that?' Bleeker asked. 'It looks like melted chocolate.'

'These are bands of thick layered deposits, thirty or forty feet thick, that surround the poles for hundreds of miles; they are made up of dust and ice, mixed up, laid down by the Martian winds. The bands tell us that the deposition process must vary, over the years. Or the millennia, anyhow. But what caused the variation? We've got three possible mechanisms. First, maybe the eccentricity of Mars's orbit changes.'

'Why should it?' Stone asked.

'Mars is a lot closer to Jupiter than we are; Jupiter's mass is capable of a lot of perturbation. Or maybe the tilt of the planet's axis changes.'

'I can see how that would happen,' Stone said. 'That bottom-heavy southern hemisphere would make a hell of a difference to

403

Mars's moment of inertia. The whole damn thing must wobble like a spinning top.'

She smiled. 'On geological timescales, yes.'

'And what's your third mechanism?'

'That the heat output of the sun changes, in some way we don't understand.'

Bleeker frowned. 'But that would change the Earth's climate.'

'That's right. And that's why the layering is a good reason for going to the poles some day. Mars is like a dusty mirror, Phil, Adam; every time we look into it, we learn something about the Earth.'

They were silent for a moment, digesting that.

York felt pleased with herself. Even if they learned nothing else, if she could puncture their complacency, make them *think* about the significance of the flight they were likely to take, she'd have achieved something.

She glanced again at her polar blow-up. It was actually of much lower quality than the images taken by later generations of probes, which had concentrated on equatorial landing-site mapping. Because of the Mars landing program, paradoxically, much less was known about the plant as a whole than might otherwise be possible.

And it was in the hands of these two guys to make it all worth while.

Adam Bleeker said, 'I'd guess the high-latitude problems would also rule out the site you've marked far to the south there, Natalie.'

'I guess. But it's another interesting site. That's the Amphitrites Patera: an ancient volcano, much older than the volcanic plains in the northern hemisphere. We don't fully understand how it was formed. Maybe the vulcanism there was sparked off by the huge impacts which created the massive impact craters in the south. You see these mustard-yellow spots in the center of the southern fields: that's Argyre and Hellas – huge, ancient impact basins, more than three billion years old. Hellas is bigger than anything we've found on the Moon – bigger even than the Mare Imbrium, for example. Hellas is where the Soviets put down Mars 9.'

Stone whistled. 'That's what you get for setting up shop next door to the asteroid belt, I guess.'

Argyre held a Stars-and-Stripes.

'You're suggesting we should try for Argyre?' Bleeker asked.

'It's a possible. Argyre is obviously very ancient, and very deep. But the basins are surrounded by concentric rings –

404

mountain chains, actually – which would be hard to negotiate or land on.

'Now,' she went on, 'you can see that the rest of the action is in the western hemisphere. This scarlet area, sprawling over into the north, is the Tharsis bulge: on average, more than five miles above the surrounding terrain. And these crimson spots are the great shield volcanoes.' She pointed. 'Ascraeus, Pavonis and Arsia Mons; and here, to the northwest, is Olympus Mons: three hundred seventy miles across its base, with a caldera fifty miles wide. Olympus is so big it pokes its way out of most of the atmosphere. So you get orographic clouds, formed when the air has to move up the slopes . . .'

'Sure,' Bleeker said, 'but I hear Olympus wouldn't be so spectacular from the ground.'

She shrugged. 'Maybe. Look at this.' She hunted about on the pin board on one wall, until she found the image she wanted. She passed it to the astronauts. It was a perspective view of a huge volcano; a cliff, sharp and well delineated, marked out its nearer rim. 'That's a computer image, an oblique view, faked up from Mariner data.'

Stone pointed to the cliff. 'How high is that?'

'The scarp? Oh, three miles.'

'*Jesus.* A three-mile-high cliff?'

'Give or take.'

They were both staring at the cliff image. Bleeker held up his hands in mock surrender.

She suppressed a grin. Astronauts were easy to impress if you pushed the right gosh-wow buttons.

Stone said, 'I see you have a couple of flags on top of those big volcanoes.'

'Yeah. Olympus Mons is the youngest, and the tallest; and the youngest lava flows on Mars emanate from it. But Olympus is seventeen miles high –'

'Too high for aerobraking,' Bleeker said. 'And I guess that would rule out the other Tharsis volcanoes also.'

'Okay,' Stone said. 'To the east of Tharsis I see a ragged blue streak, stretching along the equator. I guess that's the Mariner valley.'

'Yes. Valles Marineris. The great canyons: two and a half thousand miles long, four miles deep, and over a hundred miles wide. We know that the Valles system wasn't formed by water. A lot of the individual "canyons" are boxed in. So water couldn't have got in or out of them; we're looking at geological faulting here, like the Rift Valley in Africa.'

'The whole valley looks as if it's flowing out of your Tharsis bulge,' Bleeker said.

'Yeah. And we don't think that can be a coincidence. Maybe when the bulge was uplifted, magma withdrew from around it, which would have cracked the surface. There would have been earthquakes and extensive faulting.'

'I see we could maybe go for the Valles Marineris itself,' Stone said.

'Maybe,' York said. 'This flag is actually in a tributary called the Candor Chasma; we've seen layers in the canyon walls here, so we'd be able to get clues to the canyons' origins.'

'But I'll bet the landscape isn't too easy to negotiate.'

'No. Some of the smaller canyons there are a couple of miles deep. If you had several months to survey the place, and some kind of flying machine –'

'But we don't,' Stone said. 'Okay, Natalie. That leaves two places. Both on the border between the old stuff in the southern hemisphere and the volcanic plains in the north.'

'Yes. This one in the eastern hemisphere' – on the opposite side of the world from Tharsis – 'is called Nilosyrtis Mensa. It is what we call "fretted" terrain.' She dug out a photograph, this one a mosaic in black and white. It showed a surface uniformly crumpled.

'Christ,' Stone said. 'It looks like beaten copper.'

'We think the older, southern terrain has been eroded, here on the border, leaving this irregular, grooved landscape.'

'Looks bloody difficult to land on,' Bleeker said.

'Yes, and you'd need long traverses to achieve systematic surveys.'

'All right. So that leaves one site.'

The final flag was at the western fringe of the Tharsis Bulge, close to the border of the north and south terrains. It was in the middle of a green stripe that cut north to south across the Valles. The green, together with the blue ribbon of the Valles, made a rough upright cross, straddling the equator.

'This is a region shaped by running water. Apparently. There are channels that seem to flow out of the Valles Marineris, and across the northern plains.'

Stone smiled. 'So these are the famous water-carved features you tell us about in the Singing Wheel.'

'It's an equatorial site,' she said. 'So you get a mix of young and old geological types. And that's important to us. Most mixed terrain is complex, broken up. But here the landscape is pretty forgiving for a landing. And if you're going to find water anywhere, it's here. Maybe under the surface. And where there's water –'

'Maybe there's life.' Stone got out of his chair and walked across to the map; he leaned close so he could read the label by the little flag. '*Mangala Vallis.* What does it mean?'

'All the major valleys have been named after words for Mars. Here, to the east of Marineris, we even have an Ares valley . . .'

'And Mangala?'

'Sanskrit. The oldest language of the Indo-European group.'

'So maybe Mangala is the oldest word for Mars in the western world.' Stone smiled. 'I kind of like that.' Standing at the map, he turned to eye York. 'So you've been pushing the site selection board toward Mangala Vallis. For good operational reasons, of course. A place on which you just happen to be the world's leading expert. Right, York?'

He was grinning, and so was Bleeker.

'Still wangling to get my seat, Natalie?' Bleeker called, good-natured.

She felt chilled. *These guys see right through me.*

But maybe that's not a bad thing. If Bleeker knows I'm right on his tail, maybe he will take his geology a little more seriously.

And all he has to do is slip once . . .

She started to roll up her maps. 'What do you think? I'll give you a preprint of my next *Journal of Geophysical Research* paper on Mangala; read it and weep, fly-boys.'

'Now what?' Stone asked. 'Are we done?'

'Like hell. We're only just beginning; that was the fun stuff. Now we come to Martian climatology. Compare and contrast with Earth's, and . . .'

After some grumbling, the guys settled down again.

The day wore on, and the little room grew progressively hotter.

October, 1981

In the end, five lead companies submitted proposals to build the Mars Exploration Module: Rockwell, McDonnell, Martin, Boeing, and JK Lee's company, Columbia.

The post-presentation work of the MEM Evaluation Board was long and complicated. It was all a question of weighted scores; Ralph Gershon had never seen anything like it. There were subcommittees to evaluate the bidder's 'administrative capacity' and 'business approach' and 'technical qualification' ... Gershon was himself involved in three of the subcommittees. And each subcommittee assigned weighted scores to each bid, under hundreds of categories.

It didn't make sense to Gershon. Would all these numbers really determine the final outcome? If you could reduce decision-making to a mechanical process, the day would come when a computer could run an outfit like NASA.

In this bidding war, for instance, it was pretty obvious to Gershon that Columbia had the most plausible strategy. NASA, with the bigger players, had pissed away the best part of a decade on studies and proposals and evaluations of ever more exotic Mars landers, without ever really getting to the point. Lee's people had come in fresh and had cut through all that crap, and presented something that looked as if it could be up and flying in a couple of years.

The trouble was, the scoring didn't back up that intuition. Even though its technical pitch was well received – and the human factors stuff seemed particularly well thought through – Columbia was penalized by its status as a small experimental outfit. It just didn't look as if Columbia was capable of delivering a complete spacecraft.

When the first-cut summary sheets came in, the overall totals gave Rockwell first place, with Boeing and McDonnell tied for second, and Columbia a distant last.

Gershon argued against the scoring in the final plenary sessions. 'Damn it, you've got the results of the sims. I bust my balls trying to get a biconic to fly. We got to pick the bidder with the best chance of building something that will work ...'

He got some sympathy from Joe Muldoon. The scores went through a rethink which helped Columbia a little.

But in the end Muldoon's final report to Tim Josephson followed the scoring conclusions: 'Rockwell International is considered the outstanding source as the Mars Excursion Module prime contractor ...'

His assignment completed, Gershon went off to work at the Cape on the first of the Ares A-class missions, an unmanned proving flight of the upgraded Saturn VB.

In a couple of days he was called back to JSC to put his paw print to the final MEM report. Gershon turned up, pretty pissed with the whole thing.

Muldoon caught him up.

'Where are you going?'

'It's over, isn't it? Oh, come on, Joe. You know as well as I do that Columbia were the only outfit with a real chance of building something in the timescale. And now we're dumping them.'

'Of course I know that. But it's not over yet.'

'Are you kidding me? We've just signed off the final report, for Christ's sake. Columbia never had a chance.'

'You're learning fast, boy, but you've got a long way to go. In this game, a signed-off, final report is just the start of the negotiations.'

'What do you mean?'

'I want you to do something for me.'

A couple of days after that, a long telegram landed on JK Lee's gun-metal desk.

He called in Jack Morgan, and flipped the telegram across the desk at him.

Morgan read through the thing carefully, but he kept one eye on Lee as he did so.

The telegram had come from Ralph Gershon, one of the astronauts on the Evaluation Board. It was basically a list of questions about the Columbia bid. A lot of them were brutal, and the first was a doozie: translated from corporate speak it was, *How can a piss-ant bunch of amateurs like Columbia handle the development of a major spacecraft like the MEM?*

'Well, I guess this is it,' Morgan said, studying Lee. 'We're dead.'

Morgan had never seen Lee so low as in the last couple of months, since the MEM presentation. The release of tension, the sleep deficit, and all the rest of it had dumped Lee into a deep, deep trough of depression. And Lee's overspend on the proposal had finally come out into the open, and there was a lot of muttering against him within Columbia. During the MEM exercise Morgan had become genuinely worried about what Lee was doing to himself. Not to mention his family. Now the MEM thing was over Morgan knew he was going to have to broach the health thing with Lee, somehow. Maybe he'd try to work through Jennine.

But right now Lee, sitting back in his chair, seemed bright, alert, and his eyes had that slightly glazed, almost *high* look in them that Morgan had come to associate with Lee's major bursts of activity.

'Hell, no,' Lee said vehemently. 'Don't you get it? This damn note means we're still in the running. They wouldn't be asking us these questions otherwise.'

'What are you going to do?'

'Get the answers, of course.' Lee stabbed at his intercom. 'Bella.

I want you to start putting out calls. Get the MEM team leaders in here, as soon as you can. And book a flight for us all, out to Houston, for – let me think – two days' time.'

'But that's a Sunday, JK.'

'Here you go again with your "but but but," ' Lee said. 'I've told you about that before.'

'Yes, sir, JK.'

Morgan was aghast. 'You're not serious. It's unheard of for a bidder to make a personal visit during an evaluation process.'

'What is that, a rule?'

'An unwritten one, I guess.'

Lee arched his eyebrows. 'Imagine my concern.'

After the visit of the Columbia people to JSC, the scoring was revised again, and the senior people on the Evaluation Board took the proposal to Tim Josephson in Washington.

Muldoon's people recommended Rockwell on the basis of the scoring system, with Columbia finally showing up at third.

The Administrator listened carefully.

Then Josephson thanked the Board, and he asked Joe Muldoon, Ralph Gershon and a couple of others to stay behind.

'Tell me the truth.' His tone sounded to Gershon typically dry and bureaucratic. 'Are there any factors, other than those presented by the Evaluation Board, which I ought to take into account in this decision?'

Joe Muldoon spoke up. 'Hell, yes. You got to look again at the Columbia bid, Tim.'

'Why so?'

'Because in my opinion it's the most technically plausible. It's shallow in some areas, but overall it was the most coherent of the bids. With the support of good subcontractors, the small organizational weight of Columbia won't be a handicap . . .'

Gershon tried not to grin. As he'd watched Muldoon and Josephson and the rest work in the last few days, he'd come to believe that running an organization had a lot in common with flying a plane. You had to use your instruments, sure, but raw data, however well interpreted and analyzed, was only one input; in the end – when you had to make the decisions that could save you or kill you – there was no substitute for the mysterious internal processing that amalgamated data and experience and the *feel* of a ship in your hands.

It was just what Tim Josephson and Joe Muldoon were doing

410

now, he thought. The Columbia bid *felt* right, and that might swing it for JK Lee, even yet.

Still, it was going to be difficult for Josephson to set aside the conclusions of his formal evaluation. Two decades earlier Jim Webb had done that, when he'd plumped for Rockwell to build Apollo. And there had been muttering about corruption and back-hand deals ever since.

When Gershon left to take a plane to the Cape, the decision still hung in the balance.

Lee was getting steadily more depressed. Even though his unorthodox visit to Houston had gone well, the rumors coming out of Washington were strong and consistent: that Rockwell had the MEM contract wrapped up. *Hell,* he thought, *they always did. Who was I ever trying to kid?*

At ten a.m. on the day after getting back from Houston he found himself staring out of his office window. He was thinking of going home. He could spend some time with Jennine. And his son, Bert, was playing baseball that evening for his high school team. Maybe it would be good for Lee to show up, for once.

Then Joe Muldoon called.

'Can you come back over to Houston today?'

Lee was nonplussed. 'I don't know. The flights –'

'Tonight would be fine. I'd like to see you. Come to my office at JSC.'

Maybe Muldoon thought it would be kinder to tell Lee in person, even if it meant dragging him all the way out to Houston.

Lee thought of Bert and his ball game. That seemed a more attractive option.

He called Bella to ask her to fix up a flight to Houston.

He got to JSC in late afternoon. He'd spent the flight, and the ride from the airport, bracing himself for the axe.

Muldoon took him into his office and closed the door. He stuck out his hand and grinned. 'Congratulations. I wanted to tell you in person. You've won the MEM.'

Lee, for once in his life, couldn't think of a damn thing to say.

'Can I tell my people?'

Muldoon checked his watch, a heavy astronaut's Rolex. 'We can't make a public announcement until the stock markets close ... Well, what the hell.'

He allowed Lee to make two phone calls.

411

Lee used the phone in Muldoon's office. He thought of calling Jennine.

He called Art Cane.

And then he called Gene Tyson, at Hughes, and he took a lot of pleasure over commiserating with him.

Muldoon took Lee out that night, for a meal and a good few cold ones. Lee got thoroughly oiled, and had a hell of a time.

But by five a.m. he was up, watching the early-morning news on the TV, and packing his overnight bag.

He caught a glance of himself in the mirror on the wall of his motel room. 'By God,' he said aloud. 'I'm going to build a spacecraft to take three Americans to Mars.'

Then the TV news item broke into his awareness.

A Saturn VB had blown up. There was an image of a white cloud, tinged with orange, with Solid Rocket Boosters veering crazily out of it, trailing smoke.

The commentators said the accident would set the Ares program back years.

My God. Lee knotted his tie, his fingers frantic, fumbling, and hurried from the room.

New York Times, *Tuesday, December 15, 1981*

... Today the last remains of the tragic Apollo-N space mission have been buried, in an underground storage facility at NASA's Cape Kennedy launch site in Florida.

I spoke to Aaron Raab at the Jacqueline B. Kennedy Space Center about the problems involved. Raab was born in Tulsa, Oklahoma in 1946. He joined NASA in July 1967, just a few months after another tragedy, the Apollo 1 pad fire which claimed the lives of astronauts Grissom, White and Chaffee.

In the immediate aftermath of the Apollo-N disaster, Raab shouldered the heavy burden of 'Debris Manager.'

After being offloaded from its recovery vessel at Port Canaveral, the Apollo-N Command Module – the eleven-thousand-pound capsule which returned NASA astronauts Dana, Jones and Priest to Earth – was painstakingly disassembled and laid out for investigation purposes in temporary storage areas by a National Transportation Safety Board (NTSB) team. Under Raab's supervision, and under the watchful eye of the investigating Commission appointed by President Reagan, the components of the Command Module were arranged in their original configuration relative to one another, to assist the investigators. The components remained in this 'footprint' for almost a full year, because once the investigations were over and the reports written, NASA got down to its own internal engineering evaluation and data retrieval.

Surprisingly little equipment was used to move the components about, including a light crane, a fork-lift, and two flatbed trucks.

Because the Command Module had been recovered from the salt-water ocean, some of it required corrosion-proofing to preserve it. In addition, special measures were taken to protect Apollo-N's voice recorders. Soon after recovery the recorders were sent to the Johnson Space Center in Houston for restoration by IBM and analysis by a team led by woman astronaut Natalie York.

The Command Module's final resting place is perhaps bizarre, but practical. The spacecraft now lies deep underground in a disused Minuteman missile silo complex in a quiet corner of Cape Canaveral. The chosen site consists of one silo (Complex 31) and four vault-like underground equipment rooms.

The operation to prepare the silo as a final resting place was a tricky one. The silo complex had deteriorated badly after some ten years of neglect. The equipment rooms still housed a considerable amount of electronic equipment associated with missile operations, which Raab's team had to remove before the Apollo-N debris could be transported in. Other modifications were made to transform the underground equipment rooms, which were in a bad state of repair, into permanent storage vaults. Although there was to be no environmental control, the underground facilities had to be made at least watertight; it turned out that back in the late 1960s a burst pipe had immersed the floor of Complex 31 under several feet of water, and so the water lines were all capped off before the Apollo-N debris was moved in.

There was extensive photo-documentation by NASA cameramen, and the whole operation was conducted under a tight security cordon, with round-the-clock surveillance to deter morbid souvenir hunters.

'We got the components in the vault in a very organized manner,' Aaron Raab told me. 'We compartmentalized the components according to function and storage requirements. Primarily, we put in the larger components first, and anything we felt would be of any significance in the future was left in an accessible area. It was all logged in by our quality control personnel here at the Cape, in official logbooks. These record precisely where each component is stored.'

It would be a fairly involved operation for anyone to get back into the vault, but future investigators could go in and retrieve components after a few days of clearing work. But, says Raab, there are no plans for the periodic opening-up of the vaults to check the condition of the stored wreckage.

Today, I watched as Aaron Raab personally laid the last few poignant components of the Command Module in position. A huge ten-ton concrete cap was secured with long steel rods, and welded down over the underground vault.

A year after the accident, Apollo-N is at last laid to rest . . .

January, 1982
Washington DC

At first Bert Seger had been enthusiastic about his new post in Washington. He was, after all, given the rank of Associate Administrator, and, as a senior manager in the Office of Manned Spaceflight, he still expected to have a strong hands-on involvement in the manned program. But when he studied the new organization charts, and he saw just how far away from him were the reporting lines of the major players, like Joe Muldoon, he started to realize he'd been had. He'd been handed a sinecure, something to get him decently out of the way during the investigations into Apollo-N.

He never became comfortable at Headquarters. He had a few assignments, and some pet projects of his own to pursue, and they filled his time, but not his attention. He would find himself sitting alone in his office for hours on end, waiting for the telephone to ring, reading newspapers.

He took long walks around Washington.

He found favored benches in the big public gardens, and floated through the museums. He liked the serenity, the timelessness of the museums.

The evenings weren't any better.

Fay was still in Houston, with the boys, and Seger would fly back there every Friday. Fay didn't want to move, because of the boys' schooling, and Seger accepted that, reluctantly.

Every Sunday or Monday, when he had to get ready to fly back to DC, Fay prepared him a little bouquet of carnations. Each day

414

he'd take one for his buttonhole, but they'd be pretty faded by the end of the week, and it just wasn't the same.

He had too much time to think.

He kept on going over the events of that flight – in fact, over everything he'd done in all the years that had led up to Apollo-N.

Was there anything he should have done differently during the flight, anything he'd missed that might have saved Jones, Priest and Dana? And during the long development, how far was he responsible for the shoddiness, the carelessness which had finally destroyed the nuclear rocket?

He didn't come up with any answers. He could, in retrospect, think of a thousand things he might have done differently. But he wasn't wallowing; he knew that anything is possible with the benefit of hindsight. He'd done the best he could, at every stage of his career.

But it was no comfort. *It happened on my watch.*

In the hall of his rented apartment he had hung a small brass-framed photograph. It showed three spacesuited astronauts. *To Bert – In Your Hands.*

Seger didn't go in or out of his apartment without looking at that photo and reading the inscription.

He found a run-down little Catholic church, tucked away just a few blocks from Headquarters, and took to spending time in there. He attended Mass three or four times a week. The ancient, gentle ritual took him back to his childhood, and comforted him.

He was struck – shocked, even – by the poverty he saw around him in the neighborhood of the church, just blocks away from NASA Headquarters, here in the capital city of the richest nation on the planet.

He began to see that he'd been locked away inside NASA for too long, pursuing the organization's single goal, the Mars landing, with blinkered obsessiveness. Perhaps they all had.

He remembered how shocked he'd been by the intrusion of those anti-nuke protesters at the Cape.

The world out here, beyond JSC, had continued to evolve, and Seger felt as if he was emerging into a new, harsh light, his NASA cocoon crumbling around him.

He went to the libraries and started going through back issues of newspapers – papers he'd barely scanned when they were printed, save for sports results and NASA coverage. Now, as he stared into grainy microfiche screens, he felt as if he was learning about some

415

phase of ancient history. But this was the world in which he had lived, the story of the country which supported him.

The United States was falling apart, it seemed to Seger.

The country was deep in recession. Under Reagan, there was a kind of cheerful, simplistic optimism around. But the divisions in society seemed to Seger to be growing wider than ever. Two Americas were emerging: there was a grotesque, materialistic money-chase among the already affluent, and among the poor – particularly the non-whites, in the inner cities – there was a tailspin of drugs, crime, decaying housing projects and a failing educational system.

And meanwhile, Seger learned, in the middle of the recession, Reagan was vastly increasing the Pentagon's budget. Nuclear weapons were a key part of that build-up. Next year, cruise missiles would be deployed in Western Europe, in the face of much protest from those countries. There'd been more protest here, too, he read.

People were growing scared again. A DoD official had talked about how backyard shelters would save them all, when the bomb dropped. *If there are enough shovels going around, everybody's going to make it.*

Seger read back as far as Three Mile Island. The similarities – administrative and technical – between that disaster and the Apollo-N incident chilled him.

The general press coverage of NASA, now he looked on it with his new perspective, startled him too. He saw skepticism, anger, contempt, resentment, on the part of the people outside looking in. He remembered how Eisenhower had cautioned against the growth of military and industrial power – against an expanded space program, in fact – because technocracy was foreign to the individualistic American spirit, and grafting it on to the nation was going to do a lot of harm. Well, Kennedy had accepted that risk. And it seemed to Seger now that the country was paying the price.

The space program, he saw now, was a prime symptom of all this. What *use* was any of it? The much-lauded spin-offs were minimal and probably would have come about anyhow, if the need was there. NASA had lobbied to go to Mars, he began to see, in order to justify itself, to keep its huge teams together, after the great lunar effort wound down.

Of course, freeing up NASA's funds to other, Earth-bound projects would have been a token gesture. The money would have seeped away, Seger was sure, with no tangible benefit. But that wasn't the point. The space program was like a huge, spindly,

416

etiolated plant, pushing all its energy obsessively into one sickly Mars-red bloom, while the society in which its roots were anchored was steadily disintegrating.

It just wasn't appropriate. Any more than had been the over-ambitious civilian nuclear program, the weapons build-up . . .

The Mars mission came to seem almost blasphemous, to Seger.

A new clarity entered his thoughts, as he shaped these ideas. A new determination.

Of course he knew that he was still reacting to Apollo-N. His thoughts would be shaped by that defining incident for the rest of his life. Perhaps, in fact, he was still in some mild form of shock. It didn't matter. Truth remained truth, no matter what the form of the revelation, and he felt he was on his own road to Damascus now, seeing the space program from the outside, in its true perspective, for the first time in his working life.

He found great comfort in his new perception.

The next time he attended Mass, he asked the priest if he could give a sermon.

Mission Elapsed Time [Day/Hr:Min:Sec] Plus 313/11:33:22

313/11:33:22 CDR   . . . For my part, I want to use the opportunity of this telecast to register our awareness of the debt we owe to all those who came before us. This flight has come out of the efforts, first, of people from history, of scientists across the world, who have brought us to the point where we can meet the challenge even of a deep space trek like this across the Solar System. Next, the American people, who have expressed their will to see this great exploration adventure continue. Next, four Administrations and their congresses for having the courage to implement that will. After the Moon landings I think it's true to say that America came close to turning its back on spaceflight, and it took political courage and vision to bring us to where we are, today. And then we come to the Agency and industry teams that built the spacecraft: the Saturn boosters, the Mission Module, the Apollo, and the MEM. This trip of ours to Mars may look to you simple or easy. I'd like to assure you that that has not been the case. The Saturn VB booster system which put us into orbit is an incredibly complicated piece of machinery, every piece of which worked perfectly. This switch which I have in my hand now, if you can see that, has over three hundred counterparts in this control rack alone, and there are many more in the Command Module and the MEM. In addition to that, there are myriad circuit breakers, levers, rods and other associated controls. The MS-II, the big rocket stage on the back end of our Ares cluster, has performed flawlessly so far; and it must do so again, or we cannot return to the Earth . . . We have always had confidence that all this equipment will work and work properly, and we continue to have confidence that it will do so for the remainder of this flight. All this is possible only through the endeavors of a number of people. First, the American men and women who put these pieces of machinery together at the factory. Second, the test teams, with their painstaking work during the assembly and re-test after assembly. Third, the astronauts who flew before us to assemble the Ares components in Earth orbit. Finally, the people at the Lyndon B. Johnson Space Center, in management, in mission planning and flight control, and in crew training. This operation is somewhat like a TV news show; all you see on screen is the three of us, but behind the scenery are thousands of others – hundreds of thousands. And every damn one of them did his or her job to the utmost.

313/11:35:10 MMP   [INAUDIBLE]

313/11:35:12 CDR   And every one of them did his or her job to the utmost. To those people, we give a special thank you, and to all the other people that are listening and watching tonight. And finally we have to remember those crew, those astronauts, who have

418

lost their lives in the course of our space program. Here I want to remember both Russians and Americans. I want to tell you that I begrudge every one of those lives lost, and no such price is worth paying. But by their sacrifice, those brave men and women have made this mission possible. God bless you. And now Ralph is going to show you something, the marker we're intending to leave on the surface of Mars. Ralph?

313/11:35:45 MMP   I have it. I'll hold it up to the camera. I hope you can see that. Maybe if I turn it a little. For those who haven't seen it, I'll describe the marker. The marker is a disk of diamond, a little like a coin, about an inch across and maybe an eighth of an inch thick. It is a single-crystal diamond. An excimer laser was used to cut a message into the diamond, creating a layer of graphite in there, with a layer of diamond deposited on the top. The marker has been manufactured of diamond because that is the most durable material we know; the marker could survive for millions of years, long after our MEM and our other artifacts have been destroyed. As you know this is the only Mars flight planned for the foreseeable future. But the marker is like a time capsule, to people who may follow us to Mars; and it is, perhaps, a message to future life on Mars, to sentient beings who may emerge there some day. The marker is a little like a microfiche, with a lot of information stored on it, mostly too small for me to make out. But we have here greetings from all the nations of the Earth, and a map of the Solar System as it exists today, and information about the biological composition of human beings. And, embedded in the diamond, we have small samples of Earth rock, and of Moon rock, and human tissue. And, also on here, there is a list of all four hundred thousand Americans who have contributed to Project Ares. We think this is a fitting thing to leave there, on Mars, as a memorial of our mission.

419

313/11:37:07 CDR	Okay. Natalie, I believe you're going to tell the folks about our call signs for the rest of this mission.
313/11:37:11 MSP	Thank you. I know that sometimes our space-age jargon confuses the hell out of people.
313/11:37:15 CDR	Hot mike.
313/11:37:17 MSP	Confuses people. And it sure confuses me. For instance, our space travelers' 'calendar.' We count our days from the moment we left the ground, aboard our Saturn VB booster, from the Jacqueline B. Kennedy Space Center. So, to us, today is MET 313 days – that's three hundred and thirteen days of Mission Elapsed Time, more than three hundred days since we left Earth. While to you, it is a plain old Tuesday, January 28, 1986. And this business of the call signs is another problem. Why is it that spacecraft sometimes have call signs – individual names, like Apollo 11's *Eagle* and *Columbia* – and at other times Houston will refer to us as just, say, 'Ares'? The answer is that we need to use call signs when there is more than one separate spacecraft involved in a flight, and they need to be distinguished in our radio conversations. And that's going to be true on this flight, when we get to Mars in a couple of months' time, and we land on the surface in our MEM. Unlike the Apollo missions to the Moon, we decided not to choose the names for our separate craft until now, until after the launch, as we haven't needed them. As a crew we thought we'd prefer to spend some of the long transfer time to Mars on thinking about that.
313/11:38:18 MMP	Sure. That's what we did. Rather than watch video tapes of the Superbowl.
313/11:38:25 CDR	[INAUDIBLE]
313/11:38:28 MSP	So today I'm going to tell you what names we've chosen. I know we have a lot of children listening

420

today, at schools, and I hope this will bring alive some of the history lessons you have, and you'll be able to see how what we're doing today, in our exploration of Mars, is really an extension of the great journeys you can read about in your texts. Phil, if you . . .

313/11:38:46 CDR   Sure. We've decided to name our spacecraft after famous exploration sailing ships of the past, uh, in line with what Natalie's just said. And I'm particularly pleased with the name we've given to our Mission Module – that is, the place we're living in during the voyage – because it was from the Mission Module that we conducted our study of Venus, as we flew past that planet. And we've decided to name it after the sailing ship which Captain James Cook commanded to Tahiti in 1769, to watch a transit of Venus across the sun: *Endeavour*. Ralph . . .

313/11:39:17 MMP   Yeah. Then there's our Apollo, which we'll use to return to Earth. We've chosen the name *Discovery*. That's actually for two ships: the one Henry Hudson captained in 1610, in his search for a northwest passage between the Atlantic and the Pacific, and another of the ships Cook captained, when he visited Hawaii, and Alaska, and western Canada. Back to Natalie.

313/11:40:00 MSP   And now the MEM, the Excursion Module which will be the first ship to land humans on the surface of Mars. We're going to call it after a famous US Navy ship, which made a prolonged and very successful exploration of the Atlantic and Pacific oceans in the 1870s.

313/11:40:19 CDR   Yes.

313/11:40:21 MSP   We're naming our MEM *Challenger*.

Extracted from NASA, Lyndon B. Johnson Space Center, 'Ares Technical Air-to-Ground Voice Transcription,' January 1986, pp. 1367ff. Ares Files, NASA Historical Reference Collection, NASA Headquarters, Washington, DC

Monday, January 11, 1982
George C. Marshall Space Center, Huntsville, Alabama

The conference room was almost full, but a chair had been reserved for Udet in the front row. He took his seat, and crossed his legs with precise motions.

Gregory Dana was at the lectern, fumbling with his thick spectacles, preparing to speak. Udet had not been surprised when Dana had been selected to chair the investigating panel.

On a large screen behind Dana, an image was projected; it showed the Saturn VB stack a few minutes before launch from Pad 39B at Kennedy. The fat MS-IC first stage gleamed white in the sunlight, with its wide tail-fins and the four slim Solid Rocket Boosters clustered around it. It looked like a broken-off piece of some elaborate Moorish temple. The second stage was a squat cylinder atop the MS-IC, bone white, with the silver-gray gumdrop shape of an unmanned boilerplate Apollo capsule at the top.

Umbilicals snaked into the stack from the big, complex launch tower, feeding liquid oxygen and propellant into both the liquid stages: hydrogen for the second stage, and RP-1 – kerosene – for the big first stage. Vapor wreathed the upper levels of the booster, dispersing slowly, and Udet could see the sparkle of ice against metal and insulation.

The sky behind the stack was a gray-blue, and heat haze shimmered about the tower.

Udet felt his heart move at the sight. He had never lost his boyish wonder at the sight of such magnificent devices – these heroic machines – wrought by human hands from the raw materials of the Earth, to be hurled toward the planets.

And, of course, that sense of awe was piqued on this occasion by his foreknowledge of the fate of Booster AS-5B04, just a few seconds later.

Udet glanced around. Joe Muldoon, up on the stage with Dana, was moderating the meeting, and much of NASA's senior management appeared to be in attendance; there were staff from Marshall and Houston and NASA Headquarters, including aides of Tim Josephson, and a heavy representation from the contractors responsible for the system components under scrutiny today.

The presentation was to be a summary of NASA's preliminary internal report into the problems encountered during the launch of Saturn VB stack AS-5B04, three months earlier. Depending on the

422

reaction of this audience, and on the NASA hierarchy as a whole to the content of the report, a draft would be finalized and published within the week.

There was an air of tension, anxiety, weariness.

Coming so soon after the Apollo-N tragedy, nobody in the Agency wanted to face up to another disaster, the first loss of a Saturn. Udet had heard the muttering. *Who the hell can we blame for this one?*

Dana was speaking, in his thin, frail voice. Udet drew a little more upright in his chair.

'At six point six seconds before launch, the Saturn's kerosene-fueled F-1A main engines were ignited in sequence and run up to full thrust, while the entire structure was still bolted to the launch pad. The thrust of the main engines pushed the Saturn assembly upwards, against the restraint exerted by the pin-down bolts anchoring it to the pad. When the Solid Rocket Boosters' restraining bolts were explosively released the stack's "stretch" was suddenly relieved . . .'

On the screen behind Dana, clouds of smoke and steam billowed up around the base of the Saturn stack. Then the four Solid Rocket Boosters ignited, and yellow-white fire plumed from their engine bells. The camera shuddered, as testimony to the acoustic energy spewed out by the stack – but the film was without sound, and the brilliant launch sequence worked through in eerie silence.

The image froze. Billows of smoke stopped their evolutions, and became mounds of gray and white, solid-looking, like dirty ice cream.

Around Udet, rows of lined faces were illuminated by frozen rocket light.

An arrow pointed to a blurred patch of white near the base of the MS-IC; it was just below the 'A' of the red stenciled 'USA' on the wide hull of the booster.

Dana said, 'At zero point six eight seven seconds into the flight, photographic data shows a strong puff of vapor spurting from the lower casing of the MS-IC, just above the engine fairing.' Dana glanced over his shoulder, wrinkling his nose. 'As you can see here. The two pad cameras that would have recorded the precise location of the puff were inoperative. Computer graphic analysis of film from other cameras indicated the initial vapor came from that level of the MS-IC where the feed from the oxidizer tank exits the propellant tank.'

The MS-IC contained two huge cryogenic tanks. The oxygen tank was uppermost, and the fuel lower. Fat suction lines carried liquid oxygen through the kerosene tank for combustion in the five huge F-1A engines at the base of the stack. Dana was implying, now, that there had been some kind of problem with that feed.

The film started again, in extreme slow motion; the smoke evolved around the Saturn with glacial slowness. White arrows continued to prod at the offending vapor patches at the base of the MS-IC.

'Six more distinctive puffs of vapor were recorded between zero point eight three six and two point five zero one seconds. The multiple puffs in this sequence occurred at about four times per second, approximating the frequency of the structural load dynamics and resultant stack flexing . . .'

The wretched 'stretch'!

'You can also see shock diamonds in the F-1A exhaust, another symptom of the stack resonance. At three point three seven five seconds the last vapor was visible below the Solid Rocket Boosters. It became indiscernible as it mixed with rocket plumes and the surrounding atmosphere. Other vapors in this area were determined to be melting ice from the bottom of the MS-IC or steam from the rocket exhaust in the pad's sound suppression water trays . . .'

The film began to run at normal speed.

The Saturn tipped away from the launch tower, and rolled, as programmed, onto its back. Udet could see, between the four brilliant stars of the Solid Rocket Booster bells, the pale, almost invisible, smokeless fire of the kerosene-oxygen main engines.

Dana went on, 'At this point the first indications were received, via telemetry, of a significant reduction in propellant flow to the MS-IC main engines.'

The image froze again. The audience stirred; the sudden cessation of the launch sequence's hypnotic flow was jarring. An arrow pointed to the five main engine bells.

'The first visible indication of main engine thrust reduction was detected on image-enhanced film at fifty-eight point seven eight eight seconds into the flight. It is visible in this frame, as a dimming of the plume from the right hand F-1A bell – just here.'

'One film frame later from the same camera, the reduction is visible without image enhancement.' The engine bell had grown dark, and its four brothers were also clearly ailing. 'At about the same time telemetry showed a differential between the pressures in the main engine chambers. The right-most booster chamber pressure was lowest, confirming the growing reduction in the flow of propellant.

'At sixty-two seconds into the flight, the control system was responding to counter the forces caused by the differential thrusts from the main engines . . .'

The film ran on, slowly; the main engines flickered or died, but the Solid Rocket Boosters still blazed with fire. The stresses on the stack were enormous, as the SRBs tried to compensate for the loss of the main engines.

No change in the attitude of the complete stack was visible to the naked eye. Udet knew, however, that at this point his doomed Saturn was already fighting for its life.

Dana cleared his throat, and pushed his glasses against his face; his gestures were small, precise, almost apologetic. 'Analysis has shown that the primary cause of the malfunction evident at this point in the flight was the feeder-valves set in the underside of the MS-IC's oxygen tank, which carry oxidizer into the feeders to the main engines. Tests have indicated that under certain circumstances, the valve design could go into a "flutter" regime and effectively shut off the supply of oxidizer, resulting in a total failure of all F-1A engines. As was observed here. The frequency of the possible flutter has been shown to be close to the frequency of the launch "stretch" and to oscillations caused by instabilities in the burning of the Solid Rocket Boosters . . .'

Udet massaged the bridge of his nose, trying to control the irritation that flared within him. *We know this. My team at Marshall, and the contractors independently, determined this root cause of the fault within an hour of the malfunction.* The Saturn had already been vibrating, from the 'stretch,' at three or four cycles a second just after launch. Then one of the Solid Rocket Boosters had started vibrating lengthwise, at about the same frequency. Such oscillations had been observed before. But the coincidence of frequency was unfortunate, for that frequency, as it turned out, had been just right to set up standing waves in the valve system carrying liquid oxygen into the main engines . . .

We know all this, and we are already working to correct the problem. Have you no more wisdom to add than this, Doctor Dana?

But now Dana was continuing; he was describing how some preliminary tests, carried out during the MS-IC's design stage, had indicated the possibility of a resonant flutter – although no change in the stage's design had resulted – and he even referred to the problems encountered with the Apollo-N flight, when similar resonance problems had caused that stack to pogo.

That link with the fatal Apollo-N mishap showed Udet clearly which way the report was shaping.

It was ludicrous, of course; anyone who understood anything of the complexity of a ship like a Saturn – with its millions of moving parts – would recognize the impossibility of adjusting the design to counter *every* possible problem that could be conjured up. There was never the time, or the resources; the realistic way was to balance the risks, and exercise judgment as to what is acceptable, and what must be changed. Why, if one waited for the perfect rocket, one would never fly at all!

Udet felt enormously tired. He was sixty-eight years old now. And sometimes – especially since the death of von Braun – he wondered whether the battle was still worth the effort, whether he still had the strength for the endless struggle to convince the Americans to accept the great rockets he was building for them.

Udet had donned something of the mantle of von Braun, since Wernher's retirement a decade earlier. He had even inherited Wernher's office, here on the tenth floor of Marshall's headquarters building. But Udet had no pretensions; he knew that he was no substitute for Wernher. The Americans had adored von Braun: they responded to him, Udet thought ungraciously, as they did to evangelists, and the salesmen of cars. And, it seemed, questions about the Germans' past – possible complicity in 'war crimes' during the Peenemunde period – were irrelevant for Wernher.

Well, Wernher was dead now. And it was different for Udet. He knew that, try as he might, he could not help but project an aloofness, an aura of the disdainful Prussian aristocrat. The Americans did not trust Udet; and they appeared to find it much easier to believe ill of him than ever they had of von Braun.

And meanwhile, he had been forced to watch as Gregory Dana had risen in status and power within the organization. Being the father of the lost hero James, and the fact that his once-vilified mission mode had been chosen as the basis for the new Mars program, had raised Dana's status almost to national celebrity.

And now, Dana continued to pronounce his damning testimony on Udet's life work, his tone dry, level, like a soulless prosecutor.

Udet's dark, dwarfish twin.

'Beginning at about seventy-eight seconds, a series of events occurred extremely rapidly that terminated the flight. Telemetered

426

data indicate a wide variety of flight system actions that support the visual evidence of the photos, as the Saturn struggled against the forces that were destroying it.

'At seventy-eight point nine seconds the lower strut linking Solid Rocket Booster Number Four and the MS-IC was severed or pulled away. This failure was evidently caused by the abnormal stresses placed on the structure by the failure of the main engines. SRB Four rotated around its upper attachment strut. This rotation is indicated by divergent yaw and pitch rates between the Solid Rocket Boosters.

'At seventy-nine point one four seconds a circumferential white vapor pattern was observed blooming from the side of the MS-IC. This was the beginning of the structural failure of the MS-IC's propellant tank, which culminated in the separation of the aft dome of the tank. This released massive amounts of RP-1 from the tank and created a sudden forward thrust of about two point eight million pounds, pushing the propellant tank upwards through the motor casing toward the S-II. At about the same time the rotating SRB Four impacted the lower part of the MS-IC's liquid oxygen tank. This structure failed at seventy-eight point one three seven seconds, as evidenced by the white vapors appearing in this area . . .'

The images on the screen continued to unroll, frame by frame, their pace matching Dana's dry, analytical delivery. The pictures were blurred and shrouded by the haze of distance, and a fog of escaping vapor, but it was just possible to see how the Solid Rocket Booster was swiveling around, and its conical tip was puncturing the flank of the central first stage.

Then brilliance erupted, within the space of one frame, engulfing the image.

'Within milliseconds there was a massive, almost explosive, burning of the propellant streaming from the bottom of the failed tank. At this point in its trajectory, while traveling at Mach one point nine two at an altitude of forty-six thousand feet, the Saturn was totally enveloped in the explosive burn. The Apollo spacecraft's reaction control system also ruptured, and a hypergolic burn of its propellants occurred; the reddish-brown colors of this burn are visible on the edge of the main fireball. As you see here. The second stage also ruptured at this point, adding one million pounds of propellant and oxidizer to the fireball. The stack, under severe dynamic loads, had by now disintegrated into several large sections which emerged from the fireball; separate sections which can be identified from film include the instrumentation module, trailing a mass of umbilical lines, and the first stage's main engine section with the engines still trailing vapor . . .'

The upper sections of the Saturn didn't explode. They had fallen out of the disintegrating stack and hit air which, at such velocities, was like a wall. The Saturn was simply smashed to pieces by the air.

The screen now showed the image which had filled TV screens for days: a huge orange and gray fireball of the explosion, hovering in the Florida air; the four Solid Rocket Boosters emerging from the explosion, still burning, veering crazily across the sky and trailing their frozen lightning, plumes of white smoke.

Dana was still talking. 'At one hundred and ten seconds after launch, the Range Safety Officer caused the destruction of the Solid Rocket Boosters. Had this been a manned flight the emergency escape tower should have hauled the Apollo Command Module free on the loss of the main engines. Had the launch escape system failed, however, and arguing from the evidence of some system components later recovered from the Atlantic, it is possible that the crew capsule might have been thrown clear of the fireball intact. There is no reason to suppose that such a module might suffer an internal explosion, or significant heat or fire damage. The most severe damage would probably have come from the high forces generated by impact with the water, rather than by the explosion itself . . .'

Now, for the first time, there were rumblings of complaint from the audience.

Udet found himself on his feet.

'I must protest at the tone of this last section. This is entirely speculative. AS-5B04 was *not* manned, thank God, and if it had been we have no reason to believe the launch escape system might have failed, and I see no purpose in hypothesizing in such detail, *and in public,* about the fate of the crew of a manned flight.' He was aware of the orange light of the fireball – still frame-frozen on the big screen – gleaming on his glasses, his cheekbones.

Joe Muldoon, at his moderator's desk, said, 'Will you let me take that, Gregory?'

Dana shrugged his compliance.

Muldoon turned to the audience, his lean face underlit by the lamp on his desk. 'Now, Hans, I don't think we're in a position where we're going to be able to hide on this. We have to discuss the implications for the manned program. And we have to face the fact that there *was* evidence of potential problems on earlier VB

428

tests, with solid fuel burns inducing destabilizing oscillations . . .'

Udet found himself shouting. 'But the AS-5B04 loss was not caused by an Solid Rocket Booster failure!'

'But Solid Rocket Booster problems contributed,' Muldoon said. 'We've seen that. And it seems to me that the whole design is inherently more risky than the old liquid-fuel configurations. Remember we survived Saturn V launches in which we lost whole engines. But if you're sitting on top of those damn unstoppable Solid Rocket Boosters, it's not a question of *if* you go, just which direction. None of us is arguing that we should stop flying the upgraded Saturns; it's just that we have to be honest about the consequences of the compromises we've made in its design. Because if we don't come clean now, the folks on the Hill are going to hang our hides out to dry.'

Muldoon looked around the room, taking in all of the delegates. 'You know the situation we're in, folks; the budget deficit is running so high this year that every discretionary program – including Ares – is under pressure, all the time, every budget round. Now, you may say that isn't fair – that our mistakes get magnified out of proportion, while the much bigger foul-ups of other agencies are hidden – but we're a high-profile Agency; you have to accept it as a fact of our lives. So, we have to be squeaky clean. We'll take questions at the close, folks; I want to move this along now . . .'

Udet, still standing, did not trust himself to speak. *Compromises. You talk of compromises. We were compromised from the beginning. Our Saturn VB funding from the start has been half the projections we requested. Half! Without compromises you would not be flying into space now. And yet you bleat about the consequences, about the loss of a single launcher!*

He felt he could bear no more of this. He clambered past the people beside him, apologizing, and reached the aisle. He stalked toward the back of the room.

Dear God. Are we really reduced to such finger-pointing inanity? All I ask – all I have ever asked – is that you give me adequate tools, and I will finish the job. Achieve the dream. Even with half the resources, I will find you solutions! But what I will not – cannot – achieve is a miracle; I cannot guarantee you perfect safety and reliability. When will you people understand that?

It seemed a long way to the door. Nobody was prepared to meet his eyes.

Dana's patient presence at the podium, unseen, was like a wound in Udet's side.

Saturday, June 5, 1982
Newport Beach

It all came to a head.

It was their wedding anniversary, for God's sake. And although JK had flowers for her, and a card, and a kiss on the cheek in the morning, Jennine knew from long experience that it was his secretary, Bella, who scheduled such events in his diary and would buy the card and whatever. There was no *thought* from JK at all.

That evening they were supposed to be going out for dinner. They did that together maybe twice a year. But JK didn't come home. That wasn't so unusual. When Jennine phoned his office, she got Bella, who politely told her he wasn't at the Columbia site. That was code for: *he's out with the guys.* And so it proved. JK came rolling in, after eleven, as oiled as you like, parking his T-bird at a crazy angle in the driveway.

'You shouldn't drive like this,' Jennine said. She hated the querulous tone that came into her voice at such moments.

'Oh, God, the dinner. Honey, I'm sorry,' JK said. 'I clean forgot. We'll do it tomorrow. Okay?'

No, you idiot. It's not okay. And right now, I have the feeling that it never was.

She went to bed.

After an hour or so he joined her. He touched her face, tenderly, and ran his hand down her nightgown, until he had cupped her breast.

She turned away. She was much too tense, too upset. And anyhow she could smell the stale rum on his breath, oozing out of his pores.

But at least he was home. At that thought she softened, as she drifted toward sleep. *At least he's come home. Maybe in the morning, I might be able to persuade him not to go in quite so early for once.*

Before she fell asleep, the phone rang. JK picked it up immediately. 'Lee.'

She had followed the development of Columbia's MEM program. Actually, since JK brought work home most nights, and since he routinely held business meetings at their home – and always without any warning – she could hardly *help* but follow the program.

Once, JK took her out to Boston, where the Avco company were manufacturing the MEM's ablative heatshield. It was a fascinating place. The ablative stuff was an epoxy resin, something the Avco engineers called 'Avcoat 5026-39.' To hold this in place, the engineers constructed a titanium honeycomb, which would be bonded to the capsule's lower surface, and they pumped the epoxy into each individual cell with a caulking gun. It had to be done by hand; the engineers worked their way across the surface until they had filled in all two hundred thousand cavities. If an X-ray inspection revealed a bubble, that cell would be cleaned out with a dentist's drill, and refilled.

Jennine watched this through a glass picture window. It was a startlingly medieval scene, this slow and painstaking hand-crafting. And she wondered how it must feel to work on something – to touch and shape it with your finger-tips – knowing that it might, one day, enter the air of Mars.

Avco's testing process would start with hand-held blowtorches, and finish up with rocket-propelled power dives into the Earth's atmosphere . . .

But such occasions, when JK took the trouble to share his work with her, were the exception, not the rule. Mostly she had to endure his absences, silently hostess his business meetings.

Jennine had married JK back in 1955.

At the time he had been working for a master's in aeronautical engineering at Caltech, the California Institute of Technology, out at Pasadena.

They got married in a Catholic church close to Jennine's parents' home, in New Orleans. She had been starting to make her way as a secretary in a large law practice in the city. But she gave it all up to go with JK, to support him and his career a thousand miles away. That was what you *did* in 1955.

Jennine's parents gave them money to hire a car for a couple of weeks, and so they drove out east, through Vermont, to watch the fall coloring the leaves. Whenever the fall came now she thought of that honeymoon.

After the honeymoon they flew west, and JK drove her out to Pasadena, to the little house he'd rented.

When they arrived, there was a group of JK's pals waiting there. She thought it must be some kind of welcome-home party. But no; it turned out there was a problem in the Caltech wind tunnel.

So JK had kissed her and gone off to the lab, and left her standing in the driveway with all her luggage. JK didn't get home until dawn.

As it turned out, that honeymoon in Vermont, twenty-seven years ago, had been the last holiday Jennine and JK had taken together.

And this damn Mars program was the toughest project JK had ever worked on. JK was at heart a technician, and a hands-on manager, at his best – so Jennine thought – when working with comparatively small teams, at one site. But now he was running a national effort, one of the most complex engineering projects ever undertaken.

Even beyond the complexity of what was going on at Columbia itself there were all the subcontractors Columbia had to deal with: Honeywell working on stabilization and control (*not* Hughes, JK would point out with relish), Garrett Corporation on the cabin environment, Rocketdyne, a subsidiary of Rockwell, providing the main propulsion systems, Pratt and Whitney developing the fuel cells, and so on.

JK wanted to avoid the thousands of uncoordinated changes that had pretty much paralyzed Rockwell's development of Apollo for a while in the 1960s. So he had instigated a change control mechanism. And that had brought him endless conflict with the astronauts – including Joe Muldoon – who, in the Apollo days, had got used to ruling the roost.

And on it went.

Once, JK showed her a PERT chart for the MEM development, a project plan with all the tasks linked together in their logical order. It was just a mass of computer printout, little boxes and spidery connecting arrows.

'What do you do with all this?'

JK laughed and tipped the plan toward a waste bin. 'Nothing! Haven't got time to read it!'

The project was a monster, and JK was trying to wrestle it to the ground.

She could see that the whole damn thing was bending Lee in half. But to relax, he generally wouldn't think of coming home to her. Instead he would go out with Bob Rowen or Jack Morgan or some such, out to some Newport Beach hot-spot like the Balboa Bay Club, and he'd come home in the small hours roaring drunk, and sleep it off. He wasn't an alcoholic, she believed; the drinking was just one more example of the way JK's life was never *stable*, never *routine*, but swung constantly between crazy extremes.

And the next morning he would be back at his desk, hung over or not, with his two cups of sugary coffee inside him.

The night was so quiet that she could hear both halves of the phone conversation.

432

'JK, you'd better get down here,' Julie Lye's insect voice whispered. 'I'm at the pressure test of the oxidizer tank. We've had a failure. Catastrophic. I'm looking into the test pit right now. We had seven tons of nitrogen tet down there. Now, all we've got is a few fragments of titanium stuck in the walls.'

'All right. I'll be straight over.' JK began to rattle out instructions while he hunted for his pants. Lye was to begin with a scrutiny of the evidence of the explosion. Just by looking at the distribution of the pieces it was possible to figure out the order in which the tank had come apart. Then there would have to be more structural tests. They should pressure up other test tanks with plain water instead of the nitrogen tet. That way, they could tell if the failure was due to something mechanical – like a faulty weld – or some kind of chemical reaction to do with the propellant. And Lye should get onto the tanks' manufacturer, a division of General Motors out in Indianapolis. The manufacturers should run identical tests. That way, they could see if the failure had been caused by damage in shipment, or some kind of local phenomenon . . .

He was still barking out instructions as he left the bedroom. He threw the phone back on the receiver cradle, and left the house at a run.

He didn't say good-bye to Jennine.

Jennine lay there, trying to summon up sleep. It didn't work.

She felt as if something was cracking inside her, as if she was one of JK's goddamn oxidant tanks, pumped full of pressure.

She got out of bed and walked barefoot to the bathroom. She had a couple of bottles of tranquilizers there.

She looked at herself in the mirror. She saw a slack, sagging woman, with worry lines etched into her face and tired, graying, mousy hair.

She took the pills, popping them into her mouth like jelly beans. The image in the mirror, the little pills pushing into the small, sour-looking mouth, was like watching somebody else, someone on TV maybe. She couldn't feel anything.

When she'd done, she threw the empty bottles into the trash, and went back to bed.

Even now, sleep wouldn't come.

After a time, she reached out for the phone and dialled Jack Morgan's home number. By a miracle he was there, and not throwing rum down his throat in some bar. She told him what she'd done.

* * *

433

At around six a.m., JK came running in, with his hair mussed and no tie and his shirt sticking out of his pants.

Jack Morgan was sitting on the bed, with an overcoat thrown over his pajamas, rubbing Jennine's limbs. 'Where the hell have you been? I called you an hour ago.'

JK started talking about the oxygen tank, and batches of contaminated nitrogen tet, and all the rest of it; but Jack just glared at him.

So JK broke off, and then he started trying to take command. 'Have you called a hospital? What about a stomach pump?' It was typical JK. Arrive too late, then order everyone else around.

'She doesn't need a pump,' Jack snapped back at him. 'But she's going to sleep for a hell of a long time. She should be asleep now. And then I want her to go into hospital, for observation.' He nodded at the bedside table. 'I've left a number there.'

JK, looking restless and bewildered, sat on the bed. Then he took Jennine's hand and began to rub, as Jack had been doing, along the length of her forearm. His hands were warm, but they were trembling, and his touch was uncertain, wavering between too hard and too soft. She managed to smile at him, and he seemed to get a little confidence, and the strokes evened out.

'This is a hell of a thing,' he said, his voice thin. 'A hell of a thing.'

'Listen to me,' Jack Morgan said. 'You've got to get your head out of your ass, JK. You've got to start paying some attention to your family. And yourself, come to that. Or Jennine is going to walk out on you, and nobody's going to blame her. In fact, I'll be here to drive her away.

'I'll come back in a couple of hours. You take care, Jennine.' And he went to get his coat, and she heard the door bang behind him.

JK looked devastated. He really hadn't seen this coming, she realized.

'So,' he said stiffly. 'I guess it was a cry for help, huh.'

Oh, JK. Pop psychology slogans. She closed her eyes and thought of the face in the mirror, the steady stream of pills passing her lips. *Have I really become such a cliche?*

JK sat silently for a while, rubbing her arm. And then he began jabbering about the tank failure. 'It was amazing,' he said. 'The tanks only blew when they were filled with nitrogen tet. So we knew there had to be some kind of chemical thing going on. But the tanks would only blow here, at Newport. We ran identical tests over at the manufacturers', in Indianapolis, and zippo.

'So we started doing a trace on the nitrogen tet. It comes from a big refinery run by the Air Force. And guess what we found? The stuff we had at Newport was from a later batch than the stuff at Indianapolis. Our stuff was purer. The Indianapolis batch had impurities, a tiny amount of water in it. So we set up another lab test back at Newport. And we found that when the nitrogen tet is *too* pure – better than ninety-nine per cent – it becomes corrosive! It attacks titanium! But add a dash of water, like in the Indianapolis batch, and the problem goes away. Anyhow, to hell with it. I think we're going to switch to oxygen-methane for our propellant. The performance is okay, and it's non-toxic, and we can store it easily for months in space, even if it isn't hypergolic . . .'

Jennine lay there listening to this, with her arm in JK's hands. He was full of his story by now, with the technological sleuthing and all the rest of it, and she could feel his hand jerk around, animated by the story-telling, quite oblivious of her flesh lying passively inside his.

She thought of the immense project, the pieces of the Mars ship flowing into the Newport assembly bays from every state in the Union: fuel and oxygen tanks from Buffalo and Boulder, instruments from Newark and Cedar Rapids, valves from San Fernando, electronics from Kalamazoo and Lima. And probably every one of those pieces left an invisible trail behind it, of drunkenness, and heart attacks, and smashed-up marriages.

She thought, oddly, that JK really ought to understand what had happened to her.

It's destructive testing, JK. That's all. Destructive testing.

Tuesday, August 10, 1982
Lyndon B. Johnson Space Center, Houston

'You're not going to let me fly.'

Joe Muldoon sat back in his office chair, which creaked under his weight. There was an empty Dr Pepper can on his desk, out of place among the executive stationery and leather blotters; he grabbed the can now and crushed it with a quick movement. 'It isn't like that, Natalie. I told you; I wanted to explain all this to you in person, myself, rather than let you hear it another way . . .'

'I appreciate that. But you're not going to let me fly.'

'You're not going to be the only disappointed dude in JSC. Look, I told you: because we lost that damn Saturn VB, and because we've had our budget pared even more – goddamn it, Natalie, the whole country's been in recession for a year; that's hardly my fault – because of all that we're having to compress the schedule. And we've still got a deadline to meet, an appointment with Mars. The crew of the first E-class mission will now fly a mission we're calling D-prime, which will combine the objectives of the old D and E classes. And –'

'So the D mission, my space soak mission, is gone. Joe, I know as much about Mars as anyone in the Astronaut Office. And you're not going to let me fly.'

Muldoon made a visible effort to control himself. 'Natalie, you have to believe this. It isn't personal. Except that I don't think this is such a loss. It's precisely *because* you know so much that you're a lot more use to me here, on the ground, than hanging around in some tin can in LEO watching the paintwork yellow. I need you here, Natalie. To teach us about Mars. To remind us why we're going there in the first place.'

She thought it over, trying to contain her anger. 'All right. What choice have I got? But I'm going to continue with my training, and my time in the sims, and I'm going to grab every bit of flight experience I can. And if you're telling me now you're going to stop me doing that, I'll be walking out of that door and I won't be back. Mars expert or not.'

He held his hands up. 'Enough! You've got yourself a deal, Natalie.'

She narrowed her eyes as a new suspicion entered her head. 'ERA,' she said.

He looked baffled. 'Huh?'

'The Equal Rights Amendment. It was thrown out in June.' She felt her anger blossom inside her, an unreasonable rage. 'The political climate's changing. Is *that* why you feel able to pick on me now?'

'Fuck it, Natalie, that's got nothing to do with it!' He leaned forward, visibly angry, unhappy. 'You know, you, and the other women, would get on a lot better around here if you didn't walk around with such goddamn immense chips on your shoulders.'

She glared at him. Muldoon sat tall in his chair, trim, sharp, irritated, studying her frankly, his blue eyes empty of calculation. He really believed that he was benefiting her with such advice, she saw; he couldn't see anything wrong with what he'd said.

She didn't trust herself to speak.

*　　*　　*

436

Later, in the dingy apartment she was renting in Timber Cove, she tried to get drunk, and failed.

Her life was going steadily down the toilet. At thirty-four she was getting old as a practicing scientist, and her academic career was probably beyond repair, now; her commitment to the space program – all those hours in sims and survival training – meant the time and energy she'd had to devote to her research just wasn't enough, and she knew that her papers, briefer and sparser every year, just weren't enough to enable her to prosper, if she returned to university.

And what had it all been for? She'd just lost her one chance – limited as it was – to get some genuine space experience.

She was further from Mars than ever.

It looked as if she'd blown it, as if she'd made one damn foul-up in her life after another.

Mike Conlig was ancient history. But she was still on her own. Generally that suited her.

But, God, she missed Ben.

Monday, December 6, 1982
Headquarters, Columbia Aviation, Newport Beach

The MEM simulator here at Newport was an ungainly assemblage, without much resemblance to the sleek lines of the final spacecraft shape. It looked like a car smash, surrounded by the blocky forms of mainframe computers, all laid out in this corner of the echoing, refurbished manufacturing shop.

Ralph Gershon clambered out of the simulator, pissed as all hell. 'That fucking thing is a lemon,' Gershon said. 'A big fat lemon, JK.'

JK Lee was waiting for him at the hatch, his round face creased with anxiety. 'Christ. Talk to me, Ralph.'

'Look,' Gershon said, 'the simulator's supposed to match the real thing – that's the whole point – it's no good looking for your left-hand joystick *here* when on the real thing it would be placed over *there*. JK, you got to keep these things up to date with the changes you're making to the design.'

'Hell, I know that, Ralph. But what can I do? The MEM design is still so fluid that there are always a couple of hundred changes outstanding, and so the sim never catches up with the real thing . . .'

'Oh, it's worse than that,' Gershon said. He pulled off his gloves and jammed them in his helmet. 'This thing doesn't even make sense in itself. The changes you *have* made aren't consistent.' He looked into Lee's anguished, stressed-out face; his sympathy for the man struggled with his anger. 'Look, JK, I'm going to raise Cain about this. That's my job, damn it. It's impossible to gain genuine experience with such a flawed sim – in fact, in my view the simulator itself is a severe danger to the overall progress of the project.'

Lee led him away from the sim and lit up a cigarette. 'Oh, Christ, tell me about it. Change is my bugbear, Ralph. Change is killing me.' He painted a picture of a whole industry ploughing its way toward Mars, a vast national network of craftsmanship and expertise slowly coming to focus on a single problem, and all of it flowing through this one site. 'We're working in places no one has touched before,' Lee said. 'It's not surprising nothing is right first time. So we get a *thousand* change requests a week, from all across the country. And every time we change something, every piece that component touches has to be modified as well. And I'll tell you who are the worst offenders.' He eyed Gershon. 'Your good buddies in the Astronaut Office.'

Gershon laughed. He wasn't surprised to hear it.

The astronauts still exerted a lot of power, official and unofficial. It was their asses on the line, after all. Lee was trying to get them all to submit to his change request process, just like everybody else, to keep everything orderly. But he was also aware of the need to keep this key group sweet. So he'd set up a private lounge for the astronauts, just down from his office, with a shower and a couple of fold-out beds, a place where they could sack out and hide from the press. And he'd take them home with him and have Jennine throw swank dinner parties for them, and make a hell of a fuss of them, and laud them to the skies. And the astronauts would come away thinking JK Lee was the greatest thing to have happened to the space program since the invention of Velcro.

At least, Gershon reflected, until he bounced their next request for a change.

Now Lee spotted something else, in another part of the shop floor. He stalked over to an operator of a six-ton turret lathe, who was shaving thin slices off an intricate aluminum sculpture. The thing looked beautiful, like a work of art; Gershon, who was supposed to be an expert on MEM systems, couldn't place it or identify its function. Lee picked up the engineering drawing the guy was working from. Then he called Gershon over; Lee was agitated, and the operator avoided Gershon's eyes, obviously embarrassed. Gershon felt sorry for him.

'Look at this,' Lee said, waving the drawing in front of Gershon.

'What about it?'

'We've got a policy that any drawing with more than a dozen changes has to be redrawn. This one must have over a hundred, for Christ's sake. And that's not the worst of it.' He picked up the component the operator had been modifying. 'This fucking thing is obsolete! I know it is! Even before it's been manufactured!' He threw the thing to the floor, where it landed with a clatter.

The operator, baffled, wiped his hands on a rag and looked around for his supervisor.

Lee stalked away, a tight little knot of tension; Gershon walked with him, his flight helmet under his arm.

Lee looked quite gaunt, his skin stretched tight as if by wires under the flesh, and his posture was stooped over. Lee was a man just eaten up by nervous energy and adrenaline.

Gershon had come to spend a lot of time here at Newport as the MEM had moved through its development. He'd served as a guinea pig for the life sciences boys, and he'd crawled in and out of hatches and down ladders to sand-pits stained red like Mars dust.

He'd spent hours in plywood-and-paint mockups of the spacecraft interior, trying to imagine that this was *real*, that he was all but alone on the far side of the Solar System, trying to bring a spacecraft down to Mars. Just like Pete Conrad.

He wanted nobody to know the MEM better than he did. Right now, he was achieving his goal.

He'd become aware that the whole place, the whole of Columbia Aviation, was kind of high-octane, driven forward by the relentless, destructive energy of JK Lee. And under the high pressure, and the enormous complexity of the project, the place always seemed on the point of being overwhelmed.

But Gershon still believed, as he had at the time of the RFP, that the Columbia vision of the MEM – inspired and led by JK Lee – was the best shot they had of building something that might actually work, sufficiently well to fly people down to Mars in a few years from now.

Gershon had been tough on Columbia himself. But basically he wanted the project to succeed. He wanted to fly to Mars, damn it, not hang JK Lee's scalp on his wall.

But, even as he framed that thought, he tripped over a wire, stretched across the floor. And when he looked down he saw more wires and loose components and discarded equipment: bits of spacecraft, scattered over the floor like detritus, washed up by the overwhelming tide of specification changes.

Monday, February 21, 1983
Ellington Air Force Base, Houston

Gershon, flight helmet under his arm, walked around the training vehicle. Natalie York walked with him, her hair lifted by the breeze, her sunglasses hiding her eyes.

Ralph Gershon couldn't help himself. '*That's* the MLTV? Holy shit,' he said.

Ted Curval, from Phil Stone's prime crew, was the senior astronaut assigned to oversee them for the day. Now, he just grinned. 'Your regulation Mars Landing Training Vehicle, Number Three. Brutal, ain't she?'

The Mars Landing Training Vehicle was an open framework, set on six landing legs. Gershon could see a down-pointing jet at the center, surrounded by a cluster of fuel tanks. Reaction control nozzles were clustered at the four corners of the frame, like bunches of metallic berries, and there were two big auxiliary rockets, also downwards-pointing. The pilot's cockpit was an ejector seat partially enclosed by aluminum walls, with a big, bold NASA logo painted on the side, under a black stenciled 'three.' The whole thing stood maybe ten feet high, with the legs around twelve feet apart. There was no skin, so you could see into the guts of the thing, jet and rockets and fuel tanks and plumbing and cabling and all; it was somehow obscene, as if flayed.

In the low morning sunlight the bird's complicated shadow stretched off across the tarmac of the wide runway.

'Shit,' Gershon said again, coming back to Curval. 'It's like something out of a fucking circus.'

'Tell me about it,' said Curval. 'But it's the nearest thing we got to a MEM trainer. You want to fly a MEM, you got to learn to handle one of these things, boy.' Curval was grinning, laughing at him.

Ted Curval was one of the Old Heads. A classic astronaut profile: a Navy test pilot, he'd even been an instructor at Pax River, and he'd logged up a lot of time in space already. Now, in the endless battle to climb up the Ares selection ladder, Curval had the great advantage of being from an earlier recruitment class than Gershon, and had already accrued plenty of live, free-flying MLTV experience. While the best Gershon had managed, for all his angling and hours spent at Columbia, had been some time on the tethered facility at Langley, where a MEM-type mockup dangled from cables.

So Curval was in Phil Stone's crew, and was on his way to Mars. And Ralph Gershon was still on the outside looking in.

But what the hell. As of today, Ralph Gershon would be able to add MLTV experience to his list of accomplishments. So screw Ted Curval, and all the other complacent assholes.

As far as Gershon was concerned the contest wasn't over until the bird left the pad, on April 21, 1985.

Gershon jammed his helmet on his head. He jumped up into the MLTV's open frame. With a single twist he was able to lower himself into the single seat. 'How about that. Just my size.'

Curval stepped forward. 'Hey, Gershon –'

Gershon was strapping himself in. 'The seat's a Weber zero-zero, right?'

'Come on down from there, man, you're not prepared. You're not supposed to –'

'And the jet back there is a General Electric CF-700-2V turbofan. Come on, Ted, I know the equipment. I've come out here to fly the thing, not listen to you yack about it.' He glanced down at the control panel: a few instruments, a CRT, a couple of handsets. Just like the sims.

He found himself blinking; the sun was strong, almost directly in his face, and his eyes hurt. On the plexiglass windscreen in front of him he could see reticles – fine lines – etched in there, labeled with numbers –

But suddenly the pain in his eyes amplified. 'Yow.' He threw his arm across his face. His eyes itched unbearably, and started to flood.

'For a start,' Curval called up dryly, 'you can close up your visor. You're being hit by hydrogen peroxide leaking from the attitude controls. You *sure* you know what you're doing, guy?'

Gershon snapped shut his visor and squeezed his eyes closed. 'Let me bust my neck, Ted. It's my neck. What do you care?'

'Okay,' Curval said at length. 'Okay, you win.'

Curval, with York, went over to the control truck and clambered in the back. In a moment, Gershon heard Curval's crisp voice sounding in his flight headset. 'Okay, Ralph. What we're going to do is take the MLTV up fifty feet, twice around the block, and back

441

home again, just as nice as pie. Just to let you get the feel of her. And then you're coming out for an eye bath. You got that?'

'Sure.'

Gershon kicked in the jet, and there was a roar at his back. Dust billowed up off the ground, into his face. Vapor puffed out of the attitude nozzles, as if this was some unlikely steam engine, a Victorian engineer's fantasy of flight.

The runway tarmac fell away. The lift was a brief, comforting surge. The MLTV was like a noisy elevator.

Gershon whooped. 'Whee-hoo! Now we is hangin' loose!'

Of MLTV Number Three's four cousins, two had crashed during the last half-year. The pilots had ejected and walked away. Nobody was sure about the cause. Well, vertical takeoff and land vehicles were notoriously unstable; maybe you had to expect a percentage of failures. The hope was that these crashes weren't showing up fundamental flaws in the design of the MEM itself.

Anyhow, the MLTV itself still needed test flights. Nobody was too keen to risk it, right now, so far away from the Mars landing itself.

Nobody except somebody so desperate to get on the selection roster they'd do all but anything.

Gershon took the MLTV up to maybe sixty feet, and slowed the ascent.

The principles of the strange craft were obvious enough. You stood on your jet's tail. You kept yourself stable with the four peroxide reaction clusters, the little vernier rockets spaced around the frame, squirting them here and there. In fact, he found, he didn't even need to work the RCS control when he was trying to hold the craft level; the little rockets would fire by themselves, in little solenoid bangs and gas hisses.

He experimented with his controls. He had a full three hundred and sixty degree yaw capability, he found; he could make the MLTV rotate around its vertical axis, back and forth. He whooped as the world wheeled around him. And he had some pitch and roll control: he could make the vehicle tip this way and that. But when he tried it, of course, the thrust of his single big downwards jet was at an angle to the vertical, and he'd find himself shooting forwards, or sideways, or backwards across the painted tarmac –

Curval shouted in his ear. 'Hey, take it easy!'

—and that was evidently the way you had to fly a MEM. But

he had to take care not to tip too far in any direction, or he could feel the stability start to go.

The low sunlight got in his eyes, which were still watering, and made it hard to read his instruments.

He came to rest perhaps a hundred feet above the ground, facing the control truck.

'Maybe you should get back down here for that eye bath, Ralph,' Curval said.

'So how much fuel does this thing carry?'

'Enough for maybe seven minutes.'

'And how long would a landing sequence take?'

'Ralph –'

'Tell me.'

'Three, four minutes.'

He checked his watch; he'd been up here no more than two minutes. Time to spare.

He took the MLTV straight up in the air.

'Ralph, get your ass down here!'

'There's only one way I'm coming down, bubba, and that's by a Powered Descent.'

'You're not trained for this.'

'I've done over fifty sims. Come on, man. I know what I'm doing. This bird is working as sweet as a clock. Let me bring her in.'

Curval sounded as if he was choking. 'Goddamn it, you asshole, you smash up that trainer and I'll sue you myself.'

Gershon grinned. 'Sure.' What, after all, could Curval do? Nothing, as long as Gershon was up here, and Curval was stuck down there.

Gershon took her to three hundred feet. 'This high enough to initiate?'

He could hear Curval take a few breaths. 'Find the button for the automatic control sequence.'

Gershon found it and pushed. The jet throttled back, and the MLTV dipped briefly. Then a new, throaty rocket roar opened up, and the trainer stabilized.

'All right,' Curval said. 'Now, the secret of the MLTV is that it has *two* independent propulsion systems. Right now, your turbofan jet is throttling back to absorb two-thirds of your weight. So if everything else cut out, you'd fall under one-third of G – just like on Mars. You got that? The jet is knocking out gravity, just enough to make it feel like Mars.'

'Sure.'

443

'But you don't fall, because of the two hydrogen peroxide lift rockets under your ass which have just cut in to hold you up. And it's the lift rockets which are emulating the landing system of the MEM, and that's what you have to control to bring her in to land. You throttle down the rockets until you land. Like an ICBM trying to land on its tail.'

'Okay.'

'You got two more controls there, Ralph. Your attitude control on the right, and your thrust control on the left. You want to try those babies out?'

'Sure.'

The controls were familiar to Gershon from his sim runs. The attitude control moved in clicks; every time he turned the control the reaction rockets would bang and the MLTV would tip over, by a degree at a time. The thrust control was a toggle switch; every time Gershon closed it the lift rockets roared, to give her a delta-vee of a foot per second.

After the free-flight mode it was surprisingly difficult to handle the trainer; it was like being immersed in some viscous, sticky liquid. Because of the one-third effective gravity, he had to tip the bird three times as far as before to get the same push in any direction. And once he started moving, he just kept on going, until he changed the attitude again, and the craft took some time to respond because of the sluggishness. He found that he had to think out the simplest maneuver well in advance.

Flying like this – balancing on a rocket – was harder than he'd expected, harder than any of the sims had led him to believe. Everything he had painfully learned in a lifetime of flying planes, he realized now, was useless.

'Okay, guy. Now, you got a little computer up there running a PGNS program for you.' Curval pronounced it *pings*. PGNS was a guidance and navigation software package. 'If you're such a hotshot sim jockey, you don't need me to tell you how you got to let the computer fly you down. All you get to do is to point and squirt –'

'I know it. Come on, Ted. I'm running out of juice out here. Let me bring this thing down.'

'Okay. First off, look through your windshield and pick a place you want to come down. And you'll see a number on your CRT –'

Gershon peered out. He saw a fat number 'three' stenciled on the tarmac, maybe a quarter-mile away; it would be kind of fitting

444

to come down slap in the middle of that, in this MLTV Number Three.

He used his attitude controller to tip up the MLTV until the numbered marking on his windshield overlying the target matched the number displayed by the computer on the CRT. 'Thirty-eight,' he called out to Curval.

The MLTV started to float toward the target. Now, the PGNS program was computing a trajectory to take him to the 'three' – or rather, to a position just above it.

'I don't know the math behind it,' Curval said, 'but you got to know the basics, Ralph, to follow the logic of this thing, here.'

'I know it.'

'The PGNS works by the same system, basically, as the old Lunar Module. And there's enough equipment on the MLTV, a computer and a radar, to let you do a complete Powered Descent. What you have is your computer taking your *current* position and velocity, and your *target* vector – which will be hovering, just above the ground – and it works out a nice smooth curve between the two for you to follow. Every couple of seconds, it recomputes, and figures out another curve. And the numbers it flashes up on the CRT tell you where to look on your reticles, and you should see your computed landing site right there, behind the mark.'

'I got it.' He swept across the tarmac, smooth, easy.

'If you want to change the landing site you just use your attitude control to swivel and point your window, and the PGNS starts recomputing. You can set to ATTITUDE HOLD and just glide for a while, if you like. And you can change your down velocity by –'

'I know it, Ted. I –'

Now York came on the line. 'Ralph. It's Natalie. I think you ought to pull out.'

'Huh? Why?'

'You're coming in too fast. Too low.'

He checked over the crude instrument panel. Everything looked fine to him. It was true he was coming in low and fast, but that was intentional; he knew Curval's gassing hadn't left him a lot of time, and he didn't want to run out of fuel. 'What's your problem, York?'

'I think you're going to overload the PGNS.'

'Come on. Everything up here is sweet as a nut.'

'It's not as simple as that, Ralph.' She started talking about best-fitting polynomials and higher-order curves, and a lot of other crap that went right over Gershon's head.

He just tuned her out.

He watched the tarmac roll away under him. He swept along, the PGNS working smoothly; he barely needed to touch his controls. He felt a surge of success, of achievement. *Here's something else I can do, ma. Another step on the long fucking ladder I'm climbing to Mars.*

He'd just let her land, this first time through. He'd made his point; he didn't want to antagonize Curval too much. Maybe he could persuade Curval to get the MLTV refueled and he could take her up again. Next time he'd try changing the landing site a couple of times.

That big old 'three' started to loom up toward him, upside down as he looked at it, slightly obscured by the dust his rockets and the jet were kicking up.

Now the MLTV tipped itself back, to slow his forward velocity. He checked his numbers; the CRT display evolved smoothly to match what he saw through his plexiglass screen.

The MLTV started to drop down as the auxiliary thrusters throttled themselves back.

Maybe that dip down *was* a little sharp.

York was still yammering in his ear. He needed to think. He watched his trajectory and tried to visualize where he was going.

Something was wrong, for sure. He was coming down too quickly.

He let another couple of seconds wear away, checking his instinct. Yes: his trajectory was a tight downward curve that would bring him to the ground maybe a hundred yards short of the 'three.'

Well, so what? Maybe the PGNS was out by a little; maybe all these damn reticles on the window needed recalibrating. If he came to a smooth halt in mid-air, but short of his target, he could blame fucked-up equipment . . .

But he wasn't coming to any smooth halt. The lift rockets were cutting right back, and he was starting to fall, hard, toward the ground.

York and Curval were both shouting at him.

He watched the ground explode toward him, resolving into unwelcome detail, bits of dirt and dust and concrete ridging high-lighted by the low morning sun.

He pushed the button to disable the automatics.

He didn't waste time trying to straighten up the MLTV's attitude; instead he just throttled up the turbofan jet and let it push him away from the ground. He felt a surge of acceleration, a good

446

crisp couple of G, strong enough to keep him away from Earth's unwelcome clutch.

He pulled up maybe a hundred feet from the ground. He throttled back the turbofan, and landed softly.

York ran toward the downed MLTV.

Technicians in white protective suits surrounded the trainer. Ralph Gershon had already climbed out. His hair had been compressed flat by his flight helmet, and his face, released now from behind the visor, was round and shining with sweat. His eyes were bright red, she guessed from the dose of peroxide he'd taken earlier.

'You asshole, Gershon,' Curval said. 'I told you that if you wrecked the trainer –' Curval towered over Gershon, his hands bunched into heavy fists. He started to chew out Gershon.

In a way the anger was justified, York knew; if Gershon, with his gung-ho heroics, had got himself killed, or smashed up a key piece of equipment like the MLTV, he could have put the whole program back a long way. York decided Gershon needed the bawling out, and she let it run on for a couple of minutes.

Then she stepped forward, putting herself between the two of them. 'Actually,' she said, 'none of it was Ralph's fault.'

Curval turned to face her, still high on his anger.

'It was the landing program. I think it has a bug, Ralph. It nearly killed you.' She turned to Curval. 'We can prove it by running Ralph's trajectory through the sims a couple of times.'

Curval said, 'What the hell do you know about programming?'

She sighed. 'Not a hell of a lot. But I'm the big-brained, tight-assed college girl, remember? It's not my field, but I've done enough math to know how routines like the PGNS work.

'Look.' She mimed the MLTV coming down. 'The PGNS tries to fit a smooth curve between your position and velocity, at any time, and your destination. But it isn't magic. It's just math. And it has its limitations.

'The curves the program uses are polynomials. Smooth curves, with wiggles. The higher the order of the polynomial, the more the curve will wiggle about. You don't have an infinite choice of curves; it's like trying to fit a template out of a fixed set to suit the job. And the more complicated the data you feed the program, the more the polynomial will have to wiggle to fit your data points. You see? '

'So why is this bad?' Gershon asked with a kind of fake innocence. 'And why do I need to know about it?'

447

She struggled to keep her patience. '*Because the program doesn't know the ground is there.* It's not like a human pilot, Ralph. It's really pretty dumb. All PGNS is doing is fitting a curve to two positions in space. It doesn't care how much the curve wiggles in between. And if one of those oscillations happens to carry you down *into* the ground, and up again –'

Curval whistled. 'So because Ralph was flying low and fast –'

'The polynomial solutions, the best the PGNS could come up with, were high order. Full of wiggles.'

'Helicopter experience,' Gershon muttered.

York was confused by the non-sequitur. 'Huh?'

'Helicopter experience. That's a nice bird, and it's easy enough to fly. But it goes against everything, every instinct you build up flying a plane.' He obviously hadn't listened to her. Or maybe he had taken in what she'd said, as much as he felt he needed to know, and had moved on to his next thought, the next step of his inexorable approach to Mars. 'If that's the way the MEM is going to handle, anybody with a lot of chopper proficiency is going to have an edge. That's obvious.'

'And you have, I suppose?'

'No. But I will soon.'

His helmet under his arm, he stalked off across the tarmac, short, purposeful, bristling with determination, back toward the MLTV.

Curval scratched the back of his crew-cut head. 'What a day. What an asshole.'

Maybe, York thought. *But he looks to me like an asshole who is going to Mars.*

November, 1983
Newport Beach

As he walked into the low fieldstone building that served as office space for Columbia's executives, Gershon could all but smell the tension in the air.

The CARR was to be held in a big bleak conference room here. The CARR, the Contractor's Acceptance Readiness Review, was a major event in the life of a spacecraft, the moment when it was judged to have met the specifications of the contract and became the property of the United States government. And since Spacecraft 009 was the first MEM designated for a manned mission – the

448

man-rating D-prime flight – the pressure on Columbia Aviation to get this CARR right was intense.

There were a dozen senior NASA managers, and a lot of the top people from Columbia involved in the project: Chaushui Xu, Bob Rowen, Julie Lye and others. People Gershon had got to know well.

But the CARR was starting late.

JK Lee, the chairman for the day, hadn't turned up for work yet. In fact, the word was, he hadn't shown up at all since Friday afternoon; here it was Monday morning, and everyone knew that Lee normally worked right through the weekend. Gershon felt vaguely disturbed. This sure as hell wasn't like Lee.

Gershon got himself a coffee and a bag of peanuts from one of the ubiquitous vending machines.

Without a single article having yet left the ground for a flight test, the MEM program was suffering very visible delays and failures and cost overruns. Columbia was coming in for a huge amount of criticism: from NASA, from the Congress, from other subcontractors.

In fact Gershon knew that Joe Muldoon had gotten so impatient with what he saw as lax management of the project that he'd ordered a 'tiger team' review of the whole thing. It was a technique NASA had borrowed from the Air Force. The tiger team, led by Phil Stone, had a free hand to descend on Columbia's plant and rake through any and all aspects of the operation. Gershon knew that the tiger team was likely to be here today, even in the middle of the CARR review; and their draft summary report was all but completed. This, and the CARR, were in addition to the usual review process, which might involve as many as four hundred NASA staff out here at Newport, looking over the shoulders of the Columbia staff. It all added to the pressures, already barely tolerable, on JK Lee and his people.

Now JK Lee came bustling in at last, his tie on crooked, a fat stack of papers under his right arm. He was holding his left arm a little stiffly, Gershon thought. He dumped his papers on a lectern at the front of the room, and spent a few minutes glad-handing some of the NASA people.

Then he went up to the lectern and called for order.

'Okay,' he opened. 'This is the CARR for Spacecraft 009. It's a meeting specifically concerned with 009 and its suitability to leave the plant, here, and begin the checkout procedures and booster mating procedures down at the Cape. We should try not to get

449

ourselves tangled up with design changes; we're concerned with the specific checkout of *this* spacecraft as it is presently configured.'

He faced his audience. 'Now, it's not a meeting where I want to see us bring up old bitches. We know the ship has been moving slowly. I acknowledge that. In fact it's still not completely through all of its tests, so the CARR is in that sense somewhat provisional. But I intend to go ahead with it anyway . . .'

There was some grumbling at that, but nobody protested out loud.

Gershon picked up his thick briefing papers.

Under Lee's bustling chairmanship, the meeting began to work its way through the list of problems. Most of them were minor, and had been hashed over in previous sessions. Lee tried to keep the discussion short on each point, cutting off arguments and sum- marizing the mood of the group in a series of Action Responses for each itemized problem.

Even so, the list of items to be reviewed was so long that it was soon obvious to Gershon that the CARR was going to go on for many hours; maybe it wouldn't even finish that day.

Still, Lee was in good form today, Gershon thought. He was hyped up, but he took them briskly through the items. He arbitrated disagreements, joking and laughing. It made for a good atmosphere, relaxed and constructive and with plenty of humor.

But Lee still seemed to be having trouble with that left arm of his. He rubbed it frequently, up around the armpit, and he was having difficulty standing for long periods.

Lunch was a finger buffet. Gershon gulped down a quick plateful. Lee sought him out, and invited him to take a walk around the plant. Gershon appreciated that, and accepted. Right now it might have been more politically astute for Lee to be oiling up to the NASA bigwigs. And Gershon hadn't exactly been uncritical of Col- umbia, over the years. But Lee had evidently never forgotten the favor that Gershon had done him, by pushing the MEM RFP his way in the first place.

They reached the Clean Room. Here, the four flight test articles were being assembled, in antiseptic conditions. Lee and Gershon had to sign in, and they had to put on white coats and soft plastic overshoes and tuck their hair inside little plastic caps with elas- ticated brims. They were given strict instructions by the foreman to keep to the marked paths, and *away* from the spacecraft if you please.

The Room stretched off in all directions, white-walled and illuminated by brilliant fluorescents. Clusters of workmen, all kitted out in soft hats and overshoes, toiled at huge pieces of equipment. There was a soft murmur of conversation, a clank of metal on metal, a whir of machinery. Huge winches and cranes dangled from the reinforced roof, empty and potent.

The Clean Room reminded Gershon more of a sculptor's foundry than a factory; there was no sense of the routine here. Only a handful of MEMs would ever be built, and so everything here was new, special, a one-of-a-kind.

And in the middle of all this, four conical shapes were starting to emerge, as if crystalizing from some superconcentrated solution. They looked like religious artifacts, Gershon thought, like four pyramids in a row, with their silvery, shining skins punctured by mysterious nozzles and inscribed windows.

This was the mark of Lee's achievement, Gershon reflected. Amid all the management chaos – and blizzards of changes, and balky subcontractors, and awkward customers, and engineering unknowns, and cost overruns – JK Lee was creating something magical: four Mars ships, coalescing on a factory floor in Newport Beach.

Beside each of the cones there was a sign: *This is a Manned Spacecraft. Your PRIDE – Personal Responsibility In Daily Effort – will ensure their safe return.*

Lee grinned. 'Something I stole from McDonnell,' he said. He kept on rubbing his arm, and he looked drawn and tired, with none of the intense energy Gershon had come to associate with him. Maybe the CARR was taking it out of him.

They stopped alongside one of the four glittering spacecraft. 'Spacecraft 009,' Lee said. 'The subject of the CARR today; the first MEM intended to carry a crew. How about that.'

The MEM loomed over Gershon, all of thirty feet tall, like some fat metal teepee. The shining heat-resistant skin was incomplete in many places, and he was able to see the subsystems in the interior, exposed as if this was some big cutaway model.

He could make out the overall layout of the ship. There was the slim shaft of the ascent stage at the axis of the teepee – a spacecraft buried within a spacecraft – with the angular, truncated crew cabin at its tip. And there at the base of the MEM was the fat half-torus that was the surface shelter, with the curving access tunnel snaking upwards to the ascent stage cabin at the top of the stack. And opposite the shelter, balancing its weight, were propellant and

451

oxidant tanks: big spheres for the descent stage, squat cylinders for the ascent stage, grouped in an asymmetrical cluster like big shining berries.

A service platform, on wheels, had been set up beside the MEM. Corrugated walkways snaked over from the platform into the interior of the MEM, and Gershon could see workmen in white coveralls on their bellies in there, laboring over wiring, control panels, ducts and pipes, like little worms crawling around inside the gleaming machine.

Gershon ducked down to get a view of the interior of the surface shelter. He could see the big storage lockers, which would hold the Mars surface suits and EVA equipment. The pale green walls of the shelter were encrusted with control panels, twenty-four of them, and five hundred switches. There were warning lights everywhere. Here and there loose wiring spilled out of an open panel, but some of the panels and lights were already operational, and they glowed softly, sending complex highlights off the experiment tables and science equipment.

Gershon could have drawn this layout blindfolded. After so many years with Columbia, so many hours in simulators here and at the Cape and Houston, he knew the position of every damn switch. He could even lay claim to have designed half the panels he saw from here.

There was a scent of wiring, of lubricant, of ozone, of fresh-milled metal. The MEM was unfinished, but it had a *live* feel to it, much more so than any simulator. It was like the cockpit of a new, gleaming aircraft.

And it was *homely*. It was the kind of den Gershon would have loved to have owned as a kid, a mixture of workshop, radio station and clubhouse.

He would have no trouble living in here for a month, on Mars, he realized now; no trouble at all.

If he got himself the chance.

There was some kind of commotion going on, and Gershon straightened up to see.

Jack Morgan stalked down toward Lee and Gershon with a document in his hand. 'JK! Have you seen this?'

Gershon recognized the document as a draft summary of Phil Stone's tiger team review of the MEM program. It was a photocopy marked 'Confidential'; Gershon guessed that some sympathizer inside NASA had leaked it to the Columbia people.

452

Lee started flicking through it, speed-reading. 'Jesus Christ,' he said. 'Jesus Christ.'

Jack Morgan stood there, clenching and unclenching his fists.

Lee looked to Gershon like he was trembling, and he kept twitching that left arm, as if it was giving him severe pain. 'Listen to this. "I am definitely not satisfied with the progress and outlook of the program . . . I could not find a substantive basis for confidence in future performance . . ." Paper-pushing cocksucker! "My people and I have completely lost confidence in the ability of Columbia Aviation's competence as an organization . . . I seriously question whether there is any sincere intent and determination by Columbia to do this job properly . . ."'

Jack Morgan's own anger seemed to have dissipated as he studied Lee. 'JK, what is it with you and that arm?'

Lee waved both arms in the air. 'Screw my arms! Listen to this: "I think NASA has to resort to very drastic measures, including the possibility of shifting to a new contractor . . ."'

Morgan, frowning, grabbed Lee's right elbow. 'Listen to *me*, asshole. You're coming to my office right now.'

Lee tried to shake loose, but Morgan wouldn't let go, and with a nod he instructed Gershon to get a hold of the other arm.

Gershon, hesitantly, got hold of Lee's bony elbow.

So Morgan and Gershon frogmarched JK Lee out of the Clean Room, past goggling technicians, all three of them still in their soft shoes and their hats and white coats.

Lee waved the report around, shouting like some Old Testament prophet. '"For me, it is just unbearable to deal further with a non-performing contractor who has the government over a barrel when it comes to a multi-billion-dollar venture of such national importance . . ." And screw you too, Mr Phil fucking Stone!'

They reached Morgan's office, and Morgan pulled up a portable EKG machine.

Lee eyed the machine. 'What's this?'

'Roll up your sleeves, JK.'

'There's nothing wrong with my heart.' Lee dropped to the floor and, to Gershon's astonishment, started doing push-ups. 'Look at this!' Lee shouted up at Morgan, twisting his head. 'If I was having a heart attack this would kill me.'

Jack Morgan ignored Lee's antics. He bent down and grabbed Lee by the collar, and simply hauled him to his feet. He shoved Lee into a chair and began to strap in the EKG leads.

Lee still had the Stone report. 'Look at this! He's even put on a

453

list of the people who should be fired! Including you and me, Jack! Cocksucker!'

Morgan read the EKG trace. He looked at Lee. 'You're going to the hospital.'

'Bullshit,' Lee snapped. 'I'm in the middle of a fucking CARR.' He got up and headed for the door.

Morgan simply blocked the door with his body. He nodded to Gershon. 'Get on the phone to Mr Cane,' he ordered him. 'Tell him he has to speak to Lee.' And he turned and shouted to an assistant to send for the paramedics.

Uncertain of what he was getting himself into, Gershon picked up the phone.

Lee kept reading the report. 'Look at this shit. Missed deadlines. Late drawing releases. Cost overruns. Yeah, yeah. But don't they understand how *complex* this thing is? Or what chaos their own people create down here every time they allow through another *change*? Look, you can comb through the paper trail all you want, but you got to look at the fucking *hardware*. Sure, we're behind schedule. But this is a joke.' He appealed to Morgan. 'It's a fucking witch hunt, Jack. That's what it is. A witch hunt.'

Gershon held the phone out to Lee. 'Art Cane wants to talk to you.'

Lee took the phone.

Art Cane ordered him to leave the plant.

A couple of paramedics came running up the corridor. They had a wheelchair with them.

JK Lee looked around, bewildered, still wearing his Clean Room overshoes and plastic hat.

The paramedics got him into the chair, ignoring his vague protests, and rushed him out.

Morgan lit up a cigarette, his hands trembling.

Gershon found he was shaking too. 'Christ,' he said to Morgan. 'I didn't know.'

Morgan pulled off his plastic hat. 'Really? Hell, JK's not the only one who's nearly killed himself on this fucking program. Haven't you heard about it? They call it the Ares Syndrome.'

It had been a coronary, all right; it hit Lee soon after the medics got him to the hospital.

When Lee came to himself – a couple of days later, flat on his back in the hospital – the first thing he did was get a secure phone installed in his room, and he started calling the plant.

454

He found the place in an uproar.

The final draft of Phil Stone's tiger team report was, if anything, even more damning than that leaked early summary. And there was a lot of wild talk in the press of NASA going to another contractor for the MEM.

After a point the speculation seemed to feed on itself – Lee had even seen articles *about* the number of articles that had appeared on the MEM problems. It seemed to Lee that his people were spending more time on rooting through all the press garbage and the gossip from NASA and in-house than they were on building a spacecraft.

Well, as far as Lee was concerned it was all a lot of bull; there was no way NASA could pull out of Columbia if it wanted to preserve anything like its 1986 Mars landing target. It was just bullying, industrial blackmail.

But Columbia had to respond.

Art Cane, in Lee's absence, ordered yet another internal audit.

In the days that followed, a high-powered team went right through the whole program, interviewing hundreds of people. They had kept everything confidential; they'd even used rooms which they'd checked were clear of bugs in advance. That was supposed to reassure the employees, but Lee knew that sure as hell it would scare the life out of them.

And the early results of *that* audit looked like being as hard-hitting as Stone's.

Lee, lying there helpless, seethed. *There's nothing wrong with the goddamn program. They're pulling my organization apart for nothing. This is a witch hunt.*

And all of it while Lee was conveniently out of the office. All his people were worried about their own positions, and about the future of Lee himself.

So Lee called up Jack Morgan and told him he wanted out.

Morgan protested, of course. Lee had been in the hospital little more than two weeks.

Morgan came to the hospital, and he brought Jennine, to try to persuade him to stay.

'JK, you're stuck here for another two weeks at least, maybe a month.'

Lee was furious. His anger at the betrayal by his own body seemed to course through him like nitrogen tetroxide, a volatile substance that was burning him up. He got out of bed and started

455

doing push-ups again. 'See?' he gasped. 'For Christ's sake, what is wrong with you people? Can't you see – '

But Jennine was screaming. She had her hands clasped to her cheeks, so that her face was a thin, moist ribbon, compressed between the palms of her hands.

'Stop it. *Stop it*, JK.'

They came to a compromise. He was out of there three weeks after the attack.

The deal was that he was supposed to stay home, working if he really had to, for another couple of weeks at least.

He tried to watch TV. There was some godawful depressing thing called *The Day After*, about a nuclear attack on Lawrence, Kansas; everyone said he should watch it.

After the first hour he threw the remote across the room. He'd always hated Jason Robards, anyhow.

After two days he couldn't stand the isolation any more, and he got the T-bird out of the garage.

Jennine didn't try to stop him. She just watched him preparing to go. It made him uncomfortable to look her in the eye, to meet that bruised look there.

When he got to work the plant was in chaos. It was worse than he had expected, with NASA people still crawling all over the goddamn place, and Art Cane bouncing off the walls of his office, convinced he was going to lose the MEM contract.

So Lee tried to get a hold of his program again.

First he kicked out all the outsiders, the NASA people and the rest, whom he regarded as not strictly necessary for the progress of the MEM. It took him a day just to do that, and he had a lot of opposition from the NASA bigwigs, of course, but he did it anyhow.

Still, it worried him a little that Art Cane's backing in this was muted.

Then he spent a couple of days working through the two audit reports, and blue-penciling the politics and the waffle and the ill-informed and the downright goddamn *stupid*. And there was a hell of a lot of that.

The auditors, both internal and external, had gone for what he considered to be easy meat: schedule delays and paperwork snarl-ups and procedural problems. To Lee, schedules on paper were all very well – you had to produce them for senior management, and they were always the best guess you could make, and you had to keep a weather eye on them – but the fact was, half the time

456

Columbia didn't know what they were trying to build here, or what the latest batch of test results would throw at them, or what the latest flood of changes from the design teams at Marshall, Houston and elsewhere would bring. In a program like the MEM you couldn't expect actually to *stick* to a schedule. The delays certainly weren't a question of his people's *competence*, as far as Lee was concerned; they were more a measure of the inherent complexity of what they were trying to do here.

Columbia was building a *spacecraft*, for God's sake; and you only had to walk through the Clean Room, to see the four beautiful test articles emerging, to understand that basically, at the heart of all the paper storms, JK Lee was succeeding.

He tried to distil the reports down to what he considered to be the elements of common sense, of valid criticism, and then act on them. For instance the auditors had found poor demarcation of work areas, and sloppy handling of materials, and so forth. Well, he wasn't going to argue about that kind of thing. Lee fired off memos, and called in people to chew ass, and demanded some fixing.

After a few days of this he went to see Art Cane, and he was able to throw the two fat audit reports across the desk at Art. Every paragraph of each report had been blue-penciled by Lee, either as completed, with a fat tick, or as irrelevant bullshit, in which case he'd just scribbled it out.

Cane leafed through the stuff, looking a little dubious; but he accepted what Lee had given him, and told him to write up his responses to the reports formally.

Next, Lee got everyone at the plant involved in the MEM program – there were almost a thousand of them by now – to come squeezing into the big, roomy old canteen. The room was still used as the main conference room, and its walls were lined with multicolored schedule boards and progress charts. Lee got a photograph of their prime MEM, Spacecraft 009, blown up so it covered the wall behind him – the great complex silver pyramid made a beautiful image – and he stood on a table in front of his people. He put his hands on his hips, and glared out at the sea of pinched-up, worried faces around him.

'Now, I know times have been tough for you guys. I know you got a lot of people crawling all over you saying you don't know your butts from third base. And we did get some things wrong. But now we're fixing them, and that's healthy. And I know, deep down – and *you* know – that there's nothing fundamentally wrong with the way we're working here. And I know there's nothing wrong with the spacecraft, either. If NASA want to fly in April –' the target date for the D-prime mission, the first manned flight '– then we'll be ready for them.

'I want you to forget about everything else, now, except that first flight. We're going to focus on this one spacecraft here, and make it work; because if we can complete that flight well, believe me, all the rest of the program is going to slot into place, *bang bang bang,* just like that.

'And I know one thing more.' He looked around at their faces, all somehow smoothed out by the way they were tilted up at him, made to look younger; he felt a surge of protectiveness. 'One thing more. I know I couldn't ask for a better group of people to work with. Now, let's get back to work, and let's make history.'

Well, this was a standard spiel for Lee, a version of a talk he'd used at tough times on many projects. A standard-issue motivator. On the B-70, it had even gotten him a cheer.

But this time, although there were a lot of nodding heads, nobody cheered; and when he was done, they just turned away, and drifted back to their work stations.

He got down off the rickety table, with a hand from Jack Morgan. He had a sick feeling, deep in the pit of his stomach. He felt isolated, somehow vulnerable.

Maybe it was his heart, letting him down again.

The hell with it. Leaning a little on Jack Morgan, he started prowling around the plant, trying to pinpoint problems, bawling out technicians, riding herd on his program managers as hard as he could.

Tuesday, November 8, 1983
Lyndon B. Johnson Space Center, Houston

Joe Muldoon wasn't a happy man.

He had a decision to make, and today was the day he had to make it.

He had the three names of his prime Ares crew – the Commander, the Mission Specialist and the Mars Excursion Module Pilot – written out on a piece of paper on his desk.

CDR: Stone. MSP: Bleeker. MMP: Curval.

Less than eighteen months before Ares was supposed to leave the ground, the heat was on NASA over its crew selection – which still

458

hadn't been announced to the public – and NASA, in turn, was turning up the heat on Joe Muldoon, who was responsible for that selection.

The scientific community was going ape shit about the fact that all three astronauts on the prime Mars crew were from the military. Adam Bleeker – while he was doing fine in the freshman-standard geology classes York was mounting, and while everyone acknowledged he was an intelligent, competent, experienced astronaut – was, according to the egg-heads, a completely crazy choice for the Mission Specialist slot. The National Academy of Sciences and the US Geological Survey were throwing around a lot of crap about the fact that NASA even had a fully qualified Mars surface scientist, in Natalie York, but wasn't planning to give her even a seat on the mission. And all the other scientists in the corps, the geochemists and geophysicists and life scientists, had been overlooked as well.

It was Apollo all over again, they said.

Well, York had shown she could do a good job under pressure, on her assignment as Apollo-N capcom for instance, and she'd been putting in an impressive amount of time in the sims. She could probably handle the flight.

Muldoon knew that putting York on the mission as the MSP would shut up the science lobby for sure. And, he reflected, assigning York would have the side-benefit of closing down another couple of lobbies – the minority-interest ones – which complained long and hard about the way NASA still supposedly discriminated in favor of sending up white males.

He wrote out that list of names, now, to see how it would look:

CDR: Stone. MSP: York. MMP: Curval.

But York was a rookie.

He remembered what York herself had said, back at the time of her selection interviews. *We need to get a scientist on Mars. But a dead scientist on Mars wouldn't do anybody any good.* The fact was, you weren't talking about a trolley-car ride here but an extended deep-space mission using complex, edge-of-the-envelope technology.

Sometimes, when he reflected on what they were doing here, it grabbed at his imagination. They were planning to send three people in a fragile collection of tin cans across forty million miles – and then hope that the engineering being cooked up in Lee's ramshackle operation in Newport Beach, and whatever discipline could be adapted from a lifetime of aviation in Earth's atmosphere, were

459

capable of bringing them safely down to the surface of an alien world. Plumbing, TV cameras and all.

The scale – the audacity of it all – stunned him, when he let himself think about it. And *he*, he reminded himself, had walked on the Moon.

Maybe, as many people argued, they were going too far, too fast . . .

He shrugged that off. Be that as it may, they were going.

As far as Muldoon was concerned it was better to get *somebody* down to that surface to do at least *some* science, no matter how dumb. And, the way he saw it, the way to maximize the chances of achieving that was to send up his three best aviators: people who had cut their teeth in the most extraordinary physical situations the home planet had to offer. And hope that was enough for Mars . . .

Also, while he was impressed by York, there was something about her which unsettled him a little. *All that intensity.* She'd come into NASA with a great big grudge against the world, and it was still there, and getting bigger all the time, as far as he could see. *Those goddamn twitching eyebrows of hers.* She would drive her crewmates crazy in a month.

York wasn't ready. It was a shame.

He crossed out the draft list.

Anyhow, it wasn't the MSP but the MMP seat that was giving him the most grief at the moment.

He was hearing a lot of bad things from the mission controllers, and others, about Ted Curval's performance.

Curval was one of the best test pilots Muldoon had worked with. And Phil Stone, his commander, was intensely loyal to him. But Curval's attitude looked to be a little bit off beam.

Curval was fucking arrogant. He was taking his seat for granted. He seemed to feel it was sufficient to just turn up, and laugh his way through the training, and expect just to be able to crawl into the MEM when the time came, and everything would be fine. His performance in the sims, for instance, was well below the target the SimSups expected.

Muldoon had been on Stone's back about this; as Stone was commander of the crew, in Muldoon's mind it was up to Stone to get Curval in gear. And he knew, for instance, that Stone had been instructing the SimSups to give Curval all the help he needed.

Everybody understood how tough it was, to learn to handle a system orders of magnitude more complex than any spacecraft which had yet flown. But it was up to Curval to apply himself. And Curval didn't show any sign of improving. Or even of understanding the importance of improving.

In his own mind, Muldoon kept comparing Curval with another good pilot: Ralph Gershon.

Muldoon had kept a weather eye on Gershon for a while now. He'd shown himself to be willing to work at anything he was asked to. Muldoon had followed Gershon's performance in the sims, and he'd heard – ironically, from Ted Curval himself – how determined Gershon had been to get on the Mars Landing Training Vehicle, and then, once he was there, to make that baby his own. And he'd spent a hell of a lot of his time out at Newport Beach, working on the long, slow grind of MEM development.

Gershon was gradually putting himself into the position of being the automatic choice as MEM pilot.

He was surely aware he was doing that – he was probably even planning for it – but that was no bad thing. It showed Gershon was figuring out the system, and knew how to apply himself around here.

The contrast with the complacent Curval was marked. In Muldoon's opinion, Gershon's potential as a pilot wasn't quite that of Curval, but then Curval showed no signs of realizing the potential he had.

Flying Gershon would shut up another corner of the minority-rights lobby, anyhow. America's first black face in space ... But Muldoon wasn't about to let that influence his decision one way or the other. If Gershon was seen to be getting preference he didn't deserve – if he was appointed to a mission ahead of guys who were better qualified – then a hundred resignations would be hitting Muldoon's desk within a day. And Muldoon would be banding them together and sending them on to Josephson, with his own stapled to the front. He was absolutely clear in his own mind about that issue.

What was of a lot more concern to him was the fact that Gershon was a rookie. And, of course – and a big reason why Gershon was still grounded after so long in the corps – there was the question of Gershon's stability.

Gershon had been through Vietnam.

That was a different type of war from what some of the older guys remembered. Gershon was a loner, a bachelor, too wild and eccentric for many of the guys – particularly the older ones who, in their own way, were deeply conservative.

461

Gershon was a risk, then. But the bottom line was that Gershon could probably land the MEM in situations where a lot of other guys would abort, or even crash.

And if Muldoon bumped him onto the upcoming D-prime mission, let him fly the test MEM in Earth orbit, he could maybe prove that quickly, and he wouldn't be a rookie any more.

Muldoon wrote out three names.

CDR: Stone. MSP: Bleeker. MMP: Gershon.

It didn't look so bad. It was still a crew of pilots. All USAF, actually. You had a streak of brilliance in Gershon, which was missing in Curval, and which might make a lot of difference if it came down to the wire, forty million miles away on Mars. And, unlike Curval, Muldoon knew he could rely on Gershon to apply himself to every aspect of the mission, including all the dull shitty stuff. Like the geology.

And he could expect Stone and Bleeker, both calm and unflappable, to compensate for Gershon's instability.

Gershon, then.

It didn't go any way toward satisfying the carping scientists; but, hell, he'd just have to absorb the flak about that. Bleeker was a good man, and there was no way he was going to bounce him.

And, of course, he reflected, with Gershon being a rookie that definitely ruled out any chances of selecting Natalie York, even if he could get Gershon some experience on the D-prime. One rookie, or near-rookie, on the crew was bad enough; two would be laughable, in his opinion.

He picked up the phone and asked Mabel to set up calls to Stone, Bleeker, Gershon, and Curval.

He wondered if he should call York. He decided there was no need.

Thursday, July 12, 1984
Cheney-Palouse Scabland, Macall, Washington State

Although it wasn't yet ten a.m., the sun was already intense on Phil Stone's head and back. He could feel the sweat pool beneath his collar and under his light Snoopy helmet, and it soaked into the shirt on his back, under the heavy pack.

The ground was just black rock, it seemed to him, and the heat from the cloudless furnace of a sky came blasting straight back up

462

at him. There was nothing but rock, scrubby grass, and smashed-up gravel for miles around.

Dangling in a plastic wallet at Stone's belt there was a pack of aerial photographs of the area, together with a couple of outline US Geological Survey maps. Now he unclipped the pack; he looked around, trying to figure how the features he saw compared to the photographs and maps. The photographs had been blurred, artificially, so that he couldn't see any detail finer than would be shown in Mariner photos of the surface of Mars.

The landscape here was extraordinary. Sculpted, full of knobby hills and canyons, some cut right into the bedrock. He'd never seen anything like it.

'I don't know where the hell we are,' he admitted. 'It's damned difficult. Everything looks different, from the ground.'

Adam Bleeker, hiking beside Stone and similarly laden with helmet, pack and Mars boots, came to a halt. Bleeker was towing a two-wheeled cart called a MET, a Modular Equipment Transporter. Bleeker leaned forward, propping his hands on his knees. His blond hair seemed to be on fire in the sunlight. 'I can figure where we are,' Bleeker said wearily.

'Huh?'

'About a mile to the east of the Union Pacific. I just heard a whistle.'

Natalie York's radio voice crackled in Stone's headset. 'Say again please, EV2; I do not copy.' York was playing capcom in the comparative comfort of her tent.

Bleeker straightened up. He caught Stone's eye and mouthed an obscenity.

Stone said, 'Roger, Natalie. We're both a little weary here, on the surface of Mars. I guess we're using up our consumables at a heavy rate.'

'Then take a drink, you babies.'

Bleeker mouthed more obscenities, but Stone waved him silent. 'She's right, goddamn it. Come on.' He reached behind his head, to where two short plastic tubes dangled from his backpack. He pulled one of them to his mouth and sucked; tepid Tang squirted over his tongue.

Bleeker took a mouthful of water from his own plastic spigot, swilled it around and spat it onto the black rock underfoot, where it sizzled, running away and drying quickly.

'Try some Tang,' Stone said.

'Tang gives me the farts.'

463

'Yeah, but you need to replace the potassium you sweat out. Good for the heart . . .'

'You two heroes ready to carry on?'

'Oh, up yours, York,' Stone said.

They straightened up and walked on.

They came to a bed of gravel and clay, broad and sweeping; the bedrock thrust through it like blackened, exposed bone. 'We've found what looks like loess, Natalie,' Stone said. 'River valley deposit.' He found he was breathing hard, and he was aware that Bleeker, struggling with the heavy MET, was sweating so heavily he had soaked right through his thin T-shirt. 'I think we should go for a SEP set-up.'

'Roger, EV1.'

Damn right it's 'Roger.' Staying in one place and playing at scientists for a while was going to be a hell of a lot easier than footslogging across this goddamn volcanic battleground. After all, this was *worse* than the real thing; his Mars suit would be *air-conditioned*, for God's sake.

'Adam, why don't you scout on ahead. Go that way, up across the loess.'

'Okay.' Bleeker set down the MET's handle, hitched his pack on his shoulders, and set off along the loess, his blue Mars boots stained and muddy.

Stone dug out a set of gloves from the MET. The gloves were thick and stiffened with wire, to simulate the pressurized gloves he'd have to wear on Mars. With the gloves on he picked the SEP out of the buggy. The SEP – the Surface Experimental Package, a suite of scientific instruments – was folded up into a heavy dumbbell shape, weighted to mirror how the real thing would feel under Martian gravity.

Bleeker had walked maybe a hundred feet down the loess. 'Over here,' he called. 'This is good and flat.'

Stone began to walk toward him. 'Okay, Natalie, I'm deploying the SEP now.'

'Rog.'

It was a real effort to grip the bar of the dumbbell through his stiffened gloves, and to hold the packages away from him. After maybe thirty feet, he stopped and put the SEP down.

Bleeker laughed. 'It's only plywood, Phil.'

'Goddamn it,' Stone shouted at him, 'do you have to walk so far?'

'You know I do.'

Of course, Bleeker was right; on Mars they would have to carry the SEPs far enough from their MEM, or from the Mars Rover, that they could be sure to find a piece of surface undisturbed by the dust kicked up by their vehicles.

He pulled off the gloves, and threw them in the general direction of the MET; he didn't bother to look where they'd gone.

Bleeker whistled. 'Are you supposed to do that, skipper?'

'Sue me.'

He brought the SEP mockup to Bleeker and set it down; together, they began to deploy the instruments.

Assembling the SEP was like setting up a home barbecue. *Undo the bolts. Take the packages out of their Styrofoam blocks. Tamp down the dirt to make the ground flat* – actually that wasn't so easy here; the loess was gravely and unforgiving – *and set the instruments level. Make sure each instrument is pointed the right way, and is the right distance from the others. And don't let them get coated in dirt, goddamn it.*

When they'd finished, the SEP looked like an odd, multi-pointed star, with the radioisotope power package at the center, and the instruments set up on the ground all around it, connected by fine orange cables. The seismometer was that silvery paint tin. A little meteorology boom stuck up in the air – the SEPs would act as weather stations for the astronauts during their stay on Mars – and that spidery gold-leaf sculpture was a magnetometer. At the front of the assembly was a pair of tall, thin stereoscopic color cameras. And on top of the whole thing sat a delicate S-band antenna, pointing to an imaginary Earth.

The SEPs would be placed at a variety of sites, as the astronauts completed their traverses. There was every hope that the SEPs could send back data long after Stone and his crew had returned to Earth. It would be kind of a neat memorial to the mission; and now, looking down at the installed balsa-and-card mockup of the SEP, Stone felt a certain pride in his accomplishment, in a task done well.

'Okay, Natalie, the SEP's installed,' he said. 'What next?'

'Rog. According to our checklist, here, one of you should be setting up the CELSS, and the other taking samples.'

'It ain't time for lunch yet?' Bleeker asked plaintively.

Stone laughed. 'I'll do you a favor, Adam. You set up the CELSS, and I'll hike around for the goddamn samples.'

They trudged back to the MET, and Stone sucked a little more of the flat, tasteless Tang from the tube at his neck.

I'd sure rather be watching the Olympics with a couple of cold ones at my side, he thought. But there just wasn't the time. He'd had no time of his own, it felt like, since he'd joined the Agency.

Stone helped Bleeker haul the mockup CELSS kit out of the MET. The CELSS, the Controlled Environment Life Support System, was a small inflatable greenhouse. It came packaged as a disk of plastic. Stone and Bleeker laid the disk out on the ground and Bleeker went to work on a small foot-pump, pushing air into the ribbing of the greenhouse; soon a dome maybe four feet high had taken shape.

By the time he'd done Bleeker was sweating even harder. 'My God, Phil, it's real work operating that damned pump in these boots.'

'You want to go rock hounding instead?'

'No, no,' Bleeker said. 'Leave me to my darn vegetable patch.'

He pulled a simple aluminum spade out of the MET and began to scrape without enthusiasm at the soil. Later he'd set up a little water sprinkler inside the dome, and he'd be planting crops – soybeans and potatoes. The idea was that the carbon-dioxide-rich Martian air would be able to reach the plants through the permeable walls of the greenhouse, and the plastic dome would trap a lot of the heat of the sun. Martian soil, it seemed from the limited Soviet lander results, contained most everything needed to grow crops save for phosphorus and free water, so Bleeker would be doping the soil with a nutrient additive.

This CELSS kit was just an experiment; there was no intention of growing foodstuffs to supply the first expedition. The point was to prove that crops could be grown on Mars; it would point the way to techniques for future, longer-term missions – and even the first permanent colony, off in an unknowable future.

Likewise, Ares would be carrying another long-term experiment called ISPP, for In Situ Propellant Production. The crew would set up kits designed to extract oxygen from compressed Martian air, and maybe hydrogen and oxygen from any accessible under-surface water. If it could be shown that propellants and oxidizers for the return journey could be manufactured on Mars, the weight and costs of future trips there could be cut by more than half.

Dragging the MET, Stone began to walk, more or less north of Bleeker.

'Okay, Natalie. I'm coming off this layer of loess, now. I'm arriving on what looks like a gravel bed, loosely compacted. I can see striations. Kind of streamlined, like scour marks. It looks as if water has flowed here . . .'

York called, 'Why don't you make a sample stop?'

'Rog.'

He picked a spot, reasonably level, and set up the calibrating gnomon. He walked around the gnomon, carefully photographing it from every side. Next he worked the mechanical tests. He pressed a spring-loaded metal plate against the soil, and thrust a cylindrical probe into the ground. Then he put a lump of aggregate into a crusher, a handheld nutcracker affair. He called out readings to Natalie York as he worked.

When he'd fully documented his site he took samples from the surface. He picked up loose material with tongs, rakes and scoops, and tried breaking a piece off a larger rock with a hammer.

Actually, the landscape baffled Stone. He'd been taking a geology field trip each month for the last year, and he'd gotten familiar with the subject to some extent. But he'd never seen an area like this.

Most EVA training was taking place out in the high deserts in the western USA. At one site, in Nevada, half a square mile of desert had been faked up to simulate the Martian surface as observed by the Soviets, with fine sand raked in, large boulders set deliberately on the surface. There was even a fake MEM descent stage set up there, a mockup of wood and paint. The MEM had a compartment for a full-scale Mars Rover, which you could pull down and unfold, just like the real thing. Now, *that* was a sim exercise Stone could appreciate: bouncing across a fake, but recognizably *Martian* desert, in a four-wheel-drive Rover . . .

But he really did not know what the hell was going on here today. How was this piece of shit in Washington State, across which they were dragging this fucking Apollo-class golf buggy, supposed to relate to whatever the hell was waiting for them on Mars?

After maybe half an hour, he'd piled the MET with carefully selected – and uniformly worthless – samples of Washington State. 'Okay, Natalie, I figure I'm done here.'

'Well done, Phil. We'll make a rock hound out of you yet. But I still haven't heard much about the morphology of your site.'

He growled, and wiped sweat from his brow with a dusty hand. 'Give me a break.'

'Come on now, Phil. Taking samples isn't enough – you ought to know that by now – what's crucial for the geologists is the context. Tell me what you see.'

Stone began to walk forward again. His pack chafed at his shoulders, but now, looking around more systematically, he began to see some pattern, some logic underlying the landscape formations; and as he did so, he began to forget his discomfort.

'I see a mix of landscape here. I see what looks like bare bedrock, and sedimentary stuff that's been scoured out, and depositional material. As if left behind by running water.'

'Good.'

'The land here can't be of much value. Light pasture, maybe; there isn't much growing, certainly not in the bare rock faces. I think the rock is basalt. Volcanic, anyhow. The macroforms in the bedrock are mostly channels. The channels are pretty straight: not much sinuosity. They look as if they are basically river valleys, but widened and deepened. Maybe by glaciation?' Great tongues of ice, flattening and deepening valleys, scouring down to the bedrock –'

'Don't speculate, Phil. The goddamn Apollo astronauts speculated all the time, and they confused the hell out of everybody. Just observe.'

'Sure.' Speculating test pilots, on Mars. Natalie's number one nightmare. 'I see evidence of channel anastomosis. And uplands left isolated between the channels.'

Back at the CELSS, Bleeker looked up skeptically. He called, 'Anasto-who?'

Stone imagined York's chagrin at that remark. Bleeker's comparative backwardness at the geology wasn't surprising. The guy was under real pressure; as well as field trips like this in support of the eventual landing mission, Bleeker was also working toward the D-prime Earth-orbit mission, next month.

But then, Stone reflected, Bleeker *was* supposed to be the landing mission surface specialist.

'Anastomosis, asshole. It's all in your Boy's Coloring Book of Geology. Where a channel has been breached, and cut a branch through into another channel. Look. See the way the channels over there seem to diverge, then join up again. And you can see over there, where that bit of plateau has been left isolated. Cut off by the new channels.'

The isolated upland was like a table top of rock, stuck in the middle of the plain.

'Yeah. Okay, I see it. So what caused the breach?'

'Phil –'

'Okay, okay, Natalie. Don't ask me questions like that, Adam. I won't speculate.' *It could be glaciation, though. Must be. What the hell else could have caused so much damage to the landscape? A lava flow, maybe?*

468

'What other macroforms?' York asked.

Stone climbed on top of a rock, the heavy pack banging against his back, and peered around. 'More uplands, carved out of the sedimentary stuff. They look –'

'What?'

'Smooth. Streamlined.' Like islands, their flanks smoothed out, left stranded by the drying out of a parent river. 'And I can see what look like bars of gravel, some maybe twenty, thirty feet high. Kind of like sand banks. They seem to have formed behind outcroppings, maybe of loess, or bedrock. Like tails. The rock has grooves scoured in it. Longitudinal. The grooves flow past the islands, and the gravel bars.'

He came to a bed of loose clay and sand. 'This is more loess, I think. I see –'

'What?'

'Ripples. Kind of frozen here, in the loess. Like small dunes, I guess. The dunes are stratified. It looks as if a river has dried out here.' He stalked on over the rock. 'I got pits in the rock surface. Circular, a few inches deep, width from a foot wide upwards. Scallop pits, I think.' Gouged out by pebbles, carried by turbulence ...

'The whole place is kind of like a river bottom,' he said. 'Yeah. You basically have the topography of a dried-out river bottom – but magnified. Channels and bars and islands. All shaped by flowing water on a massive scale ...'

He looked around with a new excitement, seeing the geology with new eyes, with Natalie York's eyes: the deep-carved, breached channels, the huge deposits of loess, the carved-out islands. 'Christ. Is that it, Natalie? Is that what you've brought us out here to see? Was all of this region formed by a *flood*?'

'You're speculating again, Stone.'

'Oh, come on, York.'

'Okay. You're right, Phil. At least, that's the favored hypothesis.'

Bleeker gave up on the half-assembled CELSS, and came to stand close to Stone. 'What is?'

York said, 'In the Late Pleistocene – maybe twenty thousand years ago – much of Idaho and West Montana was covered by an immense lake. Called Missoula. Thousands of square miles of it. The lake was contained by an ice dam. The dam eventually burst, and released a catastrophic flood that swept over this area. Tens of millions of cubic yards per second, maybe a thousand times as much as the Amazon's discharge rate –'

'Jesus,' Stone said.

'Yeah. The existing streamways couldn't cope with the sudden volume, so they burst; the valleys were widened and deepened, and interconnecting channels were cut – all the way into the bedrock – in hundreds of places. Thousands of square miles were swept clean of the superficial structures, right down to the basalt bedrock, and another thousand square miles were buried in river-bottom debris.

'We're left with hundreds of cataract ledges, basins and canyons eroded into the bedrock, isolated buttes and uplands, gravel bars thirty or forty yards high.

'This is the scabland, Phil. There are only a handful of areas on Earth which show the effects of large-scale, catastrophic flooding so well.'

Bleeker pushed back his Snoopy hat and scratched his blond head. 'It's fascinating, Natalie. But I don't see what it has to do with us.'

'Okay. Phil, I've given you another pack of photographs. In the left side-pocket of Adam's pack.'

Stone dug into Bleeker's pocket and pulled out a plastic packet of black and white photographs. He leafed through them quickly, showing them to Bleeker.

Cratered plains: the images were of Mars, clearly enough. But here was a channel cut deeply into what looked like the tough, ancient landscape of the southern hemisphere. Here was a crater complex, overlaid by anastomosed channels. Here was a crater with a teardrop-shaped, streamlined island, like a gravel bar, collected in its wake; and 'downstream' of the crater, there were scour marks, running parallel to the island . . .

Stone was having trouble making sense of this. 'Are you saying that Mars has suffered catastrophic flooding – like the scabland here, in Washington State?'

York hesitated. '*I* believe so. A lot of us have argued that, since the Mariner pictures came in. I've been studying the area you're looking at, in those photos, since 1973. I guess I'm the leading expert on it, now. And it seems to me the analogy between the terrestrial scabland features and the Martian morphology is too striking to be a coincidence.'

'But not everybody agrees,' Stone hazarded.

'No,' she conceded. 'Some say the Martian "scabland" features are too big to have been formed by water. Schumm, for instance.'

'Who?' Bleeker asked.

'Schumm says the Martian channels must have been formed by tensional factors in the planet's surface. Cracks, modified later, maybe, by vulcanism and the action of the wind.'

'Sounds like an asshole to me,' Stone said, peering at the pictures. 'I'm with you, Natalie.'

'But if these Martian channels were formed by flooding,' Bleeker said, 'where the hell did the water come from? And where did it go?'

'I'll bet she has a theory about that, too,' Stone muttered.

'I didn't copy, EV1.'

'Go ahead, Natalie.'

'Underground aquifers. Contained by tough bedrock below – maybe ten miles deep – and a cap of thick ice in the regolith above. Whatever lifted up Tharsis – a convection process in the mantle, maybe – must have caused the faulting that led to the flooding. The pressure of the water got to exceed the pressure of the rocks. All you'd need would be a breach on the subsurface ice cap for the water to gush to the surface, under high pressure.'

'My God,' Stone said. 'Oceans, buried in the Martian rocks. How can we find out if you're right, Natalie?'

'What we need is for three guys to land there in a MEM, and dig a few deep cores.'

Stone started to see where all this was leading. He leafed through the photos again. 'What area are these photos of?'

'That's one of the most striking outflow channels. It's Mangala Vallis, Phil. Martian scabland: your landing area.'

Stone grinned. *She's doing it again. Mangala Vallis. On which Natalie York, leading light of the site selection committee and would-be Mars voyager, just happens to be the world's top expert.*

And Adam Bleeker still doesn't know what anastomosis is. I hope the guy's watching his back.

Mission Elapsed Time [Day/Hr:Min:Sec] Plus 349/11:14:03

Twenty days from orbit insertion, Mars had opened out into a disk. Where the line between light and dark crossed the planet, she could see, with her naked eye, wrinkles and bumps in the surface: craters and canyons catching the light of the sun.

It was remarkable how much she could recognize. Almost as if she had been here before. There was the huge gouge of the Valles

Marineris – a wound visible even from a million miles out – and the polar cap in the north, swelling with water ice in advance of the coming winter, and the great black calderas of the Tharsis volcanoes.

Mars was clearly a small world, she thought. Some of the features – Tharsis, the Marineris canyons, Syrtis, the great iced pit of Hellas in the south – sprawled around the globe, outsized, dominating the curvature.

In some ways Mars was as she had expected. It looked a lot like the big photomosaic globes at JPL. But there were surprising differences too. Mars wasn't red so much as predominantly brown, a surface wrought out of subtle shadings of tan and ochre and rust. There was a sharp visible difference between northern and southern hemispheres, with the younger lands to the north of the equatorial line being brighter in color, almost yellow.

Ares was approaching the planet at an angle to the sunlight, so Mars was gibbous, with a fat slice of the night hemisphere turned toward the spacecraft. And the ochre shading seemed to deepen at the planet's limb, and at low sun angles. These features gave the little globe a marked roundness. Mars was a little round orange, the only object apart from the sun in all the three-hundred-and-sixty-degree sky visible as other than a point of light.

In the depths of the mission – suspended between planets, with nothing visible but sun and stars beyond the walls of the craft, and ground down by the stultifying routine of long-duration flight – York had suffered some deep depressions. She'd shrunk into herself, going through her assignments on autopilot, shunning the company of her crewmates. She suspected they'd suffered similarly, but they seemed to have found ways to cope: Gershon with his love of the machinery around them, Stone with his little pet pea plants.

Already she was dreading the return journey; it loomed in her imagination, a huge black barrier.

But that was for the future. Right now she was climbing out of the pit, up toward the warm ochre light of Mars.

She spent as much time as she could just staring at the approaching globe, identifying sites no naked human eye had seen before, as if claiming more and more of Mars for herself.

As they prepared for the ignition, Bleeker had *Born in the USA* playing on the cabin's little tape deck. It drowned out the clicks and whirs of the MEM's equipment.

Bleeker said, 'Ascent propulsion system propellant tanks pressurized.'

'Rager,' Gershon replied.

'Ascent feeds are open, shut-offs are closed.'

On the ground, Ted Curval was capcom today. '*Iowa,* this is Houston. Less than ten minutes here. Everything looks good. Just a reminder. We want the rendezvous radar mode switch in LGC just as it is on surface fifty-nine ... We assume the steerable is in track mode auto.'

Gershon said, 'Stop, push-button reset, abort to abort stage reset.'

Bleeker pushed his buttons. 'Reset.'

Curval said, 'Our guidance recommendation is PGNS, and you're cleared for ignition.

'Rog. We're number one on the runway ...'

A hundred miles above the Earth, as Gershon and Bleeker worked through the litany of the pre-burn checklist, MEM and Apollo drifted in formation. The Apollo, containing Command Module Pilot Bob Crippen, was an exquisitely jeweled silver toy, drifting against the luminous carpet of Earth. And the MEM was a great shining cone, at thirty feet tall dwarfing Apollo, surrounded by discarded Mars heatshield panels and rippling with foil.

Its six squat landing legs were folded out and extended. But MEM 009 was destined to land nowhere.

Gershon stood harnessed in place beside Bleeker in the cramped little cabin of the MEM's ascent stage. He felt bulky, awkward in his orange pressure suit. In front of Gershon was a square instrument panel, packed with dials and switches and instruments. There were two sets of hand controllers, one for each man. More circuit breakers coated the walls, and there were uncovered bundles of wiring and plumbing along the floor. The cabin had two small triangular windows, one to either side of the main panel, calibrated with the spidery markings that would help guide a landing on Mars. Blue Earthlight shone through the windows, dappling the cabin's panels.

Behind Gershon there were three acceleration couches, two of them folded up. On a landing flight there would be a third crewman in here, the mission specialist, a passenger during the MEM's single brief flight.

The cabin's surfaces were utilitarian, functional, mostly unpainted, with everything riveted together, the bundles of wires lashed together by hand as if in a home workshop.

The MEM was an experimental ship: the product of hand-crafting, of thousands of man-hours of patient labor, and based on conservative designs, stuff that had worked before. The apparent coarseness of the construction was the feature of space hardware that most surprised people used to sleek mass-produced technology. It was nothing like *Star Trek*.

But to Gershon the MEM was *real*, almost earthy.

To descend to Mars, in a ship assembled by the hands and muscles of humans: to Gershon, still elated to be in space at all, there was something wonderful about the thought.

As long as the mother worked, of course.

'Coming up on two minutes,' Curval called up. 'Mark, T minus two minutes.'

'Roger,' Bleeker said. He turned off the tape.

Glancing at his panel, Gershon could see that the ascent stage was powered up now, no longer drawing any juice from the lower stage's batteries. It was preparing to become an independent space-craft for the first time.

In this test, simulating a launch from the Martian surface, the whole unlikely MEM assemblage was supposed to come apart, releasing the stick-like ascent stage with its ungainly, strap-on pro-pellant tanks.

Gershon knew this was the moment on the mission that was most feared by the engineers at Columbia and Marshall. There were too many ways for the fucking thing to go wrong. Like, the ascent stage ignition would take place with the engine bell still buried within the guts of the MEM's descent stage. What if there was a blow-back, an over-pressure of some kind, before the ascent stage got clear? . . .

Well, they were soon going to find out.

Bleeker said, 'Guidance steering in the PGNS. Deadband mini-mum, ATT control, mode control auto.'

'Auto,' Gershon responded.

'One minute,' the capcom said.

'Got the steering in the abort guidance.'

Gershon armed the ignition. 'Okay, master arm on.'

'Rog.'

'You're go, *Iowa*,' said Curval.

'Rager. Clear the runway.'

Bleeker turned to him. 'You ready?'

'Sure.'

'That mother may give us a kick.' Bleeker reminded him of the drill. 'Okay, Ralph. At five seconds I'm going to hit ABORT STAGE and ENGINE ARM. And you'll hit PROCEED.'

'Rager.'

'Here we go. Nine. Eight. Seven. Six. Five.'

Beyond the small window in front of Gershon's face, the shining blue horizon of Earth drifted by, a complex, clearly three-dimensional sculpture of cloud over sea.

The computer display in front of Gershon flashed a '99,' a request to proceed. He glanced across at Bleeker.

Bleeker closed the master firing arm. 'Engine arm ascent.'

Gershon pressed the PROCEED button.

There was a loud bang, a rattle around the floor of the cabin. Pyrotechnic guillotines were blowing away the nuts, bolts, wires and water hoses connecting the upper and lower stages of the MEM.

A weight descended smoothly on Gershon's shoulders.

'First stage engine on ascent,' Bleeker said. 'Here we go.' He smiled. 'Beautiful.'

After his unexpected, incredible assignment to the prime Mars crew, Gershon had been happy to be bumped onto this D-prime test mission. His first flight into space might not have been the most glamorous in the MEM test program – that would probably be the one remaining E mission, the attempt to bring a reinforced MEM in through the Earth's atmosphere and land it on the salt flats around Edwards Air Force Base. That had been given to an experienced crew led by John Young. But the D-prime, an eleven-day Earth-orbit shakedown flight, was arguably the more important test. In an untried spacecraft, the crew would rehearse every phase of the Mars landing mission save only the atmospheric entry and final powered descent; and, as well, they would rehearse many contingency procedures which might save future missions.

Already, in the MEM, Gershon and Bleeker had ventured as much as a hundred miles from Apollo. In a craft which nobody had tried to rendezvous with before. Which didn't have a heatshield strong enough to get them back to the ground. And on top of that, the whole flight was in low Earth orbit, where communications and navigation challenges were even tougher than on, say, a flight to the Moon.

If they got through this flight the MEM would be man-rated, with only the Mars heatshield remaining to be test-flown. It was a connoisseur's spaceflight, a flight for true test pilots.

And besides, Gershon had been happy to bury himself in the mission, to get away from the attention his assignment to the Mars crew had brought him. *The first black man in space: the first brother on Mars.* He was learning to deal with it, but it was relentless, distracting. And nothing to do with him.

As far as he was concerned he was Ralph Gershon, complete and entire, and not a symbol of anyone else's agenda.

However, the mission had been snake-bit: nothing but problems from the beginning.

It started even before the launch, in fact. Gershon had seen JK Lee's people at Columbia tearing their hair out as they tried to coax Spacecraft 009 through its final prelaunch checkout in the Vehicle Assembly Building at the Cape. There had been times when Gershon had become convinced that it wouldn't come together at all.

Then, once they had reached orbit and opened up the docking tunnel between Apollo and MEM, Gershon found himself floating in a snowstorm of white fiberglass. It had blown out of an insulation blanket in the tunnel wall. Gershon and Bleeker had spent their first couple of hours in the MEM just vacuuming all that crap out of the air, and they had finished up with white stuff clinging to their hair, their eyelashes, their mouths, until they'd looked like nothing so much as a pair of plucked chickens.

After that Bleeker and Gershon had crawled all over the MEM, putting the subsystems through comprehensive tests. And every damn one of those tests had given them problems, which had needed diagnosis and repeated testing.

There had been that odd, sour smell coming from the environment control system in the surface shelter, for instance, which they had finally traced to a piece of scuffed insulation slowly scorching behind a panel. The electrical power system had shown some severe faults, with whole panels of instruments just cutting out. Meanwhile the inertial guidance system was a pig, wallowing inside its big metal sphere, constantly losing its lock. And the MEM's big antennae complex had gotten stuck, and for a while it couldn't talk to the Apollo or the ground . . .

Relationships between the crew and the ground had gotten

strained in all of this. As they wrestled with the craft, Bleeker, as commander, had become concerned that Houston was reluctant to make any compromises in the scientific and PR elements of the flight plan – which, as far as Bleeker and Gershon were concerned, came a long way down the list in comparison to the engineering objectives of the mission. So Bleeker, showing an unexpected assertiveness, got into battles with the flight controllers. He canceled TV broadcasts, and he blue-penciled whole sections out of the flight plan.

At one point the capcom told the crew that the controllers were plotting to bring the Command Module down in a typhoon, and Gershon suspected it was only half a joke.

Finally Gershon had got so sick of the problems that he'd taken a little plastic juice-dispensing lemon from the food lockers, and hung it up between the MEM's triangular windows, in full view of the onboard TV, to show what the crew thought of their new ship.

All Gershon could hear right now was the rattling thump-thump of the ascent engine's ball valves opening and closing. The noise was oddly comforting, giving him a feeling of security, that the mission was unfolding as it should.

The Earth slid away from Gershon, as the ascent stage climbed smoothly up toward its rendezvous with *New Jersey*, the waiting Apollo; it was so smooth it was a ride in a glass-walled elevator.

There wasn't much for Gershon to do. Because the ascent stage engine had no backup – *it had to work* – it had been made as simple as possible, with just two moving parts: ball valves, to release propellant and oxidant into the combustion chamber. The engine, fueled with oxygen and methane, had no throttle or choke; all you could do was throw the master arm and turn the engine on, and it would just burn steadily for ten minutes or so, just as it was designed, to lift its crew off Mars and back to a parking orbit.

Gershon leaned forward, resting against his restraints. Through his window he could see the descent stage falling away; it was a truncated cone, with a great gouge dug out of its center. Cables and hoses, cut by the guillotines, dangled. Foil insulation had been blown off the stage by the ascent engine's blast, and Gershon could see sheets of the stuff floating away, spreading outwards in rings.

JK Lee was standing in the Viewing Room in back of the MOCR, chain-smoking. Whenever TV pictures had come down from the orbiting MEM over the last couple of days, you could clearly see the little plastic lemon, floating about under the alignment telescope. He could decode that symbol: it was a little message from the crew, from Ralph probably, meant for him.

But it didn't faze him, or dilute his elation. No, sir! Sure the crew were having problems, but they had to expect that; combing out the problems was what this proving flight was for, after all. He was a little disappointed Ralph Gershon didn't understand that, in fact. The important thing for Lee was that he was watching *his ship*, up there in orbit, glitches or not; *his ship*, delivered on time and against all the odds.

Lee felt a huge glow of triumph. It was as if, to achieve this day, he'd had to fight everybody – NASA management, the suppliers, the astronauts, half of Columbia, even his own treacherous body. But he'd made it, and the monument to his achievement was up there in orbit right now, larger than life in the big screens at the front of the MOCR, and on TV sets all around the world. What a victory! Lee had the feeling that nothing in his career from now on would mean as much to him as this triumph, right here, right now. Not even the moment when another of his babies, hatched from the Clean Room at Newport, set its pads on Mars itself.

He could care less about Ralph's fucking lemon.

He laughed out loud, uncaring who stared at him, and hauled out another cigarette.

Bleeker said, 'Twenty-six seconds. We're going to pitch over a little. Very smooth, very quiet ride.'

Gershon prepared for the MEM to pitch over. Thinking that it had reached five thousand feet above the surface of Mars, the MEM should tip up, programmed to head for a Mars-orbital rendezvous with the rest of the Ares cluster.

The horizon tilted to his right.

Gershon, already feeling heavy, was thrown against his restraints.

The pitch had been right on cue. But the tipping had felt sharper, more of a rattle, than he'd expected.

And the pitch continued; beyond his window, the cloudscape of Earth was rolling upwards, turning from a floor to a wall.

Bleeker said, 'What the fuck?'

'Hot mike, Adam,' Ted Curval called up.

They don't know what's going on, Gershon realized.

The shining landscape passed over his head now, and shadows shifted across the banks of circuit breakers. Vapor, squirting from the reaction control system clusters, sparkled past the window.

But the automatics couldn't regain control. The spinning speeded up.

'Jesus,' Bleeker said wryly. 'It's a real whifferdill. I need to cage my eyeballs.'

An orbital tailspin: Bleeker was right, Gershon realized.

Soon the MEM was twisting through a full turn every second, and Earth flashed past the windows. Sunlight strobed across the cabin, dazzling, disorienting.

Gershon's vision started to blur as he searched the instrument panel. *Time to earn your flight pay, boy.*

He started throwing switches, methodically trying to isolate the problem. Maybe an attitude thruster was stuck on; he looked at that first. Whatever it was, he had to get the spin killed quickly. The guidance systems were in danger of locking up altogether; he needed to get manual control before that happened.

He grasped his hand controller and started squirting the RCS clusters, using the Earth as a reference, trying to push against the tumble of the ascent stage and stabilize *Iowa*.

For a time the whirling got faster; it was as if the RCS motors were having no effect at all, and he started to feel dizzy. Both he and Bleeker continued to snap breakers furiously. If they didn't get the MEM under control soon, there was a danger they would both black out, and after that, even if the ship didn't break up, it would be impossible for the Apollo to dock with the spinning *Iowa*.

At last, they got both primary and abort guidance systems shut off. With the automatics offline the RCS clusters started to slow the pitching.

Bleeker cut the ascent stage engine. The spinning continued to slow.

Gershon had to eyeball the horizon to judge when he finally got the stage stabilized; his inner ear was shot to pieces by the spin.

Bleeker sounded strained, as if he was working to keep from throwing up inside his helmet. 'Jesus. You were right, Ralph. This ship is an Edsel.'

Gershon kept his eyes fixed on Earth's horizon; the sense of tumbling slowly receded from his head. 'No,' he said. 'An Edsel's a clunker, but it's harmless. This mother is downright dangerous.'

From the ground, Curval told them that Bob Crippen, in Apollo, was already on his way down from his higher orbit to retrieve them.

JK Lee hung around the MOCR through the rest of the mission, right up until the moment when Bleeker's crew returned to Earth in their Command Module.

Outside Building 30, Art Cane was waiting for him.

'Art!' Grinning, Lee went up to his boss. 'I didn't know you were coming out here.'

In his shirt-sleeves, Cane stood there in the sweltering humidity of Houston like an ancient, denuded tree. 'I wasn't intending to. Get in the car, JK.'

The car, parked in a Building 30 space, was a hired stretch limo, with a bar in the back. It was pleasantly cool, a relief after the heat of the day. Lee got in and lit up a cigarette.

Cane nodded to the driver, and the car pulled smoothly away.

Lee eyed Cane. 'Not like you to be so extravagant as this, Art.'

Cane shrugged and loosened his tie. 'I'm an old man, JK. What can I say? I can't put up with this Texas heat; I need the air-conditioning.' Cane folded his jacket neatly on his lap, and then put his hands together over the jacket, one on top of the other. 'Now, look here, JK. You know the pressure we've been under.'

'Sure.'

'That goddamn tiger team thing. And the CARR on 009, and the delays in shipping the bird to the Cape, and those problems with the busted fuel tanks. And now that business in orbit.'

'But that's all resolved, Art.' Lee launched into a bubbling description of how the whifferdill problem had already been diagnosed to a mis-set switch in the MEM's cabin. '. . . When the ascent engine fired, the switch told the abort guidance system it should start looking for the Command Module, to get a lock on for a fast emergency docking. But of course the Apollo was miles away at the time.' He laughed. 'So the MEM just started tumbling, looking for that old Command Module for all it was worth . . .'

Cane held up a hand, the skin on it so loose it reminded Lee of a plucked chicken's claw. 'Yeah,' he said. 'But it wasn't a crew mistake, was it? I mean, they thought they'd set that switch correctly. *We* had mislabeled the switch. So it was *our* fault, not theirs.' He shook his head, looking gaunt and old. 'Jesus Christ, JK, how in hell did you let something like that out of the factory? It could have killed those guys.'

'Oh, come on, Art. It wasn't so serious. It'll be trivial to fix. All of the problems we had were trivial. Finding problems is what proving flights are for. Now, I can take the D-prime records and transcripts and test results back to Newport Beach, and we can begin raking out the remaining flaws in their hardware.' He felt enthused, energetic, renewed by the flight of his machine. 'Why, I want to set a new record, coming out of this. I want 010 to show the smallest number of defects in its preflight checkout of any craft of any generation ever shipped to the Cape. Why the hell not? We're going to make history, Art. With the D-prime behind me, I'll hit the next one out of the park –'

Cane cut him off. 'Listen to me, JK. There are some things you just don't understand about this business. I'm not talking about specific problems. I'm talking about –' He waved his hands vaguely. 'A cumulative effect.'

Lee was uneasy, but baffled. 'Cumulative?'

'Things kind of pile up, one on top of another. It's an image thing. There's been a lot of comment about the performance of the Apollo hardware – the proven stuff, which brought the astronauts home flawlessly – compared to the problems of the MEM. *Maybe the contract should have gone to Rockwell after all*, is what they're muttering. With talk like that around, before you know where you are you can't do anything right. Even fixing what's wrong, specifically, isn't going to help. When you're in this kind of mess all kinds of questions get asked. Queries about the basic competence of my company.' Lee heard frustration and anger in Cane's thin voice. 'Once they've decided you're dogshit, you've had it.'

He turned to Lee, his face crumpled with anger and sadness, his rheumy eyes shining. 'And that's what's happened to us, JK. NASA, the Congress, the press – they've decided we're dogshit. That *I'm* dogshit.'

The pain in his words tore at Lee. 'Oh, Christ, Art, it isn't as bad as that.'

'You know they're talking again about moving the contract away.'

'They can't do it,' Lee said vigorously. 'You know that. Not without abandoning the schedule altogether.'

Cane was growing angrier. 'They're talking about reassigning a lot of the MEM work to Aerojet, Boeing, GE, McDonnell, Martin, maybe bringing in Rockwell project managers to Newport –'

Lee laughed. 'All the usual suspects.'

'This isn't a fucking joke, JK,' Cane snapped. 'Maybe NASA

won't do it. Maybe they can't. But they're *talking* about it. And that's the point. Goddamn it, don't you understand any of this? NASA is trying to show us – and Congress and the press – how seriously it's taking all of this.

'And heads have been rolling in NASA. Did you know that? Guys who've been jerking off instead of keeping a hawk-eye on us.' He rattled off a list of names, people at Marshall and Houston.

'Yeah, but look, Art, those guys are mostly administrator types. It won't make a damn bit of difference if they go or stay. It's engineers that count. You know that.'

'But it doesn't matter what I think. Don't you see it, JK? It's all a demonstration of intent. It might seem abstract to you, all a game, but believe me, up on the Hill, it's real. And now, in response, we have to make our own gesture.'

And suddenly, through his euphoria, Lee did see; he saw it in a flash of comprehension, all of it. 'Oh, Christ, Art. Oh, no. You can't do this.'

Cane reached out and spread his long fingers over Lee's arm. 'I'm sorry, JK. I think I have to. I'm looking at schedule and budget overruns. Shoddy manufacturing practices. A test flight that turned into a fiasco, almost a goddamn lethal fiasco at that.'

Lee looked at the back of the driver's crew-cut head, at NASA Road One sliding by beyond the car windows. He tried to focus on the here and now: the leather smell of the upholstery, the air-conditioning's crisp coolness. But he felt numb, as if he was insulated within some pressure suit, like Adam Bleeker and his crew.

'I almost gave my life for this goddamn project, Art.' *And my marriage.* 'You know how close we are to the finish line, don't you?'

'Yes, JK, I –'

'*That* close.' He held up thumb and forefinger a fraction apart. 'And it's me who got you there. The whole damn conception, the MEM design based on the old Apollo shape, all of that was *mine*, Art. And it's me who's been holding everybody's feet to the fire ever since. Now we've built it, and it's going to be the finest spacecraft ever flown. And you're yanking me out of the saddle, all at the behest of some bunch of do-nothing jerk-offs in Washington who couldn't find their asses with both hands –'

'Cut it, JK.'

'Who's going to replace me? Bob Rowen? Jack Morgan, maybe? Or –'

'No. Nobody internal. JK, I've decided we need a heavyweight program manager to follow you. A top guy, to step into your shoes –'

'Who? Who are you giving my job to?'

Cane looked away. 'Gene Tyson.'

Lee stared at him, then laughed out loud. Tyson: the slick, fat veep from Hughes who had laughed Lee out of his office during the MEM bid. 'Gene Tyson. Are you kidding me?'

'Gene's a fine engineer, and a good man.'

'Sure, Art. But he's no –'

Cane looked at him. 'No what? No *JK Lee?*'

'That's right, damn you. Anyhow, it wouldn't work. My people wouldn't work with him. They wouldn't –' *Betray me.*

Cane coughed, and avoided his eyes again. 'Tyson has already agreed to take the job. And I've spoken to your people.'

'I . . . you're kidding me.'

'Morgan and Xu and Lye and Rowen and –'

'And they agreed to go along with this?'

Cane shrugged. 'I wouldn't say they were happy about it. But –'

But they accepted it. And the sons of bitches never said a word to me.

'Listen to me, Art. Don't do this. We've got a fine ship there. And a fine manufacturing process. All we have to do is fine-tune a few items, and we can keep right on course, keep on doing what we're doing, all the way to Mars. *Nothing needs fixing*, Art. I really believe that.'

'I know you do,' Cane said. His voice was harder now, colder. 'The trouble is, JK, there aren't many people left who agree with you.'

Lee flew home, and told Jennine what had happened. He felt a stab of anger, of resentment. 'I suppose you're glad. I suppose you think this is good news.'

Her tired, slack face showed no irritation. 'Oh, JK.' She came across to him and held him.

After a while, he felt some of the tension leaking out of him, and he lifted his arms to encircle her.

The next day he went in to the plant. He drove his black T-bird into its usual parking slot, as if nothing had happened.

At her desk, Bella was in tears. He just squeezed her shoulder; he didn't trust himself to say anything.

Inside the office they were waiting there for him, lined up in front of his old gun-metal desk: Morgan, Xu, Lye, Rowen. Their faces were long, and not a damn one of them could meet his eye.

A smell of sweet-sickly cologne, of stale tobacco, wafted around Lee's office.

There – standing behind Lee's gun-metal desk – was Gene Tyson.

Lee went straight to Tyson and shook his hand. 'Congratulations, Gene. Art is showing a lot of faith in you. You've got a hell of a job, but you've got the best people in the industry here, and I know you're going to pull it off.'

Tyson gripped his hand. 'I've got one big act to follow.' He sounded sincere, his big fleshy face solemn. 'I'm going to need your support during the handover, obviously. JK –' He glanced around the office. 'You don't need to move out of here. It's not necessary. I mean –'

'No.' Lee released Tyson's hand; his own fingers felt moist from the perspiration of Tyson's soft flesh. 'No, that's okay, Gene. Just give me a day to get out.'

'Of course.'

Then, graciously enough, Tyson left the office.

When Tyson had gone the room felt empty, purposeless.

'Damn it, JK,' Bob Rowen said suddenly, and his big round moon of a face, under its grizzle-gray crew-cut, looked alarmingly as if it might crumple up into tears. 'I didn't want it this way. You know that. The MEM is your ship.'

Lee took his shoulders and shook him gently. 'Well, now you've got the ball coming out of the sky at you, boy,' he said softly. 'And there isn't a pair of hands anywhere in the industry I'd rather see under it.'

'We go back a long way, JK. All the way back to the old B-70.'

'Christ, it's not as if I'm going to Mars myself. I'll even be on site here, most days.' It was true; Cane had offered him a staff job, a way to keep his rank of vice president. 'Any time you need me, you know you've only got to pick up the phone.'

Now Rowen's face did crumple. 'I know, JK. Oh, Jesus.'

Lee felt as if he might fold up too. *Destructive testing, again.*

He stepped back and clapped his hands. The sound was loud, startling, and they all looked at him.

'Come on, guys. You've all got work to do. Let's get on with it.'

His people made attempts at good-byes, at more eulogies.

He chased them out of his office.

When they'd gone he stood there for a while, looking at his big metal desk. It looked like a piece of a wrecked battleship, stranded in the middle of a sea of blue-gray corporate-colors carpet.

Suddenly he couldn't stand it any more.

He went out, closing the door behind him. He asked Bella, who was sobbing openly, to pack up his effects and send them on.

Outside, Jack Morgan was waiting. 'Come on,' Morgan said. 'I could use a day off. Let's get down to the Balboa Bay and drown in Lemon Hart.'

It sounded like a hell of a good idea to Lee. But, there in the middle of the car park, something slowed him, snagging at him like a trapped thread.

'No,' he said. 'Thanks, Jack, but no.'

'Huh?' There was the concern of a doctor mixed in with Morgan's surprise.

Lee grinned. 'I'm fine. It's just that –'

Morgan clapped his shoulder. 'Don't worry about it. Next time, huh.'

'Sure.'

Lee walked to his T-bird. He guessed Morgan understood.

It's just that today, I think I should go on home to Jennine.

Monday, August 13, 1984
Lyndon B. Johnson Space Center, Houston

Bleeker, in blue coveralls, sat in a small padded chair, opposite Muldoon's desk. Bleeker's eyes were large and pale, and had always seemed somehow calm to Muldoon. Like windows to a church. But now little creases bunched up around those eyes, and the color drained out of Bleeker's face.

When Bleeker spoke his voice had tightened up, but it was under control. 'So tell me, Joe. I did something wrong?'

'No. No, of course not. You know that.' Muldoon tapped the fat brown card folder on his desk. 'It's just surgeon shit . . . Listen. You want a drink?' He opened the bottom drawer of his filing cabinet. 'I got a bottle of sour mash down here, and –'

'No thanks, Joe. Just tell me, will you?'

Muldoon opened the folder on his desk. It was the preliminary surgeon's report from Bleeker's D-prime mission post-flight checkup. He started leafing through it, through the metabolism graphs and radiation dosimetry charts and countersigned forms and all the rest, wondering where to begin. 'Hell, Adam. You know how it is with surgeons. You only walk out of their office two ways: fine, or –'

'Or grounded. And I'm grounded. Is that what you're going to tell me, Joe?'

Impatient, Muldoon banged the folder closed with the palm of his hand. 'Adam, you've spent a hell of a lot of man-hours in space, in Skylab, Moonlab, and now D-prime –'

Bleeker ducked his head.

'In fact, that's one of your main qualifications to be on Ares. Right? We know you can cope with long-duration missions, because you've done it already. And now you've got experience with the MEM, the new technology . . . But you know that space exposure gets to you in the end.'

'So what's the problem? Muscle wastage?' For the first time Bleeker looked vaguely alarmed. 'Is it my heart?'

'No,' said Muldoon quickly. 'As far as I can tell from this crap, your heart is fine. Adam, you've always been outstanding in adhering to your exercise regimes. Your muscle decline has been small, every trip, and you've recovered quickly.'

'What then? Calcium loss?'

'Not that. Adam – it's radiation exposure.'

'I'm within the limits,' Bleeker said quickly.

Muldoon tried to suppress a sigh. 'Yes, but they changed the rules on you, pal. To be fair to the surgeons, they keep on learning; they still don't know much about the effects of long-term low-level radiation exposure, and they keep on coming up with new ways for you to get hurt . . . Listen: what do you know about free radicals?'

Bleeker frowned.

'Free radicals are bits of molecules. Highly energetic. Like ions – with charges knocked out of their atoms – only with more horse power. They're highly oxidizing, which means they got a taste for hydrogen. They'll strip hydrogen atoms out of nearby molecules, even. And that can cause havoc if it's happening inside your cells.

'Now, we all got free radicals in our bodies. We need them for the operation of the metabolism. But there's a *balance*. Your body produces them, and absorbs them, and keeps everything together. But if you're exposed to high energy radiation, or light, or extremes of temperatures –'

'You get more free radicals.'

'Right. The balance is lost.' Muldoon looked over the report once more. 'These babies propagate. A free radical will return to normal by stealing its neighbor's electron. But that makes that neighbor into a free radical in turn. Your body has a scavenger system to fight these things, but it can get overwhelmed or inactivated. And then the damage you suffer depends on what gets hit. You can get radiation-induced cancers if a DNA base is damaged, or your system loses control of its functions if protein is damaged, or you can get internal bleeding if membrane lipids are broken.'

Bleeker frowned. '*Membrane lipids*, Joe?'

Muldoon tried to put together an answer in plain English: how free radicals contributed to aging, and cancers, and degenerative diseases of the heart, liver and lungs; how the loss of free radical balance contributed to a lot of other microgravity problems like disturbing the inner ear's balance mechanism, and bone degeneration . . .

'Look, Adam, you ever left a slab of butter out in the sun?'

Bleeker thought about it. 'Gets rancid.'

'Well, there you are. That's free radical damage.'

Bleeker, his eyes locked on Muldoon's, started pulling at his cuff, in a precise, apparently unconscious gesture.

Bleeker really did seem to have a kind of inner calm, an even temper. It had evidently got him through all that A-war shit he'd trained for, Muldoon supposed. Maybe the psychos were right, that Bleeker had a lack of imagination.

But now Muldoon could see the tension building in him, under the surface. How was he going to react to this, the worst news of his life?

'Look, Adam. You got to understand. You're not ill. It's just that because of this kind of study, they've tightened the limits. On everybody. And you, with all your exposure to space, have finished up outside the limits. If the free radical study had come in a couple of months earlier you probably would have been bumped off D-prime too. Look – you might have suffered some of this free radical damage. Or not. Or something else –'

'I've proved myself in space, Joe, and on the ground, time and again. Look how I pulled off the D-prime flight. I deserve this goddamn trip.'

'I know that, but –'

'And I know about surgeons' reports. They talk about risks. Likelihoods and percentiles. Not certainties. And besides, it isn't logical. The Ares crew is going to run up a lot more time in space than I've accumulated anyhow.'

'But starting from a lower base, Adam. Even Phil Stone.'

487

'Joe, I don't care about the risks. I want to go anyhow.'

'If it costs your life?'

'Even so.'

Bleeker lifted up his head, and there were those wide, church window eyes looking right into Muldoon, open, honest, committed.

I have to kill this, here and now. I can't leave him with any hope. And he didn't intend to tell Bleeker about the pressure he'd been under: from the flight surgeons, even from Administrator Josephson himself. He wasn't going to hide behind any of that.

'That's not the point, Adam,' he said, and he tried to get some steel into his voice. 'I can't risk having you fall ill, half-way to Mars. I can't risk sending you. Because you would endanger the mission.'

Bleeker smiled, a small motion of the muscles of his cheeks. Then he stood up, stiffly, still tugging at his cuff. 'I appreciate the way you're handling this, Joe.'

'Oh, God. Don't be kind to *me*, for Christ's sake. Adam, we'll talk later. You know I need your help now. We haven't got a lot of time to recover from this. And later – hell, there are still good careers here, on the ground.' He laughed, a little hollowly. 'Look at me. You're still in the team, Adam.'

'Sure. I know my duty, Joe. I'll do everything I can.'

Goddamn this job. This is the most competent man in the Office, and I have to bump him. 'Yeah. I know you will.'

Bleeker turned back. 'By the way. Who's replacing me? You decided yet?'

Joe Muldoon hesitated.

His orderly crew rotation system had gone out of the window, first with Curval bombing out, and now this bad shit from the surgeons about Adam. He felt an unreasonable anger at the doctors, the managers, the psychologists, all the rest of them who wanted a piece of his decision.

He felt like shocking them all, taking back the responsibility in his own two hands.

He'd already spoken to Phil Stone, the Ares mission commander. Stone had defended Bleeker to the hilt. But when he'd come to accept Bleeker was off the mission, Stone had been surprisingly clear about who he wanted to replace Bleeker.

Well, Joe, you got to pick the best Mission Specialist. The most knowledgeable: more so than Adam, for sure. And the most committed: the one who's been spending time in the sims, and trailing around trying to train the prime crew, and all of that. And –

What?

488

And someone who can maybe see things, the mission, in a way old jocks like you and me can't. A different perspective. Someone who can articulate it better, maybe . . .

Rookie or not, Phil?

Hell, yes, Joe. Rookie or not.

Muldoon found himself grinning. He knew that the candidate he had in mind had spent a lot of time working with Ralph Gershon, in the MLTV and various sims and survival exercises. But only because they were both outsiders, pushed together by circumstance. Still, they'd proved they could work together, although they would never be bosom buddies. *The goddamn shrinks will jump up and down, over having two dipsticks on one flight, with only Phil Stone to keep 'em apart . . .*

So, fuck 'em.

'Yes,' he said to Bleeker. 'Yes, I've decided. But, Adam –'

'Yeah?'

'She doesn't know yet.'

Monday, August 13, 1984
Ramada Inn South/NASA, Houston

Vladimir Viktorenko had his shoes off, and he was sipping at a miniature bottle of mini-bar malt whisky. He was in Houston to work on more aspects of the Ares training program. Right now, he was listening desultorily to the evening news and wondering what to do with the evening.

The newsreader – a stunningly beautiful young woman – said that the crew for Ares had just been announced.

Viktorenko coughed, and dropped the little bottle.

He sat up, wiping a fine spray of the liquor from his upper lip. He couldn't have heard correctly.

But no: there was a picture of Natalie herself, an official portrait in which she sat before a nondescript background, staring past the photographer's shoulder, nervously clutching a long-obsolete model of a biconic MEM.

He picked up the phone and dialled York.

'Marushka! I just heard! You are going to Mars!'

York's voice was flat, unemotional. 'It isn't true.'

'What? But I have seen the news . . .'

'Yeah. Me too. But I haven't heard anything from NASA. Until they call me, I don't know anything about it.'

489

Viktorenko felt his mouth opening and closing, like a fish's. *You are going to Mars! You should be dancing, singing!* The silence on the line stretched out.

'Marushka. You are alone?'

'Uh huh.'

Of course you are. 'Do I have your permission to come wait with you, until the phone call comes? Perhaps this will help you.'

'If you like. You don't have to. I'm fine, Vladimir.'

'Of course you are.'

Viktorenko hung up, swept up six of the miniatures from the mini bar, and ran out of the room.

In her rented apartment York was sitting on the couch, alone, with the TV running in the background. She wore a sports shirt and slacks. On the living room walls she had pinned up her old Mariner pictures, and there was work scattered over the small desk, half-finished: a new paper, evidently, on the surface properties of some obscure region of the planet Mars.

Viktorenko bustled in. 'I bring you a present.' He dug the six miniatures out of his pocket, and set them up in a row along the top of the TV set.

'What's that for?'

'For when you get the right call. Or, perhaps, in case you get the wrong one.'

He sat beside her, then, and held her hand, and they watched the TV together, without speaking. At first her hand was stiff in his, but after a couple of minutes she clung to him, and he could feel the cold dampness of her palm.

The phone rang, startling Viktorenko.

York let it ring a couple of times. Then she unwound her hand from Viktorenko's and walked to the phone. Her steps were slow and deliberate, as if she were wearing some invisible pressure suit.

'York.'

He heard her exhale, softly.

'Oh, hi, Mom. No. It's not true. Well, maybe. I've only seen the TV news, like you. NASA haven't called me. Until then I . . . No, I don't think I should call them. They know where I am. I'll just wait here until – yes, maybe you should get off the line, Mom. I'll call as soon as I know. Bye. Yes, me too. Bye.'

She hung up. She turned to Viktorenko and shrugged.

On the TV a rerun of some awful dated sitcom was showing; Viktorenko could barely follow the quick-fire accents, and found the visual business of the show cheap and unfunny.

York sat silently, trembling a little. He doubted that she could even see the TV images.

The phone rang. York got up again.

'York.

'Yes, sir.'

She fell silent, then, for long seconds.

'Yes, sir. Thank you. I'll do as best I can. Sure. Goodbye.'

She hung up the phone. Viktorenko did not dare to speak.

York walked to the TV, where the canned laughter was still rattling from the inane sitcom. She picked up one of Viktorenko's miniatures, twisted it open, threw the cap across the room, and downed the draught in one gulp.

Viktorenko couldn't contain himself. He got off the sofa and crossed the room in one great stride; he got hold of York by the elbows. 'Well? Well, Marushka?'

She looked up at him, her eyes vulnerable under those peculiar big eyebrows. 'It's true,' she said. 'Vlad, it's true. That was Joe Muldoon.'

Viktorenko wanted to dance, shout, pick her up and whirl her around! . . . But she just stood there, looking up at him, fiddling with the empty bottle; he told himself to be calm, and wait on her needs.

She picked up the phone, and called her mother. Then she suggested that they should wait a while, in case there were any more calls.

So, bizarrely, Viktorenko found himself back on the sofa, holding York's trembling hand, and watching the stupid sitcom run its meaningless course.

After a time, York said: 'I can't stand this, Vladimir.'

'What?'

She made a small gesture; he guessed she was holding herself in, tight. 'The uncertainty. The roller-coaster ride. The lack of control I have over my own life. My God, Vlad, after the space soak mission was canned I thought I was further from Mars than ever. And now – out of nowhere – *this*.'

He squeezed her hand. 'You were never in the military, Marushka. This is the military way to do things. In the military, you have no choices, no control. Perhaps your civilian NASA has more of a military streak than many care to admit.'

491

The phone rang. It was Adam Bleeker, whose seat York had taken. York spoke to him briefly, quietly.

'How is he?'

She shrugged.

They sat a little longer, but there were no more calls. No doubt those idiots in the Astronaut Office were closing ranks, punishing York – and Gershon, probably – for ousting their buddies, their preferred candidates.

Eventually Viktorenko decided enough was enough. 'No more of this! We would handle matters so much better in Russia. Come. We will go out. We will eat, we will go to a barbecue pit or a Pizza Hut or a Mexican drive-in, or whatever you like. My treat! The treat of the Soviet Union, Marushka!'

At first she demurred, but he insisted.

As they left the apartment, a fat young man with a tape recorder came running up the hall; a spotlight glared over his shoulder.

'Miss York! KNWS-TV News. How does it feel to be the first woman on Mars?'

Book 5

ARES

Ochre light, oddly mottled, shone down through the little Command Module window beside her: *Mars*, grown so huge it no longer fit into the window; Mars, sliding like oil past the glass.

'Three minutes to loss of signal,' capcom John Young called up.

'Roger,' Stone replied.

The crew sat side by side in Apollo. York's pressure suit felt hot, bulky, the angular acceleration couch uncomfortably restricting after so long in the Mission Module's shirt-sleeve environment.

'Ares, Houston, we read you as go for Mars orbit insertion. Everything is go for MOI. Two minutes to loss of signal. Be assured you're riding the best bird we can find.'

'Thank you, John. We appreciate that.'

Sure. But Young's assurances weren't all that comforting, York thought.

Right now, Ares was free-falling past Mars. Even if the big MS-II engines failed altogether, they still had enough speed to escape from Mars's gravity well, and emerge on a free return trajectory back to Earth.

But if Stone, and Mission Control, decided to commit to MOI, this Mars Orbit Insertion burn, then their final abort option would be gone. They would be committed to Martian orbit.

MOI really was the moment of truth, the moment when Ares finally cut the long, fragile ties of gravity and celestial mechanics that could draw it home to Earth again.

But Ares was about to fall around the back of Mars, into its shadow, and out of radio line of sight of Earth; and it was at that point, with Stone able to rely on nothing but the instruments in Ares, that the burn would be initiated. The crew would be on their own – isolated by time lag and the rocky bulk of Mars – when it most mattered.

According to the ground's best predictions, they were going to hit the MOI window within plus or minus ten miles of the required height above Mars.

However, who the hell believed predictions?

The MS-II was going to impose a tough acceleration, this time. So all the stack's remaining modules – the MS-II and MS-IVB booster stages, then the MEM, the Mission Module and Apollo – were still strung out along the center line of the stack, along the line of the burn. Then, after the burn was completed, and they were safely in Martian orbit – if they got there – the crew would have to go

495

through a complex repositioning exercise to prepare for the landing. It was one hell of a way to run a mission, York thought: to reassemble your spacecraft in Martian orbit . . .

'One minute to loss of signal,' said Stone.

'One minute,' John Young said, almost simultaneously. He was timing his transmissions so they arrived to match their local events. 'Ares, this is Houston. All your systems are looking good going around the corner.'

'Copy that, John.'

York could hear the tension in Stone's voice. Gershon sat in the center couch, uncharacteristically silent, pensive.

The ochre light shifted. She looked up.

Ares was dipping low across Mars.

Less than three hundred miles beneath York, a mottled, battered landscape slid by. She could see Arabia, a bright yellow circular area, and to its right an irregular, blue-black patch, the volcanic plateau called the Syrtis Major Planum. Syrtis had been the first Martian feature observed by telescope from Earth. *And now I am falling ass-backwards over Syrtis itself; I can see it before me.* It was a lurid patch the size of her hand.

She felt the hairs on the back of her neck stand up, prickling. She was so close that Syrtis slid across her field of view, falling toward her as Ares slid deeper into Mars's gravity well, moving past her fast enough for it to change the lighting conditions in her cabin.

The belly of Mars seemed to bulge out at her. Mars was a small world; in contrast to Earth, she could see its curvature prominently, even at such a low altitude.

She tried to be analytical, to separate the panorama into geological units . . . But this was a battered, tired landscape. The land was the color of bruises, inflicted by the ancient meteorite impacts: like accumulated porphyrin, which the little world was unable to break down. *Bruises on the face of a corpse, left there for all time.* It was a surprisingly depressing panorama, obviously lifeless.

'Thirty seconds,' Stone said.

York turned briefly to her own workstation. On this first pass around the planet, the science platform was working at full capacity, taking observations of the surface and atmosphere. Even the tail-off of the radio carrier during loss of signal, as Earth was eclipsed by the atmosphere of Mars, would give a lot of information about the structure of the Martian air.

These first observations were important. If the burn went wrong, and the mission turned into nothing more than a flyby, it could be that these contingency observations would be the most significant data that Ares would return.

Ares dipped lower now, and swept over the line between night and day. She was granted a brief glimpse of a line of craters picked out by the last of the sun, their wind-eroded rims casting long shadows across the ancient, resilient surface.

'Ares, Houston, coming up to loss of signal,' Young said from distant Mission Control. 'You're go all the way, guys.'

'Thanks a lot,' Stone said. 'See you on the other side, John. Ten. Nine.'

... Then the cratered contrast was gone, and Ares flew into shadow, over a land immersed in unbroken darkness. *The solar system is full of empty, unlit worlds*, she thought. *Earth is the exception.* She felt isolated, vulnerable. A long way from home.

'Three. Two. One.'

Static burst from the grilles on the science station racks, from the little speakers in her headset.

LOS had come right on time. That meant their trajectory was true.

Gershon laughed, explosively. 'How about that. Right on the button. Hey, Phil. I wonder if they just turned it off. Wouldn't that be terrific? I can imagine John saying, "They're just a bunch of uptight assholes. Whatever happens, just turn the damn thing off..."'

York could see Stone in profile, beyond the cupped headrest of his couch. He was grinning, but it was a tight grin that showed a lot of teeth. 'Let's go to the MOI checklist, Ralph. Ah, coming up on ten minutes fifteen to MOI.'

York craned her head upwards, staring at the circular patch of darkness that was Mars. She summoned up a map of the surface, in her mind. Ares was traveling over the Hesperia Planum, another volcanic plain to the east of Syrtis, close to the equator.

She could see traces, outlines, glimmers of white against the darkness. *Has to be starlight, picking out the cee-oh-two ice.*

She had seen nomads' camp fires burn, pinpricks in the night of the huge deserts of Earth. But there were no fires in this Martian desert. In fact, of all the worlds of the Solar System, only Earth – with its oxygen-rich atmosphere – knew fire.

'Five minutes to the burn.'

She was sealed into her suit, shut in with the hiss of oxygen, the whir of fans, the scratch of her own breathing. She felt isolated, cut off. *Lousy design. I need to hold somebody's hand.*

'Okay, Ralph,' Stone said. 'Translation control power, on.'

'On.'

'Rotational hand controller number two, armed.'

'Armed.'

'Okay. Stand by for the primary TVC check.'

'Pressures coming up nicely,' Gershon said. 'Everything is great . . .'

A hundred feet behind them, the big MS-II injection stage was rousing from its long, interplanetary hibernation. Heaters in the big cryogenic tanks were boiling off vapor, bringing up a pressure sufficient to force propellant and oxidizer out of the tanks, and Stone and Gershon were running tests of the sequence which would bring the hydrogen and oxygen into explosive combination inside the combustion chambers of the four J-2S engines.

In the window above her, she could see a segment of a circle: bone white in the starlight, quite precise, immense.

'. . . Oh, my God.'

Stone twisted, awkward in his suit, and peered over his shoulder. 'What's wrong?'

'*Look* at that. I think it's Hellas.' The deepest impact crater on Mars. And white, with its frozen lake of carbon dioxide. Somewhere in there, the Soviets had set down Mars 9.

Stone grunted. 'You're going to be looking at that for a long time.' He turned his back, his disapproval evident, and resumed the pre-burn checklist with Gershon.

'Thirty seconds,' Stone said. 'Everything is looking nominal. Still go for MOI.'

He placed his gloved hand over the big plastic firing button.

The whole burn was automated, York knew, controlled by computers in the cluster's Instrumentation Unit, the big doughnut of electronics behind the Mission Module. Multiple computers, endlessly checking everything and backing each other up and taking polls among themselves. It was hard to see what could go wrong. Nevertheless, Stone sat there with his hand on the button, ready to take over if he had to. To York, it looked comical – and yet, somehow heroic as well. Touching.

'Twenty seconds,' Stone said. 'Brace, guys.'

'All systems are go for MOI,' Gershon said.

York checked her own racks. 'Roger, go.'

She checked the restraints across her chest, rapidly, and settled her head against her canvas headrest. She tried to make sure there were no creases or folds in the thick layers of the pressure suit under her legs or back.

She felt her heart pound, and chill sweat broke out across her cheeks and under her chin.

'T minus ten seconds,' Gershon said.

Stone's hands hovered over his controls.

'Eight seconds.'

'I got a 99,' Stone said. He pushed a button. 'Press to proceed.'

York felt air rush out of her in a sigh.

'Six seconds,' Gershon said. 'Five, four. Ullage.'

There was a brief rattle, a sharp kick in the small of her back. Eight small solid-fuel rockets, clustered around the base of the MS-II, had given the booster a small shove, helping the propellants settle in their tanks.

Gershon said, 'Two. One. Ignition.'

The crisp ullage shove died, to be replaced by a smooth, steady push that she felt in her back, her neck, her thighs.

The force built up rapidly. The silence was eerie. She had her back to the direction of thrust, and she felt as if she was sitting up and being hurled forward, into some unknown future.

'Fifteen seconds in,' Stone said. 'Point five G. Climbing.'

After a year of zero G, the pressure already felt enormous. *So much for all those hours of exercises; didn't do a damn bit of good.*

There was a shudder, now, a vibration that set into the walls and equipment racks around her. Loose gear rattled. She heard a clatter somewhere behind her: some bit of equipment, inadequately stowed, falling the length of the Command Module. 'One G,' Stone called. 'Two.'

The pressure built up further, compressing her chest.

'Jesus,' Gershon said. He had to shout over the rattling of the walls and equipment. 'Eight minutes of this.'

'Can it,' Stone snapped. 'Two point five G. We're doing fine. Right down Route One. Three point six. Hang on, guys.'

She felt unable to breathe. It was as if the pressure suit was tightening around her, constricting her. It was a bizarre, terrifying, claustrophobic experience.

A fringe of bubbly darkness gathered at the edge of her vision.

They were utterly alone, inside a tiny artifact arcing above the

499

surface of an empty planet, reliant on the smooth working of their machines to survive.

'Four point three G,' Stone called. She could hear the rattle of the thrust in his voice. 'That's it. That's the peak. Coming up on pericenter.'

Stone and Gershon began to run through a readout of the status of the maneuver so far.

'Burn time four four five.' Four minutes, forty-five seconds. Half-way through. 'Ten values on the angles: BGX minus point one, BGY minus point one, BGZ plus point one . . .' Velocity errors on the burn were amounting to only a foot per second, along each of the three axes of space. 'No trim. Minus six point eight delta-vee-cee. Fuel thirty-eight point eight. Lox thirty-nine zip, plus fifty on balance. We ran an increase on the PUGS. Projected for a two nineteen point nine times twelve six eleven point three . . .'

York translated the numbers in her head. The burn was working. The cluster was heading for an elliptical orbit, two hundred by twelve thousand miles: almost perfect.

'Hey, Natalie.' It was Gershon.

'What?'

'Look up.'

With an effort, she tilted back her head. The helmet restricted her, and under the acceleration her skull felt like it had been replaced by a ball of concrete, tearing at her neck muscles.

Through her small window she saw the battered southern plain of Mars. And the bulging landscape above her was lit up, right at the center, by a soft, pink glow; it was like a highlight on a huge, ochre bowling ball.

It was the glow of the burn, the light of the MS-II.

For the first time in the planet's four-billion-year history, artificial light had come to the Martian night.

Friday, August 17, 1984
Lyndon B. Johnson Space Center, Houston

The questions came drifting out of a sea of lights so intense that they seemed to bake York's face dry.

'How does it feel to be on the crew?' 'What about the guys you beat out?' 'Who will be first on the surface?' 'What's it like in space? . . .'

The three of them – chaperoned by Joe Muldoon and Rick

500

Llewellyn, head of NASA's Public Affairs Office – sat on a rickety podium, with the NASA logo emblazoned behind them, and a Revell model of a Columbia MEM on the table before them. The briefing room here in the Public Affairs Office was packed, and in front of their table there was what the Old Heads called a goat fuck, an unseemly scramble of microphones and camera lenses, pushed into the faces of the astronauts.

Rarely in York's life had people been interested enough to ask her to explain herself, her background, her motives, her hopes and fears. Now, *everything* about her was significant: everything that had happened in her life, every aspect of her personality.

It was probably going to last forever. And she found she hated it.

She envied Phil Stone, with his neat, crew-cut good looks and his hint of a Midwest twang – the stereotypical astronaut hero – for the grace with which he fielded the dumbest, most repetitive questions. And the press had already taken Ralph Gershon to their hearts for his infectious grins – *the glamorous, hellraising bachelor spaceman* – and for his wisecracking, and the hint of danger, of ambiguity about him. Even if he did make Rick Llewellyn visibly nervous every time he opened his mouth. And even if there was, as far as York was concerned, an undertow of racism about the patronizing affection with which Gershon was treated.

And that left York: in her own view, the least equipped to handle the media pressure, but the one in whom most interest was placed. And all for the wrong reasons.

It started the day after her place in the crew was announced. All the outlets used the same ancient stock NASA photo of her, holding up an outdated biconic MEM model. 'This quiet, intent and dedicated scientist . . .' 'Redhead Natalie York is, at 37, unmarried and without children . . .' 'We asked beautician Marcia Forbes what advice she would give America's premier space woman. *Well, to begin, with those eyebrows, you know* . . . ' 'This mop-haired 35-year-old native of LA . . .' ' . . . A crop-haired brunette of medium height, Natalie York is said to be disconcerted by the prospect of publicity . . .' 'Her dark, close-cropped hair and her Latin good looks make Natalie a woman of glamor and mystery, but a natural for the role of America's first woman on Mars . . .'

Hair, eyebrows and teeth. It drove her crazy.

Already they'd tracked down her mother, who was loving the attention, and Mike Conlig and his new family, who weren't.

It would help if NASA had given her any preparation for handling this. Even basic communications training. Instead, the only guideline was: *Don't embarrass the Agency.*

Some of the questions were tougher, more pointed, than others.

'Doesn't the case of Adam Bleeker indicate that we're not yet ready to send humans on these immense long-duration missions? That we don't yet know enough about the effects of microgravity on the body? That, in fact, the Ares mission is an irresponsible jaunt?'

'You're surely right we don't know enough,' Muldoon said smoothly. 'But the only way we're going to find out is by getting out there and working in microgravity and studying the effects. Sure there are dangers, but we accept them as part of the job. It's a price of being first. You ought to know that Adam was broken up to be taken off the flight, medical risks or not; and I know everyone in the Astronaut Office would volunteer to take his place . . .'

'Ralph, you want to talk about your Cambodia runs?'

'Ah, that's all in the public record now, and I got nothing more to add. It's all a long time ago.'

'But how do you feel about having to distort records and maintain a cover-up that lasted for years before –'

'You can read about it in my memoirs, Will.'

Laughter.

'What about Apollo-N?'

Muldoon leaned into his microphone. 'Ah, what about it, sir?'

'I took the JSC visitors' tour earlier on. Big heroic machines. Lots of plaques about Apollo 11. Mission Control as a national monument, sure. But Apollo-N might never have happened, still less the Apollo 1 fire, for all the evidence I saw at JSC. What is it with you people? How can you pretend that everything's upbeat, that nothing bad ever happens?'

'We don't pretend that at all,' Muldoon said. 'I think the crash is uppermost in our minds, every day.'

'That's what you call it? *The crash?* The damn thing didn't crash, it exploded in orbit.'

'We have to learn from what went wrong, move forward, make sure that the losses we suffered aren't wasted. We can't afford to brood, or be deterred from our intentions.'

'Look, I'm from out of town. All around JSC I saw Apollo-N car lots and shopping plazas. There's even an Apollo-N memorial park, for God's sake. Don't you think a public reaction like that, spontaneous and visible, deserves something more from you people than "learning from what went wrong?" . . .'

Hell, yes, York thought. Some around JSC thought the malls and so forth were tacky, somehow undignified. York didn't; as the reporter was implying, such things were symbols erected by the people out there as they responded to the human tragedy. Sure, it was car lots and malls: what the hell else were they supposed to do?

But she'd also got to know the pilots' viewpoint well enough to understand it. They'd accepted the deaths, put Apollo-N behind them and moved on. Ben would have done just the same. It was difficult for an outsider to accept, but that was the culture.

York wasn't a pilot, though. She'd spent long enough agonizing over her own role here, in the wake of Ben's death. As if there wasn't already enough doubt, enough ambiguity in her mind.

She'd resolved it by determining, in the privacy of her own mind, that everything she did from this point in was for Ben. It was as simple as that.

A strident woman stood up. 'Natalie, as a scientist, how do you respond to those people who claim that the whole of the Mars expedition is a stunt, a fake? – that instead of traveling to Mars you'll just be closeted away in some studio in Nevada for a year, bounding around a mockup of the MEM?'

That did it. York was incensed. She leaned forward so her voice boomed from the speakers. 'Look, I've really no time for crap like this. We're training for a deep space mission, for Christ's sake. Why should we give up our time, put more pressure on ourselves, just to respond to dumb-ass remarks like –'

Phil Stone put his hand over her microphone.

'I understand how Natalie feels,' he said smoothly. 'Believe me. The suggestion's just implausible. I think the best proof I can offer you that our mission is genuine is this: it's probably easier to fly to Mars for real than to fake it up.'

That got a laugh, and the moment passed.

York tried to steady her breathing. She knew she was in for a lecture from Rick Llewellyn later.

'What about sex?'

Stone asked, 'What do you mean?'

A male reporter got up now, in a seedy Lieutenant Columbo raincoat, a grin on his face. 'What about sex? You're all normal, healthy adults – America's first mixed space crew – and you'll be

503

cooped up in that dinky Mission Module for eighteen months. And Ralph and Natalie aren't married . . . Come on. Two guys and one gal? What a situation.'

York felt her cheeks burn. *I could just walk out of this.* Yeah. And out of the mission.

Gershon was grinning, enjoying it all hugely.

Stone pursed his lips. 'I take it you know the official NASA line. It's in our induction handbooks. *Close coupling of crew members is to be avoided.*' He smiled, self-deprecating, completely in control. 'Some help.' Another laugh. 'But I'd say that advice is basically right. Hell, we're all adults. But a sexual relationship between crew members – or, more importantly, a special emotional relationship – would be harmful to the stability of the crew as a whole, and might compromise our ability to support the whole crew through the entire duration of the mission. And if you fully understand the potential for negative impact – you've got jealousy, special treatment, circumvention of the chain of command, recrimination and regret when you fall out, and so on – I bet this avoidance will be adopted as a group norm on future mixed flights.'

Gershon cocked his head. 'Adopted as a what?'

'Pay more attention to your psych training, Gershon.'

Another laugh. Another defused moment.

York hoped the color was fading from her cheeks. It was remarkable the way Stone could turn out the party line, though. The same bland crap, the half-lie which NASA had fed to the world since the days of Mercury.

And I'm just part of the machine now, she thought. *An accomplice in the traditional lie. I'm an astronaut, now; my human needs don't exist any more, officially.*

The reporter's question, if facetious, was actually perceptive. NASA was terrific at the technology, she thought, but stunningly bad at dealing with the needs of the soft, pink bodies they loaded inside their gleaming von Braun dream machines – unable even to recognize that those needs existed.

The questions continued to come, sliding from topic to topic. And all of them, York thought, looking for ways into the central, banal question everyone wanted to ask of an astronaut:

What does it feel like, in space? On the Moon? On Mars?

At first it seemed just dumb to her: naive, too open, without a possible answer. And the way it cropped up, in one form or another, at every conference irritated her.

Today, Joe Muldoon tried to answer it.

504

'I'm just an ordinary guy. But I guess you could say I've done something extraordinary.

'Let me tell you what it was like. When you look down on the Earth from orbit, you forget about your hassles: the bills you got to pay, the trouble you're having with your car. Instead, all you think about is the people: the people you know and care about, down there in that blue bowl of air. And you realize, somewhat, how much indeed you do care about them . . .'

Save for Muldoon's voice, the room was silent.

She watched the questioners, tough, cynical pressmen all, as they fixed on the face of the astronaut. Even the woman who'd asked about the fake-up was listening, intent, trying to understand.

Muldoon was saying, 'To see the Earth fall away behind your receding capsule . . . To stand on the Moon, and see that little world curve away under your feet: to be cognizant that you are one of just two humans on this whole world, and to be able to hold your hand up and cover the Earth . . .'

Here you had a handful of men who had done something extra-ordinary: flown beyond the air, even walked on the airless surface of the Moon – unimaginable things, things which nothing in their human evolutionary heritage had prepared them for. And York began to see that something in the press people – masked by all the banter and joshing and bluster – was responding to that. Something primeval.

You've been up there. I could never go. Don't say you're just an ordinary guy. What is it like? Tell me.

As the astronauts spoke to the public – even though, for God knew what reason, even a skilled operator like Muldoon always seemed to fall into a stilted jargon littered with 'somewhat' and 'cognizant' – a very basic and primal communication was struggling to happen, a layer under the spoken. The words of Muldoon and the rest weren't enough; they could never be. York often had the feeling that people wanted to close in and *touch* the astronauts. As if they were gods. Or as if information, sensations, memories could be transmitted through the skin.

But *she* could not contribute to this. How could she? She'd never flown higher than in a T-38.

She felt like a fake, sitting there bathed in TV lights, alongside a man who had bent down and run his fingers through lunar dirt.

... How frequently we perceive our national debates about the future of SPACE TRAVEL veering between hysterical extremes! And all of it is played out against the background of the most cynically AMORAL times in living memory.

While the 'yuppies' parade their Rolex watches and their BMW sports cars, and while our illusory economic 'upturn' is fuelled only by the President's massive rise in MILITARY EXPENDITURE – which is itself inherently inflationary, and to which the Mars mission has become explicitly linked, by NASA's supporters in politics – all of which is leading to an immense DEFICIT which we will bequeath to our children – the income gap between richest and poorest is at its widest in two decades.

And that very DEFICIT is itself a cynical manipulation of the economy by an Administration which is determined that there shall be no opportunity, because of the DEFICIT burden, for an expansion in welfare spending or other programs in the years beyond President Reagan's retirement in 1988.

At its grandest, the dehumanizing experience of SPACE can lead us, paradoxically, to a fuller understanding of the HUMANITY the astronauts must cast aside. Indeed it can teach us a truer perspective:

—CONTEMPT for our works
—VALUE of ourselves.

It is a new perspective which can lead us closer to GOD.

But all too often the experience of SPACE, certainly as portrayed to the general public by the Government information organizations and public bodies supporting and opposing the space initiative, veers between twin mirror-image idols, both of them false:

—MELLONOLATRY, that is the baseless worship of technology for its own sake

—MISONEISM, an equally baseless fear and hatred of technology.

What better argument for casting aside our rocket vessels now, with their deadly NUCLEAR hearts! ...

Excerpt from 'Mellonolatry and Misoneism: The Twin Idols of Space,' Rev. B. Seger, Church of St Joseph of Cupertino. All rights reserved.

Ralph Gershon was standing in the hatchway of the MEM mockup, his face visible behind his clear visor. 'Okay, Natalie. You want to come in now?'

'Rog, Ralph.'

York, on the faked-up Martian surface, took a deliberate step toward the MEM.

As she moved, the harness around her chest hauled at her brutally, and she was dragged upwards through a couple of feet. She tripped. The suit, pressurized at three and a half pounds per square inch, was like a balloon around her, and it kept her body stiff, like a mannequin, and she couldn't save herself.

She toppled like a felled tree.

She fell on her knees, with her gloved hands in the dirt. The soil in front of her face was dried-out Houston gumbo, sprinkled with pink gravel: she was on what the astronauts called, inaccurately, a rock pile, a simulated Martian surface. This surface was more or less flat, because flat areas were where the more conservative mission planners wanted to put the MEM down.

'Goddamn this harness.'

'You tell it, Natalie. You want any help?'

'No. No, I'll manage, damn it.'

York was lashed up to a tethered Martian gravity simulator. The harness around her chest was attached by cables to a pole above her; the cables led to pulleys which offset two-thirds of her weight. Just like on Mars. Except on Mars, there wouldn't be some ludicrous, clumsy rope hauling unpredictably at her back every time she took a step.

To get upright now, for example, she had to push at the ground, and let the harness haul her upright, and scrabble with her ankles at the soil, hoping not to tip over backwards again.

She stood there teetering on her feet, her hands outstretched for balance. Through her helmet she could hear ironic applause from the technicians.

'Ignore the assholes,' Gershon advised.

'Rog.' She took a breath. 'Here I come again, Ralph.'

'Just take it steadily, Natalie. That's my girl . . .'

She took a slow and measured step. It was actually a lot easier to take her feet off the surface than to put them back down again.

She seemed to drift in a shallow parabola through the air before each step completed, and she grounded with a crunch in the dried gumbo. It was like swimming through some viscous liquid, all her motions rendered slow, dreamlike, unstable.

At last, though, she seemed to be getting up a little momentum. The mass of her backpack tugged at her, its inertia constantly dragging her off her line; whenever she wanted to change direction she had to think four or five steps ahead.

The MEM drifted before her, remote and all but unattainable, bathed in movie-set floodlights. The mockup's hatch gaped open, the fluorescent light within revealing the hardwood-and-ply nature of its construction.

Not far from the MEM was a mocked-up Mars Rover, the TV camera mounted on its prow swiveling to stare at her with its dark lens. The camera was live. York, under its gaze, felt like some gorilla loping around its cage.

Ralph, of course, had taken to Mars-walking as if he'd been born to it.

This was actually a simulation of their second walk on Mars, the first time they would get to do any serious work. The first walk would be an hour-long solo by Phil Stone, as commander. The purpose of the first walk – according to the mission plan – was for him to test out the systems of his suit and his general mobility, to check out the status of the MEM after landing, and to resolve any glitches with the comms systems. Stone would do little science, that first time out, except to pick up a small contingency surface sample.

Of course there was a hidden agenda.

The attention of the Earth – and all of NASA's sponsors in the White House and on the Hill – would be on that first walk, the first small steps by a man on Mars. So all the ceremony – putting up the Stars and Stripes, the footprints-and-flags stuff, the speech by President Reagan (who was, right now, basking in his new landslide win against Teddy Kennedy) – could be got out of the way in that first hour. And on Joe Muldoon's advice, learning from his Apollo experiences, *everything* in that first walk was being checklisted and timelined, including Reagan's call.

After that, hopefully, the rest of the program would be free for some serious work.

It made some sense to York. She knew how such things had to be accommodated. But it still seemed odd to her, sometimes, that NASA should be planning the exploration of Mars around TV ratings.

* * *

Now she reached the MEM. She skidded a little as she came to a halt, at the foot of the ladder down from the hatch.

The simulation supervisor spoke to her over her headset. 'Natalie, this time we'd like you to try extracting a SNAP from its cask.'

'Rog.' She tried to keep the weary irritation out of her voice. That meant she had to trudge further, across to the plywood Mars Rover. She swiveled on her heel like a puppet, until her body was pointing at the Rover, and then lumbered across the crunching surface.

The dummy Surface Exploration Package was already set up, its silver and gold boxes sprawling across the surface in a spider-web of power cables and data feeds. Some of the cables still needed connecting, as did the antenna for transmitting signals back to Earth. The SNAP generator – System of Nuclear Auxiliary Power – was a box to one side of the little complex. York was supposed to activate it by inserting a little pod of plutonium into it. The pod – a dummy, one of several – was mounted in a little rack at the back of the Rover. It was a narrow cylinder, maybe a foot long, held inside a graphite storage cask.

She got hold of a handling rod. By pulling a trigger handle, she opened little jaws at the end of the handle and tried to engage them around the pod. Her pressurized, elasticated gloves resisted every movement of her hands; it was like trying to close a fist around a rubber ball.

When she had got the handling jaws open, she had to use two hands to guide the open mouth around the end of the pod.

Finally she tried to pull the pod free of its flask. But the damn thing wouldn't come.

The jaws slipped off the pod, and she staggered backwards. She could hear her breathing rasp, the rattle of the cable on her harness.

'You got any suggestions, Ralph?'

'Hold it there. Let me try that mother.'

She rested surreptitiously against her cables, while Gershon clambered backwards out of the MEM. He wasn't hooked up to a Peter Pan, so he labored under the full weight of his suit, and his movements were heavy and awkward.

He climbed down the ladder and took the handling rod. With York's help he got the jaws fitted to the fuel pod. He started to pull; he even leaned back, digging his heels into the dried-out gumbo. But the pod wouldn't come loose.

The SimSup called, 'Ah, you guys want to take a break? That thing sure is jammed.'

'Nope,' said Gershon. 'Natalie, let's try the direct approach. You get hold of the rod, here.'

'Okay.' She took it from him, moving slowly, being careful not to release the grip on the trigger handle.

'Now.' He reached over and took a geological hammer from the loop at her waist. 'Start pulling, babe.'

With both hands on the handling rod, she leaned back and dragged.

Gershon started hitting the cask with the hammer, with high, sweeping blows; his whole body had to swivel to deliver the blows.

Every time a blow landed York could feel the fuel pod shudder. 'It's not working, Ralph.'

'The hell it isn't.'

He spun like a hammer-thrower, and with two hands he delivered one final almighty blow to the cask.

The graphite split right in two.

The fuel pod came free. York stumbled backwards, her boots scuffing at the gumbo in an effort to keep upright. The cables helped her this time, giving her just enough leverage to keep from falling.

The fuel pod went tumbling to the surface, like a dropped relay baton.

Gershon lumbered across to her, his face framed by his visor. 'Hey. You okay?'

'Sure. How's the pod?'

They bent over the little metal cylinder, where it lay in the pink gravel. There was a hairline crack down one seam.

'How about that,' Gershon said. 'We busted it. We nuked Mars.'

'Well, it was only a mockup. Probably the real thing will be tougher.'

'Christ, I hope so.'

'Okay, guys,' the supervisor said. 'Both your heart rates are showing a little high. That is definitely it for now. Take five. We'll resume in an hour.'

Jorge Romero came barging into the simulation chamber. 'Goddamn it,' he stormed. 'You did it again, Natalie! You broke my damn SEP! *And* you were a half-hour behind schedule!'

York, free of her cabling, was sitting on the Rover with her helmet on her lap, cradling a mug of coffee. She smiled at him. 'Oh, take it easy, Jorge. It's only a sim.'

Romero, small, purposeful, pink with anger, marched back and forth across the fake Martian surface, sending up little sprays of gravel. 'But that's three times out of the last three that my SEP implementation has been screwed up . . .'

Her training had been intense, the compressed schedule committing her and the others to eighteen hours a day in complex exercises like this, for long weeks at a stretch. She felt her patience drawing thin, as Romero paced about. *I don't have time for these debates, Jorge.* But she owed him an answer.

'Look,' she said to Romero, 'I know how you feel. But you have to make allowances, Jorge. Out on a field trip, you can take as long as you want, days or weeks thinking over a sample if you need to. It's not like that here. The Mars-walks can last only a few hours each. They'll be even more curtailed than the old Apollo moonwalks. So we have to plan out every step. These simulations are' – she waved a hand – 'choreography. It's a different way of working, for you and me. *Real time*, they call it.'

Romero was still pissed. 'Goddamn it. I'm going to write a memo to Joe Muldoon. All these screwups. Those Flight Operations people just can't be running the mission properly.'

'But that's the point of the sim, Jorge. We're supposed to break things.' She found a grin spreading across her face, but she suppressed it. 'I'm sorry, Jorge. I do know how you feel. I sympathize.'

He glared at her. 'Oh, you do? So you haven't gone over to the *operational* camp altogether?'

She winced. 'That's not fair, damn it.'

His anger seemed to recede. He sat on the Rover, small beside her ballooning white suit. 'Natalie. I guess you should know. I'm resigning from the program.'

She was startled. 'You can't.' Romero was a principal investigator for Martian geology. If he was lost to the program now, its scientific validity would be greatly diminished. 'Come on, Jorge.'

'Oh, I mean it. I'm almost sure I'm going to do it.' He looked around at the sandpit sourly. 'In fact, I think today has made up my mind for me. And if you had any integrity left, Natalie York, you'd quit too.'

'Jorge, are you crazy? You'll have a geologist on Mars. What more do you want, for Christ's sake?'

'No. You'll be a technician, at best. Natalie, Ares is a marvelous system, *operationally*. Scientifically, it's Apollo all over again. Look at this.' He waved a hand around the sim site. 'All the stuff you'll actually use to explore Mars. Pulleys and ropes. The MET. That damn beach buggy, the Rover, with its carrying capacity of, what, a few hundred pounds? And the way you fumble with those gloves

511

and that ludicrous handling rod.' His voice was tight, his color rising; he was genuinely angry, she saw. 'Natalie, all you have to do is look around you to see where the balance of the investment has gone. Did you know they've spent more on developing a long-lasting fabric for a Martian Stars and Stripes than on the whole of my SEP?'

Operational. Romero had used the word as if it was an obscenity. Once, York thought, she would have too. But maybe she saw a better balance now. A space program, especially something right out on the edge like this Ares shot to Mars, had to be a mix of the operational and the scientific. Without the operational, there wouldn't be any scientific anyhow.

She tried to explain some of this to Romero.

'Save it, Natalie. I've gone over all this a hundred times. I'll not be convinced. And as for you –' He hesitated.

'Yes? Say it, Jorge.'

'I think you've sold out, Natalie. I supported your application to NASA. Damn it, I got you in here. I hoped you could make a difference. But you've gone native. Now we have Apollo all over again, the same damn mistakes. But this time – in part, anyhow – it's your fault. And mine. And I'm sorry.'

He climbed off the Rover, stiffly, and walked away.

York found herself shaking, inside her pressure suit, from the ferocity of his attack.

January, 1985
Lyndon B. Johnson Space Center, Houston

In addition to their rising workload as launch day approached, the crew were still expected to attend PR functions. The astronauts called it 'time in the barrel.' Usually a head of a chamber of commerce would need a showpiece astronaut to attend a reception and shake hands and pose for pictures and spread goodwill.

York was lousy at it, and she tended to be kept behind the scenes, mostly doing goodwill tours to various NASA and contractor facilities. Gershon spent a lot of his time at Newport, where even now, the Columbia engineers were struggling to comb out the MEM problems highlighted by the D-prime mission and other tests, and complete their flight article, the MEM that would land on Mars.

York was sent up to Marshall.

They put her up overnight at the Sheraton Wooden Nickel in

Huntsville, a town which the tourist information called 'Rocket City.' The next day she was taken on a tour of Marshall by a couple of eager young engineers. Marshall had been hived off into NASA from the Army Ballistic Missile Agency, but its military origins were obvious; in fact it occupied a couple of thousand acres within the Redstone arsenal. She was shown a spectacular rocket garden at the Space Orientation Center, and shown around a huge test stand used in the development of Saturn F-1 engines. Saturn stages were assembled here, and then, bizarrely, traveled by water routes to the Cape; they were shipped on barges down the Tennessee River, then moved via the Ohio and Mississippi into the Gulf of Mexico, and then around the coast to Florida where they were brought into the Kennedy waterways.

She spent most of the day in von Braun's old conference room, with around twenty engineers. Most of them were young Americans, thus confounding her prejudice about Marshall's domination by Germans. Each of the engineers got up for a half-hour, to talk about his or her specialty, while the rest of them remained in the room, half looking at the speaker, and half at her. It seemed odd. Didn't these guys have anything better to do than look at *her* looking at Vu-graphs of rockets?

She was taken to a party at the Marshall people's country club, called the Mars Club.

There, she started to understand these people a little better.

This was an isolated group, stuck out here in Alabama, and they ate and drank spaceflight. To them, an astronaut was worthy of much greater homage than you were liable to receive in, say, Houston: and the Ares crew especially, as embodiments of von Braun's thirty-year-old dream of flying to Mars. Having an astronaut come out here to Alabama made it all real – and reassuring, in the midst of the usual crisis about the overall NASA budget and the future of the centers.

Later she went out to the Michoud plant in New Orleans, where the big External Tanks were being constructed. She spent longer there; she was being encouraged to make the Tanks a specialty during the mission.

The warehouses were immense caverns, big enough to hold the Tanks in great cylindrical chunks. She watched the manufacture of a bulkhead, a huge dome which would cap the big liquid hydrogen tank. The dome came in pie-shaped aluminum slices called gores, which needed manufacturing precision far beyond the capability of

513

any hydraulic press. So a forming die, with a flat sheet of aluminum on top, was sunk to the bottom of a sixty-thousand-gallon water tank, and a pattern of explosives was laid over the top. The gore was blasted into shape by surging shock waves.

York was awed by the scale of this enterprise. As she pursued her studies she became fascinated by the Tanks, even though they were perhaps the most mundane item in the whole mission.

Each Tank contained two massive, domed canisters, of propellant and oxidizer, connected by a cylindrical ring. The Tanks were coated with four inches of polyurethane foam and reflective shielding, to reduce boiloff of the cryogenic propellants. Inside the Tanks there were zero-G screens and cage-like baffles designed to stop the liquids sloshing during engine fire; the liquids were so heavy – more than two million pounds per tank – that the whole booster cluster could be thrown out of control by a severe enough slosh. And there were anti-vortex baffles, like huge propeller blades, to prevent the build-up of whirlpools – like those above the plughole of a draining bath – that could suck bubbles of vapor into the feed pipes . . .

Because of the need for extreme reliability, and the extraordinary range of conditions a spacecraft faced, every component of Ares contained a hell of a lot more engineering than she'd expected from outside the program. Even these simple babies, the Tanks. And because of the limited opportunities to test, traceability was essential: the ability to trace the life history of the humblest component right back to the ore from which it was smelted, to aid analysis in case of a failure.

This was the kind of level of detail which passed by people – including Capitol Hill decision makers – who balked at the price of components NASA ordered. *You want to spend how much, just on a goddamn gas can?*

When she was at sites like Michoud – in the thick of the program – the discouragement of Romero's resignation, and the skepticism, even downright hostility, of some sections of the press to the mission, all fell away from her. *How could I turn down a Saturn?* It would hurl her to Mars, to perform experiments of huge importance. A billion dollars were being invested in her, a billion eyes would be on her to do a good job.

At places like Michoud, she would become convinced that the price she was paying – all the Astronaut Office bullshit, the disruption of her career, the compromises of the science, the laying waste of her personal life – all of it was justified.

* * *

514

... We see that a manned space mission may be viewed as a complex biotechnical and sociotechnical system consisting of manufactured and human parts. A thorough understanding of the psychological and interpersonal dimensions of the Mars mission is crucial for reducing the probability of malfunction of the human part of the system, independently of the structural, mechanical and electronic elements, thereby forcing the readjustment of the system as a whole. Psychological and interpersonal stresses may be reduced through environmental engineering, manipulating crew composition, and the structuring of situations and tasks ...

To York, the psych experts' pseudo-scientific lectures – and the role-playing group exercises, and the individual and group psych analyses the crew had to endure – were the worst part of the pre-mission training. They were invariably excruciatingly dull, or profoundly embarrassing, or both.

York had little experience of the soft sciences; and she was dismayed by how limited the underlying thinking was – even here, in the money-no-object space program. Some of the theories that were being applied to her and her crewmates seemed speculative at best. And it was clear that the study of group psychology – as opposed to an individual's psychology – was still primitive.

Also, more fundamentally, experience of long-duration spaceflight was still so small that there was hardly any evidence to back up the guidelines and techniques being taught to them.

A deep space mission like Ares was basically unprecedented. So, to figure out what might befall the mental state of a Mars crew, the research psychologists were having to work from case studies of analogous situations – undersea habitats, nuclear submarines, polar research stations, isolated Canadian villages – and they used data from sensory deprivation experiments, sleeplessness studies, and work on social isolation. And sometimes, it seemed to York, they pushed those analogies a little far.

She'd got used to the idea that the Ares flight would take aerospace technology to its limit. It was disturbing to her that the softer disciplines, like psychology, would be pushing at the edge of their envelope too.

It was disturbing that in this fundamental aspect of the mission, nobody actually knew if the crew could survive the flight.

Later, from Vladimir Viktorenko, York started to learn something of how the Soviets handled such matters.

Small things: the Soviet mission planners would plan the selection of food to suit the taste of the crew. Color schemes for

515

the spacecraft's walls and equipment would be adjusted carefully. There would be music, on personal players, to suit individual preference. There would be recordings of simple sounds from home: bird songs, waves on a sea shore, falling rain. Cosmonauts were even encouraged to take living things into orbit, perhaps as part of biology experiments: plants, grasses, tadpoles – little droplets of life, said Viktorenko, bits of Earth's great ocean of existence.

The astronauts tended to dismiss the Soviets as backward, technically, compared to the US. But York decided she liked some aspects of the Soviet way. They'd come up with simple, practical, homely ways of dealing with the pink bodies inside the rockets.

She started bringing Viktorenko's ideas into the psych sessions with Stone and Gershon.

'. . . The sheer magnitude of the publicity program, I might say, is unmatched by anything we've seen since Apollo 11. The Voice of America is heavily involved, of course. We estimate that the VOA can reach twenty-seven percent of the world's population outside the US. This is the biggest operation in their history. Pre-launch we'll be sending out ten thousand forty-five-minute English-language tapes and scripts, to US Information Agency posts around the world. During the key phases of the mission the VOA will be broadcasting live commentary in seven major languages, and summaries in a further thirty-six.

'We're also sending out special pre-launch press materials, in addition to the regular NASA manned mission press kits we pouch out around the world. These include ninety news wire stories and features sent in the weeks before liftoff; the *Life* feature on you and your families; a forty-eight-page "Man on Mars" color illustrated pamphlet, four hundred twenty-two thousand copies of that; and one million, nine hundred thousand postcards of the astronauts, of you three. Also we anticipate having in place at the USIA outposts overseas a million Ares lapel buttons, nine full-size Mars-walk space suits, a hundred and twenty-five Ares kiosks, with lights, music, transparencies and posters. We've got ten thousand maps of Mars, eight hundred and forty plastic Saturn rockets, two hundred and fifty sixteen-inch Mars globes . . .'

The statistics went on and on, baffling, the slides bewildering.

For someone responsible for NASA's PR, York thought, Rick Llewellyn's speaking style was oddly drab, uninspiring. It was hard to fix your attention on him for much longer than a couple of sentences at a time. It was like one of her early ground training classroom sessions: all those block diagrams, the endless, droning afternoons.

But the content of Llewellyn's slide show was terrifying, if you thought about it too hard.

'We're already planning a world tour for you guys when you get back. Over forty-eight days you will visit thirty-five countries, meeting key groups of press, television, scientists, students and educators, as well as politicians. You'll go to Mexico, Columbia, Brazil, Spain, France, Belgium, Norway, England . . .

'We set a couple of broad guidelines for the media stations around the world, a long way back in the mission planning. First, of course, Ares represents man on Mars, it's a culmination of an age-old dream, it's in the nature of man to accept difficult challenges, blah blah, all of that stuff. And then, historically, Ares is built on the achievement of many scientists, Newton and Goddard and von Braun. You know the score. And today Ares has a strong international flavor, with the overseas investigators, the open access to samples and data, the tracking stations around the world, the assistance from the Russians in your training, and so on. Additionally, of course, space is benefiting man – you have a lot of stuff here about the spin-offs – and you have the hope that Ares, spectacular off-Earth achievement as it is, represents a promise that man may eventually use his technologies to resolve the Earth's intractable problems . . .'

Ares, as the shop window for technocratic solutions, York thought sourly. *Jorge was right. It's turned out just like Apollo after all.*

But today the mood was a little darker than in the 1960s. Today, you had Reagan's Star Wars talk, of particle beams and lasers and smart bullets. Space was again an arena for flexing national muscles. And Ares was being used, blatantly, by the Reagan Administration to appease national and international sensibilities about the aggressive use of space technology. Ares had become twinned with the Star Wars initiative in the media. Ares was the dreaming half of the US space program, coupled to its threatening sibling. Maybe that had been the Administration's intention all along, when they approved Joe Muldoon's reshaping of the mission back in '81.

She could see the hand of Fred Michaels in this, still pulling strings, even from his retirement in Dallas. Michaels had locked Ares together with SDI in the mind of Reagan – and of the public and Congress. As long as Reagan kept on pumping billions of

517

dollars into military spending, some of that was going to flow into NASA, to sustain Ares. It was smart footwork by Michaels. Even if it was, she reflected, completely amoral. *Do anything, say anything – just keep the mission progressing.*

Meanwhile, every news item about her mission – every gimmick, every toy, every image – had multiple meanings, she saw: Ares, as a geopolitical symbol; Ares, as an ad for technocracy.

It would probably always be like that. To gain political advantage was the only reason, really, why any Government would fund travel into space.

And now here was she, Natalie York, the great skeptic about space, being transformed into one of the great icons of the deadly space glamor business.

She looked up at the screen, at a thousand reproductions of her own face, and shivered.

The tours, the press conferences, the photo-opportunities continued.

Her message was formulaic, coached by the Public Affairs Office people. *I need you! Do good work!*

And everywhere she went, there were *people*: thousands of them, all gazing at her, smiling, with an odd pregnant distance about them. As if they longed to touch her. And always, they applauded her.

She hadn't thought much about the future. To her, 'after the mission' was so remote it might as well not exist; it was as if her whole life was going to end, at the moment she stepped into the Command Module.

But her life afterwards would, inexorably, go on. And in a sense nothing she actually did on Mars – not even her precious geology – would matter so much as the simple fact that she was there.

She thought of the looks on the faces of the press and public, as they gazed on people who had been into space, to the Moon. *When I get back they will look at me in the same way. They do even now. And they've a right to; it's their money.*

And what about herself? Would she become like Joe Muldoon, a kind of walking ghost, her life transformed by her brief, dream-like – and forever unrepeated – interval on Mars?

She began to see a darker side to the fascination with which people regarded her. Sure, they wanted to witness this woman – this otherwise ordinary person – who might walk on Mars, take an unimaginable evolutionary step on their behalf.

But they also thought she might die.

518

The little cemetery struck York as classic small-town: neat, well-tended, the white marble gravestones gleaming in their rows. The open grave was like a wound in the cultivated soil, waiting to be healed.

Somehow, the astronauts, current and former, among the mourners at the grave side – Joe Muldoon, Phil Stone, others – didn't look out of place here, in their crisp black suits, their military bearing. Astronauts were small-town heroes to perfection, nothing more, nothing less.

The day was glorious, the sky an infinite blue, the sunlight sharp with the edge of early spring.

York felt numb, empty, unable to mourn.

Peter Priest had died a squalid death, of a cocaine overdose, at age twenty-five. He'd pissed away his life, she thought brutally, and achieved nothing; what the hell was there to mourn in that? And she shouldn't feel guilty for her absence of feeling. The kid would probably have opposed this heavyweight turnout for his funeral anyhow; it was all his mother's idea.

York remembered the little boy who'd gone running around the nuclear rocket plant, all those years ago. What did his death mean, now? Was it somehow linked to that long-ago day at Jackass Flats – to the space program in general, to its obsessive dedication to its goals – to his father's final consumption by it?

And how did this new, grisly, numbing event cast light on her own ambiguous relationship with Ben?

She shouldn't have come here. But Karen Priest had asked for her specifically: 'Ben often spoke of you. I know you were one of his good friends. I'd be honored if you would be here to remember Petey, as best we can . . .'

Peter, for Christ's sake. He wanted to be called Peter. Not much of a thing to ask.

Oddly, Karen didn't seem as distressed as York had expected. As if she'd accepted Peter's death as part of the ancient deal she'd made with her husband.

Sometimes York's lack of feeling at times like this made her wonder if she was somehow less than human. Maybe her single-minded, lifelong pursuit of her own goals had made her obsessive. Hollow inside, as people perceived the space program itself. She simply couldn't imagine how it felt to be Karen Priest, to have to attend funerals of husband and son within a few years of each other. *Maybe NASA ought to fix up a sim of it for me,* she thought sourly.

The service was over. The party broke up and people began heading back for their cars: battered Fords for the locals, big hired Chevies for the space program people.

York knew Karen was inviting people back, but she didn't think she could stand what she was feeling much longer: not grief, but this awful emptiness.

A man – short, overweight, dark – came up to her. 'Hi.' He was neatly groomed, and wearing an expensive topcoat. He smiled at her.

Although he looked familiar, at first she didn't place him. She shied away, studying his face. It wasn't impossible for press people to have got into even as private an event as this; she really, really didn't want to have to say or do anything that would be quoted right now.

His smile faded. 'You don't recognize me, do you? My God, Natalie. Well, I guess it's the new uniform –'

It was Mike Conlig.

'Mike. Jesus. What the hell happened to you?'

He grinned, and self-consciously ran a hand over his clean-shaven chin. 'You don't like it?'

'It's a hell of a change, Mike.'

'Well, needs must.'

'You still with Oakland?' Conlig had left NASA after the Apollo-N debacle and moved to Oakland Gyroscope.

'Sure.' He looked at her, calculating, as if wondering how she would receive his news. 'I'm doing fine there. In fact we're making parts for the Saturn VB. Maybe you should come visit us someday.'

'Sure,' she said vaguely.

'I've moved away from the engineering now. Management.' He laughed, self-deprecating. 'There's talk of making me a veep of technology. Can you believe that? And you – how are you?'

Me? Still playing at being a spacewoman. 'Oh, fine,' she said awkwardly. 'If you read the press you probably know more about me than I do.'

'Yeah. I was pleased for you, Natalie. Pleased you achieved what you wanted . . .' He sounded embarrassed, and he backed off quickly into generalities. 'And it's good the way interest has picked up in the mission, since your appointments were announced. I follow the news, of course. There has been a lot of hostility over the years, to the Mars initiative, hasn't there? But now that seems to be reversing. It's like Apollo 11 all over again . . .'

That seemed to be true, she reflected; a number of people had said it to her. Somehow the general, persistent opposition to manned spaceflight had dissipated, if briefly, as people focused on the three of them, the humans who would be making the extraordinary journey. When spaceflight came down from the realms of rocketry and scientific objectives, and turned into something human, people responded.

But York knew that Muldoon and Josephson and others were already worrying about what would come after Ares, how quickly this mood would dissipate.

'I think it's because of you, Natalie,' Conlig said hesitantly.

'Me? How so?'

'Because you're a woman, probably. And because you're a recognizable human being, definitely. Not one of those damn inarticulate robots they sent to the Moon. Underneath, I figure, people always did want the space program to do well. To go places. It's a basic human thing. And hell, we can afford it, when Reagan is talking about spending a *trillion* bucks on defense. But the cold, inhuman face NASA always puts up turns everybody off. But now, people want you to succeed because you are *one of us.* You know what I mean?' Conlig was studying her, his expression complex.

'Damn it, Mike. That's probably the nicest thing you've ever said to me.'

This was the first time she'd seen him since their final fight, after the NERVA thing. It was brave of him to come, she supposed. If her own feelings about Ben were so complex, so guilt-laden, God alone knew what Mike must be feeling.

But he didn't seem perturbed. Maybe he'd found some way to rationalize what had happened, his own part in the disaster. If so, she thought, she envied him.

'You should come over,' he said again. 'You ought to meet Bobbie.'

'Your wife, right?'

He did a double-take. 'You haven't met her.' He turned and pointed vaguely to a slim, blonde woman, over by the line of cars. She was holding a child, and she waved back.

'You've got a kid.'

'Two.' Conlig grinned, unselfconsciously. 'The baby's not here;

521

he's with his grandmother. You didn't know about the kids either. Hell, Natalie. And to think –'

To think they might have been mine. She turned away from the thought, and Conlig, mercifully, shut up.

She managed to get away fairly easily. Mike had become gracious.

He extracted from her another couple of promises to come visit, to tour his gyroscope plant. They parted with a handshake.

York hurried to her car, confused.

Conlig had been much more in command of himself than she remembered. All that obsessiveness, the single-mindedness, had dissipated. Maybe it had served its purpose in propelling him to where he needed to get, and had been discarded, like a spent booster stage.

Conlig looked like what he'd become, she thought: a prosperous, aspiring forty-year-old.

Mike had started a family. Set down roots. He'd put aside the obsessive, technology-oriented goals of his youth. He'd joined the human race. He'd grown up. He'd become the kind of person she always seemed to look at from the outside, but could never imagine becoming herself.

So where the hell does that leave me?

The existence of the Mars mission had distorted the whole history of the space program, she'd come to see. Right now, NASA existed for one purpose only, to land the three of them on the surface of Mars, and bring them home again. Nothing else mattered – not even whatever the hell came afterwards.

And in the same way, Mars had warped her own life, as if she was a scale model of the greater world.

Hell, maybe I could have been happy, and a lot better off, as a rock hound for some oil company somewhere. But the red glare of Mars had dazzled her, and to reach it she'd sacrificed everything: her career, her science, maybe, probably her chance of having a family, even her future after the mission.

Mike Conlig, today, was like an image of the adult she might have become. If not for goddamn *Mars*.

As she got into her car, alone, a black depression settled on her.

Building 3 was the JSC cafeteria. York, Mars astronaut or not, still queued for lunch with the rest. She took a seat at a small table by the window. The food was sticky Government issue – smothered steak with rice – washed down with soda.

The cafeteria was one of the older of JSC's buildings, a big gloomy room with small windows and ceiling tiles, done in an early-1960s style that reminded her, claustrophobically, of her high school.

Adam Bleeker sat down opposite her. 'You mind?'

She forced a smile. She hadn't seen him approach. Bleeker's face was calm, as empty of expression as ever. *Maybe he really is like that inside.* 'No. I mean, hell, no, of course not, Adam. Please.'

He nodded and sat down, with his tray. He had a vegetable lasagne, today's healthy option; he picked up bits of pasta in his fork and brought them to his mouth. The daylight made his eyes an intense blue, impenetrable.

York tried to think of something to say.

'You busy?' she asked.

He grimaced around a mouthful of pasta. 'What else? Busier than when I was on the flight, if you can believe that. They've got me in the sims more often than I can count.'

'I guess it shows how much –'

'– you need me. I know, Natalie.'

'Look, Adam, I know how you must feel. Your training goes back to the Moon landings, for God's sake. And to be overtaken by a rookie like me –'

'I've been studying space medicine,' he said unexpectedly. 'In my spare time.'

She was startled by the non sequitur. Maybe it showed something about Adam's state of mind. 'Really? Why?'

He eyed her. 'Wouldn't you? I never took it seriously before. You know what I've found out? Legally, as a spaceflight crew, you're a federal agency radiation worker. How about that. And you're covered by Occupational Safety and Health Administration regulations, when it comes to radiation doses you receive in space.'

'So what does that mean? I'll bet if we stuck to the rules, we'd never fly out of Earth orbit.'

He laughed. 'Actually, that's true. In low Earth orbit you're protected, to some degree, by the magnetosphere. Outside, you're exposed. But NASA does have an exemption, for "exceptional exploration missions."'

'So they've covered their asses.'

'Yeah. Just like the Air Force. CYA.' He looked at her, his face unreadable. 'You know, there *is* a lot of hazard out there, out of the shelter of the magnetosphere. You've got your solar particle events – solar flares, where you hide in your storm shelter – but there's also the constant background radiation, cosmic rays from the galactic background. And women are –'

'Fifty per cent more susceptible to radiation risk than men. I know, Adam,' she said.

His face was distant, inward looking. 'You know, you can *feel* the difference up there. You'll have to experience it, Natalie; I can't describe it. You can feel the blood flowing through your heart valves, into your vessels. You come home with "chicken legs," as we call them. All that goes away. But then you're hit by a kind of rapid aging . . . You know, Natalie, I'm not the only one.'

'The only what?'

'The only astronaut who's come down like this. Nobody else on the active list has been grounded specifically because of radiation exposure, as far as I know. But some of the older guys, who flew in the 1960s, are showing up now with osteoporosis. Cancer. They're turning up in their fifties and sixties, dying from risks you don't find in the normal population.'

She felt cold; she put her fork down. 'But those guys only had spaceflight records of two, three weeks –'

'Yeah. But we've spent four billion years adapting to life on Earth. For a while we thought spaceflight was easy. I guess we really do put our lives on the line, right? But then, some people seem to adapt well. They come home with trivial amounts of muscle atrophy, for instance. Maybe you'll be lucky, Natalie. Maybe you'll be an immune . . .'

'Well, if we were in a rational world,' York said, 'we wouldn't have a mission profile like Ares anyhow. The Ares plan is really a relic of the '60s.'

'Yeah. When the emphasis was just on getting there, not on what you do when you get there. If we were smart, we wouldn't plan for a thirty-day stopover; we'd look to put you up there for a year. On the Martian surface you'd be relatively protected. On your brief little trip you'll soak up almost as many REMs as on a Hohmann mission twice the duration, which would earn you five hundred days on Mars. On this one mission, you'll come close to your legal lifetime dosage.'

'According to OSHA guidelines, right?'

'Yeah. Anyhow,' he went on, 'a long stopover on Mars would probably be better for you anyway, to give you time to recover to the effects of the long zero-G transit . . .

'Ah, hell.' He pecked at his food. 'You know, you could say we're not ready to do this, yet. We've been studying Mars mission options for thirty years. Right back to von Braun. And the basic problems – the energy needed to get out of Earth's gravity well, to cross interplanetary space – none of that has changed. And we haven't come up with any fundamentally smarter solutions than von Braun's, either. We're still firing off big hydrogen-oxygen rockets, because we don't see what else we can do.'

She felt pleased, to hear someone like Bleeker talk like this. Maybe the culture was changing here, slowly. But he might have been discussing baseball scores for all the inflection in his voice.

'I can never read you, Adam,' she said frankly. 'You know, I've often thought the same thing. That we're not ready to go yet . . .'

He nodded, smiling faintly. 'I figured.'

'But it won't stop me going, anyhow.'

'No. And it wouldn't stop me, if they'd let me.'

'You're not trying to talk me out of it?' She tried to inject some humor into her voice, but wasn't sure how successful she was.

'I would if I thought I could,' he said seriously. 'Not that it would do me any good.' He shook his head. 'You know what was the hardest thing?' he asked suddenly.

'What?'

'When I had to explain to my boy – Billy – that I'm not going to Mars. Damn,' he said, and he gazed out of the window at the muggy Houston sunlight.

She couldn't think of anything to say.

He ate a little more of his lasagne.

Mission Elapsed Time [Day/Hr:Min:Sec] Plus 371/01:32:3(

Gershon gave *Challenger*'s attitude control rockets a final blip, ₂ squirt to make sure they were functional.

Solenoids thumped.

'Everything is copacetic, guys.'

525

Stone's face, behind his scuffed faceplate, was set, almost grim. 'Good. Then let's get the hell on with it,' he said.

Gershon grinned.

With a clatter of explosive bolts, *Challenger* kicked free of the rest of Ares. Then came a brief burn of the retropack, the small solid rocket cluster strapped to the base of the MEM.

The burn knocked *Challenger* into a new, low orbit around Mars.

York, strapped into her acceleration couch, tried to relax. *Challenger* would stay in its new orbit for a couple of revolutions, while the two pilots and the controllers back in Mission Control checked out its systems.

The MEM's ascent stage cabin, buried within the conical upper heatshield, was more or less a vertical cylinder, rising up above her. The three acceleration couches were crammed into its base, side by side. She could see, at an angle, the navigation and guidance panels with their big false horizon displays, and the alignment optical telescope thrusting down from the ceiling above her.

The cabin's main windows were big triangles, angled to face downwards, so the pilots, when they stood up, would be able to see their landing site. And there was a small rectangular sighting window directly above her, with a matching panel cut in the upper heatshield. York stared up at that little window; trapped between the two pilots, she felt like a prisoner, staring up at a small window in the roof of her cell.

Where the interior of the Apollo Command Module had a warm feel to it – all browns and grays and greens – this cabin was mostly unpainted aluminum, thin and delicate and somehow unfinished. She could see lines of rivets, stitching the thing together. To York, the raw look spoke of a hurried development, a less mature technology than Apollo.

Through the window York watched Ares recede from the MEM. It was the first time she'd seen the craft from the outside since the rendezvous in Earth orbit. The fat, faithful MS-II injection engine was still evidently the stack's center of gravity – though the two External Tanks were long discarded – and ahead of it was fixed the slim MS-IVB stage which would brake them back into Earth orbit. The whole of *Endeavour*, their cylindrical Mission Module with its solar array wings, had been separated from the MS-IVB, turned around and redocked nose-first; the idea was to free up the MEM from its shroud at the Mission Module's base. Meanwhile *Discovery*, their Apollo, was now docked to a lateral port, so it dangled sideways from the Mission Module, like a berry from the line of fuel-tank cylinders.

When *Challenger* returned to Martian orbit, the MEM would be discarded, and the remaining modules – booster stages, Mission Module and Apollo – would be reassembled, once more, in a straight line, for the burn home.

The cluster was a collection of cylinders and boxes and panels, crudely assembled – and clumsily repositioned since their entry into Martian orbit. All this orbital construction work – sliding modules through space like kids' construction blocks – was unnerving, to York. When they separated the Mission Module from the boosters, they were cutting themselves loose from their only ride home, for God's sake! But she understood that there were backup strategies at every stage, ways they could reassemble some kind of configuration that could tolerate a ride home, even if they lost the landing.

It's all a symptom of the clumsy way we're constrained to do this, the lousy technology. One day, maybe we'll have the power and energy to do this journey in something resembling comfort, without having to take the damn spacecraft apart all the time.

The assembled craft had none of the detailed, toy-like brilliance she had observed about ships in Earth orbit. After a year in space, the brilliant white paint of pre-launch had faded to a pale yellow; and the shadowed areas of the hull were picking up brown shading from the battered skin of Mars. The cluster looked aged, soaked in space.

When Ares had receded from view she could see nothing through the little window but darkness.

Darkness, and, occasionally, a sliver of ochre landscape.

Challenger flew over the shadowed limb of Mars.

'Thirty seconds to DOI,' Stone said. 'Everything's go.'

'I confirm a go,' Gershon said.

DOI: insertion into descent orbit – a new, low, elliptical orbit, an orbit that would intercept the surface of the planet.

York could see Gershon's hand, hovering over the manual fire button. *Challenger* was Gershon's baby, of course; this landing – the next few minutes – were the culmination of a decade of work for him. He looked keyed up to York, tense, expectant.

Sims were spring-loaded to fail. That was the point, really: to familiarize crew and controllers with all the myriad ways the mission could go wrong, and train them to cope. Now, however, York had the feeling that Ralph Gershon was spring-loaded the other way. *It is going to take a lot to keep him from landing this bucket of bolts.*

And that, as far as York was concerned, was good.

'Fifteen seconds,' Stone said. 'Ten seconds to DOI. Here we go, guys. Eight. Six, five, four.'

Gershon's gloved hand closed over the firing button.

'Two, one.'

The rockets fired in sequence. It was a muffled, rattly noise.

And then came the jolt, deep in her back.

'Retro light on.' Gershon flashed a grin. 'Beautiful! Pure gold!'

It felt as if *Challenger* had been knocked backwards. Solid rockets, she'd been told, always burned a lot more crisply than liquid.

The burn went on, with Stone counting up the time. The rockets' thrust of forty thousand pounds force was too small to shove seriously at the mass of the MEM, and so there was no rattle, no vibration, no real sense of deceleration. Just a steady push at her back, a smooth hiss as the retropack burned.

The push died sharply. Right on cue, the retropack had cut out.

Nothing felt different. *Challenger* was still in orbit around Mars, for the time being, and York was still weightless, floating within the restraints which held her to her couch.

But now the MEM was following a path that would bring it arcing down until it sliced into the Martian atmosphere, at maybe thirty miles above the surface. And the drag of the atmosphere would not allow the craft to climb out again.

Challenger was committed to Mars.

Suddenly she got an unwelcome sense of perspective, a feeling of how small and fragile this little capsule was. This was *different* from landing on Earth. On Earth you were descending toward an inhabited planet, toward oceans full of ships waiting to pick you up.

Out here there was only the three of them, jammed up against each other in this little pod, descending toward a dead world. So far from Earth they couldn't even see it. Out here, they weren't closing off their journey, coming home; out here, they were pushing out still further, into extremes of technological capability and risk, so far from Earth that Mission Control couldn't even speak to them in real time. It was like climbing the ladder one more rung.

But what York felt right now was not fear, but mostly relief. *Another abort threshold crossed.* The further the mission went, the fewer things were left to go wrong.

528

'Coming up on jettison retro,' Gershon said.

Stone counted him down. 'Three, two, one.'

York heard a muffled bang as pyrotechnic charges broke the metal belt holding the small retropack against the base of *Challenger*. Then there was a clatter against the wall, oddly like the footsteps of a huge bird: that must be the belt of the discarded pack, scraping along the hull.

Now, with the retropack gone, *Challenger* was falling ballistically, like a projectile shot out of a gun. Its heatshield gave it the form of a blunt cone, the classic Command Module shape, though the MEM was nearly three times as big as an Apollo CM.

Gershon tipped up the spacecraft, so that the blunt prow of its base, where the titanium honeycomb heatshield was thickest, led the way into the gathering air. When he fired the attitude thrusters York saw brief bursts of gray mist, beyond the small window above her.

Then the mist got more persistent, in short bursts of translucent paleness, that lingered even after Gershon had stopped firing.

Soon the mist started to turn pink. There was a thin whistle beyond the hull.

The glow was the air of Mars, its atoms smashed to fragments by impact with *Challenger*'s heatshield.

Gershon whooped. 'We're getting close! Old papa Mars has us!'

'Goddamn,' Stone said, his voice tight.

The first feather touches of deceleration settled over York: a gentle pressure inside her stomach, a faint heaviness about her legs.

A light went on at Gershon's station.

'Gotcha!' he shouted. 'That's point zero five G. This is going to be a real ride. Hang on.'

Point zero five G: the traditional threshold of atmospheric drag. And now here they were, reaching point zero five G in the air of Mars.

Now the deceleration piled up on her in sudden, brutal steps. *It's bumpier than the sims. This air is supposed to be thin, damn it.* There must be a more complex structure of layers in the atmosphere than had been realized, a sharper differentiation.

The pain at her chest was already exquisite.

She kept her eyes wide open, trying to remember every detail of this. *Every ounce of pain will tell someone, some atmospheric scientist, more about Mars.* After all she might be one of just three people in history to endure this.

Somehow, though, right now it wasn't worth it.

She heard the crisp rattle of the attitude control thrusters' solenoids.

Gershon watched his guidance display. 'Right on track. One forty-seven degrees . . .'

Challenger had to hit a precise reentry corridor. The allowable guidance error either way was only half a degree: less than fifty miles wide.

'Coming up on one G . . . now.'

Just one G? Already York felt as if her suit was made of lead tubes, as if some fat man was sitting on her chest. *Can this really be Earth-normal gravity?* After a year in microgravity, this burden seemed intolerable, like carrying a huge pack around on your back, for your whole life.

'One point five,' Stone said.

York groaned. She was pushed deep into her couch, her arms pressed into her body; the small components of the weights of Gershon and Stone which rested on her now became immense loads.

'Hang on, guys,' Stone said. 'One point eight. You've been through a lot worse in the Wheel. Two point one.'

Gershon worked at his guidance panel, his hand hovering over his RCS control.

'Two point five,' Stone said. 'Point six! . . . Point five. Point three. Hey, what did I tell you.'

The light in the small window above York had become a gray-white glow, cold and brilliant, as bright as Earth daylight. Gershon and Stone were bathed in the diffuse, unearthly light, the orange of their suits washed out, their faces invisible behind the reflections from their faceplates. It was like being inside some huge, complex fluorescent light tube.

The weight on her chest and legs began to slacken off now. She could feel her chest expand, her breath flowing more easily into her lungs.

Something went flying past the little window overhead, small and brilliant, glowing yellow. Flaming. It was a piece of the heatshield, melting off the base of the craft, carrying the lethal heat energy away from the capsule. Now more pieces came flying past, fist-sized or bigger, some of them rattling on the hull of the cabin.

York felt panic build up inside her. *Jesus. We can't take much more of that.*

This is the first chance Mars has to kill us, she thought. *I wonder if it will take it.*

From the ground, *Challenger* would look like a huge meteor, she supposed, glowing and burning and sputtering, leaving a complex, multiple trail across the dark Martian sky.

The thrusters squirted again, tipping up the nose of *Challenger*.

'Here we go,' Gershon said. 'Coming into pull-up.'

The MEM had some maneuvering capability. The center of gravity was offset, and so by rotating and pitching up, *Challenger* could be made to skip like a flat stone off the thicker layers of air, closer to the surface.

'Three, two, one,' Gershon said.

Now York felt a deep lurch, a shove which quickly bottomed out; it was like reaching the base of a loop on some huge roller coaster.

'How about that,' Gershon said. 'What a ride. Into the zoom maneuver.'

Challenger was ascending briefly, shedding its heat, before dipping once more into the lower air.

Stone tapped a glass panel. 'Hey. I got me a working altimeter. Sixty thousand feet.'

York felt a prickle at the base of her scalp. *Sixty thousand feet.* Suddenly the altitude reading had turned from miles – a spacecraft's measure – to feet, read from an air-pressure altimeter. Just like an aircraft. *We're nearly there.* There was another bang of attitude jets. The capsule tipped up again.

The glow beyond the small window faded, to gray, then to a pale pink, the color of flesh.

'Lift vector up glide,' Gershon called.

The MEM was falling again, dipping into the thickening air at the better part of five hundred feet a second. But now the rise was smooth, comparatively gentle, the worst of the heat and the Gs over. Now it really was like the sims.

Gershon unclipped his harness and threw it back over his shoulder. 'All change,' he said. He pushed himself up and climbed out of his couch. To York's left, Stone began to do the same. The crew had to stand for the last powered-descent phase of the landing.

Apprehensive, she unclipped her own harness. She stood, cautiously, on her couch, holding onto straps on the walls.

She could barely feel her legs. After her year in space York seemed to have forgotten how to stand up. Her inner ears were rotating like crazy, and the aluminum walls of the cabin tipped up around her. She felt enormously heavy.

She felt a hand on her arm. Stone's.

'Don't worry about it,' he said. 'It passes.'

That was true. But after most long-duration space missions there were ground crews to lift you out of your cabin and carry you to a wheelchair, en route to the hospital . . .

Stone slapped his gloved hands together. 'Let's hustle,' he said. He turned to his station, and Gershon did the same, and they began to rattle through a fresh checklist.

York's job right now was to support the pilots. She hauled at levers to fold up the acceleration couches, leaving the cabin floor exposed; then she fixed restraints, elasticated cables, to the waists of the pilots as they worked.

Then she took her own position, standing in a corner of the little cabin, and hooked herself up to restraint cables. *Standing room only, all the way down to the surface of Mars.*

There was a sharp crack. Sunlight streamed into the cabin, strong and flat.

The conical upper heatshield, its function fulfilled, broke into segments and fell away, revealing a complex structure of propellant tanks and antennae. A plug popped out of the bottom of the craft, exposing the bell of the retropropulsion descent engine. All around the base of the MEM, six squat landing legs rattled out of their bays.

Challenger had configured itself to land.

York could see out of the corners of the pilots' down-slanting triangular windows. She saw sunlight, a violet sky, and a tan, curving landscape.

New York Times, *Monday, March 4, 1985*
German-Born Nazi Expert Quits US to Avoid
War-Crimes Suit

Hans Udet, a German-born NASA rocket expert, has renounced his US citizenship and returned to Germany, after facing the prospect of charges of war crimes, it was revealed yesterday.

Udet was one of Wernher von Braun's V-2 rocket development team during World War Two. After the war, he came to America with von Braun to work on US space projects.

After the retirement of von Braun, Udet became one of NASA's most senior managers, and he recently directed the development of the Saturn VB enhanced rocket booster. The VB will be used to launch the Ares manned mission to Mars, and has already been launched successfully several times to deliver components of the Mars ship to Earth orbit.

Now, the Justice Department has told Udet that he must surrender his US citizenship and leave the country or face charges that he had been involved in a forced labor camp at Nordhausen in Germany where the V-2 was manufactured. The Department is apparently acting on information that has been in the hands of the Government for forty years.

Udet has apparently not been accused of committing atrocities, but of being aware of them, and failing to acknowledge that fact in his application for US citizenship. Udet maintains his innocence, but says that because of his age and financial situation he will not undertake the prolonged legal battle that the government suit would entail.

Under an agreement with the Department of Justice Udet left the US in January.

Senior colleagues within NASA have spoken out in Udet's defense, calling the Justice Department action 'cynical' and 'shabby.' The feeling is that the Justice Department stayed its hand on this matter until after Udet had served out a lifetime of useful service for the Government.

Among those who campaigned on behalf of Udet within NASA was Dr Gregory Dana, father of dead Apollo-N astronaut James Dana, and a scientist who, this newspaper can reveal, was himself a conscript laborer at Nordhausen during the war . . .

New York Times, *Friday, March 8, 1985*
Frederick W. Michaels, 76, NASA Administrator

Fred Michaels, who was NASA's Administrator during its turbulent post-Apollo decade, died Tuesday at his home in Dallas, Texas. He was 76.

Born in Dallas in 1909, Michaels received a BA in education from the University of Chicago in 1933. He studied law and was admitted to the District of Columbia Bar in 1939. He worked in private business from 1939 to 1963, save for a four-year spell in the Bureau of Budget. In this period he rose to become President of the Umex Oil Company, assistant to the President of Morgan Industries, and a member of the board of Southpaw Airlines. He joined NASA in 1963.

He served as Administrator of NASA from 1971 to 1981, when

he resigned subsequent to the loss of the Apollo-N test mission and the death of its astronaut crew.

Michaels's reign at NASA was characterized by political astuteness. His stewardship was much more worldly than that of his predecessor, the visionary but ineffectual Thomas O. Paine. Michaels effectively managed both the internal conflicts between centers which have plagued NASA from its inception, and external pressures from political, budget and aerospace interests and such lobbies as the universities.

Michaels was criticized for a lack of vision. NASA under his stewardship was a throwback to the Apollo-era organization under James Webb (1906–), in which all activities, however worthy, were valued solely in terms of their contribution to a single goal – in Michaels's case, the eventual Mars landing. NASA appeared to suffer from a lack of direction during much of the 1970s, and when a clear mission did emerge, in the aftermath of the Apollo-NERVA disaster, NASA was left with no vision of its future beyond the Ares project, and with its facilities and systems dangerously weighted to serve Ares alone. Michaels's successors will face a formidable challenge in keeping the large organization and workforce in place once the primary goal has been achieved.

However history will probably look more kindly on Michaels's achievements than do many of his contemporaries. In a time of dwindling budgets and growing hostility to the US civilian space program, he followed in the footsteps of Webb by building and maintaining a political coalition behind the manned space program, which he saw as the primary goal of his Agency.

Without Michaels's shrewd handling it is possible – as former President John Kennedy remarked this week on hearing of Michaels's death – that the post-Apollo space program would have crumbled. It is worth remembering that Mr Kennedy himself lobbied for Michaels's appointment in 1971.

Whatever one's view of this year's man-to-Mars space spectacular, it is surely ironic that its principal architect has not lived to see it.

Mr Michaels is survived by his wife, Elly; three daughters, Kathleen Lau of Wilmette, Ill, Ann Irving of Pal Desert, Calif, and Jane Devlin of Rockville, Md; and eight grandchildren.

March, 1985
Cocoa Beach, Florida

There was one final press conference in Houston, just before they were brought out to the Cape. By now the crew were in quarantine, and they had to come onto the stage wearing hospital masks, which they kept on until they were installed behind a plastic screen.

To York, exhausted, it was bizarre, unearthly, the questions and answers rendered meaningless by their endless repetition.

The *Life* issue of March 28 had a cover story called 'Ready for Mars.' Inside there was the usual domestic stuff: Stone playing catch-ball with his sons, Gershon at the wheel of his car, York – well, York in her den, wading through her correspondence, redirecting her mail, arranging for her goods to be taken into storage, smiling uncertainly at the camera. She'd generated her own cliche industry by now. *The dedicated scientist. The single woman, coping alone. The bright visionary, focused on the goal.*

She'd lost her critical faculties about the press coverage, actually. The whole thing was just a blizzard, whiting out around her. The *Life* piece could have been a lot worse. In fact the reporter had made the best he could, she supposed, of unpromising material.

A few days before the launch was due, they moved out of the Cocoa Beach Holiday Inn and into the crew dormitory, on the second floor of the MSOB at the Kennedy Space Center.

The Manned Spacecraft Operations Building was pretty comfortable, all things considered. There was a gym and a mess hall. And the crew quarters, tucked away inside what looked like a regular office building, were fairly luxurious compared to a lot of NASA facilities: from a mundane, sterile office, she walked through a locked door into a carpeted apartment with subdued lights, and separate bedrooms for the three of them.

It was the same apartment in which the moonwalking Apollo astronauts had bunked before their launches.

Her bedroom was individually decorated; it even had a TV. The three rooms had paintings hanging in them: nudes in two of them, a landscape in the third.

York got the one with the landscape. She stuck over it her grainy Mariner 4 blow-ups.

The astronauts were cut off in here. To protect the crew from infection – and to keep at bay the pressure of the media attention – only 'authorized personnel' were allowed into the MSOB. That didn't include family or friends.

There was nobody York particularly wanted to see, anyhow. Her mother had called, once, and talked about her own concerns. She wasn't planning to come to the launch; she was going to be filmed watching it by some local TV company.

But she could see that Stone and Gershon, while relieved to get out of the glare of camera spots, were soon going a little stir crazy.

This was dumb policy. Why not let families in? Sure, there would have to be some kind of quarantine. But she could see how a little contact with children and spouses could go a long way to calming the soul.

Anyhow, whatever the merits and problems of the quarantine, to York it was a great relief. When she first shut the big heavy door of her MSOB room behind her, she threw her personal bag on the floor, flopped out on the bed, and slept through nine hours.

Mission Elapsed Time [Day/Hr:Min:Sec] Plus 371/02:03:23

Ralph Gershon's mouth was dry. That was the pure oxygen, pumping through his pressure suit.

Stone stood to his right, and York, silent, was behind them both.

Gershon ran over the readouts on his station. He'd already pressurized the descent engine fuel tanks, and he'd called up the right computer programs, and he'd taken sightings through the alignment telescope to check *Challenger*'s trajectory.

Houston was silent, listening, so far away they could do nothing to help.

Challenger had turned over onto its back as it fell through the air, so that its landing radar pointed at the ground. The radar hadn't got a lock yet. All Gershon had through his window was a triangle of gaudy violet-pink sky.

Stone said, 'On my mark, three minutes thirty to ignition . . . *Mark*. Three thirty.'

Gershon set the switch to arm the descent engine.

Gershon was ready. He was in charge for the first time in the mission. It gave him a sense of liberation, of power. He could make *sure* nothing fouled up.

And besides, he'd completed this run a thousand times, in the sims, and in the MLTV trainer. He could do it with his eyes shut.

Sure you could. But this is Mars, pal. Maybe that big old world out there has different ideas.

And now, this MEM was going to have to function better than any of the test articles that had preceded it.

'I got a 63 for PDI,' Stone said quietly. *63*: a relic from Apollo, a computer query about readiness to proceed to PDI, powered descent initiation.

'Do it,' Gershon said. 'I got go.'

Stone pressed the PROCEED button. 'Ignition.'

'Right on time.'

Gershon felt nothing at first. But the gauges showed him that the descent stage engine was firing up to ten per cent of maximum, smooth as cream.

Then, after half a minute, the engine reached full thrust.

He still couldn't hear anything, but the cabin filled up with a grating, high-frequency vibration. It was uncomfortable, something like the sensation of having your teeth drilled at high speed. *Different from the sims already.*

Challenger slid down US Highway One, braking easily.

'AGS and PGNS agree closely,' Stone said. Stone was acting as the navigator now; he was telling Gershon that the redundant-pair primary and abort guidance systems were agreeing with each other. 'We're looking good at three, coming up . . . Three minutes. Altitude thirty-nine thou five.' That height reading was still only an estimate from the two guidance computers, though; the landing radar had still not got its lock. And Stone would also be able to read off heights from the altimeter, although that instrument, working on the pressure of the unfamiliar Martian atmosphere, was experimental, and its data excluded by the mission rules.

'Still go,' Stone said. 'Take it all at four minutes . . . We're go to continue at four minutes.'

'Rager,' Gershon said tersely.

'The data is good. Thirty-three thou . . .'

But now caution and warning lights were glowing on Gershon's station. The landing radar should be working by now; it should have locked onto its own signals bouncing off the ground.

But it hadn't achieved lock.

'Where's that goddamn radar, Ralph?' Stone asked.

'Punch it through again.'

'Yeah.' Stone tried.

'Come on, baby,' Gershon said quietly. 'Let's have the lock on.' But there was no change. 'Come *on*.'

537

'Does talking to it do any good?' York asked dryly.

'Shut up, Natalie,' Stone said, distracted.

Gershon felt a stab of fury. Other data was still good. Velocity looked fine, and the altitude estimates from both AGS and PGNS were in agreement. But without the radar – and even if the altimeter worked – he was screwed. The mission rules said, *No radar lock by ten thousand feet and you abort.*

Stone said, 'Try cycling the landing radar breaker.'

Gershon pulled out the radar's circuit breaker, his muscles tense with anger, and shoved it back in its slot. 'Okay, it's cycled.'

The caution lights continued to show. No lock.

He turned to look Stone in the eye. 'Fine day for a landing.'

He meant: *Fuck the rules. Fuck the radar. Fuck Houston; they're so far away we'll be on the surface by the time they know what's going down. We've come too far to quit now. I say we go for a landing, by eye if we have to. Fuck it.*

Stone stared back at him.

Damn it, you cold bastard. What are you going to do? Gershon could feel the cabin tip up around him; beyond his big window, sky and a fine edge of red landscape slid past. *Challenger* was beginning to pitch up, as it dropped closer to the ground.

'Twenty-four thousand feet,' Stone said. 'Coming up to throttle down. Mark.'

Now the primary guidance program would take the descent engine down to sixty percent thrust. Gershon could feel the thin vibration subsiding smoothly. *Right on schedule.* 'That felt good,' he said. 'Better than the sims.'

'Twenty-one thousand. We're still go. Apart from the radar lock. Velocity down to twelve hundred feet per second.'

Twelve hundred. Aircraft speed. Gershon took hold of his controls. *I'm flying, in the atmosphere of Mars.* He looked out of his window. The stars were all washed out now, and the sky was a tall dome of brown light. And he could see the ground. It was a rumpled landscape that slid underneath him. Visibility was good: the contrast, the shadows cast by the low morning sun, made everything stand out.

Challenger was approaching the landing site in a broad sweep from the south west, so it was flying over the ancient, cratered terrain of the southern hemisphere. It was almost like a lunar landing sim, with craters piled on craters, some so old and huge they were almost obliterated by newer strikes. But these craters had sand dunes rippling across their floors, and here was one big old fellow whose walls looked like they had collapsed under a stream of running water. *The Moon, it ain't.*

The landscape was desolate, curving tightly, forbidding. It was an empty planet, no ground support ... *No runway lights down there, boy. On the other hand, nobody shooting at your ass, either.*

'Seven minutes thirty,' Stone said. 'Sixteen and a half thou. Coming up on high gate. Still no lock.'

'High gate' was the point in the trajectory where Gershon should be able to see his landing site for the first time. He peered ahead.

The designated landing site was just to the north of an escarpment at the mouth of an outflow valley. The valley, according to York's descriptions, would look like a dry river bed. Gershon had studied the site from orbiter photographs and plaster of paris models until he knew it like he knew his own apartment.

But coming in now, with the sun low, and the ship tipped up still at more than fifty degrees, and the light glinting off his little triangle of a porthole ...

Nothing looked like it was supposed to. The land was complex, tortured, its nature changing rapidly. Every shadow was deep and black, and the ochre-colored surface features seemed to leap out toward him, the vertical scale magnified by the contrast.

'Fifteen thousand,' Stone said. 'Still no lock.'

Shit.

'Okay, Ralph, let's go over the abort procedure.' Stone sounded resigned.

Goddamn it to hell, he's given up.

'We pitch over, activate the ascent program ... countdown to mission abort starts at eight thousand feet –'

'No. Don't abort,' Natalie York said suddenly.

Stone looked at her. 'Huh?'

'Don't abort. We may be flying over a radar-dark area.'

'And what,' asked Stone dryly, 'is a radar-dark area?'

'Volcanic ash,' she said. 'Pumice.' She was straining in her harness, trying to see the battered landscape out of their pilots' windows. 'Low-density stuff; not many rocks. It reflects radar badly. There's nothing for the landing radar to lock onto.'

'Or maybe,' Stone said, 'the landing radar is screwed.'

'*Don't abort.*'

Stone and Gershon exchanged looks.

'Nine thousand,' Stone said. 'Still no lock.'

They'd already bust the mission rules, Gershon realized.

Stone said, 'Ralph –'

539

And then the warning lights went out. The radar lock had come in.

York gasped, an explosion of relief.

'Jesus.' Gershon slammed his fist into his control station. 'We is fucking *go*.'

'We is indeed,' Stone said tightly.

Gershon twisted over his shoulder to look at York. 'I guess we flew right on over all that pumice stone, huh.'

She stared back at him. 'I guess.'

He had no idea if she'd just been bullshitting, he realized, about the pumice stone. He didn't think York was the type to do that, but it was possible. And he also didn't know if Stone would really have pulled the plug, or let him go on and try to land without the radar.

He didn't, he realized, know his crewmates as well as he thought he did.

'Eight thousand,' Stone rattled off. 'Down velocity one hundred feet per second. We're go for the landing.'

'Rager.'

Gershon took hold of his controls. He had an attitude control adjuster in his right hand – a joystick with a bright red pistol grip – and on his left there was a toggle switch called the thrust translator controller, which would squirt the down-pointing reaction thrusters to reduce the rate of fall. It was all linked up by the electronics to the reaction control subsystem, which would do most of the steering for him.

He pulsed the reaction control thrusters; solenoids rattled comfortingly.

He handed control back to the computer. 'Manual auto attitude control is good.' He felt a surge of renewed confidence. The radar was locked in and the thrusters were copacetic. When the time came, when he had to take control of the ship for the final landing, he knew now that everything would be fine.

'Seven thou,' Stone said. 'Here we go. High gate. Right through that gate.'

Under computer control, *Challenger* tipped up a little more, tilting Gershon forward. He stared ahead. Now, speeding over the close horizon, here came what looked like an escarpment, a ridge marking out the edge of the cratered terrain. Beyond that ridge, the land looked different: smoothed over, lacking craters, kind of like mud, like a flood plain . . .

And there was a valley under his prow, snaking north from out of the southern plateau. It looked like a gouge in a woodcut, with a big wide crater just to the northeast.

It looked just like the maps and the models, in the back rooms at JSC.

Gershon crowed. 'I got it! I got Mangala! Just as fat as a goose.'

He grasped the controls of *Challenger*, ready to land.

The MEM was standing on its rockets now, drifting over the landscape, like an ICBM trying to land on its tail.

'Three thousand feet. Seventy feet per second. Everything's go,' Stone said. 'Go for landing. We're go, hang tight. Two thousand. Windspeed ten feet per second.'

Windspeed. Another hazard they didn't face on Apollo. But ten fps was low enough not to matter.

'Give me an LPD,' he told Stone.

'Forty-three.'

He looked through his window now, sighting along the forty-three-degree reticle, his current Landing Point Designator. He sensed invisible polynomial curves reaching out, in the computer's imagination, to join him to his landing site, like a smooth glass highway across the Martian air. *None of those damned higher-order wiggles this time.* Even though it shared the clunky human interface of other Apollo-based systems, the hardware and software was an order of magnitude more powerful than the antiquated shit he'd had to fly on the MLTV.

Now he could see the site where the computer was flying him, more than a mile away, closing in fast, in line with the reticle . . .

Shit.

Under the guidance of PGNS *Challenger* was heading for a point a couple of miles beyond the big escarpment, north of the mouth of the major outflow valley, just as planned. But now he saw it close up he could see the land was uneven, scoured out, ribbed with what looked like gravel bars. And there was an impact crater, low, eroded, right in the middle of it all, with a teardrop-shaped island of debris behind that.

'Scablands,' he said. 'Natalie, you're going to love it. Because it looks like you were right. It looks like a fucking river bottom out there . . .'

But he couldn't put the MEM down in that shit.

Solenoids rattled, and *Challenger* shuddered. The computer was revising its trajectory all the time, as information came in from the radar. Gershon was surprised how often the attitude jets were firing, though; it was much more frequent than in the sims.

Stone was still calling out height and velocity readings. 'Seven hundred feet, down at thirty-one feet per second. Six hundred. Down at twenty-nine. Five hundred forty feet. Down at twenty-five.'

Decision time, Ralph.

He flicked a switch to override PGNS.

He pressed the translation controller, and toggled the little thruster switch to slow the MEM's fall. *Challenger* responded smartly to his touch, with a rattle of solenoids.

Suddenly, he was piloting the ship. The response was crisp and sharp. The thrusters banged, and the MEM pitched forward. He found himself leaning into his restraints.

Challenger drifted over the surface of Mars, under his command.

He was aware of Stone's eyes on him.

'Low gate,' Stone said. 'Five hundred feet. Thirty-five degrees pitch. Coming down at twenty-one feet per second.'

The MEM was still falling, but now it was skimming forward, sliding over the broken, flooded-out terrain. *I got to get north. Away from this shit from out of the old terrain. North; that's the place to be. On the smooth lava plains beyond the flooding.*

Test pilots had an adage. *When in doubt, land long.* Ralph Gershon kept on going, looking for a place where he could land long.

'Four hundred feet, down at nine feet per second. Three hundred fifty feet, down at four. Three hundred thirty . . . Watch your fuel, Ralph.'

Watch your fuel. Sure. The mission planners had sent him all this way, looping around the sun, to make landfall on an alien planet for the first time, and they'd given him about two minutes' worth of hovering fuel to do it.

But this is what you wanted, Ralph. Isn't it? This is what it's all been about, all these years. To fly to a planetfall, just like Armstrong.

He felt his heartbeat pumping up.

Here was a place that looked reasonable, but when he got close up, he saw it was peppered with big boulders. Another gift for Natalie York, maybe, but a disaster waiting to happen for the MEM. And over there was a smoother area, but it looked crusty to Gershon, with lots of little rivulets and runs. He could imagine a footpad plunging through the surface, the whole damn MEM tipping over.

He pitched *Challenger* back again to keep it from picking up too much forward speed. Now he flew over another field of boulders; he banked to the left to avoid them.

There wasn't a runway, he thought, on the whole fucking planet.

Sweat trickled down from his brow and into his eyes; he had to blink to clear them.

New terrain advanced over the close horizon at him, rushing up toward him, exploding in sharp, unwelcome detail. Still, he couldn't see anywhere to set down.

'Three hundred feet, down three and a half, fifty-four forward.'

'How's the fuel?'

'Seven per cent.'

Shit. He was doing worse than in any of the sims. Except the ones he'd crashed.

There. A flat area, like a little plateau, off to his right: just a field of dust. On one side there was a field of big old boulders, on the other an eroded area. The flat place was no bigger than a parking lot, a couple of hundred square feet, but it ought to be enough.

He had his landing site.

He pushed his joystick. The MEM turned to the right. He lined up his marked window, and locked in the computer. He imagined those invisible curves, York's magical polynomials, snaking out to join him up to his landing site.

'Two hundred twenty feet. Thirteen forward, down four. Eleven forward. Coming down nicely. Altitude velocity lights.'

The shadow of *Challenger* came swooping across the uneven surface of Mars toward him. The shadow was a fat irregular cone; he could see antennae bristling, and at the base the shapes of the landing pads, with their long contact probes sticking out from beneath.

There really wasn't much of a gap left between him and that shadow.

And now dust, red and brown and yellow, came billowing up in big clouds from the surface, suspending itself in the thin air. Dust, and shadows. *They didn't have those in the sims.*

Guess this is for real, Ralph.

A light marked 'DESCENT QTY' came on in front of him. Low fuel. If he was too low when the descent fuel ran out he would be in a dead man's zone: too low to abort, too high to land safely. The MEM would just fall to the surface, smashing open like a big aluminum egg.

He tried to ignore the warning light. *Overdesigned crap. Let a man fly his aircraft.*

PGNS released the craft from the landing program, and *Challenger* began its final descent.

He picked a little gully, just beyond the landing point, to use as a reference for the craft's height and motion, and he stared at the gully as he worked toward killing his horizontal velocity. The MEM had to land straight down, with no sideways motion. Otherwise the touchdown might break off a landing leg.

There was a haze of dust all around the craft now, billowing up, obscuring his view, adhering to the window in great ochre streaks.

'Thirty seconds.'

'Any forward drift?'

'You're okay. Hundred up. Down at three and a half.'

The haze was all around him. And now he could see dust flying away from him in all directions, scouring over the surface. The streaks confused his perception of his motion, the way fog blowing across a runway could sometimes. But he could see a big rock, sticking up through the haze, and he focused on that.

'Sixty feet. Down two. Two forward. Two forward. Good.'

He clicked the descent toggle, killing the speed, until *Challenger* was floating toward Mars as slow as a feather.

'Fifty feet. Thirty. Down two and a half. We're kicking up a lot of dust.'

I can see that, damn it. The MEM was drifting backwards, and Gershon couldn't tell why. And going backwards was bad, because he couldn't see where he was going. He pulsed the hand controls.

'Twenty.'

Well, he'd killed the backward motion, but now a sideways drift had crept in. *Fuck.* He was pissed with himself. Right now he wasn't flying his bird smoothly at all.

'Four degrees forward. Three forward. Drifting left a little. Faint shadow.'

The shadow closed up, and dust billowed, so he couldn't see the ground any more. He struggled to get the MEM vertical.

He kept falling, blind.

'Four forward. Three forward. Down a half. Drifting left.'

Gershon felt a soft bump.

'Contact light,' Stone said. 'Contact light, by God!'

For one second, Gershon stared at Stone.

Then he killed the descent engine, fast.

The vibration that had accompanied the engine firing, all the way down through the powered descent, faded at last. He should have cut it as soon as the contact light came up; if the engine kept firing too close to the surface the back pressure from its own exhaust could blow it up . . .

Challenger fell the last five feet, and impacted on Mars with a firm thud. Gershon felt the landing in his knees, and every piece of gear in the cabin rattled.

'Shit,' he said.

Stone started to rattle through the post-touchdown checklist. 'Engine stop. ACA out of detent.'

'Out of detent.'

'Mode control both auto. Descent engine command override off. Engine arm off . . .'

They got through the T plus one checkpoint, their first stay/no-stay decision.

And then they had the ship buttoned up tight, and it looked like they could stay for a while.

Out of Gershon's window there was a flat, close horizon. He could see dunes, and dust, and little rocks littering the surface. Nothing was moving, anywhere. Without buildings, or people or trees, it was hard to tell the scale of things. The sky was yellow-brown, the sun small and yellow and low. The light coming in the window was a mix of pink and brown, and he could see how it reflected off his visor, and off the flesh of his own cheeks.

Martian light, on his face.

He saw Stone grin, behind his faceplate. 'Houston, this is Mangala Valles. *Challenger* has landed on Mars.' Gershon could hear the confident elation in his voice.

Gershon and Stone and York shook hands, and slapped each other on the back, and threw mock punches at each other's helmets.

Gershon said now, 'Houston, can you pass on my regards to Columbia Aviation. This old Edsel has brought us down. JK, you are one steely-eyed missile man.'

He checked his station. He had fourteen seconds of landing fuel left. *Well, the hell with it. Fourteen seconds is a long time. Armstrong himself only had about twenty seconds left, and nobody beefed about that.*

Anyhow it's going to be a long time before anyone comes back, to better what I did today.

Joe Muldoon squinted down as the plane from Houston came in on its approach to Patrick.

Although it was still hours to sunup, there was a steady stream of corporate planes descending on Patrick Air Force Base and Orlando Airport. And every road on the peninsula looked like a ribbon of light, locked up. He felt a knot of anxiety gather in his gut. Maybe he'd left it too late to get to the launch.

But he couldn't have got away any earlier. He hadn't got any sleep that night, and not much the night before. The logistics of the launch – the press stuff, and ensuring the NASA control centers were talking to each other, and handling a lot of last-minute crap to do with VIP passes and TV sites and such – all of it just went on and on, ballooning in complexity and detail.

Hell, was he going to have to listen to the launch on the radio of some hired car in a bumper-to-bumper queue?

The stewardess offered him a drink before landing. He refused, as he had before. Time enough for that later.

When the plane got into Patrick he hurried off. A young guy in a suit was waiting for him, holding up a hand-lettered card with his name on it.

'Mr Muldoon?'

'Yeah.'

'I'm from KSC. We got a chopper waiting for you. This way, sir.'

'Thank Christ for that.'

Muldoon had a bag to collect from the plane. He hesitated for less than one second. To hell with it; he'd buy a clean shirt when he needed it.

He walked briskly across the tarmac with the aide. The young guy said, 'We're laying on copters to bring in key people who might get stuck in traffic.' He seemed rushed, almost awestruck, just about in control. Muldoon guessed the poor guy had been doing this ferrying all night.

'That bad, huh?'

'Hell, yes, sir. All the roads into Merritt Island are jammed. It's like a car park out there. I've never seen anything like it, sir.'

Muldoon eyed him in the gathering dawn light. The kid was not more than twenty-two. So, aged about six in 1969. *He doesn't remember.* He really hadn't seen anything like this before.

Muldoon felt old, trapped, gravity-bound. Just as he'd felt after the splashdown in '69. His work on Ares was nearly done, and the depression he'd been fighting off for all these years, using that huge goal to distract himself, was seeping back.

His one landing was long ago, and he'd never walk across that snow-like surface again.

They walked more quickly, toward the waiting chopper.

Manned Spacecraft Operations Building, Cocoa Beach

There was a smart military knock on her door.

She rolled on her side and switched on her bed-side light. Four-fifteen a.m.

'Wake-up call. The night's been clear, and the weather's expected to be good . . .'

'Thanks, Fred.'

Fred Haise was right on schedule. 0415 was the first time recorded on the Ares checklist.

The clock starts ticking here. And it won't stop for eighteen months.

She pushed back the covers and climbed out. She rearranged the sheets, smoothing them out. She wasn't going to be back here for a while, and she didn't want to leave behind a mess.

She switched on the TV. She found herself staring at a still of her own face, while a commentator talked about the launch day crowds gathering around the Cape. She clicked the thing off.

She took her time over showering. She relished the sting of water against her skin, the way the lather ran away down her body to the drain. She turned the shower on cold, and stood there shivering for long seconds, feeling the blood rise in her capillaries. Showering in microgravity wasn't going to be so easy; she had the feeling that she wouldn't feel so clean as this again until she got back to Earth.

She toweled herself dry, quickly. Her hair was cropped short and dried easily. She pulled on a sports shirt, slacks and sneakers.

The sports shirt was plain blue except for a patch with the Ares mission logo. The logo was a disk circled by the name 'Ares' and their three surnames. The circle contained a stylized, pencil-shaped Ares cluster blasting toward a red star; the ship's exhaust billowed out to become the stars-and-striped wing of an American eagle, peering sternly at the departing spacecraft.

It was a clumsy, cluttered design, she'd thought from the

beginning. But the NASA PAO people had thought it appropriately patriotic in tone, and Stone and Gershon hadn't cared enough one way or the other, and that had been that. So now the badge sat high over her right breast, glaring out, kitsch and embarrassing.

When she left her room, she found Gershon and Stone waiting in the corridor. They were leaning against the wall, arms folded in almost identical poses, talking quietly. They grinned at her.

She walked up to them. Then, spontaneously, she reached out her hands to the two of them. Stone and Gershon each took a hand, and then, to her surprise, they clasped hands as well. For a few seconds the three of them stood there, joined in a circle, in the middle of the carpeted corridor, grinning at each other.

Merritt Island

Bert Seger had thought that his two mule-drawn wagons would clog up the traffic. But all four lanes of US One had been at a dead standstill anyhow. Even off the freeways the traffic was moving at slower than the pace of the mules, and the problem was going to be that the animals might grow impatient at the slow pace of the cars.

Already he had seen people giving up on getting closer to the launch, climbing on top of their cars and setting up tripods.

A row of black faces peered out of each of his wagons, at the staggering stream of traffic. Seger had brought a dozen of the poorest families here from Washington, all members of the congregation of the little church he'd founded in the capital.

Now, though, he wasn't so sure how effective his gesture was going to be.

Every gas station and coffee shop along the road – all of them open all night – was full of humanity, teenagers and Marines and factory workers and middle-aged couples and kids running around. It was a real cross-section of America. The Mars shot, he'd calculated, had cost every man, woman and child in the country around fifty dollars apiece, and it looked as if a good sample of them had come out here today to check on that investment, dumping themselves onto this flat, primitive landscape.

In all this flood of people, Seger realized with a sinking heart, his little protesting band wasn't going to make much of a splash. Anyway, there was maybe enough evidence around here that it was wrong to be sending off three Americans to Mars, while so many of their fellow citizens suffered, without the need for stunts by Seger. He'd learned that there were still cases of *malnutrition* being discovered among the poorest of the poor: here at the Cape, here at the feet of the Mars ship itself! If such things didn't turn a few heads, maybe his little gesture really wasn't going to make much difference.

But he wasn't going to give up. The effectiveness of the PR wasn't really the point. Anyway, maybe he could trade on his old NASA contacts to get closer to the pad than most of the rest. Just a little TV coverage would make his mission worthwhile.

Someone in the wagons began to sing, and the rest took it up, as the mules made their mournful way along the packed road. After a couple of words Seger recognized the song. It was the hymn the astronauts had read out from lunar orbit, to mark the deaths of their colleagues. *Abide with Me . . .*

He wondered where Fay was. Maybe she was watching on TV, out in Houston. He hadn't seen her since he'd told her, by phone, he was setting up his church. Maybe she'd forgive him, for leaving her behind like this.

On the horizon the Saturn VB was visible as a finger of white, bathed in light from every angle.

Seger was moved, unaccountably. He grabbed at the crucifix pinned to his lapel, so hard the metal dug into his fingers.

Manned Spacecraft Operations Building, Cocoa Beach

York reported to the exercise room, where a nurse weighed her, took her temperature, and checked her heart rate and breathing and blood pressure. It was all brisk, thorough, but somehow perfunctory. As if the nurse – a cheerful woman in her forties – wasn't really interested in the results. After all, NASA knew all about York's health by now; fragments of her body, scrapings and fluid samples, already lay around a dozen NASA facilities, as prized as bits of moonrock.

But it made sense on another level. This was all just part of the ritual. *Like a priest robing up*, she thought. Today, she was different from the run of mankind, and she must be treated as such.

She made for the mess hall. Here she had to sit in line with her two crewmen, at a table which crossed the head of another, longer table. There was a curtain behind her, and on the table there was a gaudy flower bowl with a ribbon which read 'Ares,' and a little display of silk and bows in the shape of the mission badge. Two rows of people sat down the longer table, looking at her, with a mundane ridge of sauce bottles and pepper pots between them.

It was like a wedding breakfast, she thought.

The meal was another pre-launch ritual: nothing on the menu but steak, eggs, juice, toast and coffee. Every astronaut, back to Al Shepard himself, had sat down to the same fare before The Flight.

York tried to eat, but the steak was thick and massive, and tasted like rubber in her mouth.

She'd fought to get this part of the ritual changed. A little muesli and canned milk would do her fine right now. But the doctors had lectured her about the importance of sticking to a 'low residue' diet before the launch. That was to reduce the volume of her solid wastes. Fine in theory, but it turned out to mean, in practice, steak with every meal, big bleeding slabs of the stuff.

She watched the other people in the room. There was Administrator Josephson, and several senior managers from NASA centers, and from the contractors. She recognized Gene Tyson from Columbia, the firm which had built the MEM, fat and corporate and beaming complacently. There were senior astronauts in here too, Bob Crippen and Fred Haise and others. And there were Ted Curval and Adam Bleeker, grinning and wisecracking as if nothing untoward had happened; but York thought she could see the tightness of their grins, a kind of hardness behind their eyes.

Stone and Gershon, sitting alongside her, were in good form, she thought. They were just two Air Force guys joshing with the other pilots, self-deprecating, almost witty. Humble, brave, relaxed. Almost bored with it. *Just another day at the office.* It was a good performance.

But, under the surface – the studied casualness, the soft clink of cutlery against china, the occasional sharp ripples of laughter – the atmosphere in the mess hall was extraordinary. Strained to the point of breaking.

York couldn't think of a damn thing to say that wouldn't sound lame. And as the hideous meal went on she began to develop a fear that if she spoke at all her voice would crack.

She stabbed a fork into her egg, but the yolk had hardened, and only a little yellow liquid oozed out onto her plate.

Fred Haise kept checking his watch. Like every other item today, breakfast was timelined.

*　　*　　*

550

The crew were released to return to their dorm rooms.

York brushed her teeth. She picked up her PPK, her Personal Preference Kit. She checked over the Kit. She wasn't planning to carry much: a calendar, a yellowing Mariner 4 picture. But now, she found, some extra stuff had been snuck in the Kit while she'd been at breakfast. There was a little card of Saint Christopher which she recognized: her father used to say that card had gone through World War One with *his* father. And there was a good-luck card from her mother, and a present from her old high school, a brooch in the shape of an orbital ellipse, with a tiny ruby to represent Mars.

And here was a squat, lumpy form: a little cosmonaut, his troglodyte face leering at her from his squashed helmet, a short chain dangling from his skull. She grinned. 'Hello, *Bah-reess*.'

There was no privacy here, of course; probably one of the maids had been bribed to smuggle in all this crap. Anyhow, she didn't care. She had only one truly private item to carry.

She lifted up her sports shirt. Pinned on the inside, hidden by the mission logo badge, was the silver rookie pin given her by Ben Priest out at Jackass Flats, all those years ago.

She slipped the pin into the PPK and zipped up the kit.

She hefted the little pack. The PPK was coated with Beta-cloth, a nonflammable synthetic material as tough as a fire hose. The PPK was just a mundane little personal item, but even the PPK was built for spaceflight.

She took a last glance around the room, with its single bed and its little window, and the color TV on the stand. She felt a surprising tug, as if she was leaving a nest. In no way was this her home; she'd been here for only a few days. Nevertheless, it was the last place on Earth she could claim as *hers*. The last place she had slept before the launch.

She took a pencil, and signed her name on the back of the wooden door. A little cosmonaut tradition, shown her by Vladimir Viktorenko.

Then, with determination, she opened the door and stepped out of the room.

Banana River

Gregory Dana had stayed overnight in the Holiday Inn. He'd been lucky to get a room. Every motel in central Florida had been booked since February. Some of them were even charging overnight rates for the use of poolside deck chairs. But the Inn management had remembered Dana, and given him the room he habitually used on his working visits to the Cape.

In the motel lobby, Dana bought up bumper stickers, T-shirts, button badges for Jake and Maria. *ARES: I WAS THERE.* The youngsters, with Mary, were with Sylvia at Hampton; both of them were teenagers now – and hauntingly like their father – and they would probably be too cool for all this junk; but Dana didn't mind. Let them save it for their own kids.

He'd hired a small cabin cruiser for the day, and he picked it up well before dawn. He set off down the river. He was aiming for an anchorage three miles south of the pad.

He could have got a pass for a grandstand, or followed the events of the launch from one of the NASA centers, of course. But this seemed more appropriate. He preferred to be alone. He needed the space to remember Jim, today of all days – the day when Jim might have been one of three Mars explorers, wadded into the tip of the huge rocket on Pad 39A.

Anyway, he liked to be on the water. It was a reason for staying in Hampton as long as he had. And he'd always been struck by the siting of this spaceport here at the border of land and ocean. It was as if three elements – land, sea and space – had come together in one place, here where the long line of stark ICBM gantries challenged the erosion of the flat landscape.

So it was appropriate to be on the water. And besides, he knew he'd have a better view of the launch at his planned anchorage than from the VIP stands.

He began to thread his way up the channel through the thousands of yachts, houseboats, dinghies, catamarans and kayaks. The waterway was almost as choked as the roads. It was going to take him a couple of hours to get to his vantage spot, but he had the time.

The sun was coming up, through the low clouds out over the Gulf Stream.

Manned Spacecraft Operations Building, Cocoa Beach

The suit room was about the size of a large hotel suite: white-walled, windowless, surgically sterile. There were three reclining couches in the middle of the room. Three orange pressure suits, their empty helmets like gaping mouths, lay on the floor. The white light was dazzling; the room looked like a futuristic laboratory, and the suits were like the cocoons of gigantic, dissected insects.

Suit techs, in their white coveralls, caps and surgical masks, approached the crew, applauding. Some of the techs wore that gentle, misty look that had followed York around her tours of the country in the last few months.

After her dorm room and the mess hall, it was the first truly inhuman environment York had entered today.

She felt her blood pool in her stomach.

She didn't want her step to falter. She was grateful for the calm, purposeful stride of Phil Stone, just ahead of her; all she had to do was follow Phil and she'd be okay.

She was taken behind a screen by a couple of nurses. Now she had to strip down. Her own warm clothes were taken away from her; she watched the little bundle being packed away, and she wondered if she'd see the clothes again.

For a moment she stood naked, bereft of all possessions, poised between the ground and the sky.

Her chest was swabbed and a biomedical instrument belt was buckled around her waist, with wires snaking up to four silver chloride electrodes that were plastered to her chest. The little electrodes were cold and hard.

Now she had to massage her backside with a salve before she slipped on her fecal containment bag, a large plastic diaper with a pee-hole in the base. It was humiliating, but mandatory. If something went wrong in orbit it could be five or six days before she could be brought back to Earth. *And you'll be stuck inside this suit for that whole time. You're going to have a bowel movement in that time, no matter how much steak you've shipped. So wear the goddamn diaper.*

So here was York, beginning her journey to Mars by rubbing zinc cream over her own skinny butt.

After the diaper she slipped her legs into a kind of jock strap, and then came a tough, comfortable sports-style brassiere, and then a set of underwear, wrist and ankle length.

She was fitted with a catheter, which led to a tube attached to a urine collection device, a thing that looked like a hot water bottle.

Now two suit techs came toward her carrying her pressure suit. It was a pristine orange carapace in human shape, its arms and legs dangling, emblazoned with the NASA logo and the mission patch. The techs sat her down and began to load her into the suit.

The suit had three layers. The inner layer was five-ounce Nomex, soft and satin-smooth against her flesh, and the outer layer was tough Beta-cloth. The middle layer, the pressure garment assembly, was a bladder of neoprene laced with a network of hoses and valves; when inflated it would compress her body with a quarter-G pressure. The suit was fitted out with pulleys and cables and joints, to help her move around when the thing was pressurized.

To York it was like climbing inside a second body, with veins of rubber, pulleys for joints, cables for muscles.

She was led out from behind the screen to the reclining couches. Stone and Gershon were already sitting there, side by side. Evidently it didn't take as long to fit a condom as a catheter.

Six techs attended her. Two led her to her couch and sat her down, and plugged tubes from metallic blue and red connectors in her chest into a small couch-side air-supply console. They lifted black rubber pressure gloves onto her hands, and heavy boots onto her feet. A second pair of techs lifted her Snoopy skullcap into place, fiddling with the microphone under her chin.

It was like an extended grooming, she thought. All this touching. Maybe there was a subtext to this preparation, something deep, something reaching back to primate history; she needed to be handled, stroked, before being sent off to impossible danger.

The last two techs approached with her helmet. It was a big goldfish bowl with a thin metal rim.

She took one last sniff of the antiseptic air, listened to the murmurs of the techs, felt the faint air-conditioned breeze on her face.

Then the helmet was lowered over her head. At her neck, metal rasped against metal.

She was sealed in. The sounds from outside were diminished, her vision distorted by the curvature of the glass of the helmet. The noise of her own breathing, and of the blood pumping at her neck, was loud in her ears.

Now she had to lie back in the chair and wait, for a half-hour that seemed much longer. Her air-supply console was filling her suit with pure oxygen, purging her system of nitrogen.

The suit techs fussed around the three of them, checking things, smiling through the glass, their faces broad and unreal. The techs moved through an intricate, silent choreography. They were like workers around three queen ants, she thought.

Ralph Gershon had a suit tech drape a towel over his helmet, and he lay back in his reclining chair with his gloved hands folded over his chest. He showed every sign of taking a nap.

*　　*　　*

554

When the waiting period was done, the suit techs covered her boots with yellow overshoes, and lifted her up out of the chair. They swapped her air hoses over to a suitcase-sized portable unit, and handed the unit to her to carry.

The three of them formed up in a line – Stone first, then York, Gershon last – for the short walk out of the MSOB to the transfer van.

It was an effort just to walk. The weight of the suit would have been bad enough, but she had to fight with every step against the grip of the inflated garment around her legs and waist; it was like trying to walk against elastic rope. It was confining, alienating.

The irony was, these bulky, clumsy, antiquated, Apollo-style pressure suits would only be needed during the launch phase, and later for the return to Earth. The suits would spend most of the mission stowed in the Command Module of their Apollo ferry craft. The MEM contained suits of a much more modern design for the EVA operations on Mars.

The halls were lined with people: astronauts and managers and NASA support staff, friends and family, all applauding soundlessly. York had to walk through a kind of corridor of faces, smiling in at her, smeared out and distorted by the helmet over her head.

They passed Stone's family, Phyllis and the two boys. Stone stopped, put down his air unit, and reached out. He hugged his wife against the huge, crumpling chest of his suit, and he let the boys grab at his gloved fingers. He ruffled their hair and blew kisses at them. The boys looked tiny, skinny, against the suit's soft orange expanse.

But York knew the suit had sealed Stone off from his family; he wouldn't be able to feel them through the thick, elasticated gloves, nor hear anything of their voices through his helmet save a muffled blur. Inside the suit, the only sound was the hiss of air, the rustle of your own breathing.

Stone was only inches from his boys, but already he might have been a thousand miles away.

They stepped out of the MSOB.

It was not yet six a.m. There were press here, beyond barriers, and she was confronted by a barrage of flashlights, popping all around her. The last photo-opportunity, before they walked on a new world, or died.

There was a little gangplank leading into the transfer van. She was startled to see Vladimir Viktorenko standing by the van door. He was dressed in his full Soviet air force uniform.

Phil Stone drew himself up and saluted Viktorenko, and she heard his voice over her headset radio. 'My crew and I have been made ready, and now we are reporting that we are ready to fly the Ares mission.'

Viktorenko saluted back. York couldn't hear his reply, but she could guess what he said. *I give you permission to fly. I wish you a successful flight, and a gentle landing.* Another little Soviet ritual.

Stone stepped forward to the van, and let the suit techs help him toward his seat.

York, in line, moved up to Viktorenko. His smile softened, and he spoke again, silently. *Marushka.*

She felt something break open inside her, something she'd been holding in, from the moment she'd woken that morning.

She dropped her air unit, careless of how it fell, and stepped toward Vladimir. His uniform pushed into the softness of her pressure suit, and his arms circled her back, tightly enough that she could feel his strength through the layers of the suit.

He stepped back, and she forced a smile. 'I found *Bah-reess.* Thank you.'

He spoke again. He dug into a pocket, and pulled out a little handful of steppe grass. He showed it to her, and tucked it into a pocket on the sleeve of her pressure suit. Then he gripped her arms one last time, and helped the techs guide her up into the van.

Newport Beach

It was a fine and clear spring morning.

JK Lee stepped out onto his porch and sniffed the air deeply; he could smell growing things, grass and flowers and such.

He found himself coughing.

His lungs seemed to have gotten attuned, over the years, to the characteristic scents of an aviation plant: kerosene, lubricant, ozone, rubber, hot metal. Now that he'd emerged from that cocoon of engineering, he found himself stranded on a planet whose atmosphere was alien to him.

He lit up a cigarette, and, behind a gathering cloud of nicotine and tar, he started to feel more comfortable.

It would be a good day to cut the grass.

So he went to his tool-shed and started fiddling with the mower, lubricating the blades and checking the plugs. The shed was warm and dark, redolent with the smell of stained wood.

He could hear the voices of commentators at the Cape, drifting out from the windows of all the houses nearby. The launch was all around him, as if it had soaked its way right into the fabric of the neighborhood. And all the other neighborhoods, right across America, this Thursday morning.

Jennine called him into the house.

She handed him the phone. Jack Morgan was calling. He asked if Lee and Jennine wanted to come over to his house to watch the launch over a couple of beers. Lee thought about it, but said no, he wanted to work on his lawn today.

Actually, Lee had been hoping for an invitation from NASA to go down to the Cape, to watch the launch. It would have been a nice touch. It hadn't come.

He and Morgan gassed on the phone for a while about the old days.

Morgan had quit Columbia now, and had set up as an independent consultant in aerospace medicine, and was making a hell of a lot more money selling himself back to Columbia as a freelance. At that he'd lasted longer at Columbia than Lee, though.

The frustration of his do-nothing sinecure had slowly driven Lee crazy, and he'd taken an early retirement.

Art Cane had died a while back, less than eighteen months before MEM 014, his company's finest product, was due to touch down on Mars. And now Gene Tyson – the smug jackass who had once taken over JK's own job – was head of the company.

Anyhow, Lee went back to his mower, and eventually he rolled the thing out into the sunshine, and when he started it up the rattling roar of the petrol engine drowned out the thin Canaveral voices from the neighborhood.

After a while, Jennine came out again. The sunlight caught the gray in her hair, making it silvery, shining. She brought him a glass of lemonade, and then she took him by the hand and led him into the house.

The TV was on, of course.

And there it was, the already familiar image of the Saturn VB stack, a bundle of white needles. The ripple of early-morning Florida heat haze betrayed the distance of the camera from the launch pad. JK picked out the pregnant bulge of the MEM shroud at the middle of the stack, above the fat first stage and its boosters, beneath the slimmer lines of the Mission Module and the Apollo spacecraft.

'Go over there,' Jennine said suddenly. She had her Polaroid in her hand.

'Huh?'

She waved her free hand. 'By the TV. Go ahead.'

He thought of the lawn, half-cut.

Then he went to stand by the TV.

Slowly, JK Lee raised his hand in salute, standing there beside the TV image of the Mars ship, while his wife took his picture with her Polaroid.

Launch Complex 39A, Merritt Island

The bulk of the eight-mile journey from the MSOB to the pad was via the regular highway, US One, the main coastal road. This section of the road had been cleared by the local cops, but even so the van, with its convoy of backup vehicles, proceeded incredibly slowly along the wide, empty freeway.

Stone glared stoically out of the windows, and Gershon's gloved fingers drummed on his thigh.

KSC was big and empty, a rectilinear complex of dusty, straight roads and alligator-infested drainage ditches. The buildings were four-story blocks, square, low and weathered – uglier than anything at Houston – with the feel of a government research establishment. In the low morning sunlight, everything was flat and dusty, beach-like.

Occasionally, beyond the cordon, York would see a little knot of people, regular citizens, waving at her and clapping. She felt numbed, isolated.

On the eastern horizon she could see the misty forms of launch complexes, the blocky gantries protruding above the grassy beach. Many of the gantries were disused and half demolished, now; they looked like relics, washed up on this scrubby, rubbish land, here at the corroding, entropy-laden margin between sea and land.

The transfer van turned off the highway, and started down the access road to the pad.

And suddenly – for the first time that day – York could see the Saturn: the central, gleaming white needle, slim and powerful, with its cluster of four squat solid rocket boosters, the whole enclosed by the massive, blocky gantry, sitting atop the pad's octagonal base. The assembly was picked out by powerful searchlights, augmenting the morning light. She could see ice coating the sides of the cryogenic fuel tanks, and there were puffs and plumes of vapors emerging from the central column, little clouds drifting across the launch complex.

The rising sun came out from behind a thin cloud, and splashed the sky with orange and gold. Light washed over the launch pad, and, beside its access tower, the Saturn shone like a pearl.

The van pulled up at the foot of the pad's concrete base. The van doors swung open, and York was helped to the tarmac by suit techs.

Up close, the Saturn, looming before her, had a gritty reality that made it stand out in the washed-out dawn light. It had almost a home-workshop quality: the huge bolts holding it together, the white gloss paint on its flanks. Its complexity, its *man-made-ness,* was tangible.

There was a sign fixed to the concrete base of the launch pad: GO, ARES!

She looked back down the crawlerway to the Vehicle Assembly Building. The VAB was a black and white block, squat on the horizon; it was impossible to judge its size. The crawlerway was a path of big yellow river-gravel blocks running straight as an arrow to the VAB, at infinity; it ran alongside the canal built for the barges which hauled huge Saturn stages up to the VAB. She could see the tracks ground into the road surface where the crawler-transporter had hauled the Saturn to the launch complex; they looked like dinosaur footprints.

Suddenly it struck her. The event they'd practised and talked about for months was about to happen. She really would be sealed into the little cabin at the top of this stack and thrown into space. *My God*, she thought. *They're serious.*

In recent weeks York had been out to the pad many times. She'd come to think of the pad as a noisy, busy place, like an industrial site: machines running, elevators going up and down the gantries, people clanging and banging and talking.

Today was different. Today, save for the crew and their attendants, there was no living soul within three miles.

After the press of people at the MSOB – the glimpses she'd had of the million-strong throng around the Cape – to be at the epicenter of this concrete desolation, with the overwhelming bulk of the Saturn VB before her, was crushing, terrifying. Like a glimpse of death.

Still carrying her air unit, accompanied by only the whisper of

559

oxygen, York followed Stone toward the steel mesh elevator at the base of the launch tower scaffolding.

Perhaps these are my last moments on Earth. Right here and now, on this blasted concrete apron. Maybe this is indeed a kind of death, time-delayed by hardware.

Jacqueline B. Kennedy Space Center

The breeze off the Atlantic ruffled the flags behind the wooden bleachers at the viewing site, close to the VAB. The grandstand crowd was more than twenty thousand, Muldoon was told, including five thousand special guests and four thousand press. There were celebrities, politicians, families and friends of the crew.

There were one million people within seventy-five miles of this spot.

JFK was there, in his wheelchair, behind big sunglasses, looking a lot older than his sixty-eight years. The rest of Muldoon's old Apollo crew showed up, and the NASA PAO people had the three of them line up – Armstrong, Muldoon, Collins – behind the frail old former President, with the Saturn gleaming on the horizon behind them.

The PR done, Muldoon sat down.

He was looking east, into the low morning sun. It was a clear, still morning, with a few scattered clouds; the PAO said the probability of meeting launch weather rules was good, more than eighty per cent.

The VAB was a huge block to Muldoon's left, the windows of the cars clustered around it glistening like the carapaces of beetles. There was a stretch of grass before him, with its clustered cameramen, the flagpole, and the big digital countdown clock, and on the other side of that the barge canal stretched across his vision. Beyond the canal was a line of trees. And beyond that – there on the horizon, made faint by morning mist – he could see the blocky, blue-gray forms of the two LC-39 gantries. 39A, the pad for Ares, was on the right.

If he turned to look further to the right he could make out more launch complexes, gaunt, well-separated skeletons: ICBM Row, stretching off down the Atlantic coast.

KSC had changed a hell of a lot since he'd first flown, in Gemini. Even from here you could see how the space program had receded. Employment here was less than half what it had been then. The launch complex he'd flown Gemini from, LC-19, was still there – used for unmanned Titan launches now – but only ten complexes out of twenty-six at KSC remained operational. The launch pads rotted, the gantries had rusted and were pulled down, and NASA executives let local scrap merchants bid to take away the junk.

But Complex 39A was still there. Once, he'd flown out of there on Apollo. And now the Ares stack was there, assembled and ready to fly.

Behind Muldoon's seat, two old ladies chatted about the launch parties they'd held over the years in their Florida gardens, as brilliant manned spacecraft had drifted through the night sky, directly overhead.

NASA had set up a series of press portakabins, and reporters in short-sleeved shirts trooped in and out carrying photocopied mission timelines, and glossy goodies from the contractors. To Muldoon's left, toward the VAB, the big network TV cabins were full of activity; their huge picture windows shimmered in the morning light.

Loudspeakers boomed with the voices of the astronauts on the air-to-ground loop, and with updates from Mission Control at Houston and the Firing Room here at the Cape. The Public Affairs Officer intoned countdown highlights. A way down from Muldoon, a girl reporter was fanning herself with a crumpled-up press release.

Muldoon, stiff and hot in his dark business suit, felt aged, restless, thirsty.

The mist was burning off the horizon. Now, at 39A, he could see the slim white needle of the Saturn, emerging from the blue haze.

Launch Control Center, Cape Canaveral

When he'd first come to work here at the Cape, Rolf Donnelly had found the LCC very different from the MOCR, back at Houston.

The Firing Room was full of the same computer consoles and wall-sized tracking screens; but there were also sixty TV screens showing the Saturn stack from different angles. And in the viewing room behind the Trench, there was a huge picture window with a panoramic view of Merritt Island, with its launch gantries poking up out of the sand, three miles away. Unlike the MOCR, the Firing Room wasn't closed to the outside world.

And at the moment of launch, the Firing Room flooded with real, honest-to-God rocket light.

The atmosphere was different here, too. The controllers here were independent of the Mission Control guys, by job description and inclination. They were more like blue-collar technicians. The LCC controllers were in charge for the first few seconds of the flight; they were the guys who had to get the mission off the ground by doing the dirty work of the launch.

It was an atmosphere Donnelly liked. He'd come out here to Florida, bringing his family, soon after the Apollo-N fiasco, hoping to rebuild his career.

As he'd feared, some of the shit flying around then had stuck to him. Well, he wasn't a Flight Director any more; Indigo Team was just embarrassing history, and Donnelly's brilliant career probably wouldn't look so brilliant ever again. But he was still here, still involved, still with NASA.

They reached T minus five minutes, and the controllers moved into the final pre-automatic check.

'Guido?'

'Go.'

'EECOM?'

'Go.'

'Booster?'

'Go.'

'Retro?'

That was Donnelly.

He glanced at his console. His vision was misty. 'Go,' he said. *Go, by God. Go!*

Jacqueline B. Kennedy Space Center

Helicopters flapped over the pads: that was Bob Crippen and Fred Haise, Muldoon knew, checking out the launch weather conditions.

At T minus ten minutes, the countdown went through the last of its planned holds. After that, there were no more holds; and for Muldoon, events unfolded with the inevitability of falling off a cliff.

At thirty seconds, Muldoon stood with the rest, and faced the Saturn. Save for occasional flags of vapor from the cryogenic tanks, the pad was still static, like a piece of a factory.

There was a moment of stillness.

Plumes of steam – from the sound-suppression water system –

squirted out to either side of the slim booster. Muldoon could see the last umbilical arms swinging aside. *Main engine start.*

Then a bright white light erupted from the base of the Saturn.

The Saturn lifted from the ground, startlingly quickly, trailing a column of white smoke which glowed orange within, as if it were burning. The booster was a splinter of bone white riding on a lozenge of liquid, yellow-white light – the fire of the Solid Rocket Boosters – light that was stunningly bright. *This*, the brilliance of rocket light, was what the pictures never captured, he thought; right now the TV images would be stopped down so much they would tame the rocket light, turn the sky dark blue, make the smoke a dull gray.

The stack arched over, following a steep curve away from the tower: the pitchover maneuver, violent, visible. Already the gantry was dwarfed by the smoke column; it looked denuded.

The Saturn punched through an isolated thin cloud, threading it like thread through a needle. The surface of the barge canal rippled, glaring with the reflected rocket light.

Now, after maybe ten seconds of the flight, the sound reached him. There was a deep reverberation that he sensed in his gut and chest, and then a clattering thunder which rained down from the sky above him, in sharp multiple slaps: that was shock waves from the booster engines, huge nonlinear waveforms collapsing and battering at each other. Through that bass pounding he could hear the people around him whooping and clapping.

Before him, silhouetted in rocket light, JFK raised up a wizened fist.

Muldoon could feel that he was in the presence of a huge release of energy: it was like being close to a huge waterfall, maybe. But this energy was made and controlled by humans. He felt a surge of triumph, a deep exhilaration . . . a huge outpouring of relief.

It was done. And after this last effort, he thought morbidly, he could get to work on pickling his liver seriously. It was a kind of release. *No more goals.*

The Saturn arced upwards, its vapor trail leading right into the sun; Muldoon, dazzled, couldn't see the first staging.

His vision was blurred. He was crying, damn it. 'Go, baby!' he shouted.

Merritt Island

Seger had been leading his group in hymns, and handing out leaflets about how Ares was carrying plutonium casks, for its SNAP generators, into space. ST JOSEPH OF CUPERTINO IS THE PATRON SAINT OF ASTRONAUTS. JOIN WITH US IN PRAYER . . .

But they were mainly ignored by the crowds around them on the road, with their cameras and binoculars, their eyes shaded by hands against the sun.

When the Saturn light burst over the road, the hymn dissolved, as the members of the group turned to look.

The white needle, clearly visible, had lifted off the ground on a stick of fire. There was no sound yet.

Seger fell to his knees, dazzled. It was the first launch he'd viewed since Apollo-N. He let his leaflets fall to the dust, and tears stung his eyes. He could see some of his congregation staring at him, amazed; but it was as if he was back in the MOCR again.

He knew now he'd never left it, really; in fact, he never would. 'This is holy ground,' he said. 'Holy, holy ground.'

Gulls wheeled overhead, crying, oblivious to the lethal noise cascading toward them.

Jacqueline B. Kennedy Space Center

Muldoon stayed in the stand until the news came that Ares had reached orbit successfully. When he got to the limousine that had brought him here – in the VAB car park, maybe thirty minutes after liftoff – the vapor stack still loomed in the sky above, a man-made column of cloud, miles wide and slowly dispersing.

Book 6

MANGALA

Through the airlock's small window, Natalie York could see stars, embedded in a black sky.

There was Jupiter, high in the sky, a good third brighter than as seen from Earth, bright enough to cast a shadow. And in the east there was a morning star: steady, brilliant, its delicate blue-white quite distinct against the violet wash of the embryonic Martian dawn. That was Earth, of course. The twin planet was close to conjunction – lying in the same direction as the sun – and was about as close as it ever got to Mars; right now it was actually a crescent in the Martian sky, with its shadowed hemisphere turned to Mars.

The constellations themselves were unchanged from the familiar patterns of her childhood. It was a sobering reminder of what a short distance they'd come: the stars were so remote that they reduced this immense interplanetary journey – achieved at the very limit of human technology, far enough to turn Earth itself into a starlike point – to a child's first step.

Today, though, they would reach the climax of this journey, when Phil Stone became the first human to walk on Mars. The MEM had already been on the surface for three days. The crew had had to spend that precious chunk of their stay time adapting from zero G.

As she'd been warned, York had found herself a few inches taller and a stone lighter than when she'd left Earth. At first, she'd had trouble walking around the MEM's tight compartments; she'd kept walking into walls and forgetting which way was down. And she had the scrawniest pair of 'chicken legs.' *Rapid aging, huh, Adam,* she thought. *You were right. We're three old people, stuck here on the surface of Mars.* But anyhow, chicken legs were all she needed in Mars's one-third gravity.

But after three days on the Martian surface, she still felt disoriented, as if the Jupiter-lit landscape beyond the window was just another plaster-of-paris sim mockup.

When she walked out there, though, it would become real.

Stone joined her at the port. Stone, like York, was wearing thermal underwear, with his Cooling and Ventilation Garment over the top. The cooling garment was a corrugated layering of water coolant pipes. York had her catheter fitted, and Stone wore his own urine collection device, a huge, unlikely condom. The two of them looked bizarre, sexless, faintly ridiculous.

567

'Pretty view, huh,' Stone murmured. 'You know, Ralph claims he can see the Moon with his naked eye.'

'Maybe he can. It's possible.' The Moon ought to look like a faint silver-gray star, circling close to its master.

Stone had brought over York's Lower Torso Assembly; this was the bottom half of her EVA suit, trousers with boots built on. 'Come on, York; enough rubbernecking.'

She stared at the suit with a feeling of unreality. 'That time already, huh.'

'That time already.'

She hooked the sleeves of the cooling garment over her thumbs; the hook would stop the sleeves riding up later. She looked at her hands, her own familiar flesh, with the plastic webbing over the balls of her thumbs; it was the first step in the elaborate ceremonial of donning the suit, and the simple act had made her heart pump.

She stepped into the Lower Torso Assembly. The unit was heavy, the layered material awkward and stiff, and it seemed to wriggle away from her legs as Stone tried to pull it up for her. She found she was tiring rapidly, already.

Now she fitted a tube over her catheter attachment. It would connect with a bag large enough to store a couple of pints of urine. There was nothing to collect shit, though; she was wearing a kind of diaper – an absorbent undergarment – that would soak up 'any bowel movement that cannot be deferred during EVA,' in the language of the training manuals.

York planned to defer.

Now it was time for the Hard Upper Torso. Her HUT was suspended from the wall of the airlock, like the top half of a suit of armor, with a built-in life support backpack.

She crouched down underneath the HUT and lifted up her arms. She wriggled upwards, squirming into the HUT. In the darkness of the shell there was a smell of plastic and metal and lint, of newness.

She got her arms into the sleeves, and pushed her hands through; the cooling garment's loops tugged at the soft flesh around her thumbs. Her shoulders bent backwards, painfully. Nothing about this process was easy. Still, these suits were a hell of a lot simpler than the old Moon suits; the Apollo crew had had to *assemble* their suits on the lunar surface, connecting up the tubes which would carry water and oxygen from their backpacks.

Her head emerged through the helmet ring. Stone was grinning at her. 'Welcome back.' He pulled her HUT down, jamming it so that it rubbed against her shoulders, and guided the metal waist rings of the two halves of the suit to mate and click together.

Now she helped Stone don his suit.

York and Stone had already been inside the cramped airlock for two hours. *Challenger*'s atmosphere was pressurized to seventy per cent of Earth's sea level, with a mix of nitrogen and oxygen, but to stay flexible their suits would contain oxygen only, at just a quarter of sea level pressure. So York and Stone had had to pre-breathe pure oxygen to purge the nitrogen from their blood.

It was a tedious ritual. And EVAs on Mars could last only three or four hours, at most. Apollo backpacks had been capable of supporting seven hours of surface working. But Mars's gravity was twice as strong as the Moon's, and Mars suits had to be proportionately lighter, and could therefore only sustain much briefer EVAs. There would also have to be a long tidy-up period after each EVA: the suits would have to be vacuumed clean of Mars dust, which was highly oxidizing and would play hell with their lungs if they let it into *Challenger*.

The brief EVAs, with the surrounding preparation and cleanups and anti-contamination swabbing, were going to occupy most of each exhausting, frustrating day on Mars.

York fixed on her Snoopy flight helmet, and over the top of that Stone lifted her hard helmet with its visor, and twisted it into place against the seal at her neck.

The last pieces were her gloves; these were close-fitting, and snapped onto rings at her wrists.

Stone flicked a switch on her chest panel, and she heard the soft, familiar hum of pumps and fans in the backpack, the whoosh of oxygen across her face. He rapped sharply on the top of the helmet, and held up a gloved thumb before her clear faceplate. She nodded out at him and smiled.

She held up her arm; there was a reflector plate stitched into her cuff, allowing her to see the panel on the front of her chest which gave her a readout of oxygen, carbon dioxide and pressure levels, and various malfunction warnings. She could see her oxygen pressure level stabilizing.

Stone tested out the radio link. 'Hi, Natalie. Able Baker Charlie . . .' His voice sounded soft and tinny, echoed by muffled sound carried through the thick glass of her faceplate.

She checked the small plastic tubes protruding from her helmet's inner surface; she sipped out little slugs of water and orange juice. The OJ was okay, but the water was too warm. It didn't matter. She pushed her suit's internal pressure up to maximum, briefly, to test for leaks. She fixed her little spiral-bound EVA checklist to her cuff.

When they were through with the suit checkout they studied each other. Stone's suit was gleaming white, with bright blue Mars overboots, and the Stars and Stripes proudly emblazoned on his sleeves.

Stone asked: 'Are we done?'

She was sealed off from *Challenger*, now: locked inside her own, self-contained, miniature spacecraft. She took a deep breath, of cool, blue oxygen. 'Yes. Let's get on with it.'

'Roger.' He looked away from her to talk to Gershon, who was up in the ascent stage. 'Ralph, we're waiting for a Go for depress on time.'

'Rager, Phil; you have a go for depress.' Gershon would monitor this first EVA from the ascent stage cabin.

Stone closed a switch on the wall; York heard sound leak out of the air, and the internal noise of her own breathing seemed to grow louder, more ragged, to compensate.

'Roger,' Stone said. 'Everything is go here. We're just waiting for the cabin to bleed enough pressure to open the hatch.'

The gauge, York saw, showed the pressure already down to two-tenths of a pound.

Gershon said, 'I'm reading a real low static pressure on your lock. Do you think you can open the hatch yet?'

Stone said, 'I'll try.'

The exit from the airlock was a small hatch, close to the floor. The handle was a simple lever. Stone bent down, twisted the handle, tugged. York could see the thin metal of the hatch bow inward. The hatch stayed shut.

'Damn it.'

'Let me try.' She crouched down, and picked at the corner of the hatch, where it protruded from the wall. Her gloves, of metal mesh and rubber, were clumsy; her hands felt huge and insensitive. But she managed to get a little flap of the hatch peeled back.

Through the sliver she'd opened up between the hatch and its frame, she could see ochre light.

'I think I broke the seal.'

Stone pulled at the handle, and this time the hatch opened easily.

York saw a little flurry of snow as the last of their air escaped into the Martian atmosphere.

They both had to back away to let the hatch swing back.

Now York could see the porch, the platform fixed to the top of

Challenger's squat landing leg, onto which Stone would back out in a moment. The porch was coated in brown grit, thrown up by the landing. And beyond the porch, she could see the surface of Mars: it looked like sand, and it was streaked with radial lines pointing away from *Challenger*, showing the effects of their descent engine's final blast.

It was just a scrap of landscape; on Earth it would look so commonplace she wouldn't even perceive it. *But it was Mangala Vallis*: now, there was only a few feet of thin Martian air separating her from the surface she'd been studying all her adult life.

'Natalie,' Stone said.

She turned; in contrast to the brown of Mars, in the mundane kitchen-light of the airlock, his suit seemed to glow white.

'There's something we forgot,' Stone said. 'From the checklist. We didn't fix these.' Stone had taken his red EV1 bands from a suit pocket. Stone, as the leader of the first EVA, was in charge of the operation; York was, officially, his backup, and Stone would wear the red bands around his arms and legs for identification by the TV cameras.

But he was holding the bands out to her.

'I don't understand.'

He was smiling again. 'I think you do. Put on the bands.'

She held out her hand, and he dropped the bands into her palm. Through her clumsy gloves she couldn't feel the bands' weight.

'You've got to be kidding.'

He said testily, 'Look, I'm not asking you to land the goddamn MEM. You've done this in the contingency sims. All you have to do, on this first EVA, is to walk around and scratch a few rocks, and talk to the folks at home about it.'

She didn't feel any pleasure, or pride, in his startling offer. All she felt was irritation. *That damn roller-coaster again.* 'This doesn't make sense, Phil. You're passing up the chance to become the first human to walk on Mars, for God's sake. What kind of asshole does that?'

'This kind,' he said, annoyed. 'This is important, Natalie. I discussed it with Joe Muldoon before the launch. We have to get this right – this first EVA most of all – for the sake of the future. The next few minutes are maybe the point of the whole damn mission. Even more than the science – though I don't expect you to agree with that. Natalie, it's going to be a long time before anyone comes this way again. But we're changing history here; even if we fall back, now, people will be able to look up at Mars and say, yes, it's possible, we can get there, live up there. We know, because somebody did it.

'Look, I know I'm no Neil Armstrong. You're more – articulate. And this is your place; your valley. Your planet, damn it. You know your way around here better than anyone alive. I think you'd do a better job of communicating this than me. And besides . . .'

'What?'

He smiled. 'I have this feeling. I might be remembered longer for being the man who passed up the chance to be first.'

'I hope she's obeying orders,' Gershon called.

'About as much as she ever does.'

They've plotted this. I've been set up.

'And take this,' Stone said.

She held out her hand; Stone dropped into her palm a small disk, like a coin, less than an inch across. It was the diamond marker. 'I think it's more appropriate for you to place it. For Ben. And the others.'

He reached out with two hands, and closed her fist over the marker. He was looking into her eyes.

He knows, she realized suddenly. *About Ben and me. He knows. They all knew, all the time.*

She dropped the marker into a sample pocket on her suit. Then, numbed, she pushed the red bands over her arms and legs, and dropped her gold visor down over her face.

Stone held the hatch aside. York got down, clumsily, to her knees, and backed up ass-first to the hatch. She started to crawl backwards, out onto the porch.

'Here we go. You're lined up nicely, Natalie. Come toward me a little bit. Okay, down. Roll to the left. Put your left foot to the right – no, the other way. You're doing fine.'

She could feel where her sides scraped against the hatchway. Coolant tubes dug into her knees.

Blood hammered in her ears.

'Okay, Ralph, I'm on the porch.' She reached out and grabbed the handrails, to either side of the porch.

She looked up. The white paint of the outer hull was stained with landing dust, and tinged yellow by the quickening Martian morning. She had got so far out that could see the whole of the hatchway before her; it was a rectangle of brilliant fluorescent light, set within the skin of *Challenger*. Inside the rectangle Phil Stone had crouched down, peering out at her, nodding inside his helmet.

She continued to move backwards, still crawling over the porch, feeling out with her right leg; eventually, her toe hit the top rung of the ladder.

Holding onto the handrails, she straightened up.

She was emerging into the shadow of *Challenger*; the rising sun was hidden by the bulk of the craft, and the sky above her was still black, though the stars were washing out. She turned, stiffly. To left and right she could see a flat, sharp, close horizon, delimiting a plain of dust and rocks. Everything was stained rust brown, like dried blood, the shadows long and sharp.

The change of scale was startling. She'd spent months inside the confines of the Mission Module, where everything in the universe had been either a few feet away – enclosed by the tight, curving walls – or at infinity. Now, the sense of height and depth, of scales opening out around her, was profound, disorienting; nothing in her training had prepared her for this. For a moment she felt as if she would fall backwards, and she hooked her hands around the handrails of the porch.

'Natalie?'

'I'm okay, Phil. It's just –'

'I know,' Stone said. 'A big moment, right?'

'Yeah.'

Gershon asked, 'Natalie, have you got out the MESA yet?'

The MESA, the Modularized Equipment Storage Assembly, was a panel on the descent stage, to the left of the ladder. York reached out and opened a latch; the panel swung down like a drawbridge, bearing a TV camera.

'Ralph, the MESA came down all right.'

'I copy that, Natalie. I'm turning the TV on now.'

The lens of the camera was dark, clean, watchful; she saw the camera swivel as Ralph worked its servo-motors, focusing on her. She felt absurdly self-conscious.

Gershon said, 'I'm waiting for the TV. Man, I'm getting a picture. There's a great deal of contrast in it – it's just splashes of color – and currently the damn thing's upside down. But I can see a fair amount of detail and – I got it, it's corrected itself. Natalie, I can see you at the top of the ladder.'

York nodded to the camera. *But they can't see my face behind this visor.* She waved.

She made her way down the ladder, rung by rung. They were big steps, and in the stiff suit she found the best way to go was to let herself drop from step to step.

The last rung was three feet from the ground, and she pushed herself away from the ladder and let herself fall. Her descent was distinctly slow-motion; it took nearly a second, she guessed, to cover that last yard. On Earth, it would have taken half that.

Her blue boots came to rest on the white metal of the descent stage's three-feet-wide footpad. It was still so dark, here in the shadow of *Challenger*, that it was actually quite difficult to see.

She held onto the ladder with her fat-gloved hands, and tried to step back up to the ladder's bottom rung. She had to make sure she could get back home. But the suit was too stiff, and she couldn't lift her feet that high.

'Fucking dumb design.'

'Hot mike at this time, EV1,' Gershon said blandly.

She gave up trying to make the step. She bent down a little and jumped. Her knees were stiff, inside the suit, and all her mobility came from her toes and ankles. The Martian gravity pulled her back, but feebly, and she overshot the bottom rung. She fell against the ladder with a clatter, but she managed to get her feet hooked over the rung.

Breathless, she dropped back to the footpad again.

She looked past the pad to the Martian surface.

'Okay. I'm at the foot of the ladder. The MEM's footpads are depressed in the surface a couple of inches, maybe three; the sides of the depressions they've made are quite distinct, sharp and clear. There's little water here, of course, and I guess the soil's cohesion is electrostatic . . .' *Don't analyze, York; tell them what it looks like.* 'The surface soil looks a little like beach sand. Wet sand. But as you get close to it it's actually much finer-grained than sand, and it's evident that it bonds well together. Here and there it's very fine, powdery.' She reached out her leg and kicked gently at the regolith, leaving furrows in the soil. 'It's easy for me to dig little trenches with my toe. The surface crunches when I kick it. I have the impression that the surface material is a duricrust. That is, dust particles cemented together by the upward seepage of water in the soil, with salts being precipitated out on evaporation.'

There had been a little Martian dust on the footpad, she saw, and now, when she lifted up her boot, she could see that a little of that had already transferred itself to her. 'The dust is clinging in fine layers to the sole and sides of my boot. So it's both cohesive and adhesive. It looks as if it will take a slope of around seventy degrees . . .'

Now Ralph Gershon said, 'Natalie, I need you to get back facing the TV camera for a minute please.'

'Say again, Ralph.'

'Rager. I need you facing the field of view of the camera. Natalie, Phil, the President of the United States is in his office now and would like to say a few words to you.'

Stone replied for her. 'That would be an honor, Ralph.'

She checked her cuff checklist. Reagan was right on cue. Trust an old actor.

She turned toward the MESA.

She imagined the TV pictures of herself now on their way to Earth: she would be a stiff, angular figure, posed on the footpad, her outline fuzzed by false colors against the crimson of Mars.

She took a still Hasselblad camera from the MESA platform. After some fumbling, she fitted the camera to a mount above her chest panel.

She turned around slowly, letting the camera snap a panoramic mosaic. Then she picked up a small TV camera, and fixed that in place on her chest, beside the Hasselblad.

The quality of the radio link changed; a Houston capcom came on the line. 'Go ahead, Mr President. Out.'

Natalie and Phil, I'm talking to you by a radio link-up from the Oval Room at the White House.

Reagan's gravelly voice was lively, interested. *He sure plays the part well.* She found herself drawing a little more upright, as if coming to attention.

Now, the NASA technical people tell me that it will take four minutes for my words to reach you, and four more before I get to hear your reply. So I figure we can't have much of a conversation. I just want to say this, as you talk to us from the Valley of Mangala. Our progress in space – continuing to take giant steps for all mankind – is a tribute to American teamwork and excellence. And we can be proud to say: We are first; we are the best; and we are so because we're free.

America has always been greatest when we dared to be great. We have reached for greatness again. We can follow our dreams to the planets and to distant stars, living and working in space for peaceful, economic, and scientific gain . . .

York – standing on the pad in the reality of the glowing landscape, and with the weight of her pack heavy on her back – endured the remote, distorted voice.

. . . Now I'm going to shut up, Natalie and Phil, but I want you

to indulge us with just a couple of minutes of your time. Please tell us how it feels to be, at last, on the surface of Mars.

Reagan fell silent, and the radio link hissed.

Stone said: 'Thank you, Mr President. It's an honor and a privilege for us to be here, representing not only the United States, but all of mankind. Natalie . . .'

Natalie, tell them how it feels.

The oldest question in the world, the most difficult to answer – and, maybe, the most important, she thought.

The one question the Apollo astronauts could never answer.

Now I must try.

In the pink sky, the sun was continuing to strengthen, and the world was a bowl of shades of red and brown, of light scattering from the dust on the ground and suspended in the air. The light from the hatchway shone as brilliantly white as before, incongruous.

'Okay, sir. The MEM is standing here on the flats north of Mangala Vallis. It's a late fall morning – we're only about eighty days away from the winter solstice, here in the northern hemisphere of Mars. The sky is uniformly ochre. The dust suffuses everything with a pale, salmon hue. The red planet isn't really so red: the dominant color is a moderate yellow brown, reflected from the land. There's no green, or blue, anywhere. If humans ever colonize Mars for good – no, make that *when* – we'll have to invent a lot of new words for shades of brown.

'I'm almost on the Martian equator. To give you some reference, the great Tharsis Bulge, with its three huge shield volcanoes, is a couple of thousand miles to the east of me; and Olympus Mons, the greatest volcano in the Solar System, is about the same distance to the north.

'We're close enough to Tharsis for this region to have been affected by the uplift of the Bulge. So, although the surface here looks as flat as a beach at low tide, I know that when I look away from the MEM I'm probably looking down a slope of a few tenths of a degree.'

She took a long, slow look around at the panorama of Mangala Vallis.

'The MEM is standing on a surface which is littered with rocks. The rocks, I would say, range in size from maybe half a yard up to two yards. The rocks show vesicles. That is, there are small bubbles in the surface of the rocks; it means the rocks are probably bits of frozen lava. The rocks are uniformly pitted and fluted, I would guess by wind erosion. I can seem smaller formations that look like pebbles, but I'm pretty sure they are duricrust aggregate. Just bits of the surface stuck together. The surface is not like sand; it's evidently much finer grained. I'm sure that the dust is the result of the slow weathering of the rocks, with much oxidation having occurred; the rocks have the characteristic deep red-brown coloration of smectite clays . . .

'I can see how geological processes are continuing to shape this landscape. The surface has clearly been scoured by wind: the landscape is eroded, and the dust under my feet has surely been transported from around the planet. From a geological point of view, there is clearly a sequence of events represented here: impact, wind, volcanic activity, possibly flooding, probably ground ice.

'The Moon is an old world; we think its story ended, essentially, a billion or more years ago. But it's obvious to me, standing here, that Mars, like Earth, is still evolving. Still alive.'

There was a long silence on the radio link.

'Natalie,' Stone said gently. 'Are you all right?'

'Yes. Yes, I'm fine, Phil.'

She thought of her words dispersing, radiating away to Earth and beyond; she wished she could call them back. *It's not enough. It could never be enough.*

But, I guess, it was the best I could do.

It was time.

She said, 'I'll step off the footpad now.'

She held onto the ladder with her right hand and leaned out to the left. She raised her left boot over the lip of the footpad, pushed it out a little way, and – silently, carefully – lowered it to the dust.

Nobody spoke: Stone, Gershon, remote Earth. It was as if the whole of creation was focused on her, on this moment. She tested her weight, bouncing on her left boot in the gentle gravity. The Martian regolith was firm enough to hold her. As she had known it would be.

She was standing with one foot on this clumsy artifact from Earth, the other on the virgin terrain of Mangala. She looked around, briefly, at the empty landscape, framed by the rounded rim of her faceplate, and she could see the play of soft ochre light over her nose and cheeks, the flesh of a human face, here on Mars.

Holding onto the ladder, she placed her right foot on the ground. Then, cautiously, she let go of the ladder. She was standing freely on Mars.

*   *   *

She took a step forward, then another.

Her boots left clear, firm prints, which showed the ridging of the soles. She wished she could take her shoes off, press her bare toes into the sand of this Martian beach, feel the fine, powdery stuff for herself.

Her suit was comfortable, warm. She could hear the whir of the twenty-thousand-rpm fans in her backpack. She had hundred-and-eighty-degree vision through her faceplate; she had no sense of enclosure, of confinement.

She took a few more steps.

She bounced across the surface. Moving on Mars was dream-like, somewhere between walking and floating. She had no real difficulty in moving around. In fact it was easier than the sims she'd performed on the ground. But she was very aware of the mass of the equipment on her back, and she had to lean forward to maintain her balance. It was difficult to bend at the knees, so that her movement came mostly from her ankles and toes; she suspected her legs would tire quickly. *But my monkey toes are strong, pawing through this Mars dust.*

Oddly, she felt as if the shades of Armstrong and Muldoon were beside her, as if she was echoing their first, famous expedition. It was a thought that somehow diminished this moment.

She turned to face *Challenger*. The MEM was an angular pyramid, huge before her, silhouetted against the light of the shrunken sun, and propped up in an unlikely fashion on its six fold-down legs. She was still in the shadow of *Challenger*. The ambient light was like a late sunset, with *Challenger* drenched in a weak, deep pink color; against that, the rectangle of fluorescent light from the hatch, framing Stone, was a harsh pearl gray, startlingly alien.

The dominant red tones came from dust suspended in the air. There was about ten times as much dust, she knew, as over Los Angeles on a smoggy day. And no rain, ever, to wash it out.

She walked away from *Challenger* now, working her way over into the sunlight, moving along the shadow of *Challenger*, toward the west. The MEM's shadow was a long, sharp-edged cone on the rocky surface before her.

She passed beyond the edge of the shadow and into the light.

She turned. Sunlight shone into her face, casting reflections from the surfaces of her faceplate.

Sunrise on Mars: the sky here was different, the way the light was scattered by the dust . . .

The sun, rising above the silhouetted shoulders of *Challenger*, was surrounded by an elliptical patch of yellow light, suspended in a brown sky. It looked unreal.

The sun was small, feeble, only two-thirds of its size as seen from Earth.

She shivered, involuntarily, although she knew that her suit temperature couldn't have varied; the shrunken sun, the lightless sky, made Mars seem a cold, remote place.

She turned around, letting her camera pan across the landscape. The Martian dust felt a little slippery under her boots as she turned.

She stepped further away from *Challenger*, her line of footprints extending on into the virgin regolith. She felt as if the long, thin line of communications attaching her to *Challenger* and her home planet was growing more attenuated, perhaps fraying, leaving her stranded on this high, cool plain.

The land wasn't completely flat, she saw now as the light continued to increase; there was a subtle mottling in the shading. And she made out what looked like low sand dunes, off to the west. But the dunes were more irregular than terrestrial sand dunes, because, she guessed, of the small size of the surface particles; the dunes were actually more like drifts in the dust.

Away to the west, she saw a line, a soft shadow in the sand. It looked like a shallow ridge, facing away from her.

She walked forward, further from the MEM.

After perhaps fifty yards she came to the ridge. It turned out to be the lip of a small crater, quite sharply defined, a few dozen yards across, embedded in the floor. But the crater walls were worn, and there was a teardrop-shaped mound behind it.

That mound had to be an erosional remnant, streamlined like the remnants found in terrestrial braided streams. And she thought she could see stratification in the sides of the remnant. It was just like the scablands, after all.

She began to step down into the crater, clumsily; her legs were stiff, and dust swirled up around her, sticking to her legs and her HUT.

· Her faceplate was misted up, her breath rapid. She leaned forward.

In the lee of the crater rim, something sparkled, something that finally banished the lunar ghosts of Armstrong and Muldoon from this moment, something that made her feel that her life's circle had closed, at last. *I guess I got to step into the picture after all.*

It was frost.

She leaned sideways, and stretched down to the crater's floor,

579

awkwardly. She scraped at the dust with her fingers. Her fingers cut easily into the surface, leaving sharp trench marks. *I'm like a kid, digging on a beach. A planet-wide beach.* Everywhere she dug, she found the same soft, powdery surface, the same cohesiveness, what looked like pebbles.

She lifted her glove to her face, to get a closer look at the dirt. It was oddly frustrating. The bit of regolith was very light, so light she couldn't even feel its weight. She couldn't even feel its texture because of the thickness of her clumsy suit. And the glare of the rising sun in her glass faceplate made it difficult to see, and the whir of pumps, the hiss of the radio, cut her off from whatever thin sounds were carried by the Martian winds.

She had a sense of unreality, of isolation. She was *here,* but she was still cut off from Mars. It wasn't like a field trip at all.

She closed her fingers over the sample; the little 'pebbles' burst and shattered. They were just fragments of a caliche-like duricrust.

She tipped her hand and let the crushed dust drift back to the surface; much of it clung to the palm of her glove, turning it a rust-brown.

She took the diamond marker out from the sample pocket on her suit. She held the little coin in her hand; it caught the sunlight and refracted it, turning its glow to a bright scarlet, jewel-like, against the ochre of Mars.

She felt a sudden, and unexpected, surge of pride. She distrusted patriotism intensely; and maybe this expedition, these few days of scrambling over Mars like rabbits, really was all a grand techno-cratic folly. But the fact was that her country had – in little more than two centuries of existence – sent its citizens to walk on the surfaces of two new worlds.

And if some calamity were to wipe Earth clean of life before anyone decided to come again, this little marker, with its flag, would still be here, as a monument to a magnificent human achievement: this, and the remnants of *Challenger,* and three Lunar Module descent stages on the surface of the Moon.

And to think we nearly didn't come here; to think, after Apollo, we might have closed down the space program.

Carefully she dropped the marker and let it float through the weak gravity down into the hole she'd dug, where it lay, sparkling, in the base of the crater.

Then, silently, she dug into her pocket again. With some diffi-culty, she drew out a small silver pin. Its 1960s design was tacky: a shooting star soaring upwards, a long, comet-like tail.

For you, Ben.

She dropped the pin into the little ditch, after the diamond marker. Then she kicked dust back into the hole, and scuffed over the surface.

The footprints Armstrong and Muldoon had left behind on the Moon's surface were still there – would remain there for many millions of years, until micrometeorite erosion finally obliterated them. But it was different here. The prints she was making today would last for many months, perhaps years; but eventually the wind would cover them over.

In a few years her footprints would be erased by the wind, the first little pit she'd dug all but untraceable.

'. . . Natalie?'

She hadn't said anything, she realized.

She turned to *Challenger*. The human artifact was a squat, white-painted toy, diminished by the distance she had come; the sun made the sky glow behind it. She could still see the pearl-gray interior of the airlock, embedded at the center of the MEM, and above that she could make out the fat cylinder of the ascent stage, with its propellant tanks clustered like berries around a stalk.

There was a single set of footsteps, crisp in the duricrust, leading from *Challenger* to where she stood, beyond the circular splash of dust from the MEM's landing rocket. They looked like the first steps on a beach after a receded tide; they were the only footsteps on the planet.

By God, she thought, *we're here. We came for all the wrong reasons, and by all the wrong methods, but we're here, and that's all that matters. And we've found soil, and sunlight, and air, and water.*

She said: 'I'm home.'

Afterword

LOST MARS

In our world, *Challenger* was the name – not of a Mars lander – but of the Shuttle orbiter which was destroyed in January 1986, killing its crew of seven. It was a disaster which brought the US space program, in 1986, to a nadir, rather than the new zenith of a Mars landing.

But it might have been very different.

After the liftoff of Apollo 11 in July 1969, an exuberant Vice President Spiro Agnew proclaimed that the US 'should articulate a simple, ambitious, optimistic goal of a manned flight to Mars by the end of the century.' And NASA had strong, feasible plans to achieve that goal.

America has never been so close again to assembling the commitment to go to Mars.

What went wrong in 1969? Why did President Nixon decide *against* the Mars option?

And how would things have worked out, in an alternate universe in which Natalie York walked on Mars?

In February 1969, a few months before the first Apollo Moon landing, the incoming Nixon Administration appointed a Space Task Group (STG), chaired by Vice President Agnew, to develop goals for the post-Apollo period. The STG was to report to the President in September. (President Nixon's initiating memo was similar to that reproduced in the novel – but *without* the handwritten addendum . . .)

Post-Apollo planning for space entered its most crucial months. And gradually, over this period, NASA lost the case for Mars.

To space proponents in 1969, *technical* logic appeared to indicate a building from the achievements of Apollo to a progressive colonization of the Solar System, including missions to Mars. But the *political* logic differed.

The Apollo era – when the efforts of half a million Americans had been devoted to spaceflight – had been born out of an extraordinary set of circumstances, which were not repeated in 1969. Just a week after Yuri Gagarin's pioneering first spaceflight in April 1961, President Kennedy sent a memo to Vice President Johnson asking for options: 'Do we have a chance of beating the Soviets by putting a laboratory in space, or by a trip around the Moon, or by a rocket to land on the Moon, or by a rocket to go to the Moon and back with a man. Is there any other space program which promises dramatic results in which we could win? . . .'

Although NASA by this time already had a schedule for a lunar program, there was no overriding logic favoring the Moon goal.

585

In fact, in private, Kennedy berated his technical advisers for not producing recommendations for more tangible, down-to-Earth scientific spectaculars, such as desalinating sea water.

So when Kennedy made his famous 1961 commitment to put a man on the Moon within a decade, the new program was not intended as a first step in an orderly expansion into space. Rather, Kennedy was reacting, to the early Soviet lead in spaceflight, and his Administration's Bay of Pigs disaster.

Thus, in 1969, there was *no* internal logic which proceeded from Apollo to Mars. This key point was evidently misunderstood by many within NASA in this period. Technically Apollo was an end in itself, a system designed to place two men on the Moon for three days, and it achieved precisely that; its political goals were similarly well-defined – to beat the Soviets in space – and had been achieved. With the completion of Apollo, there was no momentum to be carried forward to future goals – and, in 1969, no perceived threat to drive the necessary political reaction behind a new program.

Still, NASA had explored the technical feasibility of a Mars mission in as many as sixty study contracts between 1961 and 1968. But the visionaries were dealt a severe blow when the pictures of Mars returned by the early Mariners showed a bleak lunar-like cratered landscape. There were still compelling scientific reasons to go to Mars, but the opportunity for human expansion was clearly limited. NASA suffered deferments and cancelations as a result.

Meanwhile, throughout the Apollo period, NASA's overall long-range planning was weak, leaving it ill-prepared for 1969.

This was in fact a deliberate policy of James Webb, NASA Administrator from 1961 to 1968. Webb believed that Apollo's success would give US citizens great pride and encouragement, and that any evidence of commitment to an expensive long-term Mars program would lose NASA the margin of strength needed to finish Apollo.

As early as 1966, NASA budgets began to slide.

On September 16, 1968, after arguing with Johnson about the latest cuts, Webb resigned. When the STG began its work NASA's only firm funding commitments for manned spaceflight were for the Apollo lunar landings and a follow-on Apollo Applications Program.

President Nixon himself was not an instinctive opponent of spaceflight. But – as new NASA Administrator Thomas O. Paine learned as he flew with Nixon to Apollo 11's splashdown – the incoming Administration could not direct large amounts of money into space while the Vietnam War continued.

Given such strong signals, NASA's political tactics during this key period, under Paine, showed deep naivety.

Although in its STG submission NASA formally called for such worthy goals as 'commonality,' 'reusability,' and 'economy' – the program it actually envisaged was outward-looking and very expensive, including a space station, a manned Mars mission, a new generation of automated spacecraft, and new programs in advanced research and technology. These tactics were counter-productive. Even supporters of more modest programs, given a Hobson's choice of a huge Mars 'boondoggle' or nothing, backed away.

NASA also tried to talk up the benefits of state-managed R&D, but this too was a mistake. There was no doubt that NASA was an astonishing success as a giant technocratic exercise in management science and project control. And only a fifth of Kennedy's 1961 speech had been devoted to spaceflight: Kennedy had been promoting the space program as part of a greater *technocratic* solution to perceived threats and problems – eliminating poverty, resisting Communist expansion, promoting development abroad.

But by 1969 it was clear that technocracy had failed in its greater objectives. Instead there was only the maturation of the power complex of the technocratic state. Nixon seemed to understand the anti-technocratic mood of his day, and also how technocracy was in opposition to America's older Jeffersonian tradition of local politics and democratic responsiveness.

Meanwhile, during 1969, funding cuts were made in the NERVA nuclear rocket research program, which had been proceeding in Nevada since 1957. Although the Nevada test station would not be shut down until 1972, the 1969 cuts ended any hopes of flight testing nuclear rockets. Without NERVA, a component NASA believed was vital to a Mars expedition, the case for Mars was essentially already lost. (In the novel, NASA manages to fend off these cuts.)

Against this background – and without a strong and articulate champion, the role served by Jack Kennedy in the novel – the Agency was soon forced to back off from its more aggressive proposals. The language in NASA's draft report to the STG, prepared in April 1969, read: 'We *recommend* that the US begin preparing for a manned expedition to Mars at an early date.' By the published version the sentence had been watered down to: 'Manned expeditions to Mars *could* begin as early as 1981' (my emphasis).

Agnew himself was, however, a champion within the White House of aiming for Mars – even though he was booed when he spoke of the project in public. White House counsel John Ehrlichman later described how he was unable to dissuade Agnew from including a 1981 landing in the STG's list of recommendations, even though it was already clear that the Mars mission did not fit with the Nixon Administration's overall budget priorities. Agnew insisted on taking the argument in to Nixon. We do not know what Nixon said to Agnew, but fifteen minutes later, Agnew called Ehrlichman to explain that the Mars mission was being moved from the list of 'recommendations' to another category headed 'technically feasible.'

The proposals of the final STG report, as delivered to the President in September 1969, were much as depicted in the novel.

The STG proposed a series of common elements: a Shuttle, space station modules, a space tug, nuclear shuttles, and a Mars Excursion Module (MEM). The modules could be put together into a series of mission profiles to achieve a variety of goals; only the MEM would have been Mars-specific.

The earliest Mars mission would have left Earth on November 12, 1981, consisting of two nuclear-boosted ships each carrying six men. The expedition would return home on August 14, 1983, and the astronauts brought back to Earth by shuttles.

A series of funding options were presented, ranging from a maximum-pace sprint to Mars by 1982 to a lowest-level funding option which would curtail all manned flight after Apollo. Three central options were presented: Option I aiming for a 1984 Mars landing at a peak cost of $9bn per year, Option II for 1986 at $8bn/year, and Option III for no firm landing commitment at $5bn/year.

The STG proposals were designed to allow incremental near-term decision-making, while decisions on more ambitious programs – such as Mars – could be deferred.

It was widely expected that, given the heavy lobbying by NASA and the US aerospace industry, some elements at least of this vision would survive. But public and political reaction was swift and negative.

While it awaited Nixon's formal response to the STG, further pressure on NASA came in the FY1971 budget process.

Facing further cuts, Paine scrambled to reprioritize. One Skylab and the Apollo-Soyuz Test Project (ASTP) were the sole survivors of the Apollo Applications Program. Apollo 20 was canceled to free up a Saturn V for Skylab. The remaining Apollo missions, 13 through 19, would be stretched out to place two missions after Skylab. There was no prospect of a post-Apollo lunar program. Viking was postponed to 1975.

In January 1970, Nixon somberly told Paine of a Harris poll reporting that 56% of Americans believed the costs of Apollo were too great. Nixon said he regretted cuts but could not make an expansive space program a priority. Paine, however, kept up pressure on the President for a greater commitment to NASA's activities, and this led to hard feelings between them. White House officials concluded that: 'We need a new Administrator who will turn down NASA's empire-building fervor ... someone who will work with us rather than against us, and ... will shape the program to reflect credit on the President rather than embarrassment.'

In March 1970 Nixon formally endorsed the STG's third and least expensive option. His language was cautious. 'With the entire future and the entire universe before us ... we should not try to do everything at once. Our approach to space must continue to be bold – but it must also be balanced.'

Nixon set out six specific objectives: the remaining Apollo missions, Skylab, greater international cooperation in space (essentially ASTP), reducing the cost of space operations (Space Shuttle studies), hastening space technology's practical application, and unmanned planetary exploration. Nixon made mention of one 'major *but long-range* goal we should keep in mind ... to *eventually* send men to explore the planet Mars' (my emphasis). Nixon distanced NASA organizationally from its Apollo past: 'We must think of space activities as part of a continuing process ... and not as a series of separate leaps, each one requiring a massive concentration of energy and will and accomplished on a crash timetable.'

Essentially, NASA had lost the argument for Mars, and Nixon had (provisionally) chosen the Space Shuttle. In this short but crucial statement, Nixon summarized virtually all of US space policy through the 1970s.

In the *Voyage* timeline, Nixon withdraws this statement before publication; after this crux point, history diverges decisively.

Even after Nixon's response to the STG, the future of US manned spaceflight was far from assured. To save funds for future programs, on September 2, 1970 Paine cut two more Apollo missions. Paine was out of place in the Nixon Administration, and he resigned on September 15.

Congressional critics still wanted more of NASA's budget

trimmed. The familiar partially-reusable Shuttle concept emerged in response to the need to halve development costs. But even this did not win automatic approval. In November 1971 the new NASA Administrator James Fletcher sent a testy memo to the President arguing that the US could not afford to forgo manned spaceflight altogether, that the Shuttle was the only meaningful new program that could be accomplished on a modest budget, and not starting the Shuttle would be highly damaging to the aerospace industry.

But Fletcher did not know that NASA had gained a powerful ally inside the Administration in Caspar Weinberger, Deputy Director of the Office of Management and Budget, who wrote to Nixon on August 12, 1971 in support of the Space Shuttle (*not* of a Mars program!). NASA's budget was still under threat simply because it was cuttable, Weinberger said. Further NASA cuts would confirm 'that our best years are behind us, that we are turning inwards, reducing our defense commitments, and voluntarily starting to give up our superpower status and our desire to maintain world superiority.' In a handwritten scrawl on the memo, Nixon added, 'I agree with Cap.'

In December 1971 Fletcher learned that Nixon had decided in principle to go ahead with the Shuttle. The decisive factors were the arguments put forward in Weinberger's and Fletcher's memos, the fact that so many high-technology programs had already been cut, and – given the decision already to cancel the proposed Supersonic Transport (SST) project – the desire to start some new aerospace program that would avoid unemployment in critical states in the 1972 election year.

On January, 5 1972 Nixon issued a statement announcing the decision to proceed with the development of 'an entirely new type of space transportation system designed to help transform the space frontier of the 1970s into familiar territory, easily accessible for human endeavor in the 1980s and '90s . . .'

So ended the tortuous post-Apollo decision-making process. In January 1972 Nixon initiated the Shuttle project, not a Mars program.

Mars was lost. But so, nearly, had been the Shuttle – the last, compromised, element of the STG's grand vision – and with it, the US manned space program.

In the pages of *Voyage*, the survival of President Kennedy in 1963 pushed history onto a track which diverged from our own trajectory: slowly, but sufficiently far, in the end, for the US space program to reach out to Mars. The decision-making points depicted in *Voyage* closely parallel those in our own world. It could – with a small perturbation – have happened like this.

But even if the argument for Mars had been 'won' in 1969, it would have been essential to maintain a supportive coalition of political forces behind a Mars program over the years, or decades, it would have taken to implement it – a period during which downward pressure on NASA's budget was consistent. To reach Mars, NASA would have needed a Fred Michaels: another Webb – not another Paine.

And in many ways, an Apollo-style Mars program could have been a mixed blessing.

As Nixon foresaw, if the Mars program had come about NASA would have been able to remain a one-shot, 'heroic' agency, rather than move to the organizational maturity for which current Administrator Dan Goldin is still reaching. On the science side, Apollo dominated other space programs in the 1960s – often to their detriment. The Lunar Orbiter and Surveyor lander programs were effectively downgraded to serve as mappers for Apollo. Perhaps, if the Mars option had been followed, Viking might have been compromised in a similar fashion, and unrelated programs – such as the unmanned exploration of the outer planets – might have been put under even greater funding pressure.

On the other hand, the abandonment of Mars and NASA's other great plans did *not* free up funds for other projects; the funds simply did not make themselves available at all. If a Mars program had gone ahead, it would surely have brought many benefits in its wake, such as the need for the US to build up expertise in orbital assembly and long-duration missions.

And in the end, we cannot help but regret the loss of the great spectacle we should have enjoyed had Natalie York walked on Mars at Mangala Vallis in 1986.

Stephen Baxter

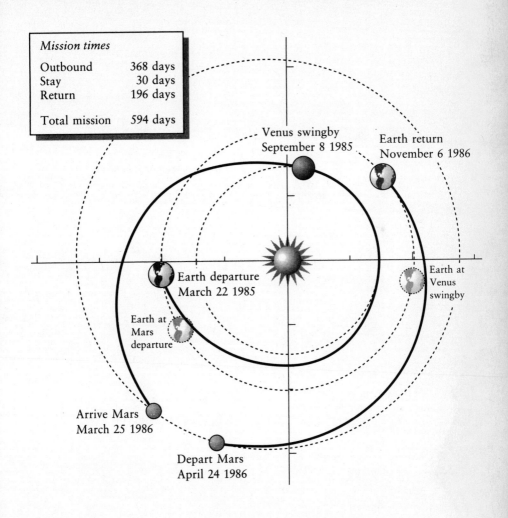

Mission times	
Outbound	368 days
Stay	30 days
Return	196 days
Total mission	594 days

Venus swingby
September 8 1985

Earth return
November 6 1986

Earth departure
March 22 1985

Earth at
Venus
swingby

Earth at
Mars
departure

Arrive Mars
March 25 1986

Depart Mars
April 24 1986

Ares Mission Profile

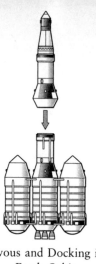

1

Rendezvous and Docking in Low
Earth Orbit

4

Trans-Mars Cruise

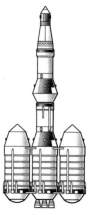

2

Trans-Mars Injection

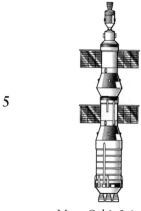

5

Mars Orbit Injection

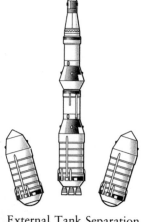

3

External Tank Separation

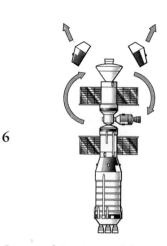

6

Command-Service Module Repositioning
Mission Module Transposition
Mars Excursion Module
Shroud Separation

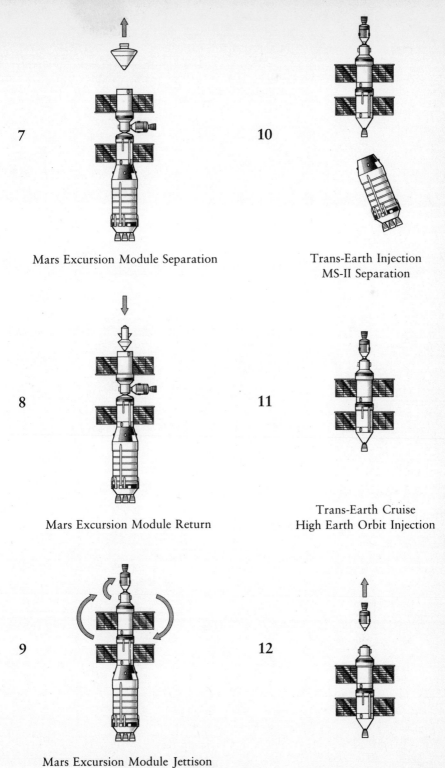

7

Mars Excursion Module Separation

10

Trans-Earth Injection
MS-II Separation

8

Mars Excursion Module Return

11

Trans-Earth Cruise
High Earth Orbit Injection

9

Mars Excursion Module Jettison
Command-Service Module Mepositioning
Mission Module Transposition

12

Command-Service Module
Separation and Reentry